Born and raised in New York, Sam Barone attended Manhattan College, graduating with a Bachelor of Science degree in 1965, with a major in Psychology. After a hitch in the Marine Corps, he became a software developer and manager. After spending nearly 30 years in the software development game, he retired in 1999 to start working on his second career: writing.

SAM BARONE

Empire Rising

arrow books

Published in the United Kingdom by Arrow Books in 2009

1 3 5 7 9 10 8 6 4 2

Copyright © Sam Barone, 2008

Sam Barone has asserted his right under the Copyright, Designs and
Patents Act 1988 to be identified as the author of this work.

This novel is a work of fiction. Names and characters are the product of
the author's imagination and any resemblance to actual persons, living or
dead, is entirely coincidental

This book is sold subject to the condition that it shall not, by way of trade
or otherwise, be lent, resold, hired out, or otherwise circulated without the
publisher's prior consent in any form of binding or cover other than that in
which it is published and without a similar condition, including this
condition, being imposed on the subsequent purchaser.

First published in Great Britain in 2008 by Century

Arrow Books
Random House, 20 Vauxhall Bridge Road,
London SW1V 2SA

www.rbooks.co.uk

Addresses for companies within The Random House Group Limited can
be found at: www.randomhouse.co.uk/offices.htm

The Random House Group Limited Reg. No. 954009

A CIP catalogue record for this book is available from the British Library

ISBN 9780099498551

The Random House Group Limited supports The Forest Stewardship
Council (FSC), the leading international forest certification organisation.
All our titles that are printed on Greenpeace approved FSC certified paper
carry the FSC logo. Our paper procurement policy can be found at
www.rbooks.co.uk/environment

Mixed Sources
Product group from well-managed
forests and other controlled sources
www.fsc.org Cert no. TT-COC-2139
© 1996 Forest Stewardship Council

Typeset by SX Composing DTP, Rayleigh, Essex
Printed and bound in Great Britain by
CPI Bookmarque Ltd, Croydon, CR0 4TD

IN MEMORIAM

This book is dedicated to the memory of Jim Jasper,
who passed away in September 2006.
He will be missed.

Empire Rising

Prologue

≡

3157 B.C.E., at the eastern edge of the great southern desert in Mesopotamia . . .

Head sagging, his face inches above the heated rubble of rock-hard dirt, Korthac struggled against the escarpment. The long ascent had scraped the skin from his hands and knees, and now every contact with the sun-seared stones burned his flesh, as he struggled another step up the slope. *Close your eyes, just for a moment.* The inner voices grew more insistent, seductive, as another wave of dizziness swept over him. *Rest! Let another lead the way.*

Clenching his teeth, he crawled on, fighting against the voices as much as the steep hillside and the pitiless sun. Korthac could not show weakness in front of his men. The desert might kill him, but it would not defeat him. He'd find water at the top, and live. Clinging to the thought, he dragged himself upward.

Water. Most of all he fought against the need for water, forced himself to ignore his swollen tongue and parched throat. *Water.* Korthac pictured streams of clear, bubbling water nestled under shady sycamore and willow trees. He forced the image from his thoughts and concentrated on wrenching himself up another arm's length. The vision and the voices kept returning. He must find water, or the desert would prevail over him, claim him and all his followers. That could not be.

The top of the ridge beckoned, just a few paces above. He moved with caution, making sure his trembling legs did not betray him. Twice in the last hour Korthac heard the death screams of men who had fallen back to the desert floor. If he lost his grip, started to slide back down, he didn't know if he had the strength to stop his fall.

His thirst drove him on. Fortune had saved him and his minions time and again in the last two months, but even the gods couldn't keep a man alive in the desert with no water. He refused to believe his destiny meant for him to die like this, hunted and herded into this barren wasteland like some wretched slave, driven mad by thirst before the death gods claimed his body.

Last night, a few hours past sunset, Korthac and his men reached the base of the plateau they'd first glimpsed three days ago. The remnants of his once mighty army fell on their faces and slept until dawn. When they awoke this morning, two men could not get to their feet.

Korthac ignored their pleading. "Kill them." He'd given the same order almost every morning for the last two weeks. Those closest drew their knives and thrust them deep into the chests of the helpless men. The rest needed no further urging. They crowded around the two dying men and cut their victims to pieces, every man shoving and pushing his way to seize a piece of moist flesh, valued as much for its thirst-quenching blood as for its nourishment. When the gory ritual ended, only the splintered bones, their marrow sucked dry, remained on the red-soaked sand. Even the skulls were cracked and the brains scooped out. Afterwards, fewer than eighty men started the climb up the sheer and treacherous slope.

Korthac ate with the rest, on his knees and pushing the bloody flesh into his mouth as fast as he could. The act no longer shocked him or any of his men. The strong fed upon the weak to gain sustenance for another day. But even a fresh-killed body didn't hold enough water to keep so many men going through the desert. They'd had no water for three days, not since a brief rainstorm sprinkled the sands and filled a few hollows in the rocks with its precious liquid. If they didn't find water atop this plateau, they'd all be dead by sunset.

His outstretched hand grabbed onto nothing, and Korthac realized he'd reached the end of his climb. Pulling himself over the crest, he rolled onto his back, breathing hard, oblivious of the blinding sun. When he heard the scraping of those following, he forced himself first to his knees, then to his feet. His men would not see him crawling about on the dirt.

Shading his eyes, he looked around. The landscape had changed. For the first time in weeks, he saw the endless sands replaced by a stony mixture of earth and clay, with scattered shrubs and bushes dotting the terrain. To the east his eyes picked out what he'd hoped to find, a line of green about two miles away that could only be trees. Where trees grew, water flowed. The gods had favored him once again. He would survive to find his destiny.

Korthac turned back to the cliff's edge and in a hoarse voice called out the news to his men. As he did so, he looked down at the desert floor, surprised at how distant it seemed. They'd climbed more than two thousand feet to reach the top of this elevation.

Hand on his knife, he made sure the first four men to reach the crest still carried their burdens, small sacks tied to their backs. Only then did he relax, counting and appraising each of his fighters, to see if any looked too weak to carry on. But the sight of the distant tree line gave every man renewed vigor. Dirty, crusted with blood and sand, their skin burned nearly black from weeks under the unrelenting sun, they looked more like demons than men.

When the last one reached the top, Korthac finished his count. Seventy-four men had survived the desert passage, less than half the number who survived the battle and fled with their leader into the wasteland. Nothing could stop them now. He led the way, his men stumbling along behind him. They headed east, the same direction they'd run, walked, and crawled for the last two months.

Halfway to the trees, Korthac caught sight of a village and changed his course. As they reached the outskirts of the small cluster of mud huts, the ground gave way to a barley field that offered its heady scent to the wind. Forcing a path through the waist-high crops, his eyes picked out the mud-ridged channel carrying water to the growing plants.

Korthac lurched into a run, his men staggering behind as best they could. He reached the edge of the irrigation ditch and flung himself down, to gulp mouthfuls of the muddy stream. His men splashed about on either side, crawling and pushing until they, too, shoved their faces into the water. Korthac drank until he needed to draw a breath, then let his face fall again into the muddy water. Only when his stomach protested did he stop.

Disgusted at showing such weakness, Korthac pushed himself to his feet, noted the flow of the water, and moved away from his men until he reached a part of the ditch still unsoiled by his followers. He knelt and drank again, but only a few mouthfuls, able to restrain himself once more. Then he washed his face and hands, and scooped the cool water over his body, rinsing away most of the dirt and blood that had crusted over him for days.

When Korthac stood up, he felt refreshed, even his hunger driven away by the fullness in his belly. He and his men would take what they needed from the village and rest there until they regained their strength.

He walked down the line of the canal, giving orders to his subcommanders, getting everyone out of the water before some fool drank himself to death. Splashing through the ditch, Korthac walked toward the huts. It seemed strange that no one had noticed their approach, that no farmers worked the field. Just before he reached the first of the mud structures, he heard a scream, a piercing cry of agony that rose above a background of laughter, the mixture of sounds close ahead. Passing into the village, he counted the dozen or so scattered huts and tents. Likely less than fifty people, all struggling to stay alive in this rocky place at the edge of the great desert.

The screams increased in intensity as they guided his steps. In the center of the huts he found a crowd gathered, their attention focused on something he could not see. A young boy dancing with excitement noticed Korthac's approach and gave a shout, pointing with his arm. Everyone turned, and Korthac saw fear and surprise on their faces as they saw his grim followers walking into their midst, hands on their weapons. A babble of sound arose at the sight of the ragged band, and the crowd parted. Korthac strode through, until he reached the center and halted, his men bunching up behind him.

Five men lay on the ground, staked out naked in the dirt. Two had died, blood pooled around their necks, their agony ended with slit throats. Half a dozen men and women knelt around the three who lived, sticks, rocks, or knives in their hands. Korthac noticed that one captive, a big man with dark hair and a gray-flecked beard, had only scrapes and bruises on his face and chest. He would be the leader, Korthac decided, saved for last so that he could watch his followers die and better appreciate his coming torment.

"What is this place?" Korthac's hoarse words silenced the crowd. He'd scarcely raised his voice, but everyone recognized the authority in his tone. "What is this place?"

One of the kneeling men stood and replied, but Korthac could make no sense of his gibberish. Korthac tried again, using all the tongues he knew, but with the same effect.

"It's called Magabad."

Korthac could barely comprehend the words, and he glanced around to find the speaker. To his surprise, the words came from the bearded man spread-eagled on the ground, the captives' leader. Lifting his bloody, sweat-soaked head from the ground, the man struggled to meet

Korthac's eyes.

"You understand the language of Egypt?"

"A few words, lord… learned from men I commanded."

"And you are…?" Korthac strained to discern the man's words.

"My name is Ariamus. I was…" The man's voice broke, and he couldn't get the words out.

Korthac turned to his subcommanders. "Cut that one loose."

With none of them understanding the foreign tongue, the villagers stood speechless during this exchange. But when Korthac's men pushed forward and started to free Ariamus, the crowd protested with a jabber of incomprehensible sounds that meant nothing to Korthac. One of the farmers stepped in front of Korthac, raising his voice and gesturing. Anger showed on the villager's face as he waved his hands in excitement, and the rest joined in to support their leader, everyone shouting at the same time.

The knife flashed from Korthac's belt and buried itself in the villager's stomach. Almost as quickly, Korthac withdrew it, then pushed the man to the ground with his other hand. The dying man clutched his belly and bled into the dirt, his face showing as much surprise as pain.

Korthac's fighters moved among the now silent crowd, shoving them back with their hands. The dozen or so adult men, surrounded by their women and children, had no chance against Korthac's seventy, even weakened by their ordeal in the arid wasteland. The few knives his followers still possessed made the crowd step back. None of Korthac's men possessed a sword. Even he had discarded his fine blade weeks ago, its weight magnified by the desert heat.

A handful of villagers turned and fled. Korthac frowned at the sight. If they kept running, they would get away. His men had no stamina to pursue.

The subcommander finished cutting Ariamus free, then pushed him to his knees at Korthac's feet.

"Water, lord," Ariamus gasped, lowering his forehead to the ground.

"Why should I give you water? Are you the leader of these captives?"

"Yes, lord. Please, lord, we've had no food or water since yesterday."

Korthac thought of his own hunger and the harsh passage just completed. "Why were the villagers torturing you?"

"We were . . . we needed food and a place to stay," the man said, his voice hoarse. "This place . . . it seemed weak and undefended."

A common bandit, Korthac decided, forced to raid outlying farms to stay alive. Nevertheless, the man sounded intelligent, and might even be useful. In this strange land of unknown languages, much might be different.

"You will serve me… Ariamus? If I give you your life, you and your men will swear to obey my commands?" His voice rang out over the village, and Korthac felt his power and purpose returning. "Serve me faithfully, or you die."

"Whatever you say…lord. Just give me water."

Korthac gazed at those surrounding him. Only fear or obedience showed on their faces, the first of those in this new land to submit to his rule. He turned to his subcommanders. "Round up the villagers. Have them bring food and water." He walked toward the largest of the nearby huts, unable to resist the shady interior any longer. "And bring that one to me," he pointed to Ariamus, still crouching in the dirt. "We have much to discuss."

Fifteen days later, the horror of the desert trek had almost faded from memory. Korthac had gained back much of the weight he'd lost and almost all of his strength. The bloody scabs on his hands and knees had closed, then healed. Belted around his waist hung a well-made bronze sword, taken from one of the villagers who had in turn captured it from Ariamus. Korthac's dark hair hung neatly around his shoulders, trimmed and combed by one of the village women.

A slight man with the wiry muscles and the endurance of a runner, Korthac knew he had to stay fit, had to be stronger and more skillful with every weapon than the men he commanded. They must fear his anger as much as they respected his cunning. It must always be so.

The day after they reached the village, Korthac set up a regimen for himself. Each morning he trained with the wooden swords the sullen villagers carved for him and his men. Then he spent three hours with Ariamus, learning the main dialects of the Land Between the Rivers, as the inhabitants called the farmlands they occupied.

Afterwards, Korthac rode for two hours, hardening his thighs and back as he forced the village's only horse up and down the steep and rocky hills until his mastery of the animal had returned. While he rode, his subcommanders kept Ariamus busy; they took charge of their newest recruit, forcing him to learn the dialect of northern Egypt. Their wooden swords served another function: to make sure their pupil applied himself diligently.

When darkness approached, Korthac returned to his language lessons with Ariamus They talked long into the night. Korthac learned not only the language and its nuances, but also the customs and beliefs of the people in this new land. This night, an hour before sunset, Korthac relaxed on a small mat under a poplar tree, his back leaning against the slim trunk. Six feet away, Ariamus sat cross-legged in the dirt. Two of Korthac's men squatted a few paces behind Ariamus.

Korthac had learned much from Ariamus, far more than the man intended to reveal. It hadn't taken long to discover his weaknesses – his lust for gold, women, and power. But Korthac trusted no one, and so his men remained nearby. He didn't want Ariamus to have any sudden change of heart, at least not until the man had given up every bit of useful information he possessed.

"So, Ariamus, tell me again about this great village of Orak."

"I've already told you everything I know, lord. My head aches trying to remember more to tell you." He looked up at Korthac, noted the frown that had suddenly formed, and quickly went on. "Lord, Orak is about two hundred miles from this place, across both the Euphrates and the Tigris rivers. A few weeks ago they drove off a mighty barbarian horde. Now Orak is the most powerful village in the land. They say that soon all villages in the countryside will defer to Orak."

"And their leader, this… Esskar?"

"An ignorant barbarian, lord. A stupid lout driven out by his own kind, no doubt for good reason. He could barely speak our language when he came to Orak, and he drank his pay as soon as he earned it. He was my least subcommander when I led Orak's guard. If it wasn't for his skill with a horse, he'd have been nothing more than a common soldier."

"Yet now you say he commands three thousand people in Orak while you nearly died here in the dirt. Doesn't that seem … strange to you?"

Ariamus squirmed and clenched his fist, uncomfortable at being reminded how far he'd fallen. "Eskkar took a witch for a wife. Some slave girl from the south who belonged to one of Orak's ruling families. She bewitched him. They say she rules Orak through him."

Korthac didn't believe in enchantments, but most of his men did, so he let the comment pass. The superstitions of Egypt had helped him there, and whatever foolish beliefs held sway in this land would do the same.

"Did she also put a spell on the men of Orak, to turn them into warriors? Or perhaps these barbarians you feared so much were such puny fighters they let a village of farmers and shopkeepers defeat them?"

"The barbarians are ferocious fighters, lord, and none can stand against them. But the villagers built a mud wall around Orak, and the barbarians could not overwhelm it. The wall saved them, not Eskkar."

Korthac noted the flush that came over Ariamus's face at the mention of barbarians, apparently wild tribes of nomadic horsemen from the distant steppes. Though Korthac had coaxed the whole story out of him more than a week ago, he kept probing Ariamus's memory, searching for more details or any hint of deception. Each retelling yielded some new fact for Korthac to ponder.

Once again, Ariamus related how a small raiding party of these wandering horsemen had ambushed him and his band of rogues, killing most of them and seizing all their accumulated loot and horses. Ariamus and a handful of men managed to escape on foot, driven to the west. They'd run and walked for over a week until they reached this miserable collection of huts called Magabad. Ariamus had taken over the village, but he didn't have enough men, and after two days of indignities, the villagers rose up in the night. They killed two of their oppressors as they slept and captured the rest, to put them to the torture. If Korthac had arrived an hour later, Ariamus would have died under the knife, along with all his men.

"You say this Eskkar was once one of these fierce barbarians, so hated by the people of Orak. Yet despite that, though you say he did nothing, Orak's inhabitants made him their ruler. Your customs for selecting leaders are very different from those of Egypt."

Ariamus bit his lip at the sarcasm, no doubt tempted to say something rash. "No, lord, not nothing. Eskkar can fight, and he has some skill with a sword."

Korthac wondered what other skills this Eskkar possessed. Not that it mattered. "Since you knew him so well, describe him again, Ariamus. Let me see him through your words, before I meet him."

Putting down his empty wine cup, Ariamus licked his lips. "He's a common barbarian, lord, one of the horse people. They tend to be taller and stronger than those of us who grew up in these lands. Riding a horse all day keeps any man fit and hard. Eskkar is taller even than most of his kind, taller than me by at least a hand's breadth, and nearly as strong."

His Egyptians considered the powerfully-built Ariamus tall, so Eskkar must be of considerable size, which might make him a formidable fighter, at least to these people. "Go on. Show me his face."

Ariamus closed his eyes for a moment. "He has straggly dark brown hair, almost black, that he usually forgets to tie back. Hides most of his face half the time. Brown eyes, and hardly any beard. A thin scar, probably from a knife, slants down his left cheek, from just below the eye. Still has all his teeth, or at least he did when I last saw him. Speaks slowly, and with a strong accent. I thought he was dull-witted when I first met him." Ariamus shrugged. "Just an ordinary barbarian, lord. I still can't believe he survived the barbarians' attack."

Despite Ariamus's dismissive words, Korthac knew better. It took more than a sword to command, and ordinary men don't rule mighty villages. He thought of the vast army he'd commanded in Egypt, recalled the final confrontation where he'd risked all and come so close to victory. One of his allies, jealous of Korthac's rapid ascent over so many, had changed sides at the height of the battle; that tipped the scales just enough to bring catastrophe and slaughter to nearly all of Korthac's men. Even now, anger made him clench his fist in rage at his unexpected defeat, though Korthac took care that Ariamus saw nothing.

"But now these barbarians are gone, the fields are ravaged, and bandits such as you roam the countryside."

Korthac smiled at Ariamus. Once the man learned his place, Ariamus would make an excellent servant. His wits appeared sharp; he spoke his mind a little too freely, but for the moment, Korthac could let such bravado pass. He knew how to correct such behavior. More important, Ariamus's brutish skills and crude desires matched Korthac's needs perfectly. The time had come to tell the man of his role in Korthac's plan.

"You are an experienced fighter, Ariamus, and I require one such as yourself, who knows the land and its people. You can help me, and at the same time take your revenge on Orak. And you can earn much gold and a place of honor in my city." Korthac noted the gleam of interest that widened Ariamus's eyes at the mention of gold.

Then a puzzled look came over Ariamus's face. "Your city, lord?"

"Yes, my city. Orak will be my city when I take charge of it. My men are powerful and experienced soldiers. They have fought many battles and survived passage through the great desert. I intend first to rule this Orak, and then all these lands, as I reigned over the cities and villages of Egypt. You will help me, and as my servant, you will have more power than you've ever dreamed of. Or have you already forgotten your oath to me?"

Ariamus glanced toward the two men standing nearby, watching and listening in silence. "You do not have enough men to conquer Orak."

"If all you've told me is true, if the countryside is still recovering from the passage of your barbarians, then the time is ripe to seize power. And do not underestimate my desert fighters. They are the strongest of those who fought for me in Egypt, and each one of them is worth two or three of your kind."

"Even so, Orak has hundreds of men to defend it, lord," Ariamus said, shaking his head. "You do not have enough men."

"No, not yet. But you will find them for me, and you will command them. Such men will prefer to follow one of their own kind, at least in the beginning. That is why I need someone from this land who knows how to fight and how to lead men. The treasure I carried across the desert will pay my new followers until all of Orak's wealth is mine. If this land is as troubled and unsettled as you claim, we will soon have more than enough men."

In the desert, Korthac's followers had taken turns carrying the four sturdy bags containing amethyst, cornelian, jasper, onyx, quartz crystal, emeralds, and other sacred stones stolen from rich merchants or looted from the temples of the Egyptian gods. His men had thrown away their weapons, their gold, even their clothing, but Korthac refused to let them abandon the last part of the wealth he'd captured. They begged him to bury it, but Korthac killed one who refused the burden, and after that, they obeyed. He knew it would be needed if they made it across the desert.

Korthac recognized the doubt on Ariamus's face. "Don't think I will ride against the walls of Orak like those ignorant barbarians. No, I will take Orak from within. One night of blood will establish my rule. And you will help me."

"What can I do, lord?" Ariamus leaned forward, greed and the desire for revenge on Orak struggling with his usual caution. "I mean… lord… how can I …"

"You can and will do as I command, Ariamus. You will help me fulfill my destiny, which is to rule this land. If the village is as rich and prosperous as you claim, its resources will supply me and my men with all that we need. Soon all the other villages up and down the two rivers will succumb to my will. I will build a mighty empire, starting with Orak."

Sufficient light remained for Korthac to see the lingering doubt in the man's eyes. He smiled at his newest follower.

"And you, Ariamus, you will have more wealth and power as my subcommander than you could ever attain on your own. In my name, you'll will command hundreds of fighters, and enjoy the choicest women in Orak and the surrounding countryside. Or are you not interested in what I offer?"

"I am interested, lord," Ariamus said. "I will be your subcommander."

Korthac smiled. As he expected, Ariamus's greed had overcome any misgivings. For wealth and power, the man would do anything.

Unlike most men, Korthac had no interest in gold and gemstones, mere tools to bind men to him. Only power, the power to rule everyone, to command their lives or their deaths, meant anything to Korthac. That destiny had guided him even before he grew to manhood, and he would not turn away from it now.

"Tomorrow we will leave this place and begin our journey east. We'll take a few villagers with us as slaves, to carry food and water. I will allow you and your men to kill the rest, as revenge for capturing you. Besides, it's best that no one know from whence we came. As we travel, I will tell you how I will capture this Orak." Korthac changed the subject with a wave of his hand. "But now, tell me more about Eskkar, this wanderer turned mighty ruler. I must learn the ways of my enemy."

"Lord, I've told you everything I can remember."

"I am sure you can remember much more, Ariamus. Or do you need some encouragement?" Korthac smiled once again and leaned back against the tree. "Take your time and start at the beginning. Tell me of when you came to Orak, what you did, how you became captain of the guard."

Korthac had heard the story several times already, but each reiteration added some new insight, some further detail that helped him better understand this land and its people. He called out for ale, all this miserable village could provide in the way of strong spirits. A woman appeared with a jar and two wooden cups. Kneeling, she filled his cup, then did the same for Ariamus before returning to the shadows.

He watched Ariamus staring into his ale cup. The man wanted to drink, but he'd learned his place and his manners in the last few weeks. Only after his new master had taken a sip would the man drink from his own cup. Korthac drank a mouthful of the bitter barley brew, then waited until Ariamus drank, gulping loudly until he lowered his empty cup.

"Now, Ariamus, tell me again of this barbarian and the slave girl who bewitched him. They stand in my way… our way now. So tell me everything, every little story you can remember, about Eskkar and his witch-wife."

1

3157 *B.C.E.*—*The City of Akkad (Orak), on the eastern bank of the Tigris River . . .*

Lord Eskkar of Akkad pulled down hard on the restive horse, as impatient as its master to begin the long-awaited campaign. He had planned to be on his way soon after sunup. Instead a missing horse, then a broken pack strap, and finally two soldiers still befuddled from too much drinking the night before prevented the early departure. At last his embarrassed subcommanders signaled their readiness.

Eskkar gritted his teeth as he yanked on the halter, turned the horse around, and took the first steps to reclaim the countryside from roving bands of marauders. A few cheers came from the small crowd of Akkadians who bothered to watch his departure, but most just stared in silence. Less than two months ago every one of them had praised his name to the gods, acclaiming him ruler of

Akkad for saving their lives and their homes. But already many chaffed at the very restrictions he established to protect them.

As he led his soldiers through the city's gates and out onto the plain, Eskkar knew that, at this moment, he cared more about getting out of Akkad than pacifying the surrounding farmlands. With each step away from the city he felt his responsibilities lessen and he longed to put his horse to the gallop. That would have been unfair to the seventy soldiers, only twenty of them mounted, who marched behind him. Eskkar restrained both himself and the eager horse until he reached the first of the low hills about a mile away from Akkad.

He turned his mount aside from the trail and urged the animal up the steepest part of the slope. At the crest, the horse snorted from the climb, then restlessly pawed the earth, as if to say it wanted to race across the soft grassland, not scramble up rocky and slippery inclines. Eskkar first studied the ragged column of soldiers moving beneath him. A small force for what needed to be done, but all that could be spared to drive off the marauders and bandits who had plagued the land for almost a year, thriving in the chaos caused by the barbarian invasion. The dreaded Alur Meriki horsemen had passed on, but turmoil and anarchy marked their passage throughout the land.

Eskkar shifted his gaze to the river, only a few hundred paces away. The midmorning sun reflected off the slow-moving waters of the Tigris, giving the wide waterway a rare pale blue tint. He took a deep breath, filling his lungs with the clean air that blew across the water, glad to be rid of the city-smell of too many men and animals living too close together. Eskkar looked back toward Akkad nestling against the great curve of the river. The tall wooden gates remained open, and rising from one of the towers that guarded them, a large banner floated in the breeze. Eskkar could just make out the stalking lion embroidered on it. The lion spirit now protected the new city, the city that had changed him from a mere soldier to captain of the guard to a fighting leader, and nearly killed him in the process.

Another horse scampered up to the hilltop and his bodyguard halted beside him. "Do you miss it already, Captain?" Grond used the old title for his commander.

"Akkad? Do I miss the stink and the noise? Or the whining and scheming? No, the place can fall to the ground for all I care. But I haven't gone a mile yet and already I'm worrying about Trella."

"Lady Trella will be well protected by the soldiers," Grond said patiently.

"I suppose she'll be safe enough for a month or so." All this had been discussed many times in the last few days. Gatus, Eskkar's second in command and the oldest of the soldiers, doted on Trella as if she were his own daughter. Officially, Gatus would command during Eskkar's absence, but everyone knew the real ruler of Akkad would be Lady Trella. Gatus, busy as ever with the training of new recruits, would do nothing without her approval.

Nevertheless, Eskkar stared at the city, with its hastily built walls that had withstood brutal attacks and still showed scars from the recent conflict. This very hilltop had served as a watching post for the five thousand barbarians who laid siege to Akkad for almost two months. A few hundred paces behind him lay the remains of the

besiegers' camp. He and his men would pass through it as
they journeyed northward.

A tug on the halter, and Eskkar's horse shifted to face
northward. He'd seen the remnants of the onslaught, still
visible everywhere around him, often enough in the last
few weeks. Blackened circles of fire-split stones still
contained scattered ashes marking the residue of hundreds
of campfires. Animal bones lay everywhere, moved and
displaced by dogs, birds, and carrion eaters. The
scavengers had gorged themselves for many weeks on the
battle-dead.

By now the easy pickings had disappeared, the bones
gnawed clean. Human and animal waste would provide
less tasty tidbits for several more weeks or until the rains
came. The city's inhabitants had gathered anything of
value weeks ago. They'd searched through whatever the
barbarians left behind, looking for whatever they could use
or sell. More than a dozen large mounds marked the burial
places of the enemy dead The common burial pits
contained those who had survived the battles but died from
their wounds, or the dead deemed important enough to be
carried back to the barbarian camp and interred in a mass
grave before being covered over.

Those barbarians who died assaulting the wall suffered
the final indignity—abandoned by their clan and dumped
in the river by their enemies, to be carried wherever by the
whim of the gods, assigned a bitter fate in the afterlife.
Everyone knew that without a proper burial, the spirits of
the unburied dead would wander beneath the earth for
eternity, prey for the shades and demons who would live
off their tormented souls.

"How many years before all this disappears," Grond said, "before the grass covers everything?"

His bodyguard's question echoed Eskkar's own thoughts. "Probably two, maybe three years," he said. "Farmers will be unearthing debris longer than that. You don't fight battles like that and not leave traces everywhere."

Eskkar turned his gaze back toward the city. His city. He could make out the scars on the walls from the thousands of arrows launched against them. Even today, almost two months after the barbarians had departed, men still labored on Akkad's repairs. So much had been destroyed, but the city and its people had survived. Most of them, Eskkar remembered soberly. Many good and brave men had died in its defense. He took comfort in knowing that the bodies of his soldiers had received the proper rites, and their phantoms would not be condemned to wander in the darkness.

Eskkar shook the black thoughts from his head. Better to think of the future than the past. "We'd best be on our way, Grond. Half the day's passed, and we've a long way to travel."

They wheeled their horses away from Akkad and rode down the slope. The horses wanted to stretch their legs as much as their masters, and the two men soon caught up to the rear of the soldiers. Once there, however, Eskkar slowed his mount, to ride behind the column instead of at its head, as was the usual custom. From the rear, he could observe the men, see how they marched, even encourage them if need be. One lesson Eskkar had grasped very well in the last year's training and fighting was that he needed his soldiers' loyalty as much as their skill.

Aware of his gaze, the soldiers at the rear of the column straightened up and quickened their pace. Eskkar knew the new men thought him a legend, the fierce warrior who had defeated the mighty Alur Meriki. The more experienced veterans knew better. They understood exactly how close they'd come to being overwhelmed by the barbarians. These recent recruits needed to master the trade of soldiering. They'd better learn quickly, Eskkar thought. They might be fighting for their lives in a week or two.

"What do you think of the men?" Eskkar said, glancing at his companion. Grond had been a slave in a distant land to the west before coming to Akkad. He'd fought well during the siege and earned the rank of subcommander, but now he filled the role of Eskkar's bodyguard and friend. A big man, nearly as tall as his Captain, Grond stood even wider across the shoulders, with massive arms that, not too long ago, had carried Eskkar to safety as easily as one might carry a child. In the last few months, the former slave had saved Eskkar's life more than once.

Grond took his time before replying. "They'll do, I suppose. But you should have brought more veterans, Captain. Seventy isn't going to be enough to reclaim a hundred and fifty miles of rough country, not with almost half of the men newly trained."

Eskkar didn't want to start that argument again, especially when he'd insisted enough seasoned men must stay behind to guard the walls and patrol the land to the south. He didn't think the barbarian horde that attacked Akkad would return, but Eskkar had too much respect for their fighting abilities and their hatred of defeat to take any chances.

"All we'll be doing is chasing after stray bandits and looters, Grond. It's not as if we'll be facing hardened warriors in a pitched battle. Besides, the recruits need battle experience, and this is the best way to get it."

In addition to the soldiers, the column included a dozen camp boys to act as servants to those who could afford to feed them. Five liverymen looked after the fifteen pack animals and the twenty horses, and three younger sons from Akkad's leading merchants represented their father's trading interests. They would help reestablish local trade wherever possible. Akkad's ruling council had also assigned two scribes to help Eskkar. They would record anything of interest and keep track of any goods or loot Eskkar and his men might acquire.

He hadn't wanted to take the scribes, but the elders had insisted. How else, they had asked, could everything be accounted for? Eskkar had looked across the table at Trella, saw her nod her head, and gave in. Now he wondered if he had enough soldiers. It seemed such a small force to establish control of all the villages and farms north of Akkad.

"Did you hear anything more about Dilgarth?" Grond said, changing the subject.

"Another trader arrived just before sunset yesterday," Eskkar said. "He claimed he saw other wayfarers being robbed near the village. There may be several bands of thieves attacking and robbing travelers on the road between here and Dilgarth."

The small village of Dilgarth lay more than forty miles north of Akkad. Eskkar planned to pass through the place on their way to Bisitun, a much larger village that was his main destination. He intended to sweep the land clear of bandits and marauders between Akkad and Bisitun, to protect the hundreds of farmers and herders who produced the food that Akkad and its busy traders depended upon.

"Well, we should be able to finish off a handful of robbers easily enough," Grond said.

"Yes, after fighting the barbarians, a few bandits shouldn't present any problems," Eskkar said. "And once we've taken control of the land around Bisitun, the countryside should start settling down."

"I hope they brew some decent ale in Bisitun," Grond said. "I'm thirsty already."

"They do," Eskkar said with a laugh. "Just don't try and drink it all."

The soldiers made good time that first day, the men glad to stretch their legs, out of the city and into the fresh air that already bore a hint of the autumn's coming coolness. By the time they made their first camp, Eskkar relaxed enough to smile and joke with his men, enjoying the freedom of the trail and putting all thoughts of Akkad and its intrigues behind him.

In his heart, he felt glad to be away, free to be himself without worrying about what some merchant or tradesman would think about him. For the last few months, he'd struggled with his changing role. No longer merely a soldier defending the village, Eskkar now had to rule nearly three thousand people, all of them demanding immediate attention to their particular problem. Nothing in his years of wandering had prepared him for such responsibility. Even with Trella's help, the weight of constant decision-making strained his patience. Unlike the preparation for the siege, when he could just make military decisions, now every conflicting claim seemed to require endless hours of discussion, which invariably turned into arguing and complaining that left neither side satisfied.

Eskkar had believed he could deal with his new position, but in the last few weeks, doubt had crept in, and he found himself growing more and more irritable and short-tempered. And that, he realized, made dealing with everyone even more difficult. So he felt glad to put down that mantle, even temporarily, and deal with something familiar—like ridding the land of thieves and murderers.

Out here in the countryside, among his men, he could be a soldier once again. That satisfaction, combined with the fresh air, the rough-cooked food, and the tiredness from walking and riding all day, let him enjoy a good night's sleep for the first time in weeks.

The next morning Eskkar rose before dawn, happy that his body remembered the old ways. He demanded the soldiers be on their way an hour after sunup, and threatened to leave anyone and anything behind that wasn't ready. The men had scarcely enough time to eat a hasty meal, care for the animals, and pack their goods before the march resumed. Almost immediately, complaints of sore feet and tired muscles rang out as they continued their way north, still following the east bank of the great river Tigris.

Today Eskkar ranged ahead of the main group, accompanied by Grond and six of his horsemen. They rode more toward the east, away from the river and into the countryside. Eskkar wanted to see for himself the devastation the barbarians had caused. Everywhere the scattered homes and fields lay barren, the crops burned. The grass had just started to return, having first been burnt by the villagers to deny food and fodder to the approaching enemy, and then the fresh growth overgrazed by the barbarian herds. This winter's harvest would be small. Still, the farmers considered themselves fortunate. At least they'd have a chance to get enough of the precious and carefully preserved seeds planted in time for next season.

As they rode farther to the northeast the farms grew smaller and more isolated, and they encountered fewer people. Many fled at the sight of them. Others stood their ground, hands clenched nervously on crude weapons or farm tools. When they learned who Eskkar was, and that he meant them no harm, they relaxed their vigilance. From these farmers he learned that the small village of Dilgarth, now only a few dozen miles ahead, had in fact been captured by bandits more than a week ago. The tales of Dilgarth's plight grew worse and worse as Eskkar's band encountered more people wandering in the ravaged fields. His face turned grim once again.

Dispatching a rider to return to the main column and order them to speed up their pace, Eskkar and his men rode as hard as they could push the horses, alternating between a fast walk and a canter, toward the village of Dilgarth. The sun had moved well past noon when they rounded a bend in the river and saw the village less than a mile away. While they rested their horses, a party of armed men rode leisurely out of the village, heading north.

"Looks like they knew we were coming," Grond commented. "Should we give chase?"

Eskkar stretched upright on his horse, counting the

distant riders, his lips moving silently. Twelve men had
ridden out, more than twice his own number and on fresh
horses. "No, we'll wait here until the rest of the men get
here." He could say that easily now, without having to
worry some might think him afraid to fight. No one doubted
his courage. And it would make a better impression on
Dilgarth's inhabitants if he entered with the whole troop.

It took another three hours before the rest of the soldiers
arrived, breathing hard and complaining of the quickened
pace. Eskkar gave them no rest. He entered the village at
the head of his men an hour before sunset.

Dilgarth was a small place, with fewer than forty mud-
and-reed houses, none with a second story. Eskkar had
visited it several times in the last few years, tracking
runaway slaves or thieves. Before the barbarians came,
more than a hundred and fifty people lived here. All of
those had fled their homes, most going to Akkad, then
known as Orak, though many passed across the river or
continued south. Some of those original inhabitants might
have already returned, but most would have abandoned
their homes for good.

Eskkar understood Dilgarth's importance. The last
sizable resting place before Akkad, the fields surrounding
Dilgarth supported many crops, with soil almost as fertile
as that surrounding Akkad. Perhaps as important,
Dilgarth's inhabitants had learned special skills in working
with their principal harvest, flax, a plant grown not for
food, but for its thin, durable fibers that could be woven
into linen and other materials.

Before the invasion the local farmers and villagers had
selected the finest fibers and woven them into quality linen

cloth. The merchants in Akkad wanted to know when the supply of linen would be restored. The barbarian incursion had created a shortage of skilled craftsmen who could fashion linen into fine tunics, dresses, or skirts. Dilgarth had thrived for years before the barbarians swept through the land. There was no reason it shouldn't be prosperous again.

As Eskkar and his soldiers rode in, less than a dozen men stood scattered about, watching the visitors in silence as they filed into the village. None greeted them. Those few that met Eskkar's eyes looked sullen or suspicious. Everyone's clothing looked ragged and filthy, covering bodies thin from lack of food. Many had bruises on their faces or bodies. He didn't see any women or children.

Eskkar rode down the narrow lane until he reached the tiny marketplace, located at the rear of the village. He saw no carts with goods for sale, no cooking fires accompanied by the smell of roasting meat, not even any dogs running loose to yap incessantly and nip at the heels of his men's horses. Once the dwellers of Dilgarth had lived happy and content with their lives. Now its few inhabitants had little more than rags to cover their gaunt bodies. Those who possessed anything more had lost it, either in the initial barbarian onslaught or to the departed bandits.

Without some hope for the future, these villagers might abandon their homes and take to the roads, perhaps even head toward Akkad. His city needed tradesmen and craftsmen, plus a steady supply of flax, not more refugees.

He took all this in as his horse reached the village well. He remained astride until his men, horses, and pack animals filled most of the square. The village's center had barely enough room for all of them, but they stood patiently, waiting for his order that would give them leave to put down their burdens. Unbidden, Trella's words came into his mind. "As you won over the hearts of your soldiers, you must win over those whom you seek to rule."

Eskkar turned toward Sisuthros, his second in command, standing in front of the men, awaiting his orders. "Sisuthros, rest the men here, until you find places for them to sleep. Keep part of the square clear." His eyes turned to Grond. "Gather all the villagers and bring them to me. I want to hear what's happened to them since they returned to Dilgarth. Don't alarm them, just bring them."

His order to rest the soldiers, rather than dismiss them for the night, meant they could put down their burdens and sit on the ground, but little else. Eskkar didn't want them wandering around, poking into people's houses, frightening the villagers even further until he knew exactly what new calamity had taken place in Dilgarth.

He swung down from the horse, handing the halter to one of the camp boys, as Sisuthros began shouting orders. Some of the soldiers left the ranks, taking the horses to the crude corral to water and feed them. Sisuthros gave further instructions, and the majority of the soldiers, along with their animals and supplies, wedged themselves around the sides of the square, leaving the center empty.

Eskkar paced over to the rough stone well in the center of the marketplace and stood there, waiting. His mind tried to sort out what had gone on here. Except on the battlefield, where he trusted his instincts, he no longer made decisions in haste. He had learned to use whatever time he had to think things through. That included understanding what he wanted to accomplish, and what words he would use to obtain his goal. So he stood there, imagining what had befallen the village, using the time to prepare and anticipate what he would do after he heard their story.

By the time Grond and a few soldiers finished searching the huts and rounding up all the inhabitants, Eskkar had his thoughts in hand. Grond escorted the last few stragglers into the market just as Eskkar ended his count. Thirty-six people stood before him. Fourteen were men or older boys fit for manual labor. Many of the women shook with fear as they gazed at the crowd of soldiers surrounding them. Others had the look of hopelessness on their downcast faces. Eskkar noted the signs of repeated rape and beatings easily enough. He didn't see any tears. Days or weeks of weeping had dried their eyes. The women had reached the point where even death might look inviting.

"Who speaks for the village?" he asked, keeping his voice calm. Silence greeted his words, and he repeated the question.

"Those who speak for the village are all dead, noble." The words belonged to an old woman, gray-haired and stooped from laboring in the fields, almost invisible in the center of the crowd. A little girl of three or four seasons clung fearfully to her hand.

"Are there any village elders, then?"

"All dead as well, noble." Her voice sounded weary, without any emotion, but her gaze met his without fear.

Eskkar scanned the crowd but every face stayed downcast, no one willing to say anything. He felt his patience wearing thin but kept his temper as he walked toward them. They shrank out of his way until he stood in front of the old woman. "And what is your name, elder?" Eskkar kept his voice low and his words polite.

"I am called Nisaba, noble one. As for these others, they are all afraid to speak to you, lest they be killed by the bandits when they return. They said they would come back as soon as you are gone."

"But you're not afraid, Nisaba?"

"They have already killed my two sons. My life is finished, and I am too old for their sport. The most they can do is kill me."

"No one is going to kill you, Nisaba, I promise you that. You are under my protection now."

He took her free hand and led her back to the well, the child following along, eyes wide and still holding fast to the old woman's hand. "Sit down, elder." He unslung his sword from his back, then joined her on the ground, sitting on the dirt in front of her and placing the scabbard flat across his knees. "Do you know who I am?"

She took her time answering him, as she gathered what was left of her ragged dress about her. "You are the Noble Eskkar, and, for now, the ruler of Orak."

He couldn't resist a smile at her use of the words "for now." In the last few months he had often thought the same thing. "It is no longer called Orak, Nisaba. Now it is the City of Akkad."

"Orak . . . Akkad . . . it makes no difference, noble one. It was called Orak when I was a child, and I see no need to change the names of things."

Eskkar tugged at the thin beard on his chin. Trella had suggested the change of names, from Orak to Akkad, to help the people identify themselves with Eskkar and a new beginning. Eskkar had warned her that the switch might not be as smooth out in the countryside as within Akkad's walls.

"Well, elder, we'll talk more of that later. For now, you are the elder of the village of Dilgarth and you will speak for the village." He lifted his eyes over her head to watch the reaction of the villagers. "Is there any other that thinks he should be the village elder?"

No one challenged his decision. "Nisaba, Dilgarth is under the protection of the City of Akkad, and all here will obey the laws of Akkad from now on." Eskkar raised his voice, and addressed Dilgarth's inhabitants. "Akkad's soldiers will soon clear the land of bandits, and you and your families will be safe in your shops and on your farms. The trade of flax and other goods will resume with Akkad, and, as before, you will be fairly paid for your goods. If you have complaints, bring them to your village elder," he nodded toward Nisaba, "and she will present them to the soldiers stationed here or bring them to Akkad. If necessary, I will make the final decision. The customs of Akkad will apply to all equally, and Nisaba and the soldiers will see that they are enforced fairly."

Eskkar felt glad to have that formality over with, though he doubted many understood what it really meant. Not that it mattered. Over the next few months, everyone in Dilgarth would soon appreciate the stability and security Akkad could provide. He returned his gaze to the new village elder. "Now, tell me about the bandits that rode off when we arrived."

The story came out slowly, as Eskkar's commanders

gathered close around their leader, anxious to hear the tale. The rest of the soldiers strained to hear Nisaba's soft words, and for a long time the only other sound came from the occasional movement of one of the horses crowded together across the square.

Two months ago, the villagers began returning to Dilgarth after the barbarian migration had moved on, slipping back to their houses by ones and twos as they started to rebuild their homes and look to their crops and animals. They had rejoiced when they heard that the invaders had been defeated and driven off from Akkad, and even more farmers and craftsmen had returned.

But a little less than two weeks ago, while Eskkar and his men remained locked behind their walls, still afraid to venture forth until the barbarians moved out of striking distance from the city, a band of about twenty bandits had ridden into Dilgarth in the middle of the night, forcing the small fence and killing any who opposed them. By dawn, they had taken what women they wanted and looted the village.

Nisaba thought they might move on after a few days of pleasure, but these raiders seemed content to have the villagers gather and prepare food for them while they enjoyed their wives and daughters. The bandits remained in the village, a few now and then riding out on small raiding parties, looking to rob any farmers trying to work their lands or searching for any weak or isolated travelers on the road to Akkad.

The intruders had been cunning enough to kill any who attempted to escape to Akkad, and so only rumors had reached the city of their activity, though enough travelers had been robbed and attacked on the roads. The bandits had commandeered all the local food while the villagers went hungry. This morning, a little after dawn, a rider brought word of Eskkar's approach. They had taken their time before riding off, insolently waiting until the soldiers from Akkad had been spotted less than a mile from the village.

When Nisaba finished, the crowd remained silent. Eskkar knew that everyone, soldiers and villagers alike, waited to see what he would do. Not two full days' march from Akkad, and already he had a problem. Dilgarth was an insignificant place, a mere way station on the road to Akkad, and no one, soldier or villager, would be surprised if he left it and its misery behind. Eskkar had urgent business farther north, at Bisitun, and he could ill afford the time to scour the countryside looking for a small party of well-mounted and well-armed bandits, or to worry about the fate of a few pathetic villagers. Eventually, the bandits would leave the area when they had exhausted its food or tired of its women. Or when Eskkar established control of the land to the north. So in a matter of days or weeks, the problem here would be solved even if he did nothing.

Nevertheless, these villagers had now come under his protection. If Eskkar could not look after these wretched people by killing a few brigands, then his own authority would be little better than any bandit leader.

But as long as he stayed here, the bandits would not return, and he could not remain here long. Nor could he leave behind enough men to protect Dilgarth properly. He would need all of his soldiers in the north. If he rode on, the bandits would return as soon as he had passed on. Without sufficient men, and even more important, without enough horses, he couldn't chase after the bandits either. Besides, Eskkar didn't know how many men they had, and he might soon find himself fighting a force equal to or greater than his twenty horsemen. So he had a problem with no easy solution, but one he needed to resolve, and quickly.

Eskkar looked at Nisaba, and he could almost see the same thoughts running through her mind. "Elder, I will think about this for a while. You and the others must eat. My men will share their food with you." He looked at Sisuthros, seated a few steps away, making sure his second in command understood the request. "Then we will talk again, Nisaba."

He stood up, and his men began to move. He heard Sisuthros give the orders to establish the camp, post the sentries, and feed the villagers. Leaders of ten assigned sleeping places to their men while others saw to the pack animals. With all the activity underway, Eskkar entered the village's largest dwelling, the home that the bandit leader had taken for his own headquarters.

Inside, Eskkar found the floor covered with discarded bones and shreds of cooked and raw flesh scattered among broken pots and furniture. Flies buzzed about, feeding on the refuse. One corner had served as a casual latrine. Blood smears covered one wall and the dirt floor in the far corner was crusted red, either with wine or more blood. An odor of something rotten hung in the air, overpowering even the smell of urine.

Ignoring it all, Eskkar found an upended stool, picked it up, and sat down facing the doorway. He didn't look up when Grond and two soldiers entered and began cleaning up the place. One of the men had found a broom, and the other carried a pail of clean sand to dump over the urine-soaked dirt. They all worked quietly, not wanting to disturb their leader. By the time they finished, Sisuthros entered, followed by one of the camp boys and two women from the village, carrying platters with some dried meat, bread, and dates, as well as a crude carved goblet containing wine. The food and wine came from Akkad; the bandits had taken what little food remained in Dilgarth when they left.

Eskkar looked up as one of the women placed the food in front of him. "I want these bandits dead, Sisuthros."

"They're probably already gone, Captain," Sisuthros answered cautiously. He had heard that tone of voice before and knew what it meant. "They've no reason to hang around here. The place is stripped bare. There isn't even any more food to be had. And the women . . ." He shrugged.

Eskkar's second in command was a sturdy young man of twenty-three seasons, seven seasons younger than his commander, but he had fought his way through the long campaign against the Alur Meriki and had earned the men's respect. More important, Sisuthros had a good head on his shoulders. Eskkar planned to leave him in charge when they reached their destination farther north, the village of Bisitun.

"They'll be back," Eskkar said quietly. "There're still some vegetables in the fields and they'll want to take some villagers with them as slaves, either to use or to sell, before they abandon this place. They left here only minutes before we arrived. They didn't even take any of the women."

"They seem to know our plans well enough," Sisuthros said. "They probably guessed we don't want to stay here. We could leave enough men behind to protect the village, at least for a while."

"If we leave men behind, we'll have to leave some horses as well," Grond argued. "And we don't have enough horses as it is."

A shortage of horseflesh had plagued Eskkar even before the siege of Akkad began.

"Nor do we know how many men to leave behind." Eskkar took a sip from the wine cup. "If we leave too few, they could be overrun." He shook his head. "No, I don't want to waste time and men defending Dilgarth. I want these bandits dead when they return from the east."

"Why east, Captain?" Grond asked. "Why not north, or south?"

"They can't cross the river here, not without boats. It's too wide. They can't enter Akkad. Gatus would seize any force of well-mounted and armed men loaded with loot, so they won't go south. And we're moving north, so they won't like having a large force of men following behind them. That leaves east, the land that the barbarians stripped bare. If they're heading that way, even for a few days, they'll need to get as much food, loot, and slaves as they can carry."

Neither man said anything, which merely meant they didn't see any immediate flaw in his logic. Eskkar had established certain rules of command, and one of these insisted that his subcommanders speak up freely regarding his plans and ideas. It was another of the many painful lessons Eskkar learned in the last six months—that it was more important to get everyone's ideas and comments out in the open, rather than have to make all the decisions himself.

"So that means they're probably watching the place," Grond said. "They'll wait until we move on, make certain we're gone, then come back, take as many villagers, food, and whatever else they want, and be off."

"Why couldn't they have taken what they wanted today?" Sisuthros asked.

"Because they don't have enough horses for the slaves and goods themselves," Eskkar answered, glad that he had asked himself the same question. "And they weren't sure if we would chase after them or not. If they were burdened with slaves and loot, we could have caught up with them easily enough. No, they'll be back. Some fool even said as much to Nisaba."

Eskkar looked toward the doorway, making certain the sentry stood in his place before continuing. He didn't want any villager to overhear his words. Nevertheless he lowered his voice to almost a whisper. "This is what we'll do."

Like all of Eskkar's plans, it seemed simple enough. And like most of his plans, there was plenty that could go wrong. Sisuthros first tried to argue him out of it, then offered to take his place, but Eskkar wouldn't hear of it.

"I know what you're saying makes sense, Sisuthros," Eskkar said, putting an end to the argument. "But I'll be safe enough. And this is something I want to take care of myself."

Sisuthros made one more attempt. "Before we left, Lady Trella asked me to make sure you didn't take any unnecessary chances." When he saw that even Trella's name wasn't going to change his captain's mind, he changed his tactic. "At least keep Grond here with you. By the gods, Eskkar, they may have more men than you."

In the old days Eskkar would have raised his voice and demanded obedience. Now he made his voice firm and his words final. "If we do it right, they won't be expecting trouble, and I'll have trained men who should easily be able to take care of a dozen or so bandits."

Grond and Sisuthros both started to protest, but Eskkar held up his hand.

"Enough arguing. Let's eat in peace," Eskkar went on, "then we'll select the men and work out the preparations. When we're ready, I'll speak to Nisaba. She and the villagers will have to play their part as well."

The two subcommanders looked at each other. They had made their arguments and heard his decision. Now the task ahead of them was to make sure their captain succeeded. They nodded their heads in resignation, and each man started thinking about his part of the plan.

2

An hour after dawn, the Akkadians marched out of Dilgarth. The villagers stood around sullenly, watching them go and waiting until the soldiers were well on their way before turning to their own tasks. Some of the men went down to the fields, others to the river. The women soon followed their men out of the ruined gate, to kneel in the mud and repair the vital irrigation ditches that carried precious water from the river to the ever-thirsty crops. A thin plume of smoke rose up from the smith's fire, and the carpenter's hammer rang out as another day's work in the rebuilding of the village began. Like the bandits, the soldiers had come and the soldiers had gone. With no other option, the villagers would attempt once again to get on with their lives.

The morning passed uneventfully. Noon arrived, and the villagers trudged back to their homes, to eat a meager meal and take a brief rest before returning to their labor. At midafternoon, despite the sun still high in the sky, they began moving back to the village, carrying their burdens or tools, walking slowly, heads downcast, their exhausted stares fixed on the dust of the earth.

When the last of them passed inside the gate, Eskkar stepped back from the edge of the square. From there he could just see the village entrance. He returned to the village elder's house and pushed open the door. For most of the day he had stood guard over the house and its eighteen occupants, mostly children or those too old or ill to work, making sure only his soldiers had gone forth to the fields. Eskkar didn't want to take any chance the villagers would betray him, either willingly or with a knife at their throat. His men had kept track of the women they took with them into the fields. Only those Nisaba vouched for were allowed to depart, and then only in close contact with Eskkar's men.

The rest of Dilgarth's men, dressed in soldiers' garb, had marched off with the rest of Eskkar's force in the morning. The tallest "soldier" in the column wore Eskkar's tunic and sat astride the captain's horse. That soldier had ridden at the head of the column, between Grond and Sisuthros, as the Akkadians departed the village and continued their northward journey. If the bandits had left behind a spy, he would report that Eskkar personally led the column.

If the spy could count, he could also declare that all of the soldiers went north. At least Eskkar hoped his departure would be reported that way. Meanwhile, the soldiers would march north until they made camp at dusk. Then the twenty horsemen would turn about and begin retracing the journey back to the village. With luck they would arrive before midnight, though Eskkar expected everything to be long over by then.

Eskkar had stayed behind with ten men, the only number he could match against the able-bodied men of Dilgarth. But he selected some of the finest fighters and archers in his troop, all eager to prove themselves at Eskkar's side, to show themselves worthy of the Hawk Clan.

In Eskkar's rise to power, many of the old ways had fallen aside and many new customs created. After one of his earliest battles, Eskkar established a new kind of clan, a clan not of blood or place, but one of fighting brotherhood. Since then, every Hawk Clan member had sworn an oath of loyalty first to Eskkar and then to each other.

In the subsequent fighting against the barbarians, the Hawk Clan grew in number, though many died in the final assault. Only those who had proven themselves in battle could be nominated for entrance to the Hawk Clan. If accepted, their past, their homeland, their old clan did not matter. Now men from the corners of the earth, many once homeless and friendless, had a clan of their own, a new family, where all stood equal in honor. The Hawk symbol grew into a mark of valor and prestige, and any soldier worthy of his sword hungered to wear the Hawk emblem. Though they numbered less than thirty, these elite soldiers formed the backbone of Eskkar's subcommanders and bodyguards, the core of fighting men who supported Eskkar's power.

Each Hawk Clan member wore the emblem proudly on his left shoulder, so that all could see the mark of bravery and distinction. Any of Eskkar's soldiers would jump at the chance to demonstrate his courage and worth, and how better to do it than to fight at Eskkar's side. Five of the ten soldiers who stayed with Eskkar belonged to the Hawk

Clan. The others hoped to earn that honor in any upcoming battle.

Without any way to know if the village remained under the bandits' scrutiny, Eskkar ordered the men back from the fields early. He didn't want the bandits riding in while his few soldiers were scattered in the fields, or heading back to the village, to be killed or captured by ones and twos. Besides, his men would need some time to rest, to prepare their weapons, and take their stations. Eskkar hoped that the bandits, if they were watching, wouldn't think the early return of any significance.

Hamati, the only other senior man in the group, walked to his captain's side. Hamati had stopped only long enough to take a deep drink of water at the well and to wash the mud and muck from his hands and face.

"Marduk's curses on these farmers, Captain, and their filthy way of life. I haven't worked so hard in years."

Legend told that Marduk, ruler of the heavens and father of the gods, had created the first farmer from river mud to till the soil. Farmers asked his blessing for their crops, even while they swore at him for making farming such a difficult labor.

"You're soft from too much easy living, Hamati," Eskkar said with a laugh. "Not even a full day in the fields and you're complaining. Be grateful you don't have to do it each day. Did the women give you any trouble?"

"No, but they kept looking over their shoulders toward the hills. Half of them wanted to run back to the village and the other half wanted to hide in the fields or along the river."

A few nervous women wouldn't arouse anyone's

suspicions. After what Dilgarth had been through, it would be natural enough for them to keep their eyes out for bandits and robbers. "Make sure your men are fed and ready, Hamati. If I were the bandits, I'd be here an hour or two before sunset. That will give them enough time before dark to gather what they need and be gone."

Or they might not come at all. Eskkar worried they could already be far away, or be planning to come back in a few days or a week's time. He had tried to put himself in their place and hoped they would do what he would have done. If he were wrong, if they had moved on . . . three days out of Akkad, and he'd look like a fool in front of his men, outsmarted by a few lazy bandits. He resolutely put the thought away. The afternoon sun promised several more hours of daylight. If they didn't come today, his horsemen would be back tonight, and he could ride out and search for them tomorrow.

If Hamati had any doubts of his own, he didn't voice them. Instead, he moved off to see to the other soldiers.

Eskkar turned to find Nisaba standing before him. She, like Hamati, was covered with dirt from the fields. The women had rebuilt an irrigation ditch a few hundred paces from the village. Even in the best of times, ditches needed constant repair as they channeled the life-giving water to the growing crops. "What do you need, elder?"

"Nothing, noble. I have already offered prayers for your success in battle. Kill all of them, noble. Avenge my sons."

Eskkar smiled at her. "Take the bravest women and keep them at work just beyond the village entrance, elder. The bandits might think it strange if they see no one outside the village. At the first sign of trouble, return to this house and bar the door."

As soon as the meaningless words left his lips, he wanted to recall them. If he and his men failed, a wooden stick across a door wouldn't stop any bandit.

She bowed and left him. He strode quickly through the tiny square, making sure the men stood ready and that everyone understood the plan. That earned him a disapproving look from Hamati, who had just performed the same rite. Nevertheless Eskkar wanted to take no chances, and his concern showed each man how important their orders were.

In his successes against the Alur Meriki, Eskkar had learned no detail was too small to leave to chance, just as no order was too simple, but that some fool would forget it in the excitement of battle. Only when he felt sure everyone was ready and in place did he go to his own station near the main entrance. He'd assigned the best archers to Hamati. While Eskkar could shoot a fair shaft, he'd never managed to match the rapid-fire pace of his best trained men. Better to help hold the entryway, where his sword might prove useful.

Once a crude gate had stood there, more to keep tame animals in and wild creatures out at night, but the bandits wanted nothing to impede a quick entrance or exit from the village. So they knocked it down and used it as firewood.

After a few moments standing about, Eskkar realized he didn't have the patience to just wait there, where he couldn't see much of anything. Swearing under his breath, he returned to the elder's house, entered, and climbed the wooden ladder to the roof.

Mitrac, the youngest of Eskkar's archers, glanced up at

his captain's arrival. The youth reclined on his elbow, studying the approaches to the village, a blanket under him and his bow and two quivers of arrows close at hand. A long dagger, almost as long as the short swords the soldiers carried, rested on the blanket. His powerful bow stretched a foot taller than any that the soldiers carried, and Mitrac's arrows were not only three inches longer, but slightly thicker—all marked with a red streak near the feathered end.

The boy's face looked even younger than his seasons, and Eskkar had to remind himself that no one who killed an enemy in battle could be considered a boy, let alone someone who had killed as many as Mitrac.

"Is something wrong, Captain?" Mitrac said, surprised at Eskkar's unexpected visit. "I thought you would be at the gate."

Eskkar sat down at the roof's edge. "No, Mitrac, I just want to see what's happening, and I could see nothing from the gate." Looking out over the flimsy palisade, Eskkar saw a half-dozen women working on one of the closest irrigation channels. Part of the embankment had collapsed, either of its own accord, or because some bandits had ridden their horses through the soft sides.

Three women stood in the ditch, in brown water reaching their knees, as they scooped the mud from the channel back onto the embankment. Only one had a shovel. The others used clay shards or even their hands to pick up the mud and pack it into place. As Eskkar watched, Nisaba came into view and stood at the edge of the ditch. She would be trying to reassure the women and keep them at their task. The village had to appear as normal as possible to the returning bandits.

"The women are frightened, Captain," Mitrac offered. "They keep looking to the hills."

"Well, they've been raped and beaten enough times." He turned to the young archer. "Are you nervous as well, Mitrac?"

"No, Captain, not as long as you're here. Where you go, I can follow. You always know what to do."

Eskkar smiled at the boy's trust. Mitrac and his bow had probably killed more barbarians than anyone else in Akkad. Eskkar hoped the young man's confidence in his leader wouldn't prove misplaced.

"Let's hope our luck holds, Mitrac." Part of Eskkar's reputation consisted of his ability to anticipate his enemies. Luck had favored him more than once in the last few months. Trella had suggested the idea of trying to think like his enemies, to put himself in their places and to anticipate their actions. No doubt those efforts had helped the gods bestow their good fortune upon him and his followers. Now that Eskkar thought about it, his young wife had turned out to be the greatest piece of luck in his life.

The women's shrill cries turned his head back to the countryside, to see the women fleeing toward the gate. It took a moment before he spotted the band of horsemen. The bandits were approaching more from the south than from the east, where Eskkar had anticipated they would appear. He watched them ride toward the village at an easy canter, cutting across the fields and angling toward the path that led to the village.

They would reach the trail in a few moments, and then

there would be only the last five hundred paces to the village entrance. They rode in barbarian fashion, shouting their war cries as they galloped, intending to frighten and panic the villagers as much as possible. Esskar stayed immobile only long enough to get an accurate count of the riders.

"Damn the gods! I count eighteen of them. Good hunting, Mitrac."

Without rising, Esskar slipped back down the ladder and raced to the main entrance. His ten men were going to be outnumbered. Today he would need all the luck the unpredictable gods could dispense. Esskar reached the gate as the last of the women, breathing hard, stumbled back into the village.

Then Nisaba walked through, still wiping her hands on her dress. She nodded at him as she passed by, letting him know that all the women had returned. Esskar took up a bow and nodded to the two soldiers on the other side of the gate. One of them had a bow in his hands, an arrow already fitted to the string, while the other man leaned against a low cart, the sort farmers used to display fruits and vegetables in the market. Esskar knelt down behind a similar cart, his shoulder against the rough stakes of the palisade, and peered through a crack between the logs. He ducked back his head and fitted an arrow to his string. The bandits were only moments away. The rush of battle tingled his nerves, and he felt his heart racing, the way it always did before a fight.

Shrilling a war cry, the first rider burst through the gate at a canter, a sword swinging easily in his hand. Esskar stayed down, counting the horses as they crossed into the village. Riders eased back their winded mounts, slowing as they entered Dilgarth. They didn't expect any resistance, and the women's panicky cries had already faded. Straggling behind, the last horse finally passed through the opening at barely a trot, its rider apparently more concerned with the animal's halter than his surroundings.

As soon as the last rider moved past the gate, Eskkar rose up and drew his bow. At the same moment he let fly the arrow at the man's back, a great shout came from the rear of the village, followed by the screams of frightened and wounded horses. Eskkar's target was less than twenty paces away, but the man's horse jumped at the noise, making for a poor shot that struck the rider low in the back instead of squarely between the shoulders. Nevertheless, at that range the shaft landed with enough force to knock the bandit off his horse.

The moment he loosed the missile, Eskkar turned and, keeping the bow in his left hand, pushed hard against the heavy cart that had concealed him, and shoved it with all his might into the space between the palisade. From the other side of the opening, the second cart bumped up against his own, blocking easy exit from the village.

Two waist-high carts didn't form much of a barricade. A really good horse and rider might even jump the obstacle, but Eskkar was determined to give no bandit an opportunity to test his horsemanship.

By the time Eskkar had strung another arrow to his bow, the second archer had fired four times at the distant horsemen, fitting and loosing shafts with a speed Eskkar couldn't hope to match. But hitting a moving, twisting target was another matter. Dust swirled everywhere, rising

high into the lane. At the rear of the village, the surprised
bandits had encountered Hamati and six of his men as they
entered the square. The soldiers would continue pouring
arrows into their confused targets as fast as they could.

Eskkar knew the bandit leader would have only a
moment to make his decision. If he dismounted and urged
his men forward, to attack Hamati's archers, things would
get very bloody. But mounted warriors rarely wanted to
fight on foot, and attacking an unknown number of men
standing behind a barricade of carts and tables wouldn't be
too appealing.

A mass of panicked horses broke out of the dust and
surged back toward the gate. From the hoofbeats, Eskkar
knew the bandit leader had decided to run, not fight.
Eskkar picked the man out, hanging low over his animal's
neck, shouting to his men, and urging his beast back toward
the village entrance.

Mitrac, standing exposed on the edge of the roof,
wreaked havoc with nearly each shaft he loosed. Only
three riders remained on their horses as they charged back
toward the main gate. Ignoring the other two, Eskkar
aimed at the leader and fired his arrow into the man's
horse, an easy target even Eskkar couldn't miss at such
close range. The animal screamed and twisted in its tracks
before stumbling to a halt, and its rider, clinging to the
wounded beast's neck, couldn't hold on and tumbled to the
ground. A second bandit went down, but the last rider put
his horse directly at the carts, and the animal leaped high
into the air. Horse and rider cleared the carts and landed
cleanly outside the fence. Then one of Mitrac's heavy
arrows struck the man high in the shoulder, and the bandit

pitched from his mount at the same moment the animal landed.

"Stop that man," Eskkar shouted. "Don't let him get away." Eskkar slid his own sword from its sheath. The bandit leader had fallen hard, but already he'd climbed to his feet, sword in his hand, and started racing toward the gate. The riderless horses all turned back at the sight of the carts, the dumb beasts racing back the way they'd come. For the moment, the area in front of the gate stood empty. Eying the horse wandering a few paces outside the gate, the bandit leader made a dash for the opening.

Eskkar blocked the way. "Put down your sword!"

The bandit chief showed himself a true warrior, and flung himself at Eskkar with all the speed and force he could muster, his sword striking at Eskkar's head. Trapped, the man knew there might still be a chance to escape, if he could get outside the village.

Eskkar's sword, made from the finest bronze, flashed up to parry the blow, and the loud clank as the two blades clashed carried over the other battle noises. In the same instant, before the man could recover, Eskkar lowered his shoulder and thrust himself into the bandit leader's chest.

The two men met with a crash. The bandit, moving at a run, had momentum behind him, but Eskkar was the bigger man, and he put the force of his body behind his shoulder. Gasping as the air was knocked from his lungs, the bandit went down, and before he could get up, one of the soldiers from the gate leapt upon him, pinning his sword arm until Eskkar could stomp his sandal on the blade just past the hilt. The man let go of the useless weapon and grabbed for a knife at his belt, but Eskkar pushed the point of his sword against the man's neck. He stopped moving, though his eyes darted from Eskkar to the sword.

Before the prisoner could change his mind, Eskkar's soldier ripped the prisoner's knife from his belt, then used its hilt to strike the man hard across his forehead. That stunned the bandit for a few moments, and before he could begin to resist, the soldier cut free the man's sandal straps, rolled the prisoner onto his stomach, and started binding the prisoner's wrists behind him. Eskkar kept the sword against the bandit's neck until the man's hands were bound.

"Captain! Over here."

Eskkar turned to see the other soldier who'd helped defend the gate. He'd scrambled over the carts and had the wounded bandit on his feet, the arrow still protruding from the man's shoulder. That prisoner grimaced in pain either from the arrow or from the fact that the guard had twisted his other arm up behind his back and had a knife at the man's neck.

Eskkar shoved one of the carts out of the way so that the two could enter.

Hamati arrived, bow in hand with an arrow to the string, his step as assured as if he strode on Akkad's training ground. He had a big grin on his broad face.

"I saw him take that cut at you, Captain," he said. "Not many men could have parried that blow."

Eskkar glanced down at the weapon still in his hand, then raised it up to Hamati. A tiny gouge in the metal showed where the two blades had met, but nothing of consequence, though Eskkar knew that a common sword might have shattered under the impact of such a ferocious blow.

"Trella's gift keeps me safe." The great sword,

painstakingly cast from the strongest bronze by the best craftsmen in Akkad, had taken months to forge. Trella had ordered it cast especially for him, and it had saved his life once before.

"How did it go, Hamati?" Eskkar asked.

"As we expected. As soon as they rode into the marketplace, we put seven arrows into the horses. That put them in a panic. The poor beasts started rearing and twisting, and two men were pitched right off their mounts. My men just kept shooting. Each of us got off at least five arrows. That took the fight out of them."

Eskkar wasn't particularly adept at counting, but some numbers came to him more easily than others. Horses, men, arrows, these kinds of things he could count quickly enough. Thirty-five arrows from Hamati and his six men, in about twelve or fifteen seconds. In those same fifteen seconds, Mitrac, standing on the rooftop, had fired at least seven shafts, since he was much faster than the others. Nearly forty-five arrows loosed into a crowd of sixteen or so bandits, since a few hadn't made it all the way into the square before the ambush started.

"Did we lose anyone?"

Hamati grunted in disgust. "One of the bandits finally got an arrow fitted to his bow and Markas took a shaft in his arm. But it was poorly drawn. It didn't even go through. The women are tending to him. He'll be fine in a few days."

Fitting an arrow to a bow, while trying to control a panicky horse at the same time, sometimes meant you couldn't pull the shaft as far back as you wanted. With the smaller bows the horsemen used, that could result in a weakly launched shaft. The bows Eskkar's men used were much larger, more powerful weapons, shooting a heavier arrow, and were as useful for hunting game as men. Their weakness was that they were too big to be used from horseback. That disadvantage didn't trouble Eskkar, since he didn't have many horses, nor men who knew how to fight from them.

The bandit leader on the ground groaned, and Hamati kicked him casually in the ribs, but not hard enough to break anything. "Captain, except for one bandit at the square who was knocked senseless when his horse was killed, these two are the only ones left alive. All the rest back there are dead or dying."

The other prisoner was shoved to the ground, alongside the man Eskkar had fought. The wounded man gasped in pain at the impact. The shank of the arrow, still protruding from his back, had brushed against the ground, twisting the shaft inside his shoulder and no doubt sending a wave of pain through the man.

"Better pull that out of him," Eskkar ordered, looking at the wound. Mitrac's arrow had struck the man's right shoulder, but looked low and deep enough to be fatal. The man would likely die, but might live long enough to answer some questions.

"Bring them both back to the square, and we'll see what we can get out of them." Eskkar glanced up at the sun and realized it had scarcely moved. The whole fight had lasted only moments.

Hamati, meanwhile, stepped over to the injured prisoner. Before he realized what was coming, Hamati gripped the shaft and ripped it from the man's shoulder.

A piercing scream erupted from the wounded man; then he fainted from the pain and shock.

Eskkar returned to the square. He counted nine carcasses, several with multiple arrows protruding from breast and neck. The rest of the animals, some of them wounded, their eyes still wide with fear and nervous from the smell of blood, had been rounded up and pushed into the same rope corral that had contained the soldiers' animals last night. The stink of blood, urine, and feces rose up from both man and beast. Eskkar didn't mind the familiar smell. He knew you had to be alive to notice it.

A horseman since he'd grown old enough to sit astride one, Eskkar hated the thought of killing such fine horseflesh. But despite the familiar pang of sorrow at their deaths, he knew that, in battle, you did what you had to do. The men remembered their training, to shoot first at the horse. When you shoot the horse, even if it's only wounded, the animal panics and the rider can't control it. When the horse goes down, the rider is usually stunned or injured from the fall. First you stop the charge, then you kill the dismounted riders. Hamati's veterans had all fought in the siege of Akkad and they had learned that lesson very well indeed. Tonight, there would be plenty of fresh meat for everyone, and Eskkar had gained himself another eight or nine riding stock animals for his men.

The other sight wasn't as pleasant. A woman, blood spattered all over her face and arms, sobbed as she knelt against the side of the elder's house. Nisaba and another woman attended her, their arms around her, trying to give comfort. The bandit captured in the square lay dead, his throat slit by the still-shaking woman. She had waited until

Hamati's men had bound the prisoner and gone off to chase after the loose horses.

Blood still dripped from the man's eyes and nose, as well as from his neck and chest. Eskkar guessed she stabbed the helpless man a dozen times before someone pulled her off him. The victim must have done some injury either to her or to her kin. Eskkar couldn't do anything about it now. He turned to Hamati, but the soldier, after shaking his head in disgust at his men's carelessness, had already given orders to guard the two remaining prisoners.

Eskkar went to the well and brought up a fresh bucket of water, drinking his fill and dumping the rest across his face. Once again, he was surprised at how thirsty he became after a fight, even one as brief as this. That was the way of most battles, he decided—a sudden, brief burst of activity with no time for thought or fear.

Then he recalled the long battles for Akkad's walls. Those fights had seemed endless, and every man had been completely exhausted when they ended. He remembered men on their knees, trying to catch their breath, some with tears running down their faces, suddenly unable to control their emotions or even to raise their arms. Eskkar shook off the gloomy vision, refilled the bucket, and drank again. His thirst satisfied, he went back inside the house, picked up the same stool he had used last night, and brought it back outside.

He sat down under a small tree barely large enough to provide a bit of shade. Hamati's men dragged the two prisoners in front of Eskkar. Both of them were bleeding and covered with dust. They were forced to their knees, the hot sun directly in their faces. No doubt they were even more thirsty than Eskkar. They had ridden a wide circle to return to Dilgarth, where they found death waiting for them instead of food and water.

"What are your names?" Eskkar asked sharply.

The wounded man answered immediately. "I am called Utu, noble." His voice cracked as he spoke, and he swayed a little from side to side. Loss of blood had drained the color from his face. "Water, noble, can I have . . ."

"Keep silent, you dog of a coward!" His leader spat the words at him, though his own voice croaked harshly as well. Before anyone could stop him, the bandit leader threw his shoulder against Utu's body, knocking him into the dirt and wrenching another long moan of pain from the wounded man who lay twitching in the dust.

This time Hamati kicked the leader with force, using the heel of his sandal. Once. Twice. And a third time, until the man let out a moan through clenched teeth.

"Bring Utu into the house, Hamati, and give him some water. Go easy with him. Keep the other here, and *keep him quiet!*" Eskkar stood, picked up the stool, and carried it back into the house.

Inside, the mud walls and roof provided some shelter from the heat of the day. Eskkar sat down again while Hamati and one of his men carried Utu inside, then held a ladle of water to his lips. Eskkar studied the man while he drank. His face had turned as white as unleavened bread, and his wound still bled, though not as rapidly as before. The man had lost much blood, and Eskkar guessed he didn't have long to live. Utu finished the water and asked for more. Eskkar nodded, then waited while the wounded man emptied a second ladle.

"Utu, you're in pain, and you'll probably be dead within the hour. I want you to tell me about your leader and what you've been doing for the last few weeks. If you do, you can have plenty of wine and water to comfort yourself. If not, you will be put to the torture. I can even hand you over to the women outside and let them toy with you. They won't be in such a rush this time."

A sob came from the man, and tears ran from his eyes. "Then I'm to die?" He whispered the words in a trembling voice.

"You *are* dying, Utu. The arrow struck deep and hard. Nothing can save you, not even the gods. Only how you die is left for you to choose." Eskkar spoke with the certainty of one who had seen many die before. Then he waited, saying nothing. The dying man needed some time to grasp his plight.

It took Utu only moments to decide. "Wine, noble! For the pain."

"Untie his hands and put something under his head," Eskkar ordered. He had done this many times before. Tell them the truth, that they were dying or would be put to death. It didn't matter which. In that state of mind, most wounded men would appreciate every comfort. Hamati untied the man, then eased him down on the dirt floor, with his head elevated by a folded blanket. Hamati brought over the last of the soldier's wine and held the wineskin to Utu's lips, letting the man drink until he coughed and spat up some of the harsh liquid.

"Now tell me, Utu," Eskkar asked, "what is the name of your leader, and how many others have been raiding the lands?"

"Shulat, noble. His name is Shulat." Utu coughed again, but cleared his throat and swallowed hard. He rolled his eyes toward Hamati.

Eskkar nodded again, and Hamati dribbled more wine into the man's mouth. "How many others, Utu?" Eskkar repeated.

Utu swallowed twice before he could speak, and even then he could barely raise his voice above a whisper. "There is another band of men up north, in Bisitun. Many men there . . . Shulat is the brother of their leader, Ninazu. He rules in Bisitun." Utu's voice gave out and he looked pitifully at Hamati, who gave him another mouthful of wine. "Ninazu . . . Ninazu wanted to know about the lands to the south, and Shulat wanted to raid the farms, so we came here a few weeks ago." The man paused to take a labored breath, and his eyes closed for a long moment.

"Give him more wine," Eskkar said, while he used the time to think. Bisitun was a much larger village five or six days' march farther north from Dilgarth. Bisitun sat on the northern edge of the lands that bordered Akkad, right at the point where the Tigris turned sharply north. It marked the outlying boundary of the lands Eskkar intended to bring under his rule.

He planned to leave Sisuthros in charge of Bisitun, after they finished ridding the surrounding countryside of bandits and marauders. With Akkad and Bisitun working together, more than half of the best farmlands on this side of the Tigris would be under Eskkar's control. Eskkar's plan, worked out with the elders in Akkad, depended on securing Bisitun.

"How many men does this Ninazu have with him in

Bisitun?" The man whimpered, but said nothing. Eskkar placed his hand on Utu's good shoulder and shook him gently, knowing even a small movement would send a wave of pain through the man and keep him conscious. "How many men, Utu?" He spoke sharply, to make sure his words penetrated Utu's weakening mind. "Tell me! Or there'll be no more wine!"

Utu rolled his eyes toward Eskkar, his face a mixture of fear and pain. But the dying man wanted the wine, wanted anything that would ease the pain and the fright of dying. "Seventy or eighty ... maybe ninety ... I don't know ... maybe more." His voice trailed off a little.

"Do they plan to stay there, or will they ride on?" Utu's eyes closed again, and he didn't answer. Eskkar looked at Hamati and a few more drops of wine were carefully dripped into the man's mouth. Another spasm of coughing took Utu and he choked on the wine. It took time before his breathing slowed and he could speak again.

Eskkar waited patiently. "Utu, do they plan to stay there, or will they ride on?" Eskkar had to lean close to hear the man's words.

"Ninazu plans ... to stay in Bisitun. He says the village is his now. From there ... he rules over the land."

Eskkar ground his teeth in anger. Another petty ruler had arisen. With eighty or ninety determined and well-armed men, it would have been easy to take control of Bisitun, already devastated by the Alur Meriki's passage. Once in power, Ninazu's force would grow steadily each day, as more and more desperate men joined him, either out of a desire for loot or simply as a way to get something to eat. Again Eskkar silently cursed the barbarians and their passage. Whatever they touched, they left in chaos. He had expected to find problems in and around Bisitun, but not a village full of fighting men who surpassed him in numbers.

Eskkar had more questions, but Utu's mind wandered now, his voice weak as he struggled to breathe. The vague answers came slower and slower. Blood seeped into the dirt underneath the man. Utu's face looked even whiter than before and now a bluish tinge showed on his lips. Finally the only word Eskkar could get out of him was "wine."

Hamati, still holding the wineskin, looked at Eskkar, who noted the nearly empty wineskin and shook his head. "No, we may need the wine for the other one. Give him water. He won't know the difference."

Eskkar stood up, picked up his stool, and walked back outside. The sun still shone bright in the late afternoon sky, and he had to shade his eyes when he left the house.

The square bustled with activity. Drakis, one of Hamati's men, sat on the ground next to the prisoner, to make sure he stayed alive and to keep him quiet. Before Eskkar could speak, Drakis began. "I've posted a guard by the main entrance, Captain, and Mitrac keeps watch from the roof," indicating the house Eskkar had just left. "The bodies are being loaded on a cart and will be dumped in the river. The rest of the men are helping the women butcher the dead horses or gather firewood. We'll have plenty of meat for the next few days."

As Eskkar watched, two soldiers lifted the last naked body and tossed it onto the cart. They'd already stripped the dead of whatever clothing and valuables they possessed. He moved farther away from the house and looked up to the roof.

"Mitrac!" he called out. "Do you see anything?"

The young archer stepped into view. "Nothing, Captain. The fields are empty. Not even any travelers on the road."

It would be too late in the day for the few travelers brave enough to venture forth. "Good. Keep a sharp watch, Mitrac," Eskkar said. He walked back to the shade of the tree, put down the stool and sat, his feet almost touching Shulat's body.

"Well, Shulat, are you getting thirsty yet?" The man had a fresh bruise on his face, no doubt a reminder from Drakis to keep silent. "It's time for us to talk about your brother."

"I'll tell you nothing, Eskkar. I'm not afraid to die."

"As I told Utu, your death is certain. Only *how* you die is to be decided."

Hamati came out of the house, carrying the wineskin in his hand, and stood next to Eskkar. "The other one is dead, Captain."

"You see, Shulat, your man, Utu, is dead," Eskkar said. "At least he died full of wine, to ease his pain. Are you going to tell me about your brother?"

"I'll be avenged when my brother takes your head." Shulat spat the words at him as a curse. "He likes to kill soft farmers and tradesmen."

Eskkar smiled at the man's words but detected the first hint of fear behind the bravado. "I'm a barbarian myself, Shulat. And my soft villagers took your men easily enough. So don't be so sure of your revenge." Eskkar turned to his second in command. "Hamati, this man needs to change his ways. Stake him out here in the square. We'll let the women have some time with him."

Looking up, Eskkar saw Nisaba standing in the shadows, watching him. Her women had already stripped Utu's corpse. Now the loaded cart stood there, awaiting only Shulat's body. Nearby, the rest of the women, eager for the taste of meat, moved about a little faster and worked swiftly to build cooking fires for the butchered horses. Eskkar walked over to Nisaba's side. "Did you hear what I said?"

"Yes, noble." Her hands fingered a small, leaf-shaped knife she'd taken from one of the dead. Blood streaked the dull copper blade.

Eskkar saw the gesture. "No knives, Nisaba. And just his hands and feet, for now. Do you understand?" Working only on the man's hands and feet helped avoid an untimely demise.

"Yes, noble, I understand." She looked toward the group of women, then back at Shulat. "Shulat killed Nitari's husband in front of her and her children, then took her. And there was . . ."

"Enough, Nisaba," Eskkar cut her off. No doubt the man had taken every woman in the village. "Just you and two women, to start with. He is not to die, only to feel pain. Can you do that?"

"Yes, noble." Her hand gripped tighter on the knife she held.

"I mean it, Nisaba. If one of your women gets carried away . . . I don't want him to die yet. You can have your revenge after he talks. Make sure they truly understand, Nisaba."

He walked over to Hamati, who supervised his men as they finished staking the prisoner. They'd cut his garment off, then spread-eagled him in the dirt, with his arms and legs spread wide apart. A hammer and some wood stakes had come from the blacksmith's stall, and the men pounded four stakes deep into the ground to anchor the ropes that secured him.

Esskar stood over him. "Make sure the ropes are tight, Hamati. I don't want him moving around." If the man could move, even a little, an accidental death might occur. That reminded Esskar of something else.

"And break his thumbs first." Esskar had once seen a man staked out like Shulat grab a woman's hand and snap her wrist. There was no sense taking any chances. With the man's thumbs broken, he couldn't grab anything. "Keep a close watch on the women. I don't want him to die."

"Yes, Captain," Hamati answered patiently. He waited until his men had Shulat securely fastened, then knelt on Shulat's right wrist, letting his knee pin the prisoner's hand to the ground. Shulat clenched his fist tightly, but another soldier added his own weight, and together they forced apart Shulat's hand, ignoring his curses and struggles. It took some effort, but Hamati finally grasped the man's thumb. A quick twist, accompanied by a popping sound, and the deed was done. The pain forced a low moan from the man, even as it weakened his resistance. The other thumb went much easier.

Esskar looked down at Shulat. Esskar knew his own presence would give the man a reason to resist, so he went back into the house and again climbed the ladder to the roof. Up there, a slight breeze blew and the air seemed free of the scent of blood and urine that lingered below. Mitrac turned as Esskar arrived. "Nothing to see, Captain. Are more bandits in the hills?"

"I don't think so, but there's a large force at Bisitun and I don't know what they're up to. I want to get back to our men as soon as possible." He gazed out over the hills, taking his time, letting his eyes slowly traverse every point of the horizon, then moving them back and forth over the intervening landscape. Eskkar knew well how to search the land for enemies. Everything looked peaceful. He decided there was nothing more he could do. His twenty horsemen would arrive later tonight, and tomorrow they'd link up with Sisuthros and the rest of the soldiers.

"Stay and watch until it's too dark, Mitrac. Hopefully our men will return soon after."

Mitrac nodded, and Eskkar went down the ladder. One of Dilgarth's women had cleaned the room and the signs of Utu's passing had vanished. Reentering the square, Eskkar heard Shulat's first cry of pain. Two women worked on his feet, each sitting on one of Shulat's legs. The women held stones in each hand, and they had started crushing his toes by smashing the rocks together. Nisaba knelt on Shulat's right wrist, doing the same to the fingers of his hand. Eskkar noticed that her hands seemed as strong as those of the two younger women.

With all the small bones in his toes and fingers crushed or broken, the pain from each subsequent blow would increase, and soon the man's extremities would be shooting waves of pain throughout his body. Eskkar lingered only long enough to make sure the women didn't get carried away, and that Hamati kept his eyes on them.

Eskkar left the square and walked back to the main gate. One soldier stood guard there, sitting on one of the carts, bow across his lap, and looking out through the gate toward the horizon. All of his fighters looked tired enough. They'd had little sleep last night as they prepared for the ambush. Then they'd worked in the fields during the day and finished with a hard fight in the afternoon. It wouldn't take much distraction for them to relax or fall asleep at their posts.

Nonetheless, the guard seemed alert. Eskkar spoke to him, reminding the man to remain vigilant. Eskkar knew the more time he spent with each man, the more he showed his trust in each of them, the more likely each soldier would do his duty properly.

Even before Eskkar returned to the square, he heard Shulat's screams. Five other village women stood a few paces away, just watching, or perhaps waiting their turn. The women had finished with Shulat's toes and fingers, and had moved up to his knees and wrists. They had fallen into a rhythm. First one would smash at him with the stones, then pause to let the waves of pain shoot through his body. Then the second woman would strike, then the third, then back to the first. Soon they would begin on his genitals, and by then, Eskkar expected Shulat to begin talking.

Eskkar stood at the man's head and watched for a moment. He'd seen many men tortured. Five years ago, in the days of his own banditry, he might have been the one staked out and put to the torture. Eskkar nodded to Hamati and walked a few steps away, out of earshot of Shulat.

Hamati joined him. "He's a tough one, Captain. But I think he'll talk."

"Just don't let the women get carried away. He'll be hoping they'll kill him."

"Nisaba understands what you want. Shulat raped both of them, and killed one's husband. Nisaba is keeping the women under control. I'll keep a close eye on them."

"We both will," Eskkar said. He walked back to the prisoner, folded his arms, and stood there. He took no pleasure from the man's suffering. It needed to be done. The man had information Eskkar needed, and Shulat would have to give it up. The hard part would be separating the truth from the lies when he did begin to speak.

The man resisted as long as anyone could, before he began to scream for mercy. By then his hands, feet, and knees were broken, swollen, and oozing blood. Nisaba worked alone now, kneeling between his spread legs, cupping his testicles in her hand. Twice she had clenched her fist, each time extracting a long scream of agony from her victim as he thrashed helplessly against his bonds. Now she looked toward Hamati and Eskkar, and waited.

Eskkar picked up the stool and sat down near Shulat's head. "Are you ready to tell me about your brother?" Before the man could answer, Eskkar went on. "Would you like some wine, Shulat?"

Hamati already knelt on the other side, the wineskin in his hands, and he shook the vessel under the prisoner's nose for a moment. Shulat's eyes stayed wide with pain and hatred, but they followed the wineskin as Hamati withdrew it.

"The wine will make the pain go away," Eskkar suggested gently. "It can't hurt to have some wine, can it? Or should I tell the women to continue?" The man's eyes moved back and forth, but he said nothing. Eskkar turned toward Nisaba and nodded. The woman's hand clenched again.

Another scream split the air as the man's body arched up off the ground, twisting and trembling helplessly as it fought against the ropes. Eskkar let it go on, waiting impassively for the man to break. It didn't take long. Shulat began to shout that he would talk. Eskkar called out to Nisaba, and she opened her hand. This time he saw blood on Nisaba's palm and fingers.

Eskkar waited until the pain subsided and the man could speak again. "If you lie to me even once, Shulat, you'll suffer for a long time. You will answer my questions instantly, or there will be more pain. Do you understand?"

"Yes . . . yes. Wine! . . . Give me wine!"

Hamati started to move the wineskin to the man's mouth, but Eskkar held him back. "Remember this, Shulat. If you lie, or hesitate, you will be very sorry."

Hamati dribbled the wine slowly into the man's mouth. Eskkar let him have as much as he could take. At this stage, the wine would loosen his tongue even as it dulled his nerves. When the man began to cough on the wine, Hamati lifted the wineskin away from Shulat's lips, and he began to speak.

It took some time for Eskkar to learn all he could. Only once did he find it necessary to turn to Nisaba and for her to clench her fist again. By then, Hamati had emptied the wineskin and Shulat was barely conscious. The wine, combined with the pain and exhaustion, had greatly weakened him, and now he drifted in and out of consciousness.

"I think that's all you're going to get, Captain," Hamati said, as the two men took a few steps toward the house.

"Yes, he's finished. How much of it is true, we'll find out

soon enough." Eskkar was thoughtful, his face grim. Darkness had fallen and the cooking fires were well under way, the smell of roasting horsemeat overpowering even the scents of death. With nothing left to do, most of the soldiers and villagers still stood there, fascinated, watching Shulat take the torture, enjoying the spectacle, no doubt wondering what they would do in his place.

"What shall I do with him?" Hamati asked.

Eskkar looked back over his shoulder. Nisaba still knelt between the man's legs, waiting permission to continue. One of the women had lit a torch, to provide more light for everyone.

"Nothing, Hamati." Eskkar took a deep breath and let it out. "Just give him to the women. They've earned their revenge. When they're finished, load him on the cart with the others and dump them in the river."

He walked away and entered the house, then climbed the ladder to the roof. Mitrac had remained there, though darkness made it difficult to see much of anything. Eskkar told him to go down and find something to eat. As Mitrac started down, the first of another long string of Shulat's screams pierced the night as the women unleashed their fury on him.

Alone on the roof, Eskkar sat there, sword across his knees, staring out toward the north, and cleared his mind. Shulat's words had given him plenty to worry about, and he thought long and hard about what to do next. Eskkar had several courses of action to consider. He could return to Akkad, to wait there until he gathered more men. He could even stay here for a while and scout out the lands to the north and east. Or he could continue on to Bisitun.

Going to Bisitun now would almost certainly mean a battle, not just a few skirmishes chasing down some ill-equipped and poorly led bandits. A fight for the village would cost men, and he had too few of those already. Eskkar's veteran bowmen had taken months to train, a huge investment in time and effort, and he didn't want to lose any of them, certainly not without some surety of success. But turning back would leave the inhabitants of Bisitun at the mercy of their occupiers, and for each day he delayed, the stronger his enemy's position would become. It might take weeks or even a month to gather and train more men, and by then, Bisitun might be beyond saving.

The consequences to Akkad might be as serious. Without a pacified countryside producing crops and herds, the city's growth might falter, and construction of the great wall itself might be delayed or even halted. That would bring ruin to Trella's plans. For most of his life, Eskkar had concerned himself with his own problems; now he had to think and plan for a whole city, even the entire countryside. Thousands of people would be affected by whatever he decided, and the wrong choice might plunge the land back into chaos or open war, as devastating to Akkad as the Alur Meriki invasion.

Eskkar didn't consider himself a quick thinker, and Trella had advised him to take his time, to take into account all the possibilities. Now he had many choices, and each choice led to yet more possibilities, all of them carrying their own risk and benefit. He went over them again and again, weighing the consequences and considering all the things that might go wrong. At last he made his decision. With that settled, he began planning, working out in his head how the entire campaign would go. Only after finishing that did he know what he would need, and how to proceed.

At last, Eskkar felt satisfied. It might not be the best course of action, but only time would answer that question. He never wanted this kind of responsibility, never dreamed that some day his decisions would affect so many people's lives. Or even bring about their deaths. Nevertheless, Trella believed in him, and he didn't want to disappoint her. Eskkar shook the dark thoughts from his mind. Right or wrong, he would continue the course he had chosen.

He stood and stretched muscles grown stiff from inaction, looking up at the star-filled sky. The little glittering points of light that moved across the night sky had fascinated him as far back as he could remember; his father had taught him the stars' names, and how to use them to travel at night. The moon had risen, shedding its own pale gleam on the land. For the first time, he noticed the silence of the night. Shulat's screams had ended long ago. No doubt the women of Dilgarth regretted their revenge had ended so swiftly. The bandit's demise had been the first of this campaign. Eskkar knew there would be many more death cries in the next few weeks. Just how many would depend on the course of action he'd chosen.

3
===

And so, Lady Trella," Drakis said, finishing up his report, "Lord Eskkar dispatched me on one of the captured horses back to Akkad, to tell you and Gatus what took place."

Trella shifted her body slightly in her chair as she listened to the soldier's tale. The meeting had lasted for some time, and her pregnancy had reached the stage where she felt uncomfortable if she sat too long. Into her seventh month, she already looked forward to the child's birth. Her body kept distracting her with one thing or another, making it more difficult to concentrate on the task at hand. Not that anyone in the room noticed. Trella had grown very skillful at keeping her emotions and thoughts under control.

In the middle of her fifteenth season, Trella's figure would have been slender except for the coming child. She was slightly above average height; her hair was her best feature, very dark and thick, reaching just below her shoulders. A thin silver headband held the tresses away from her face, leaving cheeks and neck bare. Around her neck a loop of thin leather held a small gold coin, hidden between her breasts, a gift from Eskkar for saving his life. Aside from the unadorned fillet and necklace, she wore no other jewelry, though Akkad's shopkeepers produced some of the finest bracelets, rings, and earrings sold on the river. Strangers tended to notice her eyes first, deep brown and set wide apart, which seemed to overlook nothing, as if they stared directly into your mind. Hardened soldiers twice her age often got flustered in her presence.

Not that her eyes revealed the power of her mind. Her father had trained her well, teaching his precocious daughter to listen, observe, and think. Her sharp wits did the rest. When anyone spoke, she listened intently while she watched his face, his hands, the shuffling of his feet, to better analyze his words. She perceived much by noting not only what men said, but how they said it and what they omitted. Few could hide the truth from her.

Many men underestimated her abilities at first, seeing only a young woman. Those who knew her did not. Trella possessed a presence of authority, an aura of domination. The barbarian clan Eskkar had befriended called her "a gifted one," a term that designated a woman singled out by the gods, even allowed to speak at the council fires.

In Akkad, many thought the goddess Ishtar blessed her with special insight, a fact continually reinforced by Ishtar's priest even as he took Trella's gold. Others swore she'd learned the art of witchcraft, with the power to cast spells and control men's souls. Trella smiled at all these ideas and did nothing to dispel any of them. Rather she used each to her advantage.

"And you are planning to return to my husband immediately, Drakis?"

"Yes, Lady Trella, as soon as I gather the supplies he requested. I must rejoin him before he reaches Bisitun."

Gatus leaned forward across the table. "How many men did he leave behind in Dilgarth?" Seated at Trella's right, Gatus, the new captain of the guard, commanded the garrison soldiers in Eskkar's absence. An old man, already past his fiftieth season, Gatus had trained nearly every soldier in Akkad.

"He said he would leave three men," Drakis replied. "The wounded man, plus two others. Lord Eskkar asked that you send more soldiers to Dilgarth as soon as you can, as well as craftsmen and whatever else you think best to help rebuild the village."

"And he didn't say why," Gatus went on, "he wanted the ropes and oil?"

"No," Drakis answered. "He just told me to bring ten coils of rope and as much of the black oil as I could carry on one spare horse, plus my mount."

"I hope he's not planning on burning Bisitun to the ground." Corio, one of the Noble Families that helped rule Akkad, said the words only half in jest.

Trella turned to her left. Each day at least one of the city's ruling families sat with Gatus and Trella to review any important matters. Today Corio represented the nobles at the council. Akkad now possessed seven such families, and the council room had scarcely enough space to hold all of them, though they rarely came together as a group.

A skilled artisan, Corio had designed and built Akkad's wall, the wall that enabled Eskkar and his soldiers to defeat the barbarians. Undertaking that task had changed his status and brought him into the Noble Families. Trella knew that many in Akkad, especially those critics unhappy with Eskkar, regarded Corio and his wall as the real saviors of the city.

"I'm sure that's not his intention," Trella said, smiling at Corio's words. "If it were, he would have said so."

Corio nodded agreement. Those who worked closely with Eskkar knew he was not a subtle man. "And the oil will have to go in wineskins," Corio added. "It's too easy to break pots on horseback, even if they're well wrapped."

"I don't like this at all." Gatus shook his head as he spoke. "There could be more men in Bisitun than Eskkar has with him, and this time they'll be the ones behind a stockade. Maybe we should tell him to come back to Akkad. Bisitun can wait until we have more men."

"Eskkar knows the situation, Gatus," Trella said calmly, though she didn't like it either. They had expected that Eskkar would encounter small, isolated bands of robbers and thieves, bandits who would flee before an organized force of fighting men. No one had foreseen a village full of armed men. Still, Trella had learned not to question her husband's decisions on military issues. Eskkar had been fighting one battle or another for most of his thirty-odd seasons and he often saw things on the battle-field that another man would miss. And something told him he would need ropes and oil at Bisitun. That meant he thought he could capture Bisitun without too much loss of life.

"Drakis," Trella began, "you say that after Shulat revealed his information, Eskkar remained on the roof for over an hour?"

"Yes, Lady Trella. Night had fallen, and the horseflesh was well cooked before he came down to join us. After he finished his meal, he gave me my instructions and told me to leave at dawn."

One lesson Eskkar had learned well was the need to think and work out his campaigns in advance. Trella knew that if Eskkar thought about Bisitun that long, then he must have come up with a plan, and he would have weighed all the alternatives. She sighed to herself and shifted her weight once again. Short of an urgent plea to return, Eskkar would do whatever he decided. He would take too many chances, but that was the man he was.

"You will see to Drakis's needs, Gatus?" If the man left at first light tomorrow, Trella reasoned, and the horses held up, Drakis would rejoin Eskkar just as he reached Bisitun.

"Yes, Lady Trella." Gatus softened his gruff tone whenever he spoke to Trella. "I'll make sure he has the two best horses left in Akkad, and an extra man or two for Dilgarth. And I think I'll send another man with Drakis, to make sure he doesn't fall off his horse, or wander off somewhere and get drunk."

Everyone smiled at the jest. A member of the Hawk Clan, Drakis had proved himself steadier than most.

"Make sure you carry plenty of food with you, Drakis," Trella said. "But tonight you will eat and sleep at our house. You need to rest. You'll be riding hard for at least four days." She knew the words weren't needed, that the man would do his duty regardless, but the effect achieved all she could wish.

The thought that the leader of Akkad worried about his

dinner and sleeping arrangements brought an embarrassed flush to Drakis's face. He stood up and bowed. "Thank you, Lady Trella. I will be honored." He bowed again, this time to Gatus, and left the room.

Trella, Gatus, and Corio remained seated at the table in what had come to be called the Council House, a good-sized, one-level dwelling located only a few dozen paces from Akkad's marketplace. Eskkar and the Noble Families met in the Council House to govern the fast growing city and manage its affairs. The structure contained only two large rooms: an inner chamber where the leaders met, and an outer room that functioned as a waiting area for those with council business. Three clerks worked there, to keep a record of what the council decided, and to keep track of those seeking to speak with the council. Two guards kept wary eyes on every visitor, and made sure no one brought a weapon into the inner room. Two other Hawk Clan soldiers, Trella's usual guard, waited there as well. Another soldier stood watch outside the house.

Trella leaned back in her chair as she felt the child within her moving about. At least the business of the day had nearly finished. "How are the plans for the new wall, Corio? Are you any closer to completing your design?" Trella knew he had been meeting every day for over a month with all the master builders and artisans in Akkad.

Corio stood, then moved around to the other side of the table, so he could face them more easily. A tall man with large hands, he preferred to talk while standing. "We argued all day and into the night about it, until there was no more oil for the lamps." He shook his head as he remembered. "No one is really satisfied. But based on what everyone needs and how much Akkad is expected to grow in the next few seasons . . . we finally agreed to begin."

"And where will this new great wall be placed?" Gatus asked, his voice already rising. In addition to providing soldiers to maintain order during the building process, he would have to develop and train additional men to defend the expanded city in the event of another attack.

Corio shook his head ruefully. "You won't like it, Gatus. The new east wall will be eight hundred paces from the present one. The north and west walls will remain as they are, but the south wall will also need to be shifted. The area enclosed by the extended walls will be more than three times greater than what Akkad is today."

"And how long will it take to build this wonderful new wall? Trella will be a grandmother before it's finished, I'll wager."

Trella smiled at the old soldier's words. He thought of her almost as a daughter, and considered himself one of the few in Akkad that didn't need to use a title when he spoke to her, though in formal occasions he still addressed her properly.

"The new walls will be thirty-five feet high," Corio said, "but ten of those will be belowground. With the many towers that you and Eskkar have demanded, it will take at least three years to build." The value of towers that projected above and over the wall was no longer questioned—they had learned that lesson the hard way during the Alur Meriki siege.

Trella showed no surprise, though privately she thought it would take closer to five years to complete. She'd attended many of the discussions, and knew that Akkad's need for new space would be great. It would be a huge project and take many years, and she worried more about where the gold, soldiers, and laborers would come from. With the new wall in place, Akkad would be the greatest and strongest city in the world, and her child would be safe within its mighty walls.

Gatus slapped his hand on the table in disgust. "Three years! That's if we can find soldiers and workers aplenty to work on it. More likely twice that, if you ask me. I doubt I'll live long enough to see it built."

Trella placed her hand on top of his and smiled. "You will see it, Gatus, as will all of us. Corio will build a great city for us. We must be patient." She held him in as much respect as the soldiers did, though for a different reason. The soldiers honored his experience and his years. Not many fighting men survived past their fortieth season. For Trella, Gatus had proven his loyalty to her and Eskkar more than once.

She turned to Corio. "I am glad all of you have agreed on what is needed. As always, you have done well, Master Builder." She stood, grateful for the chance to ease her back and already looking forward to returning home.

A shadow crossed the open doorway and one of the attending scribes appeared, a young man with the sallow face of one who rarely saw the sun. He had a thin beard and a high-pitched voice. "Lady Trella . . . Captain Gatus, there is one more waiting to see you, a stranger from the far west. The messenger from Noble Eskkar was brought in ahead of him. Shall I tell him to return tomorrow?"

Trella felt tempted to do exactly that, but the far west meant the stranger came from the land beyond the other great river. They seldom met travelers from the region west of the Euphrates. She saw the same curiosity on Corio's face and changed her mind. "No, we will see him now. Please send him in."

By the time she and Corio had taken their seats again, the stranger stood before them. Trella guessed that he neared his thirtieth year, though his smooth, unblemished face made him seem younger. Not much taller than her own height, the man had a slight build, though he seemed sturdy enough. His garments appeared worn but well made, his features smooth and even. Except for his gray eyes and darker complexion, nothing distinguished him from any local trader. He bowed politely, turning to face each of them as he did so.

"I thank you for receiving me, Captain Gatus." Korthac spoke softly, with a pleasant voice, and even though he had a strong accent, his meaning was clear. "My name is Korthac. I realize it is late in the day, and I saw that Noble Eskkar's messenger was unexpected. I can return tomorrow, if you wish."

Gatus turned toward Trella, but she gave no sign, just studied the stranger. The old soldier nodded formally at the visitor. "No, we can speak now. And there is no need to stand." Gatus waited until Korthac took a seat facing them across the table. "This is Corio, our master artisan, and this is Lady Trella, the wife of Eskkar, our ruler. You say you're from the lands west of the Euphrates?"

"Yes, Captain. From beyond the great desert. I arrived yesterday with a small caravan. I am a trader, and I would like to establish a House here in Orak . . . I mean, Akkad." He smiled at his mistake. Everyone seemed to have trouble getting used to the city's new name.

"What kind of trader?" Corio leaned forward on the table. The question was more than just idle curiosity. Every trader had his own contacts and trade secrets, and if this man truly came from across the desert, he might bring new trading links to the city.

"Noble Corio, I deal in gemstones and other small items that can be traded profitably. I plan to bring such goods across the great desert, and trade in emeralds, onyx, rose quartz, peridot, amethyst, and glass beads. To make a profit over such a great distance, the items traded must be small and easily carried, as I'm sure you understand."

"Jewelry made from beads of glass is very rare here," Corio mused. "They are much prized for their beauty and healing properties. And peridot is in short supply as well, since it has the power to dissolve enchantments."

"Then perhaps I shall do well in Akkad," Korthac said politely, his smile showing white and even teeth. "If, Noble, I am permitted to open a House of my own."

"There is a tax that must be paid before you can establish a trading house," Corio said, glancing at Trella before answering. "You understand, Korthac, we have just defeated a barbarian invasion, and at great cost to all of us, I might add. Newcomers must pay to do business under Akkad's protection. There are other taxes and rules as well."

A frown passed briefly across Korthac's face. "I hope that such fees will not be too great, Nobles. I have had to struggle across a great distance and my own expenses have been high."

Trella cut in smoothly. "Perhaps you can tell us a little about the lands to the west. What are they like? Are there many people there?"

"Once you get across the great desert, to the land called Egypt, there are many villages and great numbers of people," Korthac answered.

"Villages as great as Akkad?" Gatus had more than a hint of doubt in his voice. "Distant lands are always magical or mighty, it seems, but I traveled widely in my younger days and never encountered a city with as many people as Akkad."

"Oh, no, none so great as Akkad," Korthac said. "Akkad is a mighty . . ."

"Please forgive me, Korthac," Trella interrupted, "but you may speak plainly here." She knew a visitor would be expected to praise Akkad to the skies, to flatter its rulers and important citizens. "We wish to hear the truth about the lands to the west. Those few who come to us from afar are mainly lost men or desert wanderers, who understand little about the ways of village and farm. Such as those can tell us little."

Korthac looked at Trella carefully before continuing. "In truth, Lady Trella, Egypt is a vast and fertile land of many villages, some of them larger than Akkad. Egypt has much gold and silver, as well as great flocks of cattle and other beasts. The numbers of its people are beyond counting."

"Do these villages have walls around them?" Corio sounded unconvinced.

"Many do, Noble Corio," the stranger answered calmly. "Not all, but some have raised walls such as yours for protection, to keep out bandits or invaders."

"Akkad is the first village in these lands to build a fortified wall to protect itself," Corio added, a hint of skepticism showing through. "A strong wall is not such an easy thing to raise."

"I can only tell you what I have seen, Noble Corio," Korthac said, raising his hands slightly in deference. "Lady Trella asked me to speak the truth, and I have done so."

"Then we should thank you for your honesty, Korthac," Trella said, again speaking before Corio could reply. "But now, it grows late and the council still has some business to attend to. Would you be able to call upon us tomorrow, say, at the hour before noon? Then we will have time to speak with you at leisure and you can tell us much more about what you have seen in your travels and this land called Egypt."

Korthac took the dismissal gracefully. He stood and bowed respectfully. "Of course, Lady Trella, I understand. I will return at that hour."

Trella had risen when he did and she bowed as well, giving Korthac a pleasant smile as he left the room. She waited until he stepped out of earshot before she turned to Corio and Gatus. "This stranger took a great chance, crossing the desert with such valuable trade goods, with only the hope of establishing a House here in Akkad."

"Whatever his reasons," Corio answered, "he is here and with his goods. Every merchant adds to the wealth of Akkad. Let him establish his trading house, if he can pay his tax of twenty gold coins."

"No, Corio," Trella said firmly, "I think not. Tomorrow we will tell him that he must pay forty gold coins if he is to do business here."

"Ishtar's eyes, Trella," Gatus swore, "Mantar wailed for days when he had to pay twenty. He claimed he would be reduced to begging in the streets. And that only a month ago."

"Still, Mantar paid the tax," Trella said. "And remember, Korthac is a stranger. Mantar lived here all his life."

Mantar dealt in livestock, mostly goats and sheep, that supplied milk and cheese. He had complained bitterly about the amount of the tax, but he had been one of those who fled the city before the barbarians arrived, and now had to pay to reestablish himself. Trella had no sympathy for those who had refused to defend Akkad.

"And I doubt Korthac will cry as loud as Mantar did," Trella said. "I think it is important to learn as much about Korthac as possible." She turned to Gatus. "How many men were in his caravan, how many slaves, how many animals? What kind of people did he bring with him? Find out where he is staying and talk to the innkeeper. Let us all see what we can find out, and we'll meet here tomorrow at midmorning. We can speak about this before we see Korthac again. I will make sure Nicar is here as well. He sees much in men that we may miss."

The Noble Nicar had led the city before the invasion, and had entrusted the city's defense to Eskkar. Nicar had also given Eskkar a slave girl named Trella.

"What is it about Korthac that worries you, Lady Trella?" Corio sounded surprised at her concern. "He seemed polite enough."

Trella shrugged. "Nothing worries me yet, Corio. But we can afford to be cautious. And isn't it strange that a merchant would cross the great desert at such risk, before he was sure of what awaited him here? Was he unaware that the Alur Meriki were passing through these lands, killing anyone they encountered? Why didn't he send an emissary ahead of him?"

Corio opened his mouth to reply, then closed it again. In the last few months, he'd learned not to dismiss her thoughts.

"Think on it, Corio," Trella went on. "And you, too, Gatus. Let us all learn what we can. Now if you will excuse me, my body calls to me once again."

She walked into the front room, her two guards rising as she entered. Her friend and companion Annok-sur waited for her as well, getting to her feet as Trella crossed the room. The two women stepped side by side into the square and began the walk back to Eskkar's house. One guard walked ahead of them, the other behind. Both men kept their hands on their swords and their eyes moving about.

Only a few months ago Eskkar's enemies attacked Trella in the street and nearly killed her. The men who tried to assassinate her had died under the torture. In a true barbarian rage, Eskkar had threatened to burn the city to the ground and kill every inhabitant if it happened again. No one doubted him. And so the guards remained wary and suspicious, exactly as Eskkar and Gatus instructed. They didn't want to face Eskkar's wrath or their own shame should another attempt on Trella's life take place.

Annok-sur, as alert as any of the guards, stayed close beside Trella. The wife of one of Eskkar's subcommanders, Annok-sur had nearly twice Trella's seasons. Her husband Bantor and a group of soldiers had departed Akkad a few days before Eskkar left for the north. By now Bantor's force would have ranged far to the south of Akkad, carefully watching from afar the progress of the retreating barbarian migration, and making sure they did not double back for another attack on Akkad. The barbarians had been driven off, but they still had many warriors, and rumors of their presence, even as the distance grew, still frightened Akkad's inhabitants.

"Something troubles you, Trella?"

"Yes, Annok-sur, but we will speak of it when we are home."

Korthac returned to the modest inn he'd picked for himself and his men. Walking through the lanes, he ignored the open-mouthed stares of the villagers. Although the clothing he and his bodyguard wore came from these lands, their darker complexions, burnished even deeper by months in the sun, marked them as strangers and worse, foreigners. Nevertheless, Korthac smiled pleasantly at anyone who caught his eye, offering greetings and friendly nods. He needed to gain acceptance from these simple folk. There would be plenty of time to teach them proper respect later on. Then they would kneel in the dirt when he passed, afraid to lift their eyes to his lest they lose their heads.

More than a month had passed since he left Magabad. He'd entered Akkad with only sixteen men, carefully chosen to make sure they looked more like servants and laborers than fighting men. The rest of his force remained far to the west, awaiting his summons while Ariamus roamed the countryside seeking men willing to fight for gold, even with foreigners at their side.

Fortune had smiled on Korthac when it delivered Ariamus to him. Korthac couldn't image a more perfect tool. Ariamus knew the city and the countryside, knew the people, and knew how to command the rabble that would soon sweep Korthac to power. The man's desires for power and wealth made him easy to control. As long as Ariamus remained obedient and loyal, he would continue to be useful. Korthac remembered the astonishment in Ariamus's eyes when he saw the bags of gemstones. The man's greed would be the halter in Korthac's firm hands.

Korthac had brought two bags of jewels with him, more than enough to establish himself in Akkad. In a few days or a week, he would grudgingly pay whatever trivial sum the Akkadians demanded of him. After that, he'd buy a house and set up a base of operations. He would bring more of his men into Akkad by ones and twos, increasing their number while he established an innocent trade in gemstones with the local merchants. It would be lucrative business for the Akkadians, as Korthac planned to be less than astute in his dealings. That would win him many more friends even as he earned a reputation as a poor trader. And he'd bestow other gifts that would gain him more supporters.

At the same time, Ariamus would continue gathering men. In Korthac's first few talks after saving Ariamus's life, Korthac hadn't been sure that his newly acquired servant and ally could deliver the numbers of fighting men he promised. But as he traveled closer toward Akkad, Korthac saw for himself the devastation in the countryside and numbers of masterless men wandering about. Many had flocked to join Ariamus and his men, and his newest subcommander promised to recruit even more. When Korthac had enough followers, one night's fighting would see the city his.

Tomorrow his campaign would begin. He had already started learning who the important traders and merchants were, and soon he would begin buying their support with judicious and discreet bribes. Korthac didn't begrudge the gemstones that would be required; he'd make sure he got most of them back when he seized command of the city.

Akkad did impress him despite what he'd told Trella. The city bustled with excitement. Korthac saw new construction or rebuilding on every street, while freshly planted crops flourished in the surrounding fields. The inhabitants looked healthy, content, and well fed, with little illness in evidence. Even the slaves looked remarkably satisfied with their lot. Egypt might have one or two cities larger, but none matched this place in energy. No, Akkad would serve his needs perfectly. Perhaps someday he would raise an army large enough to return to Egypt and vanquish his enemies.

He put that thought out of his mind. It would take years to fully exploit Akkad, and right now he needed to concentrate on the task at hand. He'd spoken to the innkeeper and several others already and learned that Eskkar had traveled north while sending other soldiers to the south. Korthac could scarcely believe his luck. The foolish ruler had divided his forces and left the city in the care of his pregnant slave girl.

If Ariamus could raise men fast enough, Korthac would have more than enough followers to take control of Akkad. It might take only weeks instead of the months he had envisioned. While the fool Eskkar chased bandits all over the countryside, weakening his forces in the process, Korthac would husband and increase his own numbers.

Korthac reached his lodgings and passed inside. He nodded pleasantly to the innkeeper and sat down at a table. Except for the owner and his family, only Korthac and his men now stayed here. The other guests had been encouraged to seek accommodations elsewhere by the innkeeper, after a large gift from Korthac. The tiny inn normally couldn't accommodate so many travelers, but his men could bear such a minor hardship as sleeping shoulder to shoulder on the dirt floor; after the brutal weeks journeying across the desert, the inn's floor seemed almost luxurious.

Even though Korthac had selected these men with care, they still had difficulty acting as simple bodyguards instead of trained warriors. He only allowed them to carry knives, befitting their role, and kept their newly acquired swords in his room. He'd promised to kill the first man that quarreled with any of the local inhabitants. So far, they'd shown restraint, knowing their days of plunder and pillage would come soon enough.

The innkeeper rushed to his table, carrying a jar of wine and cups while his obsequious wife appeared with a bowl of dates and a chipped plate holding fresh bread. Korthac thanked them both with a smile, ignoring their filthy hands and the dirty utensils. The innkeeper no doubt imagined he would make a tidy profit from his foreign guest. The thought of someday taking it all back from the man helped Korthac's appetite. The barely adequate wine smelled of vinegar, but he drank it gratefully while he picked at the already-stale bread.

Today's meeting with Trella had gone better than he'd dreamed possible. Perhaps the fool Lord of Akkad would get himself killed and solve another problem. This Eskkar didn't even have an heir, though Korthac doubted many would rally to a son of an upstart barbarian. Korthac knew it took years of trust, years of obedience to a ruler before the people accepted without question the passing of authority from father to son.

Gatus, the temporary leader of the city, looked and acted like a plain soldier, one with little imagination. And Corio was nothing more than an artisan, only recently allowed into the company of what these locals called the Nobles. No, these simple villagers hadn't rallied around Eskkar out of choice, but out of necessity.

Eskkar had left the city, taking nearly a quarter of its soldiers. Another sixty or so had gone south, so that left little more than a hundred men here in Akkad, not even enough to defend the walls properly, not without the villagers supporting them. If the soldiers here could be eliminated, the other two forces, even if they got together, would be too weak to retake the city, especially after Korthac convinced the villagers to fight for him. There would be more than a few disaffected locals eager to gain a better place and position. Taking a sip of wine, he grimaced at the taste. He knew how to win over the rest of the villagers. Hacking a few to death in the marketplace would solve that problem.

That left only Trella to be reckoned with. She would be curious, possibly even suspicious, but a stranger with a dozen men wouldn't worry her or any of the others. Perhaps he could even win her over, keep her occupied and amused with stories of Egypt while Ariamus gathered more men. A few jewels might even do the trick.

Ariamus hadn't found out much about Trella, but the

innkeeper had plenty of stories to tell. She seemed to have her wits about her, but she was merely a pregnant girl, too young to have any real understanding in how to deal with men or rule a city. More important, she lacked experience in warfare, especially the kind of fighting Korthac had waged in Egypt. No, she and this Eskkar had attained their positions by the luck of a barbarian invasion, and in the confusion they had gained control of the biggest city on the Tigris. Korthac needed to deal carefully with her, but he would make sure she learned only what he wanted her to know. Until it was too late. Then she, too, would kneel at his feet.

He tasted a few of the dates and wished again for the fruit of the trees from the village of his youth. Somehow the food in this new place didn't seem quite as satisfying as that of Egypt. He assumed he would get used to it, however, especially when served to him on a golden platter by his new slaves. Taking another mouthful of wine to rinse his mouth, he thought more about Trella. She had little beauty, especially with her body already distorted by the coming child.

She did have a presence, a sense of command, one Korthac would enjoy breaking. He had seen how the others deferred to her, though that might be simple fear of the barbarian Eskkar. Perhaps she would make a good pleasure slave. She'd been a slave once, so it only seemed fitting to return her to her true station. He pictured her kneeling naked at his feet, begging for the chance to please him. Yes, that was something pleasant to anticipate. Almost as pleasant as the prospect of the entire city submitting to his authority, eager to satisfy his every command.

In the morning he would meet with the council, plead his case, and begin negotiations over whatever trifling taxes they demanded. Tomorrow would be the first day of his new campaign. It wouldn't be a long campaign, but when it ended, he would rule first here, then over all the surrounding countryside. Eskkar would be dead, and his woman would be Korthac's slave, for as long as she pleased him. Or she, too, would be dead.

4

Though Trella lived only a few lanes away from the Council House, the journey home always took much longer than expected. Shopkeepers and villagers filled the streets, and the sight of Trella and her guards made it impossible for her to go about unnoticed. Everyone wanted to exchange a few words with her, or even just call out a greeting.

She and Annok-sur took their time, pausing often to chat with those she encountered. Only a few months ago, Trella had walked the entire city almost every day. But now, between her pregnancy and her new role as Eskkar's representative, she had less time to wander about and meet the inhabitants. Nevertheless, Trella wanted to stay close to Akkad's people, and so she took advantage of every opportunity to speak with them.

This late in the afternoon, women, their daily chores completed, made up most of the crowd. More than an hour remained before they started preparing their family's evening repast. Few could resist the opportunity to speak with Lady Trella, the wife of Akkad's ruler. Young mothers showed off their new babies, matrons pointed out their marriageable daughters, and older women or young widows presented themselves. Many of these sought Lady Trella's help in finding a husband, a duty she had assumed during the siege, as the casualties mounted among both villagers and soldiers.

The war against the barbarians had improved the status of those serving as Akkad's soldiers, and Eskkar increased their pay enough so the more senior men could afford wives. As with every task Trella undertook, no matter how minor, she gave it her full attention. At her urging, Eskkar summoned the more experienced soldiers, and Trella met with each of them, taking the time needed to learn what kind of husband each would be, and which woman would best suit him.

She soon had a good number of marriages to her credit. Because she'd helped arrange the unions, the husbands treated their newly acquired women properly, and the brides attended to their duties. Neither wanted the Lord of Akkad or his wife to hear of matrimonial difficulties. Even newcomers to Akkad soon learned to take advantage of Lady Trella's knowledge and services, not only as a marriage broker, but also as an honest advisor for almost any situation.

By the time Annok-sur and Trella reached Eskkar's compound, she'd promised to find husbands for two more women. Two soldiers guarded the entrance, and one held the gate open for the mistress of the house. They passed into the courtyard, where the scent of jasmine hung in the air, and tulips in pots scattered along the inner walls offered some color to offset the drab mud-brick walls.

When Eskkar became captain of the guard, he had taken over this large, two-story house with its private garden and separate quarters for servants. The structure, at that time the largest in Akkad, had belonged to a wealthy merchant who valued his privacy as much as his security. Eskkar's domicile stood to the left, its second story rising up at the rear. The servants' quarters, as long as the main building, faced it across the sizable open space, and these dwellings formed two sides of the central courtyard. Man-high walls enclosed the rest.

During the siege, more than forty men had crammed themselves into the servants' quarters, though at present it housed only twenty guards, most of them Hawk Clan. Klexor, one of Eskkar's subcommanders, lived there along with his wife and children. Another room remained reserved for guests or travelers.

A large plank table with half a dozen benches capable of seating thirty rested midway between the two houses. In the hottest days of summer master, servants, and guards took their meals there. A few Hawk Clan soldiers could usually be found relaxing around the table, especially in the evening.

These warriors provided constant security for the house and its occupants. Day and night, two men guarded the front gate, while another watched the small garden at the rear of the main structure, with its single, high-set window that opened into Eskkar and Trella's second-story bedroom. In the evening, two guards took station inside the main house, guarding the steps that led up to Eskkar and Trella's rooms.

Annok-sur and her husband Bantor lived there as well.

When Eskkar became captain of the guard, Bantor and his wife had been too poor to find decent lodgings. Eskkar, with plenty of space in his new dwelling, had offered the neediest of his subcommanders one of the extra rooms in the big house.

The size of the household grew quickly, as soldiers and servants filled the rooms of both structures. Needing help, Trella asked Annok-sur for her assistance, and soon realized Bantor's wife could run the combined household efficiently and by herself. Once the two women had established the domicile, Annok-sur took over the day-to-day tasks, supervising the buying and cooking of food, cleaning the house, and washing their men's clothes in the river. Soon Annok-sur directed half a dozen servants and soldiers' wives inside the big household. With the household duties attended to, Trella helped Eskkar with organizing the village's defense, always her main task.

Weeks went by as Trella helped arrange the logistics needed to arm and supply the villagers and soldiers. Once Eskkar had that effort in hand, Trella concentrated on helping to train the villagers and get them ready for the coming siege. During the months of preparation she secretly kept to her real goal, the effort to win over the hearts and minds of the common people.

She started with the women, eager to speak with anyone who treated them with the least bit of consideration. Trella soon earned the respect of their menfolk and even the hardened soldiers, who treated her more like a sister than Eskkar's wife. In the process, and by careful use of Eskkar's newly acquired gold, Trella gradually built up a small network of spies and informers, mostly women and slaves, who kept her aware of anyone plotting against Eskkar and his new role.

Throughout the city, throughout the land, men talked freely in front of their women, whether slave or free, often treating them as furniture, something of no importance. But many women had sharper wits than their menfolk, though most had learned to keep such heresy to themselves. These women soon learned they could earn a copper coin or two by reporting anything of interest to Trella, who not only paid for the information, but actively sought the help of those who delivered it, asking their opinions and advice. She'd been raised by her father, an advisor to a ruling noble in a large village far to the south, and he'd taught her to use her sharp wits. Her days as a slave, beginning with her father's death and ending with Eskkar's ascent to power, had sharpened them even further. The information Trella's spies collected helped Eskkar survive the efforts of the nobles to replace him when the siege ended.

The siege had broken barely two months ago. That day, Eskkar and Trella stood atop the blood-stained wall, victorious over both the nobles and the barbarians. The people, delirious with joy at their salvation from death or slavery, acclaimed Eskkar their lord and ruler. At the same time, they hailed Trella as well, wanting her wisdom and guidance. They understood and respected the soldier who had saved their lives and property, but in the end, they trusted Trella to look after their well-being as much as Eskkar.

Even the nobles had finally seen the advantages of a strong ruler, though they would never have selected the blunt-speaking, barbarian Eskkar. For them, Trella smoothed the way, her intelligence and honesty giving them assurance that their own enterprises would be protected and allowed to grow. With food again on their tables, the people of Akkad relished the return of prosperity. If the bandits and thieves wandering the countryside could be driven off and the crops replanted, security and wealth would soon surpass their earlier levels.

Meanwhile, the rebuilding and expansion of Akkad continued, a gigantic task, but one Trella felt capable of accomplishing. Not a trader, merchant, or farm holder, she had no private interests to advance. The nobles and leading merchants saw everything in terms of their own wealth, did everything to increase their gold, their power, and their prestige at each other's expense.

Trella could focus on the safety of the city, something even the lowliest laborer not only understood but desired as well. As long as she treated everyone fairly and favored no particular noble or merchant, the people would support her and Eskkar. They might grumble at the taxes and some of the new rules, but everyone had learned the value of the soldiers who protected them. Just as everyone knew the barbarians would return someday, seeking vengeance.

What Trella desired most was time, time to secure their position and power. In a few years Akkad would be a strong, fortified city, and she and her child would be safe within its high walls, surrounded and protected by Eskkar's soldiers. That day remained in the future. Akkad's hastily built wall needed to be enlarged and strengthened, and more soldiers recruited and trained to defend it. Until then she would neglect nothing, overlook nothing that might threaten her plans, not even something as insignificant as a strange traveler from a distant land.

Trella and Annok-sur entered the main house, stepping into the spacious common room that held another large table where meals were served. Wooden stairs on the far wall led to the second story. They climbed to the top, where a small landing faced a stout wooden door that opened into the first of the two large rooms that made up Eskkar's private quarters.

The outer room, what Eskkar called the workroom, held a good-sized table and half a dozen chairs and stools. A tall cabinet that served both as a cupboard and sideboard hugged one wall, and two chests provided storage. Three wide, rectangular windows, cut into the walls near the ceiling and too small for even a child to crawl through, provided light and air. The wall opposite the entry had a second door, as sturdy as the first, that led into Eskkar and Trella's bedroom.

Trella passed quickly through the workroom and into the inner chamber. Though not as large as the outer room, the bedroom was spacious enough, especially compared to the cramped rooms occupied by most Akkadians. Most of them would be astonished at the idea of having a separate room just for sleeping. Trella knew a family of six or more would live, work, and sleep in this much space, and count themselves blessed by the gods to have walls around them and a roof over their heads.

Only this inner room had a true window, albeit a small one, that opened over a tiny private garden at the rear of the house. A thick wooden shutter framed this opening, with two stout wooden braces to secure it. A wide, decorated clay bowl resting beneath it held a knotted and coiled rope, for escape in case of fire. As in the workroom, ventilation came from three tiny openings on each wall, set high to let the heat of the room escape more easily. Unlike most of the houses in the city, the architect had provided no access to the roof, where the poor often slept at night to escape the heat of summer.

Eskkar and Trella benefited now from these luxurious arrangements. A smooth coat of white plaster enhanced the interior walls. The solid floor, made of sanded and joined wooden strips, stopped most sound, and Eskkar's soldiers guarded the window from the garden below.

The entire compound, with its thick and high mud-brick walls, provided a secure base in a turbulent city. The original owner had designed these rooms to keep himself and his gold secure, and his vices secret.

For its new occupants, these rooms provided one of the rarest and most valuable commodities in Akkad—privacy. Behind the stout doors in the bedroom or workroom, important matters could be discussed without danger of being overheard.

Trella went directly to the chamber pot. When she finished, she untied her sandals and lay on the bed, grateful for the chance to rest her feet and back for a few moments.

"Tired, Trella?" Annok-sur sat on a small stool next to the bed.

"Yes, though it seems strange. I tire so easily, though I've done nothing but sit and talk all day."

"Once the child comes, you'll be yourself again. Rest for a few moments. I'll tend to the servants, then come back with something for you to eat and drink."

Trella closed her eyes and joined her hands across her stomach. Already her back felt better, and as she relaxed, she felt the babe kicking gently inside her womb.

Part of her mind worried about the birth. So many women died in childbirth, especially their first delivery. She accepted the risk involved. All women did. A wife's most important role was to provide children, heirs for her husband, to carry on his line. Childbirth might be dangerous, but soldiers accepted their own risk of death in battle, and even farmers in the field suffered injuries often enough.

Still, the thought of the birth ordeal bothered her more as the event drew closer. A month ago, Annok-sur had brought the most experienced midwife she could find to see Trella. The woman lived not in Akkad, but on a farm a day's walk south of the city. To Trella's surprise, the midwife turned out to be a woman of about Annok-sur's age, not the ancient crone Trella expected. Her name was Drusala, and she'd helped deliver babies since her childhood.

Trella stood naked on two wooden blocks before the midwife, her feet spread apart and holding her hands behind her head, while Drusala and Annok-sur examined every inch of Trella's body, prodding and poking her, looking for lumps or weaknesses of flesh. Then Annok-sur had spread Trella's labia apart, so that Drusala, on her knees in front of the girl and probing with her fingers, could examine the birth channel.

"Her hips could be wider, I suppose," the midwife said critically when she finished with her examination. "But she is very strong, even though she doesn't work in the fields. I see no problems with your delivery, Lady Trella, but I'll return to Akkad when your time is near. Still, you must walk for at least an hour each day. That will help the child come out without too much pain."

Trella remembered her words of advice, and she had put them into action. Each morning, right after breakfast, she paced back and forth inside the courtyard for an hour or longer. Trella would have preferred to walk about the city, as she'd done before the siege ended, but there would have been so many interruptions she would never have finished her walk. Besides, such extended strolls had become too dangerous. An assassin had attacked Trella in the street before, and those jealous of her growing power might be tempted to strike again. She would have to be content with her courtyard excursions, at least for now.

The unborn child moved again, and this time the movement brought a smile to Trella's face. She closed her eyes and let her mind drift, thinking of the future and the heir she would give to Eskkar.

She hoped he wouldn't do anything foolish. So much depended on Eskkar. Without him, her influence and authority would vanish. The citizens of Akkad would never take orders from a woman, no matter how much they liked or respected her, let alone an outsider and a former slave at that.

Trella hadn't wanted him to go, but the countryside needed to be pacified and brought under control. And though she hated the risks, she knew Eskkar was the best choice for the task. With Bisitun taken and under Akkad's authority, the situation would be different, and she would insist he remain in the city. He hated the inactivity and petty disputes that found their way to him every day, but he would have to accept it. She needed Eskkar here, and soon his son would need his protection as well.

Trella considered finding him another girl to occupy his time. While she was pregnant, or raising the baby, there would be less time to pleasure him. She would have to select the girl carefully, of course. It must be someone who could please him without arousing too much of his interest.

Trella sighed at the thought. She didn't like the thought of sharing her husband with another woman. So far, it hadn't seemed a problem. His love for her remained ardent. But a strong man needed more than one woman, at least occasionally. If she didn't provide one, the village elders might convince Eskkar of the need to take a second wife, if for no other reason than to weaken Trella's influence. No, it would be better to do it herself, one more task to occupy her time. Fortunately, she didn't need to deal with it today. When he returned from the north, she would speak to him about it.

Now she worried about the dangers Eskkar would face. She hated being idle while her husband prepared for battle somewhere in the north. And today this stranger from the land of Egypt arrived and intrigued her. Trella closed her eyes again, and worried about the coming child.

Annok-sur slipped quietly into the bedroom, thinking Trella was asleep. But the girl stirred when Annok-sur set the tray of dates, wine, and water onto a round table scarcely bigger than the two plain stools that stood beside it. Annok-sur sat down on the one closest to the bed and ran her fingers through her brown hair, already touched with a tinge of gray though she had one more year before her thirtieth season.

"I should get up," Trella said, her voice barely above a whisper.

"No, stay there," Annok-sur said, "supper is at least an hour away." She pushed the table closer to the bed. "Eat something. The child must be hungry." Annok-sur knew that Trella did not intend to let her pregnancy interfere with her work.

Trella clasped her hands behind her head. "There is a stranger in town, Annok-sur. A trader from the lands far to the west, the land called Egypt. Or so he claims. He says the land there has many cities and villages, some with walls of mud-brick as high as our own. This man plans to trade gemstones here in Akkad."

Annok-sur had heard of the mythical Egypt from her husband, Bantor. "So the land of Egypt exists! It is said that food falls from the branches of the trees, and that gold and silver are everywhere underfoot." She shrugged at the fable. "What does it mean to Akkad?"

"Nothing, I'm sure. It's far away, and the great desert makes travel nearly impossible. Even bandits can't raid across that expanse. That's what interests me about this trader. He wants to open a merchant house here, and begin trade with Egypt."

Like Trella, Annok-sur kept her voice low, more from habit than any need. The servants had proven trustworthy, and no strangers or guests stayed in the main house. Nevertheless, outside of these rooms, spies lurked everywhere, looking to sell whatever gossip or secrets they heard to one trader or another. Women, if they had any wits, learned at an early age to whisper among themselves; the less men knew about their wives' and daughters' dealings, the better.

"Bantor told me the lands to the west of the Euphrates are wild, filled with only savage people who can withstand the desert heat. He traveled three days into those barren lands once, chasing a murderer, before turning back empty-handed."

"Yes, the wastelands are desolate and dangerous," Trella agreed. "Even Eskkar has never gone very far west of the other river. So trading across the desert will be a great risk."

"This merchant . . . what is his name?"

"Korthac. You saw him leave the Council House. He has delicate features, almost like a woman's. His eyes are sharp and miss nothing."

"Ah, yes, I remember seeing him. So this Korthac will trade gemstones." Annok-sur thought for a moment. "There's always much demand for such goods. He can sell all he wishes in Akkad, now that the boats are again moving up and down the river."

Rising from the bed, Trella sat on the other stool. She poured some wine and water for them both, careful to add just a mouthful of the spirits in her cup, as she did not enjoy the taste of wine or even the local beer.

"Yes, a steady supply of scarce gemstones would attract even more merchants to Akkad, benefiting all." Trella took a small sip before taking a date from the platter. "But I wonder what Korthac will send back to Egypt in return. Merchants must trade both ways to be successful."

The question seemed casual enough, but Annok-sur knew Trella didn't waste her thoughts on trivial matters. "Well, he would have plenty of gold," Annok-sur answered. "He might deal in linens or bronze, or perhaps . . ." Her voice trailed off for a moment as she considered the possibilities.

"When traders come to Akkad," Trella went on, as she selected another date, "they barter copper and ores for food and clothing. Or timber for tools, or cattle for leather goods or weapons." She looked at Annok-sur. "If you were a trader, what would you carry back to this rich land called Egypt?"

Annok-sur deliberated the question. Gold, of course. But gold had its limitations. You couldn't eat it or build anything with it, and its weight made it difficult to transport. Just as important, with every rich merchant making his own coins and setting their value, its worth was often suspect. So traders used gold mainly to adjust for differences in value between goods, or to represent value that could be carried more easily than bulky merchandise.

Across such a great and dangerous distance, what would one carry back? What would be worth the effort for such a trip? Food and grain would spoil on the journey. Tools and weapons weighed too much for their value. Besides, if the land of Egypt had as many riches as people claimed, it would already have these things in plenty.

"I see what you mean, Trella. But there must be something in Akkad that they lack. Or perhaps he intends to trade only in Akkad. He may have no plans to trade with his homeland." She shook her head. "We'll know soon enough, won't we?"

"Yes, we'll see what this stranger buys with the gold he gets for his gemstones," Trella answered. "But he did say he meant to trade with Egypt. So I think we should find out as much as possible about him." She finished her watered wine, then poured herself a cup of plain water. "Korthac will need furniture for his house, servants to care for him, and food for his kitchen. And he and his men will need women, especially after such a long and dangerous journey."

Annok-sur smiled. "Yes, I'm sure we can learn much about Korthac and his plans in the next few weeks."

"Be discreet," Trella said. "I don't want him to learn we are spying on him."

"As a stranger, he'll expect to be watched. But I will be careful." Annok-sur got up and moved behind Trella and began massaging her shoulders. Her fingers worked steadily, and in a few moments Annok-sur felt her mistress relax. She looked down at Trella as she nibbled at another date, separating the pit from the meat with her slender fingertips.

"You should rest, Trella, sleep a little more before dinner."

"I will." She sighed. "Eskkar is gone barely a week, and already I miss him."

"He will be away for at least a month. And the people accept your rule. They feel as safe with you as they do with Eskkar. Now rest, for the child's sake if not your own."

"You worry too much about me, Annok-sur. You're like the older sister I never had."

"After you've had a child or two, you'll know enough to rest whenever you can." Since her marriage to Bantor, Annok-sur had delivered three children. The first died stillborn, the second from fever before it reached its first year. Only the third child, her daughter Ningal, born five years after her marriage, survived, but since the long and painful delivery, Annok-sur had not gotten pregnant again.

Trella folded her hands on her stomach. "Even now, he's moving inside me. Can you feel him?"

Annok-sur reached over and placed her hand beside Trella's. "Only six months pregnant, and already the child seems strong. It will be a boy, I'm sure of it."

"Eskkar is a strong man. He will give me many sons."

"Yes, mistress, you will have many sons. And I'll help you care for all of them." She rose and stood behind Trella, her hands massaging the young girl's shoulders. Annok-sur's hands moved down Trella's arms, then brushed lightly across her breasts before returning to her shoulders. "Would you like to lie down for awhile? There is plenty of time. I could join you ... if you like."

Annok-sur's hands again reached for Trella's breasts, squeezing them gently, knowing how sensitive they would be. After a moment, she felt Trella sway against her, and knew the temptation moving through her mistress's body. She kept massaging Trella's breasts, feeling the girl relax even further.

"I shouldn't, but ... your hands feel so comforting." Trella looked up at Annok-sur and smiled. "Perhaps it would be good to lie down for a few minutes." Then she closed her eyes and let her head lean back against Annok-sur's body.

Annok-sur's smile sounded in her voice, and her hands lingered over Trella's breasts. "Let me help you with your dress, then."

"The door, Annok-sur ..."

Annok-sur stepped back and left the room. She crossed the workroom to the outer door and closed it, silently lifting the wooden bar that locked it into place. The closed door would tell the servants below that Trella wished not to be disturbed. They would assume she was taking her rest before dinner.

Trella stood up as Annok-sur returned. The older woman held her closely in her arms for a minute before she helped lift Trella's dress up over her head. Then she removed her own, while her mistress sank onto the large bed. For a moment, Annok-sur sat on the edge of the bed and gazed at the body of her mistress. Then, gently, Annok-sur leaned down and began to kiss each of Trella's breasts, enjoying the feel and taste of them. They'd already started to swell, and her milk would soon make them even larger. Annok-sur's hands went softly over the rounded belly and she could feel the child within, stirring at her touch. More pleasantly, Annok-sur could feel Trella enjoying the first wave of excitement, as her breathing grew deeper.

Annok-sur's lips began moving down Trella's body now, brushing her stomach, while her hands reached down and began stroking the girl's vagina. She sat close to Trella, their bodies touching, and used her hands and fingers to first relax, then stimulate the younger girl. Trella lay back, her eyes still closed, but her hand rested lightly on Annok-sur's inner thigh.

In a few more moments, Annok-sur had Trella's legs apart, and now Annok-sur leaned over and began to use her tongue as well as her fingers, finding and teasing that most sensitive place. Her breast brushed against Trella's thigh, and Annok-sur shivered at the contact. The young girl sighed heavily and her legs parted further, as she grew more and more aroused.

Annok-sur felt her own excitement growing. Never in her life had she felt such an attraction for anyone, man or woman. It wasn't physical beauty. Annok-sur had seen many girls and women more attractive than Trella, and never felt the slightest urge to touch any of them.

No, it was something inside Trella that attracted her, just as it attracted the men who followed her with their hot eyes everywhere she went. Trella had not only a presence, but an intellect that saw much and understood everything. More important, Trella had raised up Annok-sur's station in life, and Trella ruled the city with a power and intelligence that continued to amaze the older woman.

Now even the sight of this girl, or simply being in the same room with her, roused Annok-sur's desire, and she felt the wetness growing between her own legs. But she felt more than just desire; Annok-sur wanted Trella to succeed, wanted her to continue to exert her influence and power over the men around her. Annok-sur knew what Trella wanted, and, because of her love for Trella, Annok-sur wanted the same things. Trella and Eskkar must have many sons, and they and their children must rule Akkad for years to come. And Annok-sur would stand at her mistress's side. Then Annok-sur had no more thoughts, no words for some time, until Trella cried out softly in her pleasure.

Bringing Trella to the joy of the gods sent a wave of pleasure through Annok-sur, but she continued kissing and stroking the girl in her arms, calming her trembling, until Trella's eyes opened and for the first time they kissed. Annok-sur let herself be pulled down on the bed, and she felt Trella's hands on her own body. It seemed to take scarcely a moment before Annok-sur's own passion rocked her body, though she, too, made no sound that could have been heard outside the bedroom.

Afterwards Annok-sur held Trella in her arms, as a mother would hold a child, until the young girl fell asleep.

Annok-sur gazed at her mistress, watching her breasts rise and fall with each breath. She did think of Trella as a sister. As a child, Annok-sur had often longed for a little sister to be a companion. Instead she'd grown up with three brothers on a small farm just outside Akkad, and her parents admonished her childish request for a baby girl. Instead, they gave thanks to Ishtar for her brothers, who could share the farm's labors.

Her parents soon had their only daughter selling vegetables in Akkad's market. There Annok-sur, a plain but sturdy girl only a few months into the mysteries of womanhood, first noticed a young farmer gazing open-mouthed at her. Something about his wide brown eyes made Annok-sur smile back at him. Nevertheless, it took Bantor three days before he gathered enough courage to speak to her. A few weeks later, Bantor, only a year or two older than she, stood before her parents.

"Honorable father, I have five copper coins for a wife. It would please me to give them to you for Annok-sur."

Her father had asked for double that, but Bantor only shook his head.

"Five is a good price for a young bride," he answered stiffly. "And it is all I have."

Annok-sur's heart had faltered when Bantor turned away, ready to leave. But her father relented. The coins changed hands, and in a few moments, her future husband led her away from her family, while she clutched the few things she possessed to her breast. That day, she stood beside him facing the image of Ishtar, and became Bantor's wife.

Together they worked on his father's farm for six years, hard toil from dawn to dusk, but Annok-sur's body grew strong from the years of laboring. She was pregnant with her third child when Bantor's father died. His oldest brother took possession of the farm and, by the custom of ascension, ordered Bantor to leave. She and her husband owned nothing but the clothing on their backs and two food bowls. Desperate, they moved to Akkad where Bantor sought work as a common laborer, eager for any menial job. The birth of their daughter caused even more hardship. Raising Ningal, the three of them lived with another family, who charged them rent to occupy one corner of their single room hut. Annok-sur baked bread, worked in the market, and joined the farmers during harvest time, any work she could find to supplement her husband's efforts.

Their first two years in Akkad, they seldom had enough to eat, and Annok-sur watched her husband grow ever more dour and grim, as their life of poverty drained his spirit. When they had no coins for food, she resorted to selling herself along the riverbank with the other prostitutes. On those occasions, Bantor would look away, embarrassed at his failure to provide for them. Even Ningal proved a disappointment, as she grew into a frivolous child who complained often.

Another year went by before Bantor found work as a recruit in Akkad's guard. He hated the long days on guard duty, each dreary task interrupted only by another just as wearisome. The occasional assignment to track down runaway slaves proved more to his liking, and provided him a chance to get away from the crowded village and breathe once again the clean air of the countryside.

Annok-sur's world, too, began to shrink as the burden of life grew heavier and heavier. Once, while Bantor rode after some slaves, the captain of the guard had summoned her for an afternoon of pleasuring him. That act of humiliation tortured her for months, but she had to obey, lest Ariamus dismiss her husband. Annok-sur never spoke of that incident, but somehow she felt certain Bantor had learned about it. Whatever the cause, Bantor sank into an apathy so deep that he seldom smiled or even spoke.

She scarcely noticed when Eskkar arrived in Akkad. The tall barbarian soon took charge of the horses and most of the pursuits of runaway slaves. Eskkar and Bantor worked together often enough during the next few years, but they spoke little and showed no signs of any particular friendship. Then Ariamus ran off, as word spread of the coming barbarian invasion.

"Eskkar the barbarian will be the new captain of the guard," Bantor told her, an excited gleam in his eyes. "He has asked me to be one of his subcommanders."

Stunned, she listened as her husband explained his new duties. The night before, Bantor had told her that they must flee the city; as refugees, their desperate situation would only grow worse. Now he planned to stay and fight. For a brief moment, she thought about the coming danger, but one look at her husband convinced her; his face hadn't shown such excitement or intensity in years.

"Then you must do all you can to help Eskkar," she said, placing her arms on his shoulders. "If he can manage to defeat the barbarians, you will be one of his subcommanders, and he will remember your loyalty."

Bantor' s first test of courage and loyalty came not

against the barbarian Alur Meriki, but against one of the ruling nobles who wanted Eskkar out of the way. Instead, the rich merchant had died, and Eskkar had taken possession of the man's house. Aware of Bantor's difficult situation, Eskkar invited his subcommander to move into the spacious quarters. Annok-sur remembered the tears that came when she saw the chamber, a whole room they would have to themselves, the first such luxury they'd ever had.

Then she met Trella, Eskkar's new slave. It took only a few encounters for Annok-sur to realize how sharp Trella's wits were, how carefully she considered everyone's words, and how deep she saw into people's hearts. The gods had surely arranged the joining of Eskkar and Trella. Between them, they might save Akkad from rape and ruin.

Annok-sur soon took over the task of managing the large household, leaving the young slave girl plenty of time to work with Eskkar preparing for the siege. She had labored side by side with Trella during the assault, astonished at each task Trella undertook, and more amazed at how she achieved each goal. They'd both risked death during those evil days, helping defend the wall during the attacks, and tending the wounded afterwards. Even before Eskkar vanquished the barbarians, Trella set her mind to a new task: to ensure that she and her husband ruled Akkad for the rest of their days. To that end, Trella still labored, influencing all the men and councils of the new city to her will.

Annok-sur had joined the venture with all her heart and strength, determined to make certain that Trella succeeded. Even Bantor had changed under Eskkar and Trella's influence. Now he thought more before acting and, watching his captain's example, had learned to take heed of Annok-sur's words.

"We must follow wherever they lead," she told Bantor. "They will rule this city some day, and Eskkar will remember who stood at his side. A chance like this might never come again."

Bantor heeded her advice, and as his responsibilities and prospects grew, he'd somehow returned to the ways of his youth, softening his words and touch toward Annok-sur, and for that she gave thanks every night to Ishtar. Only the great mother goddess herself could have sent Trella to them. The two women had grown closer than sisters in many ways, working and planning together to secure Eskkar's rule over the city.

Pushing the past out of her mind, Annok-sur returned her thoughts to Korthac. She had many tasks to start in motion. The women of Akkad would begin watching the Egyptian's every move and reporting back through the network of spies and informers Trella and Annok-sur had established. Soon, she was sure, they would know all about this Korthac.

The future of both women depended on so many things beyond their control. Only moments ago Annok-sur had glimpsed the long scar, stretching from Trella's left armpit to her hip. An assassin had come within a finger's width of killing her, and anyone in Akkad with a few coins in his purse could hire a villain to do murder. Annok-sur worried every time Trella walked the streets, even though two alert bodyguards accompanied her. And now Eskkar had gone off riding around the countryside, risking his life for the chance to play warrior like any common barbarian. An arrow in the back or a knife in his ribs, and everything Trella had worked so hard for would come crashing down around them.

Well, Annok-sur could do nothing about Eskkar. The man took as little heed of his own life as he did of Trella's. Nevertheless, Trella needed Eskkar, needed him to protect not only her and the child-to-come, but Annok-sur and her husband Bantor as well. Both women realized how dangerous their position in Akkad really was. One slip, one mistake, and they could all vanish. During the siege, everyone had clamored for Eskkar and Trella to save them. Now, if Eskkar got himself killed, Trella's authority would disappear. Everyone would remember her days as a slave, and Trella's control of the Nobles and soldiers would vanish like the morning mist on the river.

In a year, even six months, Annok-sur knew things would change. Eskkar and Trella would soon have an heir, and by then the people would be used to their rule. Wealth would flow into Akkad and be shared by all of its inhabitants. The people would be happy and content; gratitude and praise would flow to Akkad's rulers.

Annok-sur sighed. When she felt certain Trella wouldn't wake, Annok-sur slipped out of the bed and spread the blanket over her mistress' body. Annok-sur pulled her own dress back on, and cleared her thoughts.

The love-making had ended, and it would not be repeated, not for some time. Trella had made her wishes plain and Annok-sur accepted them. An occasional tryst might happen, like today, but the risks were great, and neither woman could take such chances lightly. Using Trella's comb, she arranged her hair and left the bedroom, closing the door silently behind her.

5

The sun beat down from directly overhead when Eskkar and his men topped a low rise and saw the village of Bisitun in the distance, about an hour's march away. Like Akkad, it nestled against the eastern bank of the river Tigris. At Akkad, though, the great river curled halfway around the city. Here at Bisitun the river ran straight. A mile more to the northeast, and the Tigris would begin to curve sharply northward, continuing its long journey to the mountains of its birth.

Also like Akkad, Bisitun offered easy fordage of the great river. The Tigris here stretched wider from bank to bank, and the water flowed slower and somewhat shallower than at Akkad. A narrow, sandy island split the flowing water in two, and allowed travelers to rest at the river's midpoint. During the late summer season, when the depth ran even lower, a strong man could walk and swim across to the other side, though the distance reached almost a quarter of a mile. Usually small boats made of reeds carried men, supplies, and even horses on their journey. With the coming of the fall season, the river ran deeper and stronger, and its strength would continue to increase until midsummer.

Eskkar signaled a halt, and the Akkadian soldiers took their rest, glad to have reached the end of their journey. It had taken them five days to march here from Dilgarth, long days with hard traveling broken frequently by training and special drills. Those had puzzled the men, but Eskkar, ignoring their questions, pushed them ever harder. With a conflict almost certain, he wanted the iron discipline that had saved Akkad, and Eskkar demanded every order be instantly obeyed, without question or argument.

The soldiers got no respite from the drills even after dark, their rest and dinner often interrupted by subcommanders barking out orders to prepare a line of battle or form up for an attack. At least once each night, the men found themselves jolted awake, their leaders shouting that the enemy was attacking, and bellowing at them to find their weapons and places.

By the middle of the second day, a shouted command would quickly transform them into a crude square, with the pack animals and supplies in the center, ringed by ready bowmen. Well drilled by now, they would not be surprised by any attacking force. Moreover, they had the soldier's confidence in themselves and their comrades, knowing that every man knew his place and his duties.

Even the liverymen, scribes, and merchants received extra tasks, and these noncombatants drilled as rigorously as the soldiers, taking charge of the men's baggage or making sure spare arrows and extra water stood ready. That night, a few of the men had grown weary enough to complain, but they did that only once. Hamati had knocked one down so hard that the man lay unconscious for almost an hour.

By the time they reached Bisitun, Eskkar's men had achieved the mood he intended. Tired, near exhaustion, footsore—they'd transferred their anger to the men in Bisitun, the bandits who had wearied their legs and interrupted their sleep.

The Akkadians took in their surroundings with grim interest, knowing that, from today on, there would be no more drills. If the men felt worried about what would happen now that they'd reached Bisitun, they were too tired to show it. The scene before them seemed peaceful enough. The usual farms lay scattered across the landscape, crisscrossed by the ever-present irrigation canals, with the occasional brown mud houses. A single dirt pathway, well trodden, continued its way up to the village. Everything appeared peaceful, and it looked much the same as on Eskkar's last visit here, nearly two years ago.

"Well, Captain," Sisuthros said, as he rode up to the head of the column, where Eskkar and Grond had stopped their horses, "do we camp here or should we press on?"

"Let's stay here for an hour, at least," Eskkar answered. "We're in no rush now."

"They won't come out to challenge us," Grond said. "That would be too easy. Even bandits aren't that stupid."

"No, I suppose not," Eskkar said. "But the men need a rest anyway, and from now on, we have to convince Ninazu of our plan."

Eskkar caught the glance that passed between Sisuthros and Grond, but neither man said anything. The time for arguing had passed, and the next few days would resolve everyone's doubts.

So the men rested and stared at the village for over an hour before they resumed their march. They moved slowly, the soldiers walking close together, ringed at a good distance by the twenty mounted riders. During the last four days, Eskkar had drilled the men for an attack by a large, mounted band of riders. The soldiers had learned to form up rapidly, string their bows and prepare their weapons, and make ready for an attack from any or all sides.

Nevertheless the soldiers moved cautiously, every man alert, and it took another hour to reach their destination. Eskkar gave the order to halt fifty paces out of a long bowshot from the village's palisade.

Eskkar nodded at Sisuthros. His subcommander turned and began shouting orders to the men. First they straddled the road that led to the village and dropped their packs and supplies. Unencumbered, they got right to work, though every man kept his weapons close by. While twenty men stood guard with strung bows, the rest began to dig a ditch across the road. They had plenty of shovels and digging tools, most of them acquired during the last four days as the horsemen checked every farm they passed for digging implements, paying copper coins to the farmers only too eager to sell them. The rest of the men used their hands, sticks, or whatever else they could obtain. Fortunately, the sandy soil made the work proceed quickly.

Eskkar rode off a little ways, Grond at his side, and studied the village before them. The Alur Meriki in their passing must have burned a good portion of the palisade, and Eskkar could see where it had been rebuilt. No doubt the barbarians had knocked down plenty of houses during their looting, but mud bricks were easily replaced, and a peasant's hut could be rebuilt with a few days' labor. Bisitun probably hadn't changed much in the last few years. Back then more than five hundred people lived here; now that number might even be higher, with all the nearby farmers driven from their land, crops and homes destroyed. Some might have left since the coming of Ninazu, but others would still come, looking for any communal place of safety, even a village ruled by bandits.

Fresh repairs to the main gate showed plainly; no doubt the Alur Meriki had broken up the previous one and used it for firewood. All the mud houses within bowshot of the palisade had been knocked down, and the rubble broken up and strewn about, to impede the progress of any attacker. The palisade stood higher than Eskkar remembered, and appeared to have been reinforced with extra logs or planks. The new gate looked sturdy as well, though nowhere near as massive as Akkad's main entrance.

Eskkar could see the defenders standing behind the stockade, some still scurrying about, searching for their assigned positions. Most of them carried bows, with axes and swords no doubt close at hand. From the highest point of the palisade, just to the side of the gate, a small group of men stood apart and watched the soldiers from Akkad as they began to dig in.

"I'll wager that one's Ninazu," Grond commented. "Looks a little like his brother, at any rate. The tall one with the silver armbands."

Eskkar picked out the man, but his eye couldn't see any resemblance at that distance, only the polished silver glinting in the sun. For a moment that irritated him. Ten seasons ago, it would have been his eyes that spotted such details. Not that he could complain; his luck had kept him alive. Few fighting men made it to their thirtieth season, and Eskkar had survived more battles than he could remember. Still, he knew the trades of fighting and soldiering were best left to men just reaching their twentieth season.

"We'll know soon enough if that's him," Eskkar grunted. "But keep an eye on that one. We'll need to identify the leaders for later on."

"Do you think they'll come out to fight? They look ready enough."

"No, not if their leader's got any wits. Not yet, at any rate. This Ninazu probably expects an immediate attack on the village, if not today, then tomorrow. Let him watch our men dig in . . . give him plenty of time to wonder what we're planning."

"Should we ride around and take a look at the other sides?"

"When we're dug in. There'll be plenty of time tomorrow. Let's try and get a count of how many fighters we're facing."

Eskkar stayed in the same position a long time, looking at the palisade, trying to put himself in the bandit leader's place. The siege at Akkad had given him a wealth of experience in defending a village from attack. Soldiers and villagers alike had spent almost five months preparing for the Akkad siege, learning and even inventing new defenses, then endured more than a month of hard fighting against the entire Alur Meriki clan. In the end, Eskkar and his soldiers had forced the barbarians to move on, defeating them as much by denying them food as by resisting them on the battlements.

With that experience, Eskkar studied Bisitun and its wooden palisade. This time *he* would be the attacker, the one outside the walls. Put yourself in your enemy's mind, Trella would remind him. This Ninazu had the village and the stockade to protect him, and Ninazu had more men than his besiegers.

But just because a man carried a sword didn't make him an experienced fighter. The men from Akkad had trained and practiced their skills for over five months. More important, many of them had faced battle-hardened, determined fighters and beat them. No scruffy band of brigands, held together only by their love of gold and fear of their leaders, would stand up to Eskkar's men for more than a few moments in open combat. Ninazu must realize this. So there would be no sudden sortie from the village, to rush and overwhelm the attackers.

Ninazu would have other worries as well. Eskkar hadn't really needed to talk to the local farmers to know how they had been treated. And while the reluctant inhabitants of Bisitun might stand on the wall and look determined, they weren't going to fight to the death for Ninazu, a man who had taken freely their wives and daughters as well as their crops and valuables, and ruled only by force. No, Ninazu couldn't trust his villagers for long.

And if the bandit ventured out and suffered a defeat, many of his men would start thinking about taking what they had gained and slipping across the river to safety. Ninazu needed a quick victory. If Eskkar attacked and was driven off, Ninazu's position and strength would increase.

The longer the siege went on, the more confidence Ninazu's men would have. But time, which seemed to be on Ninazu's side, would soon be working in Eskkar's favor.

"This Ninazu has plenty of men," Eskkar said, "willing and unwilling. I count at least ninety or a hundred fighting men that I can see. No doubt there are more waiting behind the palisade. More than enough to attack us here. But he'll wait a few days, to see what we're up to."

"Then we'll have to show him what we can do, Captain," Grond answered. "He's in for a surprise."

"Just make sure we're not the ones who are surprised."

The rough ideas that Eskkar had first considered back in Dilgarth and reworked on the march north still had merit, and the terrain around the village seemed favorable. Now that he could study the village's defenses, he needed to give more thought to some details, but he had his plan. Tonight and tomorrow would give him more information even as he set in motion the first part of his plan.

Though not by nature a patient man, Eskkar could afford to take his time. He wanted to capture the village without losing too many men. The soldiers he and Gatus had trained were far too valuable to throw away in a frontal assault, though he already felt sure he could force the palisade, using his archers to drive Ninazu's men from the walls. But many would die, and Eskkar needed all the trained fighting men he had, not only here, but back in Akkad as well. No, he would stay with his original plan. His mind made up, Eskkar and Grond turned their horses around and headed back toward their new encampment.

By the time darkness fell, the camp's basic defense was nearly completed. A shallow ditch surrounded the men on three sides, with only their rear exposed. By early tomorrow, that opening would be closed as well. The earth from the ditch had been piled up on the inside of the camp to form an embankment, and men worked at packing it down even now. This dirt wall would stop an arrow as well as any wooden fence, while the ditch in front would hinder either men or horses, should the men inside Bisitun attempt to overrun the Akkadians.

The idea for a fortified camp such as this had come from Gatus. He and Eskkar had argued over many nights and much ale about its worth. The old soldier had a special way with training the men, and seemed obsessed with the idea of fortifications. Until this moment, Eskkar had remained skeptical, but now, watching the earthworks go up, he realized that the old fighter was right.

Sisuthros posted the guards and made the rounds to make sure they stayed alert. But Eskkar would depend more on the three men who slipped out of the camp as soon as the last of the sun vanished from the sky. They would creep up as close to the palisade as possible to keep watch. If the defenders decided to sortie out, the three sentries would give warning.

Inside the camp Sisuthros kept all seventy Akkadians busy for another two hours, before they were allowed to turn in, though a third of the men would stay awake and alert throughout the night. The tired soldiers fell asleep in moments, snoring away in blissful repose, a sound loud enough to wake the demons or the dead. Only when everything seemed secure for the night did Grond, Hamati, and Sisuthros sit down with Eskkar around a small campfire to discuss their next steps.

"From what we could see on the palisade," Eskkar began, "it looks as though Ninazu has at least a hundred fighting men, probably thirty or forty more that he's kept hidden. The rest are villagers and the local farmers, no doubt with swords at their backs as well as in their hands."

"What if they try an attack tonight?" Hamati asked. He had charge of the first group of twenty-five men who would be awake and ready throughout the night.

"I don't think they will," Eskkar answered. "He knows he outnumbers us. Why should they give up their strong position to attack us in ours? No, he'll wait, thinking we may attack tomorrow."

"We could still try something at night ourselves," Sisuthros suggested.

"We don't have the men to waste. We'll stay with the plan, for the next few days at least." Eskkar stood. "Wake me when you change the guards, Hamati. I'll want to talk to the men. Now, let's get some rest."

Eskkar arose before dawn broke. He'd slept well during the night, despite waking twice as the twenty-five defenders were replaced. Each time, he made the rounds with the new men, inspecting them, talking with them, and reminding them to keep alert.

All around him men groaned and stretched, their muscles stiff from yesterday's digging. He smiled at that. Those muscles would loosen up soon enough. There would be more digging today. A lot more. The men should be grateful. At least they wouldn't be marching anywhere.

Before the sun cleared the horizon, Eskkar stood atop the dirt embankment and looked toward the village. The palisade stood fully manned, a sign of good discipline on his enemy's part. No doubt Ninazu had expected an early morning attack, or even something during the night. With the sun behind him, Eskkar picked out the man with bright silver bracelets on both his arms. If that proved to be Ninazu, he would be an easy target, especially for Mitrac and his bow.

Eskkar studied the palisade only long enough to be sure the defenders had no plans for a morning attack of their own. When he turned away, half a dozen arrows flew into the sky, trying to reach him. All scattered themselves in the earth, the nearest of them at least sixty paces short of their target. Smiling, Eskkar waved at the bandit leader, then stepped back down inside the embankment.

After a quick meal of stale bread and hard cheese, Eskkar watched as Sisuthros gave the morning orders. His subcommander sent out ten scouts on horseback, to make sure no one surprised the Akkadians from their rear or flanks. The scouts dispatched, Sisuthros directed the liverymen and scribes to fetch fresh water from the river, and put the rest of the men to work. First they would finish the ditch around the entire camp. Then the ditch would be made deeper and the rampart higher, higher than really needed. Eskkar wanted the camp secure by day's end, and his men concealed from the defenders, so they could prepare their surprises.

The men worked steadily, only half of them laboring at any time, as the others stood guard or rested. By noon, a steep wall of packed-down dirt surrounded the camp. Only an opening six paces wide at the rear remained. Sisuthros's scouts returned, leading two wagons that could be used to block that opening if necessary. With the basic fortification constructed the men labored, on making the ditch deeper and the rampart higher. Eskkar walked around the camp once again, as he had already done a dozen times, talking to the men, encouraging them, telling them they could rest when the ditch was completed.

A shout made him look up. One of Sisuthros's scouts had appeared, riding toward the camp from the south. His slow canter told Eskkar that he bore no urgent news, so Eskkar walked leisurely to the rear of the camp. Grond, Hamati, and Sisuthros joined him, just as the rider dismounted.

"What is it, Tuvar?" Sisuthros clasped the man on the shoulder. "What did you see?"

"Just what you expected, Commander." Tuvar handed the horse over to one of the other men. Then he turned to face Eskkar. "Captain, we met five farmers from the nearby countryside. They were frightened, but they still approached us."

"Good. Where did you meet them?" Eskkar needed the local farmers. They would be an important part of his plan.

"A few miles to our rear, Captain. We were well out of sight of the village. I told them we were here to free the village from Ninazu and his thieves, and that we'd purchase as much firewood, food, and wine as they could sell us."

"And you told them . . ." Eskkar couldn't stop the smile that appeared on his face.

"I told them to bring it here. They didn't like that. They're afraid we'll just take their food and keep our silver." Tuvar smiled at the memory. "I told them that if they were afraid, to bring it a little at a time, and that we would pay for each delivery. It happened just as you said it would, Captain. They'll come, I'm sure of it."

"Since they know you, ride back to where you found them, and wait there for them. You can escort them here.

Remember, we're their friends, eager to help them get rid of Ninazu. This is important, Tuvar. Take care with them, and treat them politely."

"I understand, Captain. Don't worry. I'll bring them in." He nodded to Sisuthros before remounting the horse and cantering away.

Eskkar turned to Sisuthros. "Have men ready to greet them. You, too, Grond. Make sure you stop by and speak with them. Tell them you're looking to purchase the finest foods and wine for me."

"Yes, Captain." The two men spoke the words together. They discussed this last night and again early this morning. But Sisuthros knew his captain well. Eskkar would go over orders again and again, as much to make sure he hadn't forgotten something as to see if Sisuthros or the other subcommanders remembered them.

Another shout made them all look up again. A pair of riders had crested one of the low hills to the south, each of them leading a pack animal. Both the men and beasts looked as though they had traveled hard. Eskkar stared at the two riders, one of whom looked familiar.

"It's Drakis," Grond said, identifying the man first. "He should have been here last night."

"Who's that with him?" Sisuthros asked.

That question was answered quickly enough, and by Drakis himself, as soon as he dismounted and drank half a skin of water. The four leaders took him aside, all of them eager to hear what tidings he brought.

"Captain Eskkar," Drakis began, wiping the water from his chin with the back of his hand, "Lady Trella sends her greetings and wishes you success at Bisitun."

"Trella is well?" Almost ten days had passed since Eskkar had last seen her.

"Very well, Captain. She asked me to remind Grond to keep you safe and out of trouble."

"I will try and take care of myself, Drakis," Eskkar answered dryly. Somehow her concern made him feel proud, not embarrassed. "What else did she say?"

"Only that she wished you a speedy return. And she suggested Gatus send another man with me, with a second pack horse. So we've brought you twelve skins of oil, three bags of cotton, and all the ropes we could carry. The extra supplies slowed us down, or we'd have arrived yesterday."

Eskkar hadn't expected so much. Leave it to Trella to make sure he got double what he asked for. And he should have thought of sending two men. If one of the horses got injured, there would have been a delay in getting him what he needed. "And everything is well in Akkad?"

"Yes, and Dilgarth, too," Drakis said, anticipating Eskkar's next question. "There's no sign of any bandits remaining in the area, and the village seems to be recovering. Corio and Nicar are sending more men there, and Gatus sent a few more soldiers for protection. No doubt they've already arrived. With the extra men, Dilgarth will begin rebuilding the palisade and irrigation ditches, and helping the flax weavers get started again. Nicar says there is a great shortage of linen in Akkad."

"Good. Very good," Eskkar said, pleased to hear that Dilgarth remained safe and secure. He turned to Sisuthros. "We can begin the next part of the plan."

Grond turned to Drakis. "What about this other man? Who is he?"

"Rukor? He's one of the new men Gatus is training." Drakis seemed surprised at the sudden interest. "He's good with horses. We would've been even later without him."

Eskkar looked over toward the pack animals, where Rukor and some of the liverymen from the camp had already stripped the tired animals of their burdens and started rubbing them down. Eskkar didn't know this man and didn't want to take any chances. "We'll have to get rid of him. Rukor! Come here!"

The shout made Rukor turn, and he jogged over to where his leaders stood. "Yes, Lord Eskkar," he said, as he bowed. An older man, Rukor looked to have more than thirty seasons. He had never spoken with Eskkar before and knew little about Akkad's leader.

"Rukor, Drakis says you've done well," Eskkar said, "but I want you back on a horse and on your way back to Akkad. I have an urgent message for my wife. You will tell her ... tell her that we are encamped outside of Bisitun and waiting."

Rukor looked both confused and disappointed. No doubt he expected to get at least a few days' rest before climbing back on a horse. And the message didn't seem particularly urgent or important.

Eskkar turned to Grond. "Give Rukor two silver coins as a reward." A week's pay would make the man feel a little better. While Grond hunted in his belt for the coins, Eskkar went on. "Rukor, Drakis says you can be trusted, so I ask you to leave at once. Get a fresh horse and take whatever you need. And tell no one what message you carry. Do you understand?"

Grond put the coins in Rukor's hand before the man could answer. "Come with me, Rukor." He put his arm around the uncomprehending man's shoulder and started him moving. "I'll make sure you get a good horse and plenty of food."

When the two of them were gone Eskkar turned back to Drakis. "Now I need you to do something important, Drakis. Listen carefully. You're going to deliver the rest of the message Gatus sent to me. The message is that Gatus and a hundred and twenty men will be here in four or five days. Do you understand?"

Drakis's mouth fell open. There had been no other message. "But Captain, Gatus did not . . ."

"Listen to me, Drakis," Eskkar went on patiently, keeping his voice low. "This is very important. Gatus told you that he and a hundred and twenty men will be here in four or five days. That's what he told you to tell me." Eskkar waited a moment, to let that sink in. "Now, Drakis, tell me what message you carry from Gatus?"

Drakis looked from Eskkar to Sisuthros, who grinned broadly at the man's confusion. "Tell Eskkar what Gatus told you, Drakis," Sisuthros encouraged. "Go on, deliver the message from Gatus."

Now both Eskkar and Sisuthros waited, smiles on their faces. Drakis turned back to Eskkar. "Uh, Captain . . . Gatus said . . . that he and a hundred and twenty men would be here in four or five days."

"Very good, Drakis," Eskkar said. "Now remember well what Gatus told you. You must believe the words and say them as if it were true. When you're with the men, someone will ask you what message you carried. You will tell them what Gatus said, just as you told me. I want our men to believe that more soldiers are coming. You must believe it yourself, so that they will believe you. Can you do that, Drakis? If you can't, then you'll need to get on a horse with Rukor. The men have to believe reinforcements are coming."

"I can do it, Captain," Drakis answered determinedly. "I'm not sure what these words mean, but I can do it."

"Understanding is not required, Drakis," Eskkar said, but softened the words with a smile. "Just follow your orders. Believe the message yourself, and you'll have no trouble convincing any of the men. Now, let's go over it again."

Eskkar made Drakis repeat the message half a dozen times, until the words fell smoothly off his tongue. Finally Eskkar dismissed Drakis, letting him rejoin the men so he could get something to eat. The other men would ask for news of Akkad, and sooner or later, Drakis would "confirm" Gatus's message. Rukor had already departed, on his way back to Akkad, carrying a useless message that would raise Trella's eyebrows and make Gatus think his captain had lost his wits.

"Well, Captain," Sisuthros said, "it's as you said. The men will believe Drakis. And I expect the local farmers will be here soon. They know we've arrived, and that we'll need food."

"You deal with them personally when they arrive, Sisuthros. They're important to the plan. Remember to pay them fairly for whatever they bring, but no more. If we start paying too much ..." Eskkar glanced around the camp. "Now it's time for Grond and me to take our little ride around the village, while you do your part."

Moments later, after Eskkar had mounted his horse, a ragged cheer went up from the men. Sisuthros had just told the soldiers that Gatus and more men were on the way, to bolster their numbers. And should anyone ask Drakis, he would confirm that he had indeed delivered that message. In Bisitun, men would start wondering about the cheering. Eskkar nodded in satisfaction.

With ten soldiers riding behind him, Eskkar started his survey of the village. First they rode slowly to the west, stopping often to examine the land, always keeping at least a quarter mile from the village. When they reached the river, they paused for nearly a half hour as Eskkar studied the land, the river, and the southwestern approach to the village before they began to retrace their steps. They quickened their pace as they passed behind their own encampment, then slowed down again and leisurely inspected the northeastern outskirts of Bisitun until they reached the river once again. As before, Eskkar took his time, studying the landscape, before they rode slowly back to the encampment.

They had been gone nearly two hours and during that time, the walls of Bisitun had been filled with men, not only soldiers but villagers as well, all of them nervous and curious as to what the men from Akkad were planning. Shading his eyes, Grond picked out the man with the silver arm bracelets who followed them along the palisade from one side of the village to the other.

"Well, we got their attention, Captain," Grond said, as they dismounted and handed the horses off. "And Sisuthros makes good progress in building the ditch. It looks finished."

"Let's take a turn around the camp, just to see how it looks."

They walked slowly around the encampment but found no fault with either the ditch or the rampart. While a good rider on a strong horse might leap the six-foot-wide ditch, the animal would be jumping directly into the mound of dirt and would probably bury itself to the shoulder into the soft earth. The ditch and the earthen embankment would slow down men on foot even more. They would have to jump into the ditch, then endeavor to climb up the rampart's side, into the teeth of the defenders' bows and swords. Satisfied that his position couldn't be taken, Eskkar strode back inside the camp, thinking that, if Gatus were here, he would be pleased as well.

Eskkar repeated the inspection from behind the rampart, taking his time as he paced around the camp. The soldiers looked cheerful now, with the possibility of a fight delayed. They would have a few days' rest before Gatus and his men arrived. With another hundred men, they knew they could easily storm the village.

Eskkar spoke to many of them, always asking if they understood their orders and knew what their posts were in an emergency, always trying to remember as many of their names as he could. He wanted them to know that he depended on them. And that this wasn't the time for them to relax or forget their vigilance.

He had just finished checking the ranks when Sisuthros approached. "Captain, here come the first of the farmers."

Coming slowly down the road Eskkar saw three small farm carts, each pushed or pulled by two farmers. Either these farmers had no draft animals, or they feared the soldiers would confiscate them, a likely enough occurrence with Ninazu's men. "Well, at least we'll have fresh food for tonight."

"Do you want to meet with them?"

"No. Let them get used to dealing with you, both now and in the future. Say that I am too busy to deal with farmers. Don't forget to tell them we'll need a great deal more food in a few days."

"Do you think there will spies in this group, Captain?"

"No, not this group," Eskkar said, taking a moment to consider. "Perhaps not even the next one. But when the third group arrives . . . then I think we'll have some spies or farmers relying on Ninazu's pay."

Eskkar walked away from the rear gate and watched from a distance as the nervous farmers approached the camp. Sisuthros halted them outside the rear embankment, then spent half an hour haggling with them. At first the local inhabitants looked fearful, afraid of their goods being confiscated, or themselves taken as slaves or laborers. But with Ninazu's men taking what they wanted without paying, these farmers needed the copper coins, and their need had driven them to take the chance. So far none of these strangers from Akkad had looted anyone or raided the local farmhouses, so perhaps, after all, they would deal honestly.

That night Eskkar enjoyed good wine with his dinner, along with nuts and fresh bread. The farmers had departed, scarcely able to conceal their joy. They'd received a decent sum for their goods and they promised to spread the word, and that more food would arrive tomorrow morning.

Once again, Eskkar muttered thanks to the gods for Trella's advice. She had given him a good supply of their precious silver to win over the goodwill of the local farmers. In the old days he would have simply taken what he needed from them, no doubt in much the same way that Ninazu had. Now Eskkar understood how that would alienate them and work against him in the long run. For the next few days, he needed their help, even if unwittingly given.

Sisuthros's men kept a sharp lookout during the night, the soldiers on alert for any attack from the village. But as Eskkar expected, nothing happened. The morning sun found the land empty around them, though the sun hadn't climbed much above the horizon before a ragged column of carts, wagons, and individuals carrying whatever they could manage appeared on the road from the south. The day's trading would begin early. Eskkar resisted the urge to join Sisuthros. His commander knew what needed to be done.

After breakfast, Eskkar took Grond, Mitrac, Hamati, and half a dozen other senior men to a corner of the camp and they planned their next move. The meeting didn't last long. As soon as it broke up, Hamati put twenty men back to work, ten on each side of the encampment. They began digging out two new ditches. These would extend from either side of the camp, along the lines Eskkar had marked out yesterday.

The men had been told that Eskkar wanted to extend the ditch—to accommodate all the reinforcements Gatus would bring, and to enclose the extra food and horses. He'd told them little more, except that they could take their time and that they would be relieved every two hours. With a secure main encampment already established, Eskkar felt certain the new ditches would raise plenty of questions inside Bisitun.

Sisuthros spent the morning with the farmers as they arrived. In the beginning, as he had done yesterday, he kept them out of the camp. But soon the numbers of eager farmers multiplied, all arguing and pleading with him and the clerks, and Sisuthros grew careless. Some farmers carried their goods inside the camp, seeking private purchasers. Others, their trading completed, just wandered in, to satisfy their curiosity regarding Eskkar and the Akkadians.

Only the wine and ale remained outside the camp, away from the soldiers, except for the lucky scribes who got to taste the goods in order to determine the quality and the price. Eskkar had given clear instructions on that issue. Sisuthros had assigned his most trustworthy men to guard the wineskins. If the men got at the strong spirits, half of them would be drunk within the hour and useless the rest of the day.

The sun had climbed high into the morning sky before Sisuthros got rid of the last of the farmers and rejoined his captain. "By the gods, Captain, I hate dealing with merchants and farmers! Every one of them wanted to argue about the price, each claiming his loaf of bread or chicken was worth double what we offered."

"I told you it would be harder than you thought. Still, you'd better get used to it. Are they coming back?"

"Yes, there will be more this afternoon. But it went well, I think."

"Good. Now, tell me what you learned about Ninazu."

"Grond was right, Eskkar. He's the one with the silver bracelets. They are afraid of him, that's plain enough. He's killed anyone who's opposed him. They'd be happy if we drive him away."

Eskkar nodded grimly at that. "Yes, that would please everyone. Now, tell me what else you learned."

Part of buying and selling was talking. The farmers felt

curious about the soldiers and the new city of Akkad, and seemed willing to offer up information about Ninazu. In his turn, Sisuthros had described to them how wonderful life had become in Akkad, now that the barbarians had been vanquished, never to return again, and prosperity restored under Eskkar's enlightened and just rule. Sisuthros related the tale of the defeat of the barbarians three times, each version with more detail than the time before. Some of the farmers looked skeptical, but the individual soldiers, once they'd begun dealing with them, helped convince the farmers.

As for Ninazu, none of them knew for sure, but after much prodding from Sisuthros and the scribes, it seemed as though Ninazu had at least a hundred and twenty fighting men. As the story went, the bandit leader had waited until the village had started to reestablish itself after the passing of the barbarians. When the villagers had trickled back to their homes and farms, Ninazu had sent a few of his men into Bisitun to spy on the inhabitants.

Then, only a month ago, he and at least fifty men had suddenly ridden into the village. He'd killed the two village elders who had returned to their homes, then executed a few more brave souls who resisted or spoke out against him. At first Ninazu's men had taken what they wanted, but in the last two weeks, he'd begun restraining his followers, trying to win over the villagers and gain their support. Despite his harsh treatment of the villagers, Ninazu now had plenty of men, many of them recruited from the local countryside, while others had ridden in from the west, eager to join up and seduced by tales of easy plunder.

Eskkar knew well that old story, one he had experienced himself not so long ago, though the less anyone learned about his past the better. He didn't feel sorry for what he had done. Instead he felt embarrassed by the fact he and his raiders, half drunk and still hung over from too much ale, had been taken by surprise. A band of barbarian warriors had secretly watched him capture a village and plunder it for two days, before they swooped down on him and his band, overwhelming them in moments.

His luck had saved him again. He'd escaped, clinging to his horse and fleeing for his life, most of his men killed or captured, the rest scattered to the winds. He put that uncomfortable memory out of his mind.

"Good work, Sisuthros. Just make sure you don't make it too easy for them. Let them pick up scraps of information from the men."

"We've been very careful, Captain. The scribes are talking freely, though they still record every sale, and the price we pay."

Eskkar frowned at that. He couldn't get away from the ever-present scribes, who spent their lives counting and recording, not only men and animals, but bags of grain, loaves of bread, the numbers of swords and bows. Already one pack animal groaned under its load of small clay tablets.

"You'll have to deal with the scribes. Remember, Trella and Nicar will check every item as well. So take care, or they'll take any losses out of our pay."

That remark brought a grin to both men. Eskkar had no more coins in his purse today than when he'd first wandered into Akkad. And the only pay Sisuthros would see remained inside Bisitun, still waiting to be earned. The village would first have to be taken, then nursed back to prosperity before Sisuthros saw any gold for himself. But he would rule here, in Eskkar's name, and both men understood that, in time, the gold would come.

Sisuthros stayed with Eskkar until midafternoon, when the next ragged column of farmers appeared on the road. This group, about twenty-five men and ten women, was larger than the one this morning. Most of the same farmers had returned, their carts once again loaded with bread, fruit, vegetables, a scrawny chicken or two, and even a few skins of strong wine. Some of the women carried very little, and Eskkar guessed that what they had for sale was not necessarily what they carried in their baskets. Well, a little business of that kind wouldn't hurt his men, except in their purses.

Sisuthros repeated the process from the morning. At first he held the farmers outside the camp, until the press of business and time made discipline relax and he let them deliver their goods inside. There they mingled with the soldiers, everyone still curious about each other. This time Eskkar thought one or two of the strangers had looked toward him with more than idle curiosity.

The afternoon trading lasted almost two hours, before Sisuthros finally got the last one out of the camp and on his way. A few of the women wanted to remain, and Sisuthros had to line up the men to make sure they were all truly gone. Afterward, he had to deal with the scribes for a few moments before he joined Grond and Eskkar.

"By the gods, if I had to do that every day, I'd fall on my sword!" Sisuthros exclaimed. "I'm beginning to hate all traders and merchants. And the whores! Thank the gods they won't be back tomorrow." The farmers had been told not to come back until the day after tomorrow. The men from Akkad now had more than enough supplies to last a few days.

"You won't do very well running Bisitun with that attitude," Eskkar commented. "Did any of them seem unusual?"

"Yes, Captain. There were two or three that looked a little different. One had soft hands and looked as if he hadn't farmed in some time. He kept looking around and asking the scribes plenty of questions."

"I noticed that one, wandering through the camp and talking to the men." Eskkar knew it would take the spy or spies several hours to get back into Bisitun, now that Eskkar's men blocked the main road. Informers would have to go upriver a bit, then hug the riverbank until they reached the village. Or if they had a boat readied, they could float down to Bisitun. Either way, by this evening Ninazu would have his report. He would know his opponent's camp was strong and secure, the men confident and relaxed, and that a large group of reinforcements would be joining up soon. Now Eskkar wondered what Ninazu would do with the information.

Ninazu's choices would be limited. He could try and wait it out inside the village, trusting to his palisade to stop the Akkadians. The problem with that plan was that if Eskkar really had almost two hundred men and the skill to use them effectively, Ninazu wasn't likely to stop them. And once his followers learned of the coming reinforcements, the fight would go out of many of them. They hadn't joined up with Ninazu to cross swords in a close, desperate battle for Bisitun. No, they sought after easy loot, not a death fight.

Another choice for Ninazu would be to slip across the river. That way would always be open to him. But Ninazu wouldn't want to leave a big, wealthy village behind, one that would immediately be fortified against him. He would then be in the position of trying to keep a motley group of bandits together in lands already plundered, while having no secure base of operations. The Akkadians would start hunting him within days, while his men would start lusting after Ninazu's personal booty. That choice wouldn't look too attractive to Ninazu either.

As Eskkar saw it, that left Ninazu with only one other course of action—attack the Akkadians before the reinforcements arrived, overwhelm them, and take their weapons. Faced with such a defeat, the supposed reinforcements might turn back. At the least, Ninazu would be no worse off than he was now. A victory might even give his men the courage and resolve to resist another group of besiegers.

The rider had come from Akkad only yesterday, and it would be dark before news of the "reinforcements" reached Bisitun. It wasn't likely Ninazu could get his men ready on such short notice to attempt anything tonight. Eskkar intended to keep the pressure on Ninazu, to continue forcing him to react as Eskkar wanted. Tonight, the next step of the plan would begin, the one that would draw the noose around Ninazu even tighter.

6

As the afternoon waned, Eskkar met with his commanders and the fifteen men chosen for the initial raid. They'd had to wait until all the farmers moved well away from the camp. The carefully selected soldiers received their instructions, and Eskkar used the few hours before darkness to make sure Sisuthros and the men knew exactly what to do. Only after Eskkar felt satisfied did they gather around the campfire for the evening meal.

Nevertheless, Eskkar kept reviewing the details of the attack during dinner, speaking to each man, making sure each knew his assignment. Finally even Eskkar could find nothing wrong. He went off by himself, to try and get some sleep, leaving word to wake him when the men were ready.

Sleep came slowly. Eskkar had never sent men out on a raid before, had never delegated such a command to another. Always he had led sorties like this himself. To send others out into danger while he remained safe in camp seemed unmanly. But he knew that he couldn't risk his own life on such a small raid, just as he knew Sisuthros could easily direct the men.

At midnight, Grond woke Eskkar from a restless sleep. Sisuthros and his men stood ready, each standing by his horse. Eskkar gripped Sisuthros by the shoulder, then stood aside as his subcommander led the first two of his men out of the camp. The rest of the soldiers left, two at a time, after a slow count to one hundred, so that the horses wouldn't get nervous in the darkness and begin whinnying, or making sounds that might alert any keen ears in Bisitun. Eskkar knew horses could do strange things at night, spooking at some shadow, the moon, or even a breeze.

Each man would walk his horse a full half mile before mounting and waiting for the rest of the men to join up. When all the riders assembled, they would pace their horses at a slow step for another mile before turning north.

The last of them disappeared from sight, and nothing remained for Eskkar to do except wait. He didn't expect Ninazu to launch an attack tonight, but Eskkar wanted his remaining men alert and ready just in case.

The moon had risen late and progressed steadily across the starry sky. The scouts stationed between the camp and the village came in at regular intervals, all reporting no activity from Bisitun's defenders. Eskkar paced back and forth, checking with the men as he went, urging them to stay vigilant. Time seemed to slow the moon's journey across the night, and he thought morning would never come.

A few moments before dawn, the sound of hoofbeats came from the south. Though expected, the sentries gave the challenge. Sisuthros called out his name in a loud voice, though the approaching horses slowed to a walk a hundred paces from the camp. Eskkar gave the word, and soldiers lit torches that revealed a smiling Sisuthros leading his horse back into the encampment.

As Sisuthros and the others passed in, Eskkar grasped him by the arm and pulled him aside. "Did it go well? We heard nothing from here."

Sisuthros's grin turned into a laugh. "Yes, Captain, it went well. They never heard a thing. If we had more men, we could have forced our way in by the river. I'll wager they don't notice anything until well after sunup."

"You mean they saw nothing? And the men? All went according to plan?" By now, everyone pressed round Sisuthros and his band, who came in laughing and swaggering, pleased with themselves and the ease of their mission. "Tell us what happened."

"We walked the horses, until we were out of earshot, then rode to the northern part of the river." Men jostled each other to hear Sisuthros's words, every one eager to learn about the first action against Bisitun. "I sent the rest of the riders, with all the horses, downstream of the village, telling them to swing wide of the encampment. My men and I boarded the boats with no problems."

The scouts had found a farm a few miles upriver that possessed two small boats, probably used mainly for fishing, but each large enough to carry a few men. No doubt by now the puzzled farmer wondered who had stolen his vessels.

"We let the boats drift downstream," Sisuthros went on. "Just before we reached Bisitun, four men from each boat slipped into the water and clung to the boat's sides."

Sisuthros had chosen only strong swimmers for this raid, men who stood ready to trust themselves to the river's current to carry them to safety, if need be.

"We drifted in among the vessels at the rear of the village," Sisuthros continued. "We untied or cut the ropes mooring all the boats there, and shoved them well out into the current. It didn't take long, and we stood by in the boats to carry the men off as soon as someone raised the alarm."

"We heard no outcry here, Sisuthros," Eskkar said.

"No one gave the alarm. We could see guards walking the palisade, but they noticed nothing, and no one raised a cry. The sound of the river must have muffled the noise."

"The guards were that lax in their duties?" Eskkar couldn't believe it. "They never saw you at all?"

"No. We made certain the current took all the boats downstream. Then, with our men again clinging to the sides of their boats, we followed, making sure none of the boats had grounded. A mile downriver, we found our men and horses waiting, and rode back."

"Well done, Sisuthros! You're sure you cut all the boats loose?"

"Every one. We gave the river gods many offerings, for whatever gods and fortunate farmers live downstream!"

Everyone laughed. Sisuthros had to repeat his story in more detail, his men adding their own actions. By the time he finished, the torches had gone out, and the sun climbed above the horizon in the eastern sky. Eskkar, a smile on his face for the first time in many hours, ordered the men to get some food and rest, while he sat atop the rampart and watched the village.

So far, the plan that he had first sketched out in his mind back in Dilgarth continued to progress smoothly. When he'd learned the size of Ninazu's force, he had known that, even though he could probably take the village by direct assault, he would lose far too many men in the process. No, he knew he needed to capture Bisitun quickly, and with a minimum of casualties to his valuable men. Besides, he needed the village and its inhabitants as intact as possible. Now, in less than two days and thanks to Sisuthros's well-executed raid, Eskkar had bottled Ninazu's men in the village.

Now the next part of the plan would begin. Ninazu and his men would have plenty to worry about. They'd seen firsthand that they faced a disciplined force, real soldiers who could throw up a fortified camp in less than a day. The threat of reinforcements coming soon would make some of them think about moving on.

With all the boats gone, Ninazu's quick escape across the river would be greatly reduced. At this time of the year, a strong horse, ridden by a good rider who could swim himself if necessary, might make it across. But that rider couldn't carry much loot, and Eskkar was willing to wager that if ten good men attempted it, three or four would likely drown.

So Ninazu would have to fight or run, before his own men began to slip away. Not that Eskkar wanted them to run. He didn't want them plundering up and down the river for the next few weeks, with his Akkadians wasting their days in pursuit. He wanted most of the bandits dead, and the rest as slave labor to rebuild Bisitun.

The village shone in the morning light, as the sun moved ever higher in the sky, and Eskkar fancied he saw fewer defenders than yesterday. Everyone inside Bisitun would know about the loss of the boats, and worry, if not fear or panic, would start taking its toll. Some would be thinking about escape. The more they thought about escaping, the less willing they would be to fight. Eskkar decided to apply more pressure.

He turned back to the encampment and found Grond waiting there, a few steps behind him. "Grond, get the men on their horses. Send ten riders and ten archers to each side of the encampment. If any in the village want to make a run for it, make sure they have to fight their way out. I don't want anyone going in or out of Bisitun."

Grond relayed the orders to Hamati and the other men. It took only a few minutes to get the forty men chosen something to eat, and send them on their way. When they reached their positions, each detachment would block any escape attempt by anyone, on foot or mounted, to pass through Bisitun's back gate, and follow the river to safety.

Of course if the defenders came out in strength on either side, then the situation would change. But they talked about even that possibility. While the full force of the bandits could certainly ride through twenty men, it might take some time, and with enough time, the rest of the Akkadians from the main camp might catch them with their backs against the river.

What Eskkar thought more likely was that a hundred men would burst out of the front gate, and attempt to ride right through, or around, the encampment. He now had only thirty-two fighting men, plus the scribes, boys, and liverymen remaining to defend the camp. Eskkar had stretched his forces very thin, but he needed to act as if he had the upper hand. As soon as the men in the camp finished their meal, he had them ready their weapons and stand to their posts. With his men in place, he returned to the embankment and watched the palisade.

Once again, the man with the silver bracelets stood there, studying the Akkadians, and undoubtedly making plans of his own. Nevertheless, the loss of Ninazu's boats changed the situation, and now the ground outside the palisade, with its tumbled-down houses, worked to Eskkar's advantage. Men on horseback would only have a clear path directly down the main road, which would send them straight at the encampment, or along the river's edge, where they would encounter archers and mounted men. Ninazu would see all this, as could his men, and they would begin to worry.

For days Ninazu had assured his men that they could easily fight off Eskkar's small force from behind the palisade. Instead, the bandits could see a hard fight ahead of them if they tried to escape. Moreover, the worst worry of all would be knowing that, in two or three days, another strong force would reinforce the attackers.

Grond returned to join him. "All the men are in position, Captain. Sisuthros and Hamati are getting some sleep, but rest of the men are resting at their posts."

"Watch the walls, Grond. If they all decide to run for it, the guards on the palisade will slowly be replaced by villagers. They'll be nervous and frightened. That might give us warning."

"Do you think they'll run?"

Eskkar thought about that. "His brother was brave enough. I don't think Ninazu will give up Bisitun without a fight. Besides, he sees us splitting our force, and that will make him wonder what we will do when night falls. If he thinks that we've weakened our force here, he may fall into our trap." Once again, Eskkar went though the thought process. "I still think he will come tonight, with a large force, right at our camp."

He faced his bodyguard, who still stood there, doubt still written on his face. "I know, Grond, I have my own doubts. But if he does nothing, and another hundred men appear, he'll be trapped. His men will run if he does nothing." Eskkar shrugged. "Well, that's what I would do. But I am not him, so we'll have to wait and see."

"Are you sure that we can withstand them, if he sends everyone against us?"

"These are bandits, Grond, not Alur Meriki warriors. They have no clan or family to fight for, no code of bravery to sustain them. They are held together only by their lust for gold. If thirty of us cannot break them . . ." He shook his head and headed back to the rear of the camp.

The daylight hours dragged by, one by one, with Eskkar pacing back and forth. The camp had to appear no different from the day before, so all the regular activities continued. Men stood to their watches, cooking fires sent smoke into the sky, and anyone not standing guard relaxed on the embankment, watching the village.

The detachments on either side of Bisitun reported in, but they saw no sign of anyone trying to cross the river or escape along its banks. Sisuthros, after he had taken his rest, declared that to be a good sign—if they weren't trying to run, then they would be ready to fight.

As the afternoon began to lengthen, Eskkar, Sisuthros, Hamati, and Grond met once again, and began to prepare for the night's work. They went over everything for almost two hours, thinking of what could go wrong, what evil chance could upset their plans, what they would do if the plan failed, and even what they would do if they were beaten.

The soldiers started the evening fires and prepared their meal before Eskkar and his subcommanders finished. At least the men continued eating well, thanks to his largess with the local farmers. With dinner finished, Eskkar and his commanders met with the other senior men. The thirty men in the camp would be at the greatest risk, and Eskkar wanted them to know exactly what he expected of them. Each of the subcommanders went over it yet again, this time with their men.

Eskkar watched, looking for signs of confusion, but saw nothing but confidence. No one showed any fear, or doubted their ability to beat off an attack. The men believed in him, believed in his luck if nothing else. At last, it was time to go. "Take care, Sisuthros. And good hunting to all of us."

Grond had made all the preparations, and he and Eskkar slipped out of the camp. They took their time moving across the dark landscape, swinging wide to their rear, lest some chance flash of moonlight revealed them to any sharp-eyed guards on the village palisade. Eskkar didn't want to trip and sprain an ankle in the darkness. Finally, they joined up with the men who guarded the southern edge of the river.

The small camp had only a single fire burning in front of it, lighting the darkness between it and the village. The men sat well back from the firelight, waiting for Eskkar to arrive. They'd spent the afternoon practicing their archery, the same as they had done every day before and during the siege of Akkad, and talking over what situations they would likely encounter and how they would respond.

Every one of these bowmen could loose a properly aimed arrow every three seconds, and some even faster. Now they waited, confident in the skills and in their leaders.

Grond had briefed them earlier in the day, but as soon as Eskkar joined them, they checked their preparations again. These men were eager, anxious to go on the offensive, and ready to take their chances. Five of them were already Hawk Clan members and another seven, mostly experienced fighters, looked to prove themselves worthy of such an honor. Mitrac waited there, leaning on his bow, next to the two men he had considered his best archers, both men who had fought beside Hamati at Dilgarth. Even Eskkar felt satisfied that everyone knew what to do.

Midnight passed without event. Eskkar could do nothing to make the time pass faster, not even pace around. If Ninazu's attack came, it would likely be when the moon began to set, about two hours before dawn. Too excited and nervous to rest or sleep, Eskkar and his men just waited. Most of them lay on their backs and watched the silver orb slowly cross the night sky. At last the moon began to fade. The time had arrived.

Eskkar sat on the ground, drumming his fingers against his leg, a bad habit he had picked up during the siege of Akkad. He didn't like anyone knowing he felt nervous, and he stopped the motion the moment he became conscious of it. Except for the faint crackling of the fire, Eskkar could hear nothing. Another hour crept by, and still he heard no sign of any activity. He wanted to start moving, but he didn't dare take the chance. Any unusual sound might stop Ninazu's attack. If Ninazu even did plan to attack tonight, it should have come by now.

His doubts growing every moment, Eskkar had just decided that he had guessed wrong when a shout went up from the Akkadians' main encampment. A moment later someone hurled a torch into the sky, Sisuthros's signal an attack had begun. Shouts drifted across the black ground.

Without any commands, Eskkar and his men started to advance, trying to make as little noise as possible. They swung wide around their small fire. In single file, they moved rapidly toward the southern corner of the village, each man following the man ahead of him. Mitrac led the way. He'd studied the ground during the day, and now Eskkar and the others followed him. Behind Mitrac strode his two picked archers, trailed by Eskkar, Grond, and the rest of the men.

Time moved quickly, and they soon drew close to the village, where it came closest to the river. When Mitrac stopped, less than a hundred paces separated them from the palisade. They crouched among the rubble, and hoped no one watched this side of the village too closely. Mitrac and his chosen archers disappeared into the darkness.

Sound continued to drift in from the front of the village, though Eskkar couldn't tell what any of it meant. For all he knew, his men in the camp had been overrun and slaughtered, or they had already driven back Ninazu's men. Whatever the result, Eskkar was committed, and they hadn't much time. He hoped any sentries watching this side of the village would be lax, their attention focused on events happening in front of the main gate.

Precious moments dragged by with no movement or activity from Mitrac. Eskkar couldn't control his patience. He hated to restrain himself from action when all his instincts urged him to the attack. He started to move forward, when one of Mitrac's men slipped back to his side. "Come!" he whispered, "Mitrac killed the sentry."

Eskkar and the others began to move. Crouched over, they crept straight toward the base of the palisade, which they reached in moments. Unlike Akkad, Bisitun had no ditch to give added height to the wooden fence. No alarm had been given yet, but at any moment they could be discovered.

They reached the base of the palisade, hugging close to the rough timbers. Grond and another man unslung the ropes they carried coiled across their chests. One end of each rope had been fitted with a short block of wood, wide enough to secure the line against the top of the palisade. Mitrac had already scaled the fence, boosted up by his companion, and now stood guard atop the barrier.

Grond tossed the two ropes up, and Mitrac wedged the wooden blocks behind the tops of the logs. The two archers started climbing, the timbers creaking under their weight, though they hoped not loud enough to attract any attention.

Eskkar could barely contain himself. The sounds of fighting had increased from the direction of the main gate. Or perhaps the defenders cheered their own victory. Either way, Eskkar could no longer tolerate doing nothing. If Sisuthros had not held the camp, if he had not driven back Ninazu's men . . . no, it was too late to worry about that.

The instant the two archers disappeared overhead, Eskkar grabbed one of the ropes and began to climb. Grond pushed him from below, and the rough wood of the stockade gave Eskkar some purchase, the vertical beams creaking a little louder under his heavier weight. He reached the top, and one of the archers waiting there pulled him over.

Eskkar dropped down to his knee and looked about, until he saw Mitrac kneeling on the rampart a few steps away. The bodies of two men lay in front of him, but already the arrows had been pulled or broken off from their bodies. The silhouette of an arrow sticking out of a corpse was too easy to identify, even at night. Eskkar crept over to the archer.

"What do you see?" Eskkar asked softly.

"Two more sentries up ahead, but they face the front of the village," Mitrac whispered. He held his bow at an angle, with an arrow fitted to the string. "They're staring at the main gate."

Even as Eskkar glanced in that direction, he saw some flames shoot up into the sky. Crouched down, he couldn't see the front of the village. Suddenly a flaming arrow streaked up into the sky and fell over the wall. He grunted in satisfaction at the signal. Sisuthros and his forces had not only held the camp, they'd driven back the attackers and started counterattacking the village with fire arrows.

Using the black oil that Drakis had brought up from Akkad, Sisuthros's men had made a hundred fire arrows, wrapping cotton thickly around the shaft, binding it with linen threads, and soaking the tufts in oil. When touched to fire, the cotton would burst into flame, a flame so hot that not even the arrow's flight through the air could extinguish it.

The palisade behind him creaked again, and Eskkar turned to see Grond come over the wall, the last man to make the ascent. Eskkar looked down at the village beneath him. The inner rampart stood only about ten feet off the ground, and even in the dim starlight, he could see a lane that seemed to lead toward the front of the village. The smell of a slaughterhouse reached him, and he could see animal pens below. A few houses backed against the enclosure.

The village remained indistinct in the darkness, lit here and there by torches or watch fires, but dawn approached and already the eastern sky seemed a bit less dark. As he watched, villagers emerged from the houses, roused from their sleep by the noise, talking excitedly and all looking in the direction of the main gate.

That might change at any moment, and Eskkar had to get his soldiers off the rampart. He turned to Grond. "Get the men down now." Moving as he spoke, Eskkar grasped the edge of the rampart, and swung to the ground. His men joined him, all except Mitrac, who called softly to his two archers. Eskkar paused briefly, watching, as the three bowmen stood up, drew their bows, and launched their arrows at the sentries who guarded the next position on the palisade.

He heard a faint cry, followed by the sound of a body thudding to the earth, but nothing more, no outcry or alarm. Mitrac, followed by his two men, paced slowly along the rampart. Anyone giving them a casual glance would take them for sentries. Ignoring the rampart for now, Eskkar started off, striding with authority, followed by Grond and eleven other men. It took only a few paces before they had to push their way past the first confused villagers.

Nothing distinguished them from any of Ninazu's men. In the darkness, they would seem merely another group of

Ninazu's followers, moving toward the main gate. Eskkar
saw one man's mouth open in surprise as he shrank back
from them, but the man said nothing, and in a moment
they'd moved well past. The lane forked and Eskkar didn't
know which way to go, so he grabbed the first villager he
encountered, an older man whose white hair shone in the
dim light.

As Eskkar's hand tightened on the old man's arm, the
man froze, helpless, as much from sudden fear at these men
as the hard muscles in Eskkar's grip. "Which way is the
quickest to the main gate?"

The man's mouth opened, but no words came, and
Eskkar repeated the question, shaking the man as he did.
"Which way!"

The man pointed to the left, and Eskkar kept his grip
on the man as they resumed walking, dragging his
unwilling guide with him. The lane twisted left and forked
again, but this time Eskkar had only to look at the man, and
he gestured the way. A few more steps and Eskkar could
see his destination. He loosened his grip a little. "Return
to your house and keep silent, or I'll slit your throat!" He
pushed the man aside and increased his pace.

Fire blazed from the outer fence, and two watch fires
had been lit in fire pits on either side of the gate. Sisuthros's
arrows would have started fires in several places, and now
his men, shooting from the darkness, would be targeting
any defenders who attempted to put out the flames.

Ninazu's men had recovered from their shock. Men raced
to the ramparts, and cries for water echoed all around them.
A dozen villagers, pressed into service, carried buckets of
water from the well to extinguish the arrows in the gate.

Eskkar paid no attention to all that, his eyes searching until he saw what he wanted. A house with a low roof that faced the open ground behind the gate. The passage to the house remained closed, but even as Eskkar approached, prepared to put his shoulder to it, the door opened. An elderly woman wearing nothing but a loose shift bumped into him, obviously intending to see what all the commotion was about. Instead, Eskkar pushed her back in, his hand over her mouth to keep her silent, though she seemed too frightened to cry out.

Inside, two more women and some children had roused themselves, fearful at the sounds of fighting that now rang through the village. Grond swept them together into a corner of the hut. "Keep your mouths shut if you want to live," he ordered.

Meanwhile Eskkar climbed the flimsy ladder that opened on to the roof. From the housetop, torches and the burning fence illuminated the scene before him. He knelt down, taking everything in as he studied the situation.

The outer palisade blazed in three places, and without immediate water, the fire would soon be unstoppable. Villagers with water buckets rushed about, pouring water down the palisade. On the ground just inside the main gate a dozen men stood, two of them with arrows still protruding from them. Ninazu's men struggled to fight the fire and the attackers at the same time, while others rounded up more villagers to bring water.

Eskkar noticed plenty of men carrying weapons and standing about, talking loudly and gesturing in frustration. Obviously Ninazu hadn't lost too many in his attack on the camp. Eskkar guessed that most of the bandits had turned and run back as soon as they realized their foes waited for them. He sought to pick out the leaders, those trying to restore order to the mass of confused and panicky men.

Grond tapped him on the shoulder. All the soldiers had climbed up on the roof and knelt behind him, including Mitrac and his two men. Every Akkadian had a bow, except Eskkar and Grond, who carried only their swords. Eskkar turned to Mitrac. "There, see them, to the right of the gate. And the one at the well, and those two on the rampart."

Mitrac nodded as Eskkar pointed out the first targets. Mitrac took over, pushing in front of Eskkar and moving closer to the edge of the roof. Eskkar stepped farther back and shoved the wooden frame that covered the access hole to the roof into place. He didn't want anyone coming up behind them. The dry rasp of arrows on wood sounded, as Eskkar's thirteen archers stood up, bows drawn, as Mitrac's low voice prepared the men for the first release. Then Mitrac drew his own arrow to his ear and released.

Even after all these months, Eskkar still found himself amazed at Mitrac's skill. He scarcely seemed to aim, and yet the shaft that vanished into the darkness would no doubt find its mark, while another arrow seemed to leap from his quiver to the bowstring. The other men fired as well and immediately the screams started. It would take the defenders a few moments to figure out that they'd been attacked, and many of their leaders would be down before they turned and located their attackers.

The men Mitrac had chosen for this raid had proven themselves among the best archers in the troop, and now, despite being crowded together, they poured arrows into their enemies at a rate that made them seem like twice their number.

The roof gave Eskkar's men clear shots, and the watch fires burning at the gate provided plenty of light for their shooting. For the defenders, the shafts seemed to come out of the darkness, and at such short range, little more than forty paces, the heavy shafts with their bronze, leaf-shaped points struck with lethal accuracy.

Before a man could count to fifty, the Akkadian archers swept the area beneath the gate clear of defenders, the defenders tripping and scrambling down from the walls, some of them tossing their bows and buckets aside. Out of the corner of his eye, Eskkar made note of every time the closest archer fired. The man had released his tenth arrow before anyone spotted them, and another four volleys were launched before anyone turned a bow against them.

Eskkar couldn't count that quickly, but he guessed nearly two hundred arrows had been launched, enough to break any small group of men, let alone those still recovering from being defeated by Sisuthros at the camp. The bandits broke and ran, determined to get out of the killing zone.

With the defenders fleeing, Eskkar called out to Grond, who raised a small trumpet to his lips and blew a long blast that echoed out over the walls and into the darkness. Eskkar heard an answering sound from the Akkadians outside the gate. Sisuthros and his men now pressed their attack in earnest, the trumpet announcing that most of the defenders had abandoned the walls. They screamed and howled like wild men as they charged, every man shouting at the top of his lungs, as ordered. They carried with them the rest of the ropes, and would soon be over the palisade and into the village, even if the gate remained fastened.

Eskkar kept his eyes moving, and finally saw for what he searched. A flash of silver in the flames, and he saw the leader of the defenders on the move. Eskkar cursed the bad luck that let the man survive the archers' arrows. Now Ninazu would need to be hunted down and killed before he could escape over the fence into the darkness. No, even now, the darkness had started to give way to dawn, and the first rays of the sun already climbed slowly into the heavens. "Grond! Mitrac! Come with me!"

Eskkar ran to the side of the house and swung himself down, Grond, Mitrac and his two archers following him. Ninazu and a group of his men were moving down one of the village streets, already out of sight, and no doubt headed toward the river gate. The bandits' horses would be kept there, close to the rear gate and the river.

Ninazu had decided to run for it. The bandit leader would have no idea how many soldiers had slipped inside Bisitun, not that it made any difference. With all the casualties his men had taken, the Akkadians now outnumbered them. More important, Ninazu's men had lost the will to fight. Every bandit's thought would be on fleeing the village and saving his own skin. To stay meant death. Within hours, the villagers would turn in or denounce any of Ninazu's men still in Bisitun. Only escape could save them now.

Eskkar didn't care if a few dozen leaderless bandits escaped, but a man like Ninazu, who could organize and lead others, would only cause more trouble if he remained on the loose. Ninazu must be stopped, before he escaped.

In his younger days, Eskkar believed his strength and skill with a sword had brought men to follow him. Now he knew better. As Trella said, those skills might be useful, but they didn't make a man a true leader. A good leader, she'd told him, could think months ahead as he bent men to his will. A great leader, she added, could think years ahead.

Eskkar didn't consider himself a great leader, but he knew he didn't want to be chasing Ninazu around the countryside for the next few months. So now he and his men ran headlong down the lane, ignoring the frightened villagers who screamed and shouted in terror, panicked by the fires that lit the sky, and worried their entire village might go up in flames.

For the first time that night, Eskkar drew his sword, raising it up over his head as he lowered his shoulder to clear the way whenever some panicked villager blundered into his path. But before they had gone very far, Grond passed Eskkar, whirling his sword overhead, as he opened the way for his captain.

Then the lane widened and converged with the other, and they ran right into Ninazu and his followers. The bandits had started first, but they had the farthest distance to travel, and the two lanes joined here. Eskkar guessed Ninazu had twelve or fifteen men with him, at least three times Eskkar's group. But these confused men had only flight on their minds. Half of them kept running, screaming in fear, while the others turned, raising their swords more in surprise than anything else.

Grond struck down two of them with two rapid strokes. Eskkar slashed at another. The man parried the stroke, but the force of the blow took all the fight out of him and he turned and ran. Eskkar and Grond kept running, hardly slowing their pace and still pursuing the fleeing Ninazu and his men.

This time the narrow streets and villages worked to Eskkar's advantage. The frightened villagers slowed Ninazu's men. One of them stumbled, and Grond slashed at the man as he ran past, opening a gaping wound in the man's shoulder. Another man tried to duck into a house, but a woman peered out from the doorway and they collided. Eskkar struck at the man's back, and again a scream went up into the night, as the wounded man staggered against the doorframe. Eskkar and Grond ignored their victims. Wounded bandits would be easy to gather up later.

He and Grond burst into an open area where two lanes joined. Eskkar caught the stable smell even before he heard the animals whinnying in fear of all the shouting and the scent of fire. Someone attempted to rally the bandits at the corral. Three of Ninazu's men turned to face their pursuers, but others pushed their way into the corral, diving through the enclosure's flimsy bars.

Three men or a dozen meant nothing to Eskkar. He and Grond charged ahead like men possessed, each of them shouting at the top of his lungs. They rushed at the bandits. One raised his sword and died when Eskkar's blade struck twice, once to knock the sword aside and then a killing thrust before the man could recover. The other bandits changed their minds before Grond could reach them, one dropping his sword and diving through the corral.

The screams of horses split the darkness, and one of them reared up, crashing into the corral. The horse's weight knocked the bars loose, and the frightened animal pushed its way through the gap. Another riderless horse followed. Two more horses loomed up, men clinging to their necks, as Eskkar reached the fence. One horseman swung a sword at Eskkar's head.

He sprang aside, then dropped low as he thrust his sword into the horse's rear leg. The horse whinnied in fear and pain, then twisted as its leg gave way, stumbling into the second horse, and sending both riders tumbling to the ground. A third bandit attempted to ride through the cleared opening, but an arrow struck him square in the chest, and the man slid backward off the horse. Eskkar turned his head for a second. Mitrac had caught up to his leader, and stood to the side of the lane, already aiming a second shaft.

All the horses still inside the pen had panicked now, moving away from the entrance of the corral. After they bunched up in the rear, they turned in unison and moved forward once again. Terror-stricken animals would not be easy to mount. Eskkar tried to see past them. The night's darkness had turned to gray, and in a few more moments the sun would be up. He swore again. He wouldn't let Ninazu get away now.

"Grond! Mitrac! Shoot the horses!" With those words, Eskkar rose up, bringing the great sword up over his head and striking directly at a horse that suddenly appeared, charging right at him. The horse shied away, just enough for Eskkar to move out of its path even as he struck the blow at the beast's head. The animal's cry of agony rose up, its shoulder knocking Eskkar to the ground.

He rolled away, but even before Eskkar regained his feet, the horse had taken an arrow in its neck, the two wounds driving it beyond control. Another horse went down, then a third, their almost-human cries mixing with the noises of panic from the other beasts. But the remaining horses turned away, moving once again toward the rear of the corral. One animal, riderless, jumped the fence in panic, its hooves kicking the top rail to splinters.

Eskkar looked again into the corral. With the first rays of dawn, he had just enough light to pick out two forms, both of them struggling to hold on to their mounts. Another man lay senseless on the ground, while a fourth pushed himself up from the dirt, trying to get to his knees. One of Mitrac's arrows took him, and he pitched forward without a sound.

Then three more men from Akkad rushed up behind Eskkar, swords in hand, calling out as they did so. By now, between the dead or dying animals and Eskkar's men, any chance of escaping from the corral had ended.

"Alive!" Eskkar shouted. "Take them alive!" He wanted Ninazu in one piece if possible, to show the villagers the power of Akkad. Grond shouted something, too, and Mitrac's young voice cried out, reminding his archers to aim at the horses.

The bandit leader had not given up yet. He and his companion, each holding on to a horse's halter, pushed against the rear of the corral. In a moment, they'd knocked two of the wooden bars from their fastening. Immediately the frightened horses took advantage, breaking through this new gap. Ninazu and the last of his followers swung up onto their mounts, hugging the animal's necks as they urged their beasts into the opening. But this new passage led directly into a narrow lane, forcing the frightened horses to turn sharply. More chaos ensued as the animals jammed together for a moment. Mitrac and his archers moved forward and loosed their shafts.

One arrow, either on purpose or by mistake, struck one of the escaping men in the back. The other two struck Ninazu's horse in the haunches, and the animal whinnied in agony, reared up, and crashed into the wall of a house. The flimsy mud bricks gave way, and both man and beast half fell into the dwelling amidst a swirl of dust and crumbled mud. By then, Eskkar had raced through the shambles of the corral, ducking away from one horse that reared up at him and pushing another aside, until he and Grond reached the side lane. "Up on the roof, Grond! Don't let him escape!"

Grond stepped back, sheathed his sword, and jumped for the top of the house, pulling himself up and out of sight in moments. Eskkar shoved his way past another frightened horse until he reached the rubble of the half-crushed house, the dying animal still struggling to reach its feet. Behind Eskkar, the rest of the half-crazed horses finally broke free, hooves pounding as they made their escape from the smell of blood and death that filled the corral.

He saw Ninazu there, on his knees, barely a shadow in the darkness at the rear of the house, but a sword shone in the faint light. The bandit had nowhere to go, and even now the tip of Grond's blade glinted at the top of the ladder, the tiny house's only other exit. Ninazu was trapped.

Mitrac rushed up, as did several more of Eskkar's men. "Shall I finish him, Captain?" He had an arrow on the string.

Eskkar shook his head, but kept his eyes on the trapped man. "Put down your sword, Ninazu," Eskkar commanded. "You've no place to go."

For an answer, Ninazu leapt to his feet and flung himself at the opening. Eskkar saw Mitrac start to draw the bow and knew that he wouldn't have time. Eskkar shoved Mitrac to one side, even as he jumped to the other. Ninazu's blade flashed between them. Eskkar struck at the man's sword, but Ninazu recovered, then thrust again with his own weapon.

Eskkar's own sword countered the stroke, though he gave back half a step from the force of it. Ninazu raised his weapon to strike again, a shout on his lips, and charged forward. Then he jerked back, his balance upset, and his sword flailed wildly. Grond had dropped down from the roof, landed on his feet, and leaped on Ninazu from behind, yanking the man back by his hair with one hand as he caught the man's sword arm with his other.

Eskkar ducked through the jagged opening, his blade pointed up in the ready position. As Ninazu struggled with Grond, Eskkar struck the bandit in the face with the butt of his sword, the thick knob of bronze smashing against the man's nose, stunning him. Grond tore the sword from Ninazu's slack fingers, and struck him again with his free hand on the side of his head. Ninazu collapsed like a sack of grain, unconscious before he hit the earth. The fight for Bisitun was over.

7

The same dawn that greeted Eskkar's victory found Trella lying in her bed, awake and already thinking about Korthac. Yesterday afternoon the council had accepted Korthac's petition, and his gold, to establish a trading house in Akkad. Though he'd complained loudly enough last week when given the terms, he'd handed over the forty gold coins with scarcely a comment. To everyone's surprise, he offered up more than the coins, presenting a large peridot crystal to each of the seven council members. A small gift, he explained, to express his appreciation, show the value of his goods, and encourage further purchases from his stock.

Each of the gemstones glittered even in the dimly lit council room, the dark green crystals tinged with a hint of yellow. Trella's peridot stood out in quality from the other fine stones, much larger and with a deeper shade of green enhanced by the well-polished surface.

Trella would have preferred not to accept the costly bribe. But even she could not go against the looks and words of the other council members, who quickly took their gifts as they gave thanks to Korthac. Hers, of course, would be sold to help pay Eskkar's expenses.

Gifts for council members were nothing new, but since they all had wealth in their own right, they had little need for outright bribery. No, Trella recognized this more subtle offering. Korthac wanted friends in high places, influential friends who could assist him in the future, in a way that she still couldn't fathom.

Sleeping on it hadn't helped, and this morning the puzzle remained unresolved. That meant more positive steps would be needed to uncover the mystery. After breakfast, she waited for Annok-sur to return. Every morning, Annok-sur walked the village, giving those with information a chance to meet with her, away from their homes or places of labor. Some women dared not venture far from their husband's sight. By moving about, Annok-sur gave these women, free or slave, the opportunity to pass along what their men said or did the previous night. More than once, Trella had garnered useful information through this informal network. When Annok-sur returned, mid-morning had just passed.

Alone in the workroom, Trella fingered the gold coin that hung around her neck as she faced Annok-sur across the table. "Have we learned anything further, anything new, about Korthac?"

"Only that he's ready, today or tomorrow, to purchase a place to live. He's looked at a few houses, but he's still staying at the inn and . . ."

"Nothing from his men, nothing from the women they've approached, people he's dealt with?"

"No, nothing like that. His men keep to themselves and

stay close to the inn. Twice he's brought women back there for a few hours, to entertain his followers, but I haven't found any woman who'll admit to pleasuring him." Annok-sur shrugged. "Perhaps he prefers men or boys, though I've heard nothing of that, either."

"It's been more than ten days, and we still know little about him, except he possesses a good deal of wealth and pays well." Trella reached out and touched the peridot that rested on the table between them. "We need to learn more."

"You still think there's something amiss with him, something in his past?"

"It's not his past that worries me, Annok-sur. It's his plans for the future. He's hiding something, I'm sure of it. I've been thinking, perhaps Tammuz can discover what it is. Can you bring him tonight?"

Tammuz, barely into his sixteenth season, had ridden as a camp boy with Eskkar at the start of the campaign against the Alur Meriki. His one and only battle had shattered his arm, and he'd nearly died from his wounds. The fight also ended his dream of becoming a soldier. Before joining Eskkar's fighters, Tammuz had survived as a petty thief, but now even that life would be denied him. With little to look forward to except life as a beggar, the young man had been devastated.

Trella, always searching for friends and allies no matter what their station in life, had devised a plan for him. Four months earlier, she and Eskkar gave Tammuz enough silver to set himself up in a small alehouse in the worst part of Akkad, one catering to the poorest and most desperate inhabitants. Acting under the cover of his former profession, Tammuz joined Trella's network of spies, keeping his ears and eyes open for any plots against Eskkar's House. Gatus provided an old veteran, injured while training for the siege, to help Tammuz run the establishment, which soon became more a den of petty thieves than alehouse. Tammuz flourished better than Trella hoped, and had already supplied some minor but useful information.

"I'll escort him past the guards," Annok-sur said. "You'll want Gatus here as well, in case Tammuz needs anything from him. Midnight would be the best time."

Aside from Eskkar, Gatus, and Annok-sur, no one knew of Tammuz's new role. Even the founding Hawk Clan soldiers had already dismissed the memory of the crippled youth; warriors formed the Hawk Clan, and none of them expected Eskkar to remember his campfire promise to an insignificant boy. Since the day he left Eskkar's compound, Tammuz had returned only once, at night and with his face concealed by a cloak. Only Gatus or Annok-sur could vouchsafe an unknown person past the house guards.

"No, two hours before midnight," Trella said. "I want you to bring Zenobia here at midnight."

"Ah, then it's time to help her establish a House?"

Trella sighed. "It's past time, I think. I wish we'd helped her before, but there was no time. Now we'll have to move faster."

Annok-sur laughed. "It won't take Zenobia long to get noticed."

Trella could laugh at that. "Let's hope not."

That night Gatus accompanied Tammuz and Annok-sur into the workroom, where two lamps burned, an extravagance that lent weight to the importance of the meeting. Trella always paid close attention to people's faces when they spoke, and if that required burning extra oil, she didn't consider it a waste. She rose and bowed respectfully to the young man, reminding herself not to count his seasons, though he was much the same age as she. As Eskkar reminded her, you don't treat someone who's killed an enemy in battle as a boy.

"Greetings, Tammuz," she said. "Thank you for coming."

Tammuz pushed back the cloak that hid his face, worn more to mask his identity than keep out the nighttime chill, and bowed as well. Straightening up, he pushed light brown hair away from his face, revealing a broad smile. "My thanks to you, Lady Trella. It's good to see you again."

Trella returned the smile, remembering how Eskkar had saved Tammuz's life, then placed him in her care. When Tammuz smiled, he looked like a young boy, innocent, though she recognized his growing maturity. "Come," she said, "sit down, and tell me what you've been doing. But first, let me look at your arm."

The left arm had been broken in two places, and, out on the battlefield, none of Eskkar's men knew how to set the break properly. The ride back to Akkad had almost killed the boy. Tammuz lost most of the use of his left hand, and now the arm itself seemed shrunken, bent, and hanging at an odd angle. But the young man lived, and Trella knew that life, even as a cripple, was preferable to death.

She ignored Tammuz's embarrassment as she came around the table and helped him remove his cloak before taking his hand. "Let me see you move your fingers," she ordered. "Have you kept to the healer's advice?"

"I have, Lady Trella, though I don't think it much matters. He says . . . he says my arm will never be straight, and there's nothing more he can do. If it weren't for you and Captain Eskkar . . ." His voice trailed off as he lowered his head. "There's no work for a man with one arm."

Trella had not only nursed him back to health and made sure the healers did their best, but she'd given him a reason to live. More than that, she showed him a different way to fight, a different kind of warfare that went on each day in the shadows, where men whispered over cups of ale.

"Don't forget you are Hawk Clan, Tammuz. We are always proud of you, and you will never lack for friends." Trella lifted her hand to include Gatus and Annok-sur, sitting quietly at the other table. "Besides, what you do is more important than soldiering, remember that."

"I try to remember, Lady Trella, though it is hard sometimes."

"As is your work. You are our eyes and ears among the poor, the thieves, the prostitutes, and the murderers. With Akkad growing in size each day, there are many desperate men, men who will steal, cheat, and kill. More such will arrive in the coming months. We need someone who can mingle with these people to learn the things Eskkar needs to know. Do you have enough silver? Do you need more?"

"No, Lady Trella, not yet. I collect a share of what my customers steal, in return for letting them hide themselves and their goods in the alehouse. And I resell a few items myself, mostly small things that can't be traced back to me. Sometimes customers disappear, leaving their goods behind. It's enough to keep food on the table and ale jars filled."

Part of the arrangement with Eskkar and Trella was that Tammuz need only report on things that concerned Eskkar's House. Trella did not care about petty crimes or cut purses. Nevertheless, everyone knew that when the wealthy wanted a private murder done, they often sought out and hired desperate men, like those who frequented Tammuz's establishment.

"If you need more silver, send word through Annok-sur or Gatus." She pulled the cloak back over his arm and returned to her chair. Leaning forward, she focused her attention on Tammuz. Along with his responses, she would examine every expression, gesture, even the way he sat. Very little escaped her eyes and ears, and she knew how to take stock of what she heard and observed. "And now I have something different to ask of you. It may be dangerous."

Tammuz shrugged. "I've learned much about danger in the last few months."

"Still, I want you to be extra careful in this. Do you know of Korthac, the Egyptian?"

"Everyone knows of him."

"I want to learn more about him, especially more about his men. It's possible you may be able to find things out, overhear something, notice something." Trella told him what she'd learned about Korthac, and what she suspected.

"Don't underestimate him, Tammuz. He has sharp wits and knows how to lead men. He may have been a soldier in Egypt, possibly a leader of soldiers. Our spies have learned nothing about him, his men, or his plans, so do not think this will be easy. You must not let him be aware of your interest. Anything you can discover, even some small bit of gossip, might be useful. This is a challenge worthy of the Hawk Clan."

"When I see the Hawk Clan walking the streets, their heads held high ... sometimes, Lady Trella, I don't feel like a Hawk Clan."

"You *are* Hawk Clan, Tammuz. I know how you all swore an oath to help each other, to fight to the death if necessary." Eskkar had described the horrific fighting, and the pact the survivors had espoused; he repeated the oath for her, depicted the ceremony, the wind blowing through the dunes and the fire casting its light on each man's face as they swore binding vows to each other. No man could vouch such words and ever think of breaking his pledge while he drew breath.

"You, of course, were unconscious or delirious most of the time, but they swore for you just the same. And remember, Tammuz, someday there will be much more to the Hawk Clan than simple fighting. In the next few years, there will be more than just battles to be fought."

At their last meeting, Eskkar had reminded Tammuz that the binding oath extended both ways. He would always be a Hawk Clan, a true brother warrior to Eskkar and his clan.

"Now it is time to speak of other things. Have you thought about taking a wife?"

Tammuz's mouth fell open in surprise at the odd question. "A wife ... why ... who would want to be with a cripple?"

"You are old enough, and you own an alehouse," Trella

said, ignoring his question. "That makes you a man of substance. Annok-sur thinks you can use some help, someone you can trust, and Gatus agrees. I've picked out a slave girl for you. She's only a season or two older than you. If she proves agreeable and dutiful, we can free her for marriage. If you're not pleased with her for any reason, you can return her to me."

Gatus, watching and listening from a stool placed against the wall, couldn't repress a chuckle. "You should see your face, Tammuz. A woman isn't the worst thing in the world . . . at least not all the time."

Tammuz looked at Gatus, then back to Trella. "I don't know what to say. . . ."

"Then please me in this, and give her a chance. En-hedu is well suited to you, Tammuz, and has her wits about her. She is strong enough to work hard and free you for your other duties. She needs to be treated well; her previous owner drank too much wine and beat her often. You must be gentle with her, and patient, until she forgets her former master. She is not beautiful, but I think she will be loyal, especially if you treat her with respect. I've spoken to her several times, and told her about you."

Trella leaned back in her chair, feeling the child move within her. "Would you consider taking her?"

"Lady Trella, if you think it best, but . . . I've never been with a woman, and she might think my arm . . ."

"Bring her in, Annok-sur," Trella said. "Tell her nothing about the Hawk Clan, Tammuz. That's to remain our secret, for now at least. Other than that, you can tell her anything. And don't worry about what you know or don't know. She will guide you through Ishtar's mystery."

A few moments later the door creaked open and Annok-sur led a tall, sturdy young woman wearing a modest and patched shift into the workroom. Brown hair framed a plain but pleasant enough face, except for her nose, broken and never straightened properly afterward. Once again Trella stood, a sign of respect especially important to a slave, and Tammuz followed her example.

"En-hedu, this is Tammuz, your new master. You will obey him as if he were your husband. He needs your help, so I ask that you do all you can to assist him."

The girl looked at Tammuz shyly, showing a hint of apprehension at meeting a new master. She bowed awkwardly, then dropped her eyes to the floor. Tammuz seemed at a loss for words.

The sight touched one of Trella's vivid memories. She remembered a night not that long ago when she had been handed over, still crying, to her new master. Fear had rushed over her, fear of the unknown. That was the emotion a slave felt the most, fear of the stranger who had the power of life and death over you. Trella walked over to En-hedu, took her hand, and placed it in Tammuz's good hand.

"Be good to En-hedu, Tammuz." Trella looked at Gatus, who nodded and put his arm around Tammuz's shoulders.

"Time to let Trella get her rest," Gatus said with a yawn. "I'll take you back to the alehouse."

By the time Trella finished with the chamber pot, midnight approached, and she had only a few moments to wait before Annok-sur pushed open the door and guided Zenobia into the room. Trella rose as Zenobia approached the table. Once again, the simple gesture had its effect.

Throwing back her hood, Zenobia bowed very low, as Annok-sur closed the door behind them. Now they could talk privately, three women discussing things men should never hear.

"I thank you for coming, Zenobia," Trella said. "You are well?"

A woman of perhaps twenty-five seasons, Zenobia had deep black hair, large brown eyes, and a round face offering fine, delicate features. Trella remembered how Zenobia had looked months ago, wearing a rough shift and with smudges of dirt covering her face. Frightened and bearing marks of ill treatment, Zenobia had done everything she could to make herself look unattractive. An unprotected, beautiful woman would have been quickly taken into some man's house, never to emerge. Zenobia needed a benefactor, somebody to protect her and make sure she was not enslaved again. Trella had provided that protection.

Zenobia came from a land far to the east and had traveled many weeks before arriving at the village. She hadn't been in Akkad long, arriving only a few days before the siege of Akkad began. Shortly after her arrival, she had met Trella by chance during one of her walks. Zenobia's story had been both sad and unfortunate, but it created yet one more opportunity for Trella.

Raised as a pleasure slave since childhood, Zenobia had grown skillful at satisfying men. She'd pleased one of her patrons so much that he bought her and set her free. Despite his feelings for Zenobia, the patron saw a chance for gain and decided to establish his own pleasure house in the bountiful lands to the west. With Zenobia's help, he had purchased three slave girls to help launch the business, hired a small caravan of guards and animals, and set forth, determined to reach Akkad.

They journeyed for over a month, crossing the eastern mountains, and would have reached Akkad in a few more days. However, the patron had become thick with wine once too often and abused his guards. Tired of his ill treatment, they plotted with one of the local bandits. Together they attacked the caravan and killed the patron and his servants before turning their attentions to looting the pack animals and enjoying the women.

By then Zenobia had escaped in the darkness, running for her life, leaving the other girls to their fate. Morning found her miles away, having lost all her possessions except for a few silver coins sewn into her dress. It had taken her three days to walk to Akkad, avoiding the roads for the first two of those days for fear she would encounter the murderers or new robbers. A woman alone, especially an attractive one, would be at the mercy of anyone she met.

She reached Akkad in safety. Without a patron, Zenobia found work in one of the taverns, cleaning tables and providing sex to customers, and splitting her fees with the innkeeper. Encountering Trella one afternoon in the marketplace, Zenobia had impulsively told her tale, and the captain's slave had immediately sensed an opportunity.

Trella gave Zenobia a few copper coins and told her to find a decent inn where she could sleep safely at night. It hadn't taken Trella long to figure out how Zenobia could become an ally, assuming any of them survived the barbarians besieging the city. From time to time, she sent Annok-sur to give Zenobia more copper and to tell her to be patient a little while longer.

The siege had ended more than two months ago. Now the time had arrived.

"Zenobia," Trella began, "I've thought a great deal about you and your plight. It occurs to me that we could be of great help to each other. To serve my husband, I need someone who can gather information from the rich and powerful in Akkad. With your experience and skills, many men would whisper their secrets to you. If you are willing, I can provide protection for you and help you open a house of pleasure here in Akkad."

Zenobia's eyes went wide at the prospect as doubts rushed to her lips. "Mistress Trella ... is such a thing possible? To furnish a pleasure house with trained women would take much gold, and a strong man would be needed to oversee such an establishment. And there are the other brothels and alehouses to compete with."

"I am not talking about just another brothel, Zenobia. Nor will there be any competition. I want you to establish the finest pleasure house in the land, and fill it with the most expensive women and the finest furnishings. I have a strong protector in mind, and he can provide men to guard the house and your women."

"Who would this protector be, Mistress Trella?"

"Gatus, the captain of the guard, will be the official owner of the house, Zenobia. He will provide a soldier or two to keep order, as well as a scribe to record all the profits and expenses. He will take one-tenth of the profits, and I will take another four-tenths." She watched Zenobia's eyes grow wider. "The rest would be yours alone. There will be no man to take your share."

"But, mistress, much gold is needed to start such a business. A large house would have to be found. Girls must be recruited and trained, furnishings bought. Fine wine and exotic foods must be available. There is much that . . ."

"I'm glad you understand how difficult it will be, Zenobia. But I have considered all these things as well. To start, I will loan you twenty gold coins, more than enough to buy a good-sized house and furnish it properly. It will probably take another ten coins before you are fully established, especially if you begin your search for girls at the slave market. I'm sure there are plenty of women in Akkad who would be willing to work for you in the beginning—and for very little."

Trella paused for a moment, to make sure Zenobia understood her words. "If more gold is needed and all is proceeding well, it will be provided. Six months from now, you will begin repaying all the gold loaned to you at the rate of three gold coins each month. That is in addition to our regular profits. You will have to work very hard to make sure you are successful, and there are other conditions as well. Are you interested, Zenobia?"

The woman's head bobbed up and down with excitement. "Yes, of course, mistress, I am very interested. What else must I pay?"

"You need pay nothing further. If you work hard and the house is successful, you should be able to repay all of the loans within two years. We would charge you no interest on the loan, Zenobia." Again she paused to let that information sink in. "You would be required to train the girls, teach them the love arts, and make sure they learn how to please their customers. Can you do that?"

"Oh, yes, Mistress Trella, I have been well trained myself, and I've trained new girls for many years."

"There is one more thing, Zenobia, and this is the most important." Trella shifted her position on the chair to look directly into the woman's eyes. "Your establishment must be the best house of pleasure in Akkad. It must be the one place where all the rich and powerful men come to amuse themselves. They will come for your women, they will drink too much wine, and they will talk about many things. You will instruct your girls to report all that they hear only to you, and you will pass it all on to Annok-sur or myself. And you must do more than just listen. You and two or three of your most trustworthy women must learn to extract as many secrets as possible. You will reward those girls according to how much information they gather."

Zenobia opened her mouth, but Trella continued on, her voice harder now. "That is why we do this, to gather information, not because we wish to make a profit in a business arrangement. You must make certain that no one learns of this. No one. Only Gatus, and the three of us. If any of the girls refuse to obey, you will take whatever steps needed to make sure that they do."

"I . . . understand, mistress. It shall be as you say."

"Make very sure you understand me, Zenobia. You will tell no one what you do with the information, and you will keep silent about me. Also, you will guarantee that none of your girls tell anyone, especially their customers. They must understand the penalty for careless talk. As must you. If you fail, then you will be removed. Since you will not officially own any part of the business, you would simply disappear. So you will have great incentive to remain loyal and faithful."

Zenobia swallowed nervously but didn't hesitate. She had been in the village long enough to understand Trella's meaning. To "disappear" in Akkad meant a splash in the river in the dark of night. "I will be loyal, mistress. None will learn of our arrangement."

Trella smiled at her, then reached out and gently took her hand. When she spoke, her voice sounded soft and pleasant again. "I am glad, Zenobia. If you do this, in a few years you will be rich and respected. Starting tomorrow, you will meet with Annok-sur to begin the planning. You will report only to Annok-sur or myself. When you have listed all that you require and have an idea of the cost, we will begin buying what you need."

"Yes, mistress. Thank you, Mistress Trella."

"One more thing, Zenobia. If you hear anything about Korthac or his men, anything, you are to get the information to us at once."

"The Egyptian? Yes, of course."

"Then we are agreed." Trella pushed back her chair and stood. "You will start tomorrow. If all goes well, in a few weeks you will have the finest pleasure house in Akkad."

Zenobia stood also and bowed again, this time so low that her hair brushed the tabletop. "It will be as you say, Mistress Trella. I will learn all the men's secrets for you. I promise it."

"Then we will both prosper, Zenobia."

Annok-sur stood also. "Zenobia, it's too late to walk the streets," Annok-sur said. "Spend the rest of the night here.

I'll escort you back to your home in the morning." Taking Zenobia's hand, she led her from the workroom to one of the rooms below.

In a few moments Annok-sur returned to Trella's presence. "We'll leave the house right before dawn. With her cloak drawn, no one will notice her."

"Thank you, Annok-sur."

"I think she will do well, Trella. It will take many months, perhaps years, but Zenobia will gather much useful information. And you spoke to her with the voice of command, with the voice of someone twice your seasons. You know the ways of power and how to bend both men and women to your will."

"Yes, I have learned much in the last few months," Trella answered, a hint of bitterness in her voice. "When I was sold into slavery, I was told a slave needs to learn quickly. And so I am always learning. From Nicar, from Eskkar, from the people of the village, even from you, Annok-sur. I must be stronger and wiser than my seasons and I must hide my doubts, if Eskkar is to succeed." She shook her head to banish the dark thoughts. "Do you need any help to find the house or furnish it?"

"No, I know what is needed," Annok-sur replied. "But we should meet with Gatus in the morning, to make sure he is ready and understands his part in this new undertaking."

"I think Gatus will find this task to his liking. Perhaps Zenobia will have the girls practice their arts on him."

They both smiled at the thought of the old soldier reclining in bed, sipping fine wine, and surrounded by eager women while counting his profits.

"As long as they gather secrets," Trella said. "I just wish Zenobia were already in business. Korthac and his men would be sure to visit her."

Trella sighed. The secretive Egyptian seemed to be ever in her thoughts. Soon, she hoped, his riddle would be solved.

Tammuz and his new slave followed Gatus back to the alehouse, where he grunted his goodnight without stopping. Tammuz watched the veteran soldier disappear into darkness down the lane, hand on his sword. While anyone walking around in the middle of the night could expect to be a target for robbers, only someone blind drunk or very desperate would think of attacking the captain of the guard.

Tammuz rapped three times on the door. "It's Tammuz, Kuri. Open up."

He waited, glancing up and down the narrow lane. En-hedu still held on to his left hand, an unfamiliar sensation he found surprisingly enjoyable. He'd taken her hand when they left Trella's house, before he remembered the need to keep his right hand free and close to the knife in his belt. So he changed hands, but discovered his crippled arm couldn't hold her properly as they walked. Before he could get frustrated, En-hedu had gently withdrawn her hand from his weak grasp and taken his left hand in her own, holding him gently until they reached the alehouse.

The door creaked open at last, and Kuri stood there, looking half asleep, but holding his old copper sword in his hand. A sour odor wafted out of the alehouse; the old man smelled of barley ale, on his breath and his garment. His eyes widened in surprise at the sight of the girl.

"Fasten the door, Kuri." Tammuz stepped in, leading his charge. Even in the best of neighborhoods, you didn't stand about with the door open after dark. "No one else is to enter tonight."

Inside, he led his new slave carefully through the blackness of the main room, trying to ignore the smells of ale, sweat, and worse. His new slave would no doubt be disgusted by such a place, especially after having lived at Trella's house. Half a dozen snoring men slumbered on the floor, the heavy sleep of those who'd drunk too much ale before retiring late. None of them woke as Tammuz passed between them and into his private quarters at the back of the alehouse.

Closing the door, Tammuz placed a rickety bar across the entrance. The small room, less than half the size of Trella's workroom, had no windows, but a hint of moonlight filtered into the chamber from the roof opening. Like nearly every other humble dwelling in Akkad, the inhabitants slept on the roof during the hottest part of the summer. Tammuz unbuckled his belt, and tossed it and his knife on a table, then struggled to remove the unfamiliar cloak, a covering he seldom wore.

En-hedu's hand reached out. "Let me help you with that, master."

She untied the cloak, then folded it neatly and placed in on the table. He stood there, embarrassed at needing anyone's help to remove a garment.

"Lady Trella told me much about you, master." En-hedu kept her voice low, making sure her words could not be heard beyond the closed door. "She said you work in Lord Eskkar's service."

So she knew about his duties, just not that they considered him Hawk Clan.

"It's little enough that I do for Lady Trella," he said.

"She is a great lady. Without her help, I would be dead, either murdered by my master, or by my own hand."

Tammuz felt wide awake now, despite the late hour, and her words piqued his curiosity. He guided En-hedu to one of two stools that faced each other across the small table, the only other furniture in the room beside the narrow bed, a small chest, and the ladder that provided access to the roof. The darkness shielded them both and made it somehow easier for him to talk. "Sit down. Would you like some ale? Or wine? I have . . ."

"No, nothing, master. The hour is late. You should be asleep, taking your rest."

"I can't sleep now. Tell me about yourself. How did you meet Lady Trella?"

They spoke for almost an hour. Tammuz learned that En-hedu's parents had sold her at the slave market within days of her becoming a woman. She'd just entered into her thirteenth season, and her parents pocketed ten silver coins for their virgin daughter. Her new master, a tanner with his own shop, put in long hours at his craft, and made sure his new slave worked even harder.

When her master's labor ended at sundown, En-hedu's continued. He expected to be fed and pleasured long into the evening. The slightest fault on her part resulted in a beating, usually followed by a painful rape. She'd put up with it for three years, before she overcame her fear and struck back in desperation. That's when he broke her nose. Neighbors heard her cries, and managed to stop him before he beat her to death.

The brutal beatings continued for the next few months, two or three times a week. Some days she could hardly stand, let alone work at the tannery. A woman living nearby sought out Trella and told her the story, and the extent of the beatings.

Trella and Annok-sur arrived the next day, escorted by two Hawk Clan soldiers, and offered the tanner five silver coins for his slave. The man refused. "Very well," Trella replied. "Then I offer you four silver coins. If you do not take them, right now, tomorrow you will find that no one will purchase your leather, no one will sell you hides, no one will sell you bread or help you quench your thirst for ale. Soon no one will even speak to you. You will have to leave Akkad. Choose now."

Tammuz laughed when En-hedu told that part of the story, imitating Trella's manner of speaking. "Yes, I remember her commanding the servants and even the soldiers in Eskkar's house. It would be a brave man to stand up to her."

"I remember every word she said," En-hedu answered. "I was on my knees in a corner of his hut, where he'd told me to stay, afraid to look up. Lady Trella waited, and when my master didn't answer, she dropped four coins on the floor, called my name, and told me to come with her. Then she turned and left. I wanted to follow her, but couldn't get to my feet. One of the soldiers had to help me. I thought I'd been saved by a goddess. I couldn't stop crying."

He reached across the table and touched her hand.

"There'll be no beatings here, En-hedu. I've never had a slave before, and I'm not sure how you can help me. This place will look even worse in the morning, nothing like Lady Trella's fine house. If you wish, you can return to her service. I'm sure she can find someone . . . someone better for you."

She pondered his words for a moment. "No. Lady Trella said I could be helpful to you, and that what you do was important to Lord Eskkar and her. I will stay with you. She said you needed a woman to look after you. I'm strong, and work hard. Don't send me away."

Before he could answer, En-hedu stood up.

"Now it is time to sleep. Come to bed, master."

Tammuz heard the rustle of her dress as she pulled it over her head. Then she took his hand and guided him next to the bed. Without asking, she helped remove his tunic, then crawled into the bed, closest to the wall. When he joined her, she pulled the blanket over them both.

He felt her naked body against him, and couldn't resist reaching out his hand. She flinched at his touch, then lay still, submitting to his caress. Tammuz, his member painfully stiff, hesitated. He remembered Trella's words. "Be patient," she'd said. Taking a deep breath, he took En-hedu's hand in his, and told her to sleep. He waited a long time, staring up into the darkness, until her breathing grew rhythmic and he knew she slept. To his surprise, he found her presence comforting.

And distracting. He felt her warmth under the blanket, and his erection refused to subside. For someone who'd never had a woman—now to have a girl in his bed seemed a dream come true.

To take his mind off En-hedu, he started thinking about Korthac.

Like many others in Akkad, Tammuz had gaped the first time he'd seen the Egyptian walking about the lanes, often with only a single bodyguard. But after a few days, the novelty wore off, and Tammuz, like most of Akkad, forgot about the man. Nevertheless, Lady Trella sensed something odd, something dangerous, about Korthac, and she seldom made mistakes in such matters. Tammuz tried to remember all the things he'd heard about the foreigner.

Korthac spent most of his day at the inn he'd chosen for his home. His men stayed close by, never wandering about alone, not drinking in the ale shops, not doing much of anything, staying inside even in the light of day. Tammuz realized how odd that was. Servants, whether bodyguards or porters or household slaves, were always wandering about, trying to avoid work and their masters.

Tammuz knew all about the petty thefts servants and slaves engaged in, either from their masters or neighbors. Clothing disappeared, sandals, trinkets, dozens of small items often vanished and reappeared at the local alehouses, sometimes traded for a single cup of ale. Many brought such things to his establishment to sell, or to those traders in the marketplace who didn't ask questions. But as far as he knew, none of Korthac's men had ever entered his or any other alehouse in Akkad.

He wondered if Trella had noticed this. No, she would have mentioned it. Something like that was probably too insignificant a detail for Trella's spies, something that should be, but wasn't. Tammuz wondered if he'd noticed a small detail Trella hadn't . . . and what that might mean.

He put the thought aside for later. Lady Trella, he knew, had a keen interest in small details, always asking for more and more information. Tammuz made a mental note to ask her about it.

Tomorrow he'd take a closer look at Korthac's inn. Tammuz could ask one of his patrons to approach Korthac's men, looking for something to buy. If he could get one of the Egyptians to sell some trinket, he might be able to learn something useful about their master.

This whole business could turn out to be nothing, just misplaced curiosity on Lady Trella's part. Still, she had summoned him to her house and asked for his help. Never before had she, or anyone, for that matter, asked him for anything. He'd passed on bits of talk he heard, men grumbling over their ale, but nothing of importance had ever come to his attention. This Korthac might actually present some small danger to Akkad. Tammuz determined to solve the riddle, if for no other reason than to justify Lady Trella's asking him.

With that decided, he drifted off to sleep, again thinking about the warmth of En-hedu's body brushing against him, as she turned in her sleep. It would be difficult to restrain himself. Still, if Tammuz had learned one thing since smashing his arm, it was how to be patient.

They woke together at dawn, bodies curled against one another. Tammuz hadn't shared a bed with anyone, let alone a woman, in months. Since the day he and Kuri moved into the alehouse, he'd slept alone in the back room, enjoying the luxury of privacy he never experienced before in his life.

Nevertheless, despite the shared bed and the shortened

night, Tammuz slept deeply. Turning toward En-hedu, he saw that she'd pushed the blanket down during her sleep, exposing her breasts to the morning light. The sight made his member harden.

En-hedu, conscious of his gaze, closed her eyes and turned away. She didn't try to cover herself. She said nothing, simply lay there, waiting for him to take her. *Be patient.* Trella's advice echoed in his mind. He pushed himself up off the bed and dressed before speaking.

"The chamber pot is there. I have to wake the customers. Kuri is never much help in the mornings."

She sat up in bed, and once again he found himself looking at her body. In the light he could see scars and lingering bruises from her former master. He must have enjoyed hurting her. No one should be beaten like that. To carry bruises for so long ... her old master must be a savage, worse than any barbarian.

Tammuz remembered the countless beatings he'd had growing up. Like all boys, he expected to be beaten, and not only by his father. The older boys took advantage of the younger, the same as the strong took advantage of the weak. He'd learned that fact of life early. When he'd grown old enough to steal, he'd received a few more beatings, this time by his victims, until he learned not to get caught.

But even the worst of these chastisements left no scars on his body—more punishment than for the pleasure of inflicting pain. Then he'd joined Eskkar's men as a stable boy. He worked with horses before, knew their ways, and made himself useful to the soldiers. A few weeks later Tammuz begged his way onto the captain of the guard's first expedition against the Alur Meriki. Tammuz remembered how thrilled he'd been when Eskkar asked if he wanted to care for the horses.

Now he'd grown into manhood, and, crippled or not, no one would beat him again. The knife he wore every moment of the day insured that. When Kuri first saw him fumbling with the blade, the former soldier showed him how to use it. How to hold it, how to move with it, how to strike and counterstrike, how to retreat, and the parts of the body where a thrust would do the most damage. Most of all, Kuri taught him how to read his opponent's eyes, and how to wait for the right moment to strike. *Be patient.* Trella and Kuri apparently shared the same beliefs.

As Kuri explained, a knife fight often turned into a bloody affair for both combatants, and even the victor could bleed out. Practice hard now, the old man advised, and stay alive later. Since he'd taken over the alehouse, Tammuz spent an hour or more each day practicing, handling the knife, moving and thrusting with it. He found he had to work extra hard to compensate for his nearly useless left arm.

The patrons helped instruct him. Some had plenty of experience handling a knife, and their nimble hands and feet moved far quicker than the aging Kuri could ever do. Tammuz felt the strength and coordination of his right arm grow each day, and the quickness of his feet soon made up for his weak left arm. Those who frequented the alehouse took notice of his growing skill. No one considered him a boy anymore.

Putting such thoughts aside, he unbarred the bedroom door. Tammuz worked his way through the inn's only other room, using his foot to nudge those still sleeping awake.

Kuri, snoring loudly, slept against the door, the sword at his side. Each morning Tammuz had to wake the old soldier. Depending on how much Kuri had drunk the night before, getting him awake could be a chore.

"Get up, Kuri. It's past dawn."

By the time he had the old man on his feet, the other patrons had reached the door, mumbling and shuffling out into the lane, shielding their eyes from the already bright morning sun, to relieve themselves against the nearby walls. Tammuz turned to find En-hedu standing beside him and looking about.

"Is there food here for your breakfast, master?"

There might be, but nothing he would offer to her. He shook his head, and reached into his pouch. "Take this to the market, and buy enough for the three of us," he said, handing her a few copper coins. "Kuri, go with her, and keep her safe. Make sure everyone knows who she is."

Once those living and working nearby knew she belonged to him, she'd be safe enough. In a day or so, she could go about on her own.

While they were gone, Tammuz spoke with two men who still remained inside, men who preferred not to be seen in daylight, men being hunted by their victims or by the captain of the guard's men. Fortunately, most of the guards knew Kuri had soldiered with Gatus. That friendship usually kept any members of the watch outside, though once, while looking for a murderer, they pushed their way inside. Luckily for Tammuz, the killer had already left. The guards' leader had looked about at the poor furnishings, spat on the floor, and left.

Tammuz told the two men what they owed for food,

ale, and use of the floor to sleep. One who had the coins paid up; the other left to earn it, by whatever means he could. He knew better than to come back empty-handed. If desperate men needed a safe place to stay, they would have to pay for it, and how they got their copper didn't concern Tammuz.

Nevertheless, all of his customers had received one warning: no killing. Murderers would not be protected. Even Tammuz couldn't chance harboring a killer, exposing himself to the villagers' wrath for anyone who violated the customs by concealing such an offender.

That task done, Tammuz checked the ale supply, first to make sure none of the guests had tapped the big clay jars during the night, and then to see how much more he needed to buy. His stock needed frequent replenishing. That meant a trip to the market this morning for at least two more jars.

En-hedu returned, carrying a basket that smelled of fresh bread, with Kuri limping behind. The three went into Tammuz's room to eat their breakfast bread and sausage, and sip well-watered ale from crudely carved cups. When they finished, Tammuz gave Kuri some silver coins, and told him to buy more ale.

Kuri left, grabbing two new customers to accompany him and carry back the filled jars. A free mug of ale would pay for their labor.

En-hedu swept the bread crumbs into the basket, then faced Tammuz across the table. "What should I do, master?"

A good question, one that needed discussing, but one he couldn't talk about here, not with the door open and men hanging about. "Come, let's go for a walk."

Fortunately, during the mornings, usually nothing much happened at the alehouse, and Kuri could take care of the few customers that came. At dusk, things got busy, and Tammuz knew En-hedu would be useful serving the customers.

Once in the lane, she moved to his left side and took his hand without saying a word. He led the way down the lane. Her touch affected him, and the vision of her naked breasts flashed into his thoughts. By the time he got the sight out of his mind, they'd traversed two lanes, and reached the lane where Korthac resided.

Tammuz slowed his pace. "That's where Korthac is staying," he said, pointing to the inn a few dozen paces ahead. A bored guard stood at the door, a sword at his waist. "The Egyptian won't stay in this place much longer. He'll be moving to a fine house, away from common folk."

"Lady Trella said only Korthac's men lived inside, except for the innkeeper," En-hedu said.

The guard didn't even look up as they passed. They kept going, and soon they reached the river gate. Turning south, they walked in silence until the walls of Akkad slipped behind them, and the fresh air of the farms cleared their lungs. A flat rock near the river gave them a place to sit.

"You want to learn about this Korthac?" En-hedu pulled her knees up and held them with her arms.

"Yes. Lady Trella wants to know what he's planning." Tammuz told her everything he knew about Korthac, his tight control of his men, the way he kept them apart from the rest of Akkad.

"We should find out where his new house will be," she

said. "Perhaps I can help. It would be good to keep watch on his new home, wouldn't it?"

"Yes, but they'd soon notice anyone hanging about all day."

"Yes . . . but if I were selling something or other, like any street vendor, no one would notice me."

He looked at her. A woman normally didn't make such suggestions to a man, let alone a slave to her master. But she wasn't merely a slave. Trella had urged him to listen to her, which meant Trella believed in her wits.

"And if I set up my cart before they moved in, no one would suspect anything." She shifted on the rock, to look straight into his eyes. "This is something I can do, Tammuz. A slave has to earn her keep. It's what any servant would do for her master."

"And at night, you could return to the alehouse," he mused, "to help with the serving. Once it grew dark, I could keep watch on Korthac's home from any of the rooftops." He touched her hand. "You would do this?"

"To help you, to help Lady Trella . . . this is nothing, master. I worked from dawn to dusk with my old master, tanning hides. Look at my arms." She lifted her hands up.

Her arms looked as strong as any farm woman's who labored all day in the fields. But his eyes noted her arms for only a moment, before being drawn to her breasts. He looked away when she dropped her arms.

"Master, you need not look away. You may take me whenever you wish. I've been taken many times."

Tammuz ground his teeth at the thought of her former master. "En-hedu, I've never been with a woman. When I do lie with one, I want her to be willing . . . to want me."

The words had come out without thinking, but what surprised him more was that he remembered where he'd heard such words before: at the campfire a few days before Eskkar's return to Akkad. Someone had asked the captain of the guard about his slave, Trella. And Eskkar had answered that he no longer wanted to take women against their will, that he found it more satisfying to take his pleasure with someone who wanted him.

"Tammuz, I'm not sure I will ever want to be with a man. All I have is the memory of pain. Pain and humiliation."

Her former master again. The man should die. *And why not?* "En-hedu, Lady Trella gave you to me so that you could help me." He stood and extended his hand. "Perhaps we can help each other. But for now, let's make our plans for this Korthac, before we have to get back. Otherwise Kuri will drink all the fresh ale."

She clasped his hand, and he felt the pleasure of her touch flow through him. *Be patient*, he thought. Then he thought about her former master. *I'll be patient with him, too,* he decided, *patient until I put my knife between his ribs.*

8

The noonday sun shone straight down on Bisitun before Eskkar sat down for the first time. He stretched weary legs straight out and let himself relax for a moment. Since the sunrise capture of Ninazu, Eskkar and his men had rushed about the village, scarcely pausing to scoop a cup of water or a fistful of bread. Chaos ruled all morning, with a hundred tasks demanding his attention.

While Sisuthros worked on securing the village, Eskkar rounded up every horse he could find and put them under guard. Mounted Akkadians already ringed the palisade to make sure no bandits escaped. Sentries stood watch at the two gates as well, while the rest of Eskkar's men guarded prisoners.

Eskkar had escorted Ninazu, his arms bound tightly to his sides, back to his own house. The sight of the bandit leader being led through the lanes helped restore order to the village. Once there, Eskkar ordered one of Ninazu's legs broken, to make sure he didn't attempt to escape.

Meanwhile Hamati took a squad of men and searched

every house and hut, looking for bandits trying to hide within the dwellings or on rooftops. That took most of the morning. When they finished, they'd discovered and captured nearly a dozen more of Ninazu's men scattered through Bisitun, cowering in corners or huddled under blankets. One bandit attempted to fight his way out, killing an innocent villager in the process. Mitrac killed the bandit with an arrow when he refused to surrender.

By midmorning Eskkar felt satisfied his men had captured or killed all of Ninazu's men. Gradually a sense of relief settled over the village. The women stopped their screaming, the men their cursing. Still, most of Bisitun's frightened inhabitants stayed in their huts, wondering what new woes these Akkadians from the south would bring to them.

Eskkar dispatched men to locate and gather the village elders and leading merchants, though few enough of them remained. At the same time, three messengers on captured horses rode out into the countryside, to spread the word of Ninazu's overthrow and bring in the more substantial farmers, so that everyone could see what Bisitun's new leaders had accomplished.

As the populace realized they would not be pillaged and raped, they gathered their courage and headed for the market area, empty except for Eskkar's men and a few horses. In prosperous times, it would be filled with carts selling all manner of crops, animals, and goods, but for most of the morning, not a cart, vendor, not even a beggar, could be seen.

The marketplace, an irregular rectangle formed by dwellings of every shape and height, was accessed by half a dozen crooked lanes. That left plenty of room for the inhabitants, and soon more than a hundred people filled the square. To Eskkar's eyes, they looked little better than the inhabitants of Dilgarth. Though surrounded by fruitful farmlands, food remained scarce in Bisitun, with Ninazu's men taking most of what the local farmers delivered. Many villagers showed bruises on their thin bodies, marks from the bandit's brutal treatment. Most wore simple tunics that needed washing. Only a few possessed sandals, though Eskkar recalled that almost all of Ninazu's men had worn them.

The demands for vengeance against Ninazu and his followers mounted, with the village's women shouting the loudest. Dozens, raped by the bandits, their husbands murdered, or both, cried out for Ninazu's blood. Those outcries only stopped when Eskkar assured everyone that punishment would be meted out soon. Then the villagers pleaded for food. Ninazu hadn't bothered to secure enough provisions for the siege, and most of what he had stored went to his men, with little left over for Bisitun. Fortunately, the handful of dead horses would provide a decent meal to most. Eskkar dispatched more riders to the countryside, to let the farmers know they could once again bring in their crops with safety, while receiving a fair price.

By noon Eskkar's men patrolled the streets and lanes, the gates stood closed and guarded, and villagers labored to repair the burned-out section of the palisade. Fifty-seven of Ninazu's followers had died, and forty-one taken prisoner. Some of these, the least violent and most tractable, would become slaves. With the mark of Akkad branded on their foreheads, they would live out the rest of their lives working in the fields and canals. The rest would be killed.

No one, including Eskkar, felt the slightest sympathy for any of them. They'd chosen to live by the sword at the expense of their neighbors. The captured bandits deserved a sentence of slavery, if for nothing else than to make amends for their crimes.

Another thirty or more bandits had slipped away in the confusion. Eskkar's men had reported hearing splashes in the river, so no doubt many had risked their hand at swimming. Those that made it across the river would offer no threat to Bisitun for quite some time. One or two might still be hiding within the village, but Eskkar's men would soon discover any that remained.

Surprisingly, Eskkar had lost only six men in the fighting. Two of those had climbed the palisade with Eskkar. Sisuthros had lost the others repulsing Ninazu's sortie or storming the gate. Eight more had taken wounds, but with luck would survive. To the soldiers of Akkad, it seemed an incredible accomplishment. Outnumbered, and with minimal losses, they had defeated an entrenched and determined enemy in the space of a few hours. Eskkar's reputation among the soldiers as a canny leader who cared about his men grew even greater.

The inhabitants of Bisitun appeared as impressed. Ninazu had lied to them, told them that the Akkadians would kill everyone in the village, just as he'd told them that the village couldn't be taken.

Eskkar and Sisuthros had plenty of work to do. The scribes arrived from the encampment, and set about making lists of those villagers killed or robbed by Ninazu and his men. Eskkar sent a rider to Akkad to inform Trella and Gatus that Bisitun had been freed. He spoke with more than a dozen men imprisoned by Ninazu, and released all of them. Using one of the scribes, Eskkar made an account of the loot found at Ninazu's house. The bandit leader had taken over the largest structure in Bisitun for his residence, and Eskkar saw no reason to let it go to waste, claiming it as his headquarters.

The villagers, organized in small parties, began to bury the dead and repair the damage caused by the fighting. Nevertheless, it wasn't until midday that Eskkar felt confident enough to order everyone to the market square to hear his words. If so many villagers hadn't been killed or driven out, the square could never have accommodated them. Even then, the rooftops seemed as crowded as the streets.

Eskkar hated giving speeches, but the people of Bisitun needed to hear and see him. But they, like the villagers in Dilgarth, needed to know who he was, why he'd come, and what their role would be in the future. When he looked over the crowd, he saw shock and fear still gripped most of them. The crowd quieted when he climbed on a cart and raised his hand, as the soldiers ringing the square called out for everyone to keep quiet. He waited impassively until the chattering turned into murmurs, then into silence.

In a loud voice, Eskkar announced that Bisitun had come under the rule and protection of Akkad, and that from this day, Sisuthros would command here in Akkad's name. A new village council, to include craftsmen and farmers as well as merchants, would be established to handle local matters, including justice for the bandits and their victims. The same customs governing Akkad would be established here, and would apply equally to all, just as they did in Akkad.

"What are these new customs?" a voice in the crowd shouted out.

"The council," Eskkar said, raising his hand for silence, "will set the prices of grain and other goods. The council will also set the penalties for crimes, from theft to murder. The council will decide what rules the people in Bisitun need, and those rules will apply to everyone in the village and the surrounding farms, including the members of the council. Persons who feel themselves treated unjustly can appeal first to the council, and then to Sisuthros. He will decide anything of import, or, if he thinks necessary, Sisuthros can refer the matter to me and the council back in Akkad for a final decision. You will be governed justly and fairly."

The villagers looked at each other, no doubt wondering what that really meant, but a few cheered at Eskkar's announcement.

"The new customs," Eskkar added, "apply to my own soldiers. They've received strict instructions to take no liberties with the local people. Starting now, Sisuthros will provide soldiers for protection not only of the village, but enough to begin regular patrols of the surrounding farms. More soldiers and craftsmen will arrive from Akkad over the next few months, to strengthen the palisade and provide more security. Restoration of the farms to their rightful owners, and assistance with the canals and irrigation will be given the first priority. Taxes, in the form of goods, will be sent to Akkad on a regular basis, to pay for the protection and safety Akkad will supply."

Eskkar didn't speak long, just expanded on the same speech he'd given in Dilgarth only a few days ago. He turned the crowd over to Sisuthros, leaving him to take the brunt of the inhabitants' questions. Hours passed. Sisuthros explained the new ways of Akkad in detail, interrupted constantly to answer question after question. He had trouble keeping the crowd under control at first, but when everyone realized their voice would be heard, they quieted somewhat and learned to raise their hands when they wished to be heard.

Sisuthros consulted with the local people and trades-men, as well as the few farmers who had taken shelter within Bisitun. He took nominations for the council, and promised to begin the distribution of stolen lands and goods tomorrow morning. When he finished, he dismissed the villagers and told them to return to their homes or farms. Then, ignoring the pleas and questions that still lingered, he gathered those who would become the council of elders and departed for one of the houses a little way off the square.

Eskkar breathed a sigh of relief as he watched them go, most of the crowd following after Sisuthros. He and Grond entered Ninazu's former home. Someone had stocked the table with food and drink, and the two men emptied their water cups even before they sat. Until now, there'd been little time to eat or rest since the attack began the night before.

"By the gods, I'm glad that's over!" Grond said, as he banged down his cup. "I thought the questions would never stop."

Eskkar laughed. "They won't. Not for a few weeks at

least." He refilled his cup from the pitcher. "If they're anything like the people of Akkad, they'll drive Sisuthros crazy with their complaints and quarrels."

"I still can't believe how quickly Ninazu's men collapsed," Grond said, shaking his head and yawning. "It's going to take a day or two before everything calms down."

"Longer than that," Eskkar said, lifting his feet onto the table. "Remember, we have to settle the countryside as well as the village. We need those crops in the ground as soon as possible."

In the last few months Eskkar had learned all about the mysteries of the farm. Now he understood that real wealth flowed from the crops in the fields, that gold merely transferred that wealth from one person to another. When the farms produced in plenty, gold would flow into Bisitun and Akkad. However, without the farms, there would be little gold, no trade, and no prosperity.

The talk died out as the two men picked at the food spread before them. There was wine and bread, as well as cheese, dates, and honey. Ninazu had stocked his house well, with luxuries long absent from the villagers' tables. Eskkar mixed a splash of wine in with his water. The long night had tired him more than he would admit, and he didn't trust himself with too much strong drink.

He looked up when two women entered the room, passed in by the Hawk Clan guard who stood at the door. One carried a large wooden platter holding half a dozen slices of roasted horsemeat. The other held a small plate stacked with sweetened cakes. The women bore a strong resemblance, and Eskkar guessed them to be sisters.

The older of the two put a slice of horsemeat on each of

the men's plates, then left the platter in the center of the table. She took the sweet cakes from her sister and placed it before them as well, her eyes carefully appraising Eskkar as she did so. Then she bowed, looked at Grond, and both women left the room.

Grond cleared his throat. "Captain, I forgot to tell you, when we searched this house, we found six women here. Ninazu's women. Four have returned to their homes or families. But these two . . ." He shrugged. "They say they have no place to go."

Eskkar shook his head. He'd be dealing with Ninazu's legacy for months, one thing after another. Even the bandit's loot had become a problem. They'd found a small, windowless room in the house containing four sacks crammed with gold, jewelry, and other valuables, Ninazu's personal share of the booty. Many of the coins bore the marks of villages to the north and west, so the bandit had obviously accumulated plenty of booty even before arriving in Bisitun.

Ninazu remained with his plunder, though no doubt it gave him less pleasure today, sitting on it with his leg broken. Still, a Hawk Clan soldier stood constant guard over Ninazu and his gold. The bandit chief seemed much too crafty and resourceful, and Eskkar didn't want to take any chances with him escaping.

But until now, Eskkar hadn't heard about any women, though it didn't surprise him. Even a bandit needed someone to run his household, as well as needing women with whom to take his pleasures. Six women seemed quite a number for one man. Eskkar's opinion of Ninazu increased.

"Well, they must have come from someplace." Eskkar took his knife and sliced a bit of the warm meat and put it in his mouth. After last night's slaughter at the corral, there would be plenty of horsemeat for the next few days. The steamy flesh tasted good, and he realized how hungry he was. Cutting up the thick steak, he alternated bites with bread, sweet and fresh, washing everything down with watered wine.

"Ninazu brought these two women with him when he rode into Bisitun," Grond continued, as he worked at his own food. "Sisuthros asked me to take care of them. They offered to keep your house if they could stay here. I said that you would speak to them."

Eskkar looked at his bodyguard in surprise, but the man's attention remained focused on his plate. Grond had never offered to intercede for others with his leader, though more than a few in Akkad had sought him out, to try and take advantage of his friendship with Eskkar.

"I'll talk to them later, then," Eskkar said, as he finished the meat and selected some figs to finish the meal. He had never cared for the sweet cakes villagers devoured at every opportunity, thinking them somehow unfit for a warrior, a concept that dated back to his barbarian days. Trella had smiled when he told her about it, but she ate them only infrequently herself.

When he finished eating, he drank another cup of water, then stood up and stretched. The heavy meal sapped whatever strength remained and he felt exhausted. More than a day had passed since he'd slept, and even that had been cut short. He felt the heaviness in his legs, and cursed his own weakness.

"Grond, I'm going to get some sleep. Get some rest yourself. We'll probably be up late tonight as well, with all these villagers pestering us. Tell the guard to wake me in three hours."

Eskkar had explored the house earlier. It possessed five rooms. The common room ran the length of the house, and took up half the structure. One end contained a fireplace and a work table for preparing meals; the other held the large table where the previous owner had taken his dinner. Four chambers, varying in size, took up the rest of the dwelling, all of them accessed from the main room.

The master's bedroom occupied a corner of the house, with a solid door a few steps from the table. Inside, Eskkar found a large, comfortable-looking bed. A thick wooden bar leaned against the wall, and he used it to secure the door, knowing he'd sleep sounder with the door fastened. He heard Grond giving instructions to one of the soldiers to stand guard, more to keep anyone from bothering their leader than from any need for caution. Stopping only to unbelt his sword, he dropped gratefully on the bed, threw an arm over his eyes to block out the light, and fell asleep in moments.

The knocking on the door shook the wooden panels, and when Eskkar forced his eyes open, he realized the pounding had gone on for some time. Grond's voice called to him through the door, but it took a real effort to clear his head and force himself to sit up. A glance at the window told him several hours had gone by. He shouted at Grond to stop beating on the door, then went and opened it.

Grond had already gone, replaced outside the door by the two women who had served the meal earlier. One carried a tall pitcher of water in both hands, while the other held a large clay bowl. Both had drying cloths across their arms. They moved past him while he stood there, trying to comprehend their presence, and they placed their burdens on the small table near the bed. The older girl turned toward him and bowed.

"Lord Eskkar, I am called Lani. This is my sister, Tippu," she added, nodding to the younger girl, who bowed even lower than her sister. "Grond asked us to attend to you when you woke up." When he didn't answer her, she went on. "Would you like some water, lord?"

Still not fully awake, Eskkar tried to clear his mind. The offer of water made him realize his thirst, so he nodded. The younger girl took an ornately carved cup from the table and poured water into it, then handed it to him. He drained the cup before handing it back to Tippu.

"Lord, would you permit us to help you with your ... bath?" Lani inquired. "Your tunic is filthy and covered with blood, as are your hands. You should wash and put on clean clothing before you appear again before the villagers."

For the first time, he noticed the stink of blood and sweat on his body. "Is there a well nearby?" Eskkar asked, the dryness gone from his mouth. He certainly didn't plan on letting two strange women clean him. His thoughts flashed back to Trella, and the first time she had washed down his naked body, the first time any woman had ever done so. It had been intensely erotic, and now even the remembrance sent a shiver of pleasure through his manhood.

"Yes, lord, there is a well across the square, but right now it is crowded with villagers gossiping about the men from Akkad."

Fully awake now, Eskkar noticed how tall Lani stood, and how attractive, with a full, graceful figure, topped by soft brown hair. She'd rimmed her brown eyes with a trace of ocher, which added an intriguing reddish tint to them. Many of the wives of the well-off merchants in Akkad did the same, to enhance their beauty, though Trella never did. Lani's deep voice sounded pleasant to his ears, and she wore a dress of fine quality, no doubt plundered from somewhere by her former master. Now that he had time to study her, he guessed her age to be about twenty-five seasons.

She noticed his stare and lowered her eyes. "Your pardon, lord, but we do not know what you wish. Please, instruct us."

Either her words or her tone aroused him further, so he walked to the bed and sat. He looked down at himself and saw that, indeed, his tunic remained spotted with blood and dirt, and that his brief moments at the well earlier in the morning had not removed all the blood from his hands. Glancing at the now-soiled bedding, he decided this Lani spoke the truth. He considered going down to the river, but that would be a long walk from Ninazu's house, and no doubt he'd be pestered every step of the way by villagers. Eskkar would have to use the cloths and water bowl after all. He could do it himself, but . . .

"Is there a clean tunic I can wear, Lani?"

She pursed her lips for an instant. "You are much taller than Ninazu, but perhaps we can find something in the house." Lani turned to her sister. "See what we have here. If there is nothing that will fit, we will have to send out to the market."

Tippu put down her drying cloths, glanced nervously at Eskkar, and left the room.

Eskkar stood up, and pulled his tunic up over his head, then tossed the dirty garment on the floor. "Your sister does not talk much."

"She has been through a great deal, and is afraid, Lord Eskkar," Lani said calmly, as she poured water from the pitcher into the bowl. "As am I. We are both frightened of what is to become of us."

Eskkar watched her movements as she soaked one of the washcloths in the water, then wrung it out. Her hands were quick and sure. "You have nothing to be afraid of, Lani. No one will harm you now."

She turned to face him, looking into his eyes. "You should remove your undergarment, Lord Eskkar. I fear that needs changing as well." She wrinkled her nose as she spoke, but didn't say anything else.

For a moment, Eskkar hesitated. Damn the woman, treating him like a child. He stood, then loosened the garment and pushed it to the floor.

She moved it aside with her foot, then took the washcloth and began cleaning him. She started with his face, scrubbing hard to get all the surface dirt and rubbing his beard to clean it as well. Then she began on his neck and shoulders, rinsing the cloth again, turning him around to do his back.

Standing naked in front of this woman, he felt himself begin to stiffen. She ignored his growing erection as she rinsed out the cloth again and again, moving lower until she knelt before him, her face inches away from his now-firm manhood. But she gave it no attention, except to wipe it gently with the cloth, before scrubbing his legs vigorously.

"Please sit down, Lord Eskkar, so I can clean your feet,"

Lani said, rising to rinse out the cloth yet again. She knelt and started cleaning his feet. Tippu returned, carrying a tunic. If she thought it strange to see her sister on her knees before a naked man with an erect penis, she said nothing, didn't even meet Esskkar's eyes.

Lani turned to her. "Lord Esskkar will need a fresh undergarment. Bring one." Tippu again left without a word.

Apparently there was no shortage of undergarments in the house, Esskkar decided.

When Lani finished his feet, she asked him to stand again, and dried his body with a clean cloth, rubbing gently on his face, then briskly on his chest and shoulders, then gently again around his still-firm manhood. Again, she asked him to sit, then she wiped his feet dry.

"There, my lord, at least you're clean enough to meet your subjects." Suddenly she reached out and brushed his penis with her fingers. "If my lord would like a woman, I or my sister would be glad to pleasure you." This time she met his eyes, waiting for his answer.

Esskkar noticed a slight change in her voice, something that made the offer more than just a duty. To his surprise, he wanted her, and not only for the physical need. Something about her aroused him. "You've seen me naked, Lani. Now let me see you. Take off your dress."

She wiped her hands quickly on the drying cloth, lifted her dress up over her head, and tossed the garment over the foot of the bed. She shook out her hair to straighten it, then just stood there.

For the first time he saw her as a beautiful woman. His manhood surged as he stared at her lush body, all softness and curves.

Once again the door opened, and Tippu slipped back into the room, closing the door behind her. She barely raised her eyes to take note of the two of them.

"Bring the garment here, Tippu," Eskkar said, without taking his eyes off Lani. "Put your dress back on, Lani."

He took the undergarment from Tippu and pulled himself into it, grunting a little as he forced his still-erect penis into the clothing before lacing it tight around his waist. Tippu handed him the clean tunic, and he pulled it over his head. He noticed its quality, a fine garment more suited to a rich merchant than a soldier. Nonetheless, it fit well enough, though a little tighter than he liked, and reaching only to midthigh. By then Lani had put her dress back on, and again she knelt at his feet, this time to fasten his sandals. He helped her with the lacings, and she lifted her eyes to him as their hands touched.

A loud knock on the door startled both of them. Grond entered without waiting for permission. "Are you well rested, Captain? You slept half the afternoon."

Eskkar did feel better, much of the tiredness gone from his body and mind. A quick glance at the window showed about two hours of daylight left, still plenty of time to meet with Sisuthros.

"Yes, Grond. I think I needed the rest."

"Lord, may I speak with you for a moment?" Lani asked, her eyes downcast and her tone respectful.

He thought for a moment. No doubt Grond had told her Eskkar would speak with her. But she hadn't reminded him of it, merely asked for permission. Eskkar glanced at his bodyguard, but saw the man staring at Tippu.

"Grond, wait outside. Take Tippu with you."

While Tippu gathered up the pitcher, cloths, and the washing bowl, Eskkar fastened his sword around his waist, then sat on the bed. "Go ahead, Lani. What is it you wish to say?"

She stood in the same spot she had stood unclothed a few moments ago, but her voice remained calm. "My lord, my sister and I were captured by Ninazu and his men four months ago. My husband was killed, as was Tippu's betrothed, along with our servants. Ninazu took both of us for his pleasures. He favored Tippu, and would have turned me over to his men except for Tippu's pleadings. I made myself useful by cleaning up after him, and keeping track of his women and his affairs. After a while, he came to depend on me, and once we came here, I managed his household." She paused for a moment, as if remembering. "I think I would be dead if Tippu hadn't saved me."

She took a deep breath, as if to put the past behind her. "Here in Bisitun, we are called Ninazu's whores. The village women he took hated us as much as they hated him. This morning, one of them said we would be dead by nightfall. Ninazu's other women have returned to their families, but we have nowhere to go. Our village is many miles away, to the northwest, across the Euphrates. Even if we could return, there is no one there who would take us in, dishonored as we are, and with nothing but the clothing on our backs."

"So what do you want from me, Lani? No one will harm you here. My men will protect you from the village women."

"That is what I want, lord, your protection, that, and . . . This morning . . . I . . . I heard this morning that you will soon return to Akkad. I would ask that you take us with you. This place is hateful to us."

She saw the frown that crossed his face at her suggestion, and went on quickly. "We can be your servants, lord, as well as your concubines. I have skill at running a household, and Tippu can weave and sew. We will do anything you ask, any work. Just take us away from this place. Please, lord."

Her eyes lifted to his, and he could see her lip trembling. He saw that she held back the tears, the first time she'd shown any emotion. She might be right about the village wives. They would abuse and torment Ninazu's women, at the very least, especially one who acted in Ninazu's name. The sisters would be safer in Akkad, and Trella could find good use for someone like Lani, whose wits seemed sharp enough. Thinking of Trella made him feel uncomfortable for a moment. He hadn't thought about her much in the last few days.

Lani waited patiently, but he saw the fear in her face. She thought he was going to refuse.

"Lani, you can return with me to Akkad. And I will place you under my protection there as well. No one will harm either of you. But I warn you that I may not return to Akkad for some time, and I may have to send you on ahead. My wife, Trella, will find a place for you."

Speaking Trella's name aloud helped clear his own head, though it didn't quite drive away thoughts of Lani's body. "And you need not be a concubine for me or anyone else, Lani, neither you nor your sister."

With a small cry of relief, she went down on one knee and took his hand, then kissed it. "Thank you, lord. Thank you." Her body shook slightly, the words catching in her throat.

Eskkar stood up. Women's tears made him uneasy. He touched her head and left the room, stepping into the main chamber of the house. The common area ran the length of the structure, and the five bedrooms along the wall all faced the center of the house. The room he'd slept in, by far the largest sleeping chamber, occupied a corner of the home. The dining table stood only a few steps away. Sisuthros sat there, along with Grond, Hamati, and Drakis.

"Did you get some rest, Captain?" Sisuthros asked.

Eskkar opened his mouth to make some careless rejoinder, before he realized Sisuthros appeared really concerned about him. Eskkar saw the same look on Grond's face, and even on the other commanders'. They knew he had slept little in the last three days, and they worried about him.

He softened his voice. "Yes, Sisuthros, I slept very well. Now I'm hungry again."

Food covered the table, and the smell of horse steaks cooking wafted in from outside and made his mouth water. His stomach rumbled with hunger, even though he'd eaten only a few hours ago. He sat down at an empty place, but before he could reach for anything, Tippu arrived at his side and placed a clean earthen plate and wooden cup before him. She filled it halfway with water before leaving. Grond took another pitcher, one that held wine, and poured some into Eskkar's cup.

As he put the cup down, Lani came in from outside, carrying two steaks that still sizzled on a wooden trencher. She slid them both onto his plate, then turned to him.

"Is there anything else you need, lord?"

She stood at his side, and when he turned his head, he found her bosom only a handbreadth away. The picture of her naked body crossed his mind, and he felt the urge to take her back into the bedroom. Somehow she managed to project sexuality into a few words, words directed only at him.

"Nothing now, Lani. Thank you." He spoke the words carefully, in a neutral voice. When she stepped away, he remembered his promise and turned to Sisuthros. "I've given my protection to Lani and her sister," he told those at the table. "Make sure all the men know it, and you'd better tell these villagers, too."

"I'll tell the council today, and make sure they spread the word throughout Bisitun," Sisuthros said.

Eskkar took a sip of his watered wine. "Now, tell me what has happened while I slept."

In a moment, all thoughts of Lani vanished. Sisuthros had met again with the newly appointed village elders. By tomorrow morning the most influential farmers would arrive, and they could select the fifth and last of the council members. The elders could then start governing the village's affairs.

They would begin with the execution of Ninazu and the disposition of his men. With Ninazu's head on a lance above the gate and the worst of his followers dead, Eskkar's men would be freed up for other duties, instead of wasting time guarding prisoners night and day. As for the rest of Ninazu's men, they'd be branded and put to work.

Then the newly formed council would address the matter of the stolen property, what Ninazu had taken, and how what remained would be allocated back to its original owners. Akkad would take two-tenths of each allocation, as a restoration fee. Sisuthros guessed that it would take another day to divide the loot, including what he'd taken from the prisoners and added to Ninazu's storeroom.

With Ninazu and his stolen gold out of the way, the soldiers, villagers, and slaves would be put to work rebuilding Bisitun and the surrounding farms, clearing the land outside the palisade, repairing the damaged irrigation ditches, and any other tasks necessary to get the community back on a road to prosperity. Once that effort had commenced, the council could begin to take up all the smaller issues that would fill its days in the coming weeks, settling disputes and hearing appeals for justice.

Eskkar listened to Sisuthros's orders for the men, before speaking to Hamati and Drakis about their roles. By the time the meal ended, he announced himself satisfied with Sisuthros's plans and dispositions.

"As soon as Ninazu and his men are dead, I'll take Grond and some men and begin riding out into the farmlands. I want to see for myself how the farmers and their crops are faring, and how well the herds of sheep and goats are doing."

If any at the table thought it unusual to have the leader of Akkad visiting farmers, they kept the thought to themselves. But Eskkar knew that Trella and the nobles back in Akkad needed that vital information. They couldn't complete their own plans until they knew what could be expected from the north country, and when. Without the steady supply of flax, grain, and livestock, trade at Akkad would slow, and that must not happen, not with so much rebuilding underway. The real goal of Eskkar's efforts remained back in Akkad, not here.

Eskkar stood and stretched. He felt relaxed now, his stomach full and with enough sleep to get him through the evening. "Has Ninazu said anything useful?"

Sisuthros shook his head. "We haven't even had time to put him to the torture." Sisuthros sighed as he contemplated yet another task. "I'll talk to him."

"No, Grond and I will deal with him. You keep your thoughts on the villagers."

Grond led the way to the other end of the common room, to the bedroom farthest away from where Eskkar had slept. This windowless room had only a tiny aperture near the ceiling for light and ventilation. It possessed the only other solid door inside the dwelling, the still-fresh wood indicating a recent improvement. A soldier guarded there, sitting on a stool, but he rose up as the two men approached.

Grond pushed the door open. Inside, another guard, this one from the Hawk Clan, sat on a chest, his short sword unsheathed across his lap, facing Ninazu. The prisoner had a large bruise on his forehead, where Eskkar's sword hilt had struck, and the side of his swollen face showed cuts and bruises from Grond's fist. They'd trussed Ninazu up like a chicken, his hands tied behind his back and his arms tied to his sides. The silver bracelets he'd worn were gone, given to Grond and Sisuthros as gifts. Another rope looped around his neck, the other end knotted around a second wooden chest.

Ninazu's legs remained free, but his captors had smashed his right shinbone. The swelling on the leg had bruised to a deep blue, with blood crusted along its length. Whoever had done the work knew his job. No one bothered to set the bone straight. Ninazu would be dead long before he could walk or die from infection. For a moment, Eskkar almost felt sorry for the man, a daring bandit who had gambled for a rich village and lost.

Ninazu turned toward the door, his eyes alert, as Eskkar entered. The expensive tunic told him all he needed to know about his visitor.

"Greetings, Ninazu," Eskkar began. When the man didn't answer, Eskkar reached out with his sandal and touched Ninazu's right leg. That sent a jolt of pain through the prisoner, and he couldn't control a sharp intake of breath. Eskkar turned to the guard. "Has he been given anything?"

"Some water this afternoon, Captain. Nothing else."

Eskkar nodded in satisfaction. Give him just enough water to keep him conscious, so he could feel his pain and worry about the future.

"We'll give you more water later, maybe even some wine, if you tell us what we want to know," Eskkar went on. The man said nothing, just looked up at Eskkar with hatred in his eyes. "Your brother looked at me that way before he died, Ninazu. He took the torture for a long time, before we gave him over to the women of Dilgarth, who took hours killing him. He told me all about you and your men."

Ninazu flashed a look of hatred at his captor, but said nothing.

Eskkar leaned against the wall and looked about the room. Two chests were crammed with dozens of golden statues, bowls, and other valuable items, most of the wealth of the village. Four good-sized sacks contained gold, silver, and copper coins, as well as jewelry, gemstones, and even some fine leather goods. Ninazu remained surrounded by his loot, at least until tomorrow.

"In the morning the village elders and I will sentence you to death, Ninazu. It's up to you how much you suffer between now and then. There isn't much we need to hear from you. If you tell us what we want to know, you will be given as much wine as you can handle, and you'll feel less pain."

Eskkar paused a moment. He didn't hate the man, nor even condemn what Ninazu had attempted to do. Many others would have done the same, including Eskkar in his younger days. Now those days seemed from the distant past, the days before Trella had explained the ways of power and the mysteries of farm and village. "Or, we can just give you plenty of water, to make sure you enjoy every sensation. The choice is yours, Ninazu. Your brother chose the wine, but too late, and he suffered much."

"Who are you?" Ninazu had a deep voice, one filled with anger and hatred. "Why did you come to Bisitun?"

It would be a waste of time to explain Akkad's plans to Ninazu. "I came to claim the land for Akkad, and I have done so." Eskkar turned to the guard. "Give him as much water as he wants." He glanced about the room, filled with the bandit's booty. Such things meant little to Eskkar, now that he'd learned the ways of power. Gold had its uses, but it didn't put strength into a man's sword arm, or even crops in the earth. He nodded to the guard, and stepped back into the common room, closing the door behind him. Eskkar and Grond passed out of the house, into the village square.

The afternoon sun had dipped below the horizon, and soon another night would begin.

"Grond, there must be more loot somewhere, and Ninazu's subcommanders might have hidden their own valuables. Make sure he tells us what we want to know. Start on him in the morning, right after the morning meal. Remember he has to last into the afternoon, so not too much wine."

"This one will talk, Captain. He's finished, and he knows it. Shulat could at least hope for his brother's revenge, but Ninazu has nothing to live for. By tomorrow the fever will weaken his will."

"The sooner he's out of the way, the sooner the villagers can get on with their lives."

Eskkar spent the rest of the evening with Sisuthros. Eskkar encountered three of the new elders, but they only wanted to talk about how much they had suffered under Ninazu, and Eskkar could only stand so many hours of that kind of talk. Leaving them with Sisuthros, Eskkar and Grond, accompanied by two soldiers, toured the village, checking on the guards, the horses, and the men.

That task finished, they found a small tavern, well lit and filled with the sounds of singing and laughter. Packed to overflowing, happy villagers celebrated their deliverance from Ninazu. Eskkar and his men entered, received a drunken cheer that went on as the happy patrons made room for them. Eskkar spent an hour there, squeezed behind a table, buying drinks for everyone and talking with the common people. But he drank only one cup of ale. Grond had two, and, after the second one, mentioned that he thought Tippu the most beautiful woman he'd ever seen.

By the time they returned to the marketplace, most of Bisitun had prepared itself for bed. Even from Ninazu's house, only a single oil lamp burned. Few people had the wealth or reason to burn oil or candles long into the night, not when the moon and stars shone brightly overhead. The big well in the market square's center stood deserted for the first time all day, and Eskkar stopped to drink some fresh water and wash his face and hands.

At the house, two soldiers stood guard, and inside, he found Hamati asleep sitting at the big table, his sword beneath his hand. Eskkar stopped to check on Ninazu, and found the prisoner had fallen into a restless sleep. Nevertheless, his guards remained alert, watching their charge through the open door.

Sisuthros had taken one of the bedrooms for himself, and gone to bed an hour earlier, his snores audible in the common room.

Eskkar bid good night to Grond and entered his room. He didn't bother with the lamp, just left the door open. The soft glow from the main room gave him enough light to see the bed, covered with fresh linen. He unbelted his sword and pulled the weapon from its sheath and laid it on the low table that stood beside the bed, then sat to unlace his sandals. He went back to the door, pausing for a moment to make sure he knew where everything in the room was placed. Eskkar closed the door and dropped the wooden bar to seal it. Pulling his tunic over his head, he tossed that on the foot of the bed, and sank tiredly onto the bed.

He thought he would be asleep in moments, but instead he lay there, staring up at the faint moonlight that shone in through the tiny window set high in the wall. A long day had finally ended, but everything had worked out well enough. Bisitun would enjoy its first night of freedom. Now he just needed ... He sat up in the bed, his hand reaching for his sword.

Something moved at the window, and his hand tightened on the hilt of the sword as the movement repeated itself, a darker blackness against the night sky. The shadow moved, and he heard the thump of something landing on the floor next to the bed. Still, Eskkar had caught a glimpse of it as it jumped down.

The cat had green-gold eyes that gleamed in the faint light, and Eskkar saw them watching him. For a moment he considered taking a swing at the creature, thinking it might be some demon sent by Ninazu. Then he reconsidered. The animal seemed to think it belonged, as it sat down in the middle of the floor, a dark shadow without color, except for its eyes, which stayed focused on the bed. As Eskkar's eyes grew more accustomed to the darkness, he saw that the cat looked alert, but not frightened.

Eskkar muttered to himself and put the sword back on the table. The creature had climbed into the room. It could get itself out again. "Stay if you will. Just let me sleep." Nothing much bigger than a cat could get inside, he felt certain of that. He fell back on the pillow, let his breathing relax, closed his eyes, and soon began to drift off into sleep.

The soft knock at the door had him moving in an instant, on his feet and up from the bed, his hand again finding the sword without any fumbling. He stood by the door. "Who is it?"

"It is Lani, lord. I've brought you some wine."

She kept her voice low, and he could barely hear her

through the door. He didn't want any wine. He wanted to tell her to go away, but instead he opened the door. Lani and her sister both stood there, Lani's face flickering behind a small candle that she carried on a tray. Behind them, Eskkar saw Grond watching from the table.

"May we come in, lord?" Lani asked.

He hesitated, not sure that he wanted to see her, but he opened the door wider and stepped back. The tray that Lani carried held a pitcher of wine and a cup, while Tippu carried a bowl filled with water and some cloths. Lani stepped into the room, almost as if she worried he might close the door once again. Tippu followed, though more slowly. He watched them pass by him. The cat had vanished, no doubt leaving the way it entered, and just as silently.

"We thought you might want some wine before bed, or that you might wish to wash your hands and face." She put her things down on the table, then went to the door and closed it, though Eskkar's hand was still on it.

Before she shut the door, Eskkar caught another glimpse of Grond standing there, a frown on his face. Eskkar turned to Lani, and for the first time he noticed that she'd changed her dress from the one she'd worn earlier. A much finer garment, and one woven from something softer than the usual linen, and not one that you pulled on over your head. Instead, it looked as if it would open from the front, the two edges crossing over her breasts and tied together at her waist.

Eskkar had drunk more spirits tonight than he usually allowed himself; he didn't plan to drink anything more. In the old days he'd guzzled as much as he could afford, which had only allowed him to get properly drunk two or three times a month. Trella had changed all that, and he'd sworn never to lose control of himself again.

"No, Lani, I don't need any wine." He smiled at her. "And I washed up at the well before I returned. You and your sister can go."

She peered at him in the flickering light, almost as if checking to see if he had really washed. Lani went on as if she hadn't heard him. "Perhaps you would like one of us to stay with you . . . to pleasure you tonight? If you prefer Tippu, she is more pleasing to look at, or . . . or we could both remain, if that is your wish."

He looked at Lani, then Tippu. In the light from the tiny flame, Lani's eyes met his own, while Tippu stared at the floor. The thought of both of them in his bed sent a wave of desire through him. Eskkar had always taken a woman after every fight. Even during the fighting for Akkad, he'd taken Trella after every encounter. He remembered Lani's naked body, and the temptation surged through him. Battle did that to a man, made him want a woman just to prove he'd survived while others had died. Another thought struck him.

"Tippu," he began, and thought he saw Lani's lips compress for a brief instant, "Tippu, my bodyguard is outside. He is more than my bodyguard, he is my friend as well. And he has looked at you with longing, and told me of this. Perhaps you could spend tonight with him."

Tippu looked at her sister without showing any emotion, and waited until Lani nodded approval. "Yes, lord, I will go to your friend," Tippu said. She began putting down the bowl and cloths she still held.

"And I, lord? What should I do?" Lani asked.

He wanted her to stay, but his days of taking women against their will had passed. If she thought she had to please him to get what she wanted, he would send her away. But he didn't want to do that, not yet.

"If you like, Lani, you can stay with me tonight. But only if you want to. You already have my protection, and I don't need you in my bed to remind me of my promise."

"I will stay, lord." Lani called after her sister. "Wait, Tippu. Go to our room. I will send Grond to you there. Treat him well, Tippu." She guided her sister to the door, opened it for her, and followed her out.

Eskkar watched in surprise as Lani crossed the room and spoke to Grond, who still sat at the table. Lani spoke to him for some time, before gesturing toward the room that her sister had just entered. Grond answered Lani, then listened for another moment before nodding his head. Lani came back to the bedroom, and this time she dropped the bar across the door. She moved within arm's length, and began untying her dress.

He reached out and took her hands, then pulled her closer to him. "You don't have to do this, Lani. I don't take women against their will, or because they are afraid."

"I know, Lord Eskkar. I spoke with many of your soldiers today. They told me much about you, about Akkad, and about your wife."

She pulled her hands free from his grasp and continued untying her dress. When the knot came undone, she opened the dress wide and pushed it back over her shoulders, letting it hang from her arms as if to frame her body. "They told me so much about you that I feel safe in your care. But I also saw in your eyes today that you wanted me."

Eskkar started to say something, but she put her finger up to his lips, the movement swirling the dress around her. "There is nothing to say, Lord Eskkar. I want to be in your arms and in your bed." Lani took her hand away, and this time the dress fell to the floor. She stood on her toes and put her arms around his neck, burying her face in his shoulder.

He inhaled her hair and noticed she smelled faintly of cinnamon, a delicate perfume that mixed with the warm, musky smell of a woman. She made a small sound as she felt the pressure of his erection, and moved her hips against him.

"I do want you, Lani," he whispered into her ear. "And you are wrong. You are much more beautiful than your sister."

She lifted her head up and he kissed her, a long, lingering kiss that aroused him even further. When the kiss ended, she leaned down to blow out the candle. As the darkness enveloped them, she began unfastening his undergarment. Soon that dropped to the floor, and they lay down on the bed, their arms wrapped around each other.

In the dark, her body felt soft and full, her full breasts brushing against his chest whenever he took his hands from them. She kissed him with abandon, almost possessively, until he grew more and more aroused. At last she moved on top of him and guided him inside her moist body.

Lani gave a long sigh of pleasure when he slid deep within her and for a few moments, she stayed still. He pushed up against her and she began to move, slowly at first, then faster, stopping often to let him kiss her breasts or leaning down to find his mouth with her own, while she squeezed her muscles around his penis.

Fully aroused now, Eskkar's hands tightened around her waist, and she moved against him, forcing him deep inside her, pushing herself against him until he thrust up hard against her and cried out as he emptied his seed, both hands grasping her breasts, her hands on his chest. She stayed atop him, holding him tightly inside her, until he began to soften. Then she lay next to him, in his arms, letting him touch and caress her.

"Lani," he began, but she kissed him again to stop his words.

"Tomorrow we can talk, Lord Eskkar. Tomorrow. Now you need your sleep. Let me stay with you."

She shifted her position on the bed, wrapping her arm behind his head, letting his face fall on her breast. At first he kissed her, one hand caressing her stomach, but soon he stopped, as the long day's effort washed over him. Just before he drifted off, or in his dreams, he couldn't be sure which, he heard her voice again. "I will stay with you, lord."

9

Eskkar woke in darkness. Like most people, he tended to rise with the dawn, but this morning something had awakened him, though he heard no one moving about the house. He wondered if the strangeness of his surroundings or the unfamiliar woman beside him had cut short his sleep. Lani stirred, murmuring something into the blanket that he couldn't make out.

She lay on her side, her back toward him. He slid his arm free from under her neck. His arm felt numb, and he worked his fingers until the tingling disappeared. Lani didn't wake, just kept whispering unintelligible words in some strange language.

Eskkar glanced up at the dark outline of the tiny window. The blackness it framed seemed a shade lighter, and he knew the sun would soon be up, the household rising with it. He turned onto his side, so that his face rested against Lani's hair, and caught the last trace of her perfume, or perhaps just her scent. Her closeness soothed him, and he had no desire to arise.

Wide awake now, and refreshed by a long night of sleep,

he knew he should be thinking about the coming day, the dozens of tasks that needed his supervision. Instead he found himself worrying about Trella—what she would say about this woman, what he would tell her, how she would look at him. He knew she would not be pleased, not so much because he took a woman while away from her. That would be expected from a soldier on campaign.

No, Trella would be concerned because she would see in Lani more than a mere bed companion. In fact, Lani seemed in many ways like Trella. The similarities between the two made him uncomfortable. Perhaps he should have taken Tippu to his bed, merely to quench his lust. Tippu, who could be forgotten in the morning, a pretty face frightened for her life and eager to please. Trella would not be concerned with a woman like Tippu, any more than she worried about the other women in Akkad who offered themselves at every opportunity to her husband.

Since that first night when he'd bedded Trella, he had ignored those offers, no matter how beautiful or willing the woman. Trella had made him aware of how satisfying a strong-minded woman could be, someone who could share and understand his feelings. Lani possessed much of that awareness, yet was somehow different. Eskkar should have sent her away last night, even packed her off to Akkad, or simply given her to one of his men. But he'd sensed a quality in her, something that quickened both his desire and curiosity. He'd wanted her, wanted to keep her close to him. Now he couldn't send her away, not after she had pleasured him so completely.

Even this morning his desire remained strong. Maybe the need would lessen in a few days, when the excitement of a new woman had worn off. Eskkar hadn't slept with anyone except Trella for many months, and even longer since he'd lusted after another woman. Trella always equaled his passion as she loved him, and he had not wanted any other woman, not even for an afternoon's dallying.

Until last night. Now another woman troubled his thoughts, and what should have been a simple pleasure had turned into a problem. He looked toward the window, as the first gray light of dawn arrived, providing enough illumination to see inside the bedroom.

Lani twitched in the bed, and he knew her dreams troubled her. She spoke again, but he still couldn't comprehend the words, soft and indistinct, like a sleepy child in its mother's arms. Her head tossed about, then her arm, and she called out a word . . . a name, he realized.

"Namtar . . . Namtar." She gave a small cry and sat up, her eyes wide but empty. Her hand covered her mouth, as if to prevent herself from speaking further. Lani remained motionless, until he reached out and touched her arm.

"Oh!" She whirled in the bed, pushing herself away from him. She seemed confused to find him beside her. "Please don't hurt me! Please!"

"Why would I hurt you, Lani?" She still wasn't fully awake. "You're safe here. Nothing can harm you now."

She took a deep breath and tried to speak, but all he heard was a choking sound. "You're safe, Lani," he repeated, and this time his words seemed to calm her. "Who is Namtar?"

She jumped, as if he'd summoned a demon by speaking its name. Lani's body shook, and she started sobbing. Eskkar had seen enough women cry before, but nothing to equal what he now heard and felt. Lani fell back on the bed, hugging her knees to her chest, her whole body trembling.

Until last year he'd never wasted a moment over a crying woman, walking away from whatever sorrows plagued them. He considered leaving Lani to her misery. Instead he remembered the times Trella had cried into his chest, those nights she'd felt helpless before the barbarians. Eskkar had sworn an oath that Trella would cry no more if he could help it.

So he stroked Lani's head and held her lightly. Dawn had risen, and he heard people moving about the house. No one would disturb him, he knew, but they would hear Lani crying and wonder.

Her tears subsided, and her body sagged against him as whatever demons tortured her spirit faded with the morning's light. She attempted to sit up, but he held her close, trying to give comfort.

"I'm sorry, lord," she began, her voice so hoarse that at first he didn't understand her. "Please forgive me, lord. I did not mean to ruin your night's sleep." Again she tried to sit up, and this time he let go, but kept hold of her hands. In the growing light, he saw her face red with tears, her eyes swollen and filled with blood.

"Who is Namtar?" he repeated. She shuddered, and he thought the tears would start again.

"Namtar was my husband, lord. Ninazu killed him in front of me." Her eyes closed, as she no doubt relived the moment. "After Ninazu captured us, he said he would put Namtar to the torture, if I did not pleasure him willingly . . . give him much pleasure."

She turned her face away from Eskkar, her eyes staring

at the wall. "So I pleasured Ninazu, while his men laughed, and my husband watched, bound hand and foot to a cart." Her lips trembled as she fought back the tears. "I had to please him . . . had to . . . do many things. We had already seen men and women put to the torture. Namtar never said a word. He just closed his eyes. After Ninazu finished with me, he stood naked over my husband, letting him smell my scent on his body, then Ninazu laughed and stabbed him in the heart with his sword."

Eskkar let his hands drop from her arms. "There was nothing you could do, Lani. We've all seen men put to the torture. You saved your husband from that."

She shook her head, letting her hair fall in front of her face, as if to hide her shame. "I did not kill myself, lord. I should have killed myself, thrown myself on the same sword that took Namtar." Her voice hardened. "Or I should have killed Ninazu in his sleep. But he told me he wanted Tippu to be as willing. Ninazu said he would put us both to the torture, if we did not please him. I did not want my sister to die. Though she has not been the same in her head since that day. But she obeyed my wishes, and we lived. We stayed alive and hoped to escape someday, or for someone to kill Ninazu. The goddess Ishtar answered my prayers. She sent you and your soldiers to free us from him."

Her voice cracked with her words, and Eskkar heard the dryness in her throat. He got out of bed and looked down at the table, at the empty water cup. Lani followed his gaze.

"I'll fetch water, lord," she said, swinging her feet off the bed.

"Stay where you are," he ordered, then strode to the door, unbarred it, and stepped out into the great room.

Most of the men had risen earlier, and Sisuthros already sat at the table with Hamati, no doubt talking about the coming day's events. No one seemed surprised at the sudden appearance of their captain, naked.

"Have someone bring water to my room," Eskkar said, then turned back into the bedroom. He stood by the door, waiting, and in moments Tippu stood there, a large goblet of water in her hands.

"Bring it in, Tippu. Give it to your sister." He watched the younger girl, to see if he could detect any signs of her madness. She seemed calm, even more so than last night.

Lani took the cup and drank. He watched as she half-emptied the cup, gazing at her naked body, and he felt another stir of passion.

When Lani lowered the cup, she looked at him guiltily. "My pardon, lord. I should not drink your water."

He returned to the bed and sat down, pulling the blanket over his lap, then accepted the cup from her hands and took a few sips. A mouthful remained, so he gave it back to her. "Finish it, Lani."

She drained it and handed the empty cup back to her sister. Tippu started for the door.

"Tippu, stay a moment," Eskkar said, studying her with care for the first time. Shorter than her sister, Tippu possessed swirling reddish-brown hair that floated around her tiny face, with features as delicate as a child's. Her dress, the same one she'd worn yesterday, showed the full body of a woman. A beautiful woman, he decided, but one without her sister's sharp wits.

He knew that, given a choice, every one of his soldiers would have chosen Tippu over Lani, just as he knew that

Lani's strength of will made her more desirable, at least for him. Days and nights with Trella had spoiled him. Weak, empty-headed women, painted and perfumed, or trained only to keep house and hearth, no longer interested him. Eskkar put the annoying thought aside.

"Last night, Tippu, I sent you to Grond's bed. I did not realize what you and your sister had been through, though I should have guessed. You need not return to him tonight. I'll speak to him."

For the first time Tippu lifted her eyes to his. "Lord, there is no need to say anything. Grond did no more than hold me through the night. I am no longer afraid of being with him. He's offered me his protection."

Eskkar turned to Lani, who appeared just as surprised as her sister. That didn't sound like Grond at all, a simple soldier who enjoyed taking a woman as much as any man. Someone as beautiful as Tippu ... maybe the girl had bewitched him.

"Tippu, bring food for us both. We'll eat in here." He touched Lani's hand. "We have much to talk about, Lani. I want to hear more about Ninazu, and about you and your sister."

Eskkar sat on the bed and ate, while Lani told him everything about Ninazu. In managing Ninazu's household, she directed his servants and concubines, and served at his table. Lani knew everything. She had overheard or been present during most of Ninazu's meetings with his men. She even knew the secret place where Ninazu had buried his personal store of gold. Ninazu, like most men, had spoken too freely in his conversations around his women, a bad trait Eskkar had once possessed, until Trella showed him just how dangerous such a habit could be.

After the meal he took Hamati and a few men to retrieve the buried gold. They crossed the square and entered a well-constructed house with two rooms, big enough for a good-sized family. No doubt one of Ninazu's trusted subcommanders, or perhaps even his brother Shulat, had occupied it. It took only moments to find the hiding place, still untouched, and exactly where Lani had said it would be. A few moments of digging uncovered a good-sized sack containing gold, silver, and gemstones buried in the floor.

Eskkar hadn't expected to find such a large cache. Apparently Ninazu had been very successful in his raids even before he came to Bisitun. Added to what they had found in Ninazu's main house, there would be more than enough coins to keep Trella's wall-building going for several months, even after allocating a good portion to Sisuthros and Bisitun's elders for use in the village.

Even under torture, Ninazu might not have revealed this hiding place. So Eskkar decided he owed another debt to Lani.

Most of the morning had passed before Eskkar and Grond left the house for the second time. They took a slow tour of the village, checking on the soldiers, prisoners, and inhabitants. Reassured that his men had Bisitun under control, he decided to return to the house and visit the prisoner.

Ninazu had scarcely moved, except to soil himself. He looked weaker, and fever burned on his face. Infection had started in the broken leg. Eskkar ignored the hatred in the man's eyes.

"Are you ready to talk, Ninazu?" Eskkar began without

preamble. "I'll not ask you again, and I warn you that I already know much of what I want to know. So don't try to lie to me."

"I'll tell you nothing, barbarian." Ninazu tried to spit at Eskkar, but his parched lips produced only air. He turned his face away.

The man's words satisfied Eskkar. He'd made the offer yesterday and still felt bound by it. But the situation had changed. With the bandit's gold in hand, Ninazu now meant little to Eskkar.

"Then you'll suffer for nothing, Ninazu. Lani told us everything," Eskkar said. "We've already found the rest of your loot buried across the square."

Ignoring the man's curses, Eskkar turned to the guard. "Only water, as much as he wants."

There would be no wine to ease Ninazu's pain. With him dead and his marauders broken or enslaved, any freebooters still in the countryside would soon take heed and leave the area. If not, Eskkar would drive them away in the next few weeks, as his patrols began combing the countryside.

"When he's finished drinking," Eskkar said to the Hawk Clan soldier guarding the prisoner, "take him outside. Have the men keep a close watch on him. I don't want him killing himself to avoid the villagers' revenge. And don't let any villager, man or woman, near him. Remember what happened in Dilgarth."

Eskkar turned away and moved to the next bedroom, the chamber used by Lani and Tippu as their sleeping quarters. He found Tippu curled up on the bed and Lani sitting on a stool, waiting. She had changed back into the simple dress she'd worn yesterday. Her eyes still looked red and puffy.

"It's time for Ninazu to face the village, Lani. They'll list their charges against him."

"I will stay in my room, lord. I do not want to see his face again."

Eskkar thought about that, then shook his head. "Lani, I want you to accuse Ninazu for the deeds he committed against you, your husband, and Tippu's family. I have given you my protection, but everyone in the village and all my soldiers must know what Ninazu did to you and your kin. Otherwise some might think that you came with Ninazu willingly. Even my men might not understand."

She cast her eyes downward, and said nothing.

"It will be hard, Lani, but you need to do it. Both of you. Otherwise the spirits of your family will not rest in peace. It may even help Tippu with her memories."

"I . . . we will do it, lord," Lani said, still looking down. "When will we be needed?"

"Not for some time. Farmers are still arriving from the countryside, and there is much to discuss. Tell your sister what to say. I'll fetch you when you are needed." He started to go, then turned back. "After Ninazu is dead, the healing can start. Once you've reached Akkad, you'll both be safe."

She didn't answer. Eskkar left the bedroom, straightened his sword, and brushed the hair back from his eyes. When he stepped outside into the bright sunlight, a shout arose from his men, and the villagers echoed the cheer. "Deliverer . . . deliverer . . . deliverer."

Sisuthros had prepared well for his meeting with the village council. He'd joined four tables end-to-end, and sat in the center of the just-formed council of elders, who faced outward toward the square and the rest of the villagers. At last all of the important farmers arrived. Sisuthros called the council of five to order, and, with a loud voice, began listing the charges against Ninazu and his men.

Every soldier not on watch at the gates or corral gathered as well, and Sisuthros used them to guard the prisoners or keep the villagers back, away from the tables. Grond, carrying the last stool from the house, followed his captain outside. Eskkar took a seat behind and a few paces from the table, his back to the side of the house, determined to take as little part in the proceedings as possible.

The crowd interrupted Sisuthros after every charge, shouting approval, or calling down curses on Ninazu. At the end of the indictment, Sisuthros called for silence, then announced that the rest of Bisitun could add their own complaints to the grievances. After everyone had voiced their accusations, Sisuthros and the council would apportion justice to Ninazu and his men. After dealing with the bandits, the council would supervise the return of the stolen property to the villagers.

Sisuthros gave the order, and two guards dragged Ninazu out into the sunlight. A furious shout arose from the crowd and echoed around the square. They shouted curses at Ninazu, and it took four soldiers with drawn swords to keep the villagers back as two men half-carried the prisoner into the open space before the tables.

Another soldier pushed a low cart into the center of the square. They bound Ninazu to the side of the wagon, finishing up with a gag over his mouth, to make sure he couldn't call down curses against his accusers during the proceedings. Other guards took positions in front of him, facing the crowd, alert and determined to make sure no one seeking private vengeance attacked the helpless Ninazu with a knife or sword.

The process began, though it moved too slowly for Eskkar's liking. Each of the elders wanted to speak, and Sisuthros had to cut two of them short when they rambled on, venting their hatred. When the elders finished, the villagers came forward, pushing and shoving, one by one, to list their charges against Ninazu.

Every man and woman in the square seemed to have a personal grievance against the bandit. The sun had marched nearly to the top of the sky before Sisuthros rose and announced that the council had heard enough, and that Lord Eskkar wished to speak. For the first time the villagers quieted down, not knowing what would come next.

Eskkar stood and walked toward the elders. When he reached the tables, he climbed smoothly atop one and turned to face the people. He hated talking to crowds, but he had prepared his words while the villagers spoke. A breeze pushed his hair against his cheek, and he brushed it back, waiting until everyone stopped talking.

For the first time, the inhabitants of Bisitun got a good look at their new lord. They stared open-mouthed at the tall warrior, one hand resting on the hilt of the great sword, a man clearly born in the northern steppes, and who now ruled their lives. Eskkar's eyes slowly scanned the square, gazing, it seemed, at every single person who faced him. When he spoke, his deep voice carried even to those farthest away.

"People of Bisitun, I, too, have grievances against

Ninazu. I will speak for the people of Dilgarth, who have none here to represent their wishes. At Ninazu's order, his brother raided and killed many in Dilgarth, and their spirits cry out for vengeance as much as any here. A peaceful village, they had no fighting men to guard them. Today Dilgarth is under the protection of Akkad, as all here are now under the protection of Akkad. I tell you what I told the people of Dilgarth. The days of bandits raiding this countryside are over. From today on, they will be hunted down and killed. The few still left will soon learn to leave alone any who live under Akkad's safekeeping. You will be safe in your homes and on your farms. The prosperity that you enjoyed before the coming of the Alur Meriki will return, and this time it will be even greater because of Akkad's protection."

He paused to take a breath. Clearly in awe of him, the crowd remained silent, and he felt glad that he had left all the petty details to Sisuthros. It made it easier to play the role of a distant guardian, handing out decisions from above. "Akkad, Dilgarth, and Bisitun, as well as the other small villages, will all work together, trade together, and defend themselves together."

Eskkar turned to Grond. "Bring Lani and Tippu out." He raised his voice again. "There are two more to accuse Ninazu. I want all to hear what he has done." Lifting his arm, he pointed at Lani and Tippu as they walked into the center of the square. Grond supported Tippu, his arm around her waist, but Lani stood alone, her head high, holding Tippu by the hand. Some in the square called out their displeasure at the sight of the women, a few shouting that they, too, deserved punishment.

"Silence!" Eskkar bellowed the single word, the force of his voice shocking the crowd into stunned silence. He glanced about the square, but none of the villagers dared to meet his eyes, all of them suddenly fearful of his wrath. "Come forward, Lani."

Ignoring the crowd, she kept her eyes on Eskkar until she reached the tables. Finally the two sisters stood directly in front of Ninazu.

In a clear voice, Lani listed the crimes the bandit leader had done to her and her family. She told the whole story, what had been done to her, giving the names of those murdered and tortured. When she finished, Lani took her sister's arm, and held her while Tippu added her own grievances, the murder of her betrothed, her rape, and enslavement. Tippu's tears flowed as she spoke, and only those close by could make out her halting words, spoken in a barely audible voice.

After Tippu finished, Eskkar spoke, raising his voice to make sure everyone heard. "Lani and Tippu are under my protection. Because of them, much of the gold stolen from you was recovered, so all of you should give them thanks. And although they are not from this village, they are to be treated as honorably as anyone here."

Eskkar jumped down from the table, and this time the crowd shouted approval. He returned to his spot near the wall, while Grond escorted the two sisters back into the house. Meanwhile, Sisuthros queried each council member and asked for his decision.

"Death!" Each in turn called for Ninazu to be put to the torture until he died.

Sisuthros nodded his assent. "Death, at the hands of those

whose kin he murdered," he pronounced in a loud voice, so that everyone present could hear the council's just decision, one clearly approved by the gods. "Let the torture begin." The crowd's roar of approval filled the square.

The three villagers selected by the elders to administer the torture came forward, eager to get to their task, and wielding small knives such as used for carving, and the mallets and bronze-tipped chisels used by the tanners to decorate their leather goods; the implements would work equally as well for inflicting pain. The guards moved farther apart as the torturers began their work, so that all could see. The crowd called out their curses on Ninazu, and shouted for the pain-givers to hurry their work.

They removed Ninazu's gag and the torment began. Soon his screams echoed throughout the square. The broken leg made things easier. The slightest touch there instantly overcame any of Ninazu's efforts to hold in his pain. He passed out several times, but they always revived him by flinging a bucket of water in his face. They forced more water down his throat to refresh him, before they started in again, urged on by the crowd.

By then, Eskkar had had enough. Unnoticed, he returned into the house, followed by his bodyguard. He and Grond sat down at the big table.

"You don't feel like watching, Captain?" Grond filled two cups with water.

"I've seen enough of death and torture in the last few months." Eskkar felt glad to be away from Ninazu's ordeal. "Besides, it always makes me wonder how long I'd last under the knife."

"I was put to the torture once," Grond said. "Just

because my master caught me looking at him. Said I wasn't respectful."

Eskkar didn't bother to ask if Grond had screamed. Everyone did. Again Eskkar wondered what he would do if he were the one being tortured, how well he would stand the pain, or how long it would take before he began to plead for mercy or death. Some men resisted to the last, but most begged for the pain to stop long before the end.

The thought sent a shiver through his frame. In all his days of fighting, he'd only been captured once, and that day death had come close. The memory of being helpless before his enemies still troubled him. Eskkar swore to himself that he would never be taken alive. Better to fall on your own sword than go through that horror.

"If the assault on Bisitun had gone badly, Grond, I might have ended up dead on the cart, and Ninazu might be standing over me."

"Well, Captain, I would've avenged your death. Or at least buried your remains."

He looked at Grond and had to smile.

They were alone in the house, except for the two sisters huddled in their room, trying to block out the noise from the crowd. Everyone else was outside enjoying the spectacle. The screams from the square seemed almost as loud inside.

Eskkar finished a handful of grapes from the platter.

"Would you like some wine, lord, or something to eat?" Lani had come out of the bedroom.

"You don't care to watch Ninazu take the torture, Lani?"

"No, lord. I have seen enough of people being tortured.

Now that it's his turn on the wheel, I know what will happen."

Eskkar looked around the room. "Where is your sister?"

"In our room, her head under the blanket. Tippu cannot watch such things. It sickens her even to hear it."

Grond stood up. "Perhaps I should go to her, Lani. Do you think it would help?"

Eskkar wondered about Grond and Tippu, and what had happened last night, or not happened, as it seemed. He would ask his bodyguard about it later, when they were alone.

But Lani mentioned it herself. "I think it would be good for her to be with someone besides myself for a little while, at least until this horrible day is over." She looked at Grond. "Can you restrain yourself as you did last night, for a while longer?"

"When you've been a slave, Lani," Grond answered, "you know what is needed. I'll just hold her for a while." He looked at Eskkar. "If I may, Captain?"

Eskkar nodded, surprised at the serious tone of Grond's voice. The bodyguard left the table and went to the woman's room. Eskkar looked at Lani for an explanation.

"That's what he did last night, lord. He held her, and told her she was safe. She cried in his arms for a long time, until she fell asleep. Your bodyguard didn't take her. Was he a slave in Akkad?"

"No, not in Akkad. He told me that he'd been a slave in the lands to the west, but he never said much about it, only that he escaped. He has the marks of the lash on his back, and even in Akkad, he might have been put back into slavery, except that we needed soldiers to fight the Alur Meriki."

"But you did not put him back into bondage when the danger passed? Did not those in the village declare him a runaway slave?"

"I was born a barbarian, Lani. The ways of the village are not always my ways. Besides, he saved my life, more than once. Do you think I could repay him for that by making him a slave again?" He pushed his wine cup toward her, and she took a small sip before handing it back.

"And now you rule the greatest village in the land, so you're not a barbarian any more, else the villagers would not follow you."

Eskkar smiled at that. "They're still having trouble accepting me as their ruler. And I do not rule alone, Lani."

"It seems even stranger that the nobles of Akkad would accept a woman to rule over them."

So Lani had heard about Trella's true role in Akkad. Well, that made things easier. "She was a slave herself, given to me to help manage my household." He smiled at the thought. "Trella is what my people call a 'gifted one.' She sees much, knows the mysteries of farm and village, and understands the ways of men. Without her, I might not even be alive, let alone ruler of Akkad."

"I heard that she is young, only fifteen seasons. She must be gifted indeed. You must care for her a great deal."

Eskkar nodded. "More than you can know, Lani. She's very special to me. And she carries our child now, the child that will rule in Akkad after us."

"Then I bless her name. And I will not allow myself to be jealous of your love for her."

"Don't be, Lani. It's because of her that I am here, and that you're under Akkad's protection." He reached across the table and touched her hand. "And yet you are much like her, I think. Your wits are quick, and you understand the ways of men. How old are you, Lani?"

"In the spring, I will have twenty-four seasons, lord. But much of what I have learned is what I would soonest forget."

Ninazu's cries of agony rang throughout the square. They'd managed to ignore the noise outside for a few moments. Suddenly the screams ended, cut short, replaced by a loud groan of disappointment and disapproval from the crowd.

"Ninazu must be unconscious, or dead," Eskkar said. "I'll go see."

He went to the doorway, and called to one of the soldiers. In a few moments Eskkar returned to the table and sat down again. "Ninazu is dead, Lani. The torturers were too careless. The villagers think he scarcely suffered."

Lani bowed her head. "I'm glad he's dead. My husband's life has been avenged. Now I can bury him, at least in my thoughts."

Everyone had to deal with grief and loss in their own way, and Eskkar had already done all he could to help her. "You will not be needed for the rest of the day, Lani. Stay inside, until everything is finished." He turned away, and went back out into the square.

The crowd regained its voice. With Ninazu dead, the villagers started arguing again. Many wanted all prisoners to be tortured and killed, and Eskkar watched as Sisuthros pounded his sword hilt on the table to shut them up. Before Sisuthros finished reckoning with the rest of Ninazu's men, the sun passed midday.

The Akkadians had captured thirty-one men, and each

one needed to be dealt with individually. Esskar knew those who had committed the worst misdeeds would make poor slaves. Too ignorant or intractable, they would have to be watched and guarded for the rest of their days, always seeking to escape and more trouble than they were worth. The villagers denounced nine of these, and the council sentenced them to death. Four had committed particularly atrocious acts, and were put to the torture, giving each of them added pain before they died. A quick sword thrust to the heart took care of the others.

Sisuthros condemned those remaining, the ones docile enough to accept their punishment, to slavery, to be branded with the mark of Akkad and to labor for the rest of their lives. He ordered fifteen to be sent to Akkad as soon as possible. Akkad needed laborers more urgently than Bisitun, to work on the expansion of the walls. Corio and his builders would put the extra workers to good use.

Despite Akkad's need, Esskar shook his head at the thought of sending the slaves there. Some of his precious soldiers would be needed to guard and transport them, more food would have to be found and sent with them, along with horses, ropes, and everything else needed for at least a week's march back to Akkad.

Sisuthros spent the remaining daylight dividing up the goods and animals recovered from Ninazu. Despite recovering much of what Ninazu's men had taken, many valuables couldn't be located. Of course several villagers claimed the same items, causing arguments to erupt. Even with fair dispositions, the rightful owners argued about the part taken by Akkad.

Everyone claimed that two-tenths for Akkad was far too

great a portion, until Sisuthros threatened to take everything from the next man who protested. He reminded them that they would have nothing if the Akkadians had not rescued both them and their goods, and that Akkadian soldiers had died freeing them.

The gold and silver coins taken from Ninazu provided another source of contention, the difficulty being to establish how much had been taken from any one person. Acting together, the council made those decisions, often after appealing to the villagers, who made dispositions based on what they thought a man might have possessed.

At last the sun began to sink below the western horizon, and Sisuthros announced the end of the day's proceedings. Another assembly would convene the next day, starting at midmorning. The council of elders would meet earlier, an hour after sunup, to go over what would be the next order of business—restoring the productivity of the farms, the shopkeepers, and the merchant traders.

The crowd began to disburse, heading to their homes for supper. Even after most departed, guards were posted at Eskkar's door to keep a few overeager supplicants away from the leaders of Akkad.

"Marduk take all of them," Sisuthros said, his voice hoarse. He lifted his feet onto the table as he leaned back against the wall. "Another day like today, and I'll run off and become a bandit myself."

Eskkar felt every bit as tired. The constant arguing grated on his nerves, wearing him down. Yet he had to remain alert, to study those as they spoke, in order to determine who might be lying from those who had little skills with speech. He'd stayed out of it as much as possible, but he had intervened twice when Sisuthros looked toward him for help. Eskkar attempted to follow Trella's advice. "Be aloof. Do not deal in common matters. Leave those to your commanders. That way the people will know you concern yourself with far more important things than some farmer's cow or the innkeeper's bill."

"Tomorrow will be easier, Sisuthros. At least you've got the gold out of the way. They'll quiet down as soon as they get back to work. You'll be besieged with requests for men, to help rebuild the farms, the ditches, the shops, the boats, everything damaged or destroyed by Ninazu."

"Captain, I don't know how you and Trella stand it. Better a hard fight against the barbarians any day." He shook his head. "I don't think we have enough scribes and traders, let alone soldiers."

Lani approached the table, carrying a tray of wine, cheese, and bread, the first part of the evening meal. Eskkar mixed himself a cup of watered wine. Sisuthros was right. They would need more help, and they wouldn't be able to trust anyone from Bisitun for months.

"I'll send word back to Akkad, Sisuthros. Maybe Nicar or Corio has someone else they can spare to help you. Perhaps Trella knows of someone."

He didn't mention Sisuthros's wife. Far too shy and retiring, she wouldn't be able to deal forcefully with determined villagers.

Eskkar watched Lani as she moved gracefully about the cooking area, giving directions to the two women preparing the food. He knew she could be of use to Sisuthros, but the people of Bisitun would never accept her in that role. To them, no matter what Eskkar had said today, she would always be Ninazu's woman. Besides, he had promised her protection in Akkad.

Hamati, Drakis, the scribes, and a few of the other senior men sat down at the table, everyone hungry for their dinner. Lani and Tippu returned, carrying more trays laden with food, helped by the other women, who had done a good part of the cooking in their own homes.

No fancy fare yet. Food would remain in short supply in Bisitun until the market reestablished itself. Nevertheless, in the next few days farmers would be bringing in whatever they could spare, to sell to the soldiers and villagers. So for tonight's dinner, the men ate a stew made from two chickens, chopped into tiny chunks, and mixed with fresh vegetables. Four loaves of bread fresh from the ovens helped soak up the stew, and watered wine completed the meal. Not much food for fighting men, but most of Bisitun would not eat as well tonight. At least no villager would starve in the next week or ten days, though plenty would go to bed hungry.

The meal finished, Eskkar and Sisuthros took another walk about the village. Both men felt the need to stretch their legs after sitting or standing all day with solemn looks on their faces. Accompanied by Grond and three other guards, they spent hours poking about until darkness made it too difficult to see anything.

Eskkar took every opportunity to talk with the villagers. Such casual speech didn't come easy to him, but Trella had gotten him used to making small talk with the common folk, asking about their homes, their families, their needs, and their hopes. He'd learned that people provided the real basis for his rule, and he worked hard at building a bond between himself and those he ruled.

The three men were yawning when they returned to the square, for once empty of villagers.

After such a long and exciting day, everyone would be in bed, eager for sleep. Eskkar, Sisuthros, and Grond washed at the well, stripping down and pouring water over their bodies. It didn't feel as refreshing as a good swim in the river, but Eskkar promised himself that luxury tomorrow, come what may.

Carrying their clothes, the three of them walked back inside the house. The big room, empty of servants, held only two soldiers standing guard just inside the door. Eskkar spoke to both of them, to make sure they stayed alert. Though Sisuthros had distributed much of the loot, the house still held the gold destined for Akkad.

Eskkar had just entered his room when Lani appeared, carrying a pitcher of wine, another of water, and a single cup. She'd no doubt heard the men cleaning themselves at the well, so she brought no washing bowls. Splashing a bit of wine into a cup, she added water before handing it to him. Already she had learned that he drank his wine well watered.

"Thank you, Lani," he said, breaking the silence. She probably thought he expected her to attend him. She wore the same soft robe she wore last night when she came to him, and already he wished she would unfasten it. He took a sip from the cup.

"Lani, you don't have to be here. Your sorrow for your husband is ..."

She touched her finger to his lips. "My husband has been dead for over four months. Today ... watching Ninazu die, I put an end to my grief. Now I have to care for my sister."

"Then she'll need you tonight, Lani. Stay with her. She doesn't have your strength."

"Tonight she has Grond to comfort her." She saw the look on his face. "No, lord, she went to him willingly. It's time she ceased being afraid of men. And I think Grond is the right man for that task. He ignores her dishonor, and treats her with respect. His presence reassures her more than my words ever can. She knows no one will hurt her now."

True enough, Eskkar thought. Only a foolhardy man would offer any insult to a woman under Grond's protection.

Lani turned away and went to the door. She closed it, then placed the wooden bar across the frame. Turning back to face him, she lifted her head high. "I think it's time that I, too, went willingly to a man's bed. I would stay the night with you again, lord, if I do not displease you."

He looked at her, and his resolve vanished. She had some essence, something that made him want her, and he knew it was more than just her skill in pleasuring him. Eskkar sat down on the bed, more than a little unsure of himself.

"You know I want you, Lani. But I won't take you with a lie on my lips. My life is back in Akkad, with Trella. And I'll be going back soon enough."

"Then I only ask that you keep your word, lord, to take me and my sister back to Akkad with you. Until then, you will need someone to manage your household, care for you while you are here, and hold you in the darkness of the night."

"You do not need to call me 'lord,' Lani. My name is

Eskkar. I am just a simple soldier. One trying to rule a city and a land full of problems."

She stepped toward him, stopping just out of reach, and began to unfasten her dress. "No, Eskkar. I heard you in the square today, and saw what you did. You gave the villagers honesty and justice, something they haven't seen in many months. Despite their complaining, they already accept you as their ruler, and trust you to protect them. You are a great lord, to have such power over men."

The robe untied, she slipped it over her shoulders, letting it hang from her arms, the same as she'd done last night. She closed her eyes to his gaze, but her body trembled as if she could already feel his hands upon her.

He shook his head. No one had ever called him "great" before. If he ever ruled this land, it would be Trella who deserved that honor. He couldn't explain all that to Lani, not now. He stood and reached for her, taking her in his arms and catching her hair in his hand. He kissed her upraised lips, and heard the robe slip to the floor. She tasted sweet to him, and he kissed her even harder, letting his other hand find and fondle her breast until she caught her breath.

"What can I do to please my lord tonight?" She kept her voice low, but he could hear the passion in it.

He swung her around, and pushed her gently down on the bed. For a moment he felt tempted to leave the candle burning, but the sight of her body already burned in his memory. He leaned over and blew out the flickering light. Despite his passion, he took the time to unsheathe the sword and lean it against the wall before sliding into the bed.

They held each other, neither one saying anything, just kissing and touching for a long time, until his excitement grew. When Lani moved to pleasure him as she had done the night before, he held her down, kissing her neck.

"Oh, no, Lani. Not tonight. Tonight I will give you pleasure." He lay on his side and began caressing her, sucking and biting on her nipples while his fingers probed and teased her body. At first she seemed uncomfortable with the attention, but gradually she relaxed, letting him arouse her.

His lips moved up and down the length of her body, tasting her, kissing her, and she began to moan from the pleasure he gave her. He resisted her first pleadings, ignored the way she pushed her body against him, held back until her hand tightened so much around him that he thought he would burst.

Finally he moved atop her and slid deep into her body. A long sigh of pleasure escaped her lips, and she locked her legs around him.

He began to move against her, and she matched his movements, pushing herself against him. Before long she cried out, her arms and legs fastening themselves around him, her sounds of passion coming faster and faster until she gave a little scream into his neck as her body overwhelmed her.

Trembling, she could do nothing but hold him fast; he increased his thrusts against her and soon he, too, cried out as he gave her his seed, his face and mouth buried in her hair.

For a long time he lay on top of her, his passion spent but enjoying the touch of her body. When he moved beside her, she moaned a little. He took her in his arms and held her. Her whole body shook, and he tasted the salt of tears on his lips when he gently kissed her cheek.

"Did I hurt you, Lani?"

"No, lord." Her arms pulled tight around his neck, and she buried her face against his. "These are tears of happiness."

10

In Akkad, the days passed swiftly for Tammuz. Overnight, the addition of En-hedu to his household made the gloomy place seem brighter, and its dull routine soon disappeared, as she set about improving the alehouse. Neither Kuri nor Tammuz had ever bothered trying to keep the place clean, but she soon made up for their past neglect. She traded a few cups of ale to a carpenter who lived nearby. He labored there whenever he had no work of his own, or if he'd worked up a thirst. An hour at a time, over the course of a week, he fixed the rickety benches and tables, and built a new shelf to hold the few cups and plates the alehouse possessed.

At Tammuz's suggestion, the carpenter also rebuilt the tavern's two doors, making the outer door more solid, and repairing the inner one that led to Tammuz's private room. When the craftsman finished, the two doors hung properly, swung freely, and both could be fastened securely. For working on the doors, the carpenter asked for a payment of five copper coins in addition to his usual libations; he had to shape some cast-off bronze strips for the hinges, make a dozen nails, and rebuild the outer door's lintel. For the satisfaction of sleeping safer at night, Tammuz agreed to the sum. In his neighborhood, inhabitants paid any price for the chance to sleep in safety at night.

A few days later, when the carpenter completed his tasks and emptied his last cup of free ale, the alehouse looked much better. For a finishing touch, En-hedu, using some red dye bought at the marketplace, sketched a wine cup and the barley symbol on the outer wall, so that passersby could tell at a glance what the establishment sold.

While all this was going on, Tammuz watched in astonishment as En-hedu began ordering the patrons around. First she made them stop urinating against the alehouse's outside wall. The regular customers soon grew tired of her berating and scolding, and went down the lane and around the corner to relieve themselves. Newcomers were warned, and if anyone forgot, she told Kuri to keep them out until they learned their lesson.

In a few days, much of the rank odor disappeared from the outside of the alehouse. At the same time, with Kuri's assistance, she cut a small hole through the ceiling of the public room, giving the stale air and cooking smoke a chance to escape, a good trade-off for the occasional rain that would find its way inside. For another copper coin, two barrows loaded with clean sand arrived. Tammuz watched as En-hedu efficiently spread the contents over the dirt floor. That helped keep the bugs and insects under control.

With these and other improvements En-hedu suggested, the establishment took on a somewhat more reputable appearance. The number of customers increased as well, which not only helped profits increase, but provided more of a cover for the half-dozen or more thieves who habituated the place. Since Tammuz kept his ale prices low, his clientele soon increased, and most of the patrons knew each other. That kept the fights to a minimum, and Kuri had fewer problems keeping order.

En-hedu wanted to do more, but Tammuz, a smile on his face, told her to stop, before the place began to look too good for its customers. That made her laugh, and without thinking he took her in his arms. For a brief moment, she looked happy and alive. Then she stiffened, and he knew thoughts of her former master still troubled her.

Nevertheless he couldn't stop from kissing her. Her mouth felt warm and soft, and she didn't resist. Nor did she kiss him back. He knew she wasn't ready, not yet. The fear remained in her eyes, so he let her go. To his surprise, she hugged him for a moment before turning back to her work. Her touch gave him a feeling of contentment that lasted the rest of the afternoon.

The days went by, and if his nights still lacked the pleasure of the gods, he refused to allow the shortcoming to bother him. Be patient, he said to himself, though now he whispered it with a smile on his lips.

Best of all, the purpose lacking in his life returned. Since he'd crippled his arm, he'd held little hope for the future. Though he'd undertaken the assignment at the alehouse, he'd done so more to please Eskkar and Lady Trella than out of any conviction he would ever accomplish anything of importance. Now he saw how he could make a difference, how what he did today, and would do in the future, could help protect the vision Eskkar and Trella wished for Akkad.

Watching En-hedu day after day, he began to comprehend the mysterious ways of women. And the more he
learned, the more he understood how Eskkar commanded
Trella's affections. The tiny hint of jealousy he'd always felt
for Akkad's ruler disappeared with that new knowledge.

With the alehouse in good hands and running smoothly,
Tammuz spent several hours a day shadowing the inn
where Korthac stayed, or the river where he traded his
gemstones. One morning, after Korthac departed for his
business at the docks, Tammuz tried to enter the inn,
ostensibly to buy food, but the Egyptian guarding the door
stopped him with a hand on his chest. Before Tammuz
could even plead his case, the inn's owner, standing behind
the guard, called out for Tammuz to leave, informing him
that, at present, the inn served only Korthac and his men.

Frustrated, Tammuz decided to risk another, more
direct, approach. One of his customers, Sargat, a young
man only a season or two older than Tammuz, made his
living by thieving at night. Agile and strong, Sargat could
hang by his fingertips and pull himself up and over any
roof in Akkad. As quiet as a mouse, he could see in the dark
better than most. Sargat had slipped into many a house
without waking its inhabitants, collected what he could,
and left as silently as he entered.

In order to entice Sargat, Tammuz invented a story
about a trader who competed with Korthac, sought
information about the secretive Egyptian, and would pay
well for anything Sargat could learn.

"If you can discover anything, see anything, find out
what their plans are, or even what these Egyptians are
doing, this man will pay well for the information." As

Tammuz finished, he slid a silver coin across the table to Sargat. "And if you happen to pick up any of his goods, my patron will be glad to buy them from you."

Sargat reached for the silver, but Tammuz put his hand over the coin. "Not until you return. And you'll have to be careful. Korthac has guards everywhere, and they look as if they'd do more than just break a few bones if they catch you."

The thief nodded in understanding; he'd seen Korthac's men in the lanes.

A little after midnight that night, while Tammuz waited at the far end of the lane, Sargat took to the roofs and made his way toward the inn, vanishing into the darkness. Tammuz squatted down to wait. The better part of an hour passed without a sound. Suddenly he heard voices, then something falling with a crash, but all too muted to wake anyone sleeping nearby. Nevertheless, he knew something had gone awry.

Tammuz pushed himself to his feet, cursing at whatever unknown problem had occurred, and anxiously scanned the rooftops. A shadow blocked the moonlight for an instant, and Tammuz caught a glimpse of a dark shape running along the rooftop.

By now a light burned in the inn, and Tammuz heard the door bang open. His heart began beating faster, and he took off down the lane, running as fast as he could and trying to make as little noise as possible. When he felt sure he wasn't being followed, he slipped through the streets and back to the alehouse. Kuri waited there, the door unbarred. Sargat was already inside, his breathing still audible as he tried to catch his breath.

Tammuz led the thief into his private room, while En-hedu watched the lane and Kuri guarded the door. The two men sat in the darkness.

"What happened?" Tammuz kept his voice to a whisper. "Did you learn anything?"

"I almost got killed. They were up in a moment, looking ..."

Tammuz heard the fear in the young man's voice. "Tell me what happened. You were gone long enough."

Sargat took a deep breath. Tammuz poured the thief a cup of ale, then watched as Sargat gulped it down without pausing. The strong brew calmed him, and he took a few more breaths before going on.

"I got inside. One of Korthac's men was on guard below, watching the roof hole. But he looked ready to doze off, so I waited until his head began to nod, and I slipped past him."

Tammuz hadn't expected anyone to be guarding the roof. The flimsy wood and vine rooftops creaked and swayed with every movement, and made plenty of noise. Only someone with a slight figure, like Sargat, who knew how to move silently and with patience, could traverse the delicate rafters without waking those below. Tammuz puzzled over why Korthac would place a guard over the roof's entrance, since only an exceptional thief could gain entrance that way. "You could have been caught. You weren't supposed to ..."

"I know," Sargat went on, "but he was breathing like a sleeper, so I felt sure I could get past. Besides, there was nothing to see from the roof, just a room full of sleeping men all snoring away. But when I climbed down the ladder,

I saw two more men guarding the door, and another standing before one of the private rooms."

Tammuz felt a tingle go through him. Four guards, on watch during the night. He'd never heard of such a thing. No merchant, no noble kept that many men awake during darkness.

"Then what happened?"

"Nothing. With three or four men on guard, I decided to get out. I started back up the ladder, but the wood creaked, and the guard jumped, you know, the way you do when you wake suddenly. I scrambled up the ladder. Then I heard a crash. The guard swung his sword and nearly got my leg. He came up the ladder after me in an instant, and I ran. I heard him stumbling behind me, but I took to the ledges."

Tammuz knew the rest. Sargat could outrun anyone across a rooftop. "You're lucky you weren't caught. I told you not to take any chances."

"What about my coin? Will you still pay me the silver?"

"Yes, you've earned it. Maybe even more. Stay here, I'll . . ."

En-hedu slipped into the room. "Keep silent," she whispered. "There are men with swords in the lane, looking about. Stay here and don't move about." She went back into the common room.

Tammuz felt his heart pounding in his chest. How had they tracked him here? Could he have been followed? He heard Sargat's rapid breathing and reached out and gripped the thief's arm. "Stay still, and don't make a sound," he ordered.

They sat like that, not moving, not making a sound, until En-hedu returned. "They've gone. They're checking all the houses on the street, putting their ears to the doors, listening. Thank the gods your customers are still snoring their ale away."

So Korthac's guards hadn't followed him, Tammuz realized. They'd just headed to the places most likely to be frequented by thieves. They weren't listening for sounds, but for the absence of sounds. If they found a place without the little murmurs of slumber, they would have forced their way in. He wondered who gave them the idea, then answered the thought himself. Korthac. Only he would have the cunning to think of such things.

Something else occurred to him. "Sargat, you're not cut or anything, are you?" Tammuz, still worried about anyone overhearing, kept his voice to a whisper.

"No, the sword missed by a handbreadth, thank the lazy god who watches over thieves. Though my tunic got torn, and . . ."

"Show me," En-hedu ordered, startling both men.

Sargat fingered his shoulder. "It caught when the ladder slipped, probably on some splinter or a nail. I heard it rip."

"Don't leave the alehouse," En-hedu said. "Tomorrow I'll get you a new tunic."

"Why, what's the matter?" Sargat asked.

Tammuz took a moment to catch up with his slave. "They'll be walking the lanes tomorrow, looking for someone with a torn sleeve. If they saw that . . . you'll stay inside the alehouse for a few days. If any of the Egyptians come wandering in here, they'll find nothing."

"There's nothing else to do tonight," En-hedu said. "Kuri, Sargat, get some sleep."

Sargat emptied another cup of ale before he left, going

into the common room to try and sleep. Tammuz checked
the outer door before returning to his chamber, fastening
the inner door, and climbing into bed.

En-hedu moved against him, so she could whisper in
his ear. "If they'd caught him, they would have beat your
name out of him," she said. "I don't think you should risk
anything like that again. Korthac is leaving the inn soon.
I'll watch his new house as we planned. It will be safer than
trying to break in."

Tammuz knew she never liked the idea of sending in
Sargat, but she didn't remind him. "You're right," he admitted. "If Sargat had been captured and put to the torture, it
would have been bad. Damn the gods! I just wanted to find
out something about Korthac for Trella, something useful."

"You just did. You learned how alert his men are, and how
well he guards his secrets. Lady Trella will want to know
that, before she makes the same mistake. Now go to sleep."

He felt her thigh brush against his, and suddenly
Korthac and Trella were forgotten. The urge to take her,
mount her right now, surged over him, and he had to
struggle to keep control. *Be patient.* He had to say the words
to himself a dozen times before he finally drifted off to a
restless and uneven sleep.

For En-hedu, the days with Tammuz seemed like a
dream, a happy dream she hoped would never end. Her
brief stay at Lady Trella's house had mended her body, but
she knew her soul still needed more time to recover. Her
years as a slave had nearly ruined her mind, but Lady Trella
had assured her that, in time, her spirit would heal.

The experience of living with Trella, Annok-sur, and other strong women in Lord Eskkar's house showed En-hedu that she could make a difference, that her life wasn't entirely under the control of others. In Lady Trella's household, En-hedu saw that even slaves could be treated well, respected for their talents, and rewarded for their service. For the first time in her life, En-hedu began to appreciate the many unique and special talents a strong woman could possess, and how they might be used.

She also came to understand some of Trella's reasons for rescuing her. Pity had little to do with it; Trella wanted allies, those who could help her keep control of Akkad. She offered En-hedu the opportunity to shape her own destiny, if she could grasp it. En-hedu determined to make the most of this chance at a new life.

Her childhood had consisted of hard labor on her parents' farm, and the brutal existence she'd endured the last three seasons now helped her more than she realized. Physically strong, she could labor long hours without tiring. En-hedu soon comprehended the simple business of running an alehouse, far less complicated than the craft of tanning leather. After the first day, she took over almost all of Kuri's duties, leaving him free to assist Tammuz as needed.

Her new master helped her more than he knew. Even as he gave her the time she needed to heal, he offered something else, a life she could share as an equal partner. With each day, En-hedu grew more accepting of both him and the life Trella had restored to her.

Tammuz had almost no possessions, much less than her former master, and En-hedu owned nothing but the dress she wore each day. But he had something more valuable than goods to give her: the trust of Lady Trella. If the ruler of Akkad considered Tammuz a friend and a valuable ally, then En-hedu would devote her days to helping him, and, indirectly, Lady Trella. That common purpose helped bind them to one another.

And Tammuz listened to her. That gave En-hedu more pleasure than anything she'd known in her life. No man or woman had ever asked her advice or cared about her thoughts. Sharing her confidences with him benefited them both, and she saw that Tammuz felt much the same. One night he confided to her that, for the first time in his life, he felt happy.

For En-hedu, the discovery that someone cared for her, really cared, awakened feelings she'd never experienced. Tammuz filled her thoughts, as she knew she filled his. Slowly, almost reluctantly, she began to think about giving herself to him, to give him the one pleasure he lacked.

To her surprise, the thought seemed less repugnant than she'd expected. Now that her body had healed, she began to think more often about submitting to him, though she still had misgivings. Still, En-hedu worried that Tammuz might not be satisfied with her, that afterward he would turn from her, like her former master. She sought to banish such thoughts, but they returned, seemingly strongest the closer Tammuz and she were drawn to each other.

Nevertheless, they shared a common purpose that drew them together. As the days passed, master and slave worked equally in their effort to unravel the mystery that was Korthac. They both wished to please Lady Trella, and for much the same reason. En-hedu out of gratitude for saving her life, and Tammuz for giving his life purpose.

Their first day together, En-hedu and Tammuz talked for hours about Korthac. When they finished, they had a plan, and the next day they began the preparations necessary to set it in motion.

Taking advantage of En-hedu's experience in the tannery, Tammuz approached an older woman, Ninbanda, whose husband had died a few weeks earlier. He, too, had worked with leather, cutting, trimming, and shaping the cured hide into finished goods that Ninbanda sold in the market. But with his death, his duties had passed to his brother, who could do little to help his brother's widow. He gave her some work and a place to live, and allowed her to sell some of the poorer quality goods that came through the tannery, but she often didn't earn enough to offset the hardship to her family.

The woman quickly accepted Tammuz's offer to share in the selling of additional goods that Tammuz would provide. Ninbanda also agreed to his one condition: that she and En-hedu sell their wares not in the market, but in a particular lane and at a specific location. Tammuz, of course, didn't mention that this was where Korthac decided to dwell.

Ten days after En-hedu came to the alehouse, Tammuz received word that Korthac had finally settled on a new house. The largest houses in the better parts of Akkad remained occupied, and no amount of gold could entice their occupants to leave, to Korthac's obvious annoyance. He eventually had to compromise on his new dwelling: the Egyptian's new residence actually consisted of one large house, flanked by two smaller ones. Unfortunately for Korthac, the large central house remained occupied by its former owners, who delayed their departure an extra week or so, thereby preventing Korthac from taking possession.

Moving quickly, Tammuz established Ninbanda and En-hedu as sellers of goods, in the lane outside Korthac's residences. A few days later, when Korthac finally took possession, En-hedu had already established herself and her wares as if she'd been selling there all her life.

Each morning En-hedu rose before dawn, gathered the day's wares, and went to her post, just a few paces down the lane from Korthac's new houses. Corio, Akkad's master artisan, had offered to build a new home for Korthac, as grand as he wanted, but the Egyptian decided to wait for that, and settled for the three joined houses. He split his men between the two smaller structures, and lived in the main house with just a few servants and guards.

En-hedu and her business partner, Ninbanda, pushed their cart into the lane at dawn, then sat behind it all day, pitching their wares to all those who passed by. Sandals, leather strips for binding, belts, pouches, scabbards for knives and swords, wrist guards, and even some leather rings, necklaces, and bracelets were offered for sale. Mixed in with the goods were the occasional items stolen by Tammuz's customers, so the business actually helped her master recover some of his expenses.

With two women working the cart, the business thrived, especially since En-hedu took but a tiny part of the profits. The selling took little effort, leaving her plenty of time to chat with Ninbanda and those who lived in the lane. En-hedu soon became familiar with Korthac's men, even learning their names. After a few days she called out to them when they passed by, offering her wares, urging them to look and to buy.

She quickly learned not to attempt to speak with them when they walked with Korthac. The Egyptian showed no tolerance for those beneath him, and coldly berated any of his men who fraternized with the villagers. Of course, a woman selling in the streets was far below his notice, and after one glance at En-hedu's disfigured face, he ignored her completely.

Korthac's men, however, looked at her far differently. En-hedu knew the look of lust when she saw it, and the Egyptians all seemed to burn with it. Her broken nose didn't matter to them. And not only her, but any woman in the lane. Their hot eyes devoured each woman they passed.

Men's lusts were nothing new to En-hedu. She'd had to satisfy not only her former master, but some of his friends on more than one occasion. Spreading her legs, she'd closed her eyes and did what they commanded. Her old master had taught her to obey as soon as she reached his house. He raped her at once, not even bothering to close the door, then beat her for not pleasing him. The beatings continued every day, until she learned to obey every command instantly.

Remembering those times made her apprehensive. She knew Tammuz wanted to take her, and she dreaded the day when he could no longer restrain himself. A slave was bound to pleasure her master, and yet the thought of a man, even Tammuz, taking her, being inside her, brought back the painful memories.

After all these weeks, she'd learned to trust Tammuz, to let him hold her in the darkness, and she clasped his hand at every opportunity. Nevertheless, she wondered fretfully what Lady Trella would think, if she learned En-hedu hadn't pleasured Tammuz—that she had failed in one of the most basic duties due her master.

Aside from that concern, she looked forward to the end of each day, when she returned to the alehouse. She'd soon discovered that old Kuri needed plenty of help dispensing the ale, especially in the evening hours. He drank too much of his own wares, and easily lost track of what the customers consumed and paid. En-hedu kept a close watch on the stock, and cut down on the waste and spillage. Kuri gladly relinquished that part of his duties, and instead did his best to maintain order.

Naturally many customers wanted more than just ale, and solicitations for sex and worse initially followed her every step. Tammuz ordered one man out the first night for laying a hand on her, and Kuri did the same the following night. By then En-hedu had grown confident enough in her own strength. After she'd knocked down one drunken patron and threatened to bash his brains in with a stool, the regular patrons soon learned to leave her alone.

She was the owner's slave, and he was keeping her for himself, a not entirely unreasonable thing to do. Once the customers grasped the odd fact that she was not for sale, they accepted her as one of themselves.

For herself, En-hedu came to enjoy the time spent behind the selling cart. Being outside, breathing fresh air, and enjoying the sun with little to do except watch the cart gave her more time to heal. The long days turned into weeks, and En-hedu and her leatherwares became as much a part of the lane outside Korthac's residence as the walls, houses, and dirt underfoot, and just as unnoticed.

And so the days passed. En-hedu watched the Egyptians

with care, always challenging them to purchase something from her cart. Some of them spoke only Egyptian, but many had picked up more than a few words of the local language. They remained subdued when Korthac walked about, but a week after his arrival in Akkad, Korthac began spending most of the daylight hours at the river. He set up a trading table there, and each day offered a handful of gems for sale or trade. Many Akkadians stopped at his table, as well as travelers, boatmen, and traders journeying up or down the Tigris.

That left most of his guards—as En-hedu soon came to think of them that way—with nothing to do except wait for their master's return. She discovered they were not allowed to leave the house without Korthac or his senior assistant, a tall, bald-headed man named Hathor. Hathor also functioned as an occasional bodyguard, though there were other Egyptians who regularly guarded Korthac's person.

Forbidden to walk the lanes, Korthac's men lounged in the doorways, staring boldly at the women who passed by. For the braver ones, it only took a few steps to cross the lane and examine En-hedu's merchandise and exchange a few words with her in their halting way. She made sure they always received a warm smile for their efforts.

"They seem to be waiting for something," En-hedu said to Tammuz. Each night, they sat alone in the dark of their bedroom or lay together in the bed, leaving Kuri to keep watch in the outer chamber while the customers snored on the floor.

"We know no more than we did last month," Tammuz said, impatience and frustration showing in his voice. "Each week I send word to Trella we've learned nothing new."

"We must wait a bit longer, Tammuz," she said. "Korthac's men are becoming more friendly. He can't keep them in the houses forever." By now she'd watched Korthac's house for more than four weeks, and understood Tammuz's frustration.

"I wish I could slip into the house at night, just to listen."

"You know you cannot do that, Tammuz." Since the incident on the roof, Korthac had added another sentry on the rooftop at night, and still had the usual guards at all the entrances. No doubt another one or two would be inside the main house, alert and awake. The extra guards didn't arouse any suspicion to the rest of Akkad. Everyone knew Korthac possessed plenty of gold and gems, and naturally he would take precautions.

"Something will turn up, sooner or later," she said, taking his hand and holding it close. "We just have to be ready when it happens."

"Soon, I hope."

"Soon, I'm sure. Now go to sleep, master."

En-hedu waited as he tossed and turned, before finally falling asleep, his arm thrown over her chest. She let go of his hand, and thought about the man asleep in her arms. He needed to be pleasured, and soon. Frustrated by his inability to learn anything about Korthac, she knew Tammuz needed something else to think about. She sighed. Any day now, and she would have to do it, offer herself to him and endure the pain. Perhaps it wouldn't be so painful with Tammuz. And better a little pain than facing Lady Trella's disapproval.

11

"I tell you, Trella, this is wrong. Asurak deserves his goods, and the council should support his claim. Otherwise . . ."

"Otherwise Asurak will have to pay what he agreed," Corio cut in, the annoyance plain in his voice. "Which he should have done yesterday, instead of wasting the council's time."

The discussion, argument really, had gone on for some time, and Trella didn't need to hear much to make up her mind. The dispute started at dawn, when the trader from Dilgarth tried to deliver his goods to Asurak. The trader, Chuvash, had come down from Dilgarth yesterday with the first wagonload of raw flax. Two merchants had bid for the goods, and Asurak had proffered the higher price to Chuvash, with the goods to be delivered this morning.

Now Asurak claimed that, after a closer inspection, the goods were inferior, and only offered to pay fifteen silver coins, instead of the agreed-upon price of twenty-five. Within the hour, everyone in the marketplace knew the story. Trella, on her way to the council meeting, learned of it from Annok-sur, who'd heard it from one of the women in the market.

Rasui, the newest member of Akkad's nobles and a close friend of Asurak, supported the merchant's claim and made the argument before the other council members.

Trella spoke before Rasui could start again. "I think the council has heard enough. Both Asurak and Chuvash gave us their versions, and the council has heard the same story twice." She turned to Corio, Nicar, and then to Rasui before going on. "Asurak inspected the goods before he offered the price. He waited until the other bidder had left the city before he decided the goods were inferior."

"If the trader wants to sell his flax," Rasui countered, "then he has to sell to my ... Asurak. There are no other buyers of flax in Akkad."

Trella smiled at Rasui's logic. True enough. All the usual buyers of flax had departed for Dilgarth in the last few days, eager to resume trade and lock in prices for the first deliveries. Knowing of the temporary shortage of buyers in Akkad, Asurak no doubt felt confident the Dilgarth trader would have to accept the revised terms.

"No, the deal is revoked," Trella said. "Asurak says he doesn't want the goods at the original price. Fine. Then let him pay Chuvash two silver coins as a penalty for attempting to change the agreed-upon price. I will pay the trader twenty-five coins for the flax myself. I'm sure I can resell the goods in a few days, when the flax weavers return from Dilgarth."

Corio laughed aloud. "Sounds fair to me." He turned to Nicar. "What do you say?"

"Actually, I was about to make the same offer," Nicar

said, a hint of humor in his voice. "I don't usually deal in flax, but I have a boat going downriver tomorrow, and I can ship the raw flax south. Plenty of weavers in the villages along the river. The first boatload should fetch a good price. If Lady Trella doesn't mind, I will buy the goods from Chuvash for twenty-six silver coins."

Trella laughed. "Be my guest, Nicar. You can make better use of it, I'm sure."

Rasui muttered something under his breath. Trella couldn't hear what he said, but Corio, sitting beside Rasui, must have.

"Watch your tongue, Rasui," Corio said, disdain plain in his voice. "This council isn't here to help scheming merchants take advantage of others. Your friend should have known better."

"Well, then, at least Asurak need not pay the two silver coins as Trella suggested," Rasui argued. "Since he's getting twenty-six from Nicar and . . ."

"The two extra coins are for wasting the council's time, and the trader's," Trella said. "He pays or he can leave Akkad."

"*Lady* Trella speaks for all of us," Corio said, turning to Rasui and emphasizing the honorific. "Asurak can pay now, or leave tomorrow, whichever he prefers."

Trella had noticed Rasui's frequent omission of her simple title, a sign of respect given to her as Eskkar's wife and for presiding over the council in his absence. And while the Council of Nobles was technically a group of equals, everyone remembered when Eskkar had convened the first meeting, a week or so after the siege ended. Some newly returned shopkeeper had referred to Trella casually.

Eskkar had given the man such a look that he turned pale, and couldn't stammer his apologies fast enough. After that, no one failed to refer to her properly.

And now Rasui, caught up in the heat of the argument and trying to help his friend cheat the trader from Dilgarth, had not only forgotten her title but said something derogatory about her under his breath. If Eskkar were here, the man would already be packing his things, assuming he still had his head on his shoulders.

Trella sighed, and wished for a brief moment that indeed Eskkar were here. Her husband might hate these endless and interminable meetings, but he did have a way of settling certain disputes. Once he simply ordered a tavernkeeper out of Akkad. When the man protested, Eskkar stood and put his hand on his sword, before asking if the man wished to go for a swim in the Tigris without his head. Not very diplomatic, but, when used occasionally and with care, very effective.

Trella rose and leaned forward on the table. Resting her hands on the rough surface, she gazed directly into Rasui's eyes. "Tell your friend two silver coins to Chuvash *now*. And the council doesn't want to hear any more about this matter, so tell Asurak to keep his complaints to himself. If he can't trade honestly, he can leave Akkad. I'm sure there's room on Nicar's boat for one more."

Rasui clenched his jaw, but one glance at the two Hawk Clan soldiers guarding the door reminded him that Trella had no problem with using force.

No one spoke, and all eyes turned to Rasui. "Then it's settled," Nicar said, speaking before the silence went on too long and Rasui felt tempted to speak up. "And if there's nothing else to discuss this morning, I would like to get back to my business."

"And I," Corio agreed. "There's so much building going on, I hate to be away from my apprentices any longer than necessary."

Rasui dropped his hands on the table and nodded agreement. "As you say, Lady Trella."

Trella ignored the hint of condescension in Rasui's tone. Straightening up, she sweetened her voice. "Then until tomorrow, nobles."

Rasui left first, no doubt to give his friend Asurak the bad news and put the matter behind him. Corio nodded at Trella, but made for the door nearly as fast as Rasui. Trella and Nicar left together, her two guards forming up around her as soon as they went outside and into the lane.

"Rasui lets his tongue run away with him," Nicar commented as they walked side by side. "Asurak probably offered five coins to Rasui to help him shave the price."

"If we don't treat these traders fairly, then the goods will flow elsewhere," Trella said, repeating the policy she and the council had established weeks ago.

"Yes, but a little cheating is expected," Nicar said. "That's what we merchants do sometimes, to get the best price."

Even Trella laughed at that. "I don't recall you ever doing anything so obvious, Nicar. You always appreciate the need to keep good relationships with your suppliers."

"Perhaps I'm just more subtle in my dealings. At least, I hope I am."

They'd reached the fork in the lane, and Nicar bade her good-bye as he walked off toward his home. Annok-sur, who'd followed behind them since they left the council house, moved alongside Trella.

With only two more lanes to cross, Trella took her time, stopping whenever she saw any of the dozens of women she knew, and answering the same questions again and again about the coming child. Trella's excellent memory enabled her to keep a name with each face, and her ability to recall nearly every detail of every conversation convinced her followers that they occupied a special place in her thoughts.

In a few moments, the women and guards reached Eskkar's lane, and a few paces later, they turned into his courtyard.

"Do you need to rest, Trella?"

"No, I just want to sit outside for a while," Trella answered. "Dealing with Rasui always leaves a bad taste in my mouth."

They walked to the back of the house, and sat together on the bench between the two young trees. Only a single guard kept station there, to make sure no one slipped in over the wall, and to keep an eye on Trella's bedroom window on the upper story. The soldier, at a smile from Trella, obligingly moved away, across the courtyard. He could still see the women, but not hear them, if they kept their voices low.

"That Asurak," Annok-sur began. "He should be driven out of Akkad. He tries to cheat everyone he deals with. Sooner or later, someone is going to put a knife between his ribs."

"He's no worse than a dozen others," Trella said. "Except he has a friend on the council. Rasui encourages sharp dealing. I sometimes wish we had never accepted him into the nobles."

"Rasui had the gold to pay his way onto the council," Annok-sur said, "though how he got it, no one knows."

Before the siege, Rasui had been a minor trader dealing in slaves. Like many others too fearful to stay and fight, he'd chosen to depart the city before the Alur Meriki arrived. A few months later, after Eskkar drove off the barbarians, Rasui returned, with plenty of gold in his pouch and a steady supply of slaves. The trader paid the penalty demanded by the council for abandoning the city, and paid again to join the council itself as a noble.

Trella never cared for slave traders, not after her own experiences with them, but the reborn city required all the skills and trades it could find. She'd put aside her own distaste for Rasui and his calling, though now she wished otherwise.

"In a few months, if he doesn't change his ways, we'll send him packing," Trella said. "But not now. We still need every trader, merchant, and worker we can entice to come here."

During the siege, many merchants and craftsmen had left the city, most of them going to the south, some even as far as Sumeria. And except for war goods such as timber and bronze, much of Akkad's trade had fallen off as traders sought safer places to do business. And though many people had returned to or settled in Akkad, the number of craftsmen, herders, and farmers hadn't recovered. The situation would change soon enough, but the next six months would be critical to insure the city's continued growth. Afterward, Akkad would be stronger than before, and individual merchants and traders would be less important.

"In another week or two," Annok-sur said, "Asurak will be back before the council, answering some other complaint and hiding behind Rasui's tunic."

"Probably," Trella agreed. "But for now, I think the real problem goes deeper. These council meetings waste most of our time on petty disputes that do little to grow the city. When we first convened the council, important matters needed to be resolved. But now, Akkad has grown too big to govern in the same way as a small village. Even Eskkar knows that. We need a new way of ruling, a way that allows the city to grow while protecting its trade and its people."

"More changes," Annok-sur said. "The nobles won't like that. They've already given up much of their authority."

A breeze filled the courtyard, rustling the trees and shaking some blossoms from the limbs. Both women paused for a moment, watching the tree limbs sway gracefully.

"There are nearly five thousand people in Akkad," Trella went on. "In another few years, there may be twice as many. The number of disputes will more than double. There will be quarrels over housing, farmlands, herds, anything and everything. If there are two or three confrontations a day to be resolved now, there will be a dozen each day soon enough. No, we need to reshape Akkad's ways now, before the sheer number of people overwhelms us."

"No one likes change, Trella. People like things to be the way they've always been."

"I know. Eskkar and I have spoken about this many

times. He's visited dozens of villages throughout the land, and seen every abuse of power possible, even here. He wants to rule Bisitun in such a way that the people there are thankful to be under Akkad's control."

"He's become a different man in the last few months, because of you," Annok-sur said. "Now even my Bantor is starting to consider his choices with more care. He's started worrying about the future, too."

"New times call for new skills," Trella said. She reached down and picked up a blossom swept against her feet. "But it pleases me to see Bantor learning new ways." She thought for a moment, admiring the flower as she did so. "I think great change is coming for all of us, and if we do not lead the way, those changes will overwhelm us. With Bisitun to worry about, we must find new ways to rule there, too, ways that don't make the people there and here in Akkad hate our authority. Otherwise we'll be no better than any bandit."

"What would you change first, Trella?"

"As Eskkar says, there must be a better way to resolve disputes," Trella answered. "It would be even better to avoid them in the first place."

"There will always be disputes, Trella. The larger the village, the more frequent the arguments. One man's word against another, shopkeepers and customers alike complaining about their dealings."

"The problem, I think, is not what to change first. I think we need to change everything all at once."

Annok-sur reached out and took Trella's hand. "If anyone else said that, I'd laugh. But you . . . do you really think you can replace the customs so easily?"

"No, not easily," Trella said, "but the sooner we start, the easier it will be. Suppose we wanted to stop merchants from sharp dealing. If all the prices for everything were written down, everyone would know them, and it wouldn't be so easy to cheat."

"Most people can't read the symbols. There aren't enough symbols anyway."

"And that, I think, is another thing we must resolve. We must get the clerks together, and have them invent new symbols, ones needed to run a city. There would have to be many more symbols, and they would have to be written down, so that the scribes and clerks don't forget them."

"You'd need many more clerks, as well."

"Yes, more clerks, more symbols, more ways to record agreements, and a person in authority to settle disputes based on these new written records. So we'd have to start there, with a new school for scribes, and a new House to administer the customs." She shook her head, revising her thoughts. "No, they wouldn't be customs any longer. Once they were written down, they would become laws, something that couldn't change on a merchant's or noble's whim."

"Can the people even learn the symbols?" Annok-sur countered. "If they couldn't, they'd still be trusting some scribe or merchant to explain them."

"People would only need to know a few basic symbols. If you're a farmer, then you need to know about crops, bushels, hectares, and farm animals. A craftsman in the city would need to know different symbols, the ones that dealt with his craft. Only the scribes would need to know all the symbols. Whenever someone needed a contract, or to record an agreement or transaction, they would visit one of our new scribes. I think it would work, Annok-sur."

"There would have to be rules established to maintain order," Annok-sur said, warming to the idea. "Perhaps another House might be established, one to govern the growth of Akkad."

"Yes, next to the building where they'll teach and train the scribes, and store the records."

"That will be a large house, then," Annok-sur said, only half-jokingly.

Important contracts were written in clay, most on pottery shards about the size of a woman's hand. Once dried, they could be duplicated, stored, and even transported. The clerks traveling with Eskkar had sent back by boat several baskets containing records, all carefully wrapped to prevent breakage. Storing large quantities of such records would require many large rooms filled with hundreds of shelves to contain the shards.

Trella leaned back, letting her shoulders rest against the wall of the house. She felt the child moving about, and rested her hand on her stomach, trying to comfort the babe within. "Still, it will give the younger sons of the prosperous merchants and craftsmen something to do, a respected calling for those who cannot inherit. Perhaps parents could list their inheritors in advance, and so avoid all those family disputes."

The eldest son generally, but not always, inherited the family business, a practice that often led to quarrels among brothers. When death took the head of the household, brother often fought against brother, with the loser driven out of the family.

"You will change everything, Trella. The nobles will complain about you again."

"Perhaps. But the people, I think, would approve. As would most of the smaller shopkeepers and craftsmen. They'll see the advantage of laws that not only protect them, but provide for stable prices in the future. It's only those grown powerful enough to take advantage of others that will object."

"The people rely on you, Trella. They know you and Eskkar dispense justice, not whim. They'll trust you to keep track of their shops and farms, even their contracts, but not anyone else."

"That's why we must show the people we can control people like Asurak and Rasui."

"Still, you'd better wait until Eskkar returns. Do you think he will approve?"

"If it reduces the number of council meetings my husband has to attend, he'll approve. We spoke about many of these issues right up to the day he left for Bisitun. He wanted new ways of dealing with the people there."

"When will you tell the council?"

"I'm sure it will take several weeks to consider every aspect. You and I will start tomorrow. We'll go over everything we need, and how we think the new Houses will function. We have to be ready to answer every objection from the likes of Rasui. Even Nicar and Corio may not agree with all these ideas. We'll have to find ways to show them the advantages. Nobles Rebba, Decca, and Rasturin, with their big farm holdings, might be more amenable. Nevertheless, we'll need to have every answer prepared in advance, every problem considered, and a solution, a good solution, ready to present." Trella finished with a smile. "For Eskkar to present, that is."

Annok-sur nodded agreement.

Both women knew it would be easier for the men who made up the council to accept such sweeping new changes if Eskkar proposed them. The nobles might know that Trella conceived of the ideas, but it would still be more palatable coming from him. And with the Hawk Clan and the rest of the soldiers still solidly supporting Eskkar, the nobles would need good grounds before they dared to object.

"You'll need more gold, as well."

"Eskkar will find that, in Bisitun. The upriver trade will make the gold flow in Akkad again. Already goods are moving briskly between Akkad and the south. And the nobles and leading merchants will pay to secure their sons positions in the new Houses."

"Let's hope Eskkar returns soon," Annok-sur said, "and laden with goods and gold."

"We'll begin the planning after tomorrow's council session," Trella said. "The sooner we start, the better. And we may need to include others to help us. But I'm sure we can do this."

"More changes for Akkad," Annok-sur said, shaking her head. "When will it end, I wonder?"

12

Twenty miles east of the Euphrates, and more than a hundred miles south of Akkad, Ariamus cursed the hot sun that beat down on him and his men each day. Then he cursed the high desert where they camped, the lack of water that plagued them, the ignorant louts who whined incessantly, and the clouds of sand fleas that tormented man and beast. Finally he swore at Korthac, though Ariamus kept that oath under his breath, lest one of the Egyptians who always seemed to be shadowing his steps hear and inform the grim Egyptian. Even though Korthac had saved his life from the vengeful villagers on the edge of the desert, Ariamus found little pleasure in serving his new master, at least so far.

Ariamus would have liked to do more than curse at the two Egyptian subcommanders in the camp, but that, too, would have to wait. Takany, Korthac's second in command, spoke little, and his eyes expressed no emotion. A brutish man, he maintained tight control of the Egyptians, and they obeyed no order that came from Ariamus without Takany's approval. Nebibi, the other

Egyptian commander, proved more approachable; he spent more time with Ariamus, talking about Korthac's exploits in Egypt. Both had sworn blood oaths to Korthac, Nebibi explained one night after a little extra wine, horrific oaths neither would ever dare to break. Nebibi, at least, understood the need for the new men Ariamus recruited, and did his best to keep the two camps working together. He'd even contributed some of his fighters to help with the training.

Still, Ariamus blamed Korthac for insisting they establish their camp so far away from Akkad and other settlements. Ariamus's new master demanded a place so distant that no word could reach the city about the growing force hidden beyond the fringe of the desert. Each day the situation grew worse, as the number of men and horses under Ariamus's command increased.

Demands for food and water also increased daily. The moment he left this cursed encampment behind couldn't come too soon for Ariamus, even if it meant attacking Akkad's very walls with his bare hands.

The desolate place chosen for his camp lay well off the usual trails. Ariamus camped here twice before in his wanderings, each time for but a single night. The high desert might be a little cooler than the hell of sand and wind Korthac had crossed, but not by much. Containing only a few scrub plants and stunted trees growing among the rocks, it had little to recommend it, except for its desolation.

Worst of all, there was no water, which probably explained why wanderers seldom bothered to come near the rocky hills that circled his growing force. One of the first things Ariamus did was establish a work party for a daily trek to the nearest river, more than ten miles away, and had the men haul back as many skins of water as their horses could carry. In one respect he didn't mind assigning the backbreaking labor. It gave the men something to do, to take their minds off their training and the boredom of waiting for action. Each day, half his troop rode off to gather another day's supply of water for man and beast. Those not on the water detail practiced their riding, improved their swordplay, tended the horses, and waited. Of course, Takany's Egyptians didn't deign to do something so menial as carry water, though they managed to drink more than their share of what arrived in camp.

Ariamus spent most of his time on horseback. With a handful of riders, enough to provide protection without frightening the locals, he rode across the land looking for recruits and horses to add to his band of fighters. He stopped at every village and collection of mud huts too small even for that title. He had gold to offer, gold that first came down the river within a week of Korthac reaching Akkad. More gold arrived each week, payment for the restive force growing under Ariamus, as the Egyptian exchanged ever larger quantities of his gemstones for gold and silver in Akkad.

Korthac's Egyptians kept control of the gold, making sure that Ariamus used it only to buy men, horses, weapons, or supplies. Not that they needed to watch him. Ariamus was too excited by the prospect of looting Akkad. Nothing would please him more than returning there in power, to take revenge on the shopkeepers and merchants who had ordered him about for so many years. They would bow before their former captain of the guard soon enough.

In the initial planning with Korthac, Ariamus had been

more than a little skeptical that their forces could capture
and hold the city. But with the reports coming from Akkad,
he soon began to change his mind. Eskkar, the ignorant
barbarian, had split his forces, and if he remained out of
the city, Ariamus believed they would have a good chance
to capture the Akkad. Each week Ariamus's force grew, as
he enticed more local bandits, wanderers, and even raw
farm boys desperate for any means to escape the endless
drudgery of a farmer's existence.

A shortage of horses plagued Ariamus, but down here,
far south of Akkad, the passage of the Alur Meriki had
caused little damage to the land and livestock. In this part
of the country, marauders and other, smaller clans of
barbarians had taken their toll, but most farms and villages
had survived intact. Horses remained scarce, but not
impossible to get, if you were willing to scour the countryside and pay more than their worth in gold.

Or steal them. Twice he'd ridden into small farm
holdings at night, killed the men, and taken their horses.
He preferred not to do it, as Korthac didn't want to inflame
the countryside against them, lest word reach Akkad.
Nevertheless, Ariamus needed horses for his fighters.
Korthac's plan demanded them. So Ariamus gathered
every mount he could find, at the same time as he trained
his men to ride and to fight.

Not that most of this rabble would ever become true
fighters or horsemen, not in these few weeks. But if they
could swing a sword and ride a horse, Ariamus asked little
more. The rest, those who survived the coming battle,
would have plenty of time to improve their fighting skills
in Akkad.

He heard hoofbeats and looked up to see a rider coming toward him, raising a cloud of dust and no doubt stirring up another wave of sand fleas. Ariamus stood outside his tent until the outrider galloped up.

"Ariamus! Four riders are coming in. I think one of them is Hathor," the man shouted, as excited as a boy taking his first woman.

"Get back to your post, you useless piece of crap," Ariamus ordered. "Of course he's coming. We've been expecting him for two days."

By then the party appeared, crossing the hilly skyline, four men riding toward the camp. Ariamus didn't intend to stand there waiting in the sun, so he went inside his tent. The visitors would want water and care for their horses before they got down to business. Korthac had dispatched his third subcommander, Hathor, the last two times as well. Upon arriving, he might want to count all the men, the horses, and even the cursed weapons. And, of course, count up all the gold expended.

Ariamus had to admit that these Egyptians were thorough. Korthac wanted every man well fed, well armed, and trained in how to use a sword. And be able to use it from horseback. Korthac had stressed that point. Not many of his Egyptians could fight from horseback; they preferred to fight on foot. What Korthac demanded from Ariamus was a troop of horsemen that could be used to sweep the countryside. Those same mounted fighters would prevent the city's inhabitants from fleeing their new master, at the same time as they gathered up new recruits, willing or unwilling.

Two weeks ago, when Hathor came downriver the first

time, he'd told Ariamus how Eskkar had split his soldiers and scattered them over the countryside. That made the horsemen Ariamus trained even more important, as they might have to engage more than one enemy, and one possibly spread out over the land.

On his last visit, Hathor had even dared, in Korthac's name, to inspect the Egyptians, to see them practicing their swordsmanship, and their physical readiness. Hathor "asked" Takany to stage some mock fights with sword and knife; Hathor watched as both the Egyptians and Ariamus's men went through their drills, or charged back and forth waving their swords and shouting their war cries.

Takany's dour face had flushed a darker shade than normal at the insult, but he'd said nothing. The more than fifty Egyptians in the camp trained nearly every day, practicing with sword, axe, and knife, and they impressed Ariamus with their skill. He'd never seen better fighters, certainly not in that number of men. He had no doubt that, in a pitched battle, they would defeat an enemy two or three times their number. But Korthac also knew he couldn't hold Akkad without horsemen, and that's where Ariamus intended to impress his new master.

With a little luck, Ariamus would soon be second in command. Already he had the larger number of fighters reporting to him. That would naturally elevate him above the Egyptian subcommanders, even Takany, because Korthac, once Akkad was taken, would need Ariamus more than he needed his own forces. Besides, plenty of Egyptians were going to die taking the city, which would strengthen Ariamus's position. With a little more luck, Korthac might get killed himself. That would put Ariamus in command, since without Korthac, even hardheaded foreigners like Takany and Nebibi would realize they needed someone from this land if they intended to rule here.

If all went as Korthac planned, then Ariamus would have plenty of time to think about getting rid of Korthac. The Egyptian had taught Ariamus how to play the game, but the pupil intended to rise above the master, even if it took a year or two.

The first step was to court the Egyptian subcommanders. Takany was hopeless, but Hathor and Nebibi would see reason soon enough. Hathor was the lowliest of the three who served Korthac as subcommanders, but the one chosen for all the more difficult tasks, or whenever Korthac needed someone with more wits than brawn. The Egyptian obviously wanted men about him that he could trust, but none too sharp in the head, lest they get ideas of their own. As captain of the guard in Akkad, Ariamus had done the same himself, making sure his subcommanders followed orders without asking too many questions, let alone doing any thinking.

In some ways, Eskkar had been the perfect subcommander. A friendless loner, he kept his mouth shut and obeyed orders, spending as much time as he could away from the village, caring for the horses, and chasing after runaway slaves and petty thieves. Once again, Ariamus wondered how such an insignificant barbarian outcast had ever managed to seize control of Akkad.

Nevertheless, Ariamus didn't have time to daydream about such things now. He needed to hear the latest news from Hathor, and by now Takany would be waiting for him to come to his tent. Ariamus would have to swallow his pride once again and defer to these cursed foreigners. But not for long, he vowed. Not for long.

Hathor had just finished washing the dust from his body when Ariamus strode into Takany's tent. Hathor took another drink of water, though the warm liquid tasted more like moldy leather and horse sweat after its journey under the hot sun to this place. Out of the corner of his eye, he noted Takany looked even grimmer than usual. The man didn't like it when Hathor spoke in Korthac's name. Ignoring Takany's frown, Hathor joined the two Egyptians already sitting cross-legged on the sand, and waved his hand for Ariamus to join them.

"Greetings, Hathor," Ariamus said, his voice filling the tent. "How's the soft life in Akkad? Did you bring more gold? Are you . . ."

"We've been waiting for you," Takany said. "Do not keep me waiting again."

"Last time I came here, you kept me standing outside," Ariamus countered, as he sat. "I didn't feel like cooking in the sun while you three whispered secrets to each other."

"You presume much, Ariamus. You'd better learn to watch your tongue."

"Please, let's not argue amongst ourselves," Hathor interrupted, though he extended a small bow to Takany as he did so. Hathor did remember that last meeting. Takany had insisted on hearing everything first, and then Hathor had to repeat the same message a second time, for Ariamus's edification.

Hathor got right to his master's business. "Korthac wishes to know how ready you are, Ariamus, and how many men and horses you have. The situation in Akkad grows even more favorable. Esskar remains in the north, and the city is at ease. There are barely enough men in Akkad to maintain order."

They all smiled at his news, Hathor noted. "Now, Ariamus, how many men will you have ready to fight in two weeks?"

"Two weeks!" Ariamus sounded dismayed at the early date. "Why so soon?"

"Ariamus has almost ninety men," Takany said, speaking as if the man didn't exist, "though most of them fight like old women."

Korthac, in his wisdom, had warned Hathor about the growing conflict between Ariamus and Takany. The sooner they attacked Akkad, Hathor realized, the better. These two would be at each other's throats soon enough. Either that or Ariamus just might take it into his head to collect his men and ride off, leaving Takany to his own devices. And to Korthac's wrath.

"We must all work together," Hathor said soothingly, trying to keep the peace. "A great prize awaits us. Akkad will provide wealth and a life of ease for all of us, and the sooner we take it the better. But time grows short, and Korthac says we need to move quickly." He turned to Ariamus. "How many men?"

"In three or four more weeks, I can get another thirty or forty men. We're still a little short of horses."

"You only have two weeks, Ariamus," Hathor countered, shaking his head firmly. "Then we need to start moving toward Akkad. We'll have to travel by night, avoiding the roads. Korthac has picked a place to ford the river, and arranged for boats to be waiting for us."

All eyes turned to Ariamus.

"In two weeks . . . probably another twenty, twenty-five men. I think I can get mounts for that many, or at least most of them."

"You'll need food as well," Hathor said, "there won't be any time to scour the land for something to eat, and you must travel in secrecy. If the city gets word that a large band of men is raiding nearby, or approaching, the guards will be doubled and the defenders alerted. But if we move quickly and outrun word of our approach . . ."

The mood in the tent improved considerably at the thought of action. Hathor knew the prospect of a good fight would take everyone's mind off their squabbles. He turned to Takany.

"With our Egyptians and that number of Ariamus's men, Korthac says we will have enough," Hathor said, using his master's name whenever possible. He knew Takany feared nothing on the earth except their leader. "And weapons? You have arms for every man?"

"Yes, every man has at least a sword," Ariamus said. "We've only a few bows, though."

"They won't be needed. And there will be plenty of bows once we're inside Akkad." Hathor didn't mention that, if their men needed bows, then they were finished. He'd seen the Akkadians taking their archery training.

"And Korthac thinks we can win?" Ariamus asked the question, the only one there who would even dare cast doubt upon their master.

"Oh, yes, Ariamus," Hathor said confidently. "I know we can win. We only need to get inside." He looked around the circle. Even Takany had stopped frowning, no doubt willing to do anything to get out of this miserable camp.

"Then everything is settled. Tomorrow I'll return to Akkad," Hathor said smoothly. "Korthac will be pleased to learn that Ariamus has everything he needs, and that all of you will be ready to move in two weeks. Two weeks," he repeated. "Not one day longer. Korthac said there must be no delays, no excuses, no failures, or he will hold all of you accountable. The minute he sends word, you must be ready to move."

No one said anything. Whatever Korthac wished would be done.

"Nebibi, you are to come back to Akkad with me. Then you will return to help guide the men on the final leg of the march."

"I'll give thanks to Isis and Osiris," Nebibi said, "for getting me out of this place."

Hathor turned back to Ariamus. "I'll need four of your best men to return with me to Akkad. Men who won't attract attention, and who can follow orders perfectly and keep their mouths shut. Men who know how to kill and are good at it. Do you have any like that?"

Ariamus lifted his brow. "Yes, but I need all my subcommanders to help. . . ."

"If you need help with the training, Takany can provide it." Hathor caught the momentary frown on Ariamus's face. "I'll meet with those you select now, to see if they're capable. Your best men, Ariamus, nothing less will do. If they're good enough, they'll need good strong horses. Have them ready to ride with me at dawn."

For once, Ariamus stood speechless, his open mouth showing his dismay at losing four good men.

Hathor leaned back and smiled at everyone. His mission had gone remarkably well, and for the next few weeks, the two forces would be too busy training to cause each other trouble. Korthac had shown his wisdom once again by pushing up the date for the attack. Best of all, Hathor would be out of this unhappy place in the morning, and he wouldn't be coming back. He let himself relax.

"Now that Korthac's business is settled, what can I tell you of Akkad?"

13

Trella greeted Nicar and Corio when the two nobles entered the upper room. Seating Nicar in the place of honor at the head of the table, she took the chair across from Corio. In the days before the Alur Meriki invasion, Nicar had led the five Noble Families that ruled Orak. Faced with the city's destruction, and finding no one else willing to risk his neck, Nicar selected Eskkar as the new captain of the guard. In addition, he'd given Eskkar a recently acquired slave girl named Trella to be his helpmate and keep him out of the alehouse at night.

Those two decisions, made less than a year ago, created a future none of them could have foreseen, a future brought about by the common people, long without a voice in their daily affairs. Now they acclaimed Eskkar as their leader, and expected him to protect them not only from barbarian invasions, but also from the power and whims of the noble families.

Today Nicar remained the foremost of the Noble Families, but everyone understood who had the real power in Akkad. While Nicar might regret the loss of his authority, Eskkar and Trella had saved not only his city, but his life and that of his family, when the mob had shouted for their death.

Though their roles had reversed, Trella still felt beholden to him. A good man, she grieved that Nicar had aged much in the last six months. Nearing his sixtieth season, his only remaining son had taken charge of the family's trading ventures in the last few weeks, lifting that burden from his father. Trella planned to use that situation to her advantage.

"I hope today's meeting will be brief, Lady Trella," Corio said, ever in a hurry to be about his business. "It's already past noon, and the Feast of Ishtar has begun." He waved his hand toward the window where the sounds of celebration already echoed throughout the courtyard.

"So Ishtar's priest has reminded me every day for the last few weeks, Corio," Trella answered. "You and your family are attending the feast tonight?"

She'd arranged a major banquet, the first she'd ever given, to honor the goddess and reward those friends who had stood at Eskkar's side during the siege. "There will be an abundance of food and wine. Annok-sur has hired the finest cooks and entertainers in the city."

"Corio's family accompanied us here, Trella," Nicar said. "Now, can you tell us why you asked us here early? I assume you have something special to discuss with us?"

"Yes," Trella said, pushing her hair back from her eyes. "Before Eskkar left, he spoke about proposing a change to our customs, and I wanted to ask your advice before bringing it up at the next council meeting." Trella preferred to speak the truth whenever possible, though she'd been the one who broached the subject of how to rule

Akkad with her husband. She'd started by asking Eskkar about the customs that governed his former clan.

He told her how each clan's leader settled disputes as he chose, with no recourse. Conflicts between clan leaders, if not settled by blood, were resolved by the Alur Meriki ruler, often with the help of the full council. Eskkar compared the customs of his barbarian clan with those of the nobles of Akkad. He'd seen enough of the local customs, enforcing them for the nobles before the invasion, and knew how unjustly they could be administered. To her surprise, Eskkar had several suggestions for changing Akkad's customs and enforcing them less capriciously.

When Trella mentioned changing them into something more permanent, he not only agreed, but suggested they establish similar customs in the north. They spent several hours talking about the way Akkad, Bisitun, and the other northern villages should be ruled. Eskkar had learned the mysteries of the farm as well as those of gold and bronze from Trella, Nicar, and the other nobles, and understood that the more lightly they administered those under their rule, the more wealth would flow to Akkad.

When she'd told Eskkar what she wanted to do, he smiled and wished her luck. She spent the next few weeks preparing for this moment, waiting for exactly the right time to bring the subject before Nicar and Corio, the most influential members of the council of nobles. That time had now arrived. Today's celebration would provide the most opportune moment to launch such a new concept.

"Well, what changes to our sacred customs are you proposing, Trella?" Corio's voice held a hint of humor. "Something new and exciting, I hope."

"I want to alter the way all of our customs are administered." She saw Corio glance at Nicar in surprise. "Not so much change them, but establish them as a code of conduct, laws for all the people of Akkad. I want to set them down in writing, so that everyone can know them, and follow them without fear or worry."

Customs set penalties for crimes, determined the prices paid to the farmers for their produce, and even set the dates for feasts and celebrations. As Akkad had grown more prosperous, customs often changed, and not always for the better. But the nobles had always reserved final say to themselves, and often exempted their own families from the justice they imposed on others.

"Some of the council will object to that," Nicar commented, straightening in his chair, his voice reflecting the seriousness of her suggestion. "They've followed their ways for years, and don't see any reason to change."

"Yes, they follow custom when it suits them," Corio said. "I remember how it was. A price might be agreed upon, the work completed, then the payment reduced or even withheld. And no one to appeal to, either."

An artisan by trade, Corio had joined the ranks of the nobles when he agreed to build the wall that now surrounded Akkad. For him, the customs had not always operated fairly, something Trella had counted upon.

"It seems to me that prices vary, as well," Trella said, changing the subject before the two men began arguing about the past. "A bushel of grain set at one price when the nobles deal with each other, and a different price for everyone else." She had worked with Nicar's finances, and learned the details of his commerce. "That has led to discontent among the people, as well as disputes in the marketplace."

The child within her stirred about, and Trella shifted in her chair. She watched Nicar's eyes for any clues as to his thoughts. This would seem to him like one more way to lessen the authority of the nobles.

"Nobles," she said, "since Eskkar drove off the Alur Meriki, nearly all of his time has been spent settling disputes over prices, petty crimes, even ownership of homes. You both know him. You know he should be thinking about Akkad's defense, about building the new wall, not such petty squabbles."

Neither man said anything. They knew Eskkar had no patience for such matters. "By making Eskkar the final arbiter in such affairs, we waste everyone's time. If all the customs were written down, turned into laws that applied to all who live within Akkad's control, think how many hours laboring over such matters could be saved. And if these new laws were administered fairly, I believe trade and farming would increase, with still more benefits to the city's merchants and traders."

"And leave Eskkar in a better mood." Corio laughed.

Even Nicar found a smile at that. "Certainly that would be something to be desired. What exactly are you proposing, Trella?"

"First I want to set the prices for all the common items that are bought, sold, or traded in the marketplace. If farmers know in advance what price they will receive for their produce, they'll be easier to deal with, and can concentrate on growing their crops, and not worry about what they'll be paid for them."

"Including the nobles?" Nicar asked.

"What merchants sell their goods for on the river or in the countryside is their business. But in Akkad they'll pay one price, a fair price, with no cheating or sharp dealing."

"And if there is cheating?"

"Then, Nicar, the nobles will face the same penalties as anyone else. As the customs say, if a man tries to cheat on an exchange, he's to pay double. That would be the law of Akkad and apply even to the nobles."

"And all this would be written down? With everyone agreeing to it?" Corio looked dubious as he leaned on the table. "You'll need a half-dozen clerks just to keep track of everything."

Trella shook her head. "I think we'll probably need about twenty. To keep records of the laws, the penalties, the prices, contracts, the ownership of the land and houses . . . They'll have to invent new symbols to record events, and probably new ways of calculating sums."

"You're creating a whole new category of apprenticeship," Nicar said, trying to judge the extent of what Trella had proposed. "This will change everything."

So it would, Trella knew, and probably to a greater extent than Nicar realized. "It will change our future for the better. Akkad will be a better place to live and work."

"To train so many clerks . . . store so many records, you'll need a new building to house them, their teachers, servants, and families," Corio mused. "Clay records require large rooms with many shelves to store them." He fell silent, no doubt already thinking about how he would design and build such a structure.

"Yes, I imagine there is much more about this than I've

considered." As ever, she preferred to let others figure out what might be needed, though she and Annok-sur had spent the last few weeks going over the likely impacts on their society. Between them, they'd considered all the ramifications. At least she hoped they'd thought of everything.

"How would you pay for such an undertaking?" Nicar said. "It will be many months before Akkad returns to full prosperity, and even then, this will require much gold."

"Well, Eskkar will bring in additional taxes from the countryside," Trella said. "And those wishing to become clerks will pay for their apprenticeships in advance. That should bring enough to feed and house them." She turned to Corio. "We would need a place for them to live and work. I was hoping you would build one for us, Corio, and perhaps charge us less than your usual price?"

It took Corio only a moment to understand her meaning. If he didn't discount the price, she would find another architect. Not that it mattered. He'd still make a good profit, only a bit less than usual. "Of course, Lady Trella. I would be honored to construct a building for you, say at a discount of one-tenth?"

"That is more than generous, Master Builder. And perhaps you can help determine the prices and penalties for Akkad's other builders? Along with, of course, the other nobles." Trella accepted that he would make sure the law favored the artisans, but that would be a small price to pay. Besides, the poor didn't pay others to build for them. They built their own huts out of mud. The wealthy had more, and so they would pay more.

She turned to Nicar. "I hope you will help me draft the laws. A common set of laws that will apply to all."

"How will these laws be administered?" Nicar stroked his beard, a dubious frown on his face.

"I hoped you would tell me, Nicar. I would like the council to appoint someone to oversee the drafting of these new rules, and then preside over their administration. That someone would be responsible only to Eskkar, and would make sure the laws were applied fairly to everyone— noble, merchant, shopkeeper, and farmer alike."

Corio laughed in understanding. "You've been chosen, Nicar. You'll have to deal with it."

Nicar clearly hadn't expected this. "What you ask … why, it will take months … even years. And my business … what would I do?"

"You said yourself that your son is prepared to take over your family's business," Trella said, noting the noble's discomfort. "Perhaps he is readier than you know. Besides, who else in Akkad do the people respect as much as you, Nicar? And you'll have help. The council will provide whatever you need. I'm sure there are plenty of younger sons, men with their wits about them, who would appreciate the opportunity to serve. As Corio says, this would be a whole new House, a House of Laws, with a staff of clerks and administrators needed to ensure its honest application. You'd be deciding disputes between all of Akkad's inhabitants."

"One of my sons is more clerk than artisan," Corio offered. "He can't plumb a line to save his life. Any house he builds is certain to fall down sooner or later. But he knows the symbols, and might prefer such an apprenticeship. It would be far better for the boy to be a scribe than a builder."

"The people trust you, Nicar," Trella went on. "And the

chance to establish a new House, one of your own choosing, accepting only the best and most honest of our people. You would be honored by all."

"Accept the honor, Nicar," Corio added. "The other nobles will rely on you to treat them fairly."

"What would this new position be called?" Nicar asked with a sigh, looking as if he might be tempted in spite of his usual caution.

"I'm not sure," Trella answered. "Since you'd have to determine the truthfulness of what men say and do, it seemed to me that the title of 'judge' would be appropriate. Akkad's chief judge would be accountable only to Eskkar. He and I believe it is one of the most important duties of a ruler to give just decisions in resolving disputes. You know how much Akkad needs such an office, and who better to fill it?"

"Chief judge of the City of Akkad," Corio said. "Sounds impressive, doesn't it?"

It did indeed, Trella agreed. In a few months, certainly less than a year, the title would change to "The lord's judge," or even "The king's judge." The title of "king" meant ruler of all the land, one blessed by the gods and dispensing their favor. It had never been used in these lands, but the word "king" could wait a little longer, until the people grew ready to accept it.

"Say yes, Nicar," she pleaded, touching his hand with her own. "Your name will be remembered forever in Akkad. And think of all the good you can do."

He looked from one to the other, and lifted his hands in surrender. "When do you wish me to begin?"

"Put your affairs in order. In a week or so, we can begin

figuring out what will be needed."

"I thought I would be getting some rest in my old age, Trella. Now you'll have me working from dawn to dusk."

Longer than that, Trella thought. "Noble Nicar, I believe this will be as good for you as for the city. We'll have much to discuss, but we can start whenever you're ready."

"Since that's settled, can we get on with the feast?" Corio's tone made Nicar and Trella laugh. "I can hear my granddaughter squealing with delight even from here."

"Yes, I want to greet your wife and children," Trella said. "Perhaps I can find some extra treats for them. My thanks to you both."

When the two men left, Trella felt pleased that one of the day's more important items had been concluded. Nicar's honesty would reflect favorably on Eskkar's personal code of justice. The nobles would grumble and complain about losing more of their privileges, but they would see the benefits to themselves soon enough. And they might even believe they could influence Nicar's judgments, but she knew her former owner better than that.

No, she'd moved Akkad another step forward, this time using the nobles' self-interest to solidify and strengthen Eskkar's rule. Eventually the people would come to trust Lord Eskkar's arbiter of the laws, and, until then, they could appeal to Eskkar if they believed themselves treated unjustly. The more they trusted Eskkar and herself, the more they relied on their leaders, the safer her unborn child would be. In time, the people would accept her son as their ruler without hesitation.

Assuming, of course, that she carried a male child. If she

delivered a baby girl, then she would have to get pregnant again, as soon as possible. Eskkar needed an heir to carry on his line, just as Akkad needed that same heir for stability, to know that in the coming years, Eskkar's son, his inheritor, would be there to protect and defend them and their families.

The child's safety had become even more important than her own. Trella remembered all too well how she had changed from a noble's daughter to a slave-trader's property in a single night. Such a fate must never happen to Eskkar's sons and daughters. To protect her firstborn, she would change the customs of Akkad to ensure the people felt safe and secure under Eskkar's rule. Nothing would stand in her way, not the nobles, not the wealthy merchants, not even the soldiers. All of them must bow to Eskkar's rule, and to her design for building a mighty city.

Patting her stomach to soothe the babe, she followed Nicar and Corio to the door. At the landing, she caught Annok-sur's eye, and nodded.

With the issue of drafting new laws resolved, only two more items remained before she could enjoy the feast: her separate meetings with Gatus and then Korthac.

A few moments later, Gatus entered the workroom, closing the door behind him.

"What is it, Trella," he asked. "Is anything wrong?"

"I'm sure it's nothing, Gatus," she said, but her face remained serious as she took her seat across from the soldier. "I know your messengers returned this morning, and I wanted a word with you before the feast gets under way."

At her urging, Gatus had sent a few riders out to check on the two regular patrols guarding Akkad. The patrols rode a gradual circle around the city, returning every five or six days. He'd instructed the messengers to make contact with each patrol. Afterward, the messengers would then ride a great arc to the east and south, looking for any unrest.

"So, is everything in the countryside as it should be? How far did your riders go?"

"The patrols are about forty miles from here, one to the east and the other to the south. They say there's little trouble anywhere, especially since Eskkar went north. Even the bandits in the west and south seem to have drifted away. Perhaps they heard what happened at Bisitun, and took the lesson to heart."

"Perhaps. But I'm still troubled by Korthac. We've learned little more than what he told us himself that first day we met. The women have failed to learn anything, and even Tammuz and his customers haven't found a way to get inside his rooms."

"Maybe there's nothing to learn," Gatus said. "Just because he keeps control of his men doesn't make him dangerous."

"His treatment of his men is what concerns me. They stay inside, away from women. They don't gamble in the marketplace, drink in the alehouses, or visit the prostitutes on the river."

"So he's a hard taskmaster, but there have been no fights, no thefts. He said he didn't want them running about until they'd learned the language and customs. They've only been here a month or so."

"Actually, it's been nearly two months. But I suppose you're right." Trella wasn't convinced, but she had no facts to argue with Gatus. "Still, I want to be sure the countryside is secure."

"It's quieter than it's ever been. With Eskkar up north, and Bantor following the Alur Meriki to the southeast, the countryside has been swept clean of bandits. Even the lands west of the river are peaceful, and they were mostly untouched by the barbarians. There's never been much there except isolated farms. Have you heard anything different along the river?"

Each day, boats arrived and departed Akkad, heading for the villages downriver, some going as far as Sumeria and the great ocean.

"No, the villages on the Tigris seem peaceful enough. The boat captains report no unrest, and fewer bandits and pirates than they're used to seeing."

Gatus shrugged. "Well, what does it matter? When Eskkar returns in a few weeks, he'll bring back at least another thirty soldiers, as well as new recruits eager to join Akkad's soldiers."

Trella and Gatus had both spoken to Eskkar's messenger. He'd arrived from Bisitun this morning, bringing news that Eskkar intended to remain up north at least another two or three weeks.

"He seems pleased with his new woman," Trella said.

Gatus looked down at the floor, and shrugged. "Nothing for you to concern yourself about, Trella. And it's important that Bisitun be well secured. I'm sure he'll be back soon enough."

Trella had learned of Lani's activities even before

Gatus. One of the first messengers from Bisitun had mentioned Lani to his woman, who immediately relayed the information to Trella. At first she hadn't been concerned, but as the weeks passed, she felt her concern growing. Still, she gave no indication to anyone that she worried about Eskkar's dalliance.

"I'm sure you're right, Gatus. But since he remains away, I'm uneasy about the countryside. Could you move the patrols out farther from the city? Say another twenty or thirty miles in every direction?"

"Well, it would take more men and horses. And I'd need more messengers riding back and forth. Do you really think it's necessary?

"Humor me, then," she said, leaning toward him and touching his arm. "And you can tell your riders there will be extra silver for their labors. A few more sweeps before Eskkar returns. Have them increase their distance at least thirty miles."

"For extra silver, they'll ride an even larger circle," he laughed. "I'll send them out in a day or so. . . ."

She touched his arm again. "Send them tomorrow, Gatus, as soon as they recover from the feast."

"You're that concerned about this Korthac?"

"It's not just him. Besides, you must bear with a pregnant woman. As you say, Eskkar will be back soon, but until then, I find myself often worrying." She laughed at her own weakness. "Oh, and there's one more request. I want a rider for a special assignment, to journey to the far northwest. Do you have anyone you can trust? He'll need to be a strong horseman and have his wits about him."

"Will he have to do any fighting?"

"No, merely gather some information. You can offer a gold coin in addition to his regular pay."

"For that, I'd almost go myself. I'll talk to some of the men tomorrow, and find one to your liking."

"Then once again you have my thanks, old friend." She stood. "And now it's time to begin the feast. I've kept you away from the food and wine long enough."

She escorted him to the door, and they descended the stairs together. Annok-sur waited there, along with the servants. The workroom would also be used to entertain guests, and they needed time to prepare it. Trella planned to meet with Korthac there.

As he'd already become one of the city's more important traders, Korthac had received and accepted her invitation. The Egyptian remained a mystery, keeping to himself and staying aloof from the usual Akkadian ways. Her informers had learned nothing useful.

She wanted to understand Korthac better, to learn firsthand what drove the man. Only then would her curiosity be satisfied. Trella hoped to draw him out during today's festival. Perhaps wine and exotic foods would help loosen his tongue.

14

Korthac didn't bring any of his usual bodyguards to the feast. Instead he brought Hathor, the only one of his three subcommanders who'd accompanied him into Akkad, and the only one with the wits and self-control to act the part. Aside from Hathor's trips downriver, his primary responsibility entailed keeping the men under control, away from wine, and apart from the locals. Every day that task grew harder, and the men more difficult to keep under discipline. They'd earned their silver, survived the desert, and now wanted to take some leisure in this strange new city whose pleasures beckoned them. Fortunately the men respected Hathor, who urged them to control themselves a little longer. Korthac knew he needed to keep the men restrained.

With only a handful of men in Akkad, Korthac had too much to lose to take any chances with a drunken soldier getting into trouble. He'd ordered one whipped last week. Only yesterday Hathor had knocked another to the ground. Both Korthac and Hathor reminded their men again and again that, in a few weeks, they'd have plenty of

gold and unlimited opportunities to enjoy the women of
Akkad.

Korthac's other two subcommanders, Takany and
Nebibi, remained across the river with Ariamus, keeping a
watchful eye on the man and helping raise and train the
desperate men they recruited. Korthac felt certain he could
rely on Ariamus, at least as long as the gold kept flowing.
More than six weeks had passed since Korthac arrived in
Akkad, and he'd received a report each week about
Ariamus's progress.

Korthac's business as a trader provided a legitimate
reason to spend hours at the docks with a few of his men,
meeting ships as they arrived, doing a little trading here
and there.

Occasionally a boat carried one of Ariamus's men, who
would sit with the Egyptian and report. Korthac made sure
the messenger got right back aboard a ship heading south.
With Trella's spies everywhere, there must be no boasting
words or smug looks to give away his plan.

According to Hathor's latest report, the former captain
of the guard had already mustered over ninety men, almost
all of them mounted, and most of them claiming to have
fighting experience. Ariamus had dispensed plenty of
Korthac's gold and silver, along with promises of future
loot to recruit these men. Korthac doubted they would
come close to the quality of his Egyptians, but right now he
needed bodies. With enough men who could at least swing
a sword, Korthac would seize power in Akkad.

More than half the city's soldiers were away, either with
Eskkar or Bantor. That meant, on any given day, less than
a hundred men maintained order, watched the walls, and

manned the gates. Korthac had no doubt his seventy Egyptians could take the city from within, as long as they didn't get involved in an archery battle. He'd watched the Akkadian soldiers practice, and seen what they could do with the bow. But in close-up fighting, his men would prevail. Holding Akkad would be another matter, and for that he needed Ariamus and his men, and, equally as important, their horses.

In a few more weeks, as the entire city knew, Bantor and his men would return from the south. Korthac wanted to act before their arrival. Eskkar, proving as unpredictable as everyone said, lingered in Bisitun. Nevertheless, the barbarian might return to Akkad at any time, probably bringing with him at least half his forces. If he stayed away a few more weeks, Korthac's work would be much simpler. He'd been in Akkad long enough to understand local politics. The nobles who formed the ruling council were merely traders, men who dealt with buying and selling, not fighting, and all of them intimidated by Eskkar's soldiers. Several chafed at Eskkar and Trella's new restrictions on their authority. The people wouldn't rally around any of them. A few public executions, followed by distribution of a few gold coins, would silence both traders and nobles, and bend them to his rule.

Trella might provide such a rallying point, but he intended to take care of her when the time came. And without Eskkar here to rouse the inhabitants and give them the will to resist, the city would fall like an overripe apple from a tree into Korthac's waiting hands.

Eskkar would have to die, of course, but that could happen just as easily in the north as here in Akkad. As soon as Ariamus raised another twenty or thirty men, Korthac would strike. He'd take the city, then destroy the rest of Eskkar's forces piecemeal. Only a fool divided his forces. In his many battles, Korthac had learned one thing— concentrate his fighters and overwhelm his enemy. It had worked in Egypt and it would work here. He looked forward to teaching this Eskkar the same lesson.

Putting such ideas out of his mind, he thought about today's celebratory feast. Korthac could smile at that, the futility of the men of this land relying on Ishtar, a female deity, for protection. As foolish as the men of Akkad relying on Trella. Eskkar's wife had planned a special repast at her home to celebrate some incomprehensible aspect of Ishtar's power, though the occasion also gave thanks for the deliverance of the city from the barbarian invasion, and for Eskkar's recent success in Bisitun.

Whatever the reasons, Korthac recognized it for what it was, a chance for Trella to entertain and impress her followers with her authority. All the powerful and influential people in the city had received their invitations, a black-painted piece of pottery bearing Eskkar's mark on one side and an image of the goddess on the other. Only the lucky few bearing the invitation, and their retainers, would be admitted to Eskkar's house. The rest of Akkad would celebrate in the streets, probably long into the night. Korthac had already resigned himself to a night without sleep, with the city full of noise and revelry.

He'd received the invitation three days ago, and, befitting his new status in Akkad, no doubt one of the first to be delivered. This morning he'd coached Hathor in his role, making sure the dour soldier knew how to behave, and reminding him once again to make sure he gave no offense. Korthac had even bought a new tunic for his subcommander, something that would reflect favorably on his employer's status.

The late afternoon sun drifted toward the horizon when, wearing his finest garment and new leather sandals, Korthac strode through the streets to Eskkar's gate, Hathor at his side. Naturally his subcommander carried a sword, but Korthac went unarmed. Weapons would not be permitted inside the courtyard, the usual policy to ensure guests who drank too much didn't wind up killing each other over some perceived slight.

Of course the weapons' ban also protected Trella, and Korthac had to admit that her guards knew their business, staying alert and watching the crowds wherever she walked about the city.

Reaching Eskkar's gate, Korthac and Hathor had to wait in line, as the guards checked invitations and made sure none of the guests were armed.

"Greetings, Honorable Korthac." The guard bowed slightly as he took the clay shard from Korthac's hand. "Are there more in your party?"

"No, just the two of us." Korthac gave the soldier a friendly smile. Hathor had already removed his sword belt and handed it to another of Trella's guards. Hathor even managed a tight smile as he did so.

"Please enter Lord Eskkar's house, honored guests." The guard bowed again, already turning to greet the next in line.

Inside the courtyard, a half-dozen tables held pitchers of wine, bread covered with honey, platters of fruit and sweets. A clay bowl in the center of each table held a large spray of flowers, each table offering a different blossom. Smoke rose from the rear of the courtyard, as well as from the kitchens, and the scent of crisping meat hung in the air. On the roof opposite Eskkar's quarters, musicians played their flutes, and a juggler tossed his brightly painted wooden balls high in the air.

The courtyard, big as it was, couldn't hold everyone, and the guests mingled inside the main house as well, talking and gesturing. Servants poured the wine, mixed equally with water, and several guests appeared to be under the wine-god's spell already.

Korthac spotted several nobles from the ruling council, all of them distinguished by the dark blue trim on their tunics, a color reserved for the ruling families. He accepted a brimming cup from one of the table attendants, then moved as close to the rear wall as he could get without moving into the cooking area. Some of the guests appeared to be nothing more than common tradesmen, still wearing their ragged and dirt-stained tunics. At least a dozen soldiers were scattered about, the Hawk Clan emblem on their shoulders, mingling with the guests as if they were equals. Unlike the rest of those invited, the Hawk Clan alone carried weapons, either short swords or knives. They, Korthac noted, did not have wine cups in their hands.

Women made up almost half the crowd, wearing their finest garments, standing beside their men or gossiping together. Most did not even cover their heads with scarves, a custom Korthac still hadn't gotten used to.

"Honorable Korthac, may I offer you some of Lady Trella's best wine?"

He turned to find Annok-sur standing at his side, a small pitcher in one hand, a wine cup in the other. Korthac smiled at her as he exchanged his half-empty cup for the new one. "I thank you for your gift, Annok-sur." He took a sip. The sweet wine had a pleasing odor, a far better blend than what he had picked up at the table. "This is very good. My thanks to Lady Trella." He looked about, but didn't see his hostess. "Is Lady Trella unwell?"

"No, she's resting upstairs," Annok-sur said with a smile of her own. "She'd be pleased if you wish to visit her. She enjoys your stories about the land of Egypt."

And always interrupted each story with a dozen questions that probed for any detail of his past life, Korthac recalled. "Of course. Who would resist such a generous hostess." He turned to Hathor. "Wait here." He didn't like leaving the man alone, but it would look odd to bring him into the house.

Annok-sur weaved her way through the crowd, and Korthac trailed in her wake, annoyed that he had to follow in any woman's footsteps. He'd never been inside Eskkar's house before. Looking about, he saw the great room as crowded as the courtyard. Most of the guests stayed close to a long table loaded with wine and food, trying to get as much of the free fare as they could.

A guard kept the stairs to the upper rooms clear, but he stepped aside and nodded at Annok-sur as they passed. Another guard stood at the top of the landing. Looking about, Korthac studied Trella's private quarters as he entered, quarters that would soon be his. Benches and stools lined the walls, and a small table held pitchers of wine and water, but no food. Korthac recognized the captain of the guard, Gatus, sitting next to Trella near to the window. Corio stood nearby, with his wife and two sons, talking to one of the nobles who operated several boats that plied the river trade. Nicar, his wife, their son, and daughter-in-law stood together, talking excitedly among themselves.

Trella rose from her seat as Korthac crossed the room. Surprised by her size, he realized her pregnancy had progressed since he'd last seen her. Even the loose-fitting dress she wore couldn't conceal her condition. He'd always found pregnant women distasteful, unclean somehow. Their bloated bodies should be hidden away, out of sight, until they produced their offspring, preferably without annoying their betters. Korthac had fathered more children than he could remember, but had never cared for any of them or their mothers, either. A woman's children made her weak and easy to manage, and he looked forward to Trella's delivery.

"Greetings, Lady Trella." He bowed low to show his respect.

"Welcome to our home, Honorable Korthac." She bowed politely to him, like any respectable wife greeting her husband's guests.

"A blessing to the goddess Ishtar for your future family, and for your invitation to share in her blessings," he intoned, fulfilling the courtesy the celebration required.

"You learn our customs well, Honorable Korthac." She turned to Gatus. "Can our guest take your seat for a moment, Gatus?"

"Yes, he can have it," Gatus replied, getting up and stretching. "I need something solid to eat, anyway. I'll take your leave, Trella." He bowed to her, then to Korthac.

"Sit beside me," Trella said, resuming her seat again. "I find I tire easily, and preparing for the feast has kept me busy since early this morning."

"The city is praising your name, Lady Trella, and thanking you for the gifts of food and wine." For a city reputed to be pressed for gold, Trella had managed to buy enough food to give nearly everyone in Akkad a good meal and enough ale to wash it down.

"And you, Korthac, have you decided to remain in our city?"

He'd spread the word that he considered living in the countryside, or perhaps even downriver. The news had sent a dozen traders to his door, entreating him to stay and trade his gemstones in Akkad. The simple rumor had helped him make a dozen new friends.

"I think I'll stay in Akkad, Lady Trella." He might as well tell her the truth. She knew no merchant would willingly leave the city and all its advantages. "I'm still looking for a new house, perhaps something like this one. I heard this once belonged to a merchant?"

"Yes, but Nicar loaned it to Eskkar for the siege. Afterward, my husband paid Nicar for it."

"When does your husband return, Lady Trella? I'm looking forward to meeting him, if even half the stories I've heard are true."

She laughed. "That's what they are, Honorable Korthac, half-true. But he is a strong leader who cares for his people. I think you will like him."

"I'm sure I will, Lady Trella." I'll like him better when he's dead, which will be soon enough, Korthac thought, and then he'd wipe that smile off her face. He hated having to restrain himself around anyone, let alone an upstart young girl.

"Now tell me, Honorable Korthac, when are you going to let your men move about the city? I hear they spend all their time cooped up inside that dreadful inn."

"My servants are uncouth men. Many are not even used to living in a village, let alone a city like Akkad. But they were all I could find to accompany me on my journey." Korthac kept his tone soothing. His time would come soon enough. "I would prefer to keep them out of trouble, at least until they've learned to speak your language and understand Akkad's customs. A week or two after I'm established in my new home, they'll be ready to go about on their own."

"The merchants will be glad to see them."

"As glad as my men will be, I can promise you that." He saw a hint of disbelief in her eyes, and wondered if his words sounded too condescending.

"Have you been able to sell your gemstones for a fair price?"

"That's hard to say, Lady Trella. Some of my pieces have moved quickly enough, but others"—he shrugged—"I'm not so sure. Until one has lived in a place for some time, it is hard to know what makes for a good trade. It's difficult enough for me to know an honest price. That's why I'm keeping a close watch on my men, to make sure they aren't cheated." And meanwhile giving away most of my jewels for far less than what they're worth.

"You've picked up our language well, Honorable Korthac. You speak with only the slightest accent. It's hard to believe you've learned it so quickly."

"A trader must master many tongues, as I'm sure you know. And aside from trading, I'm spending most of my days learning your language and customs." He reached inside his tunic. "But I've nearly forgotten." He brought out a small cotton pouch laced shut with a thin strand of dark leather. "This is for you, Lady Trella. A gift from the land of Egypt."

He handed her the pouch, watching her deft hands as she untied the knot and upended the contents into her palm. An emerald the size of a man's thumb, cut into a square shape and banded with a strip of gold attached to a thick golden chain, glistened in the light.

"Honorable Korthac, this is . . . I've never seen such a stone."

Korthac relaxed as his hostess stared at the jewel, fascinated by its deep green color. As well she should, he thought. These lands produced very few of them, and those were mostly small and of poor quality. He remembered lifting the jewel from the neck of a rich merchant's wife in Egypt. On her knees, she pleaded with him not to take her favorite possession, so he handed it back to her, watching her eyes fill with gratitude. He let her hold it for a moment, until he plunged his sword into her belly. Then he took it from her and dangled it in front of her face, while she watched her blood stain the ground until she died.

"It is a beautiful gem, Lady Trella, but who else in Akkad should have it, if not you?"

"I'm honored, but I cannot accept this. It's much too valuable."

"Lady Trella, I insist. I have others, just as fine. By wearing this one, you'll encourage all the other women in

Akkad to buy my stones. And perhaps, if I need help in some matter or another, I can turn to you." He watched her eyes linger on the stone. No woman could refuse such a gift, he knew. He'd always found it so easy to manipulate women.

Trella stared at the stone for a moment, then returned it to the pouch. "It is too much, but I thank you for this gift. It's the most beautiful necklace I've ever seen." She turned to him and smiled, a smile full of warmth that he hadn't seen before. "But, Honorable Korthac, I will not wear the necklace until after the child has been born. Otherwise the gods might be jealous."

Korthac concealed his disappointment. He would have preferred to have her flaunt the jewel at today's feast, making everyone aware of his gift and his special place in her favor. But it didn't really matter. He'd take the stone back from her soon enough, and when he did, his pleasure would not be so easily satisfied.

"May your child bring you great happiness, Lady Trella." For as long as it lives, he thought.

On the other side of Akkad, no lamps or fires burned in Tammuz's alehouse. The sun had gone down moments ago, but for once the alehouse stood empty. The usual customers had departed, to partake of the food and ale that flowed freely today in Ishtar's honor, thanks to Lady Trella. A few would undertake to help themselves to goods left unattended, especially when their owners grew lax from too much wine. En-hedu heard laughter and the sound of loud voices coming from the lane, rising and falling as people passed to and fro.

Since there were no customers, En-hedu asked Tammuz if he would close the alehouse for a few hours. He suggested they walk the lanes and enjoy the crowds, but En-hedu asked him to wait. She left their chamber and went into the common room, closed the door to the lane, and set the bar in its groove. When she returned to the bedroom, Tammuz started to rise from the table.

"No, don't get up. There is something I wish you to do for me," she began, rushing the words a little more than she'd wanted.

There was just enough light for her to see the puzzled look on her master's face.

"Why, what do you need?"

She stood directly in front of him. "I want you to take me to bed." En-hedu had forced the words out, and now they couldn't be called back. She pulled her dress up over her head, and stood there, not even a step away. He'd seen her without her clothes many times, but she'd never displayed herself like this, never simply stood there for him to see. And enjoy. She took a deep breath, and moved her legs a little apart.

His eyes caressed her body, lingering on her breasts and the jutting mound of hair beneath her belly.

"En-hedu," he began, "are you sure . . ."

"Yes, I'm sure. I need to be your woman, to bring you the pleasure of the gods, and to give you children. More than that, I want to please you. You are a good man, and I want to stay with you forever."

He stood and took her in his good arm. "You will never leave me, En-hedu. I want you with me always. And you do not have to . . ."

She leaned closer and kissed him, a long kiss that silenced him. When the kiss ended, he had her breast in his hand, causing her to gasp with pleasure.

"Your clothes, master," she said huskily, feeling a wave of pleasure run through her body. Her head felt light, and she wondered if she would fall when he released her. She led him to the bed, then helped him with his tunic, for once her fingers moving clumsily instead of with their usual efficiency. Then they tumbled onto the bed, her head swimming with new sensations. This time he kissed her, and something shot through her like a tongue of fire. She felt herself grow moist between her legs, accompanied by an unfamiliar flash of warmth that excited her even more.

Now his hands roamed her body, exploring, squeezing, touching. He moved along her body, and she felt the heat of his skin against her. She moaned when he stroked her mound, and he stopped.

"Don't stop," she gasped, as surprised at her words as the speed at which she uttered them. "Don't stop." She pressed his hand against her, holding him there until his fingers slipped inside her. Never had she felt this way. There was no pain, no roughness to make her wince or cry out. Instead a wonderful feeling of warmth passed over her in waves. En-hedu heard herself laugh, a tiny sound that startled her as much as it did Tammuz. She'd never laughed in bed before.

Before he could speak, she grasped his shoulders and pulled him on top of her, spreading her legs wide, using her hand to guide him inside her.

This time she heard herself moan with pleasure, and he whispered something. En-hedu didn't hear the words, but they didn't matter. She wrapped her legs around his body and clutched him to her.

She felt him hesitate, but then he began moving against her, thrusting himself and twisting his hips faster and faster. She moaned in pleasure, arching her back, while he pushed himself deeper inside her. Then he cried out her name again and again, his body moving uncontrollably, as he drove himself into her. She heard herself cry out, as much at the pleasure she was giving as her own, though her own secret place trembled uncontrollably as it grew even more moist.

At last he slumped against her, breathing hard, still murmuring her name over and over, telling her he loved her and that she must never leave him.

"Never, master," she promised him, "I will never leave you."

When he began to move off of her, she giggled and held him tight. "No, stay where you are. I want to feel your body against mine."

"Oh, yes," he said, whispering the words in her ear. "Hold me tight. That was so good . . . so good."

She held him in her strong arms, feeling proud that she could please him so easily. Caressing his face with one hand, she felt glad the darkness hid her smile. She kissed him again, and suddenly he responded, his tongue penetrating her mouth and exciting her. She felt him growing hard again, so she slid her hands down his back and pulled him tight against her. That elicited a gasp of pleasure from him, as he buried his face in her neck and hair.

But only for a moment. He started moving again, growing firmer, each thrust sending a wave of pleasure through her, and she heard herself moan. Another wave of pleasure swept through her. This time it lasted a long, long time.

Only a single lamp burned in Trella's bedroom. The feast had finally ended, at least for Trella and her household. She sat on the bed, Annok-sur next to her, holding Korthac's emerald in her hand.

"And he asked for nothing, Trella? No gift in return?"

"Nothing. Just my favor. He didn't mention Eskkar, didn't even suggest that I tell him about this great gift. As if Eskkar didn't matter."

"What will you do with it?" Annok-sur set the precious stone down on the bed between them.

"Nothing, for now. After the child comes, as soon as I can, I'll sell it. It will fetch enough to pay Corio's builders for some time, I'm sure."

"If you can find someone with enough gold to buy it, at anywhere near what it's worth." Annok-sur sighed. "Perhaps you should keep it."

"No. If the people saw me wearing such a thing, they'd lose their trust in me. How could I ask everyone to make sacrifices for the sake of the wall, if I showed myself in public wearing a jewel worth so much?" Trella shook her head. "But this Korthac . . . something about him troubles me even more than when he first arrived. You've learned nothing new about him?"

Annok-sur sighed. "Little enough. His men are never out of his or that Hathor's sight. He bought two women in the slave market, to cook and satisfy his men, but they rarely go out. When they do, they're always escorted by one or two of his men. We've tried to speak with them, but they've been warned not to speak to anyone, and they're too frightened to disobey. They buy their goods, or wash their clothing in the river, and return to Korthac's inn. Aside from that, they seldom leave his house. I've seen them. They look wretched."

"He's hiding something, Annok-sur."

"Maybe he committed some crime in Egypt, something so horrible that he fears it even here."

"Whatever his secret, we need to discover it."

"I don't know what else to try, Trella. We watch his men, we watch him, but all he does is spend time at the trading carts along the river. Still, he can't live like this forever. Even servants need time for themselves."

Trella picked up the emerald and returned it to the pouch. "I think I'd give this away to learn what Korthac is hiding." She knotted the lace securely. Standing, she went to the bed and knelt down. Pushing hard, she slipped aside part of the leg of the bed, exposing a tiny hollow barely large enough to conceal the pouch. When she fitted the wood back in place, the jewel had vanished. Only a very keen eye and a close examination would detect the tiny compartment. There were more such hiding places secreted about the bedroom. She'd searched the room often enough, and discovered three others, but there might still be more. The previous owner had many secrets.

"Perhaps you should send word for Eskkar to return," Annok-sur said. "He's been away long enough."

"What would I say to him? That some rich trader worries me? That I can't find out if he's hiding something?

He wouldn't know any more than we do." She shook her head. "Besides, he's sent back gold as well as goods from Bisitun, and the council is happy that the lands up there are being pacified."

"And this new woman Eskkar is keeping? Suppose he begins to forget about you?"

"The child will bring him back," Trella said, though the same doubts had visited her. "Let him have his pleasures for now. He risked his life taking the village."

"At least Bantor will return soon."

"That will make both of us feel better, Annok-sur."

"Maybe we should get rid of this Korthac, if for no other reason than to stop you from worrying about him."

"No, not yet, not until we learn more. There's plenty of time, and sooner or later, we'll find out what he's hiding."

15

Ten days after the feast of Ishtar, Korthac stepped from his house and into the lane. Well past dawn, his guards had already checked the street, and today Hathor waited there as well, looking as alert as the two soldiers protecting Korthac this day. No one in Akkad questioned his need for bodyguards. Everyone knew he often carried large quantities of gems or the gold from their sale on his person, and that made him a tempting target for any thief desperate enough to risk his life. So far no one had made the attempt. Korthac's guards looked too alert, hands always on their swords and eyes constantly moving, searching for any threat.

For any thief bold enough to get past the guards, Korthac carried a long knife of his own, and no one doubted he knew how to use it. Even if a daring thief managed to cut Korthac's purse and escape, the whole city would be turned out looking for the robber. Everyone understood that Korthac had made many friends in Akkad, and its traders and leading merchants would demand the soldiers hunt down the cutpurse, even if he tried to flee the city.

This morning, however, the lane outside of Korthac's new dwelling appeared as peaceful as every other day, just the usual handful of vendors hawking their goods to those who, avoiding eye contact, hurried by. Korthac's lane didn't have much foot traffic, not with the marketplace only two lanes over. Most of the more established and better quality vendors sold their merchandise there. Away from the market, goods tended to be of more dubious quality, with correspondingly lower prices. Most of the carts and booths near Korthac's house were staffed by women, often surrounded by what seemed like gangs of children, all either shouting or crying, whose noise and antics managed to annoy anyone simply trying to get through.

Today the lane appeared relatively quiet, and Korthac started walking, one guard leading the way and the other following behind. Hathor took his usual place at Korthac's left side, and the quartet of Egyptians began their journey to the docks.

"Another fine day," Korthac said, glancing up first at the bright blue sky and then shifting his gaze to his still-tired subcommander. When Hathor and Nebibi had returned to Akkad the night before, both men reported to Korthac on Ariamus's activities. Nevertheless, ever cautious, Korthac wanted to hear it again, in more detail. His plan required careful timing, and events had to unfold on schedule to avoid failure.

"Yes, lord," Hathor said, his ever-vigilant eyes searching for danger as they walked.

They entered the marketplace, already crowded with buyers and sellers, some still arriving from the nearby farms. The most industrious rose well before dawn, to occupy the more advantageous locations in the square. Those who had farther to travel would continue to arrive for the next few hours. Nearly all of the local farmers sold their crops and animals in the morning, and started returning to their homes an hour or so after midday. Those farther away usually faced a long day, selling their goods to the boat captains visiting the city; unfortunately, many of the boats didn't arrive until well into the afternoon.

Korthac stepped with care, watching not only where he placed his feet, but also the jostling crowd. A man could get bumped by a basket of fruit, or run over by a squealing cart laden with produce. Each day required charting a different path through the market, the result of constantly changing stalls, squealing animals, even buyers and sellers. The city's local craftsmen, who usually sold their leather, tools, clay pots, and some bronze tools and bowls every day, had to take whatever space they could find, fitting themselves between farmers' carts bearing fruit or vegetables, or cages of chickens. Raucous noise filled the square, with men trying to attract customers competing with frightened animals in cages or tethered to anything solid.

Today only a few slave traders congregated at their usual corner of the marketplace. A scarce and unpredictable market, the slavers always attracted a good deal of attention from the crowd. Sellers paraded their wares, mostly women or young girls, shouting out their abilities and boasting of their skills. Some of the slaves promoted themselves, eager to find a good master and earn their keep and find a secure place to live in Akkad.

In many cases, parents sold their unneeded children, amid much crying and tears as fathers clutched a few coins and watched as their sons or daughters became the property of someone else. Dozens of gawkers, idlers, or even people just passing through, stopped and listened, always interested in the buying and selling of human flesh.

In Egypt, Korthac recalled, the slavers' market operated in much the same manner, except the snap of the whip echoed out over the slaves' cries more often. Here, a steward or head of a household watched the slaves, and little force or punishment was needed. Indeed, Korthac had been surprised to find that most of those in Akkad's slave market offered themselves for sale, hoping to find an easier life than whatever one they'd left behind on the farm or in some remote village. Even parents selling their children hoped their child would find a better life as a slave to some well-off merchant or craftsman in the growing city. Selling a daughter was less painful, since there was little difference between a slave and a wife; both obeyed someone else for the rest of their lives.

Thieves and bandits made up the last group of slaves, and these were watched and guarded more carefully. Ordered into slavery for their crimes, they knew the life they faced; they'd labor hard for the rest of their lives. And if any slaves ran away, Akkad's soldiers would hunt them down and bring them back. Apparently, so Korthac understood, Esskar himself had fulfilled that menial role not so long ago. A slave hunter who now thought he ruled a city.

But not for much longer, Korthac knew. Hathor's latest report told of steady progress by Ariamus and Takany. The number of men and horses under Korthac's command increased steadily, and soon they would be put to use.

The crowds thinned as Korthac and Hathor cleared the marketplace, and soon they passed out of the river gate.

Activity at the docks varied each day, as boat captains arrived and departed, some making more than one trip a day, others passing through Akkad and going up or down the great river on longer voyages.

Korthac reached his chosen place of business, close enough to the docks to see every arrival, but far enough away to avoid being trampled underfoot by those loading or unloading goods. Other gem traders sold in the marketplace, but Korthac needed a quieter place to run his business, away from the mob of gawkers who didn't have two coppers to rub together. Since he sold only high-quality gems, serious buyers soon learned where to find him. At least this morning Korthac wouldn't have to wait for his hired man to arrive and set out his stall. For a copper coin each day, a carpenter living just inside the gate agreed to store Korthac's narrow table, three-legged stool, and awning pole safely each night, and return it first thing in the morning.

Today everything was in place, and the carpenter stood there, grinning and waiting for his coin. Hathor handed it over while Korthac took his seat on the stool. He could have had his guards carry the load each day from and to the house, but Korthac decided that would make him a figure of fun, a rich man who traveled throughout the city with two guards carrying his makeshift stall.

Once paid, the man rushed off, eager to be about his own trade, without a word of thanks to either Hathor or Korthac. Not that Korthac really cared about words of gratitude; he intended to cut the man's ears off as soon as he took power.

Korthac settled in for another day of sham trading. As usual, he sent one of the guards to take a place near the gate, with orders to look for anyone who might be taking too much interest in Korthac's table. The other guard stood a few paces away, hand on his sword and watching everyone that passed to and fro.

Meanwhile, Korthac took his seat on the stool, sharing his morning meal of bread and hard cheese with his subcommander. Gem buyers and sellers seldom did business so early, and by now Korthac and his table attracted no more attention than any other dockside trader. He let Hathor take his time retelling his observations and conversations at Ariamus's camp, speaking between bites, as he related everything he had seen and heard. Both men spoke in Egyptian, and kept their voices low.

"So, Ariamus will be ready," Korthac said, when Hathor finished up.

"Yes, lord. He may have to sweep the land for the last ten or twenty horses, but by then it won't matter."

"And the men you brought back with you? Will they do?"

"I was with Ariamus when he chose them, lord. I tested their skills with the sword myself. They're all experienced fighters, quick and more than competent. For that much gold, they'll kill anyone."

Korthac wanted to speak to them himself, but that would be too dangerous. The four men had spent the night at a small inn only a few paces down the lane from Korthac's house, with Nebibi keeping an eye on them, to make sure they saw no one and kept their mouths shut.

"Good. Give them their gold, and get them out of the city before noon. And tell them there will be an extra ten gold coins each when they succeed."

Surprise showed on Hathor's face. "That much gold . . . they've already agreed to the price."

"I want to make sure they finish the job. I don't want them getting up to Bisitun and deciding it's too dangerous. Besides, there will be plenty of gold to pay them with by the time they get back." Korthac smiled at the thought. "And tell them if they fail, I'll offer the same gold to others to hunt them down and bring me their heads. That should help stiffen their nerve."

"I'll send them out of the city one by one," Hathor suggested. "They'll be less likely to attract attention that way. They need to buy one new horse, to replace the one that went lame."

"Make sure they know the schedule. They're to ride hard to Bisitun, and strike as soon as they can. If they delay, they're of no use to me."

"I've told them, lord. They understand the urgency. They'll strike as soon as they can."

"Good. That will mean one less thing to worry about."

Korthac glanced around, always checking to see who might be watching them. Trella's spies were everywhere, and not always easy to spot. He put thoughts of the assassins aside.

"Make sure Nebibi has time to study the land across the river this morning. Takany may need a place to hide if he arrives early, or if we need to delay. Get Nebibi on his way back to Takany as soon as the others leave. Will he have any problems traveling alone?"

"No, the land on the west bank is peaceful enough. A few farmers live there, but mostly herders. Nebibi's got a good horse, and he'll carry enough food so he won't have to stop. Less than three days' ride, if he avoids the villages."

"Let's hope he isn't murdered by bandits on the way."

Hathor laughed politely at his lord's joke. "Is everything ready here, lord?"

"Yes, I've nearly finished my list"—Korthac tapped his head with his forefinger—"of those we can use. Rasui, of course. He hates both Trella and Eskkar, thinks they're upstarts who should both be driven out of Akkad. And five or six of the city's leading traders, mostly ones who've been penalized by Eskkar or the council. I'm sure they'll all be glad to become part of the new Council of Nobles. They'll influence their friends to join us. More than enough to build upon."

"Have you spoken to them yet? I mean, did you tell them what you plan?"

"No, nothing so soon," Korthac didn't mind discussing this with Hathor, the only one of his subcommanders with the wits to see the need for subtlety. "But I've listened politely to their petty complaints, and offered my sympathy. So they consider me one of their worthy companions. The moment we've seized the city, they'll all thank the gods for the chance to become my followers and take my gold. They'll gain power and wealth, as well as a chance to pay back their enemies. The rest of the city will hate them, but that's a small price to pay."

"Is there anything that can go wrong, lord?"

"Of course," Korthac said with a laugh. "Eskkar may return, or that Bantor could arrive early. If Gatus's scouts get wind of Ariamus's force, that could change everything. But so far, everything seems to . . ."

"Lord!" The bodyguard called out to Korthac. "Lady Trella is approaching."

Korthac turned toward the gate, surprised to see Trella on her way toward the docks. Despite her pregnancy, she moved gracefully enough, head held high, surrounded by four Hawk Clan guards and walking beside a man Korthac recognized as a river trader from the south. Nicar accompanied her, and the group walked to the very edge of the river, where Trella and Nicar spoke at some length to the trader.

"Well, our mighty ruler visits even the docks," Korthac said.

"Her guards look alert enough," Hathor commented.

"She's been attacked once before. Pity she survived. Still, I suppose that worked out the best for us." Korthac studied her guards, and had to admit they knew their business. They faced outward, eyes moving all the time, watching everyone who passed by, especially those who tried to approach Lady Trella.

At last, Trella's good-byes ended. The trader bowed first to Trella, than Nicar, and trod carefully down the gangway to his boat, where his two-man crew waited, no doubt eager to depart. Trella and Nicar turned away and started wending their way back to the gate. Then Trella caught sight of Korthac, and changed her direction, heading toward him. Nicar, however, continued into the city. In a moment she and her entourage arrived.

"Good morning, Korthac," she said, bowing slightly.

"Good morning, Lady Trella," Korthac said, bowing as well. "I haven't seen you on the docks before."

"And you are Hathor," Trella said, giving him a smile. "I remember you from the feast."

"I am honored, Lady Trella," Hathor said, bowing low.

"Please, Lady Trella," Korthac said, "take my stool. And come under the awning. You should not stand in the sun."

"I'll take your shade," she said, "but I'd rather stand. You don't seem to be doing much trading this morning," she added, touching the bare table in front of them.

Korthac laughed. "I usually don't display my wares unless someone shows interest," he said. He reached inside his pouch and brought out a dozen or so gemstones, which he spread across the table. The stones sparkled in the light: a bright green emerald, three good-sized citrines, a blue sapphire, and two dark red garnets, standing out even among the others.

"The women of Akkad would love to wear any of these, I'm sure," Trella said, fingering the darker of the garnets.

"A special price for you, Lady Trella," Korthac said, smiling.

She shook her head. "No, not until after the birth. Then there will be a reason to celebrate."

"I look forward to the happy day," Korthac said. He turned to Hathor. "You should be about your duties. The sun is rising ever higher."

"Yes, lord," Hathor said, and turned to Trella. "You will excuse me, Lady Trella?"

"Of course," she said, giving him another smile. "I'm sure you still have much to do in your master's new house."

Hathor bowed to both of them, and strode off, stepping between the guards as he headed back to the gate.

"I am glad you decided to stay in Akkad," Trella said. "Your trading will bring benefit to many in the city."

"I did think about moving farther south," Korthac said, "but in truth, your city seems to be growing so fast that my business cannot help but grow with it. And your wise administration keeps the people content. I have never seen so large a city with so few thieves and beggars."

"Many people left the city before the siege began," Trella said. "Those who remained were willing to risk their lives for a new start. Still, I suppose there will always be some too lazy to work and too ready to steal. Unfortunately, they prefer to prey on the poor and weak."

"Why wouldn't they steal from the rich?"

"Look at yourself, Korthac," Trella said. "Unlike the poor, you have guards to protect you. And where could a thief sell anything stolen from you? He'd have to leave Akkad, and hope not to be caught or robbed on the road."

Anyone trying to take his gems would wind up dead, Korthac knew. He'd selected only those quick and efficient to guard his person, and his guards knew all about thieves and assassins.

"You seem to care more for tradesmen and farmers than for the wealthy traders, Lady Trella."

She laughed at that, a pleasant sound that made everyone's eyes turn in her direction. "Perhaps that's because the wealthy and prosperous need little from me. It's only those that suffer privation who need help and guidance."

Her concern was genuine, Korthac noted, surprised in spite of himself. In Egypt, rulers had claimed to lead the people as a wise father guides his family, but in truth, they'd done little more than take advantage of anyone weaker than themselves. And that, Korthac thought, was why he'd win here. The common people couldn't be depended on, didn't have the strength to endure hardship or difficulty, or the courage to face up to their conquerors. Once again he wondered about Eskkar, wondered if he, too, had the same feelings about the common rabble. Not likely, Korthac decided. Barbarians, he learned, had little use for anyone not of their own kind, anyone weaker than themselves.

"The people of Akkad are fortunate in their ruler, then."

"The city is indeed blessed by the gods," Trella said. "And, now, Honored Korthac, I must leave you. There is another meeting of the council this morning."

He bowed, and she returned the gesture, before walking away, her guards forming around her. In a moment, she'd passed through the gate and disappeared. The few laggards on the dock who'd wasted time watching their discourse turned away, and returned to their own business, Lady Trella's visit to Korthac and his tiny stall already forgotten.

Korthac swept the gems off the table and back into his pouch. Turning away from the gate, he stared at the sunlit river, not really seeing it, instead thinking of his words with Trella. She had her wits about her, he decided. Any other women in the city would have been pawing over the gems, commenting on their beauty, admiring them against the soft skin of their breasts. After a single glance, Trella had ignored the sparkling gems, keeping her eyes on his, and searching, he knew, for any hint of weakness.

Since he'd left Egypt, he had conversed with no one as an equal, but this slave girl knew something about the ways of men. If she wasn't carrying another man's whelp, he might even keep her on as his concubine, to amuse his thoughts and challenge his wits on occasion. After he trained her properly, of course. But, unfortunately for her, she was much too popular. Instead, she would play another role in his city, proving for everyone to see that he ruled here absolutely. It was a role that would see her dead at his feet soon enough.

16

Five more days went by without event, and already a fortnight had passed since Ishtar's feast. The late afternoon sun drifted toward the western horizon, and En-hedu considered packing up her wares for the day a good hour earlier than usual. This day, like all the other days and weeks before it, had brought little out of the ordinary. Business always slowed down in the late afternoon, when people, tired after a long day's work, worried more about eating their dinner than buying trinkets. She'd only sold one belt all day, and that before the noon hour, to a trader whose own had split.

She'd arrived in the lane at first light, just in time to watch Korthac head toward the river, a little earlier than he normally did. But he returned at noon, his regular hour, to take his midday meal in private. Korthac had moved into his new quarters two weeks ago, a few days after Ishtar's festival. His new residence consisted of three small houses in a row, all attached together, with the central one slightly larger than the other two.

En-hedu had started selling her wares in Korthac's lane

two days before he took possession of his new house. By the time the Egyptian moved in, she'd become just another woman selling goods, her wares displayed only a few paces away from a farmer's wife selling vegetables. At least half a dozen pushcarts lined the lane every day, sometimes blocking traffic as the vendors moved and shifted their carts and goods about, or their owners took time to gossip.

After so many days at her post, En-hedu knew the name of every one of the seventeen Egyptians, and spoke to all of them whenever they passed. But only if their master were absent. She'd soon learned not to call attention to herself, not with Korthac nearby. None would dare venture into the lane or even acknowledge her greeting.

The only small exception to that rule was Hathor. A serious-looking man who seldom smiled, he functioned as senior steward to Korthac. Or acted as occasional bodyguard, depending on the need. When Korthac left the house, Hathor took charge, and he spent his time moving between the three houses, checking on the men and maintaining order. That brought him out into the lane, and occasionally he would smile or nod a greeting to En-hedu as he passed. Twice he actually bought something from her cart. A belt one time, and a wrist guard the other. He made other purchases for the household as well, sometimes in the lane, but more often in the marketplace, which held a better selection of goods.

To her surprise, he'd picked up the local language very well, and even ventured to ask about her other wares. En-hedu tried to draw him into conversation, but he never stayed long, or spoke much. He never acknowledged her presence if Korthac accompanied him.

The Egyptian leader remained as elusive as ever. After taking his midday meal, Korthac usually returned to the docks. Boats that had started their journey toward Akkad at dawn often arrived in the afternoon hours, and trading could be brisk until late in the day. Today, though, Korthac remained within his walls. Then in the middle of the afternoon, two men she had never seen before walked up to Korthac's house. The door wardens recognized them and passed them inside, without the usual challenge. The strangers, hard-looking men in dirty tunics, remained less than an hour, then departed, walking toward the river gate.

As they did so, several of Korthac's men began passing from one house to the other, and the attitude of the guards changed. Those stationed at the doors seemed more tense, and the quick smiles they often directed at her disappeared. That piqued En-hedu's interest even more than the strangers' visitation. She changed her mind about quitting early, and began working on another belt, using a tiny bronze needle to etch a design in the soft leather. The simple pattern occupied her hands and still let her watch the lane, looking for anything out of the ordinary.

"You say Ariamus is ready to cross the river?" Seated on a small stool, Korthac's words sounded harsh in the small, windowless chamber he used when he desired complete privacy.

"Yes, lord," Rihat answered, sitting cross-legged on the floor before Korthac. "All the men are in place, hiding in the hills just across the Tigris. Ariamus said to tell you we can attack today, or wait until tomorrow, if you need more time."

"No, we will attack today, at dusk, just as we planned. You're sure no one saw our force?"

"None that we left alive, lord." Rihat licked his lips. "Ariamus was very careful. We traveled most of the night, then took shelter in the hills. We saw only a few herders, tending their flocks."

Korthac studied Rihat with care. One of Ariamus's subcommanders, Rihat appeared to have his wits about him, though he looked nervous at finally meeting Korthac face to face. Not that that meant anything. Korthac knew he made most men uneasy. The man showed the fatigue of days of hard traveling. His face covered with sweat, he gulped another mouthful of water from the cup. He glanced from Korthac to Hathor, the only other man present in the room.

"Listen to me very carefully," Korthac said, speaking with deliberation. "Tell them they're to cross today, an hour before sunset." He kept his eyes locked on Rihat, probing for any signs of inattentiveness or fear. "Then you'll approach the city from the south, and wait for my signal."

"Yes, lord. Takany and Nebibi explained everything. They made sure everything was prepared before they sent me on ahead."

Both Takany and Nebibi knew the penalty for failure to obey orders exactly. Korthac worried more about Ariamus and his men. They represented the unknown quantity, and if they failed, Korthac might be left trapped in the city.

"Lord, do you want me to return with Rihat, to make sure the men are ready?"

Hathor offered the suggestion humbly enough, and

Korthac considered the question for a moment before he answered. "No, I need you here, Hathor. Rihat can convey my orders word for word to Takany and Ariamus. Isn't that right, Rihat?"

Korthac's tone dripped with menace, and Rihat dropped his eyes to the floor. "Yes, lord," he finally answered when the silence between them stretched out. "Exactly as you say."

"Good." Korthac even permitted himself a small smile to encourage the man. "You will be rewarded when the city is ours. Now, return to Takany and tell them to make sure they get across the Tigris without being seen. Then they're to follow the river to the gate, and await my signal. They must not be late."

Korthac nodded to Hathor, who stood and extended his hand to Rihat, pulling him to his feet. The two men left the room, leaving Korthac alone with his thoughts. Takany would be the one who'd suggested waiting another day. He would have wanted to rest the men. No doubt all of them were weary after four days of hard traveling, mostly at night, to reach Akkad's outskirts unseen.

Still, Korthac knew someone in the countryside would have seen something, and a hint of his men's passage would probably arrive in the morning. Besides, the longer the men had to wait, the more likely something else would go wrong, or that Takany and Ariamus would get in some argument and blood would flow. And right now, Korthac knew he needed Ariamus and his horsemen more than Takany, a brute fighter completely loyal to his master.

Hathor returned to the room and stood in the doorway. "Rihat and his companion are on their way back, lord."

"Summon Simut. It's time to prepare."

Hathor stepped away, returning in a few moments with Simut, another one of Korthac's "bodyguards" who'd proven himself in many fights over the years.

"Gather your three men, Simut," Korthac began. "Do you know what to do?" Korthac had gone over this assignment several times with the man, so there was no need to go into the details again. "Make sure you give yourself enough time to find Gatus and kill him."

Simut nodded. "I understand, lord. He shall die in the lane returning to his house."

They'd studied Gatus's routine for over a week. The captain of the guard would finish his duties at the barracks or the council house, then visit his favorite tavern for a single mug of ale before heading back to his house just as dusk fell.

"If something goes wrong, Simut," Korthac said, "if the alarm is given, you'll have to kill him as he leaves the alehouse. The man must die, no matter how many men you lose."

"Yes, lord. I'll not fail you."

Of all the men in the city, only Gatus had the experience and presence to act as a rallying point for any resistance. With all of the other senior men out of Akkad, the rest of the soldiers and the city's inhabitants would look to him for leadership. So the old soldier had to die first, to dishearten the soldiers and the people.

"Then you'll be well rewarded when we have the city." Korthac turned to Hathor. "You'll keep the gate to Trella's house open?"

Trella's house, with its surrounding wall and force of

soldiers stationed within, would be easy to defend, given sufficient warning. And Trella would provide another rallying point for resistance. Korthac preferred to capture her alive, if possible, but dead or alive, the house must be taken before it could become a stronghold to rally the city's inhabitants.

Korthac had given that dangerous assignment to Hathor. The man could think while he fought, and he knew the importance of capturing the house.

"As soon as Takany's inside the river gate, I'll join you at the house, Hathor. Just hold the gate open until I arrive."

"Yes, lord. The gate will stay open."

"Then by tonight, we will rule in Akkad," Korthac said. He looked from one to the other. Neither man showed any sign of doubt or fear. They'd fought at Korthac's side before, and he'd always led them to victory. They understood the plan, and had no questions. They were ready.

"Prepare your men," Korthac ordered. "It is time."

En-hedu pretended not to notice Korthac's men moving about, and kept hawking her wares at every passerby, often following shoppers for a dozen steps up and down the lane, a convenient excuse to move about and study any goings-on. The sun had begun to sink toward the western hills when she noted Hathor leaving Korthac's house, accompanied by four men, two of them carrying rolled-up blankets under their arms. En-hedu thought that a little odd; she'd never seen Hathor go anywhere with more than one guard before. She called out to him, but either he didn't hear or had no time for her usual banter.

By now business at the river dock would be winding down, and certainly no boats would be setting forth so close to sundown. En-hedu still puzzled over what it might mean when Simut, another of Korthac's bodyguards, departed the house, accompanied by three more men. Again, two of them carried bulky bundles.

Unsure of what, if anything, these strange goings-on meant, she knew she must tell Tammuz. En-hedu began packing up her leather goods displayed upon the cart's frayed blanket. The blanket also served to transport the items, and in a few moments it resembled the bundles Korthac's men carried, only shorter. Using two mismatched leather strips, she fastened the ends of the blanket to seal it.

Her mind kept working, however. Weeks had gone by with nothing out of the ordinary. Now many of the Egyptians were moving about, and the change in their manner worried her.

By the time she finished packing up her goods, she heard voices speaking Egyptian, and looked up to see Korthac exit the house, accompanied by two of his men. Again, one of Korthac's followers carried what seemed a heavy bundle, this one a bit longer than those carried by the other men.

En-hedu never looked up, even when Korthac passed within an arm's length of her cart. She watched his feet through her tangled hair, and waited until he disappeared down the lane. The sight of the grim Egyptian worried her. She felt tempted to leave the cart, but an abandoned cart might call attention to herself. Best to move it as she did every night, shoving it down the lane, back to Ninbanda's house, where it would be safe. But before she could start the cart moving, a fourth group of Egyptians stepped into the lane.

Staring at their feet, she counted five of them. The number surprised her. That meant the three houses were now empty, whatever contents the dwellings contained left unguarded. In the six weeks she'd watched the houses, Korthac never had less than half of his men inside, guarding his property.

This last group, however, did not go toward the river. Instead they went up the lane, toward the center of Akkad. She watched their backs for a moment, then leaned her weight against the cart, which yielded reluctantly with a screech of wood against wood. En-hedu, alarmed now, used all her strength to keep the cart moving, unmindful of those who had to dart out of its path as it creaked and wobbled along. When she reached Ninbanda's hut, she didn't pause, just shoved the cart against the hut's entrance as she called out to the woman to attend it. En-hedu hurried down another lane toward the alehouse.

Something was wrong. She found herself running, clutching the heavy blanket of wares to her chest and dodging between the work-weary villagers plodding back to their homes. Breathing hard, she turned into the narrow lane that led to Tammuz's alehouse, ducked past two men who tried to greet her, pushed through the half-open door, and ran inside.

Kuri looked up at the noise, but she ignored his usual smile. "Where's Tammuz? Is he here?" She dropped her bundle, worried that Tammuz might have been watching the house, might even have followed Hathor or Simut's party.

But Tammuz stepped out from their private room. He'd heard the door bang and her excited voice.

"En-hedu, what's..." One look at her face silenced him.

She pushed him back into the bedroom and closed the door. Keeping her voice low, she described what she'd seen.

"These bundles... how big were they?"

En-hedu held her hands an arm's length apart. "The blankets that Korthac's men carried were longer, and thicker, too."

"Mmm, not long enough for bows." Tammuz's eyes widened. "Swords? Could they have carried swords?"

"Yes, I suppose... I didn't hear anything clanking."

Swearing under his breath, Tammuz scooped up his belt and swung it around him. From habit, En-hedu helped him fasten it, fear rising in her when she saw him loosen the knife in its sheath.

"I'm going to Eskkar's house to warn Trella," he said. "You stay here with Kuri."

He slipped through the door, then out of the alehouse, moving at a run.

En-hedu stood there, stunned. What could Tammuz do, with one good arm and only a knife? If there were trouble, he would...

She stepped back into the common room. One of the patrons saw her, and called out for another ale and something to eat. En-hedu stared at him unheedingly, then noticed his companion. The man carried a knife on his belt.

"I need to borrow this," she said, moving so quickly that she'd pulled the green-tinged copper blade from the man's belt before he even realized what she intended. "Kuri, stay here." She tucked the knife inside her dress, clutching it tight against her body through the thin shift, holding it firmly from outside, and ran after Tammuz, ignoring the voices that called after her.

People filled the lanes. Many had eaten their evening meals and looked forward to a few hours of relaxation before turning in for the night. They frowned at En-hedu as she pushed and bumped her way through their midst, following the path she knew Tammuz would take toward Eskkar's house. The sun sank below the horizon. Already the daylight colors had faded, replaced by the grayness of shadows that began to cover everything.

At this time of day it would take some time to reach Eskkar's residence, and she hurried as fast as she could, breathing hard as she weaved through the strollers. To her surprise, before she'd crossed three lanes, she saw Tammuz walking a few paces ahead of her. Relieved, she slowed to a walk. To add to her astonishment, he turned away from the lane that led to Eskkar's. She wondered what could have made him change his destination. About a dozen paces behind him, she opened her mouth to call his name, when . . .

"*Gatus!*" Tammuz yelled. "*Look out!*"

The shout froze everyone in the lane, but only for an instant. Then the dull clank of bronze on bronze shattered the peaceful evening. Tammuz darted ahead, drawing his knife. En-hedu broke into a run, fear rushing through her at what she might find.

A voice shouted in Egyptian, and she heard a man scream in pain as she reached the intersection where Tammuz had shouted. With scarcely enough light for her to see, En-hedu recognized Gatus, his back against a wall and a sword in his hand, fighting off Simut and his men. A man, Gatus's bodyguard, lay writhing on the ground, bleeding, his cries for help ignored.

Gatus, fending off three men, was about to be overwhelmed when Tammuz slipped up behind one of Simut's men and stabbed him hard in the back. The man screamed, and En-hedu saw blood gushing from his tunic. Simut saw the blow, and swung his sword at Tammuz, who ducked away from the cut. Seizing the opportunity, Gatus shifted to the opposite side, striking at the closest of his attackers. Gatus's thrust drove the man back, giving the old soldier a chance to dodge aside and escape. But before he could get clear, the other Egyptian lunged at Gatus, driving his sword into the captain of the guard's side. Gatus rammed the hilt of his sword into the man's face with enough force to shove the man back into his companion. Then Gatus, clutching his side, whirled away, and disappeared up the lane, merging with the growing shadows.

Meanwhile, Simut turned to Tammuz, to finish off the youth who'd disrupted Simut's ambush. He raised his sword and stepped toward Tammuz, slashing at his head. Tammuz stepped sideways as he jerked his knife from his victim's back. Simut's sword just missed, but the Egyptian had fought too many times to stake his life on a single blow. Moving smoothly, he followed up with a cross cut at Tammuz's head, then lunged at Tammuz's chest. Tammuz, his knife no match against his attacker's sword, twisted away, trying to avoid the thrust, but he lost his balance and stumbled.

Unable to shift his weight, Tammuz landed hard, on his

weak arm. Simut, with a grunt of satisfaction, drew back his sword and thrust downward.

But before the blow could gather momentum, Simut's easy kill turned into a hiss of pain. En-hedu, arriving at a run, had drawn the knife from her bosom, and shoved it with all her strength into Simut's back, a hand's width above his belt, feeling it sink to the hilt.

The thrust froze the Egyptian's sword. For a moment he stood there, then with a grunt of pain he turned his blade toward his attacker, mortally wounded but still able to strike. Before the blow landed, Tammuz lunged up from the ground with his knife, burying his blade under Simut's ribs.

With an incomprehensible curse, the man fell to the ground, the sword striking En-hedu weakly, but with the blade flat, before it slipped from his hand. En-hedu jerked her knife free from Simut's body, feeling hot blood gush along her arm, and reached Tammuz's side, helping him to his feet. Gatus had slipped away, his two remaining attackers vanishing after him in pursuit. Half a dozen onlookers, stunned into silence, stared openmouthed into the gathering darkness at the three men lying dead or dying before them.

Tammuz took one look around, shoved the bloody knife in his belt, then grasped En-hedu's arm. In a moment, they, too, faded into the growing shadows at a run, leaving the shocked and surprised inhabitants to wonder what they'd just witnessed.

Weaving between the unconcerned strollers, Tammuz guided En-hedu down one lane, then changed direction to another. En-hedu looked behind them, but saw nothing. They slowed to a brisk walk. No one noticed them. Here, one lane away, the commotion had gone unheard.

"We've got to get to Eskkar's house," Tammuz whispered. "Trella needs to . . ."

"What about Gatus?" En-hedu realized she still clutched her knife in her hand. She stuffed it back inside the bodice of her dress, shivering as the hot blood still on the blade dripped between her breasts. She had to force the image of Simut's face, showing a mixture of pain and hatred, from her mind. "I saw him run up the lane, with the Egyptians in pursuit."

"We can't do anything about him," Tammuz said, moving her along faster as he got his breath back. "Either he got away, or they've caught up with him by now. We need to warn Trella."

En-hedu realized they'd gone back the way they came, then closed in on Eskkar's house. The lane twisted and turned, but only one more intersection lay between them and their destination. As Eskkar's house came into sight, sounds of violence erupted from just outside the gate. They saw a half-dozen men fighting at the courtyard entrance. Tammuz started forward, then stopped, as a wall of Egyptians pushed past them from behind, knocking Tammuz and En-hedu aside in their haste. Tammuz covered En-hedu with his body and pressed her against the wall. They both watched in horror as dozens of foreign soldiers, swords in their hands, charged toward Eskkar's house. Before Tammuz or En-hedu could overcome their shock and surprise, the Egyptians had raced up and overwhelmed the Akkadians defending Eskkar's household.

Earlier, when Korthac left his house a little before dusk, he strode past the woman his men called En-hedu without observing her or any of the other vendors. Accompanied by only two guards, his eyes scanned the lane, alert for any signs of danger, but saw nothing out of the ordinary. No longer a stranger, he wended his way through the twisting lanes almost unnoticed by the people of Akkad. The few that did give him a glance didn't perceive the long knife fastened beneath his tunic.

The marketplace stood nearly deserted as Korthac passed through it, heading toward the river gate. On the way, he encountered several of Akkad's soldiers, most of them unarmed, and none of whom even glanced at him. By now Korthac knew their routine. They would have finished their duties for the day and already eaten dinner in the barracks' common room. Now they would search out their favorite alehouses, to enjoy a few hours' relaxation before heading for their beds and another night's sleep.

Arriving at Akkad's rear gate, Korthac found it half-open. Though both gates should have been sealed at dusk, the river gate often stayed open a few extra hours. The guards had pushed the one side closed, but left the other side accessible. People continued to walk in and out, some heading for the river to bathe, while others strolled along the bank, taking their ease or conducting business of a personal nature.

A watch fire burned beside the gate, next to a bundle of torches. Korthac spotted one of his other four men, sitting against the wall, as unnoticed as any beggar. The man raised his right arm in greeting, and Korthac nodded. The signal meant all of the men were ready and in place. Korthac continued on, noting that only two guards stood at the gate's entrance, watching to make sure no strangers entered after dusk.

The gathering darkness made it difficult to be certain, yet Korthac counted no more than seven soldiers manning the gate. Usually a detail of ten secured the river gate, but the number varied, and he'd found nights when as few as five walked their post. Taking his time, he climbed the steps to the right-side parapet. One of his guards followed, the one carrying the longest bundle, while the other remained below.

At the top, three soldiers stood guard, looking down toward the docks and those passing in and out through the gate. The gate commander approached Korthac. Orders said that only soldiers could mount the wall, but exceptions might be made, especially for a rich trader who wanted to see the river and didn't mind parting with a few coins.

"Greetings, Honorable Korthac," the man said, "how may I help you tonight?"

Korthac had mounted these steps at least once a day for the last few weeks, to offer his prayers to the river god, he'd explained. Each prayer session, always short, ended with a copper coin for the guard.

"Greetings to you and your men," Korthac answered with a smile. "Tonight I have to make a special offering to Enki, the river god, to thank him for the favorable cargo he sent me today." Korthac nodded to his bodyguard, who unslung the sack he'd carried across his shoulder, then turned back to the guard. "Perhaps you can help my servant with the offering?"

The other two guards, curious at this new ritual, moved closer, as the bodyguard knelt to open his bundle. Korthac stepped behind them, hand on his knife. As the blanket came open, Korthac struck, moving so quickly that he'd stabbed the two guards before either could react, and with only the sound of their moans escaping. The watch commander died at the same moment, a stunned look of surprise on his face, as Korthac's bodyguard snatched up a sword from the sack and drove it into the soldier's stomach. The man died without even reaching for his sword, and, more important, without sounding the alarm.

Pushing the bodies aside, Korthac reached down and took a short horseman's bow from his bodyguard's hand. It took but a moment to string it and nock an arrow, but there was no need. The soldiers guarding the other side of the gate had died, struck down by his Egyptians who'd moved into place just under the steps as their leader mounted. Some of the dead had cried out, but there'd been no loud clash of weapons. Nevertheless, a few citizens looked about in surprise, wondering what had happened, too confused to understand what they'd witnessed.

Korthac didn't worry about them. All that mattered was that the alarm hadn't sounded, and by now one of his men had secured the trumpet. More Egyptians guarded the two lanes leading away from the gate, ready to stop any messenger rushing toward the soldiers' barracks with a warning. Instead, Korthac leaned out over the wall and waved the bow. He couldn't see far into the darkness, but he knew his men waited there, close enough to see the signal and would relay it to Takany and Ariamus's men. Looking down into the well of the gate, he saw the rest of his men moving into position, taking station just inside the opening, to make sure no one attempted to shut the portal.

From the darkness, he heard the rumble of many sandals approaching and looked back toward the river. The moment Korthac saw his men running toward the gate, he descended the steps. Takany and Nebibi led the first group of men through without stopping. Fifty Egyptians and an equal number of recruits followed him, all moving at a run directly toward the barracks.

Ariamus, leading another forty men, followed them in, pausing only long enough for Korthac and his six Egyptian bodyguards to fall in step beside him. Korthac had belted his sword about him, and strapped on a bronze helmet, both taken from the same bundle that concealed the swords and bow. The invaders jogged steadily, moving fast enough to cover the ground quickly but not too fast to leave the men exhausted.

Korthac's force of nearly fifty men headed straight toward Eskkar's house. Korthac needed to capture it and those inside without a major struggle. He'd seen that the house was strongly built. Given enough warning, even a handful of men could hold out there for some time. His contingent had farther to go than Takany and those moving to the barracks, which were closer to the river than Eskkar's house. Hathor would be positioned there, with orders to wait as long as he could before attacking, to let his leader reach his destination.

The alarm sounded while they still had another lane to traverse. Korthac broke into a run, his men speeding up behind him. He turned into Eskkar's lane. A torch burned next to the gate, and he saw a knot of men fighting. Hathor and his men had orders to keep that gate open. A clamor rose up from behind the courtyard wall, another trumpet sending its warning up into the darkness, overriding the noise and confusion. The clash of bronze on bronze told everyone fighting raged, and inside the compound Eskkar's soldiers fumbled for their weapons and rushed to close the gate.

Two of Hathor's men died fighting, but they held it open long enough for Korthac's men to reach it. Korthac stopped just outside and ordered them in. Ariamus led the way, bursting through the opening, shouting his war cry. Korthac let a dozen men pass through, then followed them in, guarded by the same two bodyguards who helped kill the soldiers at the river gate.

Another torch still burned in the courtyard, lighting the dead bodies scattered about. Two more of Ariamus's men had died forcing their way in. The rest of Korthac's Egyptians formed up around him. He hurried along the house wall toward the house. Ariamus had orders to break in if necessary, and two of his men carried hammers and stakes for that purpose. If necessary, they would drive the stakes into the door and wrench the wood apart.

Korthac saw the tools wouldn't be needed. The thick door stood wide open. Sounds of fighting came from the house, though that noise ended by the time he reached the entrance.

Ariamus, blood on his sword, met him just inside the door. "They're in the upper rooms. We'll have to force the door." Two men pulled hammers from their packs, and rushed toward the stairs.

"Perhaps not. Bring another torch." Stepping over the

dead body of a soldier, Korthac passed inside and ascended the steps, stopping just below the landing. He rapped on the door with the point of his sword. "Lady Trella," he called out. "Tell your men to open the door. Otherwise we'll have to break it down and kill everyone inside."

Shouts answered him, and from behind the door, he heard men arguing.

"Soldiers of Akkad, the house has been taken." Korthac waited a moment, while the sounds of men cursing sounded through the door. "Lady Trella, tell your men to surrender. Your soldiers are all dead, and more of my men have captured the barracks. There won't be any help. If you don't want your followers to die, open the door."

He let the arguing go on for a few moments. They had no choice. As soon as they realized no one would come to their rescue, they'd surrender. Korthac's men filled the courtyard, some already busy looting the soldiers' quarters. Behind the door, the defenders kept arguing, their voices rising as they shouted at each other. Some wanted to hold out, others wanted to talk.

"Open the door now, Trella. You need my protection for you and the child."

"You'll let the soldiers live?" Her question carried over the bickering, which quieted at her words.

Korthac detected no panic in her voice, only acceptance of the inevitable. "Yes, as slaves. It's that or they die."

They had no choice, and it didn't take Trella long to convince her guards. He heard the sound of the table dragging across the floor, and in a moment, the bar lifting from its braces. The door swung open to reveal Annok-sur standing there. Behind her stood four men, swords at the ready. Korthac saw another man, wounded, lying against the wall.

"Tell them to put down their weapons and come out. You and Lady Trella will stay here."

"Drop your swords, and obey him." Lady Trella's voice came from behind the men.

She sounded unafraid, but he'd soon change that.

The soldiers looked at each other, then tossed their swords to the floor in surrender.

"Tie them up, Ariamus. We'll need good slaves." Korthac meant his words. A few weeks working as tethered captives under the whip would find them more than willing to join his forces. With Eskkar dead and forgotten, trained fighting men would willingly join him.

Korthac watched as Ariamus and his men secured the soldiers, binding their hands and pushing them down the stairs, to join the other prisoners. In moments, only Trella and Annok-sur remained.

"I'll send your servants up here, Trella. If you want them to stay alive, you'll remain in the bedroom."

"Why are you doing this?" Trella said.

Ignoring her question, he gave orders to have both the upper rooms searched and all weapons removed. Korthac left six of his men to watch over Trella, telling them in Egyptian to kill her if anyone attempted a rescue.

Moving downstairs, he found Ariamus and Hathor waiting for him.

"A messenger just came from Takany," Hathor said, still holding a sword dripping with blood. "He's taken the barracks and seized all the weapons. But men are holding out at the main gate."

Hathor had done well, securing the entrance to Eskkar's compound. With Takany's capture of the soldiers' quarters, the most difficult objective had been achieved. The only real resistance could have come from the barracks. With that taken, the battle had ended. Korthac's main goal had been to secure Trella alive and unharmed, so that he could use her to force the inhabitants to his will.

"Ariamus, leave twenty of your men here," Korthac said. "Take the rest and guard the river gate. Make sure no horses leave the city. Watch the boats and the river as well."

Korthac turned to Hathor. "Take your men to the main gate. Keep whatever soldiers are left penned up there. Put archers on the walls, to make sure no one leaves the city. When Takany gets here, we'll bring our men to the main gate and finish the last of the resistance. Afterward, we can begin hunting down any who've escaped. By dawn, the city will be mine."

Unsure of what to do, Tammuz and En-hedu stood there with a dozen others, even after the fighting ended, watching events unfold. Along with a few dozen of Akkad's stunned citizens, Tammuz and En-hedu had seen Korthac capture Eskkar's house. Whatever warning Tammuz might have given would likely have arrived too late. By the time he'd convinced anyone of the danger, Korthac's men would have struck.

Just when Tammuz decided they'd best return to the alehouse, armed men poured out of Eskkar's house.

Tammuz and En-hedu, like all the frightened villagers,

shrank against the wall or into nearby homes while the fierce-looking Egyptians marched by, many with blood still on their swords. After all the invaders had passed, with En-hedu holding his left arm, Tammuz followed behind them, keeping back a safe distance. When they reached the open area before the main gate, he and En-hedu could see that the archers in the towers had refused to surrender. As they watched, shafts flew at the invaders, pushing them back into the lane.

"Wait here," Tammuz said, nudging En-hedu into a doorway. He slipped as close to the rear of the Egyptians as he dared. He heard Hathor and Korthac talking, along with another man they called Takany, who seemed to be Korthac's second in command. The three men spoke briefly, but always in Egyptian, and Tammuz had no idea of what they said.

When Korthac finished, Hathor raced off back up the lane toward Eskkar's house. Tammuz watched as Korthac and Takany positioned their men, to make sure no reinforcements could reach the gate or towers, and to prevent the soldiers within from escaping. Then Korthac stood there, waiting.

Before long, Hathor returned, leading a dozen men carrying torches and escorting Lady Trella, her hands bound together with a leather thong and escorted by two grinning Egyptians who held her by the arms as they hurried her along. They took her directly to where Korthac waited. He spoke to her, then slapped her across the face before taking hold of her wrist and twisting it until she cried out.

Appearing satisfied at Trella's reaction, Korthac pushed

her into Hathor's arms. "Take her to the gate," Korthac ordered, speaking in Akkadian to make sure Trella understood his words. "If the soldiers don't surrender, kill her."

Stunned at Trella's treatment, Tammuz watched as Hathor led Lady Trella out into the open space behind the gate.

"Soldiers of Akkad," Hathor shouted, his powerful voice echoing throughout the area. "If you don't lay down your weapons and surrender, Lady Trella will be put to death, and then we'll kill everyone in the towers."

Tammuz saw that Hathor stood beside Trella, an easy shot for most of the archers in the tower. But everyone knew what would happen to Trella if an arrow struck him down. Hathor waited a few moments, then called out again. "For the last time . . . surrender now, and you will live." He pushed Trella forward. "Tell them."

"Soldiers, come down from the towers." Trella's voice carried easily to the walls. "Don't resist. Save your own lives."

Tammuz shook his head. Never had he thought such a thing could happen.

"Korthac's too wise to stand out there in the open, where an arrow could take him," En-hedu said, watching the spectacle. She'd ignored Tammuz's order to stay behind and moved up to join him. "He lets Hathor take the risk of dying."

"This is bad," Tammuz said. "The guards will have to surrender."

"We should get back to the alehouse," En-hedu whispered. "We can't do anything here. They may start killing everyone in the streets."

"As soon as I see what happens. I have to make sure."

Shouting voices came from the towers, but the debate didn't last long. The twenty or thirty men, divided between the towers and outnumbered by at least five times their strength, had no choice but to yield. Without weapons, food, and water, they couldn't hold out. At Trella's urging, they put down their weapons and filed from the tower.

By then Tammuz had seen enough. With all resistance ended, the terror would begin. "Let's get out of here, before the looting starts."

He hurried En-hedu along, his knife held tight against his side. But they didn't encounter any of Korthac's men, and soon reached Tammuz's establishment, as dark as every house on the lane. No one would burn even the smallest lamp tonight, afraid to attract any attention from their new masters.

A worried Kuri let them into the alehouse, sword in hand, and barred the door behind them. Only a faint glow from the fireplace embers gave any illumination.

Tammuz peered into the common room, but saw no one.

"I chased them all out, and told them not to return until morning," Kuri said. "They'll be busy enough, picking up whatever they can steal in all this confusion." Using a shard of pottery, he lifted a glowing ember from what remained of the fire, and carried it into Tammuz's private room, where he touched it to the oil lamp.

He blew on it gently, until a tiny flame appeared, enough to reveal another presence waiting for them.

"What's happening out there?" Gatus lay across Tammuz's bed, one hand clutching his side, his voice weak and full of pain. His still-bloody sword lay beside him, close to his hand.

En-hedu pushed past the men. She lifted the lamp and moved it closer to Gatus. "Hold the lamp here, Tammuz, while I look after his wound." Lifting his garment, she moved aside Gatus's hand and examined the gash just above his hip. She'd tended enough cuts and scrapes at the tannery, though nothing as deep as this. "He's still bleeding. His arm is cut and his side. The blade must have passed through his arm."

"An arm's not very good as a shield," Gatus said, wincing in pain. "Just tie it up. I have to go ... get to my men."

"You can't go anywhere, Gatus," Tammuz said, his voice sounding harsh in the small room. "Trella's been captured, the barracks and both gates seized. All the soldiers have been taken prisoner, except for the ones who died. Korthac rules Akkad."

"Korthac! That Egyptian dog ..."

"By dawn, half of Korthac's men will be searching for you. Simut must have had orders to kill you. Instead, we killed him and one of his men. The Egyptians will want revenge for that. They'll want you, or your dead body."

"That was you? My thanks for that stroke, Tammuz," Gatus said. "Did Kuri teach you how to fight?"

"Thank En-hedu as well. She saved both of us."

Gatus looked at En-hedu in confusion, so Tammuz recounted the fight and described Simut's death, while En-hedu cleaned the soldier's wounds.

"He can stay here," Kuri said. "I mean ... he's bleeding pretty bad."

"They'll search everywhere, including here," Tammuz said. "We'll have to find someplace else."

"We'll hide him here, on the roof," En-hedu said. She tore a piece of cloth in half and turned to Kuri. "Help me lift him." They lifted Gatus's shoulders up off the bed, enough for her to slip the cloth underneath him. She used another piece of linen to thicken the bandage, and tied it tight around his waist. Then she bound up his arm.

Straightening, she faced the two men. "They'll search here, but they won't go up on the roof. We can distract anyone who comes looking, if need be, and make sure they don't poke around too closely. He can stay up there in the hiding hole all day, or at least until they've come and gone."

"All day in the sun? He'll bake . . ."

"We'll give him a blanket to cover himself," she said. "And some water. With luck, they won't find him up there. After they've searched, we can bring him back down." En-hedu looked down at Gatus. "He needs a healer, but that will have to wait, at least until tomorrow night."

"I've been in the sun before," he said, peering from one to the other in the dim light. "One more day won't kill me." He choked off a laugh at his own words.

The roof above their heads, the solid part, had a flat space barely large enough for two people to stretch out. But what looked like the end of the roof was in reality a false wall, concealing a narrow niche where Tammuz, like the previous owner, had found occasion to temporarily hide stolen goods. It would be a tight squeeze to get Gatus in the hiding hole, but he'd be out of sight and well hidden.

"We'll have to get him up there before dawn, so nobody sees him," Tammuz said. "If they find him . . ."

"You and En-hedu should go somewhere safe," Kuri said. "Get out of the city. I'll stay here with Gatus."

"No, we're not going," En-hedu said, her voice decisive. "Why would we leave our business? They'd be suspicious at that. It makes no difference to us who runs Akkad. We should tell everyone we're glad Korthac's taken control."

Tammuz stared at her. He'd never heard such hardness in her voice. "We don't know how many men Korthac has. They may loot and rape the whole city before they go."

"They're not going anywhere," she said, still speaking with conviction. "Korthac would have struck weeks ago if he'd wanted to loot and run."

"If they stay . . . there will be rapes . . . the women . . . no place will be safe." Tammuz looked at her, worry on his face.

She reached out and touched Tammuz's arm. "So we might as well stay here."

"I won't see you taken by those men, En-hedu. I swear . . ."

"We have our knives," she said, "if it comes to that."

"And my old sword," Kuri said, patting his belt.

They looked at each other in the dim light. En-hedu raised her arms and placed one hand on each man's shoulder. "It's settled, then. We stay, and wait for Eskkar to return. And we stay alive."

Long before midnight, the last of the fighting for Akkad had ended. Korthac felt secure enough to station half his followers at the gates and let the rest get some sleep. The most serious fighting had occurred at the barracks. A few of the soldiers had managed to get their bows in play, and Takany had lost a dozen Egyptians, while almost twenty of Ariamus's followers had died.

Taking the barracks had secured the city, and capturing Trella had made the victory complete. Most of Akkad's soldiers had been in the wine shops and alehouses, and the rest taken by surprise. As important as the men, the captured barracks held almost all of the soldiers' weapons—the bows, swords, knives, and axes needed to defend the city. With the barracks and Eskkar's house taken, the remainder of the soldiers had headed for the main gate, trying to rally their forces there.

For a time the soldiers blocked the entrances to the guard towers, but without someone to lead them, they had little choice but to surrender. A few scrambled down the wall and escaped to the fields, but Korthac didn't worry about them. Ariamus would have men hunting them down in the morning.

Dawn brought a new era to Akkad. People did not leave their houses, huddling inside in fear, while Korthac's men roamed the streets, looting the shops and random homes, guzzling wine and assaulting women. After letting the pillaging go on for most of the morning as a reward for his men, Korthac issued orders to his Egyptians, and they soon had the city's inhabitants and Ariamus's ruffians under control.

The killings began just before noon. All those who had insulted Korthac during his stay in the city died, as did those who spoke out against their new ruler. The nobles and leading merchants, summoned to the marketplace under threat of death to them and their families, swore allegiance on their knees to Korthac. He promulgated a series of orders, the first of which instructed everyone to turn in any weapons in their possession at once.

All persons caught carrying or possessing a sword or bow would be put to death on the spot, along with their families. All persons speaking of Eskkar or Trella would have their tongues cut out. The process of teaching Eskkar's citizens their new place in Korthac's world had begun.

Korthac returned to Eskkar's house by midafternoon, tired and hungry. The long night and hectic morning had wearied him, but he still had one task to perform. Accompanied by Ariamus, he climbed the stairs to Trella's quarters. His guards moved aside as he stepped into the bedroom. Annok-sur and Trella rose from the bed as he entered, Annok-sur's arm around Trella's shoulders. The room seemed hot, and the smell of fear and blood lingered inside the walls.

"You are well, I hope, Lady Trella?" He kept his voice pleasant and smiled at her discomfort.

"What is it you want . . . Honorable Korthac. Why have you . . ."

"Whatever I want is what I'll have, Lady Trella, and you will not question me again, about anything. You are mine now, as much as Akkad is mine. Follow me."

He stepped back into the outer room. His men had returned the big table to its proper place, and he stood next to it. Trella moved toward him, and stopped just inside the workroom, Annok-sur a step behind her.

"Come here. Kneel before your new master."

Trella hesitated. "Honorable Korthac . . ."

Moving swiftly, he caught Trella by the hair and yanked her in front of the table. He pushed her up against it, then slapped her across the face. "You are my slave, Trella, for as long as I choose to let you live, and you will address me as 'lord.' Do you understand?"

Her hand went to her cheek, and she nodded. "Yes . . . lord."

Annok-sur stepped into the workroom, but Korthac whirled to face her. "I did not give you leave to move about." He turned to Ariamus. "Kill her if she leaves the bedroom."

"Stay inside, Annok-sur," Trella said, "don't let . . ."

Korthac turned back to her. "You do not give orders to anyone any longer." He struck her again, harder this time; blood dripped from her mouth and she slipped to her knees, as much from the blow as his order to kneel. "If you speak out of turn again, if you fail to obey the least of my orders, I'll have the child cut from your body and tossed into the fire."

He smiled as she moved herself upright, but remained on her knees. For a moment he was tempted to have her pleasure him right then and there. It would be fitting humiliation for her, in front of a roomful of strangers. But such things could wait, and he felt too tired to enjoy it properly. Besides, every day that passed would add to her embarrassment.

"Keep her in these rooms. The door is to remain open. She is to see no one, speak to no one. If she complains or gives you any trouble, kill her servants in front of her, one by one, starting with Annok-sur."

Looking down at her, he noticed the thin strand of leather hanging around her neck. He pulled it toward him, lifting a gold coin up from between her breasts. "You'll have no need for gold any more, Lady Trella." With a quick jerk, he snapped the leather, then raised the coin to his eyes. It was simply a common coin, one with Nicar's mark on it, and a thin groove. Korthac tossed the coin to one of his men. It pleased him to take it from her. Obviously the coin meant something special to her, and now it, too, was gone. She'd learn soon enough that she had nothing, was nothing.

He reached out and ran his fingers through Trella's hair, enjoying its texture. Gradually he tightened his grip until her head twisted upward, the hair pulled back from her face, her eyes wide with distress. When she started to gasp from the pain, he relaxed his hand, then gently brushed the few loose strands from her eyes. Yes, she'd give him plenty of pleasure before he finished with her.

Trella sat on the bed, trying to think. In less than a day, Korthac had seized Akkad and established himself as the city's ruler. He'd killed, captured, or driven into hiding Akkad's mighty archers. She'd become a prisoner, worse, a slave, only this time she had a child due in a few weeks. The last word from Eskkar had come three days ago, informing her yet again that he intended to remain in the north a little longer.

Her fists clenched in anger, furious at her husband for taking his pleasures in Bisitun, while Akkad and she fell into Korthac's hands. How dare he leave her like this. He should have returned weeks ago to protect her. She wanted to . . . no, she needed Eskkar, needed him to save her and their unborn child. The thought that he might abandon them to their fate, turn away from her and Akkad, frightened her. She thought about his new woman, and that image made her rage increase. Perhaps he'd choose a fresh life with his new concubine, choose to avoid a fight and continue his life in the north. That image tortured her for a long moment, until she regained control of her emotions.

No, she decided. Eskkar would not abandon her. If for no other reason than his barbarian code of honor, he would return to destroy Korthac for what he'd done. If he still lived. Trella shook her head. Without him, if he were dead, there would be no hope to escape the fate that Korthac planned for her and the child. She had to believe that he remained alive, that he would come for her. She could cling to that.

"We must get word to Eskkar," Trella whispered to Annok-sur, seated beside her. "He'll need to know how strong a force Korthac has assembled."

"Don't forget, Bantor is due any day. Together they'll . . ."

"Korthac isn't afraid of Eskkar or Bantor, Annok-sur. Did you see how many men he has? I counted as many as I could when they took me to the gate. He must have at least a hundred and fifty, maybe two hundred. More than enough to control the city and stop anyone from rising up against him. Only Eskkar can rally the people to resist."

"Assuming that he's still alive," Annok-sur said.

"He has to be alive, or we're all lost," Trella said.

"Besides, how could they kill him up in Bisitun, guarded by Grond and surrounded by his men?"

"Both Korthac and Ariamus said Esskar is dead."

"Do you believe them? They offered no proof."

Her own question made Trella stop and think. Proof would be Esskar's head, or a dozen witnesses to his death. She took her time, trying to recall the Egyptian's exact words, and comparing them to those she'd overheard from the boasting Ariamus. Korthac had claimed his men had struck down Esskar in Bisitun's lanes, but Ariamus said Esskar and his men had been killed in a fight. The slight difference might not mean much, but she needed something to give her hope.

"Korthac knows Bantor is returning," Trella said, her mind beginning to think clearly once again. "Ariamus has taken every horse he could find and ridden south. They'll meet Bantor's men on the road, long before they arrive here."

"Bantor has plenty of men, trained men. They won't be easy to defeat."

Trella shook her head. "No, Korthac must have some plan in mind. If Bantor's force is defeated, even driven off, Korthac can turn his full attention to the north. He's defeating Esskar's forces piece by piece. That's his plan." She reached out and took Annok-sur's hand. "I fear for your husband."

"Ariamus will find killing Bantor harder than he thinks. Bantor hates the man since . . . from the old days, when he was captain of the guard." She put her arm around Trella. "And Esskar isn't easy to stop, either."

"I wanted Esskar back here, but now . . . it's better that he remains up north. He might be safer there."

Both women stayed silent for a moment. Their hopes for survival depended on their husbands living long enough to rescue them.

"Is there anything we can do, Trella? I mean, can we kill Korthac somehow?"

"Even if we could, his Egyptians would cut us to pieces, then slaughter half the city. And I saw his face. He'll use any pretext to beat me, but he's looking for an excuse to kill you, to keep me in fear of him. You must not give him any reason. No matter what he does to me, keep still. Don't provoke him. I need you to stay alive. Promise me that."

"You know what he'll do to you. He'll want to show everyone in Akkad that you belong to him now, that you're nothing more than his slave."

Trella touched her swollen face, still feeling the sting in her cheek from where Korthac struck her. "Whatever Korthac wants, we'll do. We need to stay alive, at least for now. In a few days, if we find everything is hopeless, then I'll try to kill him."

"He'll use the child to control you."

"The child will have to die. I know that. He'll want no reminder of Eskkar or me left alive." She shook her head at the thought. "I'll kill the babe myself, if it comes to that."

Trella reached out and took Annok-sur's hand. "You'll die as well. He surely knows what role you played in gathering information. As soon as he thinks he's secure, then we'll no longer be needed." Trella shrugged.

"I have the birthing knife, Trella, if it comes to that. Though I prefer trying to slit his throat with it."

During the confusion, Trella had seen Annok-sur slip the small knife inside the lamp. But the tiny implement, a special gift from Drusala, and meant to be used to cut the umbilical cord, had a blade no longer than Trella's finger.

"It's not much of a weapon against Korthac," Trella said, "although it may serve to end our own lives. Keep the knife safe, Annok-sur. We may have to use it on ourselves. Until that day, we obey our new master. We must stay alive, for the child's sake, if nothing else, and to give Eskkar time to gather his forces. As long as we obey Korthac instantly, as long as he thinks we're of use to him, he'll keep us alive for a little while longer."

"So we grovel before this Egyptian."

"We grovel, Annok-sur." Out of habit, Trella reached for the coin that she'd worn around her neck since Eskkar first gave it to her. Her freedom coin, he'd called it. Now it was gone, given to another, as vanished as her freedom. "We grovel, and we wait."

17

Ariamus had hidden his sixty-three horsemen in a tiny fold of ground, a little more than one hundred paces from the trail Bantor's men were following back to Akkad. Ariamus had galloped his horse that far himself, and knew his horsemen could cover that distance in moments, long before his victims could dismount and string their bows. Horse to horse, his charging men on fresh mounts would have the advantage.

The low crest of the rise concealed fifty of Ariamus's men abreast, and the remainder formed a smaller group behind the main line. He had twenty hard-bitten fighters scattered among them. Most of these he'd recruited himself, though Korthac had added half a dozen of his Egyptians, probably with instructions to keep an eye on their commander.

Chewing his lip, Ariamus waited for the single scout who tracked the approaching column. They'd sighted Bantor's men hours ago, and they'd be here soon. Everything would work against the Akkadians—their horses would be tired from a long day's ride, they would be traveling uphill, and they expected to reach Akkad's gates and safety in a few more hours. Ariamus knew the Akkadians had shadowed the retreating Alur Meriki for over a month. That mission completed, Bantor and his soldiers were returning in high spirits to their women, plenty of ale, and a chance to sleep in their own beds. The last thing on their minds would be an ambush so close to home.

He grinned at the thought. Instead of safety, the returning soldiers would die right here, and it would be Ariamus's men who would ride through the open gates of Akkad. Korthac had planned everything with care, Ariamus admitted, though he hated to give the man so much credit.

Ariamus and his men had done well in last night's battle, capturing the river gate with a minimum of fighting. Just as important, he'd seized the boats docked there with no loss of cargo, and no vessels escaping up or down the Tigris. With both the river and the local roads under Korthac's control, at least a few days would pass before the country-side learned what had taken place in Akkad. The only thing that could have gone better was if Takany had managed to get himself killed. Ariamus had craftily made sure the thickheaded Egyptian led the fight at the barracks, where the heaviest fighting would occur, but the man had survived without even a scratch.

"You did well, Ariamus," Korthac had said afterward, grunting his approval at his newest subcommander's efficiency. "Now take your men and destroy the Akkadians returning from the south. Then you will have your reward."

Relishing the praise, Ariamus had bowed politely, gathered his men, and departed, as eager as Korthac to finish off the returning soldiers. He and his men camped for the night a few miles ride from the city, and Ariamus sent out scouts to look for the approaching Akkadians. A successful ambush of Bantor and his troops would ensure Korthac's confidence, and earn Ariamus an even bigger share of the loot waiting back in Akkad.

The moment to earn that reward had arrived. The men from Akkad marched unsuspectingly toward their fate. In a few moments, Ariamus would destroy Bantor's soldiers, leaving no organized force to rally support against Korthac. The handful of men Eskkar had with him up at Bisitun would be no problem to defeat. Ariamus knew he could raise, recruit, and train an equal number in the week or ten days it would take for Eskkar to reach Akkad. And with any bit of luck, the barbarian would already be dead, struck down by Korthac's assassins.

As soon as Ariamus returned to Akkad with the news of Bantor's destruction, Korthac's rule would be secure. The Egyptian would proclaim himself sovereign of the city, and Ariamus would stand at his side. With enough men to guard the walls, no power could force them out.

Assuming Ariamus could keep his men under control, he reminded himself. He'd readied his men for the ambush more than an hour ago. Even after yesterday's success in Akkad, many of the men looked nervous, and he saw fear on the faces of more than one. The sooner he got them into battle, the better. He wished he'd had a few more weeks to train them . . . but Korthac wouldn't wait. News of Bantor's approach had forced Korthac to move a little earlier than he planned. The city had to be taken the day before Bantor arrived. So far, everything had gone exactly as the wily Egyptian had planned.

Ariamus heard his men talking again, their voices quickly rising and threatening the whole plan. They kept testing his patience. Shifting their feet, they whispered to their neighbors and boasted about what they would do in the coming battle. His hand twitched at his sword, and he resisted the temptation to kill one as a lesson. Half-trained and lacking discipline they might be, but he'd worked with worse, and right now he needed all of them.

"Demons take you all," he said. "Keep silent!"

Gritting his teeth at the fools who couldn't keep still, he walked back and forth along the line, hand on his sword, urging them to stay ready, shut their mouths, and look to their mounts. Not that Ariamus cared how much his men twitched and worried, but he didn't want the horses picking up their riders' fears and getting spooked.

Two days ago he'd had to kill a slow-witted fool who disobeyed him once too often, and hopefully that memory remained fresh in their minds. Just so long as they followed orders. Ariamus didn't care how much they feared the enemy, as long as they feared him more.

Nevertheless, most of these bandits had little experience in attacking battle-hardened men. Fresh from Akkad's capture, they now fancied themselves fearsome fighters. Almost all had seen some fighting, or raided enough farms and small caravans to convince themselves of their bravery, but Ariamus knew they could never stand against the Alur Meriki. Even facing the soldiers from Akkad, most of this rabble would be dead in moments. Still, Ariamus had more

than enough men to do the job, and if he could surprise
Bantor, the combination would guarantee victory.

The men's talking grew louder, and Ariamus turned to
see his scout trotting toward them. At least the man, one of
Korthac's subcommanders, had remembered his orders to
raise no dust trail and to make sure he wasn't seen. Ariamus
turned back toward his still-mumbling men, and again put
his hand on his sword. They fell silent under his glare. The
sooner the attack got under way, the better.

"Well, Nebibi, are they coming?" Speaking in the
language of the Egyptian, Ariamus didn't even wait for the
man to dismount.

"Yes, Ariamus. They're but moments behind me. Their
horses look weary, and they suspect nothing. All ride with
bows slung."

"You're sure? No scouts out to the front or flanks?"

"None," Nebibi replied. "Only a rear guard of three
men. They're trailing a good distance behind the column,
but that's all."

Ariamus grunted in relief. If he and his men had been
spotted . . . Korthac had warned him not to challenge the
Akkadians' bows. If Ariamus couldn't smash them before
they could bring their bows into play, he would have to
return to Akkad and get more men.

"Good work, Nebibi. Return to your men and make sure
they know what to do. Try to keep the fools quiet." Nebibi
had charge of one-third of the men. Rihat, Ariamus's other
subcommander, commanded another third.

"Rihat." Ariamus called out to his other commander,
now speaking in their native tongue. "Get the men ready.
They're almost here."

Ariamus walked up and down the line one last time, looking each man in the eye, and making sure each knew his orders. The veterans, spread throughout the line, would steady the fools and urge them onward. They lined up the horses almost shoulder to shoulder, with the men standing beside them, waiting. Ariamus could still hear some men whispering. He swore to himself, but said nothing. Anything he did now might spook the horses even more than his men's talk. Besides, the beasts appeared to have grown used to the incessant chatter.

Nevertheless, now was not the time to take chances. "Nebibi, Rihat, I want absolute silence. Kill the next man who opens his mouth." Both subcommanders drew their swords, and Ariamus nodded in satisfaction. "Remember, men, we'll be watching you. Any man who breaks too soon, or disobeys orders, dies on the spot. Now mount up, and ready your weapons."

Their smiles disappeared, and silence came at last over the group. He smiled in approval at their fear. That fear would drive them forward, which was all he wanted. Destroying Bantor's force meant everything, and he would take any casualties to accomplish that end. Low sounds of men and horses rippled up and down the line for a few moments, before stillness again fell over the group. Ariamus scanned the line one last time—men, horses, and weapons—they were ready.

Ariamus climbed the low rise, lying flat on the ground to make sure he wouldn't be seen as he peered through the tall grass. The path Bantor followed remained empty in front of him, no other travelers or dust trails in sight in either direction. He turned his gaze to the south and waited. He checked the sun's progress and cursed at his enemy's slow approach. Dusk would be on them in little more than an hour.

At last, the head of the column appeared, as if rising slowly out of the ground. The Akkadians walked their horses two abreast, the men relaxed, talking to each other, their bows slung across their backs. They would be tired, hungry, and thirsty. No doubt all of them looked forward to an evening of food and ale in Akkad.

Behind him he heard the faint whispers of his subcommanders as they kept the men in check, each man attending to his beast, making sure it didn't whinny at the scent or sound of the approaching horses and men. No wind blew, and even the occasional breeze came from the south. He counted the men as they appeared, and ended at forty-six, with three more for the rear guard. Ariamus knew that fifty-three men had gone south with that fool Bantor weeks ago. The missing soldiers had probably returned to Akkad earlier or, even more likely, deserted.

He could hear the Akkadians now, the horses plodding along. Ariamus wanted to return to his horse, but he didn't want to move until the very last moment, to make sure none of his men charged out before the column reached the spot directly in front of them. Ariamus waited those last few moments, then slipped backward down the hill before rising to his feet and walking calmly to his horse. He jerked the halter free and swung onto the animal's back.

The whole line began to move a little, back and forth, and the animals started pawing the earth and snorting, but it no longer mattered. Ariamus tightened his knees on his horse's back.

"Attack!" he shouted, and the whole line of his fighters burst into motion. In an instant, they raced up over the top of the rise and charged at the startled column of men in front of them.

Bantor rode with Klexor at the head of the column, while Alexar, another leader of ten, rode behind the column, with the rear guard. Bantor felt as weary and thirsty as his horse. Earlier in the day, everyone had spoken of getting home, women, warm beds, hot food, and thick ale. But near day's end, the men rode mostly in silence, keeping their thoughts to themselves. If Akkad weren't only a few more hours ahead, they'd be making camp right now.

Tomorrow they'd get their pay, and each man would have plenty of silver in his pouch. The taverns would be full of cheap wine and smiling women, all glad to welcome back their men. They'd been away for five weeks, shadowing a still dangerous and much larger force of warriors, and in all those days, they had never relaxed their guard. Until today. Now, close to home, they rode easy.

The two lead horses lifted their heads at the same time, ears twitching as they rolled their eyes to the left. Bantor's eyes followed those of his horse, just as a burst of sound rolled toward them. A force of screaming men arose from what had appeared to be level ground to their left, racing their horses toward the column, flashing swords in their hands. The ground shook from the thudding hooves that threw clods of dirt and grass high into the air.

For a single moment, every man froze, the sudden

appearance of the attackers a complete surprise. Bantor felt the fear rising in his chest. "Dismount! String your bows!" He heard Klexor echoing the same orders, as both men pulled their horses around to face their attackers. "Form a line!"

Several horses reared up in terror, other soldiers began shouting, and already the attacking warriors had covered half the open ground.

Bantor saw that not all the activity was panic. Even as they'd watched the southerly progress of the retreating Alur Meriki, these Akkadians had trained for such an attack by their enemy. The men, seeing the oncoming danger, had reacted without hesitation. They flung themselves from their horses and moved to string their bows in a rush of action. All of their weeks and months of training had told them one thing over and over. They could not defeat the Alur Meriki on horseback. So they had been trained to dismount, ready their weapons, and band together.

Bantor leapt down from his horse, then smacked the animal's rump with the flat of his sword, sending the animal lumbering toward the oncoming riders. All the other riderless horses began to mill around, scattering in different directions, some of them racing toward the attackers. Their movements slowed the oncoming riders a bit, as the bandits shifted their course to avoid the frantic animals. Even so, only a handful of Bantor's men managed to launch an arrow before the wave of bandits struck them.

Bantor waited with dread for the killing flight of arrows from the Alur Meriki bows, but the arrows never came. Instead the attackers arrived in a thunder of hooves that shook the earth, a terrifying sound to those facing it on foot.

Swords slashed downward at Bantor's men, some still struggling to string their bows, others drawing swords. Screams of the wounded mingled with the war cries of the attackers. Nevertheless, the Akkadians had no time to ready themselves, and the attackers cut their way through Bantor's men. Some of the soldiers threw themselves to the ground, trying to avoid the swords that flashed down at them.

With nothing to slow them down, no line of men on horseback to impede their attack, most of the bandits galloped right through what remained of the column, swinging their swords at anything, man or beast, within reach. Some of the attacking horses jumped over the prone Akkadians, following their animal instinct to avoid stepping on anything that moved.

Not all of the soldiers managed to get flat to the ground, and many took blows from slashing swords or found themselves crushed under the horses' hooves. For the first time, Bantor realized he didn't face Alur Meriki horsemen. As he flung himself facedown on the grass, he saw his attackers rode more like bandits, not barbarian warriors from the steppes.

A man wielding a sword on a galloping horse cannot reach down far enough to strike at anyone lying on the ground. Barbarians carried lances to take care of that very problem. A trained rider could thrust the lance down to kill someone crouching or even lying prone, or hurl it at someone hugging the earth. These attackers carried neither lance nor bows, and some of Bantor's men escaped without a scratch, though fewer than half struggled to their feet after the wave of riders smashed through them.

Bantor's left shoulder burned in agony. A flying hoof had landed on him, and he wondered if his arm had been crushed. Ignoring the pain, he pushed himself to his feet, fumbling for his sword with his good hand. "Form a line on me. Hurry, before they turn. Hurry!"

It took the attackers time to slow their horses and turn them around, expecting to ride back and deliver the killing blow. But the very speed of their charge had carried them another sixty or seventy paces past the shattered column. Before the first man could goad his horse back toward the Akkadians for a second attack, an arrow reached out and struck him in the chest, then another, and another.

"Hold," Bantor shouted, as the survivors rushed together, lining up to face their attackers. "Draw . . . aim," he waited until every man had drawn his shaft to his ear. "Loose!" As the bandits finished turning their horses and began their second charge, twenty arrows flew into their ranks.

Man and beast went down, both screaming in pain, and the second charge slowed. Less than three seconds later, another wave of arrows struck, and now some of the bandits had no thought but to get away from these deadly archers. The brave few men who kept riding toward the archers died, killed in the third wave, delivered at less than twenty paces, the shafts striking with enough force at that distance to stop even a horse in its tracks.

Horses and men flopped on the ground between the two forces, and the scattered dead and dying prevented a quick assault on the line of bowmen. Again Bantor directed the men's fire, and another wave of arrows landed in the midst of a group trying to rally for another attack.

The attackers turned away, urging their horses to either

side of the bowmen. Still within range, more horses and men died before the last of the bandits galloped to safety.

Bantor had seen broken men flee before, and guessed that these attackers wouldn't be back, not for some time at least. He cursed at their backs, and flung his sword down into the earth, before sinking to his knees. The whole fight had lasted but moments from beginning to end, but more than half of Bantor's men had died, and his horses scattered over the countryside.

When Klexor reached his side, he found his leader wincing in pain and muttering one word over and over. "Ariamus!"

It took more than half a mile before Ariamus and his subcommanders managed to halt and regroup their men. Some of them had bolted for Akkad, others just raced in any direction, anxious to get away from the great arrows that buzzed like bees about their heads, striking down their companions. They circled about, trying to regroup, and Ariamus finally brought them together.

"Dismount," he shouted. "Get down off those horses."

Some refused, still frightened of the Akkadian bowmen. Most kept glancing back toward the place of ambush.

"They've no horses to follow us, you fools," he bellowed. "What are you, a bunch of cowards to run from half your number? Nebibi, Rihat, bring the men together. Kill anyone who disobeys."

Ariamus took a quick count of his riders, then slapped his hand upon his leg so hard his horse jumped in surprise. Ariamus had struck Bantor's line with over sixty men, losing only one or two to arrows before they clashed, and Ariamus doubted if he'd lost a man as they rode through them. One more charge would have finished the job.

Now Ariamus counted less than forty men, and these looked so shaken up he doubted he could drive them back for another attack. He had lost an equal number of horses, but had more than recouped that loss, since almost all of Bantor's horses had trotted after his own animals.

He stopped cursing at his men, dismounted, and squatted down on the ground to think things over, Nebibi and Rihat joining him. The rest of the men began to breathe a little easier, relaxing enough to lick their wounds or to tell their companions how bravely they had fought.

"We killed most of them," Rihat offered. "And we've got almost all of their horses."

"We're not here to steal horses, you fool! You should . . ." Ariamus took a deep breath. It wouldn't help to shout at his underling. And the man was right, they *had* killed most of Bantor's men. "How many do you think were left alive?"

Rihat closed his eyes, the better to think about what he had seen. "Twenty, maybe less. Not more than that."

Ariamus had made the same guess. So he'd killed more than half of Bantor's men. Perhaps some of the survivors had taken wounds. Damn Bantor. Ariamus had planned well, but he hadn't expected to find himself in this situation, with only half a victory. What would he tell Korthac? How could Ariamus explain that he'd left twenty Akkadians alive, when he had over twice that number still fit to fight?

"Exactly how many men did we lose, Rihat?"

Rihat shrugged, then got up and began a detailed count.

It took some time before he came back and sat down on the grass. "We've forty-one men left, not counting us. Two are wounded, but not too badly. They can still ride."

Only two men wounded, but more than twenty dead or missing. The numbers didn't improve his mood. Those arrows had struck with such force, and at close range, the shafts struck hard enough to knock a man off his mount. He doubted any of his men who'd lost their horses or gotten wounded survived. The Akkadians' arrows would have finished any survivors by now. Ariamus had lost about as many men as he had killed. Not that he cared about his losses. With Korthac's gold, they could always recruit more men.

More important, Bantor's men had been soldiers, men trained to fight, and not so easy to replace. The horses couldn't be easily restocked either. Ariamus had to scour the western lands to get the mounts he had acquired. On foot, the Akkadians wouldn't be much of a threat. Ariamus remembered seeing Bantor go down under hooves, and didn't recall seeing him get up. He recalled Bantor as a slow-witted fool anyway, and once again Ariamus wondered what Eskkar had seen in the man. Nevertheless, Eskkar's stupidity was Ariamus's good fortune.

He'd broken Bantor's men, and left them on foot. Their bows would be useless against the walls of Akkad, and from those walls Korthac and his men would have their own bows. No, the situation looked less bleak the more he thought about it. At least, it would have to sound that way when he reported to Korthac. Ariamus had promised the man he would destroy all the Akkadians, not just half of them. He started thinking about what he would say to the new ruler of Akkad.

Even more important, Ariamus didn't dare lose any more men. Without a sizable force reporting to him, Takany would overshadow him, and Ariamus, as leader of the horsemen, would lose whatever influence he had with Korthac. No, Ariamus decided, he'd already lost more men than he'd expected. Any more would be disastrous, even if he survived another attack himself.

"We must go back and finish them, Ariamus," Nebibi interrupted Ariamus's thoughts. "Korthac said we should . . ."

"Korthac isn't here, Nebibi." Ariamus cut him off. "Do you want to charge again against those bowmen?"

Nebibi's face told him the answer. The Egyptian had plenty of courage, but they both knew what kind of men they led.

"We've no bows, Nebibi," Ariamus began, lowering his voice and speaking now in the language of Egypt. "Even if we could drive this lot back for another attack . . . even if we succeed, we'll lose too many of our own doing it. And remember, those archers will be targeting anyone urging the men to the attack."

Nebibi opened his mouth, then closed it. The man might fear Korthac's wrath, but Nebibi had never seen arrows such as those, knocking horses to their knees.

"We've done what we set out to do, Nebibi. We've smashed Bantor's force. The few that survived, that escaped, let's say less than a dozen, are masterless men now, and helpless. Korthac will be pleased when he receives our report."

Nebibi thought it over, no doubt trying to balance the danger of shading the truth to Korthac compared to facing

Bantor's men again. At last he nodded uneasily. "Yes, Ariamus, only a few escaped us. Less than a dozen. Korthac will be pleased."

Ariamus smiled in satisfaction, then turned to Rihat. "Close up the men."

Moments later, the whole force of bandits clustered around their commander.

"Men! We have won a great victory. We have broken our enemies, and left less than a dozen alive, most of them wounded, and without horses. You have done well to fight so bravely."

That raised a ragged cheer from his fighters, though some of them wondered how they could be cowards and fools one moment, then heroes the next.

"Now we return to Akkad. We will join up with Korthac's men, and enjoy the city we took yesterday. The gold, the women, the horses, all the best of Akkad, will be ours."

They cheered again, as they realized the fighting had ended. He saw the smiles on their faces, and knew their confidence had returned, that they once again considered themselves ferocious fighters. So long as they didn't have to face those archers again.

That would be how he explained it to Korthac. Nebibi would support the story, or have to admit to his own failure. Besides, a few men on the loose, scattered over the countryside, wouldn't matter anyway. They'd round them up in a few days.

"Back to Akkad," Ariamus shouted, as he climbed on his horse, "back to Akkad and our gold!"

Another cheer, louder this time, went up. Nebibi looked

at Ariamus, and nodded acquiescence, tight-lipped. Their report would satisfy Korthac, at least for now.

By the time the three trailing scouts reached the column, the fight had ended. Bantor, back on his feet, shook with rage, swearing torture and death to Ariamus. Half the men had never heard the name before.

"Take it easy, Bantor," Klexor said, trying to calm his captain down. "Let's take a look at your shoulder."

Alexar walked up, carrying a water skin. "They took us by surprise, but we drove them off and killed more of them than we lost." He and the other two men acting as rear guard had rushed forward as soon as they saw the ambush, but none of the attackers had passed within a hundred paces of him. Alexar managed to dismount and tie his horse to a bush. He'd been one of the first to fire as the men rode past.

The ambush left everyone with a raging thirst, and they drank the remainder of their water with no thought to save any for later. They couldn't carry it far on foot, anyway.

"Anyone know who they were?" Alexar tossed away the now-empty water skin. "They weren't Alur Meriki, or we'd all be dead by now."

"If they were Alur Meriki," Klexor offered, "they would've finished us off with lances, the barbarian way, instead of riding through us like a bunch of old women who can't control their horses."

"Their leader was Ariamus, the former captain of the guard in Orak," Bantor said, staring at the ground. He tested his shoulder, moving his arm carefully; it didn't hurt quite as much. Perhaps the bone hadn't broken after all.

Bantor took a deep breath, still struggling to control his emotions. "The coward Ariamus ran off when he learned the barbarians were coming to Akkad, and that's when Eskkar took command of the village."

Bantor left unsaid that, a few months before his departure, Ariamus had sent Bantor out on a patrol, then summoned Annok-sur to his bed for an afternoon of pleasure. Annok-sur had never spoken about it, but Bantor had heard whispers of it from the men.

Short of stabbing Ariamus in the back, and so forfeiting his own life for killing his superior, Bantor could do nothing, so he'd swallowed his pride and pretended ignorance. He knew Annok-sur had not gone willingly, but to protect her husband and daughter.

Flexing his arm, Bantor couldn't remember a time in the last few months when he wasn't recovering from one wound or another.

"Well, whoever they were, they headed off toward Akkad," Alexar replied, "so they must be sure of being able to enter the city."

"They can't enter Akkad, not that many of them, and not carrying weapons," Bantor answered, trying to understand what had happened. No large force of armed men could get into Akkad, unless . . .

"Could they have taken the city?" Klexor asked, his mind going down the same path as his commander's.

"They must have captured Akkad," Bantor said. "They knew we were coming, and didn't want us reaching the gates."

"Forty or so bandits isn't enough to take Akkad," Klexor offered. "They must have more men inside the city as well."

"So they ambush us just before we reach Akkad," Alexar said, "before we learn what's happened to the city."

That made sense, Bantor decided. Take the city, then take the soldiers piecemeal. He wondered if Eskkar's force to the north might be next, if they hadn't already been crushed.

"Damn the demons below," Bantor swore. "We can't just walk up to the gates and ask what the hell is going on! These bandits may have had enough fighters to capture Akkad from within."

"Well, what are we going to do?" Klexor sounded worried. "If this Ariamus has captured Akkad, he may come back with more men. We can't just stay here."

A good question, Bantor thought, and he didn't know what to answer. What would Eskkar do, he wondered. Eskkar always knew what to do on a battlefield. Bantor thought about that for a while.

"How many horses and men do we have?" he asked abruptly.

Alexar had already taken the count. "Counting us, we've twenty-five men, six of them wounded, and seven horses." He glanced at the soldiers gathered around their leaders. The men looked alert, some tended to the wounded, while others salvaged what they could from their dead companions or the bandits. "We may get a few more horses if we're lucky, but darkness is coming on . . ."

Bantor thought that over. He took longer to work things out than some of his men, but he'd survived plenty of fights. One thing he knew for certain. He didn't have enough information to decide what to do. If he picked the wrong course of action, they might all be dead by noon tomorrow.

So he would get information first. He looked up to find his men watching him, waiting for him to speak.

"Here's what we'll do. Alexar, take the four best horses, and one other rider. Start north for Bisitun at once. We've got to make sure Eskkar and Sisuthros know what is happening. Get far enough away from here before you rest for the night, then keep going as fast as you can, changing mounts as often as you can. Ride the horses until they drop, if you have to. You should be able to get to Bisitun in five or six days, maybe less, with two horses for each man. Tell Eskkar what's happened, and that it was Ariamus who led the attackers. Make sure you remember that name. Ariamus. Take anything you need for the trip."

He waited until Alexar nodded understanding, then Bantor turned to his other commander. "Klexor, put the wounded on the other three horses, and send them south, back the way we came. We passed some farmhouses a few miles back. Maybe they can hide there until they recover."

"And the rest of us, where are we going?" Klexor asked.

Bantor shifted his shoulder, wincing at the pain, but he could move it. He'd have to hope it mended itself in a few days. "We are going to take what we can carry and head north ourselves, as if we were heading for Bisitun as well. We'll walk all night, and tomorrow morning. Then we'll cut over to the river. If any follow us, they'll think we've crossed over to the west bank. We'll see if we can find some boats to take us south, back to Akkad."

"Back to Akkad!" Klexor questioned. "What can less than twenty do against the city?"

"Nothing. Don't worry, we won't be going into Akkad, just to the farms north of the city. Rebba's farm, that's where we'll go. He has a jetty on the river, and plenty of room to hide twice as many men. He can tell us what the hell is going on."

Bantor turned back to Alexar. "Tell Eskkar that's where we'll be, and to get word to us at Rebba's farm. Get ready to move out."

They all picked up their weapons, gathering up all the spare arrows they could carry. Alexar picked a young archer to ride with him, a man no taller than a boy, departed on the four strongest horses and started moving north at an easy canter. A few minutes later, the injured started south, walking their horses to ease the wounded. The rest of the men closed in around Bantor, waiting for the order to move out.

Klexor broke the silence. "Why didn't this Ariamus come back to finish us off?" The others moved in closer, eager to hear their commander's words.

"Because the coward knew we'd kill most of his men before they overran us." Bantor pulled his sword from the earth, knocked the dirt off, and returned it to its sheath. He didn't like admitting defeat, or that Ariamus had still enough men to finish the job. "But I know one thing. I'm going to kill him myself, if it's the last thing I do. I'm going to rip his heart right out of his chest."

No one said anything, and Bantor went on, talking as much to himself as his men. "We'll have to wait, at least until Eskkar gets word about what's happened. If we can join our force with his, we'll have enough men to face Ariamus, and I can spread his guts in the sun."

The men looked at each other. Bantor rarely spoke with such passion, but all could see that hatred and a desire for revenge possessed the man, just as they could hear it in his voice. They, too, wanted their revenge. Ambushed like raw recruits, they'd seen their friends and fellow soldiers killed. Worse, their dead would have to lie unburied, while their comrades fled for their lives.

Hands tightened on sword hilts and bows. Counting Bantor, they numbered seventeen. They looked at each other. The fight wasn't over. For these men, the battle had just begun.

Bantor looked up at the descending sun, slipping halfway below the horizon. It would be dark soon. He had thought they'd all be drinking in a tavern by then.

"All right, men. Get what you need, and let's go. We've a long walk tonight." Ignoring the pain in his shoulder, he picked up a bow and a full quiver, and started north.

18

Once the moon rose, they had enough light to make out the flat terrain. Bantor drove the men hard all night. They'd alternated between jogging and walking, and the threat of Ariamus and his horsemen not only drove them onward, it kept them looking over their shoulders. Except for an occasional farmhouse, they saw little. Twice they stopped at a farmer's well for water. The first time they went unnoticed, but at the second, the dogs awoke everyone with their barking, and Bantor had to order the family back into their house, warning them to say nothing to anyone.

By the time he gave the order to halt, only a few hours remained before dawn. Exhausted, sore-footed, and hungry, the men had covered twenty miles and reached the trail that led north to Bisitun. Everyone fell asleep in moments, falling to the earth without regard to comfort. When the sun woke them, no one felt rested. They'd slept only long enough to sustain them.

The road posed even greater danger. Travelers and traders would be coming along, some on horseback, and it wouldn't be long before word of their passage got back to Akkad. Even more worrisome, Ariamus might send any number of riders up the road, to prevent their escape to the north. Bantor determined not to lose a moment.

As soon as he started walking, the pain in his shoulder returned. Sleeping on the hard ground hadn't helped; the brief rest had stiffened it, and each step made him wince in pain. The soreness seemed worse than the day before. Klexor examined him and declared that nothing seemed broken, and for that small comfort, Bantor gave thanks.

By midmorning, they'd walked and jogged another ten miles, and every tired step took them farther from Akkad. They began to encounter travelers, most heading in the opposite direction, toward Akkad, and all of them on foot.

"Shouldn't we warn them there might be danger in Akkad?" Klexor asked, the first time they passed some travelers heading toward the city.

"If we do, they'll spread the word, and soon half the countryside will know we're heading north. They'll have to take their chances at Akkad. Otherwise any scouts Ariamus has in the area will know we've passed this way."

"They may mention us anyway, when they arrive."

"Or they may forget all about us in the excitement." Bantor had anticipated this during the night's walk. More important, he'd learned from Eskkar the need to appear confident before the men, even when uncertainty gripped your insides. "Besides, it will take them hours to reach Akkad, maybe even until sunset. We'll cover a lot of ground before then."

Bantor turned to face Klexor. "Tell the men to say nothing to anyone we pass. Not a word."

Klexor grunted, and began to pass the word down the line.

Not that anyone wanted to speak to them anyway, Bantor decided. He and his heavily armed men looked gaunt, dirty, and dangerous, and the few wayfarers they encountered shrank aside, staring openmouthed and with fear in their eyes, as the soldiers strode past in silence.

They rested every hour, all of them trying to ignore the pangs of hunger that rumbled in their bellies. Just before noon, Bantor gave the order to halt. The men sank to the ground, too tired to complain about their hunger.

"Klexor, we're about thirty miles north of Akkad." Bantor wiped the sweat from his face, as his men grouped themselves around their leaders. "It's time to cut over to the river. I know a farm that has some boats. We'll wait until the road is clear, then we'll move west."

"We're nearly halfway to Dilgarth. We could be there by early morning, if we push hard."

"I'd like to, Klexor, but we don't know what might be waiting for us in Dilgarth. And even if we made it there, we'd never be able to get back to Akkad." Bantor shook his head. "No, I think the river is safer for us. We can find something to eat at the farm, too. If things are really bad, we may be safer on the other side of the Tigris anyway."

Klexor shrugged, but didn't have anything better to offer. "Then let's get off the road now, while it's clear."

One by one, they slipped off the dusty trail, leaving as little trace of their presence as possible. They stumbled along as best they could on the uneven terrain, until they'd passed well out of sight of anyone traveling on the road.

They covered the last stretch to the river at a slow walk, the only pace they could manage.

When they cleared a low hill and saw the farmhouse ahead, nestling a stone's throw from the river, Bantor felt close to exhaustion. The pain from his shoulder, combined with the unfamiliar effort of walking, had tired him more than he would have expected. His men looked no better, and he decided he'd made the right choice; traveling on the road, they would never have reached Dilgarth before riders caught up with them. Spreading his men out to avoid leaving tracks, they stepped down into the nearest irrigation ditch, and splashed along its winding course down to the river.

The farm, a large one with several separate buildings surrounded by fields of wheat and barley, belonged to a man named Hargar. Children playing under a tree noticed them approaching, and ran to warn the adults. The family barricaded themselves inside the main building. Bantor knew the appearance of so many armed men would frighten any farmer.

When they reached the sheep pen, Bantor climbed out of the ditch. "Wait here," he told the men. "Klexor, come with me." The two men walked side by side to the house.

"Ho, Hargar! No need to hide in your cellar. It's Bantor, commander at Akkad, and we need your help."

Nothing happened, so Bantor and Klexor sat in the dirt under a fruit tree in front of the main house, a few paces from the door. Bantor leaned gratefully against the tree and hoped nobody in the house decided to launch an arrow at him. After a long moment, they heard shuffling at the door, and a young man stuck his head out and stared at them, eyes wide and mouth open.

"Who are you?" Bantor called out.

"I'm Hargar's son, Hannis. My father has gone to Dilgarth to sell a goat. Is it really you, Bantor?" His voice sounded fearful, but he stepped outside and slowly approached the men sitting on the ground. "By the gods, it is you. What are you doing here? Why did you approach through the ditches?"

"It's a long story, Hannis. But something's gone wrong at Akkad. Have you heard any news from there?"

"No, no one's gone to market in over a week," Hannis said, still looking nervous at the sight of the rest of Bantor's men.

"Well, we need your help. If we wanted to slit your throats, you'd all be dead by now. I need food and drink for my men." Bantor reached into his pouch and took out the last of his silver coins. "Knowing your father, I suppose I'll have to pay for it." He tossed the coins to Hannis. "Give these to Hargar when he returns."

An hour later, Bantor and all his men, full of food and a few mouthfuls of ale, had fallen asleep behind a storehouse nestled next to the river. Klexor stood watch, as much to make sure no one left the farm as to guard against anyone approaching.

A little before sundown, Bantor and his men ate again, filling themselves on bread, cheese, and several tasteless sausages Hargar had been planning to sell in the market at Akkad.

"We're taking your boats, Hannis," Bantor said. "Don't bother complaining. You'll be paid when things settle down in Akkad."

"And if they don't settle down, then I'll be out two boats," Hannis answered. "Can't you pay me now?"

Bantor smiled. "You've learned your father's ways. I would if I could, but you've already got the last of my silver. Besides, you'll probably get the boats back anyway."

"Where are you going?"

"We're going upriver to Dilgarth. It's better than walking, and there's no place nearby where we'll find enough horses."

"What's going on in Dilgarth? Has Eskkar returned from the north?"

Bantor took the last piece of bread from the platter and stood. "Stay away from both Akkad and Dilgarth for at least a week. And Hannis, make sure no one in your family says anything about us being here or taking the boats. Or I'll come back and take that silver out of your hides. You'll wish the Alur Meriki had returned if I find you've told anyone we were here or where we're going. Do you understand?"

Bantor walked away without waiting for a reply. At the river, two boats bobbed in the water, tied to posts sunk into the bank. One was little more than a skiff, and used as much for working in the irrigation ditches as on the river. The other craft was larger, and sturdy enough to ferry crops and animals to the markets in Akkad.

Four of Bantor's men knew about boats, and he told them to take charge. They emptied the vessel of ballast, and positioned the men with care. Seventeen men could barely squeeze aboard, and both boats rode dangerously low in the water. Even Bantor could see it wouldn't take much to capsize them. The sun had just gone down when they pushed off, heading north. Without a breeze, they didn't bother to raise the tiny sail on the larger craft.

Powering the overloaded boats upstream took plenty of muscle, and the men handed off the small paddles to one another whenever they tired. They paddled until well away from the farm. Only when the darkness of night covered everything did Bantor order them to turn toward the shore, satisfied no one could see them. If anyone came to the farm and put a knife to Hannis's throat, the farmer could honestly say that Bantor had gone north, up the river.

They rested, watching the stars appear, before turning the boats around and heading back toward Akkad, with four men working the oars.

The paddling went easier downstream, and they made better time. Bantor wanted to go faster, but the boatmen refused to speed up, afraid of a spill in the darkness, in an overweighted boat paddled by clumsy oarsmen.

Most of the men sat immobile, afraid to move. No one wanted to go for a swim in the river at night, with a good chance of drowning in the bargain.

Bantor watched the shoreline, and soon the dark outlines of Hargar's farmhouse slid past. He saw no one, and anyone watching the river would have to be standing at the edge of the riverbank to notice the vessels' silent passing.

The moon rose, climbed, and began to fall, as they made their way down the Tigris. Bantor guessed they still had another hour or so before dawn when the boatman called out that they were approaching Akkad. Bantor couldn't see anything, except the river glinting in the moonlight. No lights showed anywhere along the river. He knew all the farmers would be fast asleep, thriftily saving their oil and candles. Torches would be burning in Akkad, but Bantor knew they would have to be farther downriver to see those.

The boat edged closer to the eastern shore, though he couldn't make out anything, and had no idea what landmarks the boatmen recognized. Though he'd lived near Akkad all his life, the river remained a mystery to him. Bantor flinched when the bottom grated on the sand, then thumped against a small wooden jetty protruding a few feet into the river. In the faint moonlight he could see another boat tied up there as well.

The boatmen swung onto the jetty and secured the boats fast. The men disembarked one at a time, taking care not to swamp the listing riverboats. Bantor climbed ashore last, breathing thanks to the gods that he, his men, and their weapons stood on solid earth again.

The soldiers moved inland, stringing their bows as they went. Noble Rebba's farm, a combination of houses and corrals, lay a few hundred paces from the river. They stopped a good distance from the nearest house, crouching down behind an irrigation ditch. The farm, one of several that Noble Rebba owned, was a rich one, and he had both dogs and men to protect his herds and crops from petty thieves and robbers. It would be too dangerous to approach at night. Bantor decided to wait there until dawn. He told the men to take what rest they could, but to keep their bows strung and at the ready for any confrontation.

When the sun's first rays crossed the horizon, Bantor advanced toward the farmhouse. He had grown up on a farm, much smaller than this one, of course, but he remembered the ways of dogs and animals. So he headed first to the path that led to Akkad, then followed that toward the main house. A dog barked, joined at once by another, and Bantor saw two men step into the sunlight in front of the main house. They looked at him in surprise as he approached, and in a moment a third man appeared, carrying swords that he handed to the others.

Bantor knew he looked like a bandit in his ripped and tattered garment that showed the mud of the river. The dogs surrounded him, growling and sniffing, but one of the men called them off, and Bantor walked right up to the door.

"Where is Noble Rebba, master of the house? I am Bantor, commander of the guard of Akkad."

Rebba appeared at the door. An old man, already past his sixtieth season, he had long white hair that flowed past his shoulders. His wits remained sharp despite his years, however, and Rebba looked keenly at Bantor, then stepped closer, as if to make sure his tired eyes had seen correctly. "So, it is you. You look very well for a dead man." He smiled at Bantor's reaction. "Come in."

Inside the main house, two frightened women and three small girls with big eyes huddled together. They stared at Bantor for a few moments before resuming their preparations for the morning meal. Bantor frowned at them, and Rebba interpreted the glance.

"Adana, take Miriani and the girls outside."

With the women gone, Bantor examined the main room, hand on the hilt of his sword, then moved to the other rooms, looking inside to make sure they were empty. Satisfied, he went back to the doorway and checked that all of Rebba's people had moved out of earshot before turning back to the old noble.

"Well, Rebba, can you tell me what is going on? On my way to Akkad yesterday, my men were attacked by a group of bandits. They were led by Ariamus. You remember that coward, I'm sure."

"Bandits? Well, I wouldn't call them bandits, exactly," Rebba said with a grim laugh. "And Ariamus? He's one of the new rulers of Akkad."

Not too long ago, such words would have infuriated Bantor. But too many men had died in the siege, and death had brushed by him too many times to worry him now. "Is he? So who else rules in Akkad?"

Something in Bantor's tone gave Rebba pause, until he remembered that this man had been away trailing the barbarians for more than a month. "Who else but Korthac."

Rebba noted the puzzled look. "Ah, yes, that's right. Korthac arrived after you left for the south. He claims he's a merchant, a trader, but he has the look of a soldier about him. He arrived about six weeks ago, just after Eskkar headed north. Korthac comes from the distant west, possibly even from the land of Egypt. He's taken control of Akkad. It seems that Trella's spies failed to uncover the plot."

"And when did all this happen?" Right now Bantor had no interest in anyone's spies.

"Two nights ago. Just after sunset, Ariamus rode up to the river gate from the south. Korthac had men waiting inside, near the gate, with weapons hidden in bundles. They killed the gatekeepers and captured the gate without anyone raising the alarm. Ariamus and more than a hundred men ran in uncontested. Joining with Korthac's Egyptians, they attacked the barracks and caught many of the soldiers asleep. At the same time, they overpowered Trella's guards and seized her house. By now, Korthac has at least a hundred and fifty bandits and thieves in his service, with more swearing allegiance to him every day. He's paying well for men willing to follow orders, and killing anyone who disobeys his commands."

"Only a hundred and fifty!" Bantor exclaimed. "There are more than three thousand people in Akkad. Surely they won't submit to this Korthac and a few bandits."

"Most of the soldiers are dead or captured, Bantor. A few may be in hiding. Anyone who speaks out or even raises his eyes is killed. Korthac holds Trella prisoner in her own house. Korthac's house, now, I suppose. I don't know what happened to Gatus. My grandson brought word of all this last night, along with a midmorning summons for me. All the big farm holders are ordered to come into Akkad today, to meet with our new master, Korthac."

"Will you still go?"

"Of course I must go. I was getting ready to leave when you arrived. I want to get there early, to see Nicar first and find out what he thinks. He'll know more of what is happening." Rebba looked closely at his visitor, who stood there looking blindsided at all these happenings. "Are you alone?"

The question brought Bantor back to the present. "No, I'm not alone. I have sixteen men with me, and they're all looking for vengeance. So go to the city, Rebba, and talk to Nicar, but don't tell anyone we're here. Not even Nicar. Not if you want to keep your family alive." He fingered his sword. "Ariamus will die, and any that stand with him. I've sent word to Eskkar. He will be here in a few days. With his seventy men, we'll brush aside this Korthac like a fly."

"They say Eskkar's dead, and his men butchered. Even

if he's alive, he'll be outside the walls, the same walls that just held off thousands of barbarians."

Bantor laughed, throwing his head back, but the sound had a trace of danger in it. "Eskkar's not easy to kill. Besides, do you think the wall will stop him?" He smiled grimly at the old noble's reaction. "Tell me, who would you rather have as your enemy? Eskkar, or this Korthac? Do you really think these bandits will stand up to Eskkar's soldiers?"

"Didn't these bandits kill most of your men?" Rebba countered.

"We were ambushed by sixty or seventy men, caught by surprise on tired horses. Even so, we killed more of them than we lost. We drove them away, Rebba. They ran from us, remember that."

"That's not how Ariamus described the battle." Rebba sighed. "Anyway, many in Akkad have no love for Eskkar and Trella." The noble paused, considering his words. "But many more will follow him, that's true enough. If he's still alive." He sat down on a stool. "Let me think a moment."

Bantor bided his time, gripping his sword hilt and staring at the master farmer, as the moments passed.

"You have forced the choice on me, Bantor. I was going to Akkad to find out which way the wind blew. Now I must throw in my lot with you and Eskkar. Even if you didn't hold my family hostage, Korthac would never trust me again, once he finds out you and your men came to me. He'll be looking for any excuse to confiscate land and property, to execute a few landowners as an example. So I can't tell him you're here." He shook his head at his predicament, then stood. "I have to go. The sooner I know what's going on, the better we'll know what to do."

Bantor didn't like having to trust the old noble, but this Korthac had summoned Rebba, so he must go, before someone came out looking for him. No important land-owner could ignore such a summons, and Korthac would certainly notice if Noble Rebba didn't appear as ordered.

"Gather your family first, Rebba, and talk to them. I'll keep all of the women and children here in the house. I'll kill them myself, Rebba, if you betray me."

"Save your threats, Bantor. I know what must be done. Still, the women and children will be safer indoors for the next few days anyway. I'm sure Ariamus's men will be wandering the countryside, looking for loot and women."

"Then I'll make sure they're safe, Rebba," Bantor said.

"And I'll explain everything to my sons." Rebba started toward the door, then stopped to stand directly before Bantor. "I'll assure them you're here to protect them. Remember that, before you do anything foolish. I think you would be wise to wait for Eskkar, if indeed he is coming." Without pausing for a reply or approval, he walked past Bantor and stepped outside, calling to his sons and grandsons.

Bantor followed him and waved his arms toward the river. His men appeared, alert, with their bows strung, and moved toward the house.

As Bantor stood there, Rebba explained the situation to his family. His sons and grandsons, their women and the frightened servants, all glanced apprehensively first at Bantor, then at the dirty, hard-looking armed men striding past them, hands on their weapons. Every man's eyes remained watchful and wary. Rebba, finishing with his sons, called the older women to his side and spoke to them as well. When he finished, the women gathered up the children and moved back toward the house.

Rebba, accompanied by two of his sons, began his journey toward Akkad. The city lay just beyond the curve of the river, little more than two miles away, but it would take them most of an hour to reach it, at the old man's slow pace.

As he watched them depart, Bantor felt the helplessness that comes when another controls your fate. Then a young girl, barely old enough to walk on her own and oblivious of his frown, slipped away from her mother and ran up to him. The mother, carrying another child on her hip, looked at Bantor nervously as he scooped the giggling girl up and carried her into the house.

Inside, another girl, a few years older, asked him if he and his men had eaten this morning.

"No, girl. We've not eaten since last night." Bantor lowered the little girl to the floor and let himself relax. He glanced down the trail through the doorway and took one last look at Rebba, walking south. Bantor had done all he could do, and would just have to wait. The last of his men filed into the house. The siege of Akkad had begun.

Bantor tried to rest as the long day dragged by. One of the women examined his shoulder, and declared nothing broken, though the pain felt as sharp as ever. He spent most of the afternoon pacing back and forth between the main house and the sentries he'd posted around the farm's outskirts, watching the path to Akkad. He'd expected Rebba to return by midafternoon, but as the sun began to set, the noble hadn't returned, and Bantor wondered if the old man had betrayed him. He met with Klexor; they spoke about what they'd do if attacked, and how they'd fight their way to the boats and cross the river.

His men, taking their cue from their commander, waited, weapons at hand. Worry spread to the rest of the household. Everyone grew more frightened with each passing hour.

As dusk descended, the dogs gave the first sign of some-one approaching. They began barking before the sentry caught sight of the returning men. Bantor recognized the yapping of dogs welcoming their master's return, not the deep growls that would warn of strangers prowling about in the night.

Nevertheless, Bantor ordered Klexor to take some men and scout the fields, to make sure no one followed Rebba. Bantor had been ambushed once. He'd not be caught a second time.

Rebba, slow of step and tired from a long day, reached his house, to the joy of his family. Bantor stood by and watched in silence as Rebba greeted his kin and accepted a cup of wine to refresh himself. At last Rebba told everyone to go inside the house. He and Bantor walked a few steps to the big willow tree that grew alongside the house. They sat on benches, facing each other in the gathering darkness across a table, its top scarred and rough from years of chopping vegetables and small game. Two dogs, their master's favorites, arranged themselves at his feet.

"The news is bad, Bantor," Rebba began, reaching down to stroke one of the dogs. He kept his voice low, though no one stood close enough to hear their words. The dogs would alert them if anyone tried to approach them in the darkness. "Korthac controls the city. His men have killed or captured most of the soldiers."

Bantor expected that news. If this demon Korthac didn't control the city, Bantor wouldn't be here hiding in the dark. "How many men does he have, Rebba?"

"Not many, I think, though Ariamus claims to have hundreds of men under his command. Both Korthac and Ariamus are offering silver to any man who follows their orders, and already some have joined him, either for the silver or to take part in future lootings. That, also, Ariamus has promised to them."

Bantor ground his teeth at Ariamus's name, but then repeated his question. "How many men?"

"I'd say a hundred and twenty at most. Apparently you did kill many of them, and others died fighting the soldiers at the barracks. I think he had less than a hundred and fifty when he attacked. Of course, others have joined up with him."

Bantor relaxed for the first time all day. A hundred bandits, even a few more, would not stop the trained soldiers who had beaten the Alur Meriki. "Once Eskkar gets here with his men, if we can get into Akkad, we have more than enough to fight them. As soon as we begin, the villagers will join us."

Rebba shook his head. "Don't be so sure. The rumor is true. Eskkar is dead. He was killed a few days ago in Bisitun by Korthac's men. Without Eskkar's name to rally the villagers, few will join you."

Eskkar dead! And Trella, what would happen to her?

"What about Lady Trella? Is she dead, too? And Annok-sur?"

"No, Korthac captured Trella, along with your wife. His men stormed the house and killed the guards, except for a handful that escaped or surrendered. Now he resides there, with Trella and Annok-sur under guard and confined to the bed chamber."

"And Annok-sur, is she . . ."

"I didn't see her, but I'm sure she's safe. Korthac has no reason to kill either her or Trella. That could be the one thing that might inflame the villagers to resist him. So he'll keep Trella alive, for now at least."

Bantor felt relief wash over him. He and Annok-sur had suffered many hard years together, and it angered him to think that her life depended on another man's whim. If anything happened to her, he'd kill this Korthac himself. "What about Gatus? Is he dead, too?"

Rebba laughed in the darkness. "The old soldier slipped past his assassins, though one of his men was killed at his side. Korthac's men claimed they wounded him, and that he must be dead by now. But they haven't found his body yet."

Bantor slumped back on the bench. This sounded bad. Eskkar's house and Trella captured, the barracks stormed, Gatus wounded or dead, and Eskkar murdered. With Eskkar gone, the soldiers would not rally around any of the nobles. He remembered his wife's words. The one thing Annok-sur had feared more than anything—an attack on Trella and Eskkar. Without their protection, Bantor and his wife would have no future in Akkad. They would have to flee the city. Somehow he would have to snatch his wife away from Korthac, then slip away with his men. It would . . . A new thought crossed his mind.

"Rebba, how did Eskkar die?"

The old farmer had to think about that. "I'm not sure. Korthac didn't say much about it. I believe Ariamus said he was killed by a sword. Yes, that's what he said."

"And the men who brought word of this? How many men did Ariamus send to kill Eskkar?"

"Just a handful, I think. He didn't say. Only that they had killed Eskkar a few days ago and just returned from Bisitun."

Bantor's smile returned. Eskkar had been declared dead at least three times before. "Well, Rebba, let's talk about that. Korthac and Ariamus sent some men up to Bisitun. They slipped past Grond and Sisuthros, and all of Eskkar's Hawk Clan guards, murdered him, then escaped back here with the news, without being killed or captured by Eskkar's seventy men. Did they bring back his head, as proof of their story?"

"Hmm, I see what you mean," Rebba said softly. "Yes, that does sound too easy, doesn't it. How good were the men with Eskkar?"

"Many of them rode against the barbarians. It would take more than a half-dozen bandits to escape those men, Rebba. Even if Eskkar were murdered, I don't think any would get away from Sisuthros and his men to tell the tale."

Rebba put both hands on the table, as if searching for support from the strong wood. "If Eskkar is not dead, then he will be here in a week or so, with his men. With your soldiers, he could quickly raise another hundred men who would follow him."

"More than that, I think."

"Don't be so quick to count your victory, Bantor. You would be outside the walls, and in a week, Ariamus and Korthac can enlist plenty of men from among the rogues and villains in the city and countryside. Korthac has plenty of gold to pay them. And despite what you say, it will not be easy to get past the gate. It's guarded even better than before. And remember, Korthac has Lady Trella. If I know Eskkar, he won't do anything that will get her killed."

"My rider will reach Eskkar in two more days," Bantor said, as if thinking out loud, "even if he has to kill the horses. With a forced march, Eskkar and the men can be here five days later, faster if he comes ahead by horseback."

Rebba nodded. "Yes, that sounds right. So it seems you will be my guest for at least that long. What are you planning to do?"

The question caught Bantor by surprise. So far, he hadn't thought about anything other than waiting for Eskkar. "I'm not sure, Rebba. I'd like to find Gatus, if he is still alive. But I dare not go into the city."

"Yes, you would be recognized." Rebba sighed. "I can't search Akkad in your place. Besides, Korthac's men are hunting for Gatus, and I am sure they'll find him sooner or later."

"What else did you learn?" Bantor asked.

"I learned my future place in Korthac's plans. I will be allowed to pay an additional tax of gold that will probably ruin me, and I am to continue working on the harvest. In return, my family will be permitted to keep my holdings, though I am sure Korthac will take most of my crops and livestock. I also had to swear on my knees to Korthac that

I would obey his authority. For that, he will leave me alone, at least for a while."

Hearing about Rebba's plight prompted another thought. "What about Nicar, Rebba? And Corio? What have they agreed to?"

"Much the same, Bantor, and with as much choice as I did. Nicar did not like it, and Ariamus struck him across the mouth when he protested. Ariamus quartered some of his bandits in Nicar's house, to keep an eye on him."

"We need to know more, Rebba, and you're the only one who can get it in safety. You must learn all you can about this Korthac and his men." Bantor leaned across the table toward the old noble. "We'll wait here for Eskkar to arrive. He'll know what to do."

Rebba sat back, digesting Bantor's suggestion for a few moments. "Bantor, your presence here puts me and my family in great danger. For the next two or three days, you'll be safe enough, but after that, the risk will grow each day as Korthac takes greater control. If Eskkar does not arrive in seven or eight days, or if we hear that he is truly dead, then you must take your men and depart."

Bantor heard the force in the old farmer's words. Rebba spoke the truth. They couldn't stay here forever. "If Eskkar doesn't come, or we haven't heard from him by then, we will leave." In that case, Bantor decided, he'd find some way to rescue his wife, with as many men as would follow him. "Meanwhile, perhaps you can find out about Gatus."

"I am to return to Akkad the day after tomorrow. Things should be settling down by then, and I'll have two wagonloads of fruits and vegetables for my grandson to sell in the market. Do you have any idea of where Gatus might be hiding?"

Bantor closed his eyes and let himself think about the old soldier. Where would the man go to hide? Ariamus knew the city well enough, so all the usual places would be well searched. A new place seemed more likely, one Ariamus wouldn't know. Then Bantor recalled some words that Annok-sur had spoken once. Something about a friend of Gatus setting up a small alehouse with that thief of a boy, Tammuz. He remembered the look Annok-sur had given him when he asked about it. She'd looked away, and told him it meant nothing, her tone of voice telling him not to probe further. He knew his wife kept many secrets.

Perhaps it did mean nothing, but he knew all about Annok-sur's network of spies. At least it might be a place to start looking. He made an effort to push thoughts of Annok-sur and her plight from his mind.

"An old friend of Gatus was injured during the siege," Bantor said, picking his words with care. "He couldn't fight any more, so after the battle, Gatus set him up in a small alehouse, along with a crippled boy who once rode with Eskkar. Maybe that is where Gatus has gone."

"There are many houses that sell ale, Bantor. I'll ask around, but not until the day after tomorrow. And only if Gatus isn't discovered before then, or found dead."

"I thank you for your efforts, Rebba. Gatus is a friend." He hesitated, then added, "You know that Eskkar will reward you for this, when he returns."

"I need no gold from Eskkar, Bantor." The old noble stood up, stretching to ease the stiffness in his bones. "But I did not like the way Ariamus struck Nicar, nor did I like

19

Eskkar had scarcely noticed the passing of time, as days turned into weeks. At first the village occupied most of his time, however much responsibility he delegated to Sisuthros. The people of Bisitun, recovering from Ninazu's terror, soon protested their rule by Akkad, no matter how reasonable or peaceful the intent. It took Eskkar more than a week to figure out why.

When the Alur Meriki threatened Akkad, the nobles ruling the city had selected Eskkar to save them. During the crisis, the inhabitants came to know both him and Trella as people they could trust with their lives. More than that, they understood that neither he nor Trella valued gold, slaves, or the other trappings of noble life. In short, the villagers accepted them as people long before they accepted their rule.

In Bisitun, such trust did not come easily. Even though Eskkar and his men rescued the village from bandits, no one in Bisitun had invited them to do so, and more than a few of the villagers longed for the days when they ruled themselves. Instead, they found themselves ruled by distant

Akkad, their daily lives governed by Sisuthros and his soldiers even more effectively than Ninazu and his bandits.

The villagers also knew they'd be tithing a portion of their earnings to support Akkad, and that Akkad, as the more important of the two villages, would always come first. That made for plenty of tension between villagers and soldiers. Incidents soon arose on both sides of the fine line that Eskkar trod each day.

He needed to rule them fairly and justly. There could be no accusations that Ninazu and his bandits had simply been replaced by another tyrant. So the soldiers had to be kept under control. Eskkar and Sisuthros warned each of them, time and again, not to take advantage of the inhabitants, especially their women. Eskkar reminded them that they had plenty of silver in their pouches. They could buy whatever they wished, but take only what the villagers offered freely.

But soldiers, he knew, acted much like children. They nodded in understanding at Eskkar's words and swore to behave, then filled themselves with wine, started fights, and chased after the women.

Eskkar kept his word. He punished offending soldiers in the village square, with the elders present. He softened the punishments as much as he could. He didn't want to alienate his men, but he could not afford to offend the villagers. So he made the punishment fit the crime as much as possible, and Eskkar soon found laughter to be as effective as manual labor or the lash.

One soldier who fondled a girl in the square had to carry water for the village's women for a day. Another knocked down a farmer, and received a day's work in the irrigation ditches. Only one soldier had to be lashed, and that for a fight that led to a villager's death, although the villager had provoked the conflict and attacked the soldier first.

Eskkar's biggest source of friction came from the innkeepers and other sellers of wine. They had a penchant for overcharging his soldiers, especially those who'd drunk too much. Both innkeepers and shopkeepers often substituted inferior quality goods on the unsuspecting soldiers. Those merchants found guilty received fines, and Eskkar turned the gold and silver over to the council of elders, to help pay for the rebuilding.

The elders banished one trader found to be a little too sharp in his dealings. Watching the unhappy man pack his family and goods, then take to the road, sent a clear message to all the other merchants to be more honest in their bargaining with both soldiers and villagers.

By the end of the second week, a grudging appreciation of each others' roles developed between the two factions. During that time, Eskkar and Sisuthros spoke at length to all the merchants in the village, listened to their complaints, and did what they could to resolve them. Progress remained slow, but steady. As the villagers came to accept the fact that Sisuthros and his men would remain, they settled down and got back to the business of farming, trading, and shopkeeping.

Every sundown, Eskkar ceased his role as ruler, refusing all requests for his time. He spent his evenings with Lani. During the day she took care of the household, smoothing the process for Eskkar and Sisuthros. She arranged food for the men, supervised the women hired to cook, looked after the cleaning, and worked with the two clerks keeping track of all the expenditures.

After dinner she took her rest, bathing and preparing for her nights with Eskkar. They enjoyed sitting in the square, talking about everything that happened during the day. Other times they went up onto the roof above Eskkar's house, where they could talk with even more privacy. They sat holding each other, or with Lani leaning back against him, so that his hands could touch her hair, her breasts, or other more intimate parts.

When they retired for the night, safe behind the barred door, they had little to say, speaking only with their bodies before falling into a deep and restful sleep. For Lani, weeks passed before her nightmares ended. Until then, she would wake up in a panic, unable to breathe, too frightened to scream, often unaware of where she was. Over time those terrors faded away, if not gone, at least banished from her dreams for longer and longer periods.

At first those dreams unsettled Eskkar. He'd never helped a woman with her private terrors before. Trella, too, had been frightened, but Trella had never known the horrors of a man like Ninazu, and Trella's fears of the future centered about the unknown. For Lani, the unknown had proven all too terrible in reality, a reality that had gone on far too long. As he discovered more about her, he helped calm her fears.

It took time for Eskkar to comprehend all this, but as the weeks drifted by, he realized he understood more not only about Lani, but about Trella as well. Often he found himself comparing the two women, their emotions, their lovemaking, even their hopes. And so when Lani fell asleep in his arms, Eskkar often remained awake, wondering about himself.

Again and again he cursed his own weakness. He loved Trella no less, and he knew it was only because of her that he could understand Lani. But as the nights went by, he saw his feelings for Lani grow, not lessen.

Two weeks after its liberation, Bisitun settled into a routine. That let Eskkar ride out each morning to inspect the countryside. Taking along Grond and a handful of men, they started with the surrounding farms, widening the circle around the village. For the first few excursions, they returned each night. But as the circle widened, they camped overnight under the stars, then continued on their journey the next day. After a few such camps, Eskkar realized how much he missed Lani's lovemaking, and after that, he made sure nearly every day's journey ended back at Bisitun.

The next day, they would change horses and ride out again. One by one, Eskkar visited every farm and every herdsman within a day's journey from Bisitun. He talked to farmers and their wives, asked about the land and the crops, and explained Akkad's role to humble peasants who'd never traveled more than a day's walk from their place of birth. To his surprise, Eskkar found this more satisfying than capturing a dozen villages.

Everywhere they went, Eskkar found the farmers and herders much the same. At first frightened, then curious, then eager to talk with the warrior who had beaten the barbarians and driven Ninazu away. Eskkar spoke with all of them, and he learned more about the problems of the small farmers and herders than he ever thought he could comprehend. Thus he gathered ideas from many sources, ideas that would make life safer and easier both on the farm and in the village. He went over these with Sisuthros each night during the evening meal.

One impressed farmer questioned Eskkar, asking how a soldier came to know so much about farms and crops. Eskkar smiled, remembering the days when he'd known nothing about the mysteries of earth, water, and seed. Trella and Noble Rebba had spent a whole day showing and explaining the secrets needed to bring forth wealth from the earth.

Twice Eskkar and his men encountered small parties of men on horseback, who took one look at them and fled. They caught up with one of these, three men whose only business looked to be thieving or raiding. Grond and the soldiers made short work of them, and the local people again gave thanks to their deliverer.

Six weeks after Ninazu's execution, peace covered the land around Bisitun. By then Eskkar had met with almost all of the farmers, not only met them, but he'd spoken with them, discussed what they needed, what they feared, what they hoped for. No one had ever heard of such encounters before. The people were amazed someone from as far away as Akkad would not only want to protect them, but that he actually listened and showed concern for their lives and their problems.

Of course many complained about the new tax to be charged when they brought their goods to Bisitun for sale, but most declared themselves willing to pay if Eskkar could keep the bandits and raiders away from their farms and families.

Trella had set the amount of the tax, set it low enough so as not to cause hardship. She had explained to Eskkar before he left for the north that the real taxes would be paid by the merchants and traders in Bisitun and Akkad. They would still grow wealthy, but they, too, had to pay for the walls and soldiers who protected them and their dealings.

In Akkad, Trella had begun changing the customs. Each week Eskkar listened to her messenger describe her plans for establishing new laws, creating a new House for the clerks, and inventing new symbols to aid the farmers and craftsmen. Once all this would have overwhelmed Eskkar, but now he not only saw the need for such changes, but understood what impact they would have on Akkad's inhabitants.

In the clans of his youth, life seldom changed. The people knew their role, their place in life, and the duties they owed to clan and family. Men hunted, and followed their clan leaders into battle. Women raised children, gathered and prepared food, and managed the herds and wagons. Each day resembled the one before, and the one to come tomorrow.

Villages, Eskkar now realized, couldn't be ruled like a steppes clan. Every village changed constantly, with new people arriving or departing. More people required more food and more craftsmen to serve the surrounding farmers and herders. Even the crops varied from year to year, with abundance often replaced by scarcity. Akkad, with so many more people living within its walls, had become ungovernable by the old ways.

No, Eskkar knew, the old practices must yield to new ways of thinking. And what better place to begin than in Bisitun. And so laws replaced the old and vague customs of the past, and the ruling council of Bisitun settled disputes fairly, without favoring the leading merchant and nobles.

By now Sisuthros governed the village efficiently, and complaints became fewer in number and minor in nature. The villagers created a new, more permanent council of elders, and they worked with Sisuthros and his clerks each day to insure farmers sold their produce peacefully, craftsmen worked in safety in their shops, and merchants resumed trade not only with one another but up and down the great river.

Eskkar had accomplished what he'd set out to achieve. For the first time in almost a year, there were no barbarians to drive off, no bandits or marauders to chase and destroy, and the people of Bisitun had started putting their lives back together. With nothing of import to do, he took his ease, something he'd never done before, letting himself relax and enjoying the peaceful days.

Eskkar knew he should return to Akkad, to help Trella manage the city's burgeoning growth. Instead he remained in Bisitun, watching the days slip by. Of course, he told himself Sisuthros still needed him, that he stayed in Bisitun to help organize the village. In truth, the thought of returning to Akkad with all its scheming and petty problems weighed on him, and he wanted to postpone his return as long as possible.

Instead, on the days he didn't travel the countryside, he spent more and more of his time with Lani. They started their day after the common breakfast, when Sisuthros went off to deal with the problems of the day. Lani and Eskkar usually found time to return to their bedroom for a few more hours of ease. After the noon meal, Eskkar would stroll around the village, talking to the shopkeepers and craftsmen, and, more often than not, Lani would accompany him, though she would leave him early enough to prepare for the day's supper. Before the evening meal, Eskkar and Grond would wash up at the well in the square, along with their bodyguards, all of them getting the dust of the village off their bodies.

After supper Eskkar spent time with his soldiers, talking and joking, as they, too, relaxed from their labors. But after an hour or two, Eskkar would leave the men with their ale and their women, and he and Grond would return to their house and their women.

Lani and Tippu would be waiting, and the four of them would sit out under the stars facing the square, talking, laughing, or sitting quietly, with an occasional sip of well-watered wine to keep them refreshed. The nights had grown cooler, but it remained pleasant to sit beneath the starry sky and enjoy the night air. Eskkar held Lani close to him, his arm either around her shoulders or slipped inside her dress to enjoy the feel of her skin, and just as often her hand would rest between his legs, stroking him gently until he grew aroused, then whispering promises in his ear for later in the evening.

Sometimes Sisuthros or one of the other senior men joined them, but mostly Eskkar and Grond had the nights to themselves, as the others sought their own companions at day's end. As the darkness increased, if no one was around or watching too closely, Lani would kiss him. Once she even leaned over and took him into her mouth for a few moments, a more certain reminder of what would come later.

During most of those nights, another visitor would join them. The dark gray cat that had appeared in Eskkar's room that first night would cautiously prowl its way to their table. Where it spent its days, no one knew. Lani had befriended the animal weeks before Eskkar's arrival, and now it stayed nearby, or came into the bedroom searching for her. Always alert and constantly looking around, the scruffy male cat would search out Lani's hand for a brief stroking, then poke her with his paw until she gave him something to eat.

In time the cat permitted Eskkar to pet it, though the hint of a growl would be heard if Eskkar rubbed too hard or too long. After the cat had eaten whatever scraps they had to offer, it often sat on the table and dozed, its legs tucked underneath its body, but ready to dart away at any moment. If the food had been good and plentiful, it might even purr for them, the low sound only lasting a few moments before the animal remembered it was supposed to be a fierce hunter.

Eskkar never spent much time with cats. As a young boy in his camp, dogs had kept his family company, but cats were almost unknown in the lives of barbarians. Cats couldn't follow a wagon a dozen miles each day, and Eskkar had rarely seen them until he came to the villages.

Nevertheless everyone knew that a cat came blessed from the gods, and brought good luck. Cats were plentiful on the nearby farms and in the villages, appreciated for their ability to hunt the rodents that ate and soiled the stored grain. Lani's cat, as Eskkar called it, seemed sure of its place, and in the last few weeks, Eskkar had come to enjoy its company.

Tonight the stars shone gleaming white overhead. Eskkar and Lani sat side by side, facing the square, their backs to the wall of the house, at a small table. Grond and Tippu had their own table, a discreet distance away, where they, too, whispered to each other. A single guard watched at the entrance to the house, twenty paces away. The rest of the square stood empty at this time of night, and the incessant creaking sound from the well as people drew up the water had finally stopped.

Lani's cat reclined on the table between them. It had dined on chicken scraps, then washed its face and paws, and now dozed lightly. Eskkar glanced up at the heavens, and knew it would soon be time to go into the warm house and warmer bed, to spend another hour making love, before falling asleep in each other's arms.

"Tell me more about Akkad," Lani urged, her arm around Eskkar's neck and one hand stroking his manhood.

"I've already told you everything there is, Lani," he answered. She asked the same question every night.

"Tell me something new, then," she insisted, her hand tightening around him. Eskkar sighed, then found some new detail to talk about. She listened carefully as he spoke about the city, its people, the farms, the traders, even the wall surrounding it. Whatever he told her, sooner or later involved Trella, and then more questions would arise.

"Do you miss your wife so much, Eskkar? Are you not happy here?"

"I have to go back to Akkad, Lani, you know that. My son will be born soon, and I must be there. I've already stayed away longer than I planned. In another two or three days, we'll start for Akkad."

"You will take us with you?"

She asked that question often. "Yes, Lani, you will come

with me. Though I'm not sure what I will do with you there. Trella will not be pleased with you."

"As long as you do not forget me, Eskkar. I could not bear that."

Trella's reception of Lani had bothered him more than he admitted. He needed to keep seeing Lani, but wanted Trella as well. As the time to return to Akkad grew closer, the problem had become more confusing. Now even talking about Trella made him uncomfortable.

"I will take care of you and your sister." He kissed her cheek and her ear. "And I will come to visit you as often as I can."

"Do you promise, Eskkar? I don't want to be apart from you."

He reassured her again, and finally she seemed satisfied. The questions stopped and she relaxed, snuggling against him, her head on his shoulder. His right arm reached around her, his hand inside her dress as he held onto her breast. He rolled her nipple between his fingers, and felt her shiver from his touch. She had very sensitive breasts, and he had discovered that he could sometimes bring her to arousal merely by playing with them. It was a new and erotic experience that never failed to excite him.

Now he leaned back, enjoying her presence and her touch, his head resting against the rough mud-brick of the house. He reached out slowly with his left hand, and gently stroked the cat's neck, just behind its ear. Eskkar had learned not to make any sudden movements around the animal. Not much tamer than a wild creature, even after all this time, it remained skittish and always ready to show its claws.

Tonight it let him stroke its rough fur, though the cat lifted its head toward him, as if to reassure itself, before lowering its head once again before settling down, its feet folded under its chest.

Eskkar's hand was knocked aside as the cat's head snapped up and to its left. Before Eskkar could follow the movement, the cat launched itself off the table with a blur of motion too quick to be seen. Eskkar turned toward whatever had alarmed the cat. Though used to the darkness, he saw nothing at first, then a faint reflection of something silvery moving toward him.

For a big man, Eskkar could move rapidly when he needed to. He shoved Lani away with his right hand, using his left to reach under the table and fling it up and between him and his attacker. "Grond!" he shouted at the top of his lungs, and then dropped to a crouch as the sword slashed the air where his head had been an instant ago. Chunks of dried mud sprayed from the wall where the blade struck. The table had hindered the stroke, not by much, but just enough to buy one extra moment of precious time.

Eskkar threw himself to the left, away from Lani, and found himself at the feet of another assailant. That man's sword missed as well, an overhand swing that sliced into the air where Eskkar had just been, the attacker expecting Eskkar to move away, not at him. Before the man could thrust down with the weapon, Eskkar gathered his feet under him and drove his shoulder into the man's stomach, and this time they both went down.

The attacker attempted to use his sword, but Eskkar rolled away with two quick turns, regained his footing, and made sure the wall protected his back. On his left, he

heard Grond shouting for the guards. Not that Eskkar had
time to worry about Grond. Eskkar saw two shadows
advancing toward him, but at least he had time to draw
his sword. He used the motion to move back to his right,
closing in with the closest of his attackers, the blade
slashing at the man nearest the wall. Bronze clashed on
bronze, and Eskkar felt something burn against his left
arm. Again he used his body, moving forward, lowering
his shoulder and thrusting himself into the man before he
could recover and swing again.

As Eskkar rebounded from his assailant, he flung himself
back into the first attacker, again ducking under another
cut, and pinning the man to the wall for an instant with his
body.

The second man proved quick in his reactions. A hand
struck Eskkar in the face, a thumb nearly in his eye, and
Eskkar was pushed back before he could thrust with his
own blade. He dropped to his knees, swinging his sword as
he did so. The attacker grunted as Eskkar's blade struck
the man across the leg, but the tip of the sword struck the
wall, weakening the blow. Still, it did enough damage to
allow Eskkar to dart away, this time back toward Grond.

The shouting and clash of swords in the square had
raised the alarm, and even in the confusion, Eskkar heard
men stumbling about inside the house behind him. He half
expected the assailants to flee, but these two men were
determined, and they again pressed the attack. From the
darkness, Lani threw herself in front of one of them,
tripping him up. That one cursed as he stumbled and fell,
though Lani's cry mixed with the assassin's oaths.

The other man kept coming, and Eskkar swung his

sword at the assailant's head. The man parried the blade, but Eskkar took control now, his feet firmly planted as he disengaged his blade, rolling it around his opponent's weapon with a motion trained in hundreds of hours of practice, and thrust hard, brushing aside the parry and sinking the blade deep into the man's chest.

He didn't dare risk a moment to withdraw it, just ducked immediately to his right, half expecting another blow from the other man, but Grond arrived now. He had no weapon in his hand, but he caught the second man from behind, his arm around the man's neck. Grond twisted him against his hip and flipped the man over. The sound of the man's neck breaking carried over the rising din in the square.

Eskkar wrenched his sword free and looked up, as a tiny bit more light filtered into the square from the main house as the door flung open. Another assailant stood there, backing away from the opening as men stumbled out, swords in their hands. The man looked toward his fallen companions, then turned and raced away, but Sisuthros and two men burst from the house and pursued him.

The assassin ran for his life, dropping his sword and taking to his heels. With a burst of speed, he darted down one of the lanes. But a doorway opened ahead of him and a woman stepped out to see about all the commotion. They collided, both crashing to the ground. The man got up in a moment, but Sisuthros had closed the gap and flung his sword at the running man's back. The blade landed nearly true, and the blow, while not deep enough to be mortal, made the runner cry out and stumble. Drakis and another man dashed past Sisuthros and even across the square, Eskkar heard the sound of the blade as it crunched into the man's shoulder. A scream rent the air, cut short by another blow, and then it was over.

Eskkar stood in the same spot, breathing heavily, his back to the wall, the great sword held out in front of him. He heard Lani crying on the ground, and remembered that she had managed to trip one of his attackers. Grond moved toward him, gathering up Lani as he came to Eskkar's side, then pushed her roughly behind them. He'd picked up the fallen man's sword, and the two of them stood in front of Lani, swords glinting in the starlight as the blades weaved back and forth in the empty space before them.

Another soldier came out of the house, a newly lit torch in his hand, its flame reaching full illumination as he raised it above his head. In the flickering light Eskkar could see the bodies of three men. He saw Tippu huddled against the next house, her hands up over her head. More of Eskkar's soldiers rushed into the square, those who had not gone to the local taverns and alehouses rushing out of the nearby houses where they were quartered, swords or knives in their hands.

In a moment a line of men stood in front of Eskkar, and he allowed himself to relax a little. He turned and found Lani slumped to the ground, her back against the wall. He reached down and picked her up with one hand, then pulled her along the wall until they reached the house's entrance. She stumbled and would have fallen if he hadn't clasped her around the waist. Inside, he saw blood oozing from her forehead and cheek. Someone lit another lamp inside the house, and it gave him enough light to see. He pushed her hair aside to examine her injury. Eskkar found a welt and a bloody scratch, but no wound, so he carried her into the bedroom. Someone brought Tippu inside, and she rushed to join her sister.

"Take care of her, Tippu. Close the door!"

When Eskkar went back outside, Sisuthros rushed up to him. His subcommander had recovered his sword, and Eskkar saw blood still on it. Drakis, a few steps behind him, dragged the body of the assassin who had nearly escaped. Eskkar remembered that Drakis had been the first one out of the house at the sound of the attack; he hadn't bothered with any clothes.

More torches flamed up, and Hamati arrived at a run from the local alehouse with another dozen men. Sisuthros shouted an order, and the trumpet rang out, its notes summoning every soldier to the house. Lamps and candles started to burn in all the houses around the square, adding their light to that of the flickering torches.

Soldiers dragged the four bodies from where they had fallen and lined them up next to the table Eskkar had flipped over. Another body lay near the doorway, that of the guard stationed at the door to the house; he'd attempted to reach Eskkar, but had been struck down from behind by the fourth assassin.

Eskkar grabbed the arm of a soldier bearing a torch, and ordered him to hold the light over the bodies. Eskkar studied each face closely, as did Grond and Sisuthros, but they recognized none of them. The torchlight showed that all the dead men looked hard and fit. They certainly had not backed off in their attempt to kill him, even after their initial attempt had failed.

"Sisuthros, get men out on horseback. They must have had horses hidden somewhere. Find them. Use torches to check for fresh tracks around the village. And secure every horse in Bisitun. I don't want anyone getting away. If any have left the village, ride them down at first light, if you have to kill every horse."

"I'll do it," Hamati said. He issued orders to his men, and they all raced off toward the stable.

Eskkar nodded and turned back to Sisuthros. "Have the rest of the men take a look at the bodies, see if anyone recognizes them. First thing in the morning, get every innkeeper . . . shopkeeper . . . no, get everyone in the village to look at these bodies. Somebody must know who they are, or where they stayed."

"Yes, Captain." He hurried off, giving orders to waken every member of the village council. The sound of hoofbeats rang out, and a single rider came back into the square, shouting for torches. He took two in his hand, struggling to keep control of the nervous horse spooked by the crackling and flickering torches. But the man retained his seat, and in a moment the horse steadied, and they galloped off down the lane.

"Grond, have a guard stationed behind the house tonight. And search inside, to make sure no one's hiding with the women."

Drakis came from the house, now dressed, with his sword belted at his waist. "Captain, why don't you go back inside and let the women look at that arm. There's nothing more you can do out here. I'll send a healer to you."

Eskkar stared down at his left arm, and found it dripping blood. He'd moved aside, but not quite fast enough, and the thrusting sword had lanced the outside of his arm. Looking at the wound, Eskkar realized it stung painfully. "I'll go inside." He looked at the other guards, their eyes wide with excitement. "You men sweep the square and the nearby houses. Make sure there are no others hiding inside."

Grond followed him into the house, and once there, Eskkar saw that the palm of Grond's left hand was bleeding as well. He must have grasped a blade during the struggle. Lani came out of the bedroom, still shaking a little but insisting she was all right, and sat down at the table. Tippu followed her, trying to wash the cut on her sister's head. Another woman came up and ordered all of them to sit. In a moment she'd brought wine and cups for the four of them.

Eskkar took two mouthfuls of wine, then set the cup back down. He needed to think clearly, and he'd already had one cup of wine during his dinner.

The healer arrived, rubbing the sleep from his eyes, a big wooden box of implements slung from his shoulder. An old man, he'd no doubt gone to bed early and heard nothing of the disturbance. He attended to Eskkar first.

"I need more light, Lord Eskkar," he announced. Another woman fetched a lamp from Sisuthros's room, and placed it on the table. "And a cup of wine, if I may. And a bucket of fresh water from the well. Now, Lord Eskkar, put your arm on the table." While the healer spoke, he pulled the two lamps close to Eskkar's left side.

Eskkar leaned forward, his arm outstretched and flat on the table. Pushing up the tunic's sleeve, the healer looked closely at the wound, moving the separated skin around and causing Eskkar to flinch, though he made no sound.

"It's nothing serious, Lord Eskkar. Let me look at the others." He spent more time with Grond, and a few moments with Lani. As he finished with them, a soldier came in carrying a bucket of water. The healer took an empty wine cup from the table, filled it with water, then poured the contents over Eskkar's arm, dribbling the water into the wound, his face inches above the gash as he examined it. The blade had sliced along the outer forearm, carving a furrow nearly a hand's width long.

"Nothing inside the flesh, lord. That's good. I don't think it will even need to be stitched. Binding will do. A clean wound, bound up in its own blood, should heal quickly enough."

Eskkar felt relieved, though the gash stung even more after the healer's examination. The old man dipped another cup of water from the bucket and again washed the blood away. Another woman arrived with clean binding strips, and the healer looked at them carefully before selecting one. Then he took the cup of wine that had been poured for him and clasped his other hand firmly on Eskkar's wrist. "Don't move now. This will sting."

A lance of pain went through Eskkar as the wine trickled into the wound, and he had to bite down hard to keep his arm immobile. The pain faded after a moment, but the healer continued until he emptied the cup. He wiped the excess from Eskkar's arm, and with considerable dexterity for an old man, tightly bound the long cloth around the lower arm, pulling firmly as he did so.

"I'll need to change that in the morning, Lord Eskkar," he said. "Try to move the arm as little as possible until the flesh has time to heal."

Eskkar grunted at the man's advice. Lani came over and sat next to Eskkar, holding on to his hand while the healer examined her head. When he finished, he merely washed it out with water from the bucket. "Nothing to do here," he said. "Just a bad bruise."

Grond's hand didn't take long. The healer rinsed it clean with a cup of water, inspected it carefully, then made Grond open and close his fingers several times. The healer treated the cut with water and wine, then bound it up, using enough wrapping to make sure Grond wouldn't move it for a few hours. "Keep it bandaged until it heals," the healer ordered. "And change the bandage every day."

The healer finished up and slung his unneeded box of instruments back over his shoulder. While he was doing this, Lani went into Eskkar's room. She returned in a moment, with two silver coins in her hand. The healer took up the wine cup and refilled it. This time it didn't go to waste, as he drank it down in four loud gulps.

"That was good wine, Lord Eskkar. Perhaps I should have spilled less on the floor." He took the silver coins from Lani and bowed thankfully. "I'll return first thing in the morning, to see to the wound and change the bindings. You should be more careful in the future, lord. It would be a shame for you to be killed so soon after having rescued us."

Eskkar thanked the man, but didn't say anything else until the healer had left. When the door closed, Eskkar turned to Grond.

"Well, what do you think?"

"Those men ... they were good. Very quick. If you hadn't shouted ... I'd have been butchered, and probably Tippu, too."

"Don't thank me, Grond. I never heard a thing. Those men knew how to move quietly. The damned cat heard them creeping up." Eskkar shook his head in disgust. Angry now, he cursed himself for a fool, taking his ease, his hands on a woman, while two men with naked swords in their hands walked within six paces without him noticing. He turned to Lani, put his good arm around her, and pulled her to him for a moment. "Tomorrow, I want you to feed that cat a whole chicken, Lani."

"You'd better sacrifice something to Ishtar, then, for sending the creature to guard you," Grond answered. Everyone knew he didn't care much for animals. "Now I'll have to bow politely the next time it hisses at me."

"No, I'll thank Lani instead. She threw herself in front of one and tripped him up." He kissed the top of her head.

"We were lucky, Captain. We've been idling and careless. I should have been more alert."

Shouts from the square made both men look up, and in a moment Sisuthros came striding into the room. "Hamati found the horses. There were four of them, tied up about two hundred paces from the palisade, near the river, near the southern road. And one of the guards found a rope fastened to the fence, just opposite where the horses were."

"Could there have been more men? There might have been one with the horses."

"Hamati didn't think so. The horses were well tied. He's still out there looking. We'll know for sure in the morning. It's too dark to see tracks now." He noticed the bandages for the first time. "Are you well?"

"Well enough," Eskkar answered. "Now we have to find out who to kill for this."

That reminded Sisuthros of something. "I found gold on the men, Captain. On all of them. One man had ten gold coins, the other three had five each. Someone with wealth wanted you dead, it seems."

More than enough gold to buy anyone's death, Eskkar knew. And that meant . . . What did it mean? He didn't know. "That's a lot of gold for anyone in Bisitun to pay for a murder."

Sisuthros picked up Eskkar's empty wine cup, poured himself some wine, and sat down facing his captain. "Twenty-five gold coins . . . nobody in Bisitun has that kind of gold, Captain, not after the Alur Meriki and Ninazu. Believe me, I've worked with every merchant and trader in the village. Even if someone wanted you dead . . . Besides, you've treated everyone here fairly, more than fairly." He shrugged. "They'd be more likely to try and kill me."

"And Ninazu didn't have any other kin," Grond offered, "and even if he did, they wouldn't be the kind to spend gold to get their revenge. They'd do it themselves."

"Akkad. That much gold had to come from Akkad," Eskkar said with understanding, his lips tightening. "What about the marks on the gold?"

Sisuthros shook his head. "At least ten different merchants, and I only recognized about half of them. No way to tell from that."

"Something must be going on there," Eskkar said.

"There's nothing happening in Akkad, Captain," Sisuthros said. "Yesterday's messenger said the city was quiet. And Bantor is due back any day. He might even be back by now."

Eskkar had talked to the messenger himself. It had been one of the regular couriers, carrying routine messages, even a personal message from Trella. "Sisuthros, make a head count. See if anyone is missing. Check the scribes and traders, too."

The sons of Akkad's merchants that accompanied them to keep the records might be involved in some scheme or another. Damn the gods that they hadn't taken one of the attackers alive. Even one would have been enough.

Sisuthros got up. "I'll take the count. Is there anything else we can do before daylight?"

Grond looked at Eskkar and shook his head.

"No, I can't think of anything else," Eskkar said. "We'll know more in the morning." He stood up as well. "I need to think about this. Wake me an hour before dawn."

When he and Lani were alone in the bedroom, the door barred, Lani sat on the bed, trembling, and he saw the tears glistening in her eyes. "Don't be afraid, Lani," he said. "We're safe enough. There are two men standing guard right outside the door."

"I am not afraid, Eskkar. But now the fighting will start again. You will go off to kill your enemies."

"That's what I have to do." He sat beside her and put his arm around her shoulders. "I'll take care of whatever has happened in Akkad, then I'll send for you. You saved my life tonight, Lani. I won't forget that. Now, put out the lamp and lie beside me. I need to think, and I'll do it better in the dark."

Eskkar had already finished dressing when the guard knocked on the door. Lani had cried herself to sleep while Eskkar lay beside her, questions churning in his head. He hadn't slept much, dozing and waking throughout the night. In the end, he couldn't wait for the summons to arise.

In the outer room one lamp burned. Sisuthros sat at the table, talking to Grond and Hamati. Sisuthros looked weary, and Eskkar knew he'd stayed awake all night as well. One of Lani's women had built a fire and heated water, so the men would have something warm with their day-old bread. Glancing out through the open door, Eskkar saw half a dozen soldiers gathered beneath a flickering torch, all of them alert and ready.

Taking a seat, Eskkar faced Sisuthros across the table. "Anything new?"

"Not much," Sisuthros answered with a yawn. "We didn't find any more horses, and there was no sign of a trail heading south. I had men walking patrols throughout the village. We'll do another sweep at dawn, when we round up the villagers."

"That should turn up something," Eskkar said. "Whoever else wanted me dead might still be in Bisitun."

"And if there are more outside the village, they might not know the attack failed."

That news helped Eskkar breathe a little easier, and he forced himself to eat some bread. By the time he'd finished, the sun had risen. Taking a piece of bread with him, Eskkar walked out into the square. Grond and two soldiers stayed beside him as the first villagers arrived to view the bodies. Eskkar insisted they wait until the sun had cleared the horizon and the torches could be put out.

In the daylight, Eskkar stared at the dead men again, but neither he nor any of his soldiers recognized anyone. The village elders came next, and Eskkar and Sisuthros watched their faces carefully, looking for any indication of nervousness or recognition, but no one claimed to know the men. The first sign came from one of the innkeepers who identified the men as having stayed at his inn for the last two nights. The tavern owner had provided food and quarters for them, but he insisted he knew nothing else about either them or their business.

"That's all I know," the innkeeper repeated in a high-pitched voice, "except for that one's name." He gave a kick to one of the bodies, the man who'd come straight at Eskkar. "He called himself Ziusudra. The four of them sat in my inn yesterday afternoon, and he was the one doing all the talking and complaining about having to sleep on the floor. They had plenty of silver for wine and food, but they said nothing about themselves or their business." He shook his head. "They weren't even interested in any of my girls."

Sisuthros questioned the man further as Eskkar watched, looking for any hint the man might be lying. But the innkeeper had nothing else for them. The line of villagers passing the bodies moved forward again, trickling by the bodies until an old man, his grandson at his side for support, stopped and announced that these men had quartered their horses in his corral. But he, too, could divulge nothing, except that they'd possessed four good mounts. After a few more questions, Sisuthros sent him on his way.

By the time the last of the villagers left the square, Eskkar knew only that the men had arrived three days ago, spent two nights at an inn, then rode out of Bisitun just before sundown. They'd slipped back into the village somehow, but no one admitted either seeing or helping them.

The stable owner's words gave Eskkar an idea, but he kept silent until all of the villagers disappeared. "Bring their horses around, Sisuthros, and let's see if any of the soldiers recognize them."

Good horseflesh required plenty of care, and such animals would be noticed. Two of Eskkar's men thought one of the horses, marked with a stripe of white across its shoulders, came from Akkad, but didn't know the owner. He grunted at the news, and went back into the house. Sisuthros, Grond, Hamati, and Drakis went with him, and they took seats at the table in the common room.

"There must be trouble in Akkad," Eskkar began quietly. "I'll take half the men and horses, and start back. I should have returned there ten days ago."

"If those men came up from Akkad," Sisuthros pointed out, "and they've been here three days, they must have left eight or nine days ago. If you'd been in the city, they might have had better luck."

"Those men were determined," Grond added. "They didn't run after the first rush failed, not even after the alarm was raised."

"Well, they had bad luck," Eskkar said. "But it doesn't matter. I'll take the men and start back to Akkad today. If I push the pace, I can be there in four or five days." He turned to Hamati. "Can we get half the men ready by noon?"

"Half the men?" Sisuthros looked surprised. "Why only half? If there's fighting in Akkad, you'll need all of us."

"We just fought a major battle to capture this place and

pacify the countryside," Eskkar answered, a hint of anger in his voice. "I'm not going to walk away from this place and let some other bandit take it over again." He shook his head. "Besides, the people here need to feel safe and to accept the authority of Akkad. If we abandon them at the first sign of trouble, they'll never trust us again."

Sisuthros opened his mouth, then closed it again. He looked around the table, but no one said anything. "Well, why don't we leave just enough men here to keep order, say a dozen or so, and take the rest back with us?"

"You're not going back, Sisuthros," Eskkar said firmly. "You're needed here. You've worked long and hard to get the villagers' trust, and we're not going to undo that. Besides, if there is an armed enemy in Akkad, we may need a secure base back here."

"Captain," Sisuthros began, his voice rising, "let me come back with you. Hamati can . . ."

A shout from the square interrupted him. On their feet in a moment, they pushed through the doorway just as one of the soldiers from the main gate reached them, wheeling his horse to stop its movements.

"Captain," he called out, as soon as he caught his breath, "there's a rider coming from the south, riding hard."

"Bring him here as soon as he arrives," Eskkar said. No sense in rushing down to the gate. They'd be surrounded by a crowd of excited villagers, and couldn't talk privately there. Besides, the man would probably need food and water. The guard nodded, then rode off to meet the oncoming rider.

No one moved or left the square, and the time seemed to drag before three men arrived. Two soldiers from the gate, half-carrying a dirty and ragged man between them, reached the doorway before Eskkar recognized the one in the middle. He hadn't seen Alexar in almost two months.

They brought him into the house, and Lani put a cup of watered wine into his hand. Alexar emptied it in one draught, then slumped back on the bench, resting his head and shoulders against the wall. His eyes drooped and he seemed to have trouble focusing. Lani took the cup, and refilled it for him. Alexar looked up at the five men standing around him, but didn't say anything until he had drained a second cup.

Eskkar sat down next to him on the bench and put his hand on the man's shoulder. "Can you talk, Alexar?"

"Yes, Captain," he answered, his voice hoarse. "I haven't stopped for anything since noon yesterday. I've ridden five horses into the ground in three days to get here."

"Three days!" Sisuthros exclaimed. "From Akkad?"

"From just south of Akkad. I was with Bantor. We were ambushed just a few hours from the city."

"The Alur Meriki attacked you so close to Akkad?" Eskkar's fear welled up at the thought of the barbarians' return. "By the gods . . ."

"It wasn't the Alur Meriki, Captain," Alexar interrupted. "Bantor said it was someone named Ariamus. He said you'd know the name. We were surprised by sixty or seventy riders, and they killed half of us before we drove them away."

No one said anything for a moment, thinking about friends who might be dead. Grond broke the silence. "Who's Ariamus?"

Eskkar ignored the question. "And Bantor?"

"Bantor survived. He sent me and another rider, with extra horses, to find you here. I left the other man behind me on the road when I needed his horse. I was to tell you that Bantor would be at Rebba's farmhouse, waiting for you."

"How many men are with Bantor?"

"Sixteen. We sent a few wounded men south to hide, but that's all that survived the ambush. We lost most of our horses, and gave the rest to the wounded, so Bantor, Klexor . . . everyone's on foot."

"What's going on in Akkad?" Eskkar asked.

Alexar shook his head. "Don't know, Captain. We thought everything was fine until the ambush. Bantor thinks Ariamus must have already seized control of the city. They headed that way after we drove them off. There must be more men in Akkad helping him."

Akkad! Trella waited there, with a baby due any day. Eskkar's fist clenched and he tapped it slowly on his leg. He'd wasted time here, and left Trella in danger. Not only Trella, but others as well; his men had kin and friends in the city, too. No one said anything, but the unsaid thought remained.

Lani returned with a plate of bread and cheese that she handed to Alexar. The man held it in his hand, but didn't eat anything.

"Bantor was sure it was Ariamus?" Eskkar's voice was grim. When Alexar nodded, he went on. "And he thought he could reach Rebba's place in safety?"

"Yes. Bantor said he would march north, then cross the river and double back to Rebba's farm. He expected to find a boat somewhere along the Tigris to take him there."

"Bantor has done well," Sisuthros said. "He's kept his men together and brought them somewhere safe, at least for a time."

"Yes, he has, unless they track him down," Eskkar agreed. "Someone has tried to seize control of Akkad in our absence. That means there's been fighting in the city as well. Trella must have ... If anyone has injured Trella, they'll pay for it." He tightened his lips. "Well, we'll just have to move faster when we march. Let's start picking the men. We'll leave at noon. We can still cover plenty of ground before it gets too dark."

Sisuthros glanced up at the sun. "Captain, you don't know what you're facing down there. You may need every man. Let me go with you."

"I need you here, Sisuthros. Besides, I'll have Bantor and his men. That should be enough to take care of Ariamus. If not, then what I said before is even more important now. We may need Bisitun as a secure place behind us, if we need a refuge."

"No one will want to stay behind," Grond said. "Most of the men have wives and families in Akkad."

That started another argument. No one wanted to remain in Bisitun, but Eskkar wouldn't change his mind. "Now let's get the horses and men ready to go."

They rose from the table, then stopped when Lani spoke up, her voice firm. "Lord Eskkar, may I say something?"

"Yes, Lani, what is it?" She'd sat quietly, away from the table, and Eskkar had forgotten her presence, all his thoughts turning to Trella.

"Have you thought about the river?"

"The river?" Eskkar answered, a touch of annoyance in his voice. "What about the river?"

Sisuthros picked up her idea right away. "Of course! She's right. You can be there in less than three days if you take the boats. And we have plenty of vessels here, more than enough to hold forty men."

A horseman first and last, the thought of using the Tigris to transport soldiers had never occurred to Eskkar. "Rebba's farm has its own jetty," he mused as he thought about the idea. "Can we put the men and arms on the boats?"

"Yes, but you won't be able to bring the horses. Still, if you reach Akkad, you won't need them. What you'll need is a way to get into the city. Maybe Rebba and Bantor will have figured out something."

"We don't know how to sail the boats," Eskkar said, still not sure about this new mode of travel. He had journeyed on a boat for a day once before, and hadn't liked the experience. He knew the small craft, built mostly of reeds, capsized easily. Cargoes got lost, and men drowned often enough.

"For gold, the boat captains will take you anywhere," Sisuthros said, his voice rising in excitement. "With extra boatmen along, the boats could go day and night. You'd travel much faster than by horseback."

The thought of being on the river at night made Eskkar nervous. But if it would get him and his men there in two or three days, instead of five . . . He made up his mind. "You know the rivermen, Sisuthros. Get them here, and arrange for use of their boats." He thought of something else. "And make sure no boat has left since last night. I don't want word of the attack, or our coming downriver, to get ahead of us."

"You'll need to pack the weapons, the bows, the arrows, and food," Sisuthros went on, expanding on the idea. "You'll probably want men who can swim, just in case. And you'll need a way to keep the bowstrings dry. Mitrac will know about that."

Eskkar looked around the table. Grond nodded, but Hamati said, "I can't swim."

"I can," said Alexar, "but even if I couldn't, I'm going back to help Bantor, even if I have to walk the whole distance."

Eskkar put both hands down on the table. "Then we'll leave as soon as possible. Sisuthros, start with the boats, and get some men on the docks to guard them. Hamati, line up the men and find out who can swim. Grond, figure out what we'll have to carry. Ask Mitrac what else the archers will need. Make sure we have everything. We won't be stopping along the way."

20

Eskkar strode out of the house and into the market, his subcommanders trailing behind him. The rest of his men waited there, all regular duties forgotten. One glance at their leaders' grim faces warned them that bad news was coming.

"Sisuthros. Are all the men here? Everyone?"

"Except for those posted at the gates."

"Get them. I want everyone to hear the news." Better they should hear it from him, rather than picking it up in bits and pieces from each other.

It took only moments. The men guarding the gates arrived at a run, bunching up along with the rest of the troop that had marched here from Akkad. Even the scribes and merchants waited to hear Eskkar's words.

Eskkar stepped to the nearest merchant's cart, and climbed onto it, letting his eyes sweep the gathering. "You know what happened here last night. This morning word came that Bantor has been ambushed, and half his men killed. It may be that some enemy has seized control of Akkad."

His words shocked them into silence. He went on before the questions could start.

"I'm taking forty men with me to Akkad, all volunteers. I intend to kill whoever started this. The rest of you will stay here with Sisuthros, and . . ."

Shouts rose up, everyone speaking. They all wanted to go.

"Silence!" Eskkar put all the force he could into the word. "Listen to me, men. I know you all want to go. But you can't. First of all, there aren't enough boats. And I'm only taking men who can swim. The rest of you will have to stay here and fortify the village. There may be more attacks here, and the villagers will need your protection. Sisuthros and Hamati will be staying in Bisitun, and will need your help."

"But what about my family?" The voice came from one of the younger archers. "My wife and . . ."

"The men I bring with me will protect all your families, I promise you that. You'll have to trust them as you've always trusted each other. They won't fail you. And I pledge that we will do everything we can. You've trusted me before. Don't fail me now, when I need your loyalty and courage."

Groans of disappointment filled the market as the men realized that some would have to stay behind. Eskkar let the rumblings go on for a few moments, then raised his hand.

"Whatever has happened in Akkad will be dealt with, I swear it," Eskkar said. "Our city will not fall into an enemy's hands."

A shout of approval echoed around the square.

"The time for talk is over," he said. "Now it's time to avenge Bantor's dead and rescue our kin. The faster we can get started, the sooner we'll reach the city. Are you with me?"

A roar of assent followed his words, and for a moment Eskkar thought five hundred men had answered him, and the clamor continued until he held up both hands.

"Then let's begin."

Soldiers and villagers worked like slaves for the rest of the morning. Eskkar and his commanders selected the men who would accompany him, a process that took longer than he expected because a few soldiers tried to claim they could swim. Everyone wanted to join him and recapture Akkad. To his surprise, many of the soldiers had lived on and around the river for most of their lives, and more than a few knew how to swim.

Obtaining the boats proved more difficult. Even for gold, two boat owners refused to help, and Sisuthros simply commandeered their boats. In the end Sisuthros selected six boats. Each vessel would need a crew of two, and could carry at least half a dozen men, plus their equipment. Crewmen utilized every rope and cord they could find in Bisitun, to lash down swords, knives, sandals, food, anything that could be lost. That way, even if the boat capsized, a not unexpected event, the food and weapons would be secure.

Mitrac ordered the bows coated with grease, then wrapped in rags and bound with cords. A short immersion in the water wouldn't weaken them too much. The master archer packed all the bowstrings into two small clay jars, then sealed them with plenty of wax and bundled them with blankets and straw, much the way the traders shipped beer or wine. The jars, too, were fastened down throughout the craft, in the safest and most secure places. The bowstrings had to be kept dry at all cost. If they got wet, it would take most of a day to dry them out, and the bows would be useless during that time. A little water wouldn't hurt the arrows, Mitrac decided. Nevertheless, they stored them in jars as well, though they didn't bother sealing these as tightly.

All this took time. The village square and the docks looked like a serpents' pit with everyone scurrying around. Lani organized the women to cook as much food as possible. Every chicken they could lay their hands on ended up on a spit, and the aroma of roasting meat wafted throughout the dockside. The men would eat a big meal before they left and have more to take with them. The women fired up the morning ovens once again and began baking more bread. Lani supervised the collection of fruits, dates, and any other edible items that wouldn't be ruined by water, gathered them together, and sent them to the boats.

Counting Eskkar, Grond, and Alexar, thirty-nine men assembled at the jetty, ready to board. Eskkar mustered all those selected. "Quiet now," he ordered. "Yavtar will speak to you. Listen carefully to what he says."

Yavtar owned two of the boats, and would command one of them. Sisuthros had dealt with the ship owner turned trader several times during the last month, and suggested Yavtar be put in charge of the whole expedition. A big man, with thick arms from years of handling an oar, Yavtar pushed his way into the center of the Akkadians. He had dirty blond hair tied at the back of his neck, and wore nothing but a skirt and a belt holding a knife. When he spoke, his deep voice carried across the docks.

"You men are going on my boats," he began, "and you'll follow my orders exactly. Anyone who doesn't will find themselves swimming. My orders, remember that, not Lord Eskkar's, not anyone else's. On the river, you'll answer only to me." He paused to stare at Eskkar, who nodded agreement.

"All these boats will be heavily loaded," Yavtar continued, "and I don't want some fool tipping one over. No one is to move without asking permission of the boat captain. All of you will be given paddles, and you'll be expected to use them. Your lord here," Yavtar pointed to Eskkar with his thumb, "has promised me a bonus if I get all of you to Akkad as soon as possible. So you'll paddle when I tell you, you'll sleep where, when, and if I tell you, and you will not move about unless I tell you."

Yavtar turned back to Eskkar. "Is that as we've agreed, Lord Eskkar?"

Eskkar raised up his voice. "All of us will do what we're told by the boat captains. Obey them as you would me. We want to get to Akkad as soon as possible."

Yavtar glanced at the sun, already approaching its high point, then turned to his men, who stood lined up against the water's edge. "Get the men onboard," he ordered, and walked off. The embarkation of the soldiers began. The boatmen had already stowed and lashed down the food and weapons.

Eskkar felt a hand on his arm and turned to find Lani there. "Lord Eskkar, take this with you. You may want it later."

The basket held more food, collected at the last

moment. Eskkar hadn't spoken to her since early morning. Taking her hand, he led her away from the jetty. The sounds of activity rose up all around them, but no one paid any attention to the couple.

"Lani," he began, "I don't know what will happen at Akkad. But I'll send for you as soon as I can. Otherwise, Sisuthros will make sure you're cared for, and . . ."

Lani shook her head. "Eskkar, you needn't worry about me. Secure your wife's safety. She needs you now. Do what you must. I'll wait for your summons."

He pulled her to him for a moment, felt her hands go around his back as she pressed herself to him. Then he stepped back and met her wet eyes. "I will take care of you, Lani, for as long as you want me to. Remember that. You have my word."

He turned and returned to the boats. Yavtar stood waiting for him, and the sailor extended his hand to guide Eskkar down into a rocking craft, the largest of the six vessels.

"Can you swim, Lord Eskkar?"

"Well enough," Eskkar said, grateful for the skill learned as a boy. "But I prefer to do my swimming near the riverbank, not out in the current."

"Then I'll make sure we only capsize near the shore," Yavtar said with a laugh.

With Eskkar aboard and seated, Yavtar took one last check to ensure that the heavily loaded craft rode evenly in the water. He took his position at the stern, and gave orders to those still standing on the docks. The boatman at the prow cast loose the last of the ropes, and coiled it back into the boat, even as the men left behind waded into the water, pushing the boat out into the river's current. Eskkar breathed a sigh of relief: under way at last.

Half the men with Eskkar had some experience with boats, another quality Sisuthros searched for while sorting out those who would go. These men, at Yavtar's order, began paddling, using slow and even strokes. Yavtar's crewman hauled up the small sail the vessel carried amidships, grunting until he'd raised the heavy linen to its full extent before lashing it in place.

Gradually the boat began to speed up as it edged into the middle of the river. "We'll be safer here," Yavtar explained, "where the current is swiftest. There aren't many rapids between Bisitun and Akkad, and it's easier to control the boat."

Once in the center of the channel, they glided along, and Eskkar reckoned the pace to be equivalent to a horse's fast walk. Glancing behind, he saw the other five boats strung out, each raising its own sails.

Yavtar spent plenty of time inspecting the sail and gauging the trim of the boat, moving the men around slightly, and showing them how and when to row. The experienced rivermen didn't need the lesson, but no one said anything. Yavtar didn't trust any of them to hold on to a paddle. He made sure a rope fastened each oar to the boat.

By the end of the first hour, they began to settle down. Everyone soon learned not to make any rapid movements, and if one man had to change positions, the others held still. To Eskkar's relief, the boat seemed stable enough, and he gradually stopped worrying about capsizing. The desultory wind blew from the north, helping to push the boats downstream, and they cut through the water at a steady pace.

Though the boat held nine men, it carried little cargo, so the craft responded well to Yavtar's handling. With everyone paddling, even with light strokes, the boat fairly flew along, picking up more speed when helped by the wind, which held steady until sundown. Then it changed direction, and Yavtar ordered the sail lowered.

Eskkar opened his mouth, then shut it again.

Yavtar saw the look. "It's too dangerous at night, Captain," he explained, a little more talkative now that he knew the soldiers could follow orders. "Hard to see rocks or anything else floating in the water. We would have lowered it anyway. We'll paddle easy until moonrise."

Eskkar grunted a little at that news. By now he knew that even light strokes moved the boat at a good pace. He learned to use a smooth, feathering stroke that took little effort. The paddling served as much to guide the boat and keep it centered in the river as to move it along.

When the moon rose, Yavtar picked up the pace. "I've never sailed through a whole night before, Lord Eskkar. It'll be interesting to see how much river we can cover by dawn."

In the moonlight, Eskkar could scarcely make out the boat behind them, still keeping its station and holding its distance. He hoped the other boats followed behind, all at their proper intervals.

Whether he rowed or rested, Eskkar kept his thoughts fixed on Akkad. The possibility that Trella might be dead kept disturbing his thoughts, filling him with anger and anguish. He remembered the fear that had numbed him when she'd been stabbed in the street. She had almost died that day. He remembered how he'd turned away as the healer dressed her wound, unable to watch her suffering.

At least then he could turn his thoughts to vengeance. Now he faulted his own actions for whatever might have befallen her. Eskkar had overstayed his trip to Bisitun. He'd taken his pleasure with Lani, with hardly a thought to Trella, her well-being, or even the coming child. Whatever fate had befallen her, it would not have happened if he had returned earlier. Instead he'd postponed his return again and again, telling himself Trella had everything under control, that he could do more good in Bisitun. Staring down at the river, he blamed himself for whatever evil had arisen, his thoughts as black as the parting water.

Grond must have known what thoughts troubled his leader. "Captain, there was nothing you could have done. The assassins left Akkad ten days ago. If we'd been in Akkad, if four men suddenly attacked you in the street, we might both be dead. Staying in Bisitun may have saved your life."

"And what of Trella? I don't know if she's alive or dead. I just hope she's still safe."

"What you should be thinking about is how this plot came about," Grond countered. "How did this happen without Trella's spies learning of it? Who could put such a plan together, gather enough men, ambush Bantor, and send assassins after you? None of the messengers, including the Hawk Clan riders, had mentioned even a rumor of a problem."

Those same thoughts had plagued Eskkar. "It takes gold to bring that many men together, even with such a prize as

Akkad at stake. I know of no one in Akkad who could devise such a plan."

"And I don't think anyone in Akkad could do this without some word getting to Lady Trella," Grond offered. "Perhaps it's this Ariamus. Who is he?"

He told Grond about Ariamus and the gloomy days in Akkad before the Alur Meriki. Grond grunted when Eskkar finished, but said nothing. Nevertheless, talking it all over with Grond helped clear Eskkar's mind. For perhaps the first time since the attack last night, he started thinking clearly. He kept paddling, the slow, deep strokes occupying his muscles and soothing his mind, while he began running what little he knew in his head.

Bantor attacked on the road, a few hours from reaching Akkad. That would destroy any organized force of soldiers outside the city. Assassins trying to kill him in Bisitun. Eskkar's death would certainly have disrupted the soldiers, and might have slowed down any response to word of trouble in Akkad. So someone wanted to keep soldiers away from the city, no doubt while they consolidated their control. His death, even the ambush of Bantor's men, meant nothing without taking power in the city.

And Grond spoke the truth. Little went on in Akkad that Trella didn't learn of sooner or later. Ariamus wouldn't dare show his face in the city. Despite the former captain of the guard's fighting skills, he wasn't capable of outwitting Trella. Ariamus, Eskkar decided, would need an ally inside the city, someone who could put together a grand scheme to seize power over the thousands that now lived there. That meant there must be someone else in Akkad, a disgruntled noble or wealthy merchant, even possibly a newcomer. Eskkar swore under his breath. He needed more information.

"There is nothing to do now, Captain," Grond said, hearing the curse, "except get to Bantor and Rebba. They'll tell us what's been going on."

So Grond had come to the same conclusion.

"We'll need to be careful, Grond, when we get to Rebba's place. There might be a trap. Bantor and his men might have been captured days ago and put to the torture."

Yavtar called out from the stern, telling them to take a break. Eskkar lifted the wet paddle and rested it across his knees. He wanted to keep rowing, to not waste a moment in delay, but the others needed their rest. The boat kept moving, gliding with the current, every moment bringing him closer to Akkad.

The night passed quickly enough. When the men didn't row, they slept at the oars. Eskkar checked his wound several times, but noticed no signs of bleeding. The pain had gone, though the arm felt stiff and sore.

Dawn found them many miles downstream from Bisitun. When Yavtar worked out how much they had traveled, he smiled for the first time since the voyage began. "We're doing well, lord," he announced. "More important, we haven't capsized, lost any paddles, or drowned anyone, at least not yet. Your men aren't bad sailors. I think we can pick up the pace, after the men have eaten."

They ate without leaving their positions, hunks of dry sausage washed down with water scooped directly from the river. Bread completed the meal. Yavtar slowed the boat and waited until all the other craft had caught up with his. After checking with the other shipmasters, he shouted out some incomprehensible orders about how much faster they would travel today, his voice booming over the river. He ordered the sail raised, and the men back to their paddles.

Eskkar scarcely noticed the extra effort demanded by Yavtar, but the boat moved much more rapidly. The morning sun brought a slight but steady breeze from the east, so they quartered the sail in the wind's direction, and that alone would have kept them going at a good pace. With six men working the oars, the boat appeared to move twice as fast as yesterday afternoon, the water curling noisily from its prow. He asked Yavtar about their speed, wondering if they could move even faster.

"Not likely, lord," Yavtar answered, sitting back in the stern with the steering oar under his arm. "Everyone will be tired enough by the end of the day at this pace, I promise you. Better pray the gods don't shift the wind any further, or it will hold us back instead of pushing us along."

To keep his mind occupied, Eskkar studied the wind, noticing how Yavtar's sailor kept adjusting the sail to meet the breeze. By noon, Eskkar thought he had the knack of it, and could have handled the sail himself, even without Yavtar's orders.

The midday sun slackened the wind. Yavtar began eying the riverbank, searching for landmarks, until he found what he sought. A small island appeared near the west bank, with two poplar trees growing on it. Yavtar turned his rudder and put the boat directly into a sand spit that hissed beneath Eskkar as the boat ground to halt. The sudden cessation of movement felt unnatural after being in constant motion for over a day. Before Eskkar could question the delay, Yavtar spoke.

"We'll rest here while I check the other boats, and rearrange our cargo. We can all stretch our legs."

One by one, the other boats beached themselves on the soft sand as they pulled alongside Yavtar's craft. As soon as the men settled onshore, Yavtar called the boat captains together and spoke with each of them. When he finished, the boatmen went into the water, checking the hulls for leaks, tipping each craft from one side to the other to inspect all they could see. Afterward, Yavtar made sure each boat captain had what he needed, and understood his orders.

As soon as his men had checked the boats and made any needed repairs, Yavtar ordered the food unpacked. The constant labor in the fresh air had given all of them a huge appetite, and they devoured nearly half their food. After they finished eating, they had to wait until the sailors rearranged the goods and weapons, lashing everything securely. Only then did the soldiers climb back aboard the boats, to take their carefully arranged positions. With a single grunt, Yavtar ordered them downstream.

"We've had our big meal for the day, lord," Yavtar said a little later, still chewing on a piece of bread. "Supper tonight will be day-old bread as we row, and we'll try to keep this pace."

"How far have we come, Yavtar?" Eskkar asked.

"Farther than I thought we could. Your men have strong backs, I'll say that for them. I always wondered how fast a trip could be made by sailing through the night, but I never thought I'd make such a voyage. Too risky for the cargo." He laughed at that thought, but then lapsed into silence.

The land on either side of them flowed steadily by, and

those on the land took little if any notice of their passage. A handful of farmers paused to stare at them with open mouths, and once some shepherds tending a small flock of sheep ran along the riverbank, calling out greetings and shouting in excitement as the ships glided by. Those on the shore had probably never seen so many boats passing at one time. Nevertheless, except for some women gathering water or washing clothes, not many people labored at the river's edge. Eskkar tried to see the trail that paralleled the river, but in most locations, it ran nearly half a mile away.

Hopefully, Eskkar told himself, no travelers journeying on horseback would pay much attention to their passage. If someone saw them, by the time the tale could be told, the boats would be far down the Tigris, moving faster than any horse.

They didn't stop again until dusk. Yavtar used the last of the day's light to beach his boat once again, this time on the eastern bank. While he inspected the craft, Eskkar checked the casks that held the bowstrings, to make sure the seals looked dry and tight. One of the smaller boats had capsized earlier in the afternoon, after brushing against some rocks; the men had righted it soon enough, and managed to catch up with the others, none the worse for the experience. Other than that, no mishaps had occurred.

"Make sure the men finish the food, Grond," Eskkar ordered. There'd be plenty to eat at Rebba's farm. Either that, or they'd be fighting for their lives.

They ate in silence. This time Eskkar and the others forced themselves to swallow as much of the food as they could. They might be fighting before they got to eat again, and only a few loaves of bread remained when the men reboarded the crafts. They hadn't stopped for longer than needed, and darkness again covered the river as they pushed off. This time Yavtar slackened the pace at the oars a bit. The river narrowed somewhat as they drew closer to Akkad, and the current speeded up. Still, Eskkar felt his arms aching from the constant strain.

They rowed steadily, picking up the pace again when the moon rose and Yavtar raised the sail. The boat captain kept his crewman attending to the sail, ready to drop it to the deck should any problem arise. They rowed for nearly four hours before Yavtar called for another break; this time he moved down the boat to squat next to Eskkar.

"Lord, I think we're a little more than three hours from Rebba's jetty. If nothing goes wrong, you'll be ashore not long after midnight. That should give you enough time to rest and stretch your limbs."

"My thanks to you, Yavtar. I still cannot believe we covered so much distance so quickly. It would have taken days on the road to reach Akkad."

Yavtar's teeth flashed in the moonlight. "I've enjoyed the trip more than you know. I always wanted to race the river, and you've given me the chance, and paid me for it as well. In less than two days, we've covered nearly a hundred and thirty miles. No man, no river captain has ever accomplished such a thing."

"You've made me think about using the river to move men in the future, Yavtar. I'll not forget what I've seen and learned on this trip."

The boat captain focused his attention on the river for

a few moments, and Eskkar thought the conversation ended.

"Lord Eskkar," Yavtar said, "when you go ashore, I want to come with you."

Eskkar blinked in surprise. "I thought you planned to return to Bisitun. We'll be fighting for our lives at Akkad."

"I was going to, but I've changed my mind." Yavtar grunted, as if surprised at his own decision. "In my years, I've seen more bandits, brigands, robbers, and thieves up and down the length of the Tigris than you could imagine. Sometimes I ferried them from place to place, and I fought them off more than once. But your soldiers are different. I've watched you and your men for the last two days. They show no fear, no doubt. They don't brag about what they've done or what they'll do. They follow your orders without thinking or worrying about the danger."

"They're good men," Eskkar answered, trying to understand the meaning behind Yavtar's words. "And they're well trained. Perhaps that is the difference."

"Yes, perhaps. But you trained them, didn't you, and gave them a home and a clan. That's why I think you'll win at Akkad, Captain, no matter what the odds. And that's why I want to fight with you. I think I want to be part of your victory. And it would be nice to have a clan of my own, for when I get too old to ride the river."

Eskkar considered the man's words for a moment. Yavtar didn't look much older than himself, so the sailor could be sailing the Tigris for many more years. Still, every man wanted a home somewhere, a place of safety to raise his family and spend his declining years. "I welcome you to the fight, Yavtar," Eskkar said, using what he thought of as his formal voice, "the Hawk Clan always needs good men."

"Thank you, Lord Eskkar." He moved back toward the stern. "Keep rowing, men. We don't want to lose any time."

True to his word, before three hours had passed, Yavtar started guiding the boat closer to the eastern bank. He ordered the pace slackened, and the other boats soon caught up with them, staying just far enough apart to avoid a collision.

Eskkar wondered how Yavtar could be certain of their location. The deeper darkness of the land looked the same to him, even with the moon up. Moments later, Yavtar angled the boat toward the riverbank. Eskkar still couldn't see anything, and Yavtar's mate had caught the jetty before Eskkar even saw it. Both Yavtar and the crewman slipped over the side into the river, ropes in their hands, and lashed the craft tightly to the jetty.

The jetty had room for only the one vessel; two small boats, no doubt belonging to Rebba, occupied the remaining space. So the other craft moved carefully alongside, until men could push them ashore, struggling in the current to move the now-clumsy boats as far up onto the bank as possible. The moment each ship came to rest, men with their gear climbed carefully over the side and started moving inshore, until every man had landed. Grond slipped away first, and had already moved inland. For a big man, he could move without a sound when need be. All the men from Eskkar's boat followed, armed only with their swords, and fading into the darkness, to make sure no one lurked in ambush.

Eskkar swore at the noise they made. The men

stumbled about in the dark. He hoped the river muffled the sounds, and maybe the din wouldn't be heard above the normal bubbling of the flowing water. At last everyone stood on firm ground once again, though now it felt strange enough to Eskkar's shaky legs.

The boat crews passed out the bows, all bundled together, and then handed out the jars containing the bowstrings. Eskkar cursed again as the sound echoed out over the river. He felt certain they could be heard all the way to Akkad.

At last all the weapons had landed. The soldiers spread out, all the men stringing their bows and readying their arrows and swords. By then Grond returned.

"Captain, nothing suspicious. I went as close as I dared. Any closer and I would have awakened the dogs. But there was nothing."

"No sentries, no guards, no horses?"

"No, no horses except the three or four that Rebba would have in his corral."

"Well, we'll have to chance it. I'll go ahead and see what . . ."

"No, Captain," Grond interrupted. "I've thought about this. Let's send Alexar, and have him approach as if he came from Akkad. If all's well, he can report back to us. If not, we can still use the boats."

Eskkar bit his lip. Grond spoke the truth. Eskkar's old instincts made him want to rush ahead, but Grond and the others wouldn't let him go, and there was no sense arguing over it.

"I'm ready to go, Captain," Alexar whispered. He had seen Grond come back and stepped over to join them. "I'll know if there's anything wrong. I'll bring Bantor back with me."

"You know about the dogs?" Eskkar asked. "The dogs will start barking as soon as they hear you."

"Yes. It can't be helped," Alexar answered. "But they'd waken anyway, so we might as well get it over with. The sound won't carry to the next farmhouse."

"Be careful," Eskkar said, putting his hand on Alexar's arm. The moment the words left his mouth he swore at himself for wasting his breath; no one needed any orders to take care. He watched them disappear into the darkness, Grond leading the way, to show Alexar the location of the road and the farmhouse.

Clenching his fist at the inaction, Eskkar moved forward, until he could make out the cluster of buildings that made up Rebba's farmstead. Moments later, the dogs began barking. The noise went on and on, for what seemed like far too long, before a light appeared in the window of the main house. But the glow went out almost immediately, and the dogs stopped their challenge. After what seemed like a lifetime, he saw two men looming in the darkness, heading toward the jetty.

Still worried about an ambush, Eskkar squinted against the darkness, looking for any other movement, his hand resting on his sword hilt. Relief flooded over him when he heard a familiar voice call out. Then Bantor rushed the last few steps and wrapped his arms around Eskkar, hugging him tight and pounding on his back.

"Thank the gods, Captain, but I'm glad to see you. Let's move up to the house."

With Alexar and Bantor leading the way, Eskkar gave the orders and started the soldiers moving toward the farmhouse. They went in single file, to leave as little trace of their passing as possible. The dogs barked a few more times, nervous at the approach of so many men. Eskkar heard voices, no doubt Rebba's farmers, chiding the watchdogs to keep silent, and keeping them away from the soldiers' approach.

Bantor guided his captain and Grond to the main house, while Alexar led the rest to another building. When the door opened, Eskkar saw that a small lamp burned. Heavy leather strips covered the windows and prevented the light from showing.

Rebba stood there, waiting. He had already sent the rest of his family to the other house. Inside, Rebba motioned them to the benches at the big table, lighting a second lamp, a larger one that provided plenty of light, though it smoked quite a bit. Rebba sat at one end, while Eskkar sat at the other. By then Mitrac, Alexar, and Klexor had joined them and, to Eskkar's surprise, Yavtar. The sailor had followed silently behind the soldiers. Eskkar noticed that Yavtar had laced sandals on his usually bare feet, and carried a short sword at his waist.

"Is Trella all right?" Eskkar had to know, though he dreaded what he might hear.

"She's alive, a prisoner in your house," Rebba answered.

Eskkar felt relief wash over him. He still had time to save her.

"How many men have you brought, Lord Eskkar?"

Rebba's voice sounded frail, but the urgency of his question took Eskkar's mind off Trella.

One of Rebba's daughters came into the house, carrying a fresh jug of water. She began pouring it, looking nervously about the table, as the men eased themselves down, shoulder to shoulder, around the table.

"Thirty-nine, no, forty now, counting me, Noble Rebba," Eskkar answered. He saw the looks of disappointment on Rebba and Bantor's faces. "We came by riverboat, and it would have taken us another three or four days to march here with more men."

Rebba shook his head. "You don't have enough soldiers. There are many men inside Akkad who now follow Korthac." He saw the question on Eskkar's face. "Ah, yes. You don't know the man. He came less than a week after you left for Dilgarth." He looked at Bantor for a moment. "Perhaps we should start when you left Akkad."

Eskkar held his tongue as much as possible, resisting the urge to interrupt with questions. The telling of the events took nearly an hour, with Rebba speaking of what had happened in the city, and then Bantor describing the ambush on the road. Rebba finished with what had happened since.

"So now," Rebba said as he wound up his tale, "the forty or so soldiers still alive are used as slaves, and kept under guard at the old barracks. Korthac's men, and now he has close to two hundred of them, terrorize the villagers. There have been many rapes and much looting. Any that resist are killed horribly in the marketplace. All the merchants and craftsmen must pay a tax just to stay alive and remain in business." He looked across the flickering lamp at Eskkar. "You must gather more men, then find a way to drive them out."

"I intend to do that, Rebba," Eskkar said. "But you haven't seen Trella?"

"No, but she is in her room, with Annok-sur, giving birth." Rebba saw the look on Eskkar's face and realized he had left something out. "Lady Trella went into labor this afternoon. I don't know how . . ."

"Trella is well, you say?"

"Yes, that's what I heard today," Rebba replied. "But we hear only rumors from the servants. Trella and Annok-sur are confined to the upper rooms of your home. Korthac uses the outer room during the day, but sleeps downstairs at night. He has taken a few young boys and girls as bedmates, they say."

"I don't care who he sleeps with," Eskkar said, his hands clenching into fists. "He'll be dead as soon as I get my hands on his throat."

"It won't be easy, Eskkar." Rebba shook his head. "The gates are heavily guarded and the walls are patrolled day and night, as much to keep the people in as intruders out."

Bantor rapped his fist on the table. "We just need to get inside, Captain. Ariamus's men spend their nights in the alehouses, drinking their fill. We'll kill them easy enough. My men have practiced each day with bow and sword."

"You said Gatus is in hiding with Tammuz?"

"Yes. Rebba's men found him there two days ago," Bantor said. "Gatus sent three men out here as soon as he learned we were here."

"What else did he say?" Eskkar knew Gatus well enough.

"Two days ago, he sent word that Tammuz has been watching the sentries. Gatus says that Butcher's Lane is the way in. He'll help us, if we send word."

Eskkar smiled at that. Butcher's Lane was where, during the siege, the Alur Meriki had almost carried the wall in a night attack. He'd considered using the same location to scale the wall on the journey downriver. But there was no time to send word. They could be discovered at any moment. He counted the men he had at his command. "So we have your twenty men, Bantor, and my thirty-nine. That gives us . . ."

"Sixty-two men, Captain," Yavtar broke in before Eskkar could complete the sum in his head. "That includes me, and two of my boatmen, willing to gamble their miserable lives for a fistful of gold. The rest will stay with the boats, in case we need them. I told you I intend to fight with you. I know how to swing a sword."

"I'm sure you do, Yavtar," Eskkar said, then he stopped for a moment. He had been struggling with ideas about how to get into Akkad, how to climb the wall. He doubted he could get sixty men inside without alerting Korthac's sentries, no matter how many throats they slit in the darkness. Yavtar's presence suggested another, better way.

"Then, Yavtar, I have a task for you, if you're willing. A dangerous task." He looked around the table. "Here's what I want you to do."

He explained his plan, his men leaning closer, intent on every word. Eskkar had thought about little else most of the day, and now Bantor and Rebba had supplied the final bits of information he needed. Yavtar's volunteering to join the battle provided yet another option.

When Eskkar finished, his commanders began to fill in their parts. They had all fought together before, working on defenses during the siege, and planning attacks on barbarians and bandits. They knew what to do and what to suggest to each other.

Eskkar said little while they spoke, and Bantor, Alexar, and Mitrac all made their suggestions and asked their questions. The whole process didn't take long. The subcommanders knew how to prepare their men. In less than an hour, they were all ready.

Rebba listened without speaking during the process. Now he shook his head as they began to get up from the table. "You really think this plan will work? Why don't you wait until tomorrow night? That way we can get some help from Gatus and others inside the city who are willing to fight."

Bantor answered even before Eskkar could speak. "No. Eskkar is right. We must go now. Anything can happen in a day. We might be discovered here, or word might reach Korthac that Eskkar is on the way. If they suspect we're here . . . no, we must attack tonight."

"It will work, Rebba," Klexor added. "Those men are bandits, and they're not even from the same clan. Half of them will run at the first sign of trouble."

"Even if half do run," Rebba answered, "you'll still be outnumbered. And Korthac's men are trained fighters, not bandits. They won't run. If we wait another day or two, we can get many of the citizens to join with us."

"We'll be discovered," Bantor said, his fist again striking the table. "Besides, we don't need them. We just have to get over the walls, and when we do, I will put my sword in Ariamus's guts and watch him die for what he did to my men."

Eskkar stared at his subcommander, surprised at Bantor's intensity. He remembered the gossip about Ariamus and Annok-sur; he'd forgotten about it until now. Eskkar realized the anger that must still burn inside the man's heart.

"At least keep your forces together, Eskkar," Rebba pleaded. "Splitting them up will . . ."

"No, Rebba. What's important is to get inside Akkad." Eskkar spoke with certainty. "If we stay together, and can't get in, then we've failed. This way, even if only half of us succeed, we can rouse the city. Besides, you say that Korthac's men are scattered all over Akkad. The more places we attack, the greater their confusion."

And gives me the best chance to rescue Trella. Eskkar had made that decision on the river, too. If he could get her out safely, he didn't care if the rest of the attack failed. The people of Akkad could live with the demon Korthac for all he cared.

Silence settled over the table. Either none of Eskkar's commanders found fault with his plan, or they just wanted to get on with the fight.

"Then I will go with you," Rebba said, the sound of resignation in his voice. "No matter what happens, I'm committed. If you fail, I will be killed and my estates confiscated. So I'll walk the streets, to rally the people behind you, even as you fight Korthac's soldiers. The people will recognize me, and many will heed my words, when I tell them Eskkar has returned to free them."

Eskkar understood Rebba's situation. If Eskkar failed, Korthac would learn of Rebba's involvement. They would all risk their lives tonight. He looked about the table, but no one said anything further.

"Tell your men to kill the Egyptian soldiers first," Eskkar said, picking his words carefully. "The rest of the rabble will break. Make sure our soldiers shout their heads off. Let your battle cry be 'Let None Escape.' That will strike fear into the hearts of these bandits."

"We need another one," Klexor offered. "'Eskkar has returned.' I think that will rouse the people."

Eskkar nodded his approval. "Good. Two battle cries will make us sound even stronger."

The night was slipping by, and the time for words had passed. "Then let us begin. We still have things to prepare, and I don't want our enemies enjoying too much sleep before we awaken them."

21

Korthac woke a few hours after he'd finished taking his pleasure with the young girl, who still lay in a heap on the floor, her legs streaked with blood. He'd told her not to move, and enjoyed the satisfaction of seeing she'd learned obedience.

Too young for the love act, she had sobbed at the pain. He'd enjoyed that, too, watching the fright in her eyes that terrorized her as much as the suffering. For the last four nights he'd taken a fresh young bedmate, alternating between sexes, enjoying at last the opportunity to satisfy himself without restraint. Not that Korthac ever felt driven by such basic needs, as most men were. He'd spent months in the desert without companionship of any kind, and considered it only a minor inconvenience. Nevertheless, now that he had all of Akkad at his feet and eager to please him, he intended to make up for being deprived.

When he grew bored with the young children of the nobles and richer traders, he would start with their daughters and wives, keeping a half-dozen or so on hand as concubines until they became pregnant. When that happened, he would send them home to their families and watch their faces as they reared his children. Korthac determined to fill the city with his offspring, so that, in the years to come, everyone could see the power of his conquest.

Tonight's diversion had been less than satisfying. The room he'd taken on the lower floor of Eskkar's house two days ago had no door, just a heavy curtain for privacy. In another day or so, he would move into the upper rooms and banish Trella to this humble chamber. She would sleep on the floor, sharing a blanket with her servant Annok-sur. After a few days, Trella would have the blanket for herself; Korthac planned to hand over Annok-sur to his men before putting her to the torture.

He had let Trella keep her quarters, more as a gesture to the people than out of any concern for her comfort. Korthac knew that many in Akkad felt compassion for Trella. His men controlled the city, but there was no reason to give its inhabitants something else to complain about, at least not for another few days.

Though tonight, Korthac felt tempted to order Trella out. Earlier in the day, he'd visited her again, and decided her eyes still showed traces of disrespect. He'd slapped her hard a few times, until real pain showed in her face and blood flowed from her mouth. When she assumed a properly servile manner, he ran his fingers through her hair, enjoying the fear that she could no longer conceal. On her knees and in tears, she'd scarcely crawled back to her room when her labor began.

Since then, through the evening meal and continuing long into the night, servants had crept past Korthac's room, moving up and down the stairs to her quarters. Even now her muffled groans echoed throughout the house, diluting his pleasure and upsetting his sleep. He'd be glad when she dropped the babe, or died in the delivery.

Not that he wanted her to die. He planned to keep her beside him, to show the city's inhabitants that he possessed complete control over their lives. Perhaps he wouldn't need her for much longer. Since he'd seized power three days ago, his men had killed more than a hundred people, and the brutal lessons appeared to be working. The last two nights had seen Akkad quiet down.

Anyone who protested, anyone who failed to show proper respect, anyone who failed to yield to his men as they walked the street, all met the same fate: torture and death in the city's marketplace. The people of Akkad had taken the first step to their proper place in his world—on their knees and at his feet.

As for Trella, he would wait until she became fit to bed. He wanted to enjoy the look in her eyes when he took her. Her child would be the means to keep her respectful, and he intended to turn her into the most obedient and pleasure-giving slave in the city. Yes, that would satisfy him for some time, perhaps even a few months. When he grew tired of Trella, she would pleasure every one of his men. Only then would he toss the child into the flames, in front of her.

Unable to sleep, Korthac rose from his bed as he contemplated that pleasant future. He often went through days when he found it difficult to sleep at night, and had learned not to fight against it. Better to just get up and walk around.

Another muffled moan from upstairs recalled Trella to his thoughts. As soon as she gave birth, he'd move her out of her quarters and into this room. Then, at last, he would have privacy and a quiet place to sleep at night. Korthac had examined all of the larger residences in Akkad, and Esskar's home came closest to his ideal. It would do for a few months, until his new slaves built him a much grander residence.

He frowned at the faint voices drifting down from above. The lamp burned low, and he ordered the guard standing just outside his door to refill it. Fully awake, Korthac pulled on his tunic and belted the sword around his waist. The guard returned with more oil, and the room brightened again.

Korthac, wide awake now, noticed the forgotten child still staring at him from the floor, her tear-streaked face showing both fear and pain. "Go home," he ordered. "Tell your family that you failed to please me." That would bring terror to her parents, who would wonder what horror would befall them next.

He went outside, taking a deep breath of the fresh night air. His room had only a small aperture high in the wall for ventilation, and its air easily grew stale. A glance at the heavens told him midnight had already passed. Korthac walked around the compound, checking the guards at the courtyard gate, and stopping at the soldiers' quarters to make sure they stood ready.

Not that he expected trouble. After the bloodbath of the first day, he had crushed every look or word of opposition. His men executed two entire families, dragging them to the marketplace so that all could witness his power. One man dared to protest the new tax, and the other had struck one of his Egyptians. Korthac determined to kill any that failed to show respect.

Meanwhile his followers grew more numerous with each day, paid for with the tax he demanded from the nobles. Most of his newest followers appeared little better than rabble. Once again he wished for another hundred of his Egyptian fighters. Not that it mattered. He had enough men, and Ariamus continued to gather more. In three or four weeks, all in Akkad would have forgotten all about their previous lives.

Feeling refreshed by the night air, Korthac sat at the big table in the garden, glancing up at the starry sky. A nervous servant brought water and wine out to him, and Korthac listened with half-interest to the report of the night-watch commander. The city remained quiet, its inhabitants in their homes where they belonged, afraid to step out on the streets at night. Since the first day of the city's capture, he had given his men free rein after darkness fell. That meant they could stop any man or woman they encountered away from their homes. After that first night, the streets and lanes were deserted, as families huddled together in their huts.

That didn't protect them for long. His men soon began entering houses at random, pulling wives and daughters from their families' arms. Korthac knew that he would have to restrain his men somewhat after a few more days, but for now, they kept the inhabitants paralyzed with fear while they indulged themselves in the spoils of war.

Another cry came from the house. Annoyed, Korthac finished his wine and went back inside. He climbed the stairs and entered the outer room. One of his Egyptians waited there, detailed to guard Trella and keep her in her chamber. Korthac paused at the bedroom door. Two lamps burned inside, adding the bitter tang of heated oil to the dank, warm air that smelled of sweat and birthing blood.

Annok-sur sat on a stool next to the bed, holding Trella's hand. She lay there, legs apart, moaning in pain. Sweat covered her naked body, and her hair hung limply over her face. Even in her suffering, Trella knew better than to try and cover her body from her master's eyes. Two other women attended her, one of them he recognized as the midwife. Korthac remembered how Annok-sur, on her knees before him, begged him to grant the midwife safe passage into Akkad and back to her home after the birth. It had pleased him to agree.

Trella's body contracted. Her back arched, as she struggled to force the child from her womb. Eyes wide, she looked at him, unable to control either her body or the pain.

"You're keeping the household awake, Lady Trella." Korthac enjoyed using her former title. He leaned against the doorway, enjoying her helplessness. "How much longer will I have to hear your whining?"

"The child is coming, master," Drusala said, her voice humble. "It won't be long now. Please forgive us."

At least the midwife knew her place, Korthac decided. Not that he intended to keep his promise of safe passage back to the countryside. His men wanted women, and soon there would be plenty of need for her skill in Akkad.

Trella's body heaved again. The contraction forced another moan of pain from her clenched lips, despite her effort to remain silent. Korthac peered at her belly. Yes, the infant's bloody head now showed. The birthing had started.

Without a word, he turned away from the oppressive atmosphere. "Call me when the child is born," he said to the guard. "I want to see it, to make sure it's fit to live."

He went downstairs and back outside, to the fresh air. The servant brought more wine, but he took only a sip. If the child survived, he'd let Trella nurse it for a few days, just long enough for her to grow attached to it, before he took it from her. Her milk would dry up after that, say in another week or so, and she'd be ready to begin serving him properly. Not that he intended to wait that long to begin her training. He'd already thought of many things she could do to please him.

22

As Eskkar and his men slipped through the darkness and approached Akkad's north wall, he refused to dwell on the countless things that could go wrong. He had to get into Akkad. If he could accomplish that task, the most difficult part of the plan would be behind them.

To scale the wall, Eskkar brought with him Grond, Mitrac, Alexar, and two of Mitrac's best archers, the same bowmen who had followed him over the palisade at Bisitun. Mitrac with his keen eyesight led the group down into the ditch. They crept in silence across the empty space, bent over as much as possible to reduce their silhouette.

A hundred paces behind them, Drakis waited, out of sight and hopefully out of earshot, with twenty-eight more soldiers. They would approach the wall only when Eskkar and his own group reached the top. Bantor had taken the rest of the men, leading them off toward the river gate, ready to support the handful who'd gone ahead with Yavtar.

Eskkar put everything out of his mind except the need to move without making a sound and without stumbling over some obstacle hidden by the darkness. He couldn't see any sentries on the wall above him, but they would be there.

With his handful of men, Eskkar reached the base of the wall, at the exact spot where the Alur Meriki had launched their night attack months earlier. Eskkar led the way out of the ditch, and one by one, they spread out along the base of the wall, hugging its rough surface as much as possible.

Except for the three archers with their bows, neither Eskkar, Alexar, or Grond carried any ready weapons that might clink against the wall and give them away. All their swords and knives had been wrapped in a blanket Alexar carried. Eskkar bore a ladder, and Grond had two coils of rope slung around his neck. The ladder and ropes had come from Rebba's farm.

They had gotten this far without seeing anyone, following the riverbank from Rebba's house before cutting across the fields. Now Eskkar and his men knelt in the dirt, freezing into immobility when they heard the sentry's footsteps above their heads. Time dragged by as they waited, listening to the sentry's tread as he walked along the parapet above them. He strolled back and forth a few times, then the sounds faded away. Eskkar couldn't tell if the guard had moved along, or simply sat down to rest his feet, no doubt leaning his back against the wall.

Only Mitrac, waiting in the center of the ditch and covered with a dark cloak, could see the sentry. Eskkar and the others waited, still pressed flat against the wall. As long as they made no noise, they wouldn't be discovered. The guard would have to lean out over the wall to see directly beneath it.

Eskkar heard footsteps again as the sentry returned,

walking slowly, until once again his footfalls faded away. Still they waited, and Eskkar stared into the ditch, looking for Mitrac's signal. In the heavens, the three-quarter moon had begun to descend, but it would still shed some light until nearly dawn.

Grond's hand suddenly tightened on Eskkar's arm. "The signal, Captain."

Eskkar swore to himself. He hadn't seen Mitrac give the sign, but that didn't matter any more. "Hurry, then. The moon is sinking fast."

Grond took the ladder hidden beneath them and leaned it up against the wall, taking care not to make any sound. Eskkar grabbed one side of it, Alexar grasped the other, and between them they held it firmly against the fifteen-foot-high wall. Eskkar had measured the ladder before they left and found it just short of ten feet. Rebba's men used it mainly for picking fruit from trees. The soldiers had selected the sturdiest one on the farm, then tightened and reinforced its bindings and steps; a snapped rung might ruin the attempt to scale the wall.

Under Grond's weight, the ladder sank a little into the sandy soil, and Eskkar leaned on it with all his weight to keep it from twisting. Grond mounted the rungs until he reached the highest place on the ladder, then reached up with his arms.

With his head twisted upright, Eskkar saw that Grond's fingers were still short of the top by nearly an arm's length. Grond merely bent his knees, taking care not to disturb his balance, then straightened them with a rush. For a moment, Eskkar thought the man had missed and would come tumbling back down on top of them. But Grond caught one hand on the top, then the other. He hung for a moment before pulling himself up. Once he had an elbow atop the wall, he jerked his body and swung a leg up and over the top.

Grond disappeared from sight. No one had raised an alarm, and Eskkar breathed a sigh of relief. He let go of the ladder and stepped back, glancing along the wall in both directions. He heard no sound or outcry. Grond carried no weapon with him, nothing but his bare hands, but Eskkar had no doubt as to the outcome if a sentry encountered Grond.

The faint rasp of a bow being drawn made him turn around. Mitrac had moved forward and joined the others at the base of the wall, his bow ready. By now all three archers knelt in the dirt, arrows pointed toward the top of the wall.

Grond called down to them in a whisper, and Alexar straightened up and threw the first rope up and over the wall. As Eskkar watched, the rope and Grond vanished from sight. A moment later, the rest of the rope slithered up the mud-bricks. The thick hemp strand, knotted every arm's length, would making climbing easier. Grond's head reappeared, and he waved his hand.

Instantly, Mitrac replaced his arrow back into his quiver, climbed up out of the ditch, and stepped up to the ladder. He handed his bow and quiver to Eskkar, who took them in one hand as his weight leaned against the ladder. The young archer moved nimbly up the ladder, then took hold of the rope and pulled himself up the last few feet.

The rope made a rubbing noise against the wall, loud to Eskkar's ears but slight enough not to be noticed from above. The instant Mitrac went over the top, the next archer started moving, clutching bow and quiver in one hand. Reaching the top of the ladder, he paused and handed up his weapon, then reached down, took Mitrac's from Eskkar, and passed that one up as well. When the archer started up the rope, he slipped. For a moment he hung there, his feet scratching the wall for purchase, until Grond leaned down and caught the man's arm and pulled him up the last few feet. The third archer had already reached the ladder and began climbing, the tip of his bow nearly poking Eskkar in the eye as he handed it up before seizing the rope.

At last it was Eskkar's turn, with Alexar holding the ladder. Eskkar pulled himself up the rope, though he welcomed Grond's help when his friend reached down and caught him under the arm. Once over the wall, Eskkar found no one there but Grond.

The archers had disappeared along the parapet, following Mitrac's orders to eliminate any sentries, leaving Grond and Eskkar to work the rope. They called down softly, and Alexar tossed up one end of the second rope. Attached to the other end was the blanket containing their weapons; it, too, was quickly drawn up the wall. The men's swords and knives had been carefully rolled inside, as well as Alexar's bow and quiver.

Only Alexar remained on the ground. He lowered the ladder, too unsteady to use without being braced, against the base of the wall, then wrapped the first rope around his waist. A moment later, Eskkar and Grond pulled him up and over the wall, to stand beside them on the parapet.

The first part of the plan had succeeded—six men had scaled the wall, and no one had detected them.

Eskkar's eyes searched the parapet as Grond untied the bundle and distributed the weapons, the three men crouched low against the wall. Alexar took his bow and vanished down the steps and into the darkness to watch the lane, leaving Grond and Eskkar alone on the parapet. Eskkar breathed a thanks to the gods, then dangled his sword carefully alongside the wall and waved it back and forth. There would be just enough moonlight for Drakis to see the signal.

Meanwhile Grond fastened the second rope to a wooden brace a dozen paces away from the first one, then tossed the trailing end over the wall. Eskkar looked up and down the parapet, but saw nothing. Turning toward the ditch, he watched as Drakis urged his men forward and began sending them across the ditch, ten at a time. They lined up five to each rope and began pulling themselves up the wall. Eskkar ground his teeth at every noise, certain they would be discovered at any moment.

The head of the first soldier appeared over the wall and Eskkar dragged him up and over with all his strength, both of them almost falling to the parapet from the effort. But with the two of them working together, the next man came over easier and with less noise.

Eskkar took a moment to make sure he had his bearings and that no one wandered the lanes. Reassuringly, the lane remained empty. He whispered to the soldier, to make sure the man knew where to send the men when they climbed the wall. Before Eskkar left the parapet, he glanced out over the ditch, but he could scarcely see Drakis's men as they slipped across the open space facing the wall. Turning toward the village, he heard only silence. The sentry would be dead by now, killed by one of Mitrac's arrows, or he would have returned, making his rounds.

Stepping away from the edge of the wall, Eskkar descended the steps from the parapet and entered the city of Akkad. He crossed the space at the bottom of the wall. During the siege, this open area once measured about thirty paces wide, but since the Alur Meriki had been driven off, villagers had rebuilt or extended their houses, once again encroaching on the wall. Less than a dozen paces of open space remained at the base of the parapet. Butcher's Lane ended there. Its familiar smells recalled the memory of how they had ambushed the Alur Meriki exactly at this spot, slaughtering their proud warriors like sheep caught in a pen.

Eskkar went to the end of the lane and waited for his men to catch up. His eyes strained in the darkness, and he listened for every sound. Then Grond reached his side, with three more men. Looking back toward the wall, Eskkar could just make out the moving shadows as they climbed over the wall. To his ears, they sounded as loud as a herd of horses, but so far, no one had raised an alarm.

Mitrac returned, along with his two archers, at the same time that Drakis, breathing hard, came down the steps to join him.

Eskkar put his hand on Drakis's shoulder. "You know what to do, Drakis? Wait here until all your men are with you. Then get to the gate as quickly as possible."

"Yes, Captain," the man replied in a whisper. "We'll be there."

"Good hunting, then." Eskkar clasped his arm, then turned away, Grond, Mitrac, and five more Hawk Clan following, all of them experienced archers. Eskkar resisted the urge to rush, forcing himself to walk along at a regular pace. Counting himself, he had eight men, not as many as he preferred, but Bantor and Drakis would need every man. Besides, if Eskkar had to fight his way into his house, Trella would likely be dead before he could reach her.

They had several streets to cross as they turned and twisted their passage toward their destination. He glanced up at the fading moon. It would be dawn soon. The light of the moon had almost disappeared.

At last Eskkar reached the lane where he lived. Spacious structures lined both sides of the street, almost all of them hidden behind man-high, irregular walls that formed the passage. His house, by far the largest, loomed above the others, near the center of the lane. A faint glow emanated from the upper story, and he wondered who guarded his workroom.

Mitrac touched his shoulder, and Eskkar let the master archer slip past. Mitrac's eyes would be almost as keen at night, and he had the hunter's ability to move noiselessly. Only moments went by before he stepped back to Eskkar's side.

"There are two of them, Captain. One's leaning against the wall. I think the gate is open, but I can't be sure."

The gate should have been closed, but, of course, these bandits had already grown careless. "Quickly, then, Mitrac. Get your men in position."

He watched as the archer eased across the lane, to the side opposite Eskkar's house, and then walked slowly down that side of the street. Eskkar could scarcely see Mitrac's path in the darkness. The archer disappeared from sight, vanished into a doorway. Two archers followed his lead, one by one. As soon as the last man reached his position, Eskkar turned to the others.

"Grond and I will start in. You three wait until we're at the gate. Make sure no one comes up behind us."

Eskkar turned the corner, and started moving toward the house, Grond at his side.

They walked slowly, talking loudly to each other, weaving every few steps as if from too much ale. Eskkar wanted to draw all attention to themselves, to keep the guards' eyes focused on them, not the shadowy figures on the other side of the lane.

The guards heard them and straightened up, but did not draw their swords. They had no worries. In the last few days, Akkad's inhabitants had learned their place. Besides, behind these sentinels, in the two houses that made up Eskkar's residence, more than twenty of Korthac's desert fighters took their rest. Rebba said he'd seen at least that many there.

As Eskkar approached, he saw that the gate indeed stood ajar. A closed and fastened gate would have been another problem. He guessed that more men would be in the courtyard, probably taking their ease at the table, helped by an occasional drink from a wineskin. The rest of Korthac's men would be asleep inside, but the nighttime watch would end soon, and these guards would be looking forward to getting some sleep of their own.

Eskkar stopped about ten feet away from the guards. Just then a muffled shout reached his ears. From its direction, he guessed that Bantor's men had reached the river gate. Hopefully the guards would not know what it meant. Before the men could react, Eskkar turned to Grond, raising his voice.

"Did you hear that? Sounds like women screaming. Maybe we should go and see if there's room for two more."

"No! We have to get back before Ariamus finds us. We're in enough trouble already."

The distant shouting faded away, and the two guards seemed confused. One took a step toward them, but the other turned in the direction of the noise.

"I think I'm going to be sick," Eskkar said loudly, and dropped down to one knee, by now only a few paces from the sentries.

"Let me help you," Grond said, slurring the words and stooping down beside him.

The instant he was down, three arrows flashed out of the darkness and struck Korthac's men. One of them made a strangled gasp, but Eskkar laughed to cover the sound. He and Grond reached the men, catching them before they could fall. Neither guard had a weapon in his hand, making it easy to lower them silently to the ground.

A bench scraped in the courtyard, and Eskkar began speaking again, raising his voice to cover the small sounds as Mitrac and his two archers slipped up beside them. "Maybe we should wake Korthac and tell him. That's good, let's ask him to settle it." The words meant nothing, but Korthac's name should give the guards inside pause.

One arm around Grond's shoulders, Eskkar pushed the gate inward, keeping his other arm extended to make sure the gate stayed wide open as he weaved drunkenly into the courtyard.

"Who are you?" came a voice from the darkness.

"We come from Ariamus," Eskkar said, slurring his words as if from too much wine.

"Get out of here, you drunken Akkadian scum. Come back after dawn."

The words, spoken with a strong accent, came from the big plank table placed between the two dwellings. So at least that hadn't been moved. "Ariamus sent us," Eskkar said humbly, bowing his head. "We have a message for Korthac." Looking up, he saw faint flickers of light coming from the upper story, from both rooms.

"But we can't remember what it was," laughed Grond, and slapped Eskkar on the back.

Moving forward as he spoke, Eskkar saw the guards, two darker shadows sitting at the table, one with his feet up on its surface, the other leaning back with his hands behind his head. Their eyes shone whitely in the faint light. Glancing around the garden, he saw no one else.

Eskkar stepped away from the gate, moving sideways toward the main house. "Is Korthac awake yet? We have a message . . ."

The sound of many voices shouting at the tops of their lungs interrupted him. This time Eskkar realized the noise came from the west, not the river gate. That meant Bantor had entered the city and reached the barracks. The two men at the table started to move, one dropping his water cup, but they were already falling, three arrows flashing into their bodies as Mitrac and his archers stepped in from the gate.

Nevertheless, one of the Egyptians cried out as the arrow struck him, loud enough to give a warning. Eskkar ignored the dead or dying guards, certain Mitrac's men's arrows would finish them or anyone else issuing from the soldiers' quarters. Instead Eskkar burst into a run, and in three giant strides reached the main entrance and flung himself with all his weight against the door.

But the portal, built to withstand just such an attack, held firm, and he bounced back, his left shoulder tingling from the impact. He'd hoped the door might not be barred or securely fastened. To his left, he heard another crash as Grond hurled himself at the kitchen entrance. But that doorway, too, was closed, and instead of a quick entry, all they'd managed to accomplish was to awaken those sleeping within.

23

"Hail, Akkad!" Yavtar's voice carried easily over the black water, alerting the guards at the river gate well before they saw or heard the boat's approach. The current pulled at the craft, and he had to lean hard on the steering oar while his two crewmen paddled furiously to bring the vessel alongside the jetty, out of the river's rush. Ignoring the questions from the men guarding the gate, Yavtar leapt onto the dock and secured the stern.

When he straightened up and looked toward the gate, a half-dozen heads appeared atop the wall on either side, and one of them held a torch over the wall, casting just enough light to reach the boat rocking against the wharf.

"Who goes there?"

Ignoring the challenge, Yavtar waited until his crewmen had hooked on the bowline, leaving the craft securely moored to the dock. That done, he turned to face the gate, where twice as many men now stood watching. Even before Yavtar finished his count, the men had bows in their hands, arrows at the ready, and a second torch appeared and added its light to the scene.

"Who goes there? Answer, or I'll cut you down!"

"I'm Yavtar, shipmaster, and I've a message for Korthac. Pass me in, or send someone to fetch him." He strolled down the jetty as he replied.

A third torch joined the others, this last one held forward from the wall, illuminating the base of the gate. More men appeared atop the walls on either side of the opening, these newest arrivals shaking the sleep from their eyes. Yavtar's count now estimated about fifteen defenders.

"You know the gate is closed until dawn. Get back in your boat and stay there until then. If you step off the dock, I'll have my men put an arrow into you."

Yavtar had reached the end of the jetty, so he stopped and put his hands on his hips. "It's nearly dawn. What does it matter when you open the gate?" Behind him, the boat rocked loudly against one of the wooden support piles sunk into the riverbed. Yavtar had deliberately used more rope than needed to fasten the stern, leaving plenty of slack; the noise of the boat slapping against the jetty might help conceal any other sounds.

"No one's admitted until dawn, and then only if . . ."

"Fine. I'll stay here until Korthac arrives. Send someone to bring him here. I have a message for him from Ziusudra."

"It will wait until morning. Stay on your boat until then."

"It will *not* wait until morning." Yavtar spoke loud enough to waken half the city. "Send word to Korthac *now*, or I'll make sure you'll find the lash on your back." Since taking power, Korthac had applied his favorite punishment to many, including a few of his own men. Back at the farm, Rebba had described Korthac's wrath at any that annoyed him, and his favorite punishment.

The watchkeeper thought about it for a moment. "Where's Ziusudra?"

Yavtar smiled at that bit of luck. So this man knew Ziusudra, but not likely his mission. "Ziusudra's dead. You'd better hurry, man, or Korthac will be very angry, I promise you. He'll want to hear my words, and see what I have for him."

"Tell me the message . . . What's your name?"

"Yavtar. Shipmaster Yavtar, as you should know. I've delivered cargo here often enough. And my message is for your master, not you." Without waiting for a reply, Yavtar turned back toward the boat, and spoke to his crewmen. After a moment, he walked back toward the dock.

"Stay on the jetty," a voice shouted, but it was not the watchkeeper's voice.

Again Yavtar stopped at the dock's edge, and let out a loud sigh that carried all the way to the gate. "I'm sorry me and my two men frighten you so much. But we've been on the river for days, coming from Bisitun. Anyway, I've got three prisoners for Korthac, and you might as well take charge of them." He turned back toward the boat. "Bring the slaves to the gate."

During this exchange, the watchkeeper had returned. He'd checked his men, making sure all of them were at their posts, weapons ready. "I've sent word to Korthac," he called out.

"Fine. I'll stay here. You can watch these slaves for me just as well from up there." Yavtar turned back to his men, and they pushed forward three men, each with their hands bound in front of them. Their ragged clothes hung loosely about them. Covered with dirt, their heads hung slackly on their necks.

"Get forward, and stand at the foot of the gate," Yavtar ordered, hoping no one would shoot them. For a moment the prisoners did nothing, so Yavtar grabbed the nearest by the shoulder and shoved him roughly on his way. The other two followed. When they reached the base of the gate, they sank wearily to the ground, heads still downcast.

On the wall, the watch commander saw Yavtar taking his ease. The gatekeeper worried about what to do. A glance down at the three slaves showed them to be harmless, unarmed and beaten men. When the messenger from Korthac arrived, Yavtar would likely be summoned to Korthac's house, and that would be the end of it. Perhaps it might be better to bring them inside the gate, then escort this Yavtar directly to Korthac himself. That way he might earn a silver coin himself, or at least Korthac's gratitude.

The watchkeeper took a torch from one of his men and leaned out over the top of the gate, then looked up and down the length of the wall. He saw nothing unusual, and the jetty showed only Yavtar and his two boatmen. Dawn approached, and he'd be opening the gate soon enough anyway. He might as well open it early for this Yavtar. He turned away from the river.

"Open the gate. Bring Yavtar in."

Alexar had never run so hard in his life. But now he waited in the darkness, his men beside him. The first five men who climbed over the wall, after Eskkar and his archers, had joined Alexar in his race to the river gate. They knew they had to hurry. Even if Yavtar talked the gate open, he'd need their help. They'd rushed through the lanes, making as little noise as possible, until, breathing hard, they reached their destination.

The huts here encroached closer to the portal than at Akkad's main entrance. Hidden in the deeper shadow cast by a house wall, Alexar and his men stood close enough to the rear of the gate to hear every exchange. They'd reached their position only moments after Yavtar docked his boat, and now Alexar, still breathing hard, stood listening, staring up at the guards manning the gate, waiting for the commander of the watch to react.

The gatekeeper took his time, talking to his men and ordering extra torches lit.

Rebba had told Eskkar that the river gate wasn't as well guarded as Akkad's main entrance. Using his fingers, Alexar counted sixteen men as they took their stations on either side of the gate. Sixteen against six. Even with surprise, it was going to be bloody if Yavtar couldn't convince the watchmaster to open the gate. Alexar knew it took at least two men to lift the heavy beams that secured the gate closed, and if they had to fight off anyone . . .

"If they don't open the gate," Alexar said, "we'll have to kill them all. Keep shooting no matter what, then make sure that gate gets opened."

Gripping his bow, he listened as Yavtar and the chief guard exchanged words. Then the watchkeeper grabbed one of his men by the arm and spoke to him before returning to the top of the gate. The man nodded, then began jogging toward the lane.

"Stand ready," Alexar ordered, and moved to his right, staying in the shadow of the houses, and converging on the same lane the messenger would take. Eskkar had warned

Alexar about the possibility of the watch commander
dispatching a messenger. Hugging the wall, Alexar watched
as the messenger turned the corner; once out of sight of the
gate and its commander, the man slowed to a walk and
started up the lane, heading toward Eskkar's house.

When Alexar turned the same corner, only a few paces
separated him from the shadowy messenger. Alexar drew
his bow, and sent an arrow into the man's back. His target,
knocked to his knees by the force of the shaft, gasped in
surprise as he pitched forward. By then Alexar had reached
the dying man's side, drawn his sword, and pushed it into
the man's neck, ending any possibility of a call for help.
Snapping off the arrow, he rolled the body against the
nearest wall.

He paused to look about. Everything seemed quiet, and
perhaps no one had heard or seen anything. Alexar returned
to his men, just in time to hear the watchkeeper give the
order to open the gate. Alexar breathed a sigh of relief.
Yavtar must have succeeded in convincing the watchmaster.
Half a dozen guards put down their bows and descended the
steps to the base of the gate. In moments, they struggled with
the heavy wooden beams that secured the portal. With a
loud creak, the right side of the gate began to swing inward.
Then Yavtar stood in the opening, scratching his head.

"That's the signal," Alexar whispered. "Bantor's men are
ready. Take the guards on the wall first, anyone with a bow
in his hands." Alexar nocked a shaft to his bow. By now the
other half of the gate began to swing open as well. The
firelight showed Yavtar stepping forward. He paused,
remaining one stride from the opening, still talking to the
gatekeeper, who stood there with four of his men.

"Fire!" Six arrows flashed out of the darkness, striking at the men looking out over the wall or down at the ever-widening opening. Before anyone could react, the second wave of shafts flew toward the gate, taking almost half their enemies by surprise. The gatekeeper died, crying out in surprise as two arrows knocked him from his feet. A guard atop the wall shouted a warning, but more arrows flew, and he pitched forward, falling with a loud crash onto a small cart beneath the wall.

By then Yavtar and the three "slaves," knives in hand, had forced their way through the opening, striking down two more men, and making sure the heavy gate stayed open. Still hidden in the shadows, Alexar and his men picked their targets, selecting anyone attempting to close the gate, or trying to give the alarm. A few shouted for help, but the heavy shafts whistling through the air soon silenced the voices.

An arrow skipped off the wall behind Alexar, the guards' first attempt to strike back. But the gate's defenders couldn't see their targets well, while the dropped torches and watch fire gave Alexar and his men plenty of light for shooting.

Then it was too late. The heavy portal, once opened, couldn't be easily closed. Yavtar's two crewmen rushed to his side, carrying extra swords, but they weren't needed. Both sides of the gate burst apart, pushed aside by a wall of men. Bantor and his thirty men, hidden less than a hundred paces away from the gate, had sprinted forward the moment Yavtar gave the signal. The few surviving guards turned and ran, scattering in all directions. Alexar and his men, shooting as fast as they could, dropped a few more, but darkness soon hid their targets, and at least two or three escaped into the night.

Alexar stepped forward, holding his bow above his head. "Eskkar has returned," he called out, just loud enough to be heard. Bantor recognized him, and the two forces joined together.

"Yavtar," Bantor said without stopping, "you and Alexar must hold the gate." Bantor had no more time for words. At a run, he and his men departed for the barracks less than four lanes away, their feet pounding against the dirt the only sound to mark their departure.

Yavtar strode over to Alexar, his two boatmen following. Together they watched the last of Bantor's men disappear up the street. "I don't want to stay here, Alexar. There won't be any more fighting in this place."

Alexar didn't want to miss the fighting either. "We're supposed to make sure no one gets away. That's what Eskkar said."

"No one will try to escape this way. They'll go over the wall," Yavtar countered. "Besides, Eskkar is going to need every man."

The more Alexar thought about it, the more he decided Yavtar was right. "We could bar the gate, and hammer it shut. That should keep it sealed."

Yavtar frowned. "Where would we get the tools?"

Alexar turned to the crowd of onlookers gathering about them. Sleepy citizens from adjacent houses had heard or seen the fight, and now peered out from doorways, the braver ones stepping forth cautiously from their houses. Their voices contributed to the babble of sound that increased every moment.

"We won't need tools," Alexar said. He raised his voice just enough to carry to those nearby. The time for silence had passed. "Akkadians! Eskkar has returned to bring vengeance to Korthac. Keep silent, and bar the gate! Hammer it shut. Find weapons and keep the gate closed. Make sure no one leaves the city! Get moving. Eskkar has returned."

Eskkar's name emptied the nearby houses, and a few cheers from the rooftops floated into the night, praising Eskkar's return.

"Keep silent, you fools!" Alexar's voice stopped the cheering.

"Should we go to the barracks?" Yavtar glanced up at the night sky. "It'll be dawn soon."

"No, Bantor has enough men for that. Let's head for the main gate. Maybe we can help Drakis."

"Lead the way," Yavtar said, fingering his sword. One fight was as good as another.

Drakis led his men at a fast walk. Enkidu brought up the rear, spacing the men five paces apart to keep their passage as quiet as possible. With luck, no one would hear them pass along the dark lanes. If he were going to surprise the defenders at the main gate, Drakis needed to get there without arousing attention.

Fortune had favored them so far. First they'd slipped over the wall with scarcely a delay and without alerting Korthac's men, a feat thousands of Alur Meriki warriors had failed to accomplish in more than a month's fighting. Earlier, Drakis worried that he might be fighting his way up this very street. Instead, he strode purposefully, his bow held close against his side. If the gods smiled a little longer, he'd have the chance to strike first.

Luck in battle. Drakis, like everyone else, knew Eskkar had more than his fair share of it. The warrior gods always seemed to smile on him, and, of course, he had Lady Trella at his side to whisper in his ear. Drakis would have preferred going with Eskkar to rescue her, but his own mission might prove just as important and probably more dangerous.

Eskkar had given him twenty men. Never before had Drakis commanded so many, and this time he would be on his own. He vowed to succeed, even if he and every one of his men died doing so. Shaking away the dark thought, he quickened his pace, recalling his meeting with Eskkar right after they left Rebba's house.

With Bantor at his side, Eskkar had asked Drakis to choose one of his twenty men to be second in command. Drakis had immediately named Enkidu. Eskkar nodded approvingly, then called out for Enkidu to join them.

"Drakis, you and Enkidu must plan everything as best you can, in the little time you have. I want you both to think of what can go wrong, and how you'll respond. Each of you must choose another to replace you should you be killed. At every step, make sure your men know what they are to do, and how they are to do it. Think now about what you will do when you reach the towers, how you will attack them, and how you will defend them, where you will position your men. And when you attack, remember to scream your heads off as the barbarians do. You must make your twenty men sound like a hundred. Nothing frightens men more at night than shouts of death and destruction."

Eskkar had spoken for only a few moments, but Drakis and Enkidu still struggled to resolve all the questions and decisions their leader raised. Drakis recalled his captain's final words. "Hold the gate, Drakis. It'll take the backbone out of our enemies if they think we're trying to keep them trapped in Akkad. Keep shouting those words, that none must escape alive. That will send half of them scurrying across the wall, fleeing for their lives."

Drakis nodded his understanding, and put his hand on his leader's shoulder. "I'll hold the gate, Captain."

"It won't be easy. But if you can hold, Drakis, no one on horseback will be able to get away, and those who go over the walls will be easy prey to mounted men in the morning. But your danger will be great. If Bantor and I succeed, every bandit in Akkad will be rushing toward you, trying to escape, and desperate to fight their way past you and your men, to reach the safety of the countryside. Stop them, Drakis. Kill them all."

Thinking back, Drakis realized that Eskkar had paid him quite a compliment, giving him a command and assuming that Drakis could work out the rest of the details himself. He'd watched as Eskkar next went to talk with Bantor, Klexor, and Yavtar. Their assignment was to force and capture the river gate. Afterward, they would attack the barracks, to endeavor to liberate the soldiers held captive there. If Bantor succeeded, he'd drive the rest of Korthac's men toward the main gate, straight at Drakis, who'd have to keep them at bay until help arrived. If he lived that long.

Drakis lengthened his stride. He and his men had the greatest distance to cover, nearly the width of Akkad, and he wanted to get there before the alarm was given. But he'd lived in the city for years, and knew its winding lanes and streets, even in the dark.

With one lane to go, Drakis muttered a curse when he heard a rush of noise from the direction of the river gate. It lasted only moments, stopping almost as soon as it began, and silence again settled over the darkened city. More important, no trumpet, no general alarm sounded. Perhaps the inhabitants had grown used to screams and the sound of fighting, even after dark. The streets were deserted at this time of night, but anyone might be awake and see them from a doorway or rooftop. Rebba had assured Eskkar that the townspeople wouldn't give them away, but it would take only one enemy or some stupid fool to raise a cry.

Clenching his teeth, Drakis prayed to the gods, asking for a bit more time, and held his bow tighter to his side. Lengthening his stride, he felt his heart thumping. At last he saw the lane widen in front of him, turning slightly into the broad space, empty now, behind the gates. He'd reached his objective.

The two tall wooden portals faced him, closed and barred, flanked by square towers that rose above the highest part of the gate by another fifteen feet. Each tower had an opening at the base that provided access to the interior, but had no connection to the wall that extended away on either side. The towers themselves were mostly empty space, with a few cots for guards to sleep on, and weapons-storage areas under the steps that hugged the walls as they rose to the battlement, the open space at the top of the tower.

Drakis stopped and held up his hand. In moments, his men took their positions on either side, lining up facing the gate, readying their bows and waiting for the order to attack. They didn't have much time left. The moon had faded to a dim, barely noticeable glow in the sky, but the tower guards had built a small fire at the base of the left tower, about seventy paces away. More than enough light for night archery at that distance, he knew. His men's arrows would strike from the darkness.

Three of Korthac's men stood around the flickering fire. Drakis didn't know how many more guards would be inside the towers, but Rebba had guessed that twenty or thirty men attended Akkad's main entrance day and night, more to stop anyone from leaving than to protect the city's inhabitants from outside marauders.

The alarm might sound at any moment, and the sooner Drakis captured the two towers, the better. From their vantage, his archers would make sure the gate stayed closed. So far they hadn't been discovered, and he wanted to keep that advantage as long as possible, at least until he had drawn first blood and . . .

A roar went up into the night behind him, a din that reached even where they stood, the sound followed by the piercing note of a trumpet that lingered faintly in the night air. Drakis ground his teeth in anger. They had been so close to surprise, and now they would have to fight their way in.

"We'll take the left tower first. Spread out, and stay even with me. Let's go."

No one had noticed them yet. Another guard stepped out of the right tower, looking about and calling out to those tending the fire. Fortunately, one fool started tossing more fuel on the fire, and the flames shot up, providing even more light for Drakis's archers.

He nocked an arrow to his bowstring as he stepped

forward into the cleared ground. Alongside him, his men did the same, spreading out to either side as they advanced. In moments, his men stretched across the open space, all striding swiftly toward the gate. Drakis took a dozen steps before he gave the order to halt and fire.

The line stopped, ready arrows were drawn to each man's eye, and the flight of shafts flew on its way. Even as he issued the order, a shout from one of the towers rang out to warn the defenders of the approaching archers, and several peered toward the street just as the arrows struck the still-confused men. Too late for them. Those tending the fire died, riddled with arrows. More guards stumbled out of both towers, looking stupidly around them, trying to understand what had happened.

Before Drakis's shaft reached its target, he started jogging forward, his men taking their lead from him. "Halt!" He nocked the shaft he'd drawn. "Fire!"

Another wave of arrows swept toward the gates' defenders. More men went down, pierced by the heavy shafts powerful enough to knock a man off his feet at this distance. The screams of wounded men added to the confused shouting. By now Drakis had crossed more than half the distance to the gate. Again he halted, just out of the fire's light. "Halt!" The dragging rasp of arrow against bow sounded loud to his ears as he drew back the shaft. "Fire!"

This time he aimed high, at the man shouting atop the tower. The shaft whistled up into the night, but he didn't bother to see if he'd struck his target.

All those guards caught outside the towers died in the third flight of shafts, launched from less than forty paces.

The instant his shaft had flown, Drakis burst into a run, heading directly toward the left tower, gripping his bow in his left hand and drawing his short sword with the other. "Eskkar! Eskkar has returned!" Drakis shouted, letting the name no one had dared speak aloud echo around the walls. "Let none of the traitors escape!"

Angry and confused outcries came from the men atop the towers, and a shaft from above hissed past him. Now Drakis and his men showed clearly in the firelight, splitting into two groups as they charged toward the towers. They needed to get inside, before they became targets themselves.

Panic and confusion took control of the defenders at the sound of Drakis's war cry. For nearly a week they'd lorded it over the city, laughing and taunting those who dared to speak Eskkar's name. Now, accompanied by hissing arrows, that name struck fear into their hearts. Many forgot their orders, others abandoned their duties. A few broke and ran, disappearing into the darkness along the walls, escape the only thought in their heads.

Drakis kept shouting at the top of his lungs. "Eskkar has returned! Death to all traitors!" His men took up the cry, screaming the words into the darkness as they raced to the leftmost tower, Drakis raising his sword as he ran. He hurtled over the dead bodies just as four men burst out of the tower's entrance, swords in their hands.

But two of them saw what looked like a hundred demon shadows rushing at them, and darted back inside the tower. The others raised their swords, and one swung his blade at Drakis's head. Drakis screamed his war cry even as he parried the thrust. Then he let his momentum carry him into the man's chest, and he used his shoulder to knock the man to the ground, then thrust hard with his sword.

Wrenching his sword free, Drakis flung himself inside the tower's dark opening. A shadow moved before him, and he struck at it, screaming "Eskkar! Eskkar!" The words rang up into the darkness. Here, deep within the tower's base, almost no light penetrated. Normally a torch burned inside the doorway, to light the steps that led to the top. The careless guards had let it go out, too lazy to replace it with dawn approaching.

Drakis pushed forward; he needed to destroy the defenders as quickly as possible, before they could regroup, before they realized that they still outnumbered their attackers.

The guards inside the tower reacted slowly. They'd been caught relaxing, most of them asleep. Jolted awake, unsure of what was happening, the gatekeepers fumbled for their swords, trying to fend off what seemed like a horde of ferocious attackers. Some fled up the stone steps, bumping into those trying to come down.

Drakis reached the base of the steps, and saw a man coming at him, stumbling in the dark. Drakis had the advantage—anyone in front of him must be an enemy. He lunged upward, arm extended, and felt the sword bite deep into muscle.

His victim screamed as the blade pierced his thigh, and Drakis felt hot blood splatter his arm and chest. The stabbed man tried to step back, but the wounded leg failed him, and he pitched off the steps, crying out as he fell.

The other defenders stopped their descent, bunching up at the first landing. Drakis never hesitated, pushed on by his men sounding their war cries behind him. He hurled himself up the steps, toward the guards, still screaming Eskkar's name, the confines of the tower amplifying his voice into something inhuman, something full of menace.

Another guard turned away, to scramble back up the steps, but lost his footing and fell to the stairs. Drakis swung his sword down viciously at the man's back, ignored the scream as the blade cut deep into the man's shoulder, knocking his opponent to the steps. The rest of the guards fled back the way they came, anything to get away from the demons charging at them. Drakis stepped on the wounded man's back, and raced up the stairs two at a time.

Behind him, his men filled the tower with a wall of sound. An arrow launched by one of Drakis's men hissed by, followed by a scream as another guard pitched off the steps, falling heavily to the ground below. Drakis ignored it all, shouting his war cry and sprinting up the last stairway until he reached the opening at the top of the stairs. Another guard met Drakis at the top of the stairs, a sword in his hand, but Drakis struck at him so quickly that the man didn't even have time to attempt to parry the stroke. Knocking the wounded man aside, Drakis, breathing hard, pushed his way out of the darkness and onto the tower's battlement. He saw shadows moving about and naked blades glinting in the starlight, as the tower's defenders rallied their forces. "Eskkar has returned!" he shouted, and charged straight at his opponents.

24

Ariamus woke before dawn, a lifetime habit that had served him well, whether for fighting or fleeing. He'd gone to sleep late last night, once again in Korthac's new residence. Ariamus would have preferred sleeping in his own house, the one he'd appropriated for himself. Nicar, the former ruler of Akkad, had lived there for more than ten years. Ariamus had enjoyed ordering him out. Now the wealthiest noble in the city and his entire family lived in a wretched one-room mud hut, and counted themselves lucky to have even that.

Unfortunately, Korthac wanted Ariamus close by, and Ariamus had swallowed his objections and accepted his leader's "invitation" to take a room in the big house. In many ways it had turned out to be a good idea. Ariamus had a half-dozen subcommanders who pestered him constantly with questions and petty problems. Having to pass by Korthac's Egyptians, grim men who spoke little and fingered their sword hilts often, helped Ariamus avoid his men in the evenings.

He thanked all the gods he'd ever heard of that Korthac didn't have a few dozen more Egyptians. Instead,

Korthac needed Ariamus and the men he'd recruited. Not that Korthac trusted Ariamus or his men. Ariamus didn't have much faith in them either. He had few enough experienced fighters, men who could do more than follow orders and swing a sword. In a few more days it wouldn't matter. He'd be riding out into the countryside, recruiting more displaced and desperate men willing to do whatever he told them for a chance to eat and earn some silver. With enough followers, even inexperienced ones, they could hold the city indefinitely.

Dawn still hadn't risen when Ariamus finished dressing and stepped out of his room, the one closest to the kitchen. To his surprise, he heard Korthac's voice coming from the upper rooms. Climbing the stairs, he found the Egyptian seated at the big table, a lamp casting a soft glow around the big room. The ever-present guard stood a few steps behind his master, watching the inner room but keeping one eye on Ariamus as well.

"Did the slave deliver her child?"

"Yes, about an hour ago." Korthac frowned at him. "You haven't heard her screams? She woke the whole house when she finally delivered."

"A woman screaming in the night?" Ariamus laughed, a booming noise that filled the room. "Never keeps me awake."

Korthac cut the laughter short with a look. "Are you ready to ride out today?"

"Yes, lord." Ariamus managed to look properly subservient. "I'll ride to the east. I should be able to get another ten or twenty farm boys to join up with us, one way or another." Ariamus planned to take a dozen men and begin visiting the big farmhouses surrounding Akkad. The local farmholders had plenty of silver, women, and other valuables, and Korthac wanted to make sure they felt no safer on their farms than did the city's inhabitants. Ariamus intended to pick up some more booty along with the recruits, after enjoying their women.

"Make sure you're back by sunset," Korthac said. "And I want you to ride north, toward Dilgarth, not east. I haven't heard from Ziusudra, but I expect this Eskkar is dead by now. Just in case he isn't, I want more patrols along the road, if he tries to move against us."

Ariamus shrugged. "Even if he's alive, what can he do? With less than seventy men? I wouldn't be surprised if he stays where he is, or runs to the west."

Korthac sighed, a long breath that made Ariamus regret his lighthearted words. "No, the barbarian will come here. I've learned much about him in the last few weeks. He won't give up such power without a fight. And there is something about his whore"—Korthac inclined his head toward the bedroom—"that will bring him back."

"Ziusudra's a good man, more than good enough to take care of Eskkar," Ariamus said, shifting his feet and wishing he'd been invited to sit down. "You've promised him plenty of gold for the job. Even if he fails, it will take Eskkar a few days to figure out what's happened, so we'll have plenty of time to prepare."

Annok-sur appeared at the bedroom door and bowed low, keeping her eyes on the floor. "Master, may I fetch fresh water for Trella?"

Ariamus looked at her and grinned. "Maybe you can carry something for . . ."

A crashing sound echoed throughout the house, coming from below. For a moment, Ariamus and Korthac looked at each other. Then a shout in Egyptian came from the courtyard, and even Ariamus had no trouble understanding the message. He moved to the landing and looked down into the darkened room below. The main door remained closed. Then heavy steps echoed from the kitchen area, and again he heard men shouting Eskkar's name. Louder footsteps sounded below, and Ariamus ground his teeth with an oath.

Stepping back from the landing, he yanked the door shut, then dropped the heavy wooden bar across the braces.

"What is it?" Korthac rose to his feet, though he remained behind the table. The guard moved beside him, hand on his sword.

"We're under attack! Eskkar has returned." Ariamus heard heavy footsteps on the stairs, then the door shuddered. A voice he recognized called out "Trella" again and again.

Ariamus backed away from the door. "It's Eskkar! He's here!" Something heavy pounded on the door, making it shake against the braces. Ariamus pulled his sword from its sheath. Damn the barbarian. How had he managed to get into the city, inside the compound? Not that it mattered. He turned to face the Egyptian. "Where are your men, Korthac?" Almost in answer, the sound of men fighting rose up from the courtyard.

"Stop her!"

Korthac's voice made Ariamus turn. He saw Annok-sur, who'd shrunk against the wall when the noise started, dart past him toward the door. Ariamus lunged to catch her, but she slipped beneath his arm, reached the doorway, and flipped the bar up from its catches, shouting Eskkar's name. Ariamus caught her by the hair and dragged her back, but the door burst open, crashing against the wall and outlining a looming shadow holding a long sword.

Cries of alarm sounded across the courtyard. Eskkar knew Korthac's men would be spilling from the doors behind him, swords in their hands. "Keep them pinned inside," Eskkar shouted, hoping Mitrac's archers could contain that threat. Then over all the clamor, Eskkar heard Grond's voice, bellowing out to him.

"Captain, come here."

Hearing the urgency, Eskkar abandoned his assault on the main entrance and rushed to his bodyguard's side. The kitchen door stood open. A half-asleep servant had opened it, either to let the attackers in or just to find out about the commotion. Whatever the motive, Grond had already pushed his way inside, and Eskkar followed behind him. The two men rushed through the kitchen, knocking a stool aside, toward the dark corridor that led to the main room. They'd barely cleared the cooking area when two shadows stumbled into the hallway from one of the sleeping chambers.

One of them cried out as Grond struck the first man down and grappled with the other. Eskkar ignored them, pushing both men aside. He knew the house even in darkness, and he ran past the other two doorways, turned the corner, and took the steps that hugged the wall two at a time. At the landing he pushed against the door to the workroom, but found it, too, fastened. Nevertheless, he flung his weight against it, but this barrier, as strong as the one below, scarcely budged. Calling out Trella's name at the top of his lungs, he pounded on it with the hilt of his sword.

To his surprise, he heard a woman's voice call his name. The sound of the bar rasping against the door caught his ear, and he shoved the thick planks, pushing the door open. Light from the upper room illuminated the landing, and he saw Annok-sur there, struggling with someone who reached out to slam the door closed. Eskkar shoved his shoulder against the thick wood and forced his way in.

The man stepped back, knocking Annok-sur down with his fist even as he raised a sword in the other. Only a single oil lamp burned in the outer chamber, but the wavering flame gave more than enough light for Eskkar to recognize his opponent.

"Ariamus!" All of Eskkar's anger and hatred went into the name. He'd despised the man every day that he served under him, and now Ariamus stood here, in Eskkar's private room. His sword lunged out, a straight, quick thrust that should have pierced his enemy's heart.

But Ariamus sprang back, then countered with a powerful thrust of his own. Another man, black bearded and dark skinned, no doubt one of Korthac's guards, appeared at Ariamus's side and thrust his sword as well. Eskkar knocked it aside, but yielded a step, the long sword cumbersome in this kind of fight, with no room to swing the blade. Both his attackers pressed forward and Eskkar, weaving the blade between them, had to take another step backward as he fended them off. One more step and he would be back on the landing, the door closed in his face again.

Suddenly Ariamus cried out in pain, stumbled, and fell to his knees with a curse. Annok-sur clung to Ariamus's leg, her teeth fastened to his calf. The distraction gave Eskkar the moment he needed. He took a half-step back, ducked down, then lunged forward. The foreigner shifted to parry the blow, but Eskkar stretched out his arm and extended his body into the thrust. The guard managed to deflect the point from his stomach, but the blade buried itself in the man's side, and he gasped in pain. Eskkar tried to free the sword, but the man staggered against the wall, his body holding the blade fast.

Eskkar twisted the hilt and the man shrieked in agony, dropping his sword as his hands clasped the blade that burned within him. Eskkar rushed forward, lowering his shoulder into the wounded guard and knocking him backward. At the same moment, Ariamus smashed the hilt of his sword on Annok-sur's head, freeing himself from her clutch. He drew back his sword, but before he could thrust forward, Eskkar leapt toward him. He slammed into Ariamus, pulling the big sword free from the dying Egyptian as he did so.

They grappled. Too close to use his sword, Eskkar dropped his weapon and seized Ariamus in both arms, pinning the writhing Ariamus before his enemy could bring his weapon into play. Something blocked the light for an instant, and Eskkar knew someone moved behind him. Keeping his arms locked around Ariamus, Eskkar whirled around, keeping Ariamus between him and whatever danger threatened.

Eskkar caught the flickering flash of the blade in the lamplight, and Ariamus screamed as a sword pierced his upper arm. Lifting Ariamus off the floor in a burst of rage,

Eskkar threw the man at this new attacker, stopping the third man's advance for an instant, until he shoved Ariamus hard against the wall. The former captain of the guard slid to the floor, dazed and clutching at his arm.

By then, Eskkar had reached down and scooped up his sword. This must be Korthac. No one else would be in these rooms. Only Korthac stood between him and Trella. But the door stood open behind him, and Korthac's men might be here at any moment. Eskkar raised his bloody blade and moved forward.

A top the tower, the stars and moon provided barely enough light for Drakis to see his enemies, milling shadows outlined against the night sky. Screaming like a demon, he hacked left and right, striking at anyone who wasn't shouting Eskkar's name. His men burst through the opening behind him, shouting their war cries. They'd driven the confused defenders up the steps, out of the tower, and onto the battlement, but Korthac's followers still had to be killed. Drakis had no thought except to swing his sword, yelling Eskkar's name at the top of his lungs, as he struck and struck at the enemy before him, not caring where his blade landed.

The defenders, panicked and thinking themselves outnumbered, lost the will to fight. Caught by surprise in the night, their thoughts turned to flight. One man died, then another, before the rest dropped their swords and fled. They scrambled to get away, shouting for mercy and leaping to the parapet that butted against the side of the tower, a fifteen-foot drop to the parapet below. Those who managed it ran for their lives, thanking their gods for their escape. One man went over the outer wall into the ditch, falling nearly twenty-five feet. A scream of pain announced his landing.

Gulping air into his lungs, his chest heaving, Drakis shook his head to clear his mind. He'd taken the tower. Looking around, he saw bodies strewn about. An arrow whistled past his head, and he realized that it came from the other tower. His excitement disappeared as he ducked down. The other tower still remained in enemy hands, guarded by men with bows of their own.

More battle sounds came from below. By now, most of his men had reached the tower's top. "Get down! Watch for enemy bowmen on the other tower," Drakis called out, as he grabbed one of his men and yanked him to safety below the rampart. Frustration set in an instant later when he realized Enkidu had failed to take the right tower.

"Use your bows to clear the top of the other tower, then cover the gate! Make sure it stays closed. I'm going back down." Shoving his way back into the tower's blackness, Drakis trod carefully down the now-bloody stairs, making sure of his footing. He reached the bottom in a rush, stumbling over the last few steps.

The base of the tower had no door, and little in it, except for the steps that wound their way along the walls and up to the battlement. He found Enkidu and his men standing beside the entrance, using their bows, shooting at anything that moved.

"What happened? Why didn't you—"

"They blocked the doorway with a table before we could reach it, Drakis. They spoke a strange language . . . must be

Korthac's men. I lost two men trying to force it." Enkidu paused to take a breath. "So I ordered the men here."

"Damn the gods."

Grunting in rage, Drakis peered out into the open. The plan to take both towers had failed, but he could still control the gate with one tower, if he could hold it. At least he would have all his men together.

The fire outside still burned, but the flames had started to die down. Enkidu had given him an idea. If he could barricade the door with something, they could hold both the tower and the gate. This tower had no table, nothing, in fact, except for a few blankets strewn on the floor. Drakis peered out the doorway. Down the street, following the wall toward the north, he could just make out the usual carts and tables, pushed against their owner's houses for the night. One object loomed up larger, even in the dim light—a country wagon, with its wheels nearly as tall as a man. If he could bring it here, it would make a formidable barrier.

"See that wagon up the lane? We'll drag it here and use it to block the doorway."

Enkidu looked out the opening. "They'll be shooting at us. Korthac's fighters are gathering near the other tower. Their archers are already targeting this entrance." As if to give emphasis to Enkidu's word, an arrow clattered off the side of the opening.

"I'll go for it. I'll take three men. Send some of your men to the top. Cover us from there. Hurry."

Ignoring Enkidu's protests, Drakis grabbed three men and told them what he planned. Putting down his bow, he stepped close to the doorway and studied the lane.

Confused shouts sounded everywhere, and men darted about the cleared space, but no one had dared to approach the tower as yet, and the lane to the north appeared empty. Still, it wouldn't be long before someone took charge and the counterattack began.

"Come!" he said, and burst through the opening, running as fast as he could. Glancing behind him, Drakis saw his men following and even caught sight of Enkidu and another man standing inside the doorway, arrows at the ready.

The wagon stood a good hundred paces from the tower, and, once there, they'd have to push the cumbersome vehicle back. Breathing hard, he reached the wagon and found it facing the wrong direction. They'd have to turn it around, or it would be even more difficult to get moving. Drakis ran past the back end of the wagon, then knelt and lifted the long wooden tongue, grunting at its weight.

One of his men joined him, and together they lifted the heavy wooden trace from the ground and pushed it higher and higher, until it fell backward, landing on the top of the wagon with a loud crash. His other men had already slipped alongside the house wall and started shoving. Drakis grasped the edge of the front wheel and added his weight. Slowly, with much squeaking and protesting, the heavy conveyance began to move.

As soon as they cleared it from the wall, Drakis called his men to the rear of the wagon. All four of them picked up the back end, straining under the weight, and simply walked it around, so that the wagon's front pointed toward the tower.

"Put your shoulders into it," Drakis said, his breathing labored from the effort, and shoved his body against the rear of the clumsy wagon. Creaking loudly, it started to move. Drakis cursed himself for not bringing more men; two full-grown oxen normally moved a wagon this size. After a few steps it rolled more easily, but they couldn't get it going faster than a slow walk, and no amount of effort seemed to increase its speed. Still, they'd covered half the distance to the tower before the first sign of anyone noticing their movement. An arrow slammed into the wagon with a twang, and from its angle Drakis guessed it had come from the other tower.

"Keep the wagon between us and the tower," he commanded, and his men shifted a little more to the left. Another arrow whistled over their heads. Then a voice cried out from above them.

"Look out behind you!"

The warning came from the rooftop beside them, where the still half-asleep citizens of Akkad had retreated, some for safety, others to watch the spectacle. Drakis glanced over his shoulder and saw four men nearly upon them, swords flashing as they ran.

"Behind us!"

He pulled his sword from its scabbard and lifted it high as he readied himself. A few steps before the attackers reached them, one of them stumbled and went down, a cry of pain echoing through the night. Drakis saw an arrow sticking in the man's leg. It meant one less man, and it gave the attackers a moment of hesitation before they struck, and by then Drakis and his men stood ready.

Swords clashed. Drakis, the fighting madness still on him, screamed Eskkar's name with all his might, swinging his sword as he struck back at his attacker, mixing thrust and cut with a savagery that put fear into his opponent's heart. His opponent broke off and ran. Another lay dead or dying, and the last attacker turned and fled into the darkness.

Drakis didn't even pause for breath. Sword in hand, he lowered his back against the wagon and pushed with his legs. His heels dug deep ruts into the dirt, and he slipped again and again, but at least he could watch their rear.

It took a long moment to get the wagon moving again, and now they had to guide it slightly to the left, in order to point it toward the tower's opening. The wagon slowed even more as it turned. Suddenly it began to move faster, and Drakis realized two more archers had come from the tower and started pulling on the left front wheel, helping the unwieldy wagon along and guiding it straight at the tower's entrance.

That made them easy targets. The front of the wagon stood exposed not only to Korthac's bowmen in the other tower, but to those men Drakis saw assembling on the other side of the square. He heard an arrow glance off the base of the tower, then felt two more shafts strike into the wagon itself.

Then the wagon wheezed past the opening. "Everyone inside!" Drakis followed them in, his legs trembling so much from the exertions that he stumbled and nearly fell. The fighting and the heavy wagon had drained his strength, and he needed a moment to catch his breath. He heard Enkidu giving orders, so he just watched for a moment.

His second in command had six men struggling with the wagon, this time using their efforts to tug one of its great wooden wheels into the doorway. One man crawled under the wagon and back out into the lane, then swung himself up and into the wagon's bed. Drakis had expected the cart to be empty, but now he saw two thick stakes stored there, no doubt used to lever the wagon out of mud or soft sand. The quick-thinking soldier handed them down to Enkidu, arrows whistling about him, before diving headfirst back into the tower. The two lengths of wood, as tall as a man, would help jam the wagon against the wall.

Drakis leaned against the doorway. The wagon blocked the entrance and provided a shield wall to protect his archers. His men could defend the tower for now, at least. He dragged more air into his lungs. "Ready your bowmen, Enkidu," Drakis said. Unlike the rabble he'd caught by surprise and driven from this tower, Drakis knew he'd next be facing disciplined Egyptian fighters, and that real fighting had just begun. "They'll be coming for us soon."

Unlike the rest of the alehouse patrons, En-hedu awoke well before the dawn, the habit acquired since she'd first started watching Korthac's house. Since the Egyptian had left that house behind the day he took power, En-hedu had given up selling her wares. The need to watch Korthac had passed; he ruled here now, at least until Eskkar returned. Until then, Tammuz and she waited, glad for the first time that almost no one knew of his real activities.

Nevertheless, the habit of early rising remained, though now she used the brief interval for another purpose. En-hedu turned on her side, facing Tammuz, who still slept soundly. She couldn't get out of the bed without crawling over him, so she decided to wake him. That had become a new experience for her. Not waking a man, she'd done that often enough for her former master. Waking Tammuz, in the last few weeks, had become a pleasure instead of the start of a day's new degradations.

She moved closer to him, raising herself on one elbow and letting her breast fall upon his bare chest. He stirred, but didn't wake, so she reached between his legs and began stroking him. Still asleep, in moments he grew hard, and when she grasped his rising manhood he moaned in pleasure.

"Wake up, master," she said, whispering the words into his ear. "It's almost dawn."

Startled, he lifted his head, but her hand, still holding him fast, kept him from rising.

"What . . . En-hedu . . ." He sighed in contentment and let his head fall back on the bed.

She tightened her grip, and began moving her hand up and down. Since she'd saved his life that day when Korthac took over, her feelings for him had changed, grown even deeper and stronger. Now she wanted to please him, care for him, keep him as close as possible. She still felt the wonder at his gentleness, and she'd grown bolder and bolder each time they made love. Unlike her former master, Tammuz felt different, tasted different. What had been degrading before had turned into something as exciting as it was pleasurable.

After a few days of lovemaking, she found herself so moist that her juices ran down her thigh. Now she squeezed him again, then leaned over him, pushing the blanket away. She kissed his erection, brushing it with her lips before taking him in her mouth. The sounds he made when she did that always excited her, and she thrilled at her power over him, at his need for her touch and her body. This morning would be special, she decided, and she felt herself growing excited in anticipation.

Suddenly she stopped, and sat up in the bed. "What was that?"

"What? Nothing ... nothing ... don't stop ..."

"No, it's something," she insisted, letting go of Tammuz. "Men shouting ..." The noise came again, louder this time.

Tammuz sat up, pushing the blanket to the floor, both of them now clearly hearing a clamor of men, followed by the blare of a distant trumpet sounding its alarm.

Overhead, they heard Gatus moving about, and knew he'd heard the same sounds. Tammuz swung his legs down and moved away from the bed. "Gatus," he called out softly toward the loft, "what is it?"

She heard the ladder creak, then the stars disappeared as the soldier's bulk blocked the opening for a moment, before Gatus descended the ladder into their room.

"Fighting," Gatus said, as he stepped from the final rung. "Men fighting near the barracks. I heard some calling Eskkar's name."

That name had not been spoken aloud in days, not since Korthac's bloody edict.

By the time Gatus reached their midst, En-hedu had risen from the bed. Fumbling in the darkness, she found the knife Tammuz had given her. The thin copper blade, sheathed in soft leather, fitted to a belt she fastened around her body, just under her breasts. Then she pulled her dress over her head. If she walked with her arms crossed, the knife was well concealed.

"Can he have returned so soon?" Tammuz asked, slipping on his tunic and taking up his own blade.

Gatus laughed as he bent down and fastened his sandals. "Eskkar knows how to move fast when he has to. No one else could rouse these cowards. He must have been on his way here when word reached him."

"Korthac has men watching the roads," En-hedu said. "They would have sent warning."

"Eskkar could have slipped by them," Gatus grunted. "He knows the countryside better than anyone . . . as long as he's here, it doesn't matter how. It's time to fight. I'm heading toward the barracks. You two stay here." He opened the door to the common room and moved rapidly to the alehouse entrance.

"Not likely," Tammuz said behind the old soldier's back, already lacing on his own sandals.

En-hedu helped Tammuz fasten his belt around his waist. By the time Tammuz and En-hedu left their room, half the sleepers had departed, awakened by the steadily rising sounds of battle that nearly masked the shouts of Eskkar's name. Only the drunks remained, still in their stupor from too much ale. Outside, several of Tammuz's customers stood beside the alehouse door, asking each other what all the commotion was about and talking excitedly to anyone who would listen.

"Where shall we go?" En-hedu brushed against Tammuz as they stood in the doorway.

"To Trella's house. We may be of some help there. You should stay . . ."

"I'm going with you," En-hedu said. She knew Tammuz didn't want her to come, but they'd already discussed that before. Wherever he went, she was determined to be at his side. Without another word, she pushed past him and began walking down the lane, heading toward Lady Trella's house.

"Any of you rogues want to fight, follow me," Tammuz called out over his shoulder, as he followed after his woman.

Dawn would be upon them soon, En-hedu realized, looking at the fading stars overhead. All around them she heard the sounds of people jabbering to each other, asking what was happening, what they should do. Over all the noise, they heard the sound of people cheering and shouting Eskkar's name, and the occasional clash of weapons.

Tammuz caught up with En-hedu, taking the lead and weaving his way through the growing crowd. Three of Korthac's men burst out of an alehouse in front of them, and stumbled down the lane, heading in the same direction. The lane soon crossed another, and the first man turned left, toward the barracks. To the right lay the way to Eskkar's house.

She watched in horror as Tammuz put on a burst of speed, overtook the last of the three, and plunged his knife into the man's back. Without pausing, Tammuz turned to the right, leaving the wounded man stumbling along for a few paces before he fell to the earth, crying out in pain. His two companions, disappearing into the darkness, never even noticed.

En-hedu ran as fast as she could, and managed to keep on Tammuz's heels. Together they turned into the lane, to see Eskkar's house just ahead. Tammuz stopped suddenly. The street was filled with Korthac's men, most of them Egyptians, roused from the nearby houses where they'd been housed. She watched them rush into Eskkar's courtyard, and the sounds of fighting and men shouting rang out over the walls.

She caught Tammuz by the arm and held him with all her strength. "You can't. There are too many of them." She felt frightened that he would rush headlong against them, his knife useless against so many swords.

"I see them," he said with a curse. "Let's go back."

They turned and retraced their steps down the lane, away from the house. Overhead, the stars were winking out, as the first rays of true dawn began to break above them. Men milled about, and she saw two more of the invaders, swords in their hands, pushing their way through the crowd, heading toward Eskkar's.

"Stay behind me," Tammuz ordered.

En-hedu reached inside her dress, pulled the knife from its scabbard, and held it against her thigh. She felt her heart beating wildly against her ribs.

Tammuz shrank against the wall as the first of Korthac's men ran past, but pushed himself out into the lane, into the second man's path. Before the cursing Egyptian could shove Tammuz aside or raise his sword, Tammuz's knife flashed upward into the man's stomach, penetrating just under the rib cage. The man grunted, as much in surprise as pain at the unexpected blow. Before the man slid to the ground, Tammuz had already slipped beyond him, rushing down the lane, En-hedu at his side, looking back over her shoulder to make sure no one followed.

They found an open doorway and stepped within,

watching the crowd move back and forth, everyone shouting and asking each other what to do. Sounds of fighting increased, and En-hedu realized the noise was coming from several different directions.

Then she heard furious voices shouting in Egyptian, and she peered out to see a band of men moving down the lane, heading toward the gate. She recognized Hathor's voice rising above the din. The man's speech seemed calm and controlled despite the chaos, as he gave orders and pushed the men along.

"Someone is ordering them toward the gate," she said.

"There must be fighting there as well." They crouched down as the force of invaders pushed by their doorway, breathing hard, cursing and yelling at each other. Before they could do anything, another half-dozen or so men ran past, following the first group and heading to the gate.

Tammuz pulled his hand free, and En-hedu knew what he planned. When the last of Korthac's men passed by, Tammuz slipped out behind the straggler, caught up with him in three strides, and struck him down.

With enough light to see now, and to her horror, she realized more foreigners were still coming. Tammuz saw the first one, who shouted out in Egyptian as he raised his sword and struck.

Tammuz ducked away from the blow, took another step back, and when the man moved toward him, raising his sword with a shout, Tammuz lunged forward with a blur of motion, extending his right arm and burying the knife into the man's chest. The man cried out in pain, as the sword fell from his grasp, Tammuz's knife striking true beneath the breastbone.

But the mortally wounded man collapsed forward, his momentum taking him into Tammuz, and knocking her master backward to the ground. En-hedu heard the crunch as Tammuz's head struck against the base of the wall as he landed, stunned, with the dead or dying man's body nearly covering him.

Two more Egyptians ran up, one shouting something incomprehensible to the other. One swerved around his fallen comrades and kept going. She saw Tammuz, dazed, trying to push the dead man off his chest with his one good hand. The second Egyptian raised his sword as Tammuz, still clutching his knife, struggled to free himself from beneath the body. The collision with the mud wall had stunned him, and the knife slipped from his trembling fingers.

En-hedu screamed as she jumped forward, raising her knife. The man saw her and dodged aside. He swung around, the sword cutting toward her head. She threw herself beneath it, rolling in the dirt and landing beside Tammuz, losing her grip on her own knife in the process. She twisted to her knees and threw herself across Tammuz, getting between him and the Egyptian. He would have to kill her first. She reached for the knife she'd dropped, but fumbled with the hilt, her eyes locked in horror on the man above her, watching as the sword swung down toward her head.

25

As Grond raced up the stairs, he heard the clash of swords and the sounds of fighting rising from the upper room. He'd killed two men on the lower floor, wasting precious time as his captain disappeared up the stairs. Luckily, he didn't encounter any more guards. Now reaching the top of the landing, Grond found the door nearly closed, but ajar.

Just as he reached for it, the door flew open, jerked wide by someone within. Before Grond could react, a body slammed into him, knocking him backward onto the landing. To keep from falling off, Grond grappled with the man, who struggled with surprising strength, dropping underneath Grond's arms and trying to push him off the landing and break free at the same time.

Grunting, Grond dropped his sword, unable to use it effectively, and wrapped both arms around the man. They spun around, perilously close to the landing's edge, each man trying to twist free, neither able to use a weapon. Behind him, Grond heard footsteps on the stairs and men shouting in Egyptian. Enemy soldiers must have gotten past Mitrac and entered into the house. Grond redoubled his efforts to break free.

Instead his foot tripped on something and he fell to his knees. His attacker broke his grip and lurched toward the stairs. Grond flung himself at the man, caught his arm, and jerked him back, wrapping an arm about him. Off balance, the man stumbled, but managed to drive a fist into Grond's face. With a shout of rage, Grond reached out to grasp his assailant, who twisted violently. The effort took Grond past the edge of the landing, and he lost his balance. He fell, clutching his assailant and taking him with him.

Holding each other, they dropped nearly six feet. They crashed together onto the long table below, its solid planks doing little to break their fall. Momentum carried them off the table, and they rolled onto a bench and then to the floor, Grond taking most of the impact. He felt his breath knocked from his body. By the time Grond could move, his attacker had trod on his chest and reached the front door. The man unbarred it, shouted for help, and vanished into the courtyard.

Cursing the evil luck that took him off the landing, he untangled himself from the bench. Grond struggled to his feet and pulled the knife from his belt, to see three Egyptians burst through the now-open front door. But an arrow struck the first down. He saw Mitrac nocking another shaft, at the foot of the stairs.

Ignoring this fresh wave of foes, Grond swung himself onto the steps. "Cover me!" He could just make out two more of Korthac's men on the top landing, one of them pounding on the door with his sword hilt and shouting in Egyptian. They must have rushed up the stairs while he and the unknown man had fallen from the landing. For the first time, Grond realized that someone had secured the door again. The other man heard Grond's footsteps and turned toward him, swinging his sword with a swift motion, no doubt expecting to strike before Grond could get close enough to use the knife.

Instead, one of Mitrac's arrows feathered itself in the man's shoulder, knocking him off balance, and the sword dropped from his hand. Grond scooped the bronze blade up with his left hand, and stepped over the dying man. Grond thrust low with the sword, his face brushing the topmost step, as the other Egyptian deflected the blade aside. Still moving forward, Grond shoved his knife into the man's leg, eliciting a grunt of pain. The man's counterthrust met only air as Grond jerked his body away. The Egyptian took a step back, but his leg gave way and he tumbled down right in front of Grond's knife. A quick stab finished the man.

"Grond, give us room!" Mitrac had climbed the landing and now stood beside Grond, but turned his attention downward, toward the main entrance. Grond saw Mitrac had to tilt his long bow to the side as he attempted to notch another arrow. A second archer stood on a lower step, and two more of Eskkar's men began backing slowly up the stairs, as dark shadows slipped through the outer doorway toward them, gathering for the attack.

Grond moved aside to give Mitrac room, then bent over and pitched the dead bodies off the landing with two quick heaves, before turning his gaze back to the door. "Open the door!" He heard the rasp of bronze from within. "It's Grond!"

He pounded on the door with his sword hilt, then threw his shoulder against it, but the door held firm. He'd seen the thick panels enough times to know it couldn't be forced, not without tools or more men. An arrow thudded into the wood beside Grond's head, ripping out a lock of hair as it passed, and he heard Mitrac's bowstring twang in response.

Grond knew he didn't have time to force the door, not with all these Egyptians rushing toward him. Eskkar had found a way inside somehow, and might be trapped there, but Grond couldn't do anything about it. He looked down toward the dim chamber below. Gray silhouettes milled about just outside the house's entrance, shouting in the language of Egypt. They'd be joining those inside soon, he knew. Grond and Mitrac would have to hold the stairs until help came.

"Take the top, Mitrac," he ordered, and moved down the steps, past his men, his sword in one hand, the knife in the other. "Let them come to their deaths." He repeated the words, in Egyptian this time, as he tightened his grip on the sword.

A fresh wave of men burst into the house from the courtyard as Grond reached the bottom of the steps. Some carried spears, deadly weapons at close quarters, especially against swordsmen packed together. One of Mitrac's arrows struck down the leading spearman. The spear fell from its owner's dying hand and skidded along the floor to land at Grond's feet. Dropping his sword, he scooped it up just in time to meet the charge.

"Eskkar has returned," he shouted, lunging forward with the weapon, and Mitrac's archers took up the cry, firing

arrows as fast as they could fit them to their strings, as the
battle for Eskkar's house began.

Inside the workroom, Eskkar lunged with his sword, but
Korthac knocked the blade aside and, in the same motion,
drove his blade toward Eskkar's face. Surprised at the speed
and strength of Korthac's arm, Eskkar barely managed to
jerk his head aside as the weapon's point stung its way past
his ear. He moved back a step, recovering his guard and
keeping his sword in front of him. The clash of swords
behind him reminded Eskkar he had little time.

"My men are behind you, barbarian. You'll be dead
soon, like your . . ."

Ignoring Korthac's words, Eskkar lunged again, this
time trying to thrust low under Korthac's guard. But
Korthac countered the stroke easily, and for a second time
Eskkar barely managed to avoid being skewered by the
counterstroke, and again he moved back half a step. He
realized that he faced a master swordsman.

"You fight like a clumsy ox, barbarian." Outlined against
the flickering lamp, Korthac's face was a dark shadow, and
his voice sounded like that of a demon from the underworld.

Eskkar knew better than to listen to his opponent, to let
himself be distracted by the man's words, then cut down
by a sudden thrust. Man or demon, the sword would finish
him. Moving to the side, Eskkar snapped the long sword
out, thrusting with every muscle to keep his arm rigid and
the blade straight.

Korthac parried the lunge, but had to move aside to do
so. Eskkar never paused. He thrust again and again, short,

quick jabs, aiming for the man's face, his stomach, even his legs, any part of the body, using the sword like a lance, striking as fast and hard as he could at any opening, never stopping, never giving his adversary the chance to counterattack.

It was the way to beat a superior swordsman, and here, inside the house and with no space to swing the long horse sword, he knew Korthac had the edge. So instead of trying for a killing blow, Eskkar used his blade's tip, jabbing it at his opponent so fast that Korthac had no time to strike back. Wound and weaken your enemy. A dozen cuts would bring down any man, as sure as one fatal thrust. His clan fought that way, the barbarian way.

"Your slut begged at my feet for a chance to pleasure me."

This time the words sounded rushed, the foreign accent stronger. Eskkar shook the sweat from his eyes, watching his foe for any weakness. Korthac retreated a step, weaving lightly from side to side, striving to get past the sword tip that kept jabbing at his face and neck, waiting for Eskkar to tire and leave himself vulnerable to a solid counterstroke.

Eskkar kept advancing, taking small steps and keeping his balance, sliding his feet across the floor to avoid stumbling on something, jabbing and lunging, turning aside Korthac's counters, and gradually forcing his enemy back toward the center of the room. Suddenly Korthac dropped low, swinging his sword at Eskkar's legs. The unexpected maneuver stopped Eskkar's advance for a moment, and in that instant Korthac leapt backward, abandoning the attack and darting through the door that led into the bedchamber.

The Egyptian slipped through the opening and tried to fling the door shut, but Eskkar, reacting almost as fast as his enemy, rammed his blade into the door, keeping it open before Korthac could bring his weight to bear and seal the door. Then Eskkar threw his shoulder and all his weight against the panel just as Korthac's second effort tried to force the door shut. Eskkar's bulk and momentum drove the door back into Korthac's face. The Egyptian staggered back with a curse, knocking over a small table and sending a water jar crashing to the floor, as Eskkar struggled to force his way inside the bedroom.

Off balance, Korthac brought up his sword, but, with no time to swing the blade, he tried to hammer the hilt into Eskkar's face. Eskkar caught his attacker's wrist in his left hand, enough to deflect the blow, but the pommel's rough edge ripped along Eskkar's head, and a splash of blood spattered against the doorjamb.

Eskkar dropped his useless sword and reached for Korthac's throat with his right hand. Before Eskkar could grasp Korthac's neck, the Egyptian caught his hand and held it with a grip of bronze. Struggling and twisting, they stumbled back into the outer room, grunting and gasping for breath as they fought. They thudded hard into the wall, sliding along its smooth surface, the Egyptian moving so quickly that Eskkar couldn't get any leverage.

Korthac still held his sword in his right hand, and he kept trying to free his wrist from Eskkar's grasp. Korthac stood a good foot shorter in height, but to Eskkar's surprise the Egyptian's muscles not only resisted his own but nearly managed to bring the blade back into play. They crashed against the table, sending it skidding across the floor with a loud screech. Esskar's leg took the brunt of the collision, but he shouted in rage and forced the smaller man back by sheer strength. Suddenly Korthac smashed his forehead into Esskar's cheek with such force that Esskar almost let his grip slip on the man's sword arm.

Esskar knew he'd be dead the instant his enemy got the sword into play. Turning his face away to avoid another head-butt, they struggled again, twisting and grunting. Esskar spun on his heel, using all his strength to unbalance Korthac. Nevertheless, Korthac kept his feet, and the two of them slammed into the wall, bounced off, then crashed back into the half-open door of the inner room. This time they fell through the opening and landed in a heap on the floor.

Another lamp burned here, giving off a dimmer light that barely illuminated the smaller room. Esskar caught sight of Trella crawling on the floor.

"Esskar, the baby," she cried out, pain sounding in her voice.

Trella said something more, but Esskar couldn't make out her words. The baby's wailing added to the confusion.

Esskar rammed Korthac's hand against the doorframe, and grunted in satisfaction when he heard the man's sword clatter on the floor. Esskar must have loosed his grip on Korthac's wrist, for in the next moment, the Egyptian had twisted his wrist from Esskar's grasp and lunged away. Esskar tried to rise, but he slipped on the wet floor. Korthac reached his feet first, a knife appearing in his hand as he moved forward, weaving quickly from side to side, like a snake readying to strike.

Reaching for his knife, Esskar found the sheath empty,

the blade lost in the struggle. Weaponless, Eskkar moved back, his hands extended, but he found himself forced backward into a corner.

"Now you'll die, barbarian," Korthac said, his voice hoarse from effort.

But as Korthac stepped past Trella's prone body, she lifted herself on one hand, and Eskkar saw her drive a small knife into Korthac's calf.

Korthac flinched in pain. He looked down, then slashed at Trella with the knife. But Eskkar needed no better opening. The instant Trella struck, he rushed the man, covering the short distance between them so fast that Korthac couldn't react fast enough. Once again Eskkar caught Korthac's wrist as their bodies crashed together and they tumbled heavily to the floor, and this time it was Korthac who landed on his back.

Eskkar found his face pressed against Korthac's stomach as the man squirmed, writhing along the floor, striving to get away and at the same time attempting to force his knife into Eskkar's side. They struggled, rolling back and forth across the floor. Eskkar lunged forward and clamped his right hand on Korthac's neck and squeezed, trying to choke the man enough to weaken his hold on the knife. They'd jammed themselves against the wall, near Trella's dressing table. From above their heads the baby continued to cry, its tiny wails competing with the men's grunts of rage.

Korthac's free hand searched Eskkar's face, trying to find his eyes, but Eskkar ground his face deeper into the man's stomach as he dragged himself up the shifting body and closer to Korthac's face. The Egyptian used his feet and knees, snapping them up and down with all the force he could muster, searching for Eskkar's groin, all the while trying to dislodge Eskkar's hold on his knife hand.

With a savage heave, Korthac loosened Eskkar's grip enough to bring the knife into play. The Egyptian's blade seared along Eskkar's arm. But the pain only enraged Eskkar, and he redoubled his efforts against the man who'd seized his wife and threatened his child. Eskkar tightened his grip on Korthac's right wrist, putting all his force into squeezing the man's bones together, harder and harder, as the blood pounded in Eskkar's ears. Korthac twisted and jerked his arm, but he couldn't break Eskkar's grip, and with a low gasp, his fingers dropped the knife.

Instantly Eskkar released his grip on the man's neck and levered himself up onto Korthac's chest, using his weight to keep the man pinned to the floor. Korthac's fingers groped for the knife and managed to grasp it, but Eskkar, with a brutal surge, slammed his knee onto Korthac's forearm, pinning his foe's right arm against the floor. Eskkar shifted his weight, caught Korthac's other wrist, then raised his fist and struck the Egyptian in the face with his left hand, once, twice, a third time.

The third blow slowed his opponent and gave Eskkar the chance he needed. He heaved his other leg up and used it to pin Korthac's free arm. The smaller man now had Eskkar's full weight upon his body and Eskkar took only a moment to draw back his fist and strike Korthac with his right fist.

This blow, driven with all Eskkar's pent-up rage, stunned his opponent. Before the man could recover, Eskkar seized Korthac by the hair, pinning Korthac's head to the floor, while with his other hand Eskkar smashed him again and again, aiming each blow at Korthac's left eye, putting all his force and hatred into the attack. At the fifth blow the man went limp. Taking no chances that his opponent feigned unconsciousness, Eskkar raised his fist like a hammer and pounded the heel of his hand against Korthac's forehead.

A burst of blood splattered up, but the man lay still. Eskkar gasped for breath, the blood pounding in his head, every muscle trembling with exhaustion. Never had he fought such an enemy before. He searched for Korthac's knife, groping along the floor with clumsy fingers until he found it, then grabbed it by the bloody blade. The weapon shook in his hand. Eskkar reversed it and put the tip against Korthac's throat. Only then did he lean back and gulp air into his lungs. Still astride Korthac's chest, he took a quick look over his shoulder.

Their bedroom, still lit by the oil lamp that somehow remained upright during the struggle, showed Trella on the floor a few feet away, her body shuddering. She pulled herself toward Eskkar, a tiny, bloody dagger still in her hand, but she could scarcely move, and her sobs had joined with the sounds of the baby crying.

The sight of her made Eskkar want to plunge the blade into Korthac's throat, but the thought that he might need the Egyptian alive stayed his hand. Korthac appeared unconscious, but Eskkar wanted to make certain; he jabbed the tip of the knife into Korthac's throat, just enough to draw blood. The man didn't react, so Eskkar raised the weapon and struck down on the man's forehead with the hilt. The Egyptian's body stayed limp.

Satisfied that his enemy wouldn't be moving for at least

a few moments, Eskkar pushed himself to his feet. His legs trembled and blood from the side of his head still dripped on his chest, joining with the blood that flowed from the cut on his arm and all the scratches on his face from Korthac's efforts to gouge out his eyes.

Eskkar lifted his shoulder to wipe the blood from his face on his tunic, and felt the muscles in his arms twitch from the strain of the fight. It took a moment before he could see clearly. Taking a deep breath he reached down and gathered Trella with one arm and lifted her from the floor.

Keeping his eyes on Korthac, he guided Trella back onto the bed, easing her down. She struggled to speak, but her body shook as much from the tears as from her wound. Blood flowed from an ugly cut above her hip, and he took her hand and pressed it against the wound.

"Keep your hand steady, Trella," he said. "I'll get help."

Looking around the room, he saw the stool that normally sat before Trella's dressing table. Knocked on its side, it lay against the wall. He scooped it up, and keeping it on its side, lifted Korthac's left foot and slid the stool underneath it. Then Eskkar raised his sandal and smashed it down on the man's shin.

Eskkar grunted with satisfaction as he heard the bones break. "That's for Trella and my child, Egyptian," he said. For the first time, Eskkar felt certain Korthac wouldn't be doing any more fighting tonight, even if he regained consciousness any time soon.

"Eskkar . . . Eskkar . . . is the child all right?"

He had to strain to make out the words, but he understood her uplifted arm that pointed toward the still-wailing child. He realized she still held the small knife, covered with Korthac's blood, in her hand. Taking it from her fingers, Eskkar dropped it next to her on the bed. His breathing slowed, and he started moving with more confidence. Eskkar stepped over to the cradle. He picked up his crying child, hands still clumsy with fatigue. Keeping Korthac's knife in his hand, Eskkar carried the infant carefully to Trella.

"Stay here. Don't try to move." Looking down at her stomach and legs, he saw more blood, and fear went through him. "Are you wounded? Where else . . ."

"No, not wounded . . . the baby . . . your son . . . he came only a few hours ago . . . I was . . ."

She hadn't realized that she had taken a cut across her hip from Korthac's blade. Blood oozed from the cut, seeping between her fingers; but she kept her hand pressed tight against her side where he'd placed it. She sounded weak, and the wound needed bandaging.

"Don't get up," he repeated. "I'll be back."

Korthac's knife still clutched in his hand, he stepped into the workroom. The flame from the lamp in the outer room burned low and didn't provide much light, but Eskkar picked it up and held it aloft. Only two bodies greeted his eyes. The dead Egyptian bodyguard lay where he'd fallen, but Annok-sur's body had moved. She lay motionless, directly in front of the outer door, now shut and bolted. Ariamus had vanished. Annok-sur must have closed and barred the door with the last of her strength before she passed out. Eskkar set the lamp down, retrieved his sword from the floor, and put it on the table.

Sounds of fighting came from beyond the door, and reminded him that he had left Grond and the others behind, and that he might not have much time. He lifted Annok-sur from the floor, and she groaned at his touch. As he carried her back to the bedroom, she started to struggle in his arms.

"Rest easy, Annok-sur. It's Eskkar. Can you stand?"

"Yes, I think . . . yes."

He felt her relax, saw her head start to sag. "Don't faint yet," he ordered, practically shouting the words into her face as he lowered her feet to the floor; he needed her conscious. Annok-sur nodded, and Eskkar set her down inside the bedroom and let her lean against the wall. "Bar the door and don't open it. Bandage Trella's wound, before she bleeds to death."

Eskkar put Korthac's knife in her hand, and watched her eyes narrow at the sight of the prone Egyptian. "No. Not until we've finished killing these vermin. Can you do that? Just watch Korthac. After you've tended to Trella, keep the knife at his throat. If he moves, or anyone tries to force the door, then kill him."

He pulled the door shut behind him and scooped up his sword before crossing the outer room. Behind him, he heard Annok-sur drop the wooden bar into place. The women would be safe in there for now. Ariamus's sword lay near the entrance. Annok-sur's body had hidden it. He picked it up with his left hand and went to the door. Taking a deep breath, he lifted up the thick bar and yanked the door open.

Shouts and the twang of a bowstring sounded through the doorway, and the backs of Mitrac and another archer filled the opening. Both heads swiveled just long enough to see who stood behind them. He had to squeeze behind

Mitrac to get out onto the landing. Dawn had arrived and light filtered through the open doorway and windows to illuminate the scene below.

The landing had barely enough space to hold the three of them. Mitrac stood beside Eskkar, bow drawn, blood pouring down his left arm. Eskkar saw that only two arrows remained in his quiver. On the top steps two more archers crouched, extending swords that passed on either side of Grond's body for protection; empty quivers on their belts explained the swords. His bodyguard wielded a sword and a spear, and kept at bay three or four rogues on the lower steps. Five or six more foes waited below, just inside the door to the courtyard, preparing for another rush. Bodies lay strewn about on the floor and steps, arrows protruding from most of them.

Eskkar took another quick look down as the others below looked up. One of them called out something in Egyptian, but all Eskkar understood was Korthac's name.

"Korthac is dead," Eskkar snarled, putting all his rage into the words. Everyone froze at the news. Eskkar raised his voice even louder and bellowed out his words, so that even those outside the house would hear them. "Korthac is dead!" Eskkar extended the long sword in his right hand, pointing at those beneath him, the blade stained with blood as if in proof. Fury possessed him, the same emotion that had filled him as he fought against the Egyptian. "Korthac is dead, and now you will all die as well."

Without any hesitation, he ducked underneath Mitrac's arm and jumped off the landing, his feet aiming for a clear space directly under the stairs. Eskkar went to one knee from the jump, but he rose up swinging the big sword as the first of Korthac's men rushed toward him. Grond shouted a war cry and led the way down the steps, the others following. With a weapon in each hand and the battle frenzy upon him, Eskkar attacked Korthac's suddenly disheartened followers.

The long sword struck one man across the face, and Eskkar parried a counterstroke from another attacker with the short sword in his left hand, then struck again with his right, wielding the heavy blade with renewed energy. The unexpected counterattack unnerved the Egyptians, despite their greater numbers; two of them bolted for the open door, and the rest hesitated. Grond's war cry boomed again within the room, and Eskkar heard the snap-hiss as the last of Mitrac's arrows struck his target.

Within a dozen heartbeats, four men had died, and the rest of Korthac's men fled into the courtyard, driven back by half their number. More men gathered there, getting ready to join the assault. Nevertheless, many heard Eskkar's words and more than a few of Korthac's men began repeating that Korthac was dead.

One of the Akkadians took advantage of the enemy's confusion to slam the front door shut and drop the bar across it.

"The servants' entrance ... secure the door." Grond gave the order, though his voice sounded weak.

Eskkar faced Grond and saw blood covering his bodyguard's neck and chest; the man was swaying on his feet.

"Mitrac," Eskkar said, "the other door ... better see if it's closed and barred."

The master archer raced down the corridor to bar the

second entrance, while the other two archers moved from body to body, wrenching arrows out of the dead to replenish their quivers. Eskkar put his arm around Grond's waist and guided him toward the stairs. "Rest here a moment," Eskkar ordered.

Taking a deep breath, Eskkar forced himself to control his shaking arms. He had only three men who could still fight. If the Egyptians forced the outer door, Eskkar could retreat to the upper rooms.

He took stock of the situation. He'd reached Trella, and both she and the baby were safe. And captured Korthac. They could hold the house for the moment. Now everything depended on Bantor and his men. If they failed, if they couldn't come to Eskkar's rescue in time, Eskkar planned to use Korthac to bargain his way out. If that didn't work, if the Egyptians broke in, Eskkar would kill Trella and the child with his own hand, before falling on his sword. No matter what happened, he couldn't let either of them fall into these foreigners' hands alive.

He shook the gloomy thought away. He wasn't dead yet. They'd just have to hold out until help arrived. "Shove that table against the door," Eskkar ordered, reaching down to pick up a spear. It was time to get ready for the next fight.

26

Hathor woke with a start, the unexpected but always familiar sound still echoing in his ears. Instinctively he grasped the sword that lay on the bed next to him. The noise that had awakened him resolved itself into a mixture of men shouting and the occasional clash of bronze on bronze, the din rising and falling, but steadily growing louder and more urgent. Already on his feet, he moved to the window, leaning outside to hear what was happening.

The last of his sleep disappeared as he peered through the darkness toward the adjoining dwelling. The noise came from Korthac's courtyard, separated from the one Hathor and Takany occupied by only a single high wall that extended to either side of the main structure. A man screamed in pain, the cry of agony rising up over the shouts and curses. Men were dying just beyond the wall, and that meant someone had attacked Korthac and his guards. No alarm had sounded, but fighting had erupted. . . . His mind finally made sense of the shouts. "Eskkar has returned!"

Hathor felt a chill pass over him. Eskkar! He was supposed to be dead. "Osiris take us all," he swore, pausing only to pull on his tunic before dashing out of the bedroom.

"Eskkar has returned ... let none escape!" The shouts from Korthac's courtyard could now be heard even inside the dwelling.

"Takany!" Hathor shouted, stepping into the common room. Korthac's second in command slept in the next bedroom. "Takany, get up!" Hathor shouted into the darkness, moving inside the man's chamber.

Takany lay in his bed, still snoring and besotted from last night's drinking and wenching. He'd spent the first part of the evening at Zenobia's, terrorizing her and her women, and forcing all of them to pleasure him. Hathor had to remain awake until his superior returned, and Takany had brought one of Zenobia's women with him, leading the shivering girl naked through the streets. Now she sat up, no doubt frightened and confused by Hathor's interruption and the noise outside.

"What ... what's happening? ..." Fear sounded in her voice.

Ignoring the wide-eyed girl, Hathor grabbed Takany's arm, shaking the man out of his sleep. "Get up! There's fighting next door." Without waiting, Hathor moved toward the doorway. The half-dozen soldiers sleeping in the house had already gotten to their feet, fumbling for weapons in the dark and asking each other what to do.

"Sound the alarm," Hathor ordered, pushing his way through the gathering crowd. "Get your swords and follow me to Korthac's."

The front entrance of this residence opened directly

into the lane that provided access to Korthac's compound. Hathor ran down the passage, stumbling once in the darkness and wishing he'd had time to put on his sandals. Behind him, a trumpet at last began to sound its warning, the shrill blast repeating the notes that would summon every soldier.

The guards supposed to be standing sentry at Korthac's gate were lying in the dust, arrows protruding from their bodies. Clenching his sword, Hathor pushed his way through the gate.

Someone had lit a torch, and in its flickering light Hathor saw half a dozen bodies strewn about the courtyard, arrows jutting out at odd angles.

"Hathor," a soldier called out. "Amun's dead ... men forced their way through the gate ... they got inside the house and drove us out. They've archers ..."

Amun had been in charge of the soldiers stationed in the courtyard.

"Enough," Hathor said. "Get your men together and make sure they've all their weapons. Guard the doors. Don't let anyone leave."

"What's going on?" Takany's booming voice cut through the confusion. He hadn't bothered to put on a tunic, and now he stood naked and barefoot, a sword in his hand.

The soldier had to repeat the story while Hathor twitched with impatience.

"You say this Eskkar is inside, alone with Korthac?"

Yes, that's what he just said, Hathor wanted to shout. But he knew better than to challenge Takany's authority, even if the man's thought process was as slow as an ox. Precious moments passed while Takany sorted things out.

"You fools," Takany said, his rage displacing any remaining trace of last night's wine. "You let a handful of men drive you from the house!" He grabbed a man backing away from the house and struck him with the flat of his sword. "Get in there and fight," he ordered. "Hathor, gather the men. We'll break down the door to the upper room and free Korthac."

Before anyone could start moving, a man burst in through the gate, and every man's eyes turned toward him. "Takany . . . Hathor," he shouted, stumbling as he reached their side, and trying to catch his breath. "Men are attacking the main gate. They've captured one of the towers and barricaded themselves in. They're shouting that Eskkar has returned to kill us all."

"Order the men from the gate to fall back and meet us at the barracks," Hathor said, facing Takany. "We should head there as well. We need to collect all our forces in one place. Then we can . . ."

"Leave Korthac! Abandon the gate?" Takany shouted, as if disbelieving his ears. "If they get the gate open, we'll have a horde of men pouring into the city."

"Eskkar's soldiers are already *in* the city," Hathor countered," and our men are scattered all about. We need to get the men together and . . ."

"No, we need to rescue Korthac *now*," Takany snapped. He grabbed Hathor by the arm. "You take a dozen men and go to the gate. Take Ariamus," Takany pointed with his sword across the courtyard, "and half his scum with you, too. If he and his men won't fight, kill him. I'll recapture the house and free Korthac. You make sure the gate stays shut."

Hathor looked across the courtyard to where Ariamus stood, surrounded by a dozen of his men, getting his arm bandaged.

"Ariamus! Is it really Eskkar?" Hathor had to raise his voice to carry over the babble of noise, though Ariamus stood only a dozen paces away.

"Yes, it's him," Ariamus said. "He was fighting Korthac and his guard when I saw them last."

Takany was right about Ariamus and his men, Hathor realized. The traitor had recruited most of these boasting thieves and bandits, and the weaklings wouldn't charge into battle without Ariamus's orders. Hathor wanted to know more about Eskkar and Ariamus, but couldn't take the time now.

Hathor hesitated, but one look told him it would be futile to argue. Takany's decision might be wrong, but they'd wasted too much precious time arguing over what to do next. The man feared nothing that walked the earth, or under it for that matter, except Korthac. Takany knew his master's wrath would be on him for this failure. Only this evening at dinner Hathor had listened while Takany assured Korthac of the city's complete submission. Now Korthac might already be dead, according to Ariamus. The upper door was bolted, and unknown archers defended the steps to the bedroom. By now the whole city had awakened, and half of them had already taken to the rooftops to shout Eskkar's name.

Better a bad plan than none at all, Hathor decided, knowing there was nothing he could do.

"All right, Takany. You free Korthac." Hathor turned to the messenger, still awaiting instructions. "Get back to the gate. Tell them I'm bringing reinforcements and to make ready to recapture the tower. Make sure the gate stays closed, no matter what."

The man nodded, and ran out of the courtyard.

"I'll take my men to the barracks." Ariamus had joined them, a fresh bandage on his arm.

"How did this happen?" Takany shouted, pushing himself right in Ariamus's face. "How did you . . ."

"Don't try and blame this on me. Your Egyptians were supposed to be guarding Korthac," Ariamus yelled right back, "when Eskkar walked right into the workroom. Your men are the ones who failed."

"Stop it," Hathor said, forcing his way between the two of them. "We've no time for this. Korthac's either trapped inside or he's dead. Either way, we've got to put down this uprising."

He pushed Ariamus away from Takany, no doubt saving the man's life. One more word and Takany would have gutted him. Hathor had witnessed Takany's rage before.

"We should go to the barracks," Ariamus said. "The extra weapons are stored there."

Hathor detected a hint of fear in Ariamus's voice. Something had unhinged the man, made him eager to get away from this house.

"Take half your men to the gate," Hathor said. "Tell the rest to obey Takany. No arguing, just go."

Ariamus opened his mouth as if to argue, then shrugged. "I'll get them moving." He strode off, shouting out orders to his men and dividing them up. In moments they started gathering at the entrance to the courtyard.

Takany had heard something in Ariamus's voice, too. "Kill him when this is over," Takany ordered, his voice cold with fury. "I don't want to see him alive again. Understand? The coward will sell us out the first chance he gets." Takany turned away and readied his own fighters for the push to regain the house.

Hathor did the same, grabbing the first twelve men he saw and ordering them to follow. He performed a quick check to see that they carried bows as well as their swords. By then Ariamus's men had departed, disappearing out into the lane. Hathor ordered his own men to follow.

Before he passed through the gate, he took one last look at the courtyard. Takany had organized his force of about twenty men. In a few moments, he'd begin the assault on the house. Hathor stepped out into the lane and began running. He hoped he wouldn't need those twenty men at the gate.

Bantor raced toward the barracks. Days of being cooped up, hiding from his enemies and unsure of what to do, had filled him with rage. Thoughts of Ariamus tormented his mind day and night since the ambush. Ariamus, who had taken his wife for an afternoon's diversion. Ariamus, who ambushed and embarrassed him in front of his men. Ariamus, who had laughed at him a dozen times in the old days. Bantor swore once again to see his nemesis dead, preferably by slow roasting over hot coals. The man must die, and more with him. Bantor planned to avenge himself and his men killed in the ambush. The faster he liberated the barracks, the sooner he could begin hunting Ariamus.

Bantor had been the first man to reach the river gate, but by then Yavtar and Alexar had taken care of most of those guarding it. Bantor's men finished off the rest, leaving him no one to kill. He waited but a moment, until certain all of his men passed inside, before moving ahead through the twisted lanes, straight toward the barracks. His sword clenched tight in his hand, he yearned to encounter his enemy.

Halting before the last turn, he let his men catch up. Counting himself, Bantor only had twenty-four soldiers, since he'd left Alexar and Yavtar to hold the river gate. According to Rebba, there were at least forty or fifty Egyptians at the barracks, along with another twenty or thirty misfits recruited by Ariamus. To have any chance against such odds, Bantor needed not only to set free the prisoners, but to capture the weapons storehouse, as much to deny Korthac's men access to them. For all this to work, Bantor had to catch his enemy by surprise.

Keeping within the shadows, he peered around the corner. The soldiers' barracks, a collection of low huts formed into a half-circle around the training ground, looked peaceful enough. The remains of a watch fire flickered a few paces outside the leftmost structure, a handful of guards standing around it. Farthest away and facing him, he could just make out at least four guards walking posts at the smaller barracks, the building that, according to Rebba, held the prisoners.

Most of Korthac's men slept in the main barracks, the only structure large enough in Akkad to hold so many men. Bantor saw three more guards a few paces from the barracks' entrance, tending the fire that now barely glowed. As soon as dawn rose, those guards would wake the sleeping foreigners inside, so Bantor had to move now. One guard looked toward the lane that led to the river gate, no doubt curious about the occasional shout coming from that direction. But not yet curious enough to sound the alarm.

"We're ready," Klexor said moments later, his voice a whisper in Bantor's ear.

"Take your men straight to the small barracks," Bantor said. "Free the prisoners. Ignore everything else. I'll take care of the Egyptians."

Bantor had given Klexor ten of the men, leaving himself with only fourteen to face the Egyptians.

"Good hunting, then," Klexor whispered, as he strung a shaft to his bow.

Bantor took a deep breath, and broke into a run, heading straight at the fire. The moment the first guard looked up, Bantor voiced his battle cry. "Eskkar has returned! Death to the invaders!"

Behind him, his men took up the war cry, heavy feet pounding the dirt in the lane. The guard tending the fire reacted slowly, staring wide-eyed into the darkness for a moment before fumbling for his weapon. The man's sword hadn't even cleared its scabbard when Bantor cut him down, feeling the blade he'd sharpened each day bite deep into the man's shoulder. Wrenching it free, he whirled on the next man, blocking his stroke and slashing at his face. The first screams of the night pierced the air, mixing with the confused shouts of disoriented men. Bantor's soldiers pushed past him, and the last guard broke and ran, ducking back into the barracks.

The main barracks, capable of domiciling forty men, housed Korthac's foreigners. Bantor ran toward the opening, just as a handful of men stumbled out the door, weapons in hand. An arrow killed one in the doorway. Then Bantor reached the Egyptians, swinging his sword with fury and striking at every man in his path.

The foreigners, still half asleep, pushed their way through the barracks door by sheer force of numbers and attempted to form a line. But arrows flew from out of the shadows, cutting them down before they could organize themselves. At such close range, the archers had little need to aim, and the lethal shafts flew off their bowstrings with such rapidity that the Egyptians thought they faced a hundred archers.

His fury raging and ignoring the arrows flashing past his head, Bantor fought his way through, determined to fight his way into the barracks. With each kill, he shouted Eskkar's name.

The Egyptians recoiled before battle-crazed Bantor and his men, abandoning the effort to form a battle line. Five more of the enemy died before they managed to retreat back into the barracks and slam the door shut.

Cursing, Bantor threw himself against the door, but it didn't move, and he knew at least half a dozen men stood behind it, holding it fast. He heard the sounds of pallets being shoved against the door. From within, a trumpet rang out, sending its muffled warning notes into the night, waking the city and announcing to all that Akkad was under attack.

Bantor glanced about him, as his men, bows drawn, watched the two narrow ventilation windows set high in the wall. The surprise attack had trapped the Egyptian fighters inside, and now Bantor was determined to keep these foes penned in. Stepping away from the barracks' entrance, he looked first down the lane, then at Klexor's men. In the lane he saw no one, certainly no armed and trained reinforcements rushing to aid Korthac's men. Less than fifty paces away, Klexor and his bowmen poured arrows into anything that moved, attacking the smaller barracks. Bantor saw men running away into the darkness, a good sign, for now.

Bantor had to hope that Klexor's force succeeded. He'd felt certain that at least half of the bandits and farmers recruited from the countryside by Ariamus and quartered in the two smaller structures would flee at the first sign of trouble, some toward Eskkar's house, others toward the main gate. They didn't matter, not right now. Bantor had to destroy these Egyptians before they could organize a defense or escape.

"Surround the barracks! They may try to break through the wall. Get to the roof," Bantor shouted. "Use fire on the roof. Burn them out! Don't let any escape. Hurry!"

A soldier raced to the fire pit and began tossing more wood on the fire. The low flames dimmed for a few moments, then the fresh wood caught and the flames began to build. The archers fanned out, all of them facing the structure with their bows ready. The barracks had only the one entrance, and the single window on the opposite side was too small for a man to climb through.

Shouts of rage came from within the barracks. Bantor couldn't believe his luck. He'd trapped forty or so of these Egyptians in a single building. If he could hold them there a few moments longer . . .

"Cover the door," he shouted. "And get some archers on that roof." He pointed with his sword at the soldiers' storehouse, a smaller structure open on two sides. Battle-axes, shields, spears, and other weapons were stacked within, only a few paces away from the main barracks. Meanwhile, the watch fire crackled under its load of fresh fuel, and thick smoke began to trail up into the sky, already showing a rosy glow to the east. It wouldn't be long before the flames took hold.

The barracks' door suddenly flew open. Three arrows flashed out into the Akkadian line. One shaft flew right past Bantor's ear, and an archer two steps away groaned and fell to the ground. His men returned the fire, but the door had already been pulled closed, leaving nearly a dozen shafts protruding from the wooden portal.

Bantor opened his mouth to berate his men, but they'd already adjusted, some cursing at themselves, others shifting positions and readying for the next attack. They'd not be caught so easily next time.

"Bantor! Is it you?"

He turned to find three men stumbling toward him. It took a moment before he recognized Jarack and two other Hawk Clan members from Eskkar's household guard. They appeared unsteady, and marks from the lash covered their nearly naked bodies.

"Give us weapons, Bantor," Jarack demanded, his hand on Bantor's arm. "We can fight."

"Take charge of those we've freed," Bantor said. "Arm yourself from the storehouse. Bring out shields and spears for my men. We'll need them in a moment."

"No, we want . . ."

Bantor grabbed Jarack by the arm and pushed him toward the storehouse. "Go!"

The barracks' door flew open again, but this time Bantor's archers were ready. Their arrows flew into the darkened interior. Only one shaft, aimed high, came out. But a wave of men burst out, the ones in front carrying shields, and they hurled themselves toward the Akkadians, shouting war cries.

From the storehouse roof above them, four archers who had just reached their positions fired their shafts into the Korthac's fighters' backs, knocking down the first two shielded men emerging from the barracks. That gave Bantor's archers more targets. They brought down another two men before the leader of the charging Egyptians reached Bantor's sword.

He caught the savage overhand thrust on his own weapon, then used one of Eskkar's favorite tactics, stepping forward and slamming his shoulder in the man's shield, halting the man's advance. Before the man could regain either his balance or his momentum, Bantor's short sword swept over the top of the shield and thrust deep into the man's chest, at the base of the neck.

With a scream the man dropped his sword, clutching at his wound. Wrenching his blade free, Bantor faced another attacker, but this man was already dying, another shaft flashing down from the storehouse roof into the man's back. Their charge broken before most of them got clear of the doorway and their leader dead, the Egyptians fell back once again to their barracks. Again the door slammed shut, leaving one cursing man trapped outside, pounding on the door for entry, before two shafts in his back brought him down. The body slumped directly before the opening, and Bantor grunted in satisfaction. The Egyptians would have to step over their own dead to reach his men next time.

"Bantor, the fire's ready," a voice called out.

"Burn the roof, then."

Jarack returned carrying a large wooden shield and three spears, another three or four former prisoners carrying similar burdens behind him. More men appeared, all carrying weapons of one sort or another, and Bantor realized some villagers had entered the compound and helped themselves to the same weapons supply.

The first firebrand mounted up into the sky, to fall downward onto the barracks' roof. Another followed in its trail, then more smoked their way onto the roof, flung by the hands of arriving villagers. These alighted on the structure, and the mix of wood and straw ignited almost at once. Fresh fire shot up into the sky.

Bantor glanced down at the ground before him, counting the dead Egyptians. Eight bodies lay in the dirt, most with arrows protruding from them. Three carried shields, something that wouldn't normally be kept in the crowded barracks. So the Egyptians had their swords and knives, a few bows, and not much else.

Another villager arrived, this one carrying a spear. He knelt on the ground right beside an archer, angling the spear point up, protecting the bowman, and no doubt well trained in how to rise up and thrust the weapon at any charging foe. Another villager arrived and did the same, and Bantor saw Jarack standing back at the storehouse, directing more villagers while he handed out more weapons.

With a loud snapping noise, a wave of fire engulfed the barracks' roof, and the bright flames added their light to the deepening dawn.

Klexor arrived, bringing most of his archers with him.

"The prisoners are free, Bantor," he shouted, already having to raise his voice over the crackle of flames. "We lost a few men, but the rabble fled."

"Spread your men out," Bantor ordered. "Get a few more up on the storehouse roof. The Egyptians will be coming out soon."

Bantor saw nearly twenty liberated soldiers stumbling behind Alexar. Most of them looked exhausted and scarcely able to stand, weakened by long hours of slave labor with little food.

"Give them your bows," Bantor ordered. Even in their weakened condition, these men would still be able to loose a shaft. At this distance, a bowman didn't need to draw back an arrow very far.

He stepped away from the front line, and took a moment to look around him. More townspeople were joining the fight, carrying makeshift weapons or swords they obtained one way or another. The freed prisoners would help, too. If the blaze didn't roast the Egyptians alive, his men, shooting down into the house, would start killing them. Korthac's vaunted fighters were going to be slaughtered.

"Klexor, finish off the ones here. I'll take my men and head toward Eskkar's house. Follow when you can."

Calling out to his men, Bantor turned and jogged off, half the soldiers falling in reluctantly behind him. They wanted to see the Egyptians burn. The first section of the roof fell into the barracks, mixing with the screams of men trapped beneath the burning sections. From the rooftops, the archers began firing, shooting at anything that moved inside. Bantor ignored it all, shouting for his men to follow him. Ariamus wasn't inside. Bantor would have recognized the man's bellow anywhere.

This time Bantor ran as hard as he could, twelve of his original fourteen men close on his heels. The alarm had sounded, and now speed mattered more than anything else. Men would be fighting at Eskkar's house, and Korthac's men would be rallying there. Bantor hoped he had enough men.

A man, sword in hand, stepped out of a house into his path. Bantor struck him down, hardly slowing, and not caring if he were friend or foe.

Every moment counted. He must get to Eskkar's house. If Ariamus wasn't at the barracks, he would be there, or nearby. Bantor knew the man's character. Ariamus would look to his leader Korthac for direction. He'd fight hard enough, but only while he felt certain he could win. The moment the fight became too risky, Ariamus would do what he always did when danger got too close—melt away into the darkness. This time Bantor intended to make sure the wily former captain of the guard didn't get away.

So Bantor pushed the pace, covering the narrow lanes, his sword flashing up and down in the moonlight, while behind him his men filled the streets with their battle cries. "Eskkar has returned. Let none escape!"

Eskkar counted on him to break into the compound. Eskkar and his handful of men, if they still lived, couldn't hold out long, not against all of Korthac's fighters quartered there. "Faster, men," he shouted, lifting the sword high to lead the way.

27

Drakis watched as Enkidu and his men used the stakes taken from the wagon to brace the bottom of the cart's wheel, levering it halfway into the opening, creating an effective barrier against anyone trying to enter.

Satisfied that the wagon couldn't simply be pulled aside, Enkidu turned toward him. "Are you wounded, Drakis?"

"No, just out of breath. Can you hold the base of the tower?"

"Yes, for now. They'll not be able to force it easily, if our archers can cover us from the top of the tower. Leave me five men, and take the rest up top."

"Is that enough to hold here?"

"Any more would just get in the way," Enkidu said. "And we found some spears in the corner."

Spears could be even more effective than swords at close-quarters fighting. Taking a precious moment to clasp Enkidu on the shoulder, Drakis turned toward the steps, as Enkidu's men kept shoving and pushing, trying to wedge the wagon tighter into the tower entrance. By now, most of the front wheel stood inside the opening. Enkidu was right. Even with plenty of men, the wagon wouldn't be easy to drag aside, especially if defended. Already two men had taken up their bows, standing ready on either side of the barricade, searching for targets. Another returned lugging an armful of spears, then leaned them against the wall, ready for use.

"Hold them off, Enkidu. Send word if you need help."

Leaving five men with Enkidu, Drakis led the rest back up the stairs, warning them to keep their heads low when they emerged on the battlement. To his surprise, the night's darkness had given way to dawn's first light, and he looked toward the east to see rays of gold pushing up into the sky, the sun itself just below the horizon.

The streets below remained dark, sheltered from the rising sun by the wall and tower. An arrow hissed over his head. On the battlement Tarok, Drakis's second in command and a seasoned veteran, had organized the men, all of them crouched below the battlement facing the opposite tower.

"We've lost two men, Drakis. One dead, and the other has an arrow in his arm. Useless. But we've killed five or six of them. They must be Korthac's Egyptians." Tarok sneaked a quick look over the battlement for a moment, then turned back to his leader. "What's happening below?"

"We've blocked the entrance with a wagon. Enkidu will hold the doorway, if we can support him from here."

"We're almost ready to begin," Tarok said. "I've been waiting for dawn, so we could see them better. They'll make easy targets. You keep watching the ones below."

Drakis looked eastward. A rosy red glow lit the horizon,

and the sun's edge would be flooding the land with light any moment now. He took a quick count of the men. Counting himself, he had fifteen archers who could draw a bow.

In a soft voice, Tarok explained to the latest arrivals what he planned to do. Then he arranged the men in two ranks of seven, arrows strung, waiting for the order to attack. Tarok nocked his own shaft and readied himself alongside the first rank.

"Now," Tarok said. The first rank rose up as one man, picked their targets, and fired, ducking back down as soon as the shafts flew free. In the same motion, the second rank stood, arrows already drawn to their ears. These men searched for targets before shooting.

The first volley disrupted the men in the other tower. Now the second volley, carefully aimed at any target that showed itself, targets less than thirty paces away, snapped out across the gate.

Drakis had under his command most of the best archers in Akkad, second only to Mitrac and his chosen few. Drakis's marksmen had no trouble hitting a man's head at that distance, even at first light. He peered across the wall. The first volley might not have struck anyone, but the second killed two or three of the enemy. Again the first rank rose up, shafts drawn, but found nothing to shoot at.

Korthac's soldiers might be fierce fighters, they might even be using the same bows that Drakis's men carried, but the Egyptians hadn't practiced hours each day for months. Today they faced archers schooled in volley firing, with muscles strong enough to hold an arrow to the ear while counting to fifty, if necessary. More important, months of training had given the Akkadians pride in their skills, and they weren't about to cower before some foreigners holding bows.

Drakis saw something move on the other tower and heard the snapping of bowstrings as seven arrows flashed across the open space between them.

The archers ducked down again, to nock another shaft. The second rank took their place without a word, searching for targets. But there weren't any, and Drakis gave a sigh of relief. Perhaps this would be easy enough after all.

"Tarok, can you sweep the tower with half the men? I need the rest to cover the entrance and the gate."

"Yes, for now. If I need help . . ."

"You'll have it," Drakis said. In a moment, he had his men moving, shifting them to the rear of the battlement, where they could look down into the square. Because their flank would be exposed to fire from the other tower, they would have to depend on Tarok's bowmen to protect them. Drakis didn't like fighting like this, with his flank unprotected, but at least he could cover the approach to the tower.

As Drakis searched for enemies below, an arrow struck the wall a foot beneath his head before glancing off the tower. Below him, a mix of bowmen and men carrying swords jostled about, getting ready to rush his position, gathering in nearly the same spot Drakis had used to launch his own assault.

"We have to hold them off, keep them from forcing the entrance below," Drakis said, as he lined up his men on either side. "Aim for the archers first." Picking up his bow and stringing a shaft, he gave one last look toward the other tower.

"Now!"

They rose up together and loosed eight arrows into the bandits assembling below. Some fired back. A few arrows rattled against the wall, but most flew overhead. It would take them a shot or two to find the range, and Drakis, like every archer, knew how difficult it was to shoot uphill. His men ignored the counterfire, and kept launching shafts into the enemy fighters, pouring shafts down as fast as they could, and trying to kill off anyone carrying a bow. Under that rapid fire, the exposed men below scattered, some running back down the street, others ducking into houses or hiding behind anything they could find.

The Akkadians fired a few more arrows at anything that moved. Finally Drakis saw nothing to shoot at, and he let his bow go slack as he studied the square beneath him. He couldn't see anyone, but knew his enemy was gathering just out of sight. If he'd captured both towers, his archers could have swept the lane with arrows. Again he cursed the fates that hadn't let him arrive a few moments earlier. Still, he thanked the gods that only bandits had defended this tower, not Korthac's desert fighters.

He wondered about Eskkar. In the distance, he could hear the shouts and battle cries rising and falling, most of them coming from the direction of the barracks. Hopefully, Bantor and his men would be in the city. If things did not go well for Bantor, Drakis and his men would be trapped up here, cut off with no way to escape. He tightened his grip on his bow. He'd know about that soon enough. Right now there was nothing Drakis could do, except wait for the next attack.

Takany watched Ariamus and Hathor leave the courtyard, glad to be rid of both of them. If Ariamus survived this night, if Hathor didn't kill the man, Takany vowed to kill both of them himself. Even if Hathor did kill Ariamus, Takany decided he wanted Hathor dead anyway. The man had questioned his decisions before, and now wanted to leave Korthac behind. Takany knew one thing. The gate must be defended. Without control of the gate, they couldn't stop more troops from entering Akkad. This Eskkar might have hundreds of men out there, just waiting for the gate to open.

Shaking his head, he put both men out of his mind. Instead, he cursed the evil demons who'd attacked the house at night, catching everyone still asleep or lax at their posts. These Akkadians were too cowardly to challenge his men in daylight, when his men could slaughter them with ease.

Looking about, Takany found the last handful of men still gathering up weapons and lacing on sandals. To his satisfaction, with the number of men in the courtyard halved, the situation improved. The twenty or so fighters remaining knew their work. They'd recapture the house soon enough. Takany knew he had to move quickly, before something happened to Korthac, though in the back of his mind Takany started considering life without Korthac.

If these weaklings had killed Korthac, Takany would take charge of Akkad, and he swore a curse on the city's inhabitants for this attack. He'd kill so many that none of them would ever dare rise from their knees again.

Leaving a handful of soldiers to guard the kitchen door and prevent any escape that way, Takany readied his men, moving those carrying shields to the forefront. Spearmen followed behind them, and six or seven archers would bring up the rear. Hathor had taken most of the bowmen with him. Bows wouldn't be of much use inside the house.

"Once we start in," Takany shouted, moving up and down in front of his men, "there must be no hesitation. Go straight up to the landing and kill everyone in your path." He took a deep breath, hefted his shield. "Now!"

Six men stood ready with the courtyard table. They'd positioned it a few paces from the door. Now they picked it up and charged the door, using it as a battering ram and smashing it against the door with all their strength. The heavy table, made of thick planks, split part of the doorway with the first attempt. Takany heard men shouting behind the door. They knew what was coming.

"Good," Takany yelled. "Hit it again."

The men battered the door again, the sound of ripping wood adding to the din. The third time smashed the door open, snapping the bar that braced it, and knocking aside a table the defenders had shoved up against it.

Arrows flew through the splintered doorway. One of the men closest to the door sank to his knees, a shaft in his chest. The rest of Takany's soldiers moved back.

"Shields, get those shields up front," Takany shouted.

Other men moved forward, carrying shields and holding swords, ready to face the danger they knew lay within. A few carried the heavy Akkadian bows. Once inside, if they could get their weapons in play, they'd wreak havoc on any defenders trapped on the landing.

"Attack!"

The men surged forward, the human wedge knocking the last of the door from the frame as they rushed inside. Arrows struck down the first two men through the doorway, head shots that slowed the Egyptians only for a moment. They knew the fastest way to end the battle was to rush in and kill everyone, so the Egyptians ignored their losses.

Standing just outside, Takany made sure the last of his fighters had surged through the door before following him inside. Raising his shield, Takany followed his fighters in, shouting at them to push ahead. "Kill them all," he roared, "get close and finish them."

His men took up the cry, the fearful words echoing throughout the chamber. "Kill them all!"

Muttering a curse at Takany's stupidity, Hathor stepped through the courtyard gate, pushing along the last straggler of those he'd ordered to the main gate. The fool had knelt in the dirt to fasten his sandal. "Leave that, you ox," Hathor ordered, shoving the man into a run. He'd sent ahead more than twenty-five men, more than enough to recapture the tower. Unlike Takany, Hathor had decided that Eskkar and his men numbered far fewer than the supposed "hundreds" that Takany feared lurked outside the gate. Otherwise Eskkar wouldn't have let himself get trapped inside Korthac's house. Probably Eskkar had slipped into the city with a few men, and hoped to raise the inhabitants.

By the time Hathor broke into a run, most of his men had already disappeared up the lane. He wanted to catch up before anything else went wrong. Turning the corner, Hathor and the soldier nearly stumbled over the dead body of one of his men lying in the lane.

Hathor slowed for a moment, looking down at the body, but a shout raised Hathor's eyes, and he saw another of his soldiers take down some Akkadians, both of them falling against the side of a house.

"Look, he's killed one of our . . ."

"Forget him," Hathor ordered. "Get to the gate." He shoved the man ahead with one hand and drew his sword with the other as he approached the two bodies. The downed Egyptian appeared dead or unconscious, but the weight of his body still pinned his stunned attacker to the ground. Hathor raised his sword, but someone screamed behind him. Whirling around, he saw a young woman, a knife in her hand, rushing at him. Off balance, he swung the sword at her head, but she ducked beneath, darting past him and throwing herself across both bodies, trying to protect her man. The knife had fallen from her hand as she landed, and now she fumbled in the dirt trying to recover it.

Although surprised at her courage, Hathor didn't care. They would both die. He took a step and raised the sword. As he did so, the woman gazed up at him, her eyes wide with fear.

"En-hedu," he said, recognizing the leather seller from Korthac's lane. He even remembered her name.

"Hathor. No!" She raised her arm to protect herself, as her eyes locked on to his.

Speaking his name wouldn't save her. The sword came

down. At the last moment, however, he turned the blade aside, striking the ground a finger width from her ear and knocking the dirt of the lane into her face and hair. For an instant, they stared at each other.

Hathor broke the spell. "Get back to your house, you fool!" The words surprised him as much as En-hedu, who looked up at him in bewilderment, her mouth open.

Then a stone, flung by someone in the crowd, flew past his head and rattled against the wall. A few villagers approached, shouting curses and threats at him. Another stone cracked against the wall. He had no more time to waste. Cursing himself for a soft-hearted fool, he raced away, heading toward the gate.

Behind him, cheers arose as the crowd saw the Egyptian running away.

Shocked, En-hedu watched him go, her heart still pounding with fear. She knew how close to death she'd come. A man and a woman reached her side, and lifted her up. Her legs felt weak and she could scarcely stand. Together they pushed the dead Egyptian aside, the one Tammuz had killed. En-hedu wrapped her arms around Tammuz. More people joined her rescuers, and two men gathered up Tammuz. Blood flowed from a large gash over her master's temple. A woman beckoned them from the doorway of the nearest house, and in a moment, En-hedu and Tammuz found themselves dragged inside its cool walls. For Tammuz and En-hedu, the fighting had ended.

Inside Eskkar's house, Mitrac fired shafts as fast as his fingers could snatch the arrows from his quiver and fit them to the string. The enemy had burst in and driven them back to the landing. Already Grond was hard-pressed at the base of the stairs. An arrow smacked into the door, just missing Mitrac's face, and another struck one of his archers on the step below. Mitrac heard the man cry out as he fell from the steps. But forced back onto the stairs, his back to the door to Eskkar's private quarters, Mitrac had nowhere to hide.

He knew his only chance lay in killing all the Egyptian archers before they killed him. So Mitrac picked his targets carefully, first selecting the enemy archers, making sure they launched no arrows of their own, but still shooting so fast that he and his last two men seemed like a dozen. Despite his haste, Eskkar's words always rang in his thoughts. "Shoot the leaders, Mitrac, and the men will lose heart."

Another shadow blocked the entrance to the house for a moment. Mitrac glanced up just as the doorway cleared. A lone warrior, a man as tall as Eskkar, stood behind the attackers, shouting in a booming voice and driving them onward, ordering them to press the attack.

Without hesitation, Mitrac shifted his aim from the spearman he'd been about to kill to the enemy leader. That warrior carried a shield held high, just below his eyes. Without conscious thought, the shaft flew from the twanging string, the arrow gliding a hand's width over the lucky spearman's head and slipping under the upraised shield by a finger's breadth, before burying itself into the man's belly, just beside the hip bone.

Before the shaft landed, Mitrac had drawn another, killing a man with a spear trying to skewer Grond at the foot of the stairs. Mitrac never noticed the Egyptian commander stagger back against the doorframe, dropping his sword to grasp at the arrow feathered low in his belly.

With a scream of pain and rage, Takany bent double, trying to grip the heavy shaft that clutched and burned at his insides as if someone had shoved a torch deep within his body. He stumbled back through the door into the courtyard, then tripped and fell, the shaft brushing against the dirt and sending another wave of pain through his body. Agony seized him, and he cried out for help, but his words disappeared in the confusion, as inside the house, his men still sought to fight their way up the stairs, most of them unaware of their leader's wound.

Takany tasted dirt of the earth in his mouth even as he breathed its dust into his lungs. The pain increased, and a wave of dizziness went over him. His own blood, as hot as if it came from a fire, covered his hands. The gods of the underworld had called out for his spirit, demanding that he come to them. Takany knew he was dying here in this foreign place, after all the fights and all the years of killing, dying with the strange taste of an unfamiliar land in his mouth.

He opened his mouth to call out, but he could no longer control his voice. Despite the dawn's growing light, his eyes refused to focus. He stopped moving, suddenly light-headed, as if he were falling from a great height. All he could do was gaze upward toward the sky, unable even to blink, watching the dawn beginning to burst over the city. He felt his blood soaking his hands and stomach, pooling between his naked legs, his life's blood pouring out into the dirt. It was the last thought he ever had.

Takany died unnoticed by his men, who fought on against the few Akkadians still standing between them and the doorway. They could feel the defense weakening, and only two bowmen remained on the landing. The storm of arrows had nearly ended, as the Akkadians emptied their quivers. Step by step, the Egyptians fought their way up the stairs, sensing victory within their grasp.

Suddenly the door behind the archers opened, a rectangle of soft light illuminating the landing. Everyone's eyes lifted to see who stood there. One glance answered the question. A tall, blood-spattered warrior holding two swords that glinted in the growing light appeared, slipping behind the archers and pointing a long horseman's sword at them.

"Korthac is dead," the warrior roared, the words filling the room. The fighting paused for a moment, just long enough for the warrior to repeat his words. "Korthac is dead!"

Every Egyptian flinched at the sound, knowing an evil omen filled the house. "Korthac is dead, and now you will all die as well."

Not all the Egyptians understood the meaning, but all of them recognized Korthac's name, and they all comprehended the truth of the message. Korthac must be dead, or he, not this barbarian demon, would stand before them.

The warrior bellowed something unintelligible, then jumped off the landing, practically in the midst of the

Egyptians, attacking them with a fury that saw two men struck down in as many heartbeats. The Akkadians, arrows exhausted and about to be overwhelmed, took heart, and began their own counterattack. Disheartened, the Egyptians fell back. The battle gods had turned against them. No one wanted to face the certain death awaiting anyone who dared to challenge their battle-enraged opponent.

In moments, the common room emptied, as the Egyptians shoved and pushed their way through the outer door and into the courtyard. The last man had barely cleared the door when someone picked up the table knocked over when the door was forced, and shoved it upright against the doorway, blocking the opening.

In the courtyard, less than a dozen of Korthac's fighters remained alive, plus an equal number of Ariamus's men. They'd seen Eskkar come out of Korthac's room alone, proclaiming their leader's death. A handful of battle-crazed archers had somehow driven them from the house, shooting shafts so quickly that they seemed like twice their number.

The Egyptians shouted at each other in confusion. Meanwhile, the sound of Eskkar's name rang through the city, taken up by hundreds of voices, a nonstop chant that filled the lanes and echoed across the rooftops, rattling their nerves. Takany, in a pool of blood, lay dead at their feet, an arrow buried in his stomach. Hathor and Ariamus had departed for the gate. Nebibi was at the barracks. Most of the senior men were dead.

Without anyone to give orders, the Egyptians began to argue. Some wanted to charge the house once again, others wanted to link up with Hathor at the gate. More than a few just wanted to flee. Korthac's death unnerved them. Korthac had survived a hundred fights. If he could be killed, then who might be next? Without a leader, they started drifting toward the courtyard gate, and in a moment all of them began moving. They rushed out of the courtyard and into the lane, heading for the main gate. Before they'd taken a dozen steps, they ran directly into Bantor and his men charging up the lane.

The street outside Eskkar's courtyard erupted with the Akkadians' battle cry. Bantor led his men up the lane, his bloody sword flashing in the morning sun, his men strung out behind him. The charging Akkadians in front had no time to draw their bows; instead they snatched swords from scabbards and smashed into the surprised Egyptians before they could form a line. For a moment Bantor's attack slowed, as bronze clashed upon bronze, men cursing as they fought. Korthac's men still outnumbered their attackers.

Bantor, engaged in a furious sword fight with a thickset Egyptian, lifted his voice. "Archers! Aim for their faces!" The archer struggling behind Bantor finally got his bow in play. The shaft nearly took off Bantor's ear, but the Egyptian screamed as the arrow took him in the mouth; the wounded man staggered back.

With a scream of satisfaction, Bantor pushed ahead. "Aim for their faces! Kill them all!"

Another arrow struck, then another. Rapidly fired arrows launched at point-blank range struck down the Egyptians, while Bantor and a handful of men up front protected the bowmen from assault. The shafts, many launched directly into the enemy's faces, took the fight out of them.

Unable to close with the archers, some of Korthac's men abandoned the fight and started to retreat up the lane. Already more than half of them had taken wounds or been struck down. The rest broke, turned, and ran back toward Eskkar's courtyard. Some fled past Eskkar's gate, disappearing from sight as the lane twisted and turned, but others ducked back inside, seeking safety. Before they could shut the gate, an arrow brought down the last straggler, an Egyptian already wounded, and the man's dead body blocked the opening.

Bantor, his face covered in blood splatter, flung his shoulder against the gate even as the surviving Egyptians struggled to shut it. In a moment the rest of Bantor's men added their weight and forced the gate open. Bantor stumbled through, ducking under a wildly swung blade and falling to his knees. Before his attacker could recover, Bantor had thrust his sword into the man's stomach.

Bows were forgotten as the Akkadians forced their way in, sword clashing against sword. Outnumbered now for the first time, the Egyptians fought back, knowing their fate should they be defeated; for a moment, they stopped Bantor's advance, and the sound of clashing arms rose up throughout the courtyard.

"Eskkar! Annok-sur," Bantor bellowed, the words echoing off the compound's walls. He wanted those in the house to know that help had arrived. "Eskkar!" he yelled again, as he redoubled his efforts against those facing him.

Arrows began killing Korthac's followers from behind. Most of the Egyptians fought to the end, but those recruited by Ariamus had no stomach for this kind of close-in fighting. They ran, throwing away their weapons and scrambling up and over the courtyard wall. Desperate to escape, they fled through lanes and even houses, searching for any path, as long as it led away from the fighting.

Bantor killed the last Egyptian facing him. Glancing around the courtyard, his eyes searched the dead, looking for Ariamus.

"Ariamus!" he shouted. "Where are you?"

It must be Bantor," Eskkar said. The clash of men fighting out in the lane sounded clearly even inside the house. "Shove that table aside."

With Mitrac's help, Eskkar cleared the hasty barricade erected only moments ago from the door, while the two surviving archers stood behind, bows at the ready. Grond tried to move to Eskkar's side, but slipped to the floor, his wounds weakening him. Mitrac nocked his bow as Eskkar lifted his sword, then shoved the table clear, ducking back as he did so.

One glance told Eskkar all he needed to know. The courtyard was filled with men fighting. Some bellowed war cries and others screamed in pain from their wounds, but this time more than half the combatants were shouting Akkadian war cries. He started forward but Mitrac caught his tunic.

"No, stay here," Mitrac said, pulling Eskkar away from the doorway. He stood just inside the doorway, and fired an arrow into the back of an Egyptian standing only a few paces away. The other two archers moved up behind him, and added their shafts, shooting over Mitrac's head. Standing with his sword ready, Eskkar watched as Mitrac and his bowmen started the final slaughter, the three of them picking off targets. With every shot, an enemy died, as the carefully aimed shafts took down any who still sought to stand their ground.

A voice rose up over the clamor. "Eskkar! Annok-sur!"

Eskkar saw Bantor leading the attack, his sword slashing at everyone before him. "Cover him," he ordered Mitrac, who shifted his bow to put a shaft into Bantor's opponent. A few more shots from the doorway, and the Egyptians broke, unable to withstand swordsmen in front and archers behind. The last of the enemy ran for the rear, frantic to scale the courtyard wall before an arrow took them. A few attempted to make a stand in the quarters across from Eskkar's house. But without solid doors, the soldiers' quarters provided only temporary security. More of Bantor's men brought their bows back into play, shooting through the doorways and windows.

Overwhelmed, the last few Egyptians died or threw down their swords, calling out for mercy, their cries for leniency barely audible against the roar of cheering men. A few ran back into their quarters, desperate to regroup, but most dropped to their knees, pleading for mercy, begging to be spared, anything to avoid being killed by their battle-mad opponents.

Eskkar stepped out from the doorway, Mitrac at his side, an arrow still nocked on his string, his eyes searching for danger. The courtyard seemed covered in bodies, most of them with arrows sticking out of them. Nearly all seemed to be Egyptians. Bantor, his chest heaving and his eyes wild from the battle madness, finally recognized his leader.

Bantor stood there, blood covering his right arm and splattered all over his face and chest. But his smile belied the blood, and he raised his sword high as the cheering men rushed past him to Eskkar's side. Their jubilation turned into a deafening roar at the sight of their commander.

With the fighting ended, at least at Eskkar's house, the dirty, bloody, and battle-weary men looked at each other in the bright morning light. Their voices turned into a chant that grew in volume, as the men shouted "Eskkar! Eskkar! Eskkar!" at the top of their lungs. The cheer went on and on, until Eskkar thought it would never end. Half the city could hear the words, and would know that Korthac had been defeated.

The wounded needed to be tended, and the fighting wasn't over yet. Eskkar saw Klexor, who'd just reached the house, and pulled him away from the delirious soldiers.

"Take charge here," Eskkar ordered. "Get the men organized and secure the courtyard."

His smile never changing, Klexor nodded and began bellowing orders.

Eskkar grabbed Bantor's arm and led him back inside the house. Mitrac was already there, tending Grond's wounds. Covered in blood, most of it his own, Eskkar's bodyguard appeared ready to collapse. The fighting had raged back and forth across the room. Wreckage of the big table littered the floor, and one of the benches had been smashed. But Eskkar found one still whole, and righted it as Mitrac and Bantor lifted Grond up and laid him out on the bench. Just enough light filtered in to show three separate wounds.

"Find the women and the healers," Eskkar said. "They must be nearby. Get them here at once." He grabbed one of Bantor's men. "Stand here and guard these steps. Trella and Annok-sur are above."

Bantor, his bloody sword held loosely in his hand, approached. "Annok-sur, where is she? Is she . . . ?"

"She's upstairs, with Trella, guarding Korthac. She's all right, only a knock on the head," Eskkar said. "Did you find Ariamus?"

"Isn't he dead?" Bantor's voice hardened and he straightened up, the fatigue dropping from his shoulders. He stopped moving toward the steps. "Tell Annok-sur I'll be back. I'll take some men and start hunting Ariamus down."

Eskkar's eyes narrowed at the tone of Bantor's voice. "No, Ariamus can wait. What's happened to Drakis? Is he still holding the towers?"

Bantor hesitated, then shook his head. "I don't know."

"Take your men to the main gate," Eskkar ordered, his voice firm. "Drakis may need you. If some of these Egyptians escape . . ." He saw Bantor hesitating, and shook his head. "Ariamus is wounded. In an hour the whole city will be looking for him. Drakis needs you now."

"Can't you go . . ."

"No, I'm staying here." With Korthac upstairs and this place recaptured, Eskkar knew his remaining soldiers would be coming to him, looking for orders. Besides, he didn't want to leave Trella and the child. He'd left Trella alone for weeks; he didn't plan to leave her again,

not to chase down a handful of foreign fighters whose cause
was lost.

"Damn the gods," Bantor said, rage back in his voice.
"I'll go to the gate. But I swear Ariamus won't get away
from me this time." Bantor shouted for Klexor. They
collected their men, nearly twenty of them, and jogged out
into the lane, heading for the gate.

As Eskkar turned back toward the stairs, Ventor the
healer entered the house, his eyes wide in amazement as he
took in the carnage and death. His frightened apprentice,
glancing nervously in every direction, followed carefully
behind, carrying his master's box of instruments. Eskkar
took Ventor by the arm and guided him toward the steps.
"Have your apprentice care for Grond. You attend to
Trella. She's upstairs, wounded."

Eskkar took the instrument box from the apprentice,
and used his other hand to half-carry the old healer up the
stairs and into the outer room.

"Annok-sur," Eskkar shouted, the sound filling the now
quiet workroom. "It's Eskkar. Open the door."

He heard the bar scrape, then fall to the floor with a
thud. The door swung open. The lamp still burned, but the
sun provided more than enough light. The baby had
stopped crying, held close and nursing in his mother's
bloody arms. Korthac lay where Eskkar had left him, still
unconscious. Annok-sur looked weak, but she still held
Korthac's knife over his motionless body. She nodded to
Eskkar and moved back to the foot of the bed, to maintain
her watch on the Egyptian.

Trella's eyes looked up at him. She seemed to have
trouble focusing, but then she recognized Eskkar and smiled.

"You're safe now, Trella," he said, kneeling next to the bed and taking her hand. "Korthac is taken and his men are being hunted down."

She nodded, and her body seemed to relax. Tears formed in the corners of her eyes. "Stay with me, Eskkar."

"I'll not leave you again, Trella, I swear it. Now let Ventor tend to you."

"Is Bantor alive?" Annok-sur asked, leaning over and holding her head with both hands, still holding the bloody knife.

"Very alive," Eskkar said. "He's gone off to hunt down Ariamus."

"Look at your son, Eskkar," Trella said, her words calling him back to her side.

Ventor moved to the other side of the bed. "Give me the child for a moment, Lady Trella." He gently lifted the child from her arms, then offered the babe to Annok-sur. She handed the knife to Eskkar, then took and held the infant close to her breast.

"Let Ventor tend to your wound, Trella," Eskkar said, stroking her hair for a moment.

She nodded, and her head fell back onto the bed. "Look at your son."

Eskkar took a step to Annok-sur's side, and peered down at the infant for a few moments. The child, its cheeks red and eyes screwed shut, looked very small.

"He looks well, Trella," Eskkar said, not sure what to say.

A moan from the floor turned his attention to Korthac, still lying there unmoving. Eskkar reached down and grasped the unconscious man by the shoulders and dragged him out of the bedroom, pulling him across the workroom

until he reached the top of the stairs. The soldier Eskkar
had ordered to guard the stairs still held his post at the foot
of the stairs. Just then two of the household's servants
stepped through the remains of the door, moving gingerly
past the bodies of the dead, their eyes wide at the sight of
all that blood and death.

"Get this filth out of my house," Eskkar said, letting
Korthac slump to the landing. Eskkar resisted the urge to
roll Korthac off the landing; the fall might kill him, and
that would be too easy a death. "Find three men to guard
him. They're to stay within arm's length of the Egyptian. If
he gives you any trouble, or anyone tries to rescue him,
kill him."

The soldier nodded.

Eskkar called down to the servants, and told them to
bring fresh blankets, water, and anything else they thought
Trella and Annok-sur would need. He turned back inside,
pushing the door closed to lessen the noise from the
courtyard.

Annok-sur didn't even look up when he returned, just
rocked slowly back and forth, trying to soothe the baby.
Ventor had pulled back the blanket from Trella's hips and
leaned over to examine her wound, his face inches from
the still-oozing cut.

"I'm afraid you'll need to change the bedding when I'm
done, Lord Eskkar," the old man said. "There must have
been much blood lost during the birthing."

Another woman, one of the regular servants, came into
the room, but left almost immediately as Ventor called for
bandages and fresh water.

Eskkar stood there, unsure of what to do. He wanted to

ask Ventor if Trella would live, but he knew better than to interrupt the healer with questions; the man would tell him as soon as he knew. The baby began to cry, and Annok-sur whispered soothingly to the infant. Ventor began wiping the blood from Trella's side, and Eskkar saw the wound from Korthac's knife. The slashing blow had struck a little above her hip.

The servant returned with water and linen. Ventor washed the gash, then wiped the blood from Trella's body before pressing the cloth against the wound. "She's still bleeding from the birthing, but not heavily. The wound is only a deep cut, and she won't be walking for a few days. I believe she will recover."

Eskkar exhaled a long sigh of relief. His wife would live. That was all that mattered.

Ventor's touch calmed Trella almost as much as his words. Her eyes closed, and she seemed to fall into a light sleep.

The healer worked swiftly. He cut up a clean part of the blanket and used it to bind Trella's wound. Then he washed the rest of the blood from her body.

Eskkar handed him the second blanket, and Ventor draped it gently over her, leaving only her head and shoulders exposed.

"She needs to rest for a few hours," Ventor said. "We'll know more then. I'll go tend to the other wounded." He stood and went to Annok-sur, gazing down at the child. "The baby seems healthy, though a bit small."

"The child is safe, Eskkar," Annok-sur said, ignoring Ventor's comment. "And so is Trella. The wound is not deep. But she's lost a lot of blood."

Eskkar muttered thanks to the gods. His wife would live, and he had a son. He'd captured Korthac, broken his men, and retaken Akkad. Eskkar started to shake, as much a reaction from worrying about Trella as from all the fighting. Suddenly his legs felt weary.

Annok-sur recognized the signs. Wincing from the effort, she lifted the baby up onto her shoulder. "Come outside, Eskkar. You can do nothing here. Let her rest for a few moments, to regain her strength."

Giving Trella one last look, Eskkar followed Annok-sur out of the bedroom, peering over her shoulder at his son's tiny face. For the first time, Eskkar felt the stirring of pride. He'd fathered a son, Sargon, who would carry on not only Eskkar's name but his descendants', those who would come afterward, down through the ages. The thought surprised him. Eskkar had never thought more than a few days ahead before, but now, the future appeared to stretch before him, the child showing the way. Somehow that seemed more important than Korthac's defeat.

28

Hathor and his Egyptians had finally gained control of the mob milling about the main gate. A handful of the cursed Akkadian archers had slipped into the city and captured the left tower, but his men still held the right. They reported no activity in the countryside outside the gate, no horde of fighters waiting for the gate to be flung open. Once again, Takany had chosen an unwise course of action. For a moment Hathor felt tempted to take his men and return to Korthac's house, but that would have provoked Takany beyond all reason. Better to finish the business here and then return, with the gate safe and under Hathor's control.

He had a rough count of the enemy who'd taken refuge in the tower, and knew he faced less than twenty men. Now Hathor needed to come to grips with them, to kill these intruders before the city turned against him.

He didn't have much time. Eskkar's name sounded everywhere around him, growing louder every minute as more and more people of Akkad took up the cry. Dawn had broken over the city's walls, exposing the full extent of the carnage at the gate. Bodies littered the open area, most with arrows protruding. Wounded men cried out for help, or tried to crawl to nearby houses seeking safety.

Hathor didn't know how Korthac had lost control of the city so quickly. No word had come from Nebibi, who'd slept at the barracks, or from Takany, since he'd ordered Hathor to the gate. He'd dispatched two runners, one to the barracks and one back to Korthac's house, but neither had returned and Hathor had no idea whether Korthac's men remained in control at either location. Not that it mattered. Right now, and for his own protection, Hathor needed to retake the gate from these Akkadians. He had more than enough men, but the longer Eskkar's men could hold Hathor at bay, the greater the danger to all of them.

One loud voice kept bellowing out Eskkar's name as a battle cry from the tower's top, the man's powerful lungs sending the name over half the city. The booming voice rattled his men, another evil omen that weakened their nerve. Hathor knew it wouldn't be long before all these cursed Akkadians rose up against them. If he failed to destroy these men in the next few moments, he, Korthac, all of them, might be overwhelmed by the city's enraged citizens. The last thing Hathor wanted was to be trapped inside Akkad.

Reinforcements kept arriving, swelling the number of fighters under his command. That would have reassured him, until Hathor discovered most of them had fled from fighting elsewhere. Apparently battles had been fought at the barracks as well as at Korthac's house. Hathor swore briefly at this demon Eskkar, and wondered how he and so many men had sneaked into the city.

Nevertheless, Hathor's veterans gathered all of Korthac's remaining followers who arrived, forced them to stand ready, and ordered them to obey his commands. Hathor, striding up and down before them, promised to kill any man who started to flee or who refused to fight. Already he had more than fifty men, half of them carrying bows, and the number continued to grow.

"We must recapture the tower," he called out in the language of Akkad. "From there we'll control the city." In Egyptian, he gave different orders. "Drive the cowards toward the gate. Let them take the arrows. Then we'll force the doorway." He still had men in the other tower, and they would add their efforts to his.

Hathor took one last look. He had enough men, and his own bowmen would at least keep the archers atop the tower pinned down. The sun's rays bathed the towers in a golden light. He gave the order, and, with a shout, they charged around the corner, everyone racing as fast as they could across the killing ground. Men fell, struck down by arrows, but only a few, and Hathor's fighters surged across the open space, calling out Korthac's name. The battle for the gates of Akkad had begun.

Drakis swore when he saw them coming, a horde of armed men that vastly outnumbered his force. At least the waiting had ended. His archers' arrows flashed out over the cart. Behind him, Enkidu waited on the first landing, with four archers standing single file on the steps below him, hugging the wall. If the Egyptians forced the opening, Drakis planned to retreat up the stairs fighting every step of the way, using bowmen to cover his retreat. They'd make their last stand atop the tower, where they could still control the gate.

The enemy surged across the open space and succeeded in reaching the base of the tower, ignoring their losses. The wagon shuddered in the opening, as the first of the attackers reached it, bodies slamming against its sides. Arrows flew, spear points flashed in the ever-growing sunrise, and wood creaked as a dozen of Korthac's men made every effort to muscle the wagon aside. But the thick wheel filled the entryway, and the strakes that braced it held fast. A spear hurtled through the opening, and one of Drakis's men screamed as the weapon took him in the chest. Another Akkadian wrenched the spear from the dying man, and flung the weapon back through the opening. The archers fired at any target—exposed faces, hands that tried to push the wagon aside, even their enemy's legs. But more took the place of those that fell wounded or dying, and Drakis realized that the barrier wouldn't keep them out much longer.

The wagon moved, stopped, and moved again. Drakis heard wood snapping, and knew the men outside were tearing the wagon to shreds with their bare hands, using force of numbers to pry it loose. The smell of blood rose up in the confined space, mixed with the heavy breath of men shouting and cursing at their enemies. The Akkadians shot at anything that moved, any target they could see, killing shots at such close range. But despite the havoc his archers inflicted, another man always took the place of those who died.

With a lurch, the clumsy cart shifted. A moment later, the last brace tore loose, and the rear of the cart wagon lurched a pace forward, dragged away from the opening with a loud screech of wood on wood. For a moment, that gave his archers better targets, and even as the opening grew wider, they poured arrows into the crowd of men outside, snapping shafts into their ranks.

Drakis had no idea how many they killed, but the attackers began to waver. Shouting encouragement at his men, he urged them to hold the barrier, even as he plied his bow, shooting at any target that offered itself. But by now Hathor's bowmen had reached the base of the tower. More than anyone, they understood that safety lay in forcing the entrance. They began shooting shafts through every opening.

The man beside Drakis dropped without a sound, an arrow through his eye. Drakis stepped up into the breach and shot three arrows as fast as he could. A scream of pain rewarded him, and he kept firing, shooting at anything he could see, an arm, a leg, even a sword. He had to hold these men off, drive them back, hold until relieved. Nevertheless, half his men had fallen or taken wounds, those unable to draw a bow moving up the stairs to safety.

With a loud cracking sound, the wagon lurched away from the tower, and daylight filled the opening. Arrows from the stairs held them for a moment, but the attackers, driven from behind by Hathor, had taken on a blood rage of their own. They pressed forward into the doorway, climbing over the bodies of their own dead. Drakis shot his last arrow, then dropped his bow and drew his sword.

"Fall back," he shouted and struck aside a spear thrust toward him. "Fall back."

Swinging the sword like a madman, knocking away spears and swords, Drakis retreated slowly, found the first step with his heel, and started climbing upward. For a moment, Enkidu's archers, farther up the steps, held the enemy back, but then an arrow flashed into the tower, and an Akkadian archer fell off the steps, groaning from his wound.

To his dismay, Drakis realized the situation had worsened. The sun's rays now reached the tower's arrow slits, illuminating the interior. From the cover of the doorway, the enemy archers could fire at his men, exposed on the steps. They'd be picked off one by one if they continued to fight like this.

"Up the stairs. Everyone up the stairs."

Two arrows struck him as he continued to back up the steps, one grazing his ribs and the other ripping into his left arm just above the elbow. He stumbled and would have fallen off the steps, but Enkidu reached down and grabbed him. They scrambled up the steps to the second landing, out of sight of the doorway for a moment. Cursing at his wound and shaking off weakness, Drakis kept his feet moving upward. He heard Enkidu directing the men, telling them to form another line, even as his subcommander pushed him up the steps.

"Get to the top," Enkidu shouted. "See what's happening there. I'll hold them here."

Wincing with pain, Drakis climbed the steps, practically falling as he reached the battlement atop the tower. The sun had cleared the horizon, and the blue sky shimmered in the morning air. The fresh scent of the morning river washed over him, driving the stench of blood away for a moment. He slipped to his knees, and leaned back against the wall.

"Sit still," Tarok said, kneeling beside him while he took

a quick look at the arrow protruding from Drakis's arm. "It's in the bone. Stay here and I'll bandage . . ."

"Rip it out," Drakis ordered, his eyes shut tight against the pain washing over him. He opened them, and stared at Tarok's sweating face, a hand's breadth from his own. "Rip it out now."

Tarok didn't argue. With a grunt, he put his knee against Drakis's shoulder, then took the wounded arm in one hand and pushed it against the wall. Tarok grasped the arrow with his other hand. Drakis flinched when Tarok gripped the shaft, but before the pain could mount, Tarok twisted the arrow and yanked on it with all his strength. A wave of agony shut out the sunlight, and Drakis couldn't hold back the moan of anguish that forced itself from his lips. But the bloody shaft came free, bits of flesh still clinging to the arrowhead.

"Still good," Tarok said, tossing the arrow toward the archers behind him. "Don't move. I've got to bind it up, or you'll bleed to death." Using his knife, Tarok cut open Drakis's tunic, tore a long strip from it, and used it to bandage the wounded arm, stretching the cloth tight to stop the bleeding.

Drakis blacked out for a few moments. When he opened his eyes, Tarok had gone, and Enkidu, blood streaming from his leg, had backed the men into the opening at the top of the battlement. Drakis struggled to his knees, found his sword, and crawled beside Enkidu. One man had found a shield, and they used that to cover themselves as they dared quick looks down the steps.

"We're killing them," Enkidu said. "The stairs are covered with bodies, but they keep coming. These Egyptians know how to fight. How goes it up here?"

Drakis glanced about him for the first time. "I don't know. Can you hold . . ."

"I'll hold them. See if help's coming."

Tarok, his red hair glinting in the sunlight, had returned to his men. Drakis saw that less than half of his original force remained, and most of those had taken wounds. Using his good hand on the top of the battlement, he pulled himself over the rough surface toward the archers still facing the other tower. A loud booming noise told him something had just struck the gate, shivering the massive wood logs. Risking a look over the wall, Drakis saw a half-dozen men trying to unbar the gate.

"Tarok! Stop those men. The gate must not open." Drakis had lost his bow, but he picked up one lying under the battlement. When he attempted to draw it, his wounded arm refused to bear the strain, and he dropped the weapon. Cursing at his own weakness, he drew his sword again.

Tarok recognized the danger. "Don't let them open the gate. Pin those archers down," he shouted, jerking his head toward the enemy archers in the opposite tower. Then he stood, leaned over the wall, and began firing. He emptied his quiver, shooting his last six arrows so rapidly that Drakis could scarcely follow his movements. Ducking back down, Tarok moved to Drakis's side.

"I drove them off, but they'll be back."

"Do what you can. Keep the gate closed." His left arm was useless, but Drakis could still hold a sword. Keeping low, he crawled back toward the tower's entrance. Enkidu and four men defended the doorway, all of them bleeding from one wound or another.

"They're getting ready to rush us," Enkidu said. "Any sign of help?"

Drakis had forgotten to look toward the barracks. He moved to the other wall, pulled himself up, and endeavored to focus on the lanes leading to the gate. An arrow flew past his head, but he ignored it. A plume of thick black smoke, wavering in the morning sun, trailed up into the sky from what appeared to be the barracks. That must mean Bantor had broken through the river gate and attacked. From his vantage point, Drakis could see two of the lanes that fed into the expanse behind the gate. Men ran toward the gate, but whether friend or foe, he couldn't tell.

He went back to Enkidu's side, kneeling next to the opening. "Men are coming, but ..."

A roar went up from inside the tower, as four or five arrows flashed through the opening, miraculously striking none of the defenders. Then the Egyptians, shouting their war cries, rushed the last few steps separating them from their enemies.

Staying on his knees, Drakis used his sword, thrusting at anything that appeared on the landing. Tarok's men, crouched over to avoid arrows from the other tower, took their time, using the last of their arrows against those attackers trying to force their way onto the battlement. Swords clashed, spears shoved and prodded, and men screamed in each other's faces. The attackers surged toward the opening again and again, but each time they faltered. Only a few men could approach on the stairs at one time. After the third attempt, the Egyptians halted their efforts, returning to the safety of the landing to regroup.

Drakis looked about. Enkidu had taken another wound, and leaned against the battlement, trying to catch his breath. Tarok, sword in his hand, had taken his place. It took only a moment to count those able to fight. Five men remained, and only one had a bow in his hands. That one scrambled about, picking up any stray shafts that lay about.

One more attack, Drakis decided. One more rush and they'd be finished, overwhelmed. He heard the attackers gathering inside the tower, taking their time now that the Akkadians had exhausted their arrows. Suddenly Korthac's war cry echoed eerily throughout the tower, as the Egyptians' followers raced up the last flight of steps, and hurled themselves at the opening.

Alexar paused when he reached the main gate, studying the situation while he struggled to catch his breath. The sounds of battle echoed from the left tower, and he guessed that Drakis and his men had taken refuge in there, no doubt fighting for their lives. The expanse now held plenty of panicky men, most of them heading toward the gate itself. In a few moments, they'd have the gate open.

The right tower, only a few dozen paces away, seemed deserted except for some of Korthac's bowmen on the battlement above. He made up his mind. Eskkar had said to keep the gate shut, and clearly Drakis didn't have enough men.

"We'll take the other tower. Let's go."

Alexar, Yavtar, and their men burst out of the lane, running at full speed toward the tower's entrance, mixing in with the crowd of frightened villagers and bandits rushing toward the gate. Alexar never hesitated or slowed. He dashed into the tower, sword in his right hand, bow in his left. No one challenged him, so he sprinted up the stairs, expecting resistance at each landing, but finding no one to oppose him.

At the top, he broke into full daylight, never stopping. Almost a dozen men, bows in their hands, faced away from him, searching for targets on the opposite tower. Alexar was on them before they knew he was there, dropping his bow and striking at a dark-skinned Egyptian.

At such close range, swords were more useful than bows, and he had two men down before they could react. By then Yavtar and the others were beside him, all of them hacking and shouting Eskkar's name, making the battle cry again echo over the city. The Egyptian archers, taken by surprise and with their bows in their hands, couldn't react fast enough. They clutched at their swords, but by then Alexar and his seven men had joined the fight.

Pinning their opponents to the tower wall, the Akkadians wielded their swords like men possessed by demons. Two men fell screaming over the wall, to land with a loud thud just in front of the gate. In a few savage moments, Alexar's men swept the battlement clean.

Alexar's lungs burned with every breath. The dash up the tower steps, the furious, close-in fighting, had sapped his strength. Gathering his bow from where he'd dropped it, Alexar peered over the wall toward the other tower. He saw men struggling there, and picked out Tarok, his red hair waving, fighting with a sword. Drakis must have retreated to the top of the battlement, and the Egyptians must be about to swarm over the Akkadians.

"Men, get your bows ready. Stop those men before they slaughter Drakis."

Alexar launched the first arrow, the shaft clearing Tarok's head by a hand's span, and flashing into the opening. Two more arrows snapped across the space between the towers, just as Tarok and those defending the doorway were about to be pushed aside. Alexar's next volley stopped the assault, five men firing together, pinning two bodies in the opening. The Egyptians disappeared back into the tower's confines.

Enkidu's face appeared above the wall, a bloody sword in his hand. He shouted something, and it took Alexar a moment to comprehend the words.

"Yavtar, take half the men to the other tower. Help them."

Yavtar nodded. He and his men carried no bows, and they could do nothing more from up here.

Alexar moved to the corner of the tower, and glanced down at the gate, just in time to see the last of the huge beams that barred it shut come down. A crowd of men massed against the wide wooden strakes in their panic, for a moment the press of their own bodies the only thing keeping the gate closed.

Alexar jumped onto the battlement, directly above the gate. Placing his feet with care, he drew a shaft and picked his target. An Egyptian trying to get the mob to move back died first. A second foreigner followed, then another, this one waving a sword. At such close range, shooting straight down from less than twenty paces, Alexar could scarcely miss. He stood alone, exposed on the battlement, but no bowmen opposed him, and he kept shooting, whipping the arrows from quiver to string to his ear so fast his movements never seemed to stop. And with each twang of the bowstring, a man died or fell wounded.

Panic erupted below. Some still worked to force the gate open, but others turned and ran, desperate to escape the deadly arrows that hissed down upon them. One of Alexar's men joined him, adding his shafts to the carnage below. Bodies lay atop one another, forming a fresh barrier to anyone striving to open the gate.

Just as he nocked his last arrow, Alexar realized he had no targets below. The mob had broken and turned back.

"Keep watch. Kill anyone that tries to get out," Alexar ordered, then jumped down and went back to where the three archers stood, bows drawn, still waiting for targets to appear in the doorway opposite them. Across the open space, the doorway to the other tower stood empty. A man leaned on the wall, waving a red-stained sword at him. Alexar had to stare before he recognized the bloody figure of Drakis.

Before Alexar could wave his bow in reply, he heard a rush of noise from below. Moving to the tower's edge, he leaned over and saw Bantor and more than twenty soldiers jogging into the open space, bows ready, looking for targets. Following them was a wall of men, hundreds of them, all shouting Eskkar's name and waving whatever they could find as a weapon, filling the lanes. The inhabitants of Akkad had finally rallied in force to support their liberators. The last of Korthac's fighters threw down their weapons and dropped to their knees, crying for mercy.

Alexar laid his bow across the battlement and stared down at the sight. The battle for the gate had ended. The soldiers and the people of Akkad once again ruled their city.

29

Bantor and ten men galloped through the main gate, heading south. All were bone-weary after a long night without sleep, but no one complained. Every one of them had a score to settle with Ariamus, and Bantor had no trouble finding volunteers. Each man led a spare horse, and carried his bow slung across his back.

After Bantor put down the last resistance at the gate, the city had gone wild, with all the inhabitants out in the streets, cheering and praising their deliverers, and generally getting in the way. He wasted close to an hour before he finished searching the dead and wounded that surrounded the towers, looking for Ariamus. Bantor even spoke with the prisoners, wounded or those who surrendered, asking for Ariamus, but no one knew the whereabouts of the former captain of the guard; Ariamus had vanished, like a night demon with the coming of dawn.

When he'd learned that no one had seen Ariamus, alive or dead, Bantor knew the man would run, making his break over the wall. Little more than an hour after the last of the fighting, Bantor stood in Eskkar's courtyard, surrounded by the pandemonium of rowdy soldiers and exuberant citizens celebrating their deliverance.

"He'll head south," Eskkar said, raising his voice over the din. "He won't chance encountering anyone coming down the northern road, not if he's got any of the Egyptians with him. He'll want to cross the river as soon as he can. Take whatever men you need and go after him."

"I'll run him down," Bantor said. He'd already worked through what Ariamus must be thinking, and had come to the same conclusion. Moving through the crowd, Bantor found Klexor sitting on the ground, feet sprawled out in front of him, his back against the house, and drinking wine straight from a jug.

"We're going after Ariamus. Get nine men who can ride and meet me at the stable."

Klexor's eyes widened in surprise, but he put down the jug. The chance to pay back Ariamus pushed all thoughts of rest and merrymaking aside.

Bantor cursed the time wasted to round up enough horses, wrench the men away from their celebrations, and move his force through the celebrating crowds that filled the lanes.

On foot, Ariamus would head south, following the river. The land there contained many farms, and some of those farms might have a plough horse or two hidden away. Once mounted, Ariamus would disappear, eventually crossing the river to head west. He would expect pursuit, but maybe not this fast, and not supplied with extra mounts.

Once outside the city walls, the quiet sounds of the countryside returned. At first Bantor didn't bother looking for tracks. Ariamus would have followed the endless, interconnected canals, moving slower through the water channels, but leaving no obvious trail. Instead, Bantor followed the main road south for a mile, until the farms began to spread out, before he moved his men toward the river.

At the riverbank, Bantor spread his line of men wide, looking for tracks as they moved southward, and anchoring the line at the river himself, searching the ground for any sign of a group of men entering the water. He stopped every confused and still-frightened farmer they encountered. Had anyone seen fugitives running from Akkad? Anyone missed any horses? No one had seen a band of men on foot, but the farmers all wanted to know what had happened in Akkad. Except for a brief statement that Eskkar had returned, Bantor refused to answer any questions about what had happened to Korthac and his men. All this took time, and Bantor grew more and more impatient, as he swept his men back and forth across the most likely routes.

"Bantor! This way," Klexor shouted, his bellow covering a quarter mile of wheat and barley fields that separated the two. Bantor turned the horse and applied his heels, racing through the crops until he joined his subcommander atop a low rise.

By now they'd traveled about three miles from Akkad. Up ahead, a good-sized farm nestled in a grove of palm trees, near a broad canal that carried water from the river. Thin wisps of smoke rose from one of the three structures. Bantor saw the roof missing from one, and guessed what had happened.

He waved his bow to show his men the way. Taking care, they converged on the farmhouse, weapons at the ready; Bantor did not intend to be ambushed again. As he drew closer, Bantor saw the tracks of men for the first time, fresh mud showing where they'd come out of the canal. Approaching the farm, they saw no one, no farmer, wife, or child, not even a dog.

Bows strung and arrows nocked, they covered the last hundred paces, stopping when they reached the first body. It was a young boy, an arrow protruding from his back, shot down trying to escape to the fields. By then Bantor knew they'd find the farmhouse empty, except for the dead. He sent his men to circle the farm, looking for fresh tracks.

"Over here ... men and horses going south, commander." Klexor dismounted, dropping to his knees and studying the ground with care. "Looks like eight or ten men, but I only see tracks for two horses."

"How long ago?"

"Not long. Maybe an hour. Less than two. They're moving at a run, following the horses."

Bantor thought it over. The horse trail went southwest, slightly away from the river. That meant Ariamus led the men. Only he would be crafty enough to head somewhat away from the river, knowing that boats might have already been dispatched north and south, to give warning of what had happened in Akkad and alerting every village to hunt down any escaping fugitives. So Ariamus would be riding one of those horses, and probably leading these fugitives; if there were any Egyptians among them, they would need someone who knew the land.

"Follow their trail, Klexor," Bantor said.

They watered the horses at the canal, then resumed the pursuit, following the recent tracks. These renegades, desperate for horses, food, and weapons, would kill anyone in their path. If they managed to pick up more horses, the whole lot might scatter, and Ariamus might yet escape.

Bantor set the pace at a strong canter, his men spread out, with a clear trail to follow. The sun marched across the sky as morning prepared to give way to noon. They pushed the horses hard, changing mounts often, but always studying the land to make sure they didn't ride into an ambush. The tracks grew fresher. Bantor looked up at the sun. They'd have them all by early afternoon, he decided.

"Fresh tracks here," Klexor said, halting the men and again dismounting to study the ground. His fingers traced the hoofprint in the dirt, getting the feel of the dirt as it hardened. "They're not far ahead now."

They rode on, passing fewer farms as they moved farther away from the river. The land became brown, the grasses sparse, with more rocks and gullies to slow them down. But the hoofprints and sandal tracks grew fresher with every stride, and Klexor no longer needed to dismount to read its message. They rode until the horses needed changing, then rested while Bantor talked to the men.

"When we catch up with them, I'll take Naram-tanni and go after Ariamus and whoever's riding the other horse." Naram-tanni shot an excellent shaft. Bantor figured that would be all the help he needed. "Klexor, you take charge of the rest of the men. Kill all the Egyptians."

Not long afterward, Bantor and his soldiers crested a hill and saw the enemy more than a mile away, walking now, heads down with fatigue, plodding a hundred paces behind two horsemen. Bantor grunted in satisfaction. He kept to a steady pace, not pushing the horses, waiting until they'd been spotted, and using the time to study his quarry. As far as he could tell, only two of the fugitives carried bows, and both bowmen were on foot.

The Akkadians closed the distance to less than a mile before anyone turned around to spot them. The fugitives broke into a run, while the two horsemen, after watching for a moment, put their horses to a gallop.

Bantor held his men to a trot, and the gap between the two groups briefly widened. But the men on foot couldn't keep up the pace, and the group began to straggle out, as the weaker men trailed behind the stronger. Bantor grunted in satisfaction. He'd learned that Alur Meriki tactic from Eskkar. If he'd rushed down on the men at first sight, they'd have banded together to resist. If they thought they could get away, they'd keep running, exhausting themselves at the same time fear gnawed at their insides.

Bantor's men spread out into a wide line that stretched a hundred paces across. The hindmost of the fugitives ahead of them stumbled and fell. He got to his feet and staggered on, but couldn't keep up the pace. He turned to face his pursuers, sword in hand.

Bantor's horsemen closed in. Their larger bows couldn't be used effectively from horseback, but they could still be drawn, though not fully extended or aimed accurately. Nevertheless, at such short range, it didn't matter. A hail of arrows flew at Korthac's man, and he went down, his body riddled with shafts.

Another straggler died the same way. By then the Egyptians realized they couldn't escape. The last six stopped and turned to face their enemy.

"Finish them, Klexor," Bantor shouted. Then he and

Naram-tanni, each still leading an extra horse, swung wide around the fugitives and galloped on.

Since two of the Egyptians carried bows, Klexor decided to take no chances. He called out new orders, the Akkadian line compacted, and they dismounted a hundred paces from the Egyptians. Three of Klexor's men gathered up the horses and held them fast, while the others started shooting.

The Egyptians, tired from the day's running and not used to the heavy bows, couldn't find the range. One enemy bowman went down in the first volley. Another took up the fallen man's weapon, but Klexor's five archers poured volley after volley of arrows at them. Both enemy bowmen went down by the third volley. The next volley struck down two more. One Egyptian killed himself, falling on his sword rather than be captured. The last three, one of them wounded, charged at their attackers and died, the deadly shafts taking them down long before they could close the distance.

Bantor and Naram-tanni ignored the fighting behind them. They kept moving, racing at full speed after the two horsemen, by now almost out of sight. The gap began to close. Bantor's horses might not be as fresh as the ones Ariamus rode, but the best horseflesh always wound up in Akkad, and these mounts now proved their quality over the stolen farm animals. When the horse Bantor rode started to tire, he slowed to a walk and leaped onto the second animal without dismounting, and broke into a gallop, abandoning the tired horse to be recovered by Klexor's men.

The distance had closed to less than three hundred

paces when one of the horses ahead of Bantor stumbled and went down. The rider, caught looking behind at his pursuers, landed hard. Bantor saw the man's dark skin and galloped ahead. "Kill the Egyptian, Naram-tanni," Bantor said as he swung wide around the dismounted man and galloped after Ariamus.

Naram-tanni pulled his horse to a stop about a hundred paces away, nocked an arrow, and waited, watching his quarry. The Egyptian looked fit and hard, and Naram-tanni didn't want to waste shafts trying to hit a dodging target. He decided to wait. Klexor and the rest of the soldiers would be arriving soon.

The Egyptian drew his sword and stood there, waiting for Naram-tanni to advance. Moments passed, until he realized the horseman wasn't attacking. Suddenly he burst into a run, coming straight toward the mounted archer.

Before the Egyptian had covered half the distance between them, Naram-tanni turned his horse aside and cantered off, glancing back to make sure he stayed just ahead of the Egyptian.

Exhausted by the chase, the Egyptian stopped and waited. Naram-tanni guided his horse back until another hundred paces separated them. He sat there, staring. Naram-tanni had plenty of time, and the Egyptian wasn't going anywhere. The sound of hoofbeats floated over the grass, and Klexor and two other men rode into view, each of them leading a spare horse.

"The other bandits are all dead," Klexor said, when he reached Naram-tanni's side. "Let's take this one alive."

"I don't think this one is going to throw down his sword," Naram-tanni said.

"Put a shaft into him," Klexor ordered, readying his own bow. "That'll change his mind."

Looking a little dubious, Naram-tanni dismounted. He handed the halter to Klexor, and started walking forward.

The Egyptian, determined to sell his life, charged again, lifting his sword and shouting something incomprehensible.

Naram-tanni waited until the man closed to within a dozen paces before shooting. His shaft flew at the man's legs, but the Egyptian leapt aside, and the arrow hissed by. But before he could change his path again, a shaft from Klexor's bow followed, this one reaching the charging man a moment before he could close the gap between him and Naram-tanni.

Struck in the leg, the Egyptian went down. He struggled to stand, but his leg gave way. Before he could recover, Naram-tanni, sword in hand, closed in. With a savage over-hand thrust, Naram-tanni knocked the Egyptian's weapon from his hand.

With Naram-tanni's sword's tip at his chest, the exhausted and wounded man yielded. Naram-tanni held the prisoner that way, until Klexor joined him.

"What's your name, Egyptian?" Klexor put his sword point at the man's throat, as Naram-tanni sheathed his weapon, took a halter rope, and moved toward the prisoner. He pushed the Egyptian down, and began tying his hands in front of him.

"I asked you for your name," Klexor repeated, this time jabbing the sword tip into the man's chest just enough to draw blood, and loosen his tongue.

"Hathor, leader of thirty, in the service of Korthac."

"You speak our language well, Egyptian dog," Klexor

complimented him. "And you'll get to see your Korthac soon enough."

"Korthac is alive? We thought . . ."

"Oh, he's alive. Lord Eskkar broke his nose, half-blinded him, and cracked his leg." Klexor laughed when he saw that the man didn't believe him. "By himself. They fought man to man in the upper room. Your Korthac didn't fare too well in the encounter."

For the first time, Klexor saw defeat in the man's face. By then, the rest of the men had reached them. "Pull that arrow out of his leg and bind it up. Then put him on a horse. Eskkar may want to talk to him. So make sure he stays alive."

Picking up his bow, Naram-tanni mounted his horse. "I'll go after Bantor. He may need help."

Klexor grinned. "Wait for me."

Bantor rode steadily, carefully watching the ground before him. A misstep, a broken leg, and Ariamus might get away. The distance narrowed faster now, as Ariamus's weary horse stumbled more and more often. Bantor saw Ariamus glancing behind every few paces.

When the gap shrank to less than a hundred paces, Ariamus gave up. He slowed the tired horse to a stop and drew his sword. "Well, where's Eskkar?" he called out. "Was he afraid to face me himself? Or did the Egyptian kill him?"

At twenty paces, Bantor pulled up his horse and drew his own sword, noting the bloody bandage wrapped around Ariamus's left arm. "Eskkar is well and sends his greetings.

He asked me to bring you back alive, but I think I'd rather kill you myself."

"I'm here, Bantor, waiting for you. Or are you afraid, too? Even your wife wasn't afraid. She got down on her knees fast enough, and begged for more."

"Your horse is finished, Ariamus. I'll fight you on foot. If you win, you can take my horse before my men get here. Otherwise I'll wait, and we'll bring you down like any jackal, with arrows."

Ariamus looked around. He didn't like the offer, but he had no choice. Bantor's men couldn't be far behind. He slid off the horse. In a fit of anger, Ariamus smacked the sweat-soaked animal with the flat of his blade, and the startled horse lumbered off a few steps before halting again, its weary legs splayed out, blowing air from its nose.

Dropping his bow, Bantor dismounted. He tossed the halter rope to the ground and walked toward the former captain of the guard.

"You're an even bigger fool than Eskkar," Ariamus said, baring his teeth in a wide grin. "There never was a day you could beat me with a sword." With a shout of rage, Ariamus closed the distance, swinging the sword high in a feint, then sweeping the blade low toward Bantor's legs.

Bantor moved a step to the side, letting Ariamus's blade pass within a handsbreadth, and countered with his own stroke.

The clash of bronze rolled over the land, sending a flock of birds squawking into the sky. Ariamus fought with the desperation of a wounded animal trying to escape a trap, determined to get rid of his opponent; he knew the rest of Bantor's men would be close behind. If Ariamus hadn't taken a wound, he might have done better. But Bantor met every stroke and knew every trick. Like all the Akkadian subcommanders during the siege, he'd practiced against Eskkar and other top swordsmen for months.

The minute he sensed Ariamus tiring, Bantor swung wide, leaving an opening for his opponent. But when the blade flashed at his stomach, Bantor slipped aside and hammered down, aiming not at his opponent's body, but where the sword arm would be.

In a gush of blood, the blade clove deep into the forearm bone. Ariamus screamed, and his weapon fell from his nerveless fingers. Bantor never stopped. Another stroke took Ariamus in the knee, staggering him to the ground. A hammer blow descended on the man's collarbone, shattering that. Then a low thrust into his right side pierced his lung. Ariamus, blood gushing from his mouth, fell onto his back, eyes bulging, unable even to cry out in pain.

Standing over his opponent, Bantor spat in his face. He put his own sword aside, and picked up Ariamus's. "This is for Annok-sur. And for me." Holding the hilt with both hands, Bantor raised the weapon up, then thrust it down with all his strength, shoving the point into the man's groin, driving it right through his body and deep into the earth. That elicited a lingering scream that echoed over the empty countryside.

Bantor let go of the sword and watched the former captain of the guard of the village of Orak bleed to death as he writhed in agony, clutching at his own blade with hands already streaked with blood.

30

Eskkar spent the first part of the morning making sure his compound stood ready for any further attack. When he felt certain that the house and Trella would be safe, he moved to the barracks, seeing to the wounded men recovering there, and making sure the soldiers had regained control of the weapons. Then he took a quick tour of the city, before finally returning to his courtyard. By then it was apparent the resistance had collapsed. Eskkar set up a command center to direct the soldiers and citizens clamoring for his attention.

Everyone claimed an urgent need to see him, and this time Eskkar had no one available to sort out the trivial from the more urgent. Bantor had ridden out to hunt down Ariamus at midmorning, and only the gods knew when he would be back. Gatus arrived, and sought to help, but he still hadn't fully recovered from his own wound. That left Alexar as the only senior man still standing. Eskkar promoted him to subcommander, and ordered him to take charge of the gates.

The three of them spent the morning organizing the

soldiers, issuing weapons to the nobles' guards, establishing patrols, and directing the search for any remnants of Korthac's force. Fortunately the stables and horses survived intact, and Alexar soon had mounted parties of men searching the countryside, looking for those who escaped over the wall. Finally things quieted down enough for Eskkar to slip away. An hour before noon, he left Gatus in charge and climbed the stairs to his quarters.

Standing in the bedroom doorway, he saw Trella and Annok-sur lying side by side on the bed, both asleep. Trella looked pale from loss of blood. Korthac's cut and the ordeal of childbirth had exhausted even her sturdy frame. Most of Trella's servants had returned, including those driven off by Korthac. Already they had replaced the broken furniture and exchanged the bloody blankets for clean ones. The room looked almost the same as the day Eskkar rode north. Except for the cradle.

He'd visited the bedroom several times before, just quick checks to reassure himself of Trella's well-being, and to make sure she and Annok-sur had everything they needed. On the last visit, Trella took his hand. She tried to speak, but he knew she needed rest, so he simply squeezed her hand and told her to sleep.

Now Eskkar looked into the bedroom and saw an unknown woman with a large bruise on her cheek sitting beside the cradle, rocking it gently, her eyes on the infant. She rose and came toward him, motioning him to follow her through the doorway.

"Your wife needs her sleep, Lord Eskkar," she whispered. "The babe needed to be fed, and his crying woke her. Now they both need their rest."

For the first time Eskkar noticed how quiet the house was. Even the soldiers in the courtyard kept their voices low out of concern for his wife. "You are . . ."

"My name is Drusala. I was midwife to Lady Trella." She stepped back inside, picked up the cradle, and returned, holding the cradle in both arms and turning it so he could see the child's face. "This is your son. He was born last night, a few hours past midnight."

Eskkar stared in fascination at the tiny infant, his eyes shut and face still red from crying. Eskkar had scarcely had time to look at him since he'd carried the babe to Trella after the fight. This time he gazed not at a baby, but at his son, his heir that Trella had promised him months ago.

"Have you decided on a name, lord?"

Eskkar spoke without hesitation. "Sargon. His name is Sargon of Akkad." Eskkar and Trella had chosen the name months ago, in fact the very day the Alur Meriki were driven off. Now he looked in wonderment at the heir who would bring the city together in a way that even Eskkar and Trella, both strangers to Akkad, never could. His son would become part of that future, would carry Eskkar's line down through the ages.

"The child . . . he seems so small." Eskkar reached out and touched the infant's fingers, amazed at their softness.

"The babe . . . Sargon came earlier than we expected. That's why he is so small. But he is healthy, and I expect he will grow as tall and strong as his father."

"Was the birth . . . difficult, Drusala? I mean, did Trella suffer much?"

"The presence of Korthac made it . . . He complained about the noise. He threatened . . . he said that . . ."

"He'll make no more threats, Drusala," Eskkar said. "Is there anything you need, anything at all?"

"No, lord. I'll stay and watch over your son. Lady Trella will need to feed Sargon again soon enough. We will have to find someone to help nurse the child. The early birth caught us unaware, and we didn't have time to arrange a wet nurse. Right now it's best to let Lady Trella sleep as much as she can."

The mention of Korthac's name reminded Eskkar of his prisoner. "Keep my son safe, Drusala." He reached out and gently touched the child's cheek again. A strange feeling passed over him, as if the gods chose that moment to forge a bond between the child and the father. Eskkar found himself smiling. "Send word when Trella wakens."

He left the room, descending the stairs and crossing the courtyard to the smaller house. Three soldiers guarded the room that held Korthac. They stepped aside as Eskkar entered. He looked down at the figure lying on the floor. The sun didn't provide much light in the low-ceilinged chamber, but he saw blood still covered the Egyptian's face. They'd bound his hands behind him.

Eskkar considered having the man dragged outside, but didn't want another spectacle. "Bring a torch," he commanded. He found a stool and moved it closer to Korthac, eying the man who'd nearly killed him. A soldier returned, carrying the torch, and handed it to Eskkar.

"Leave us. And draw the curtain."

When they were alone, Eskkar lowered the torch and used its light to examine his prisoner's face. Korthac glowered back at him, using his one good eye. Blood had crusted over the other, the one Eskkar had smashed during the fight. Korthac struggled to breathe, thanks to the broken nose. His lower lip was swollen and split, and he squinted up at the torch held just above his face.

"You are Eskkar?"

"Yes, Korthac. I'm the man whose wife you tried to steal."

"Eskkar has returned." Korthac tried to laugh, but the sound turned into a painful fit of coughing, and it took a few moments before he could stop. "You fought well . . . for an ignorant barbarian. And you should have died on my blade. No man ever defeated me in battle. Only your slave saved your life."

The words came out slowly, each one spoken with care. Even through the man's pain, the voice sounded melodious, with just the trace of an accent.

"Perhaps," Eskkar said, "but I remember you running into the bedroom, trying to put the door between us."

Korthac grimaced at the reminder. "You handled your long sword well enough. Did you never lose a fight, barbarian?"

"Just once, that I recall," Eskkar said, "but fortune favored me, and I survived."

"You should have died in Bisitun." This time Korthac's voice held a trace of bitterness that he couldn't conceal.

"Yes, your assassins missed their chance there."

"So I see. You must tell me what happened. I was supposed to get word, even if they failed. Ariamus swore they would kill you, but . . . you made it so easy for me. You divided your forces while you enjoyed your pleasures in the north. A child could have taken your city."

Eskkar felt a pang of anger at the truth of the remark. Everyone seemed to know about his dalliance in Bisitun.

"Rebba told me much about you, Egyptian. Trella's asleep now, but when she awakens, I'll hear the rest."

The torch sputtered, and Eskkar moved it away from Korthac's face. "Most of your men are dead or prisoners. Only Ariamus got away, with a handful of others, but Bantor will run them down soon enough. In a few days, the city will be cleansed of your memory."

"Akkad will be a great city someday. It was worth the gamble."

"If that were the only thing between us, I'd give you a quick death. But you terrorized Trella and threatened even my son. You'll take the torture for that. Tomorrow will be your last day of life, Korthac. You'll be weak from your wounds, and you'll suffer greatly."

"You'll get no satisfaction from torturing me." Korthac struggled to keep his voice firm and his words even. "Your slave-wife and her whelp were mine. She knelt before me . . . begged for my mercy. I only regret that I didn't kill her when I had the chance."

Eskkar reached out with his foot and gave Korthac's broken leg a shove. The injured man couldn't control the gasp of pain that wrenched from his mouth.

"I think, Korthac, that you should have stayed in Egypt."

"You won't rule here long, barbarian. You're not wise enough, even with your slave woman whispering in your ear."

The words hung in the air, as if in prophecy, and Eskkar felt a chill pass over him. He took his time thinking about them. He knew that Korthac still fought, that he still searched for any way to inflict harm on his captor. That made him a worthy opponent, fighting to the last breath, seeking to give some worry to his enemy.

"Perhaps what you say will happen. But Trella says I learn from my mistakes, and the people of Akkad have learned something, too. We'll be more careful in the future." Eskkar stood up and pushed the stool away. He paused in the doorway, and turned back toward his prisoner. "I know one thing, Korthac. My son will rule here after I am gone. That the gods have promised. Think of that when you take the torture."

Outside, Alexar and a handful of soldiers stood there, curiosity on their faces, no doubt wondering about what had passed inside. Eskkar shoved the torch into the dirt to extinguish it, then handed the still-smoking stick to the nearest man.

"Watch him closely. No one is to visit him or hurt him. Keep two men with him at all times. He must not kill himself. We want him alive, to take the torture in the morning. Give him plenty of water and a few mouthfuls of wine. Food if he wants any. I don't want him passing out too soon."

"We'll watch him, don't worry about that," Alexar said.

Eskkar went to the well at the back of the house, drew up a bucket of water, and washed his hands and face. By the time he finished, a servant joined him, carrying a clean tunic. A soldier drew up more water and Eskkar washed the rest of his body, taking his time and scrubbing away the last traces of blood and dirt.

Feeling refreshed, and dressed in a clean tunic for the first time in days, Eskkar returned to the workroom and sat down, the first chance he'd had to take some rest since leaving Rebba's farm. He'd hardly slept from the time he left Bisitun. The servants had left pitchers of wine and water on the table, next to day-old bread. No one in Akkad had the thought or time to bake this morning. Eskkar soaked the bread in his wine cup before eating, but drank only water to wash it down. Too much wine, and he'd be of little use to anyone.

For the first few hours after the fighting ended, everyone sought to speak, plead, or advise Eskkar. But as soon as he knew Akkad had been secured, he refused to deal further with anyone. He ordered Gatus and Alexar to keep everyone but the subcommanders, healers, and servants away from the upper rooms. A dozen Hawk Clan guards, released from the barracks and still weak from their ordeal, stood guard over the house, directed by Mitrac, whose arrows had brought down the last of the insurgents within Akkad an hour after sunrise.

With something in his stomach, Eskkar felt himself relaxing. It was good to just sit and rest.

Steps sounded on the stairs and Gatus limped into the room and closed the door behind him. He took the seat across the table. A fresh bandage wrapped around his body above his sword belt. "How are they?" He kept his voice low, and inclined his head toward the bedroom.

"Good. Both asleep, along with the child."

"Thank the gods for that, Eskkar." Gatus kept his voice low, even though the door stood closed. "I wanted to help her, but . . . I couldn't even get word to her."

"There was nothing you could do."

The old soldier picked up a cup with hands that trembled a little, filled it with wine, and took a sip. "If it weren't for Tammuz and his woman, I'd be twice dead. Now we both owe him."

"His woman?" He remembered seeing Tammuz and a girl

earlier in the day, just a glimpse in the lane outside the house.

Gatus laughed. "You remember the slave girl Trella rescued, the one being beaten half to death by her master? She gave the girl to Tammuz. You should have seen the boy's face. He was more scared of her than any three barbarians. She killed at least one bandit that I know of, maybe two. Tammuz killed a few more during the confusion."

"I'll have to thank him, then. There are so many to thank ... especially you. Then Drakis, Annok-sur, even Rebba, they all put their lives at stake."

Gatus ignored the praise. "Not me. All I did was hide, then kill a few rogues in the confusion. By the time I got to the barracks, Klexor had finished off most of the Egyptians. The rest surrendered." He sighed. "Anyway, I set up a command post at the barracks. Corio is there, working with Rebba and the nobles still alive. They're finding those who collaborated with Korthac, and locking them in the same prison the Egyptian kept our men. What will you do to them?"

Eskkar shrugged. The traitors could be dealt with later, when order was established and the council reconvened. "When Trella recovers, she'll decide who should be punished. How is Nicar?"

"He took a nasty knock from Ariamus, but he's back in his house, carried there by his friends and family. He'll be up and about in a few days."

"What else?" Eskkar's legs ached from weariness. His eyes felt heavy again, and the need for sleep passed over him like a wave.

"There's been at least a dozen murders since the

fighting stopped, people taking their revenge against those who supported Korthac."

"To be expected, I suppose," Eskkar said. "Anyone I should be concerned about?"

"No, not really, just . . . I did recognize one of the dead. A tanner, who also happened to be the former owner of Tammuz's new slave. Old Kuri found the body, it seems."

Eskkar shrugged. No one would concern themselves over a drunken and unpopular tanner.

"Drakis lost most of his men," Gatus went on. "He took several wounds, but seized and held the gate despite being greatly outnumbered. He had the worst of the fighting, but because of him, Bantor slaughtered most of Korthac's men and captured the rest. They never got the gate open, and the ground there was covered with bodies."

"Will Drakis live?"

"So Ventor says. And Grond is resting downstairs. He should recover in a few weeks. The man's made of bronze."

"He not only saved my life, he found the way into the house, Gatus."

"You'll have to raise his pay again, I suppose."

Eskkar smiled for a moment before he drained his water cup and refilled it. "I told Alexar to take charge here. He's organizing the search parties, looking for any of Korthac's stragglers."

Gatus shook his head in admiration. "Not a scratch on the man. Fought at both gates, killed at least a dozen men, and didn't even get his tunic dirty."

"Did you meet Yavtar? I gave him some men and told him to guard the docks, and to make sure that no boats leave Akkad."

"Yes, he fought at the main gate, too. I've given the same order to those at the main gate. No one is to leave until we've rounded up all of Korthac's men and our own traitors. I've got men riding around the walls, looking for anyone trying to slip away."

Hundreds of angry Akkadians seeking revenge had joined in the search for the remnants of Korthac's men. The Egyptians, recognizable by their darker skin color, proved easy to find. Some of the men who Ariamus had brought into the city still had to be unearthed. Together, soldiers and citizens searched house by house, and one by one, were rounding up the bandits who had terrorized Akkad.

"Good. When Bantor returns, we can start patrolling the countryside."

"The soldiers searched Akkad for Ariamus, but no one saw the traitorous filth. His body wasn't among the dead. Finally a boy came forward and said that he saw Ariamus and some Egyptians go over the south wall."

Eskkar yawned. "The battle rage is still on Bantor. He won't be back until he finds Ariamus. I told him to bring him back alive if he could."

Gatus finished his wine and ripped a handful of bread from the loaf. "Bantor fought well. Do you think he'll catch Ariamus? The man's like a snake in a swamp for hiding."

"You wouldn't ask that if you'd seen Bantor."

"I'll be just as happy to piss on his body," Gatus said. "Ariamus strutted around Akkad, looking pleased as any rich merchant with three fat wives." Gatus leaned across the table. "Your eyes are closing. Why don't you get some sleep? I'll relieve Alexar and keep watch downstairs."

Before Eskkar could argue, Gatus was on his way,

closing the door to the upper chamber behind him. Eskkar tried to finish his bread, but he had no appetite. His thoughts wandered, so he lowered his head on his arms and closed his eyes, to rest for a few moments.

He fell into a deep sleep within a dozen heartbeats. So deep that he didn't hear the servants passing to and from the inner room, nor his son waking and crying to be fed.

When he awoke, his neck and arms felt stiff, and his back complained when he straightened up. His throat felt parched, and he drained his water cup, then stretched his arms until the stiffness went away. Rested now, a glance at the window told him he'd slept for more than an hour. The door to the bedroom stood open, and he heard Trella's voice. The chair scraped loudly when he arose, and in a moment Drusala appeared.

"Lady Trella is asking for you, Lord Eskkar. Can you come to her?"

Trella, her head propped up by a cushion, smiled at him when he approached. Annok-sur had gone. Sargon nestled in Trella's arm, nursing, and a bandage covered her side. Drusala slipped out of the room, leaving the two of them alone.

"Have you seen your son, Eskkar?" Her voice sounded stronger, and she reached out toward him with her hand.

He sat on the edge of the bed, taking care not to disturb the child. "Yes. The midwife told me of his delivery, and what you suffered. Are you in pain?" He took her hand in his.

"Ventor and Drusala say I will recover. The pain is passing now that you and Sargon are both here."

"Trella, I'm sorry. I should have come sooner." The words came out in a rush.

"We'll speak of it later, husband. All that matters is that you returned to save Akkad."

"I didn't come back for Akkad. I came for you. The moment I heard . . . I came as fast as I could."

She squeezed his hand, and tears formed in her eyes. "You saved our son's life. That's all that matters. Korthac would have killed us both soon enough, after he'd taken his pleasures."

The thought of the humiliation she'd endured wrenched at him, and he held her hand tighter. "As Korthac reminded me, you saved my life last night. Without your little knife thrust . . . Where did you get such a thing?"

"The birthing knife. A gift from Drusala. We'll have to repay that debt." The baby squirmed at her breast for a moment before settling down again, and she stroked his head. "We knew Korthac was concealing something, but I never thought . . . none of us suspected anything like this." She shook her head at her failure. "He laughed at me, said I was just an ignorant girl trying to play at ruling men. He made me . . . I had to . . ."

Eskkar reached out to touch her lips with his finger, stopping the flow of words. "I've fought many men, Trella, but no one with Korthac's skills. Never. But for the luck of the gods, and your help, he might have won. It's no disgrace to battle a worthy opponent."

She blinked back the tears. "Your luck still runs true, then. The gods continue to favor you."

"The gods favor me because of you." He gazed down at the child in wonder, and his voice softened. "Now they'll have to watch over Sargon as well. He seems . . . so small and helpless." Eskkar touched the child's cheek with his finger, fascinated by the boy's soft skin.

"Sargon will need your protection and strength for many years, husband. He will rule over our city someday. Who knows what he will accomplish?"

"He and Akkad will need your wisdom. Just as it needs Corio's new walls to defend it."

"Long after we are gone, our voices will linger in these walls, for as long as this place remains. Let us hope our son honors us both."

The child had stopped nursing and fallen asleep. Eskkar stroked its fine black hair, feeling a pride grow inside him that he'd never known before. His son. The son who would carry on his line, who would make Eskkar live on through the ages to come, lay before him, nestled safely in his mother's arms.

"You seem pleased with our son. I hope you will teach him many things. How to rule, how to fight, how to lead."

"He will learn more from you than I can ever teach him. You speak of fighting, but fighting a war is easy. Destroying is easy. Building a new way of life out of what is left is hard. That's what he will learn from his mother."

"Then we will teach him together, husband."

"Yes, together." He leaned down and kissed her, taking care not to awaken the child. But her lips were warm, and still held the promise he'd always found there, the gift of love and tenderness that had won him over months ago. Eskkar put his arms around both of them, holding them close. Trella had more tears on her face, but this time he knew they were tears of happiness, and he kissed them away.

31

Hathor woke to pain, pain that possessed every part of his body. It had started yesterday with the arrow in his leg, the heavy shaft tearing into hard muscle above the knee before lodging in bone, but thankfully missing the big blood carrier. He'd fainted for a few moments when they held him down and tore the shaft from his body. When Hathor regained consciousness, he found his wound bound with a piece of tunic taken from one of the dead. Rough hands lifted him onto a horse. Dazed from the wound, he clutched at the horse's mane with both hands, struggling to stay on. If they thought he couldn't ride, they'd tie him across the animal's back, and the pain would be even worse.

One man held the halter while another rode alongside, in case Hathor started to fall off. They rode at an easy pace, laughing and talking among themselves, all except for their leader, named Bantor, who rode at their head in silence. Another horse carried the corpse of Ariamus, the only body the Akkadians bothered to bring back with them.

This Bantor apparently had some personal grudge

against the traitor Ariamus. No doubt Ariamus's body would be displayed next to that of Korthac. The bodies of Hathor's men remained where they had fallen, left to animals and carrion eaters.

Thinking of Korthac made the anger bubble up inside Hathor. He'd seen the wave of Akkadian soldiers jogging down the lane to attack the main gate, followed by hundreds of the city's inhabitants. One look at their sheer number had stopped him in his tracks. Hathor had nearly recaptured the gate, but the sight of hundreds of angry citizens carrying makeshift weapons and rushing to support their liberators told him the effort had failed. Sounds of battle from the other tower made Hathor look up, and he saw that more Akkadians had captured that one as well.

Ariamus had seen the same thing, and reached the same conclusion even faster. All was lost. The wily bandit deserted first, slipping away, running toward the southern wall, escape the only thought in his head. At that moment a chill of fear had come over Hathor, the first time he'd felt fear in years of fighting, as he thought about his fate.

Ariamus could possibly escape. He could blend in with his countrymen. But the Egyptians, wearing the mark of the west on their features and in their speech, had no place to hide. Hathor knew his only hope was to run.

With that realization, Hathor turned and sprinted after Ariamus, cursing himself as a coward for abandoning his men and refusing to fight to the end. Without a word of protest, the handful of men standing alongside Hathor followed. Korthac, even if he still lived, had lost the city and everyone knew it. Now they had to save themselves.

Ariamus had dodged through the back lanes, leading

them away from the fighting. Their swords clearing the path, they reached an unguarded portion of the south wall. They climbed the parapet and hung from the wall before dropping to the ground. Then they ran, as hard and fast as they could.

In an hour they'd managed to cover more than three miles, and reached countryside untouched by the chaos behind them. They kept moving, and with every step, Hathor felt more confident. When Ariamus led them to the farmhouse, he shouted that everyone must die, lest anyone give the alarm. Hathor's men, without even a glance to their former leader, obeyed the Akkadian, slaughtering the family in moments. Nevertheless, after they secured the two broken-down plough horses, Ariamus handed the halter of one of them to Hathor.

Once mounted, Hathor felt certain they would be safe. Ariamus knew where to flee and how to hide. It would be days before the troubles in Akkad settled down, if anyone even bothered to chase after them.

Hathor remembered the shock that went through him when he turned and saw the horsemen, riding purposefully after them. Somehow, in spite of all the confusion and fighting in Akkad, the cursed soldiers had managed to find men and horses, organize pursuit, and pick up their trail.

Less than an hour after catching sight of his pursuers, the Akkadians had run him down. Contemptuously, they'd refused his attempt to die fighting. The arrow had taken the strength from his body, and, before Hathor could even kill himself, they'd captured him.

From what he heard spoken by the riders around him, this Eskkar had taken Korthac just as easily. The barbarian had stormed Korthac in his house, surrounded by his

Egyptians, and made him a prisoner. Hathor still found it
hard to believe his cunning leader had been defeated, not
only defeated but captured alive. Nevertheless, as Hathor
clung to his horse, he slowly realized that what his captors
said must certainly be true. These men rode too relaxed,
unconcerned about any danger; they must have retaken
Akkad and killed all those who'd opposed them.

Thoughts of how swiftly they'd killed his men still
rankled Hathor. The Akkadians hadn't lost a man, not even
taken a wound, and they'd finished off his Egyptians and
taken him prisoner. Bantor had personally killed Ariamus
with scarcely a fight, then stood over his victim to watch
his death throes. Hathor knew Ariamus could handle a
sword better than most, and yet the leader of these men,
by himself, had challenged Ariamus without hesitation.
And this Bantor, according to Ariamus, was reckoned to be
the slowest of Eskkar's subcommanders. Hathor nearly
wept in shame, but the thought of humiliating himself
further in front of these warriors halted his tears.

They stopped twice on the return journey. A burly
soldier named Klexor checked Hathor's bandage each
time, and gave him water, a gesture that worried Hathor
even as he gulped it down, unable to resist the need to
quench his thirst.

By the time they reached Akkad, the sun had started to
touch the horizon, marking the end of a long day of
fighting and running. Hathor, growing weaker with each
step of his horse, remembered moving through streets and
lanes already lit by torches and filled with revelers. People
shouted and cheered at the sight of Bantor and his riders.
That turned into a roar of approval as one of the soldiers

reached down and lifted Ariamus's head into view, its mouth hanging slack in the torchlight.

Some Akkadians even recognized Hathor, and yelled curses in his direction. Bantor's men kept them away, and the soldiers led him back to Korthac's house. When the soldiers pulled him down from the horse, Hathor was unable to stand, and he fell to the ground, helpless. Laughing, the soldiers lifted him and carried him to one of the soldiers' rooms across from the main house. Hathor, filled with shame and weakened from loss of blood, had collapsed, grateful only for the end of the punishing ride. His hands still tied in front of him, the celebrating soldiers dropped him to the floor and went off to join the festivities. The celebrations went on and on, long into the night, while Hathor lay in the dirt, fighting the throbbing in his leg and contemplating the torture that awaited him.

When he woke, not sure if he'd fallen asleep or passed out from the pain, Hathor found a yawning guard watching him, outlined against a low fire in its dying throes burning in the courtyard. Twisting his head, Hathor caught a glimpse of the night sky, and realized dawn approached. At first he couldn't believe that he'd slept through most of the night, but his wound must have exhausted him more than he realized. The coming dawn explained the silence surrounding the house, and the city; the inhabitants must have celebrated their liberation long into the night, before finally returning to their beds; aside from the occasional crackling of the fire, Hathor heard nothing.

The sky began to lighten, and thoughts of what the day would bring shook the last remnant of sleep from Hathor's mind. Today would be the last day of his life. In a few hours the torture would begin. Today he would die. The laughter, the jeers of the onlookers, would fill his ears as they enjoyed the spectacle of his torment. Hathor would make every effort to be strong, but he knew a wounded man rarely kept his courage and his strength. The pain they would inflict would join with that already flaring in his leg, and he would soon beg for mercy. The torture would increase, until he begged them to kill him. They wouldn't, of course, and that would make the pain and humiliation truly unbearable.

The courtyard fire died out, but moments later the first rays of the sun brushed aside the last of the darkness. Hathor swallowed, his throat dry again, as he attempted to prepare himself for the ordeal to come. The household stirred, with people getting up and about. He heard someone moaning, a low sound he could barely detect. He struggled to sit up, finally leaning his back against the wall, facing the doorway and the soldier watching him. The low, murmuring sound continued, and Hathor realized it had been going on for some time.

"Who's that?" he muttered at the guard, a dry rasp in his throat.

The guard, who'd sat there watching him without expression, broke into a smirk. "That's Korthac, your leader. He's in the room next to yours. You two are the last Egyptians alive in Akkad."

The words sent another tremor through him. If Korthac was already unable to control his pain, Hathor, too, would soon be screaming for death. Which of us, he wondered, would scream louder?

When Eskkar woke, the morning sun had already climbed well over the horizon. He'd slept in fits and snatches during the night, despite the tiredness in his body. The tension of the last few days couldn't be erased in a single night. Celebrating citizens and soldiers had filled the streets, shouting, drinking, and singing for much of the nighttime hours. The unusual noises had troubled him. The middle of the night had long passed before Eskkar finally fell into a deep sleep. Then he slept right through sunup, waking to the sound of a baby crying for its mother.

He hadn't wanted to disturb Trella and the child; he'd slept in the outer room, on a blanket. Trella and the baby slept together, both under the watchful eye of Drusala, who apparently stayed awake throughout the night. As she'd explained to Eskkar earlier, because Sargon came before his time, he needed to be watched constantly.

Entering the bedroom with a yawn, he found Trella nursing the babe. He put his arm around her shoulders, and felt a thrill when she leaned against him, then reached up and touched his cheek.

"You look terrible, husband," she said, her voice still weak. "Your face . . ."

Korthac's fists had bruised and bloodied Eskkar's face, leaving it swollen and covered with scratches. He could only imagine what he looked like.

"You look beautiful, wife," he answered. She smiled at him, the way she always did when he told her how beautiful she was. "How is the pain?"

"Better. But I feel so weak, like I could sleep the whole day." She touched the infant at her breast. "But Sargon has other ideas."

"So I see."

Annok-sur arrived, a bandage wrapped around her head, carrying breakfast for them both.

"Gatus is looking for you, Eskkar," she informed him, setting the tray down on the bed. "He wants to know if you plan to sleep the whole day away. You should eat something now, before he takes up all your time."

"I'd better go see what he wants," Eskkar said. "I'll come back as soon as I can." He tore off a hunk of bread and filled a cup with watered ale from the tray, and went downstairs. By the time he reached the courtyard, the cup was empty.

Eskkar found Gatus sitting at the head of the table, hard at work. Apparently the captain of the guard had taken his post well before sunrise.

"About time you woke up and got to work," Gatus said. "You look terrible. How are you feeling?"

Eskkar sat down and helped himself to the water jug resting on the table. "Not too bad. I could use some more sleep, but there's time for that. What's happened during the night?"

"I've put Klexor in command of the walls, gates, and docks," Gatus said. "He's to make sure no one leaves the city without our approval. Alexar took twenty men and as many horses and is already patrolling the walls, looking for any of the rabble that escaped. Mitrac is going house-to-house, searching the city and making sure none are still hiding under some old woman's bed."

"We'll have to promote them to commanders, then," Eskkar said.

"Already did that. Told them you'd confirm it when you finally woke up."

At least that was one less task to do today, Eskkar thought to himself with a smile.

"I just sent Bantor down to the barracks," Gatus went on. "He's taken charge of the prisoners, those guarding them, and the horses. He's working with Rebba and the other nobles to make sure the dead get buried. Too bad he had to burn the Egyptians out of the barracks. We could use the space."

"How'd he look?" Bantor had returned last night, with Ariamus's body. Bantor hadn't said much, just a quick report of the number of Egyptian dead, before he went to Annok-sur. They closed the door to their room, and hadn't ventured out all night.

"Better than he did when he got back," Gatus said. "The look on his face could've shattered stones. You'd think killing Ariamus would have cheered him up."

Eskkar knew the story about Annok-sur, and the gods only knew what other deviltry Ariamus had done under Korthac's protection.

"And the wounded?" Eskkar glanced around the courtyard. The soldiers' quarters held most of the wounded, with others put up in nearby houses. Even now, more than a half-dozen bandaged men rested in the courtyard, most of them watching Eskkar.

"Ventor's with them now," Gatus said. "Got here a few moments ago. He'll do what he can. Some are going to die. Those Egyptians were tough fighters."

"Korthac trained his killers well," Eskkar said, thinking that if the Egyptians were half as skillful as their master, they would indeed have made formidable fighters.

"Only one thing left to do," Gatus said, as he finished

reporting. "And here they come," he added, the distaste sounding in his voice.

Eskkar looked up to see Corio and Rebba enter the courtyard. Corio's right arm hung in a sling, and a large bruise covered the left side of his face. Rebba looked old and tired, but had a warm smile for everyone.

"Good morning, Lord Eskkar," Corio said, speaking first and in a loud voice. "Once again, let me offer praise to the gods for your return. You were sorely missed."

"The gods favored us, Noble Corio," he answered, smiling at the architect's obviously insincere words. Corio believed in the gods about as much as Eskkar did.

"We've come for the usurper Korthac," Rebba said. "We've been meeting at Nicar's house with the other nobles. Nicar is still unable to get about, but he sends his thanks and his greetings, as do the others."

"And Korthac? . . ." Eskkar looked at Rebba.

"Unless you want the pleasure of killing him yourself," Corio said, "he's to die under the torture in the marketplace, to pay for his crimes against all of us."

The nobles and rich merchants had suffered greatly in the last few days, Eskkar knew, and they'd lost most of whatever gold they had hoarded. Fortunately, Korthac had stored most of the loot right here in the house. Still, it would take weeks to sort it all out, and this time Eskkar would have to arbitrate the distribution. "Take Korthac whenever you want," he said, nodding toward the guards watching the Egyptian.

"Also, we need your soldiers to arrest the others," Corio interrupted, "the men who joined up with Korthac, who willingly took part in his schemes."

"And what's to become of them?"

"They're to die with their leader, curse them all," Corio answered. "They deserve to take the torture, but I'll be satisfied just to see them all dead."

Eskkar had never seen the master builder in such a bloodthirsty mood. "And Nicar, and you, Rebba, you all agree to this?"

Rebba nodded. "We spent most of yesterday arguing over their fates. Five are to die, their property confiscated. Another seven will have their property taken, and then be exiled from Akkad."

More blood to be shed, Eskkar thought. For this decision, however, there was no urgency. "Gatus, have your men take these ... twelve men prisoner. Send them down to the barracks and tell Bantor to guard them well."

He turned to Corio. "In a few days, when Trella is well enough, we'll review the charges against these men."

Both men started to protest, but Eskkar cut them off. "There's no need to rush their punishment. Better to let them worry about their fate, while we make sure each one gets exactly what he deserves. Remember, Trella was here, and she heard every word Korthac said. She'll know who merits what punishment."

Eskkar stood and faced Gatus, who'd remained expressionless during the discussion. "Round up those twelve. Then take charge of Korthac and make sure he gets to the marketplace. The sooner he begins his journey to the underworld, the better."

"What about the other one, that Hathor?"

"Him, too," Eskkar said. "All the Egyptians deserve the torture."

Gatus stood as well. "Let's go, Corio. The sooner we catch up with the men on your list, the happier we'll both be."

Eskkar left the table and walked over to check on Korthac. The man looked even worse today than he had yesterday. Korthac glared at him, but said nothing. Eskkar glanced in on Hathor, but had nothing to say to the Egyptian subcommander. He didn't know the man, and hadn't encountered him during the fight. But he'd fled with Ariamus, and that alone was enough to condemn him.

As he turned away from Hathor, Mitrac and a few others from the Hawk Clan entered the courtyard. They surrounded Eskkar, eager for news and equally eager to tell him what they'd accomplished. Eskkar spoke with them for some time, answering questions, laughing, and listening to the latest rumors from the streets.

They left him, still laughing, proud men who knew they'd won a great victory. Ignoring the other activity around him, Eskkar washed himself at the well, then visited the kitchen to find something more to eat. His appetite had returned, a good sign, he knew. He leaned against the wall, out of the way of the cook, and munched on some bread and sausage, enjoying the idle moment.

"Lord, Lady Trella asks for you."

He turned to see Drusala bowing to him. "Is everything all right?"

"Oh, yes, lord, but she asked if you could attend her."

Wiping his fingers on his tunic, he climbed the stairs, Drusala following behind. But she stopped at the landing, and shut the door as soon as he passed through. Surprised, Eskkar crossed the empty workroom and entered the bedroom.

Annok-sur waited there, along with another woman, a young girl, really, her plain face marred by a broken nose. Eskkar had to stare at her for a moment before he recognized her, the girl Trella had rescued and brought to the house a few days before he'd left for Bisitun.

Trella sat up in the bed, the baby asleep beside her. "Eskkar, we have a favor to ask of you, a very great favor." She kept her voice soft, so as not to waken the child.

Trella's use of "we" warned him something unusual was coming. He looked closer at the girl, struggling to remember her name.

"This is En-hedu," Trella went on, "soon to be wife to Tammuz. At least, as soon as we set her free from her servitude."

En-hedu bowed deeply to him, but said nothing. When she lifted her head, he saw the worry in her face.

"Tammuz . . . Gatus told me he'd taken a woman."

"I gave En-hedu to Tammuz more than a month ago. She's been helping him all that time. They both risked their lives, trying to learn more about Korthac. They helped hide Gatus, and she and Tammuz both fought in the battle against Korthac."

"Then you have my thanks, En-hedu," Eskkar said, bowing his head to her.

"I will tell you all about it later, husband," Trella said, "but for now, En-hedu wishes to ask a favor."

En-hedu bowed again, her hands clenched together nervously. "Lord, please, can you spare the life of the Egyptian Hathor? He saved my life and the life of Tammuz as well. We would both be dead if he hadn't spared us."

"Hathor is to die with Korthac," Eskkar said, shock

and surprise in his voice. "He was one of Korthac's subcommanders . . . he escaped with Ariamus."

"Hathor came from the desert with Korthac, it's true," Annok-sur said. "But I didn't see him kill or do injury to anyone here in Akkad."

"Please, lord," En-hedu rushed the words, "his men would have killed Tammuz and myself. Hathor stayed his hand against us. Can you not spare his life for that?"

"What does Tammuz say?" Eskkar asked. "Does he want this man to live?"

"Yes, Lord Eskkar," En-hedu said, "but he will not ask for Hathor's life. He is too loyal to you and Lady Trella."

"In serving Korthac, who knows how many evil deeds Hathor may have accomplished in the past. He may have . . ."

Trella dropped her eyes, and Eskkar's voice trailed off. Without saying anything, she reminded him of another who had done things in the past, things better forgotten.

"No one has accused Hathor of evil deeds," Annok-sur said, filling in the silence.

"Not yet," Eskkar countered. "Today, in the market-place, I'm sure many will come forth to confront him." He shook his head. "Still, I have no quarrel with him. He can spend the rest of his days as a slave, working on the wall."

"When Korthac amused himself at my expense," Trella said, "Hathor was the only one who looked away. He did not take pleasure in my suffering."

Her words told him she wanted Hathor to live, and not as a slave.

"Perhaps there is another way," Trella continued. "Perhaps you can make use of him."

"Use him?"

"You always say how you look for men who can command. Hathor is one such. Even Korthac thought so. With Korthac gone and the rest of the Egyptians dead, Hathor has no one else to turn to. In Akkad, every man's hand will be against him. Such a man might prove useful to you, Eskkar, if you held his loyalty."

Eskkar looked from one woman to the other. Annok-sur nodded slightly, to show her approval; En-hedu's lip trembled as she watched him, as if fearful of an outburst of anger.

Trella stroked little Sargon, tracing his cheek with her finger for a moment, then lifting her eyes to Eskkar's. "It is something to think about, husband. There is no rush to put him to death."

As always, she gave him time to make up his mind, to think things through in his own way.

"I'll consider it," he answered. "Is there anything else?"

"No, nothing. You'll do what's best."

The words sounded humble, but he caught the gleam in her eye.

"But perhaps it would be good to speak to him yourself," Trella added. "Can you have him brought here?"

"Up here? Now?" He regretted the words the moment he uttered them. He knew Trella too well. Once she made up her mind, she always acted quickly.

"I can have him brought up, Lord Eskkar," Annok-sur offered.

Now Bantor's wife was calling him "lord."

"No, I'll bring him." Eskkar needed the time to think, and he certainly wasn't going to win any arguments here, not with the three of them united against him. Shaking his head, he turned and left the room, wondering what they would say with him gone.

In the courtyard, the command table stood empty. He knew Gatus had gone with the council members to gather up the traitors.

Eskkar walked over to the guards. He nodded to the one watching Hathor, and ducked his head as he entered inside.

Hathor looked up when he entered, but said nothing.

"Do you know who I am?"

"You are Lord Eskkar. I saw you yesterday when I was brought here."

The man spoke with a strong accent, but Eskkar had no difficulty understanding his words.

"Are you ready to die, Hathor?"

"As ready as any man, lord." He pushed himself up a little straighter against the wall. "I would have killed myself rather than been captured, but your men took me before I could fall on my sword."

Eskkar grunted at that news. So this all could have been avoided if Bantor's men hadn't been so efficient. He stared at Hathor. Despite the Egyptian's strong words, Eskkar saw the trembling in his hands that betrayed his fear. No man wants to die alone, surrounded by enemies and strangers. A warrior expected to die in battle, often looked forward to it; better to end that way than a lingering death from illness or old age, alone, perhaps begging in the streets.

Another long-forgotten memory returned, of a time many years ago when Eskkar had sat bound and bloody against a cave wall, death pricking the skin at his throat, afraid, yet too proud to beg for his life, while a group of women decided his fate. Women had spared him then, and now women wanted him to spare this man. Perhaps Eskkar owed the gods a debt, one that must be repaid. Ishtar, the earth goddess, was a woman, after all.

"Guard, get some water for the prisoner." Eskkar used the time to think.

The guard returned with a skin filled with water. Eskkar took it from his hands, cursing at the old memories; he should feel hate for the Egyptian, not pity. He handed the skin to the surprised Hathor and let him drink his fill, much of the water dribbling down his chest as the man held the skin clumsily with his bound hands.

Eskkar turned to the guard, still standing in the doorway. "Bring him to the workroom. And wash the blood from his hands and face first."

Ignoring the soldier's surprised look, Eskkar returned to the upper rooms. He sat down at the big table and waited. Annok-sur summoned Drusala to watch the baby; the midwife closed the door to the inner room after Trella and En-hedu joined Eskkar in the workroom. The two women guided Trella to the seat beside her husband, then stood behind her.

It took two men to bring Hathor up the stairs, and by the time he stood in front of Eskkar, a sheen of perspiration covered his face. At least they'd cleaned most of the blood off.

"Put him on the stool," Eskkar ordered, "then leave us."

"Lord, one of us should stay, in case . . ."

"I'll watch him myself," Eskkar cut the man off. He stood up and moved to the other side of the table, then sat on the corner, between Hathor and the women, fingering the knife on his belt.

Trella waited until the guards had left, closing the door behind them. "Do you remember me?" Her voice once again held the power of command, no matter how weak she might feel.

Hathor nodded, his eyes darting from husband to wife.

"Tell me of Korthac," Trella said. "Tell me what he did in Egypt."

The question caught Hathor by surprise. "Why do you wish . . . to know about Korthac?"

"It cannot matter now to answer my questions." Trella kept her voice even, a polite request to a guest.

Eskkar said nothing, just stared at the man. If Hathor refused to speak, he would go to the marketplace and suffer with his leader.

Hathor dropped his eyes. "It matters not, I suppose . . . Lady Trella."

So the Egyptian wasn't a complete fool, Eskkar thought.

Hathor's story came out haltingly. The years spent pillaging the land, gathering forces, two mighty armies battling to control the land of Egypt. The conquests, the battles, the villages taken and burned, the lands devastated, the final conflict that saw Korthac defeated and driven into the desert with the last of his men, all of them lucky to escape with their lives.

To his surprise, Eskkar found himself listening with interest. When the man ended his tale, Eskkar had a question of his own. "Tell me about the battle here in Akkad."

Hathor made a noise that might have been a laugh. "You were too clever for Korthac. He knew you didn't have enough men. He never thought you would divide what little you had to slip inside and raise the city. Or that Akkad would rise up, even for you."

"My men didn't think much of the idea at the time," Eskkar said, remembering the arguments at Rebba's farmhouse.

"Your men follow where you lead, Lord Eskkar. I see that they don't fear you, the way we all feared Korthac. You speak to them as an equal. You must be a great warrior to hold so much loyalty."

Eskkar stared at the man, not sure what to make of the words of praise. "Go on, Hathor. Tell me of the battle."

The Egyptian began again, relating how they'd been surprised at the strike here at the house, how they hadn't expected Eskkar to arrive so soon, and the confusion that broke out among them, even the hatred Takany felt for Ariamus. Hathor spoke for some time, but then his voice gave out. He tried to continue, but Eskkar held up his hand.

"Enough for now." Then he leaned closer to the helpless man. "Would you like to live, Hathor?"

"As a slave? No, better to die and get it over with."

"You might change your mind when the torture begins. But I meant something else. My wife has asked me to spare your life."

A look of shock came over the Egyptian's face.

"And this girl, En-hedu, pleaded with Trella. Do you know En-hedu?"

"Yes, I know her. The seller of trinkets outside Korthac's house." His eyes widened in comprehension. "Was she one of Trella's . . . Lady Trella's spies?"

"Why did you spare her life? And the boy's?"

"She was ready to die to protect her man. I thought . . .

She'd spoken kindly to me often enough." He shrugged, lifting his bound hands. "I thought there'd been enough killing of women and helpless men. Whether we won or lost, their deaths wouldn't have mattered."

"Yes, there's been enough of killing," Eskkar agreed. "Now there must be a time of building. The land must be freed of bandits, and the people protected from the clans of the steppes people. I need men who can help me build, Hathor, as well as fight my enemies. Loyal men."

Hathor stared not at Eskkar, but at En-hedu, unable to speak.

"Or, when you've recovered from your wound," Trella said, "we can give you a horse and let you depart. You can even return to Egypt. The choice is yours."

"You would give me my life?"

Eskkar nodded. "A life for a life. Yours for En-hedu and Tammuz's. You did no hurt to Trella, and no one has come forth to accuse you of murder or rape. If you had ... it might be different."

"I have nothing to return to in Egypt." He lifted his eyes to Eskkar, then to Trella. "The vow I swore to Korthac ends with his death. If you will accept my oath, I will serve you faithfully, lord. I swear it."

The Egyptian meant his words, Eskkar decided. He looked at Trella, who nodded. Taking his knife from his belt, Eskkar cut the knot from Hathor's bonds.

"I'll take him downstairs, Lord Eskkar," Annok-sur said, putting her arm around his shoulders. "And summon the healer for his wounds."

A knock on the door sounded, and Gatus pushed his way into the room. "I've got three of the men denounced

Epilogue

Nine days later, Yavtar once again guided his boat toward the dock at Akkad, though this time he arrived just after midday instead of the dead of night. He captained a different ship as well, a fine vessel newly purchased, and one of the largest that plied the river. It boasted a bright white sail twice as tall as a man, a long steering oar extending from the stern, and carried a crew of two men and a boy to work the ship. Today Yavtar's cargo differed as well; instead of grim fighting men and their weapons, he carried passengers and trade goods.

Only a single berthing place stood empty at Akkad's dock, and another boat, this one coming upriver, also wanted to land. Yavtar's curses echoed across the rapidly diminishing gap between the two ships, as both captains sought to secure the berth. The two craft nearly collided before the other vessel's captain yielded, as much to Yavtar's bellowing as to the Hawk Clan banner flying from the masthead.

The wet oars flashed in the bubbling current as they caught the sunlight, struggling against the river's force as the boat crept closer to the shore. With one last frantic pull of the oars, Yavtar's boat slid into the berth, its journey ended.

Yavtar grunted in satisfaction when his new ship bumped against the jetty, safe at last from the river's motion. One crewman leaped nimbly onto the wharf and fastened the holding ropes fore and aft to the well-worn stanchions. The other crewmen stowed the sail around the mast, clearing the way to unload passengers and cargo.

His latest voyage completed successfully, Yavtar intended to get decently drunk for a few days while he enjoyed the spoils of war. The great battle to liberate Akkad had proved lucrative to the old sailor. He alone of Eskkar's force had entered Akkad with a well-filled sack of gold, payment received in advance for the use of his ships and for transporting the soldiers. The day after the battle, while most of the soldiers filled the alehouses and rejoiced at their victory, Yavtar had visited the countryside, and used his new riches to buy a good-sized farm a few miles outside the city. He then traded one of his two ships, plus a stash of gold and silver coins he'd managed to loot unnoticed from a dead Egyptian in the tower, for the proud craft he now commanded. If nothing else, this war had made Yavtar a wealthy man.

"Safe and sound, a smooth voyage just as I promised," Yavtar said, his voice brimming with pride.

"So you did, master boatman," Alexar agreed, standing in the prow of the craft and trying to stay out of the crew's way. "But I'd rather travel by horseback any day, or even walk."

"The more fool you, then," Yavtar said, his smile

softening his words. "I'll see you tonight at Zenobia's. You can pay for the wine, too." He leapt lightly to the dock, and searched for the dockmaster to declare his cargo and complete his business. The crowded dockside bustled with afternoon trading traffic, busier than usual since Korthac's attempted coup. Yavtar had purchased two dozen sacks of grain while in Bisitun, and he expected to sell them for a good profit, an extra bonus to supplement the generous fee Lord Eskkar offered for the boat's hire.

Alexar, shaking his head, watched Yavtar disappear into the throng of activity. For a moment he ignored the crowd of idlers enjoying the spectacle of the river and the men working it, and stared at the city wall and gate. From here, no sign of the recent conflict remained. Already the fighting seemed something from long ago.

Alexar had dwelled in Akkad for the last two years, laboring at any task he could find, and more often than not, going to bed hungry. When the Alur Meriki swept toward the city, he joined Eskkar's soldiers, as much to secure a steady source of food as to fight against the barbarians. To his surprise, Alexar found that soldiering agreed with him; he trained hard and listened to his instructors. In little more than six months, he'd risen from recruit to soldier to leader of ten, and now to the lofty position of commander, one of those reporting directly to Lord Eskkar and a member of the elite Hawk Clan.

Like many of his Hawk Clan brothers, Alexar had wandered through many lands before he settled in Akkad. Now he thought of the city as his home and knew he would never leave its crowded and noisy lanes, always bustling with activity and purpose. Unlike most of the other villages he'd seen, dreary places where most people struggled even to survive, here in Akkad a man could improve his life, plan for the future, and perhaps leave something of himself behind someday. Whatever the coming years might bring, he would follow Eskkar's path, no matter where it led.

For now, however, Alexar followed Yavtar's example. He, too, jumped onto the jetty, grateful to feel something solid underfoot, then looked down into the boat to inspect those entrusted to his care.

"Up you go, then," a crewman said as he guided Lani up onto the narrow plank pushed into place by the ship's boy and connecting the boat with the shore.

Alexar extended his hand and took Lani's as she stepped cautiously onto the shifting gangplank.

"Thank you," Lani said, when she reached the safety of dockside.

Alexar repeated the process for Tippu, who gazed nervously at the raucous villagers. After both women disembarked, he relaxed for the first time since leaving Bisitun with his charges, grateful that the voyage had ended.

Alexar's first assignment after his promotion to commander took him to Bisitun. Eskkar had asked him to escort Lani and her sister to Akkad, as soon as a suitable vessel could be found. The easy errand gave Alexar the chance to rest for a few days. He knew his new duties in Akkad would soon occupy all his time. Eskkar had an army to rebuild and a city to defend, and Alexar knew much would be expected of him.

The two soldiers who'd accompanied him upriver followed the two women ashore, each soldier carrying a large cloth sack that contained the women's belongings in addition to their own weapons. The ever-helpful crewman leaned over the boat's side and handed up the last piece of cargo to Alexar: a good-sized cage containing a miserable-looking cat that hissed at its latest indignity. With a prayer of thanks to the river gods for his safe deliverance, Alexar led the little cavalcade off the jetty.

The trip downriver from Bisitun had gone without incident, but it had still taken three days, and Alexar felt anxious to deliver his charges to Eskkar's house, and start his new duties.

After he finished his commission, Alexar, too, intended to spend the rest of the day and evening drinking wine at Zenobia's Pleasure House. For the first time in his life, he had enough gold in his pouch to pay for the exotic services Zenobia's girls provided. Zenobia had just opened her business when Korthac seized the city, and his Egyptians had commandeered the establishment for their own gratification. Takany, one of Korthac's commanders, had forced Zenobia to service him, before taking most of the other girls. Alexar found the Egyptian second in command dead in Eskkar's courtyard, one of Mitrac's arrows in his belly.

Despite all the chaos, Zenobia had somehow reopened her pleasure house for business the day after Eskkar's return, after gathering her girls and spending a whole day cleaning her establishment of its "Egyptian stink." That was the same day the council put Korthac and the other traitors to the torture, and Alexar had commanded the soldiers who guarded the Egyptian. Zenobia, accompanied by three of her girls, had joined the chorus of those denouncing Korthac, though she and her girls would have preferred torturing Takany. One of the girls, a brown-haired beauty named Malika, winked enticingly at the newly promoted Alexar, so that evening he visited Zenobia's for the first time. Malika kept him awake most of the night, and in the morning he'd barely reached the dock before Yavtar sailed, his pouch considerably lighter after enjoying the good food, fine wine, and Malika's pleasant and energetic company.

Thinking of Malika made him quicken his steps. The sooner he delivered his passengers, the sooner he could avail himself of her services.

On the riverbank, an old woman sat in the shade of the wall and watched the passengers disembark. For two days, Uvela had waited there, observing boats come and go, an agreeable enough assignment from Lady Trella. Uvela's daughter, Shubure, stopped by occasionally to keep her company. Uvela was proud of Shubure, the very first person in Akkad to acknowledge Trella as the head of Eskkar's household. Shubure, now pregnant and married to a prosperous shopkeeper, still worked in secret for Lady Trella, gathering information.

Uvela had never met the two women who walked together, holding hands and glancing around in fascination at all the activity. Nevertheless, she recognized the Hawk Clan emblem on Alexar's shoulder, and knew these must be the passengers Lady Trella sought. Before Alexar and his charges reached the gate, Uvela stood in his path.

"Good day, Commander Alexar," she said with a bow, her voice quavering a little. A scarf struggled to contain the long gray hair that flowed around her head, but her lively eyes more than made up for a weak voice. "My name is

Uvela. Are these the women from Bisitun summoned by Lord Eskkar?"

"Yes, elder," Alexar replied politely, surprised that anyone at the dock would know his business. "Why do you ask?"

"A place has been prepared for them by Lady Trella. I am to take you there."

Alexar looked more closely at the woman. He'd never seen her before, but guessed she must be one of the many women working for Lady Trella.

"Then we'll follow you, elder," Alexar said, giving her a nod. He trailed Uvela away from the docks, through the rear gate and into the city of Akkad, the women and soldiers following behind.

They wound their way through the narrow lanes, passing the barracks area before moving into the better quarter of the city, toward Eskkar's house. As they drew closer, Alexar thought Uvela intended to take them to Eskkar's home. But a few doors away, the old woman turned left instead of right, and passed into a walled courtyard.

A bored young soldier stood guard a step inside the narrow gate. He smiled at Uvela, then straightened up and greeted Alexar respectfully when he recognized him. They entered a private garden scented with jasmine, and scarcely big enough to hold all six of them. Despite the diminutive garden, Alexar knew this must be one of the better houses in the city. He didn't see a private well, but that minor inconvenience didn't detract from the house. In this part of Akkad, with living quarters scarce and expensive, his charges would enjoy pleasant surroundings.

Alexar put down the cage and dismissed his men; he escorted Lani and Tippu inside, carrying their possessions himself, and depositing their sacks in the chamber Uvela indicated. The residence, a medium-sized, single-story structure, enclosed four small bedrooms set off from a comfortable-sized communal room.

"Good-bye, Lani, Tippu," he said. "I must report to Lord Eskkar."

"My sister and I thank you for your help, Alexar," Lani said. "You have been more than kind. May the gods keep you in their favor."

"Lord Eskkar is not in the city," Uvela offered. "But at this hour Captain Gatus should still be at the council house."

"Then I will find him there." Alexar bowed to all of them and disappeared into the garden.

"These two will be your rooms," Uvela began as soon as Alexar left, indicating two adjoining rooms farthest away from the kitchen area. "I suggest you take the larger one, Lani."

So Uvela knew who Eskkar had chosen. Lani wondered what else the people here knew about her and Tippu.

"This house is owned by Lady Trella," Uvela went on, "and is reserved for important visitors and guests. One room is vacant, and the other is occupied by a trader from the south. He will be leaving in a few days, so you should have the house to yourselves. Lady Trella asked me to meet your boat, bring you here, and help with whatever you need."

"You are most kind, Uvela," Lani answered courteously, "but what we both need more than anything is a bath, if such a thing is possible. We have been journeying in the company of men for more than three days."

Uvela nodded her understanding. Traveling for women remained a difficult and dangerous task, even by river. "It's best to bathe in the Tigris." She gathered up two blankets from a small table next to the bed. "Leave your things here. They will be safe. The guard is always here, and no thief would touch the property of Lord Eskkar. Follow me."

"The cat," Lani said, "Lord Eskkar said to bring the animal. Can we get food and water for the poor creature? It's been caged up the whole trip."

Uvela nodded. "I'll tell the guard. But it might be better to keep it in the cage for a few more days, until it gets used to its new surroundings and learns its new home." She told the guard what was needed, and they left the garden.

As the three women walked back toward the river gate, Lani looked about at the crowded lanes, filled with people and animals, all busy about their own business. She'd never seen a city so large. "How many people live here, elder?"

"They say almost five thousand now," Uvela answered, moving steadily through the throngs.

Lani wanted to know more about Akkad, but that could wait until later. "How long have you served Lady Trella?"

"Since she first came to live here, Lani. It was called Orak then. My husband died, my only granddaughter fell ill, and we had nothing to pay a healer. We couldn't even feed ourselves. Lady Trella sent a healer to us and paid the bill herself. Thanks to her, my granddaughter recovered."

"Lady Trella must be a great lady. Does she help many in the city?"

Uvela slowed and turned to meet Lani's eyes. "She looks

after those who are her friends. Those she dislikes find it better to leave."

Plain enough, Lani decided, but she had one more question. "And where is Lord Eskkar today?"

"Lord Eskkar rode out with some soldiers this morning." Uvela saw the disappointment on Lani's face, and softened her next words. "I don't know where he is, but I think he's expected back tonight or tomorrow."

Lani felt her sister's hand tighten. It took only a glance at Tippu to know what she wanted. "Uvela, do you know anything about Grond, Lord Eskkar's guard? My sister . . . We heard he was wounded in the fighting."

Alexar had known of Grond's wounds, but could only tell Tippu that Grond was still alive when he left for Bisitun.

Uvela saw the look of worry on Tippu's face. "Grond lost much blood, but he is recovering from his wounds. The healer said Grond would heal faster away from the city, so Lord Eskkar had him carried to Noble Rebba's farm to recover. It's just a short distance from the city," Uvela added, "and I'm sure you can visit him tomorrow, if you like."

"Thank you," Tippu said, the relief plain in her voice, but her hand still clutched Lani's.

By then they had returned to the river gate. Once past it, Uvela turned to the left, away from the crowded docks, and guided the women about two hundred paces downriver. The Tigris turned in here, out of sight of the docks, and an eddy pool, bounded with hedges that marked the women's area, provided a somewhat private place to bathe. A half-dozen women stood in the water, washing themselves, their children, and even some clothes. No one took any particular notice of Uvela or her companions.

Leaving Uvela on the bank, Lani and Tippu disrobed and entered the water. Both girls could swim, but heeding Uvela's warning, they stayed close to the riverbank and within the eddy pool. When they finished cleaning themselves, Uvela helped rub them dry with the blankets.

After the sisters dressed, Uvela guided them back to the house. Lani realized she could never have found the place by herself. Her mind couldn't comprehend Akkad's size in such a short time.

"You both should remain inside, until you are summoned," Uvela said. "I will return shortly." The old woman left, stopping at the gate to speak to the guard.

So they would be summoned. Lani expected it. Wherever Eskkar might be, Lani realized that she and her sister were in Lady Trella's power. For weeks she had asked everyone she met about Akkad, Eskkar, and, of course, Trella. All accounted Trella as being a fair and decent woman, and more than a few depicted her as the city's real ruler.

And soon Lani, Eskkar's new concubine, would be presented to the second most powerful person in the city. Lani did not think she would be welcomed with open arms by her lover's wife.

Nevertheless, she and Tippu made good use of their time. Vigorous toweling with another set of blankets Lani found within the house dried their hair, and Tippu used the big wooden comb to arrange her sister's soft brown tresses. Lani clothed herself in her best gown, the one she had worn the first night for Eskkar.

From her bag Lani extracted her pot of ochre, and she and Tippu took turns applying the stain to their eyes. Another vial provided perfume for each, and a small sachet held a store of mint leaves that they both chewed to sweeten their breath. Lani added a simple ring to each hand, and a single gold pin in her hair.

Tippu examined her sister and proclaimed her ready. As for Tippu, she needed little artifice to enhance her own beauty.

They finished their preparations just as they heard Uvela's voice outside, speaking to the guard. Lani saw the look of fear in Tippu's eyes. "Don't worry, Tippu," Lani said. "Whatever happens, Eskkar will see you safely to Grond."

"And you? What will happen to you?"

"Whatever is meant to happen," Lani answered, trying to sound more confident than she felt. "Remember, Eskkar sent for us."

By then Uvela had entered their room. "Lady Trella wishes to see you both," Uvela said. "I'll take you there."

Lani didn't know what to say, so she forced a smile to her lips.

As they stepped into the lane, every man's eyes turned toward them, admiring their beauty and wondering who these unfamiliar women might be. It took only a few steps before they reached the courtyard of Trella's home. Lani could not help but be impressed at the size of the house, almost hidden behind a wall taller than her own height. Two soldiers guarded the big wooden gate. Freshly painted and decorated, it swung open for them, and they passed into an expansive courtyard that seemed large enough to hold half a hundred people.

Uvela gestured them toward the main house. They entered into a large communal room, empty now, except for two servants who stared curiously at them. Lani looked in wonder at the stairs that led to the upper chambers. She'd never entered a house with a second story.

Single file, Lani and Tippu followed Uvela up those stairs and into a spacious and well-ventilated room that held two beautifully carved tables and a half-dozen chairs. Three walls showed fresh plaster, a soft white color that soothed the eyes, while the fourth wall, with its door leading to another room, had been colored a pale blue. Two women sat behind the larger table, their backs to the second doorway, waiting.

For a brief moment, Lani could not trust her eyes. The dark-haired girl looked so young that Lani found it hard to believe this was Lady Trella. She didn't even look as old as Tippu.

Lady Trella wore only a silver fillet to hold back her hair, but her dress boasted a soft weave as fine as the one Lani wore, a deep crimson that complimented Trella's hair and skin. She wore no makeup of any kind, no rings or bracelets. But her tresses had been combed and brushed into a lustrous wave that cascaded about her shoulders and onto her full breasts. Trella stood as the three women approached the table.

"My thanks to you, Uvela. You have done well. Please wait downstairs."

Trella sat back down, but did not offer chairs to her guests. Lani realized the gesture of respect had been intended for Uvela, not as a greeting to her visitors. Trella's voice surprised Lani. Not the voice of a girl but of a woman full grown, one with the force and habit of command.

Uvela left the room, closing the door behind her.

Lani felt Trella's gaze upon her. Akkad's ruler took her time, examining Lani at length before she turned to study Tippu, an inspection that lasted only a few moments. Trella returned her eyes to Lani. "You are Lani, from Bisitun?"

Lani bowed respectfully. "Yes, Lady Trella, and this is my sister, Tippu. May we give thanks to you for the rooms you provided?"

For the first time Lani looked directly into Trella's eyes, and Lani saw this was no mere girl who faced her. Trella's face revealed no trace of emotion. Instead Lani saw strength there, and power, but no hint of what she might be thinking. And whatever Trella's age might be, her eyes announced that she saw everything, knew everything.

Trella ignored the polite question. "This is my friend and advisor, Annok-sur. She is also the wife of Bantor, commander of the gate." Annok-sur did not stand, but nodded her head the slightest amount. "She is still recovering from a wound she received in the struggle."

Bowing to Annok-sur, Lani saw no kindness there, only determination and toughness. She recalled the story she had heard from Alexar about the fighting that had taken place in this house, in this very room. Annok-sur, too, had fought against the usurper. Lani looked around for any signs of the struggle, but nothing remained. Still, Korthac had been wounded and taken captive right in this very spot. "I heard there was a great fight in the house of Eskkar. Alexar said that Lady Trella was also injured?"

Trella smiled briefly. "Yes. It is twice now that I have been stabbed since I came to Akkad. Soon I will have as many scars on my body as Eskkar."

Lani saw no sign of any wound, but Trella's loose-fitting gown revealed little, though she did look a bit pale. Alexar had mentioned that Lady Trella had lost a lot of blood during the birthing, in addition to the wound. Still, the battle had ended ten days ago, and both women had time to heal. Lani started to speak, but the soft cry of a baby in another room interrupted her.

Annok-sur rose from her seat, wincing as she did so. "I'll tend the child, Lady Trella." She passed behind Trella's chair and went into the other room.

"May I offer felicitations on the birth of your son, Lady Trella?"

Trella acknowledged the compliment with another brief smile. "Sargon grows in strength each day. He will bring honor to his father, I am sure." For a moment she turned toward the inner room, but the crying stopped, so she again faced the two sisters.

"Eskkar has told me the story of your plight, Lani, and you, Tippu," she said, acknowledging the younger sister for the first time. "You both have suffered much at the hands of villains, and I'm glad Eskkar was able to release you from your captivity."

Lani lowered her eyes at the mention of her past but quickly lifted them again. "Lord Eskkar freed us from . . . our captor, and protected us from the wrath of the villagers. We owe him our lives."

"You seemed to have repaid him well enough, Lani. I learned of your . . . activities weeks ago."

Lani lifted her head a little higher. "I do not regret what I have done, Lady Trella. Lord Eskkar had fought a hard battle. He needed someone to look after him and take charge of his household. It is not so strange that he should want a woman to comfort him."

Trella sighed and pursed her lips for a moment. "A woman to comfort him I can understand, Lani. But somehow you managed to do more than that. Not to mention that you saved his life."

So Trella knew about the fight in Bisitun. Lani shook her head. "It was little enough that I did, Lady Trella. I fell to the ground and one of his attackers tripped over me."

"Eskkar described it somewhat differently. And he also told me that he cared for you."

A thrill went through Lani at the words. "As I care for him, Lady Trella. He saved more than our lives." Lani bit her lip, then decided she might as well say everything on her mind. "You are the one he loves, Lady Trella. The moment he heard that you might be in danger, he had no thoughts for me or anyone else." She paused. "He has never told me that he loves me."

"And what do you feel toward my husband, Lani? Do you merely seek his protection? Perhaps you just wanted someone to comfort *you* in the night? Or do you love him?"

"When I was with Ninazu, I swore that if I escaped somehow, I would never let a man touch me again. When the soldiers came and I pleaded for mercy, Lord Eskkar looked at me, the way any man looks at a woman. But instead of taking me or Tippu, or giving us to his men, he put his protection around us. That surprised me, Lady Trella, that a great warrior could want someone, but not take advantage of our weakness. So I went to him, just to serve him, and . . . he was tired and dirty . . . and somehow I knew he was different . . . from the others."

Her voice trailed off, and Lani realized she had avoided answering Trella's question. She lifted her chin and spoke firmly. "Yes, Lady Trella, I do love your husband."

She watched Trella shake her head, as if in disbelief, but then Trella smiled, and for the first time her face showed the warmth of a young woman.

"A man should be more than just an animal. Isn't that right, Lani?"

Lani felt confused, both by Trella's smile and her strange words. "I do not understand, Lady Trella. I . . ."

"No, of course not. But I do understand, Lani. I once had much the same feelings toward Eskkar myself. I think it's the barbarian in him that appeals to women. The savage horse fighters apparently honor and respect their women more than city dwellers, who seem to be crueler and harsher to us than any barbarian."

Annok-sur slipped back into the room, partially closing the inner door so that the conversation would not wake the child. "Sargon is asleep, Trella, but I think he will need to nurse again soon." She stared at Lani, but said nothing.

Trella's eyes brightened at the thought of feeding her child. "We will be finished soon, Annok-sur." Then she turned to Lani again. "Do you have any children, Lani?"

The question caught Lani by surprise. "No, Lady Trella. Ishtar has never blessed me with a child, though I sacrificed to her often when . . . when I was married."

"Perhaps the fault was with your husband," Trella offered.

Lani's eyes widened. The scandalous words could never be said in front of a man. Every husband knew that if a woman didn't conceive a child, it was her fault.

"No, I was his second wife. His first wife died in childbirth, and the babe was lost." Then Lani understood. Trella wanted to know if she might be carrying Eskkar's child. "I carry no child, Lady Trella. The moon has risen for me since Lord Eskkar left Bisitun."

Trella said nothing, just sat there for a long moment, staring down at the table. When she spoke, her voice took on a gentler tone. "I am sorry to have kept you standing, Lani, and you, too, Tippu. You must both be tired after your long voyage. Please sit down." She turned to Annok-sur. "Give our guests some wine, Annok-sur, and a small cup for me."

The other table held two pitchers and a half-dozen dark green glass goblets.

Lani and Tippu glanced at each other, then took seats across the table from Trella. Something must have satisfied Trella, Lani decided. Servants and inferiors stood in the presence of their betters. Annok-sur poured wine into a pair of goblets, diluted them with water, and handed them to Lani and her sister, before pouring a third glass for Trella.

"Welcome to Akkad, Lani ... Tippu," Trella said, her voice low.

Lani looked down at the dark wine glinting in the green glass, and wondered if it contained poison. She saw Tippu's hand trembling with the same thought. Trella had not raised her glass. Still, Lani had no choice, not really. If Lady Trella wished them both dead, they would die, one way or another.

Lani lifted the glass to her hostess. "To Akkad," and

drank deeply, emptying half the contents before she put the goblet back on the table. Tippu watched her for a moment, then took a small sip from her own glass. "Drink up, Tippu," Lani said. "The wine is very good."

"You do not fear poison, then?" Trella asked drily.

"No, Lady Trella. If you wish to kill me, then I am in your power and at your mercy. But I would remind you that my sister has done nothing to offend you."

"You are both safe, Lani, though I must admit there were nights when I was jealous of my husband in your arms. Would you like to know what I did about it?"

"Did about it? I don't understand?"

"No, you could not. As soon as I learned you were more than a casual bed partner and that Eskkar was growing attached to you, I sent a rider to your birthplace. I wanted to learn about you. The rider returned only three days ago. Do you know what he told me?"

"I . . . My land is very far away. How could you send . . . I don't know what to say, Lady Trella."

"He reported to me that your husband was an honorable man of a respected family, and that you were reputed to be a good and decent wife, who prayed each day at Ishtar's feet for a child. Your whole village mourned when they heard of Namtar's death and your capture. They thought you dead as well."

The mention of her husband's name sent a tremor through Lani's body. Then she understood the full import of Trella's words. This girl had dispatched a rider on a long and dangerous journey of nearly three hundred miles, simply to gather information. All this at the merest hint of a rival for her husband's affections.

For the first time Lani realized that all she had heard about Trella must be true, that the ruler of Akkad had sharp wits and would be dangerous to offend. More important, she had the power to do whatever she wished, even to send forth a man on such a difficult errand. Lani recalled how easily Alexar had turned her and her sister over to Trella's woman. He had done it without question, so certain of her authority.

"And I've spoken to many from Bisitun about you, Lani," Trella went on when Lani didn't answer. "You are important to my husband, so I needed to learn as much about you as I could." Trella paused for a moment, giving Lani time to comprehend. "Now I have some questions for you, Lani. And let me say that Eskkar and I have spoken much about you, and he asked me to make whatever arrangements for you that I saw fit."

Lani nodded her head in understanding. As soon as Alexar turned her over to Trella's woman, she knew her fate rested in Trella's hands, not Eskkar's. He had risked his life to rescue his wife and his newborn son. He wasn't likely to offend her now, not over some captive, ill used by Ninazu for his amusement.

"So, what is it you wish to do now that you are in Akkad? Would you have me find you a new husband? There are many good men in Akkad who would look with favor on you, and you could have your pick of several. Or do you want to live by yourself for a time? That, too, can be arranged. Eskkar has set aside enough gold for you to do whatever you choose."

Gold meant freedom, protection, even for two women alone. Lani could get a house, servants ... she could choose her own life. It sounded too good to be true, and yet . . .

Trella waited a moment, but Lani said nothing. "Or do you wish to remain as Eskkar's concubine?"

Lani didn't hesitate. "Lady Trella, if I could be permitted to remain as Lord Eskkar's concubine, I would pay anything, do anything . . ."

"There is nothing to pay, Lani, and the gold is yours already. However, there are rules if you are to be his concubine. So you must think hard about this."

Trella leaned forward, and her voice took on a harder edge. "There must be no issue from your womb, Lani. If you become with child, you must take the herbs to force the child from your body. If that fails, and a boy is born, you must give it up. Sargon is to be the only heir to his father." She waited for Lani to speak.

"That is very hard, Lady Trella." Lani felt the tears start and bit her lip to stop them. She would not cry in front of this girl. "But I do not think I will conceive . . ."

"No, Lani, that is not what you must say," Trella cut in, her voice firm. "You will not be a wife, and there will not be a son. You must agree to that. If you hope for a child of your own, then you must give up Eskkar and seek another man to father it."

The tears started, and this time Lani couldn't stop them. To never have a child was a terrible curse for a woman. The only thing worse than such an evil would be to give a child away.

She looked up at Trella, surprised to see sadness and sympathy in her eyes. Trella had just delivered her own baby, and knew what she asked. But Lani hesitated only a moment.

"I will take the herbs, Lady Trella. If I bear a son, I will give him up."

"I am sorry to do this to you, Lani, but I must. Sargon needs protection, as do Eskkar and I. As will you, if you are to be his companion. We still have many enemies. You must swear to do all that you can to protect and serve all three of us."

"What can I do to protect you and Eskkar?" Lani heard the confusion in her voice. How could she do anything to protect anyone?

"More than you realize, Lani. Much is at stake here, too much to tell you about now. But you know we barely survived a siege by the barbarians, and then this attempt by Korthac to kill us all and seize control of Akkad. There will be more such strife in the future, and I . . . we will need all the help we can find."

"I will do whatever you ask, whatever I can to protect all of you. What else must I do?"

"As Eskkar's concubine, you will see no other man, only him. And you will only see him once or twice a week, or when the moon does not permit me to be with him. Your role will be to share pleasure with him, to soothe and comfort his body, and ease his mind. I love him too much to give up more of his spirit."

So Lani would become a consort, a pleasure girl, little better than a hired prostitute or slave, whose only business would be to please and satisfy her lover. It would be a bittersweet role to play. Trella would be his wife, his lover, his companion, the mother of his children. Lani would be almost nothing, have nothing.

Trella saw the struggle in Lani's eyes and leaned

forward across the table. "You do not need to accept this, Lani. I know this is very hard to bear. All I can say is that, if you do accept, you will be helping Eskkar and myself. If this role becomes too difficult, you can stop being his concubine, and we will find another place for you, another task, or a husband of your own."

Lani heard the words. More important, she realized that, for some unknown reason, Trella wanted Lani to agree to this, wanted her to continue as Eskkar's concubine. It must mean a great deal to Trella, though Lani didn't understand why. She could turn down this role, but that thought was too awful to bear. Lani remembered the pain in her breast as Eskkar sailed away from Bisitun, likely going to his death. She'd been willing to kill herself at that moment, rather than face life without him. At least this would be better than that fate. And if it helped Eskkar . . .

"I will do whatever you ask. I will be his concubine, if he so chooses." The words came out almost without volition. Lani's love for Eskkar gave her no choice. She watched Trella lean back in her seat, a hint of fatigue in her face. Lani remembered that in the last few days, this girl had delivered a baby practically in the midst of a battle, been wounded, and then had to fight to save her own life and the life of her child.

"Then I'm glad you're here, Lani. I welcome you to Eskkar's household. There will be much for you to do, and much to learn. We will speak often in the coming days. Go now and rest. Tonight, when Eskkar returns from the countryside, I will send him to you. Now, dry your eyes."

Lani's tears came without stopping. She felt Tippu's arm

around her shoulders, but still Lani found it difficult to stand.

Trella turned to Annok-sur. "Can you help her, while I attend to Sargon?"

Annok-sur arose and took a square of linen from her dress. "Your eyes are very beautiful, Lani," she said, her voice surprisingly gentle, the hardness gone from her face. "Your tears will spoil your eye coloring." She dabbed gently at Lani's cheeks. "I'll take you back to Uvela."

Somehow Lani got to her feet and let herself be escorted to the door. Blurred by tears, her eyes refused to focus properly. She had to hold on to Annok-sur's arm to make sure she did not fall going down the stairs, Tippu following anxiously behind them. Lani struggled to hold back most of her tears until they left the house, keeping only one thought in her mind—that Eskkar would come to her bed tonight, and that once again she would be safe in his arms.

Trella sighed when the door closed. She regretted hurting someone like that, a good woman who had done nothing wrong, but it needed to be done. From her own sources, from Eskkar, and from what she had just seen, she realized that Lani possessed a strong mind, with wits sharp enough to see what the future would bring.

Trella didn't like sharing Eskkar's affections, but anyone could see that Lani loved Eskkar, and Trella saw just as clearly that Eskkar possessed more than a little love for Lani, even if, as she claimed, he had never said the words.

In the coming days, as Lani learned more about the ever-present dangers that surrounded them all, Trella knew Lani would do everything in her power to protect Eskkar, and that would soon include Trella and the child. In a few months Lani would become a firm supporter of Eskkar's House, and she would be useful in many other ways. Eskkar had told her about Lani's skills in running the household, and of her suggestion that he use the river to return to Akkad. And for that alone, Trella might owe Lani her own life, and the life of her child. Another few days' delay in reaching Akkad, and Korthac might never have been toppled.

After a time, Lani might even tire of being Eskkar's concubine. Still young, she would want children of her own. When that day came, Trella would make sure the right man stood beside her, someone who could give Lani the happiness she deserved. But until that day, Lani would join with Annok-sur, Gatus, Bantor, and even Corio and Nicar, and others, all those who depended on Eskkar's continuing reign over Akkad.

Lani would fit in well with Trella's plans. There were few enough Trella could trust, and she had to make the most of each of them. She searched constantly for sharp-witted women like Lani who could think for themselves. En-hedu gave promise to be another such one, and Trella had already worked out a new role for her and Tammuz.

And it would be good for Eskkar to have another woman once in a while. A strong and powerful man, her father used to say, needed more than one woman anyway. But in the future, Trella would ensure Eskkar took only women that she approved of, pliable ones that she could bend to her will. She would speak with Zenobia about supplying just the right kind of woman every few months.

Empty vessels, her father called them—women with beauty but few wits, docile and easily forgotten. Men of power or wealth always found themselves sought after by every woman eager to expand her own prestige or influence. With Lani, this would never happen, because her only goal would be to make Eskkar happy, and Eskkar could be truly happy only with his wife and son.

So even Lani would help bring about Trella's vision of the future, the future that Trella and Eskkar would build for their son, Sargon. Five years, she decided. In five years, their position would be secure. Akkad would grow great and powerful, and everyone in these lands would attribute their wealth and safety to Eskkar. The expansion and consolidation of all the farms and villages between Akkad and Bisitun would hasten that process, and all would benefit from the new prosperity and security. With a code of laws established and honestly enforced, the people would soon forget the old and confusing days when powerful merchants ruled unchecked. More than half the city's inhabitants had arrived within the last year, and had little connection to the old days.

Five years from now, everyone would have forgotten about Eskkar's barbarian origin and her own days as a slave. The people of the city would look to Sargon as their future ruler, one of their own and born in Akkad. When that day finally arrived, she and Sargon would be safe, surrounded by the new and still-unraised walls and hundreds, no, thousands of soldiers to protect them.

From the other room, she heard the baby crying. She stood, stretching her back, and went into the bedroom. She took the mewing child from its cradle, ignoring the pain in her side as she bent over to lift him, and sat down on the bed. Trella slipped one arm out of her dress, wiped the tears from Sargon's eyes, and let the boy nurse, enjoying the feel of him against her breast as the milk began to flow. She gently rocked back and forth, thinking about his future.

Tonight she would be alone with Sargon, and she would spend the time resting and talking to her son. Tonight Eskkar would be with another woman, but he would return to her in the morning. With a certainty that she couldn't understand, she knew he would always come back to her. They had been through too much together, had fought and bled together. The gods had interwoven their life-strands, created an alliance between them stronger than any bonds of family, friendship, or even the marriage bed. The road ahead might be perilous and uncertain, but their spirits and blood had strengthened the very walls of Akkad, and nothing could separate them, either from each other or from their fates. She and Eskkar would rule together, or not at all.

She smiled at the suckling child and leaned down to kiss his head. The helpless infant in her arms would reign one day, perhaps over an even greater expanse than Trella could envision. More important, Sargon would carry their blood down through the ages yet to come. She'd seen the look in her husband's eyes when he held their child. The boy's birth had changed Eskkar yet again, made him stronger, even as it drew him closer to her. And that was as it should be. Eskkar had risked his life for her and their son, and she knew their love for each other remained strong. She would give up one or two nights each week to ensure her husband's love and affections went no further.

Acknowledgments

For some inexplicable reason, I assumed that my second book would be easier to write than the first. As usual, I was wrong. In many ways, *Empire Rising* required more work and more revisions than *Dawn of Empire*. So once again I want to give thanks to all those who gave their time and effort to make sure that the book you hold in your hands would be worth the time you spent reading it.

First thanks go to my agent, Dominick Abel, whose casual suggestions did much to improve readability. Then to my editor at HarperCollins, Sarah Durand, whose ideas forced quite a bit of soul-searching and debate about several key areas of the story. Her efforts helped tighten the book and keep the focus on the action.

Extra thanks are due to my critique group NovelsInk, those intrepid writers who gave of their own time to polish the rough drafts and point out all the flaws and mistakes invisible to me or any author. Sharon Anderson, Martin Cox, Deb Ledford, Sally Mise, and Thelma Rea all played a big part in making the story work through the endless drafts and revisions. In 2006, we lost Jim Jasper, our biggest supporter, who succumbed to a sudden illness. We all miss him.

Of course, it's impossible to forget my writing felines, Gracie and Xena, who took turns sitting on my lap while I tried to type. For realism, they insisted I add a cat to the story, and naturally I had to accommodate them.

Sam Barone
Scottsdale, Arizona
January 2007

ALSO AVAILABLE IN ARROW

Dawn of Empire

Sam Barone

Three thousand years before the birth of Christ. An epic conflict is about to begin. The price of victory? Civilization. The price of defeat, a return to the dark ages.

The hopes of civilization rest on one man's shoulders: Eskkar, once a barbarian, now a warrior in charge of defending a small town which lies in the path of a vast barbarian war party. The last time the invaders came to Orak, they spared no one and the tiny candle of trade and agriculture that had begun there, the first in all of human history, was extinguished.

But Eskkar and Trella, the beautiful slave girl he has been given by the grateful townsfolk, and the raggle-taggle army he has inherited are not going to flee. They will fight against the overwhelming odds with foolhardy bravery, subtle ingenuity and the last drop of their blood. On this tiny band the lathe of history will turn: victory or darkness?

'What a cracking story. I've lost two days of writing time because of it and I don't regret it at all. This is a brilliant, fast-paced epic, bringing an ancient people back to roaring life. Superb.'
Conn Iggulden

arrow books

ALSO AVAILABLE IN ARROW

The Mosaic of Shadows

Tom Harper

Byzantium, 1096. When a mysterious assassin looses his arrow at the emperor, he has more than a man in his sights; the keystone of a crumbling empire, he is the solitary figure holding its enemies in check. If he falls, then the mightiest power in Christendom will be torn apart. Aware of the stakes, the emperor hires Demetrios Askiates, the unveiler of mysteries, to catch the would-be killer.

But Demetrios is entering an unknown world, a babbling cauldron of princes, slaves, mercenaries, pimps and eunuchs. From the depths of the slums to the golden towers of the palace, and from the sands of the hippodrome to the soaring domes of Ayia Sophia, he must edge his way through a glittering maze of treachery and deceit before time runs out. Nor are all the enemies within the city walls. With the Turks rampant across Asia, the emperor has sent to the west for mercenaries to reinforce his position. He gets more than he bargained for, however, when a great army, tens of thousands strong, appears before the gates. The first crusaders have arrived, intent on making their fortunes in war, and they have no allegiance to an empire they eye with jealousy and suspicion. As the armies of east and west confront each other, and the assassin creeps ever closer to his prey, Demetrios must untangle the golden web of intrigue which surrounds the emperor before the city – and the empire – are drowned in blood.

'Gripping from the first page . . . a fast-paced and exciting debut'
Ink

arrow books

ALSO AVAILABLE IN ARROW

Knights of the Cross

Tom Harper

1098. The armies of the First Crusade race across Asia minor, routing the Turks and reclaiming the land for Christendom. But on the Syrian border, their advance is halted before the impregnable walls of Antioch.

As winter draws on, they are forced to suffer a fruitless, interminable siege, gnawed by famine and tormented by the Turkish defenders. The entire crusade is on the verge of collapse. His lord, the ruthlessly ambitious Bohemond charges Demetrios Askiates to find the killer. But as Demetrios investigates, the trail seems to lead ever deeper into the vipers' nest of jealousy, betrayal and fanaticism which lies at the heart of the crusade.

Praise for Tom Harper:

'Tom Harper writes with strident clarity in this epic tale of murder and betrayal, bloodshed and romance. Gripping from the first page, the reader is swept up in this colourful and convincing portrayal of an Emperor and his realm, under siege. Well-researched, and cinematic in its imagery, this is a fast-paced and exciting debut.' *Ink*

'Harper effortlessly draws the reader into the court intrigues and conspiracies of 11th-century Byzantium in his outstanding debut.' *Publishers' Weekly*

'Scholarly but speedy narrative, steeped in medieval horrors ranging from flogging to famine, all anchored in what feels like a passion for history and spelling out the way things were.' *Literary Review*

arrow books

ALSO AVAILABLE IN ARROW

Siege of Heaven

Tom Harper

August, 1098. After countless battles and sieges, the surviving soldiers of the first crusade are at last within reach of their ultimate goal: Jerusalem. But rivalries fester and new enemies are massing against them in the Holy Land.

Demetrios Askiates, the Emperor's spy, has had enough of the crusade's violence and hypocrisy. He longs to return home. But when a routine diplomatic mission leads to a deadly ambush, he realises he has been snared in the vast power struggles which underlie the crusade. The only way out now leads through the Holy City.

From the plague-bound city of Antioch to the heart of Muslim Egypt, Demetrios must accompany the army of warlords and fanatics to the very gates of Jerusalem where the crusade climaxes in an apocalypse of pillage, bloodshed and slaughter.

'Scholarly but speedy narrative, steeped in medieval horrors ranging from flogging to famine, all anchored in what feels like a passion for history and spelling out the way things were.'
Literary Review

arrow books

THE POWER OF READING

Visit the Random House website and get connected with information on all our books and authors

EXTRACTS from our recently published books and selected backlist titles

COMPETITIONS AND PRIZE DRAWS Win signed books, audiobooks and more

AUTHOR EVENTS Find out which of our authors are on tour and where you can meet them

LATEST NEWS on bestsellers, awards and new publications

MINISITES with exclusive special features dedicated to our authors and their titles

READING GROUPS Reading guides, special features and all the information you need for your reading group

LISTEN to extracts from the latest audiobook publications

WATCH video clips of interviews and readings with our authors

RANDOM HOUSE INFORMATION including advice for writers, job vacancies and all your general queries answered

Come home to Random House

www.rbooks.co.uk